HAWKMOON

BY MICHAEL MOORCOCK

Hawkmoon
by Michael Moorcock

Published by:

White Wolf Inc.
780 Park North Boulevard, Suite 100
Clarkston, GA 30021

Cover Artwork by John Zeleznik
Jacket Border by Henry Gordon Higginbotham

White Wolf Fiction

Editor: Stewart Wieck
Assistant Editor: Staley Krause
Sales: Michael Krause
Marketing: Wes Harris
Art Director: Richard Thomas
Graphic Designer: Michelle Prahler

BY THE SAME AUTHOR

THE TALE OF THE ETERNAL CHAMPION
Special Editor: John Davey
New Omnibus Editions, revised and with new introductions by the author

1. The Eternal Champion
2. Von Bek
3. Hawkmoon
4. A Nomad of the Time Streams
5. Elric: The Song of the Black Sword
6. The Roads Between the Worlds
7. Corum: The Coming of Chaos
8. Sailing to Utopia
9. Kane of Old Mars
10. The Dancers at the End of Time
11. Elric: The Stealer of Souls
12. The Prince with the Silver Hand
13. Legends from the End of Time
14. Earl Aubec
15. Count Brass

Other novels

Gloriana; or, The Unfulfill'd Queen
The Brothel in Rosenstrasse
Mother London
Blood (forthcoming, Morrow)
Fabulous Harbours (forthcoming, Morrow)
The War Amongst the Angels (in preparation)
Karl Glogauer novels
Behold the Man
Breakfast in the Ruins

Cornelius novels
The Cornelius Chronicles (Avon)
A Cornelius Calendar
Colonel Pyat novels
Byzantium Endures
The Laughter of Carthage
Jerusalem Commands
The Vengeance of Rome (in preparation)

Short stories and graphic novels

Casablanca
Lunching with the Antichrist (Mark Ziesing)
The Swords of Heaven, The Flowers of Hell (with Howard V. Chaykin)

The Crystal and the Amulet (with James Cawthorn)
Stormbringer (with P. Craig Russell, Topps, forthcoming
etc.

Nonfiction

The Retreat from Liberty
Letters from Hollywood(illus. M. Foreman)

Wizardry and Wild Romance
Death Is No Obstacle (with Colin Greenland)
etc.

Editor

New Worlds
The Traps of Time
The Best of New Worlds
Best SF Stories from New Worlds

New Worlds: An Anthology
Before Armageddon
England Invaded
The Inner Landscape
The New Nature of the Catastrophe

Records

With **THE DEEP FIX:**
The New Worlds Fair (forthcoming, Griffin Records)
Dodgem Dude
The Brothel in Rosenstrasse etc.

With **HAWKWIND:**
Warrior on the Edge of Time
Sonic Attack
Zones
Out and Intake
Live Chronicles (Griffin Records, USA) etc.

Also work with Blue Oyster Cult,
Robert Calvert, etc.

For further information about Michael Moorcock and his work,
please send a stamped, self-addressed envelope to
The Nomads of the Time Streams, P.O. Box 5201 Pinehurst, NC 28374.

C O N T E N T S

INTRODUCTION

Dear Reader,

This is the first chance I have had to present the Hawkmoon story in a single edition for U.S. readers. The books were written rapidly in the mid-sixties and I think I'm wise enough, these days, not to interfere too elaborately with work which, if it lacks polish, carries the unmistakable mark of a time when we all, young and old, seemed to have more energy and a perhaps naïve belief that we could swiftly improve the world for everyone. The revisions here are mostly technical rather than stylistic.

In a spirit consciously at odds with the jingoism of the day, I chose a German for a hero and the British for villains, while here and there the reader will find a few references to such personalities of those times as The Beatles or well-known politicians.

Because of these elements some critics have been pleased to find a sophisticated political message in the book and it might save them further time if I say that the moral element in my fantastic romances is as straightforward as it was in most of my rock and roll lyrics and bears as much weighty examination. These were written as popular entertainments, with the same ambition, I hope, as a good popular song. A critic who, detecting some metaphor, a bit of irony, parody or conscious symbolism in this work, has no more discovered profundity here than a French intellectual at a Jerry Lewis retrospective. As with rock and roll, I was attracted to this form because, originally, it did not absorb the interest of academic critics. The books were written in the hope that they would help readers pass their time without feeling they were wasting it, in much the same spirit as I performed on stage.

The correspondences between this volume and the music, in particular, of Hawkwind are well-known but I was especially flattered when Sam Shepard, the writer and actor, told me he had named one of his verse collections after

Hawkmoon. Later, on our album *The New World's Fair*, my band Deep Fix featured Shepard's lyrics in a song by Steve Gilmore. *Song for Marlene* gave me my only chance to do my celebrated imitation of Marlene Dietrich in *Shanghai Express*, an opportunity for which I shall always thank Sam to whom, with my friend Mr Ian Kilminster, I dedicate this particular edition which is also the first to include examples of James Cawthorn's legendary graphic versions of the first two books, which have been hard to come by for some years and are my favourite versions of the story. Mr Cawthorn has also drawn a new, more accurate map of Hawkmoon's world.

Yours,
Michael Moorcock,
Lost Pines,
Texas.
September 1994

THE JEWEL IN THE SKULL

For Dave Brock

B O O K O N E

Then the Earth grew old, its landscapes mellowing and showing signs of age, its ways becoming whimsical and strange in the manner of a man in his last years...

— The High History of the Runestaff

O N E

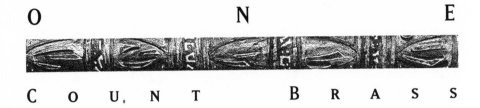

C O U N T   B R A S S

Count Brass, Lord Guardian of Kamarg, rode out on a horned horse one morning to inspect his territories. He rode until he came to a little hill, on the top of which stood a ruin of immense age. It was the ruin of a Gothic church whose walls of thick stone were smooth with the passing of winds and rains. Ivy clad much of it, and the ivy was of the flowering sort so that at this season purple and amber blossoms filled the dark windows, in place of the stained glass that had once decorated them.

His rides alway brought Count Brass to the ruin. He felt a kind of fellowship with it, for, like him, it was old; like him, it had survived much turmoil, and, like him, it seemed to have been strengthened rather than weakened by the ravages of time. The hill on which the ruin stood was a waving sea of tall, tough grass, moved by the wind. The hill was surrounded by the rich, seemingly infinite marshlands of Kamarg — a lonely landscape populated by wild white bulls, horned horses, and giant scarlet flamingoes so large they could easily lift a grown man.

The sky was a light grey, carrying rain, and from it shone sunlight of watery gold, touching the count's armour of burnished brass and making it flame. The count wore a huge broadsword at his hip, and a plain helmet, also of brass, was on his head. His whole body was sheathed in heavy brass, and even his gloves and boots were of brass links sewn upon leather. The count's body was broad, sturdy, and tall, and he had a great, strong head whose tanned face might also have been moulded of brass. From this head stared two steady eyes of golden brown. His hair was red as his heavy moustache. In Kamarg and beyond, it was not unusual to hear the legend that the count was not a true man at all but a living statue in brass, a Titan, invincible, indestructible, immortal.

But those who knew Count Brass knew well enough that he was a man in every sense — a loyal friend, a terrible foe, given much to laughter yet capable of ferocious anger, a drinker of enormous capacity, a trencherman of not indiscriminate tastes, a swordsman and a horseman without peer, a sage in the ways of men and history, a lover at once tender and savage. Count Brass, with his rolling, warm voice and his rich vitality, could not help but be a legend, for if the man was exceptional, then so were his deeds.

Count Brass stroked the head of his horse, rubbing his gauntlet between the animal's sharp, spiral horns and looking to the south, where the sea and sky met far away. The horse grunted with pleasure, and Count Brass smiled, leaned back in his saddle, and flicked the reins to make the horse descend the hill and head along the secret marsh path toward the northern towers beyond the horizon.

The sky was darkening when he reached the first tower and saw its guardian, an armoured silhouette against the skyline, keeping his vigil. Though no attack had been made on Kamarg since Count Brass had come to replace the former, corrupt Lord Guardian, there was now some slight danger that roaming armies (those whom the Dark Empire of the west had defeated) might wander into the domain looking for towns and villages to loot. The guardian, like all his fellows, was equipped with a flame-lance of baroque design, a sword four feet long, a tamed riding flamingo tethered to one side of the battlements, and a heliograph device to signal information to nearby towers. There were other weapons in the towers, weapons the count himself had had built and installed, but the guardians knew only their method of operation; they had never seen them in action. Count Brass had said that they were more powerful than any weapons possessed even by the Dark Empire of Granbretan, and his men believed him and were a little wary of the strange machines.

The guardian turned as Count Brass approached the tower. The man's face was almost hidden by his black iron helmet, which curved around his cheeks and over his nose. His body was swathed in a heavy leather cloak. He saluted, raising his arm high.

Count Brass raised his own arm. "Is all well, guardian?"

"All well, my lord." The guardian shifted his grip on his flame-lance and turned up the cowl of his cloak as the first drops of rain began to fall. "Save for the weather."

Count Brass laughed. "Wait for the mistral and then complain." He guided his horse away from the tower, making for the next.

The mistral was the cold, fierce wind that whipped across Kamarg for months on end, its wild keening a continuous sound until spring. Count Brass loved to ride through it when it was at its height, the force of it lashing at his face and turning his bronze tan to a glowing red.

Now the rain splashed down on his armour, and he reached behind his saddle for his cloak, tugging it about his shoulders and raising the hood. Everywhere through the darkening day reeds bent in the breeze-borne rain, and there was a patter of water on water as the heavy drops splashed into the lagoons, sending out ceaseless ripples. Above, the clouds banked blacker, threatening to release a considerable weight, and Count Brass decided he would forego the rest of his inspection until the next day and instead return to his castle at Aigues-Mortes, a good four hours' ride through the twisting marsh paths.

He urged the horse back the way they had come, knowing that the beast would find the paths by instinct. As he rode, the rain fell faster, making his cloak sodden. The night closed in rapidly until all that could be seen was a solid wall of blackness broken only by the silver traceries of rain. The horse moved more slowly but did not pause. Count Brass could smell its wet hide and promised it special treatment by the grooms when they reached Aigues-Mortes. He brushed water from its mane with his gloved hand and tried to peer ahead, but could see only the reeds immediately around him, hear only the occasional maniacal cackle of a mallard, flapping across a lagoon pursued by a water-fox or an otter. Sometimes he thought he saw a dark shape overhead and felt the swish of a swooping flamingo making for its communal nest or recognized the squawk of a moorhen battling for its life with an owl. Once, he caught a flash of white in the darkness and listened to the blundering passage of a nearby herd of white bulls as they made for firmer land to sleep; and he noticed the sound, a little later, of a marsh-bear stalking the herd, his breath whiffling, his feet making only the slightest noise as he carefully padded across the quaking surface of the mud. All these sounds were familiar to Count Brass and did not alarm him.

Even when he heard the high-pitched whinny of frightened horses and heard their hoofbeats in the distance he was not unduly perturbed until his own horse stopped dead and moved uncertainly. The horses were coming directly toward him, charging down the narrow causeway in panic. Now Count Brass could see the leading stallion, its eyes rolling in fear, its nostrils flaring and snorting.

Count Brass yelled and waved his arms, hoping to divert the stallion, but it was too panic-stricken to heed him. There was nothing else to do. Count Brass yanked at the reins of his mount and sent it into the marsh, hoping desperately that the ground would be firm enough to hold them at least until the herd had passed. The horse stumbled into the reeds, its hooves seeking purchase in the soft mud; then it had plunged into water and Count Brass saw spray fly and felt a wave hit his face, and the horse was swimming as best it could through the cold lagoon, bravely carrying its armoured burden.

The herd had soon thundered past. Count Brass puzzled over what had panicked them so, for the wild horned horses of Kamarg were not easily disturbed. Then, as he guided his horse back toward the path, there came a sound that immediately explained the commotion and sent his hand to the hilt of his sword.

It was a slithering sound, a slobbering sound; the sound of a baragoon — the marsh gibberer. Few of the monsters were left now. They had been the creations of the former Guardian, who had used them to terrorize the people of Kamarg before Count Brass came. Count Brass and his men had all but destroyed the race, but those which remained had learned to hunt by night and avoid large numbers of men at all costs.

The baragoon had once been men themselves, before they had been taken as slaves to the former Guardian's sorcerous laboratories and there transformed. Now they were monsters eight feet high and enormously broad, bile-coloured and slithering on their bellies through the marshlands; they rose only to leap upon and rend their prey with their steel-hard talons. When they did, on occasion, have the good fortune to find a man alone they would take slow vengeance, delighting in eating a man's limbs before his eyes.

As his horse regained the marsh path, Count Brass saw the baragoon ahead, smelled its stench, and coughed on the odour. His huge broadsword was now in his hand.

The baragoon had heard him and paused.

Count Brass dismounted and stood between his horse and the monster. He gripped his broadsword in both hands and walked, stiff-legged in his armour of brass, toward the baragoon.

Instantly it began to gibber in a shrill, repulsive voice, raising itself up and flailing with its talons in an effort to terrify the count. To Count Brass the apparition was not unduly horrific; he had seen much worse in his time. But he knew that his chances against the beast were slim, since the baragoon could see in the dark and the marsh was its natural environment. Count Brass would have to use cunning.

"You ill-smelling foulness!" (He spoke in an almost jocular tone.) "I am Count Brass, the enemy of your race. It was I who destroyed your evil kin and it is thanks to me that you have so few brothers and sisters these days. Do you miss them? Would you join them?"

The baragoon's gibbering shout of rage was loud but not without a hint of uncertainty. It shuffled its bulk but did not move toward the count.

Count Brass laughed. "Well, cowardly creation of sorcery — what's your answer?"

The monster opened its mouth and tried to frame a few words with its misshapen lips, but little emerged that could be recognized as human speech. Its eyes now did not meet Count Brass's.

Casually, Count Brass dug his great sword into the ground and rested his gauntleted hands upon the cross-piece. "I see you are ashamed of terrorizing the horses I protect, and I am in good humour, so I will pity you. Go now and I'll let you live a few more days. Stay, and you die this hour."

He spoke with such assurance that the beast dropped back to the ground, though it did not retreat. The count lifted up his sword and walked impatiently forward. He wrinkled his nose against the stench of the monster, paused, and waved the thing away from him. "Into the swamp, into the slime where you belong! I am in a merciful mood tonight."

The baragoon's wet mouth snarled, but still he hesitated.

Count Brass frowned a little, judging his moment, for he had known the baragoon would not retreat so easily. He lifted his sword. "Will this be your fate?"

The baragoon began to rise on its hind legs, but Count Brass's timing was exactly right. He was already swinging the heavy blade into the monster's neck.

The thing struck out with both taloned hands, its gibbering cry a mixture of hatred and terror. There was a metallic squeal as the talons scored gashes in the count's armour, sending him staggering backward. The monster's mouth opened and closed an inch from the count's face, its huge black eyes seeming to consume him with their rage. He staggered back, taking his sword with him. It came free. He regained his footing and struck again.

Black blood pumped from the wound, drenching him. There was another terrible cry from the beast, and its hands went to its head, trying desperately to hold it in place. Then the baragoon's head flopped half off its shoulders, blood pumped again, and the body fell.

Count Brass stood stock still, panting heavily, staring with grim satisfaction at the corpse. He wiped the creature's blood fastidiously from him, smoothed his heavy moustache with the back of his hand, and congratulated himself that he appeared to have lost none of his guile or his skill. He had planned every moment of the encounter, intending from the first to kill the baragoon. He had kept the creature bewildered until he could strike. He saw no wrong in deceiving it. If he had given the monster a fair fight, it was likely that he, and not the baragoon, would now be lying headless in the mud.

Count Brass took a deep breath of the cold air and moved forward. With some effort he managed to dislodge the dead baragoon with his booted foot, sending it slithering into the marsh.

Then Count Brass remounted his horned horse and rode back to Aigues-Mortes without further incident.

T W O

Y I S S E L D A   A N D   B O W G E N T L E

Count Brass had led armies in almost every famous battle of his day; he had been the power behind the thrones of half the rulers of Europe, a maker and a destroyer of kings and princes. He was a master of intrigue, a man whose advice was sought in any affair involving political struggle. He had been, in truth, a mercenary; but he had been a mercenary with an ideal, and the ideal had been to set the continent of Europe toward unification and peace. Thus he had, from preference, leagued himself with any force he judged capable of making some contribution to this cause. Many a time he had refused the offer to rule an empire, knowing that this was an age when a man could make an empire in five years and lose it in six months, for history was still in a state of flux and would not settle in the count's lifetime. He sought only to guide history a little in the course he thought best.

Tiring of wars, of intrigue, and even, to some extent, of ideals, the old hero had eventually accepted the offer of the people of Kamarg to become their Lord Guardian.

That ancient land of marshes and lagoons lay close to the coast of the Mediterranean. It had once been part of the nation called France, but France was now two dozen dukedoms with as many grandiose names. Kamarg, with its wide, faded skies of orange, yellow, red, and purple, its relics of the dim past, its barely changing customs and rituals, had appealed to the old count and he had set himself the task of making his adopted land secure.

In his travels in all the Courts of Europe, he had discovered many secrets, and thus the great, gloomy towers that ringed the borders of Kamarg now protected the territory with more potent, less-recognizable weaponry than broadswords or flame-lances.

On the southern borders, the marshes gradually gave way to sea, and sometimes ships stopped at the little ports, though travelers rarely disembarked.

This was because of Kamarg's terrain. The wild landscapes were treacherous to those not familiar with them, and the marsh roads were hard to find; also, mountain ranges flanked its three sides on land. The man wishing to head inland disembarked farther east and took a boat up the Rhone. So Kamarg received little news from the outside world, and what it did receive was usually stale.

This was one of the reasons why Count Brass had settled there. He enjoyed the sense of isolation; he had been too long involved with worldly affairs for even the most sensational news to interest him much. In his youth he had commanded armies in the wars that constantly raged across Europe. Now, however, he was tired of all conflict and refused all requests for aid or advice that reached him, no matter what inducement was offered.

In the west lay the island empire of Granbretan, the only nation with any real political stability, with her half-insane science and her ambitions of conquest. Having built the tall, curved bridge of silver that spanned thirty miles of sea, the empire was bent on increasing her territories by means of her black wisdom and her war machines like the brazen ornithopters that had a range of more than a hundred miles. But even the encroachment of the Dark Empire into the mainland of Europe did not greatly disturb Count Brass; it was a law of history, he believed, that such things must happen, and he saw the ultimate benefits that could result from a force, no matter how cruel, capable of uniting all the warring states into one nation.

Count Brass's philosophy was the philosophy of experience, the philosophy of a man of the world rather than a scholar, and he saw no reason to doubt it, while Kamarg, his sole responsibility, was strong enough to resist even the full might of Granbretan.

Having nothing, himself, to fear from Granbretan, he watched with a certain remote admiration the cruel and efficient manner in which the nation spread her shadow farther and farther across Europe with every year that passed.

Across Scandia and all the nations of the North the shadow fell, along a line marked by famous cities: Parye, Munchein, Wien, Krahkov, Kerninsburg (itself a foothold in the mysterious land of Muskovia). A great semicircle of power in the main continental land mass; a semicircle that grew wider almost every day and must soon touch the northernmost princedoms of Italia, Magyaria, and Slavia. Soon, Count Brass guessed, the Dark Empire's power would stretch from the Norwegian Sea to the Mediterranean, and only Kamarg would not be under its sway. It was partly with this knowledge in mind that he had accepted the Lord Guardianship of the territory when its previous Guardian, a corrupt and spurious sorcerer from the land of the Bulgars, had been torn to pieces by the native guardians whom he had commanded.

Count Brass had made Kamarg secure from attack from outside and from menace from within. There were few baragoons left to terrorize the people of the many small villages, and other terrors had been dealt with also.

Now the count dwelt in his warm castle at Aigues-Mortes, enjoying the simple, rural pleasures of the land, while the people were, for the first time in many years, free from anxiety.

The castle, known as Castle Brass, had been built some centuries before on what had then been an artificial pyramid rising high above the centre of the town. But now the pyramid was hidden by earth in which had been planted grass and gardens for flowers, vines, and vegetables in a series of terraces. Here there were well-kept lawns on which the children of the castle could play or adults stroll, there were the grapevines that gave the best wine in Kamarg, and farther down grew rows of haricots and patches of potatoes, cauliflowers, carrots, lettuce, and many other common vegetables, as well as more exotic ones like the giant pumpkin-tomatoes, celery trees, and sweet ambrogines. There were also fruit trees and bushes that supplied the castle through most of the seasons.

The castle was built of the same white stone as the houses of the town. It had windows of thick glass (much of it painted fancifully) and ornate towers and battlements of delicate workmanship. From its highest turrets it was possible to see most of the territory it protected, and it was so designed that when the mistral came an arrangement of vents, pulleys, and little doors could be operated and the castle would sing so that its music, like that of an organ, could be heard for miles on the wind.

The castle looked down on the red roofs of the town and at the bullring beyond, which had originally been built, it was said, many thousands of years ago by the Romanians.

Count Brass rode his weary horse up the winding road to the castle and hallooed to the guards to open the gate. The rain was easing off, but the night was cold and the count was eager to reach his fireside. He rode through the great iron gates and into the courtyard, where a groom took his horse. Then he plodded up the steps, through the doors of the castle, down a short passage, and into the main hall.

There, a huge fire roared in the grate, and beside it, in deep, padded armchairs, sat his daughter, Yisselda, and his old friend Bowgentle. They rose as he entered, and Yisselda stood on tiptoe to kiss his cheek, while Bowgentle stood by smiling.

"You look as if you could do with some hot food and a change into something warmer than armour," said Bowgentle, tugging at a bellrope. "I'll see to it."

Count Brass nodded gratefully and went to stand by the fire, tugging off his helmet and placing it with a clank on the mantel. Yisselda was already kneeling at his feet, tugging at the straps of his greaves. She was a beautiful girl of nineteen, with soft rose-gold skin and fair hair that was not quite blonde and not quite auburn but of a colour lovelier than both. She was dressed in a flowing gown of flame-orange that made her resemble a fire sprite as she moved with graceful swiftness to carry the greaves to the servant who now stood by with a change of clothes for her father.

Another servant helped Count Brass shed his breastplate, backplate, and other parts of his armour, and soon he was pulling on soft, loose trousers and shirt of white wool and wrapping a linen gown over that.

A small table, heavy with steaks of local beef, potatoes, salad, and a delicious thick sauce, was brought up to the fire, together with a flagon of mulled wine. Count Brass sat down with a sigh and began to eat.

Bowgentle stood by the fire watching him, while Yisselda curled up in the chair opposite and waited until he had taken the edge off his appetite.

"Well, my lord," said she with a smile, "how went the day? Is all our land secure?"

Count Brass nodded with mock gravity. "It would seem so, my lady, though I was not able to visit any of the northern towers but one. The rain came on, and I decided to return home." He told them about his encounter with the baragoon. Yisselda listened with wide eyes while Bowgentle looked somewhat grave, his kind, ascetic face bowed and his lips pursed. The famous philosopher-poet was not always approving of his friend's exploits and seemed to think that Count Brass brought such adventures upon himself.

"You'll recollect," said Bowgentle when the count had finished, "that I advised you this morning to travel with von Villach and some of the others." Von Villach was the count's chief lieutenant, a loyal old soldier who had been with him through most of his earlier exploits.

Count Brass laughed up at his dour-faced friend. "Von Villach? He's getting old and slow, and it would not be a kindness to take him out in this weather!"

Bowgentle smiled a little bleakly. "He's a year or two younger than yourself, Count..."

"Possibly, but could he defeat a baragoon single-handed?"

"That is not the point," Bowgentle continued firmly. "If you traveled with him and a party of men-at-arms you would not need to encounter a baragoon at all."

Count Brass waved a hand, dismissing the discussion. "I have to keep in practice; otherwise, I might become as moribund as von Villach."

"You have a responsibility to the people here, Father," Yisselda put in quietly. "If you were killed..."

"I shall not be killed!" The count smiled scornfully, as if death were something that only others suffered. In the firelight his head resembled the war mask of some ancient barbarian tribe, cast in metal, and it did seem in some way imperishable.

Yisselda shrugged. She had most of her father's qualities of character, including the conviction that there was little point indulging in arguments with such stubborn folk as Count Brass. Bowgentle had once written of her in a private poem, "She is like silk, both strong and soft", and looking at them now he noticed with quiet affection how the expression of one was reflected in the other.

Bowgentle changed the subject. "I heard today that Granbretan took the province of Köln not six months past," he said. "Their conquests spread like a plague."

"A healthy enough plague," Count Brass replied, settling back in his chair. "At least they establish order."

"Political order, perhaps," Bowgentle said with some fire, "but scarcely spiritual or moral. Their cruelty is without precedent. They are insane. Their souls are sick with a love for all that is evil and a hatred for all that is noble."

Count Brass stroked his moustache. "Such wickedness has existed before. Why, the Bulgar sorcerer who preceded me here was quite as evil as they."

"The Bulgar was an individual. So were the Marquis of Pesht, Roldar Nikolayeff, and their kind. But they were exceptions, and in almost every case the people they led revolted against them and destroyed them in time. But the Dark Empire is a *nation* of such individuals, and such actions as they commit are seen as natural. In Köln their sport was to crucify every girlchild in the city, make eunuchs of the boys, and have all adults who would save their lives perform lewd displays in the streets. That is no natural cruelty, Count, and was by no means their worst. Their entertainment is to debase all humanity."

"Such stories are exaggerated, my friend. You should realize that. Why, I myself have been accused of —"

"From all I hear," Bowgentle interrupted, "the rumours are not an exaggeration of the truth but a simplification. If their public activities are so terrible, what must their private delights be like?"

Yisselda shuddered. "I can't bear to think…"

"Exactly," Bowgentle said, turning to face her. "And few can bear to repeat what they have witnessed. The order they bring is superficial, the chaos they bring destroys men's souls."

Count Brass shrugged his broad shoulders. "Whatever they do, it is a temporary thing. The unification they force on the world is permanent, mark my words."

Bowgentle folded his arms across his black-clad chest. "The price is too heavy, Count Brass."

"No price is too heavy! What will you have? The princedoms of Europe dividing into smaller and smaller segments, war a constant factor in the life of the common man? Today few men can ever know peace of mind from cradle to grave. Things change and change again. At least Granbretan offers consistency!"

"And terror? I cannot agree with you, my friend."

Count Brass poured himself a goblet of wine, drank it down, and yawned a little. "You take these immediate events too seriously Bowgentle. If you had had my experience, you would realize that all such evil soon passes. A hundred years will see Granbretan a most upright and moral nation." Count Brass winked at his daughter, but she did not smile in return, seeming to agree with Bowgentle.

"Their sickness is too ingrained for a hundred years to cure it. That can be told from their appearance alone. Those jeweled beast-masks that they never doff, those grotesque clothes they wear in even the most extreme heat, their stance, their way of moving — all these things show them to be what they are. They are insane by heredity, and their progeny will inherit that insanity." Bowgentle struck his hand against a mantel pillar. "Our passivity is acquiescence in their deeds. We should —"

Count Brass rose from his chair. "We should go to our beds and sleep, my friend. Tomorrow we must appear at the bullring for the beginning of the festivities."

He nodded to Bowgentle, kissed his daughter lightly on the forehead, and left the hall.

T H R E E

B A R O N M E L I A D U S

At this season, the people of Kamarg began their great festival, the summer's work being over. Flowers covered the houses, the people wore clothes of richly embroidered silk and linen, young bulls charged through the streets at will, and the guardians paraded in all their martial finery. In the afternoons the bull contests took place in the ancient stone amphitheatre on the edge of the town.

The seats of the amphitheatre were of granite, arranged in tiers. Close to the steep wall of the ring itself, on the south side, was a covered area consisting of carved pillars and a red slate roof. This was hung with curtains of dark brown and scarlet. Within it sat Count Brass; his daughter, Yisselda; Bowgentle, and old von Villach.

From their box, Count Brass and his companions could see almost the whole of the amphitheatre as it began to fill, could hear the excited conversation and the thumps and snorts of the bulls behind the barricades.

Soon a fanfare sounded from the group of six guardians in plumed helmets and sky-blue cloaks on the far side of the amphitheatre. Their bronze trumpets echoed the noise of the bulls and the cheering crowd. Count Brass stepped forward.

The cheering grew louder as he appeared, smiling to the crowd and raising his hand in greeting. When the din had quieted, he began the traditional speech that would open the festival.

"Ancient people of Kamarg who were preserved by Fate from the blight of the Tragic Millennium; you who were given life, celebrate life today. You, whose ancestors were saved by the fierce mistral that cleansed the skies of the poisons that brought others death and malformation, give thanks in this festival for the coming of the Life Wind!"

Again the cheering broke out, and the fanfare blew for a second time. Then into the ring broke twelve huge bulls. They stampeded round and round the arena, tails high, horns gleaming, nostrils dilated and red eyes shining. These were the prime fighting bulls of Kamarg, trained the year through for their performance today, when they would be matched against unarmed men who would try to snatch the several garlands that had been wound around their throats and horns.

Next, mounted guardians galloped out, waving to the crowd, and herded the bulls back into the enclosure under the amphitheatre.

When, with some difficulty, the guardians had got every bull into the enclosure, out rode the master of ceremonies, clad in a rainbow cloak, broad-brimmed hat of bright blue, and a golden megaphone through which he would announce the first contest.

Amplified by both the megaphone and the walls of the amphitheatre, the man's voice almost resembled the great roar of an angry bull. He announced first the name of the bull — Cornerouge of Aigues-Mortes, owned by Pons Yachar, the famous bull breeder — and then the name of the principal toreador, Mahtan Just of Arles. The master of ceremonies wheeled his horse about and disappeared. Almost at once, Cornerouge appeared from below the amphitheatre, his huge horns digging at the air, the scarlet ribbons that decorated them flying in the strong breeze.

Cornerouge was a huge bull, standing over five feet high. His tail lashed from side to side like a lion's; his red eyes glared at the shouting crowd that honoured him. Flowers were thrown into the ring and fell on his broad white back. He turned swiftly, pawing at the dust of the arena, trampling the flowers.

Then, lightly, unostentatiously, a slight, stocky figure appeared, dressed in a black cloak lined with scarlet silk, tight black doublet and trousers decorated with gold, knee-high boots of black leather, embellished with silver. His face was swarthy, young, alert. He doffed his wide-brimmed hat to the crowd, pirouetted, and faced Cornerouge. Though barely twenty, Mahtan Just had already distinguished himself in three previous festivals. Now the women threw flowers and he gallantly acknowledged them, blowing kisses even as he advanced toward the snorting bull and drew off his cloak in a graceful movement, displaying the red lining to Cornerouge, who took a few dancing steps forward, snorted again, and lowered his horns.

The bull charged.

Mahtan Just stepped aside and one hand reached out to pluck a ribbon from Cornerouge's horn. The crowd cheered and stamped. The bull turned speedily and charged again. Again Just stepped aside at the last possible moment, and again he plucked a ribbon. He held both trophies in his white teeth, and he grinned first at the bull, then at the crowd.

The first two ribbons, high on the bull's horns, were comparatively easy to win, and Just, knowing this, had won them almost casually. Now the lower ribbons must be taken from the horns, and this was much more dangerous.

Count Brass leaned forward in his box, staring admiringly at the toreador. Yisselda smiled. "Isn't he wonderful, Father? Like a dancer!"

"Aye, dancing with death," Bowgentle said with what amounted to self-mocking severity.

Old von Villach leaned back in his seat, appearing bored with the spectacle. It might simply have been that his eyes were not what they had once been and he did not want to admit it.

Now the bull was stampeding straight at Mahtan Just, who stood in its path with his hands on his hips, his cloak dropped in the dust. As the bull was almost upon him, Just leaped high into the air, his body grazing the horns, and somersaulted over Cornerouge, who dug his hooves into the dust and snorted in puzzlement before turning his head at Just's laughing shout from behind him.

But before the bull could move his body, Just had jumped again, this time onto the back and, as the bull bucked madly beneath him, turned his attention to hanging onto one horn and disentangling a ribbon from the other. Just was soon dislodged, flung down to the ground, but he displayed another ribbon in his waving hand, rolled over, and just managed to get to his feet as the bull charged at him.

A tremendous noise broke out from the crowd as it clapped, shouted, and flung a veritable ocean of bright blooms into the ring. Just was now running lightly around the arena, pursued by the bull.

He paused, as if in deliberation, turned gradually on his heel, and seemed surprised to see the bull almost upon him.

Now Just jumped again, but a horn caught his coat and ripped it, sending him off-balance. One hand came down on the bull's back, and he vaulted to the ground but fell badly and rolled as the bull charged.

Just scrambled away, still in control of himself but unable to rise. The bull's head dipped, a horn lashed at the body. Droplets of blood sparkled in the sunlight, and the crowd moaned with a mixture of pity and bloodlust.

"Father!" Yisselda's hand gripped Count Brass's arm. "He'll be killed. Help him!"

Count Brass shook his head, although his body had moved involuntarily toward the ring. "It is his own affair. It is what he risks."

Just's body was now tossed high into the air, arms and legs loose like a rag doll's. Into the ring came the mounted guardians with long lances to goad the bull away from his victim.

But the bull refused to move, standing over Just's still body as a predatory cat might stand over the body of its prey.

Count Brass leaped over the side of the ring almost before he realized what he was doing. He ran forward in his armour of brass, ran at the bull like a metal giant.

The riders pulled their horses aside as Count Brass flung his body at the bull's head, grasping the horns in his great hands. Veins stood out on his ruddy face as he pushed the bull gradually back.

Then the head moved, and Count Brass's feet left the ground, but his hands kept their grip and he shifted his weight to one side, bearing the bull's head back so that gradually it seemed to bow.

There was silence everywhere. From the box, Yisselda, Bowgentle, and von Villach leaned forward, their faces pale. All in the amphitheatre were tense as Count Brass slowly exerted his strength.

Cornerouge's knees shook. He snorted and bellowed and his body bucked. But Count Brass, trembling with the effort of holding the horns, did not relent. His moustache and hair seemed to bristle, the muscles on his neck bulged and turned red, but gradually the bull weakened, and then slowly it fell to its knees.

Men ran forward to drag the wounded Just from the ring, but still the crowd was silent.

Then, with a great wrench, Count Brass flung Cornerouge over on his side.

The bull lay still, acknowledging its master; acknowledging that it was without question beaten.

Count Brass stepped back and the bull did not move, simply looked up at him through glazed, puzzled eyes, its tail shifting slightly in the dust, its huge chest rising and falling.

Now the cheering began.

Now the cheering rose in volume so that it seemed the whole world would hear it.

Now the crowd rose to its feet and hailed their Lord Guardian with unprecedented acclaim as Mahtan Just staggered forward clutching at his wound and gripped Count Brass's arm for a moment in gratitude.

And in the box Yisselda wept with pride and relief, and unabashed, Bowgentle wiped tears from his own eyes. Only von Villach did not weep, but his head nodded in grim approval of his master's feat.

Count Brass walked back toward the box, smiling up at his daughter and his friends. He gripped the wall and hauled himself back to his place. He laughed with rich enjoyment and waved at the crowd as they cheered him.

Then he raised his hand and addressed them as the cheering died.

"Do not give me the ovation — give it to Mahtan Just. He won the trophies. See" — he opened his palms and displayed them — "I have nothing!" There was laughter. "Let the festival continue." Count Brass sat down.

Bowgentle had recovered his composure. He leaned toward Count Brass. "So, my friend, do you still say you prefer to remain uninvolved in the struggles of others?"

Count Brass smiled at him. "You are indefatigable, Bowgentle. This, surely, was a local affair, was it not?"

"If your dreams of a united continent are still with you, then the affairs of Europe are *local* affairs." Bowgentle stroked his chin. "Are they not?"

Count Brass's expression became serious for an instant. "Perhaps..." he began, but then shook his head and laughed. "Oh, insidious Bowgentle, you still manage to confound me from time to time!"

But later, when they left the box and made their way back to the castle, Count Brass was frowning.

As Count Brass and his retinue rode into the castle courtyard, a man-at-arms ran forward, his pointing arm indicating an ornate carriage and a group of black, plumed stallions with saddles of unfamiliar workmanship, which the grooms were at that moment removing.

"Sire," the man-at-arms breathed, "there have come visitors to our castle while you were at the arena. Noble visitors, though I know not if you'll welcome them."

Count Brass looked hard at the carriage. It was of beaten metal, of dark gold, steel, and copper, inlaid with mother-of-pearl, silver, and onyx. It was fashioned to resemble the body of a grotesque beast, with its legs extending into claws, which clutched the wheel shafts. Its head was reptilian, with ruby eyes, hollowed out from above to form a seat for the coachman. On the doors was an elaborate coat of arms displaying many quarterings in which were strange-looking animals, weapons, and symbols of an obscure but disturbing nature. Count Brass recognized the design of the carriage and the coat of arms. The first was the workmanship of the mad smiths of Granbretan; the second was the coat of arms of one of that nation's most powerful and infamous nobles.

"It is Baron Meliadus of Kroiden," Count Brass said as he dismounted. "What business could bring such a great lord to our little province?" He spoke with some irony, but he seemed disturbed. He glanced at Bowgentle as the philosopher-poet came and stood beside him.

"We will treat him courteously, Bowgentle," said the count warningly. "We will show him all Castle Brass's hospitality. We have no quarrel with the Lords of Granbretan."

"Not at this moment, perhaps," said Bowgentle, speaking with evident restraint.

With Yisselda and von Villach behind them, Count Brass and Bowgentle ascended the steps and entered the hall, where they found Baron Meliadus waiting for them alone.

The baron was almost as tall as Count Brass. He was dressed all in gleaming black and dark blue. Even his jeweled animal mask, which covered the whole of his head like a helmet, was of some strange black metal with deep blue sapphires for eyes. The mask was cast in the form of a snarling wolf, with needle-sharp teeth in the open jaws. Standing in the shadows of the hall, his black cloak covering much of his black armour, Baron Meliadus might have been one of the mythical beast-gods that were still worshipped in the lands beyond the Middle Sea. As they entered, he reached up with black-gauntleted hands and removed the mask, revealing a white, heavy face with a well-trimmed black beard and moustache. His hair, too, was black and thick, and his eyes were a pale, strange blue. The baron was apparently unarmed, perhaps as an indication that he came in peace. He bowed low and spoke in a deep, musical voice.

"Greetings, famous Count Brass, and forgive this sudden intrusion. I sent messengers ahead, but they arrived too late to reach you before you left. I am the Baron Meliadus of Kroiden, Grand Constable of the Order of the Wolf, First Chieftain of the Armies under our great King-Emperor Huon..."

Count Brass inclined his head. "I know of your great deeds, Baron Meliadus, and recognized the arms on your carriage. Be welcome. The Castle Brass is yours for as long as you wish to stay. Our fare is simple, I fear, in comparison with the richness I have heard may be sampled at the board of even the lowliest citizen of your mighty Empire."

Baron Meliadus smiled. "Your courtliness and hospitality put those of Granbretan to shame, noble hero. I thank you."

Count Brass introduced his daughter, and the baron advanced to bow low and kiss her hand, evidently impressed by her beauty. To Bowgentle he was courteous, showing familiarity with the poet-philosopher's writings, but in reply Bowgentle's voice shook with the effort of remaining polite. With von Villach, Baron Meliadus reminded him of several famous battles in which the old warrior had distinguished himself, and von Villach was visibly pleased.

For all the fine manners and elaborately embellished statements, there was a certain tension in the hall. Bowgentle was the first to make his excuses, and shortly afterward Yisselda and von Villach discreetly left to let Baron Meliadus discuss whatever business had brought him to Castle Brass. Baron Meliadus's eyes lingered just a little while on the girl as she passed out of the hall.

Wine and refreshments were brought, and the two men settled themselves in heavy, carved armchairs.

Baron Meliadus looked over the brim of his wine cup at Count Brass. "You are a man of the world, my lord," he said. "Indeed, you are that in every sense. So you will appreciate that my visit is fostered by more than an urge to enjoy the sights of a pretty province."

Count Brass smiled a little, liking the baron for his frankness. "Quite so," he agreed, "though for my part, it is an honour to meet so famous a servant of the great King Huon."

"That feeling is shared by myself toward you," Baron Meliadus replied. "You are without doubt the most famous hero in Europe, perhaps the most famous in her history. It is almost alarming to find you are made of flesh, after all, and not metal." He laughed, and Count Brass joined in the laughter.

"I've had my share of luck," Count Brass said. "And fate has been kind to me in seeming to corroborate my judgment. Who is to say whether the age we live in is good for me, or I am good for the age?"

"Your philosophy rivals that of your friend Sir Bowgentle," said Baron Meliadus, "and supports what I have heard of your wisdom and judgment. We in Granbretan pride ourselves on our own abilities in that direction, but we could learn from you, I believe."

"I have only details," Count Brass told him, "but you have the talent to see the general scheme." He tried to guess from Meliadus's face what the man was leading toward, but the face remained bland.

"It is the details we need," Baron Meliadus said, "if our general ambitions are to be realized as swiftly as we should like."

Now Count Brass understood why Baron Meliadus was here, but he did not reveal that; he only looked a little puzzled and politely poured more wine for his guest.

"We have a destiny to rule all Europe," Baron Meliadus said.

"That seems to be your destiny," Count Brass agreed. "And I support, in principle, such an ambition."

"I am glad, Count Brass. We are often misrepresented, and our enemies are many, spreading calumnies across the globe."

"I am not interested in the truth or falsehood of those rumours," Count Brass told him. "It is only your *general* activities I believe in."

"You would not, then, oppose the spread of our Empire?" Baron Meliadus looked at him carefully.

"Only," Count Brass smiled, "in particular. In the particular case of this land I protect, Kamarg."

"You would welcome, then, the security of a treaty of peace between us?"

"I see no need for one. I have the security of my towers."

"Hmmm…" Baron Meliadus glanced at the floor.

"Is that why you came, my lord Baron? To propose a peace treaty? To propose an alliance, even?"

"Of sorts," nodded the baron. "An alliance of sorts."

"I would not oppose or support you in most senses," Count Brass told him. "I would oppose you only if you attacked my lands. I support you only in my attitude that a unifying force is needed in Europe at this time."

HAWKMOON

Baron Meliadus thought for a moment before speaking. "And if that unification were threatened?" he said at length.

Count Brass laughed. "I do not believe it can be. There is none powerful enough to withstand Granbretan now."

Baron Meliadus pursed his lips. "You are right in believing that. Our list of victories becomes almost a bore to us. But the more we conquer, the thinner we spread our forces. If we knew the Courts of Europe as well, for instance, as yourself, we should know better who to trust and who to distrust and thus be able to concentrate our attention on the weaknesses. We have the Grand Duke Ziminon as our governor in Normandia, for instance." Baron Meliadus looked carefully at Count Brass. "Would you say we are wise in our choice? He sought the throne of Normandia when his cousin Jewelard possessed it. Is he content with the throne on our terms?"

"Ziminon, eh?" Count Brass smiled. "I helped defeat him at Rouen."

"I know. But what is your opinion of him?"

Count Brass's smile grew broader as Baron Meliadus's manner became more intense. Now he knew exactly what Granbretan wanted of him. "He is an excellent horseman and has a fascination for women," he said.

"That does not help us know the extent to which we may trust him." Almost impatiently, the baron put his wine cup on the table.

"True," Count Brass agreed. He looked up at the large wall clock that hung over the fireplace. Its golden hands showed eleven o'clock. Its huge pendulum swung slowly back and forth, casting a flickering shadow on the wall. It began to strike. "We go to our beds early in Castle Brass," the count said casually. "We live the lives of country folk, I am afraid." He rose from his chair. "I will have a servant show you to your chambers. Your men have been placed in rooms adjoining the main suite."

A faint shadow clouded Baron Meliadus's face. "Count Brass — we know of your skill in politics, your wisdom, your comprehensive knowledge of all the weaknesses and strengths of the European courts. We wish to make use of that knowledge. In return, we offer riches, power, security..."

"I have all I need of the first two and am assured of the third," Count Brass replied gently as he pulled a bellrope. "You will forgive me if I claim tiredness and a desire to sleep. I have had an exerting afternoon."

"Listen to reason, my lord Count, I beg you." Baron Meliadus was making an effort to appear in good temper.

"I hope you will stay with us for some time, Baron, and be able to tell us all the news."

A servant entered.

"Please show our guest to his chambers," Count Brass told the servant. He bowed to the baron. "Good night, Baron Meliadus. I look forward to seeing you when we break our fast at eight o'clock."

When the baron had left the hall following the servant, Count Brass let some of his amusement show on his face. It was pleasing to know that Granbretan sought his help, but he had no intention of giving it. He hoped he could resist the baron's requests politely, for he had no wish to be on bad terms with the Dark Empire. Besides, he quite liked Baron Meliadus. They seemed to share certain beliefs in common.

F O U R

THE FIGHT AT CASTLE BRASS

Baron Meliadus remained at Castle Brass for a week. After the first night, he succeeded in recovering his composure and never again betrayed any sign of impatience with Count Brass for his persistent refusal to listen to the inducements and requirements of Granbretan.

Perhaps it was not only his mission that kept the baron at Castle Brass, for it was plain that he gave Yisselda much of his attention. With her, in particular, he appeared agreeable and courteous to such an extent that it was plain that Yisselda, unfamiliar with the sophisticated ways of the grand courts, was not unattracted to him.

Count Brass seemed oblivious of this. One morning as they walked in the upper terraces of the castle garden, Bowgentle spoke to his friend.

"Baron Meliadus seems not only interested in seducing you for the cause of Granbretan," he said. "He has another kind of seduction in mind, if I'm not mistaken."

"Eh?" Count Brass turned from the contemplation of the vines on the terrace below. "What else is he after?"

"Your daughter," Bowgentle answered softly.

"Come now, Bowgentle!" The count laughed. "You see malice and evil intention in the man's every action. He is a gentleman, a noble. And besides, he wants something from me. He would not let the ambition be jeopardized by a flirtation. I think you do Baron Meliadus an injustice. I've grown rather to like him."

"Then it is high time you involved yourself in politics again, my lord," said Bowgentle with some fire, but all the time speaking softly, "for it would seem your judgment is not as sharp as it was!"

Count Brass shrugged. "Be that as it may, I think you are becoming a nervous old woman, my friend. Baron Meliadus has behaved with decorum since his arrival. Admittedly, I think he wastes his time here and wish he would decide to leave soon, but if he has intentions toward my daughter I have seen no sign of it. He might wish to marry her, certainly, in order to make a blood tie between myself and Granbretan, but Yisselda would not consent to the idea, and neither would I."

"What if Yisselda loved Baron Meliadus and he felt passion for her?"

"How could she love Baron Meliadus?"

"She sees few men as handsome and sophisticated in Kamarg."

"Hmm," grunted the count dismissively. "If she loved the baron, she'd tell me, wouldn't she? I'll believe your tale when I hear it confirmed from Yisselda's lips!"

Bowgentle wondered to himself if the count's refusal to see the truth were sponsored by a secret wish to know nothing at all of the character of those who ruled Granbretan or whether it was simply a father's common inability to see in his child what was perfectly evident to others. Bowgentle decided to keep a careful eye on both Baron Meliadus and Yisselda in future. He could not believe that the count's judgment was correct in the case of the man who had caused the Massacre of Liege, who had given the order for the Sack of Sahbruck, and whose perverse appetites were the horror of every whispering scullion from North Cape to Tunis. As he had said, the count had lived too long in the country, breathing the clean rural air. Now he could not recognize the stink of corruption even when he smelled it.

Though Count Brass was reticent in his conversations with Baron Meliadus, the Granbretanian seemed willing to tell him much. It appeared that even where Granbretan did not rule, there were discontented nobles and peasants willing to make secret treaties with the agents of the Dark Empire, in promise of power under the King-Emperor if they helped destroy those who opposed Granbretan. And Granbretan's ambitions, it seemed, extended even into Asia. Beyond the Mediterranean there were well-established groups ready to support the Dark Empire when the time came for attack. Count Brass's admiration for the tactical skills of the Empire increased every day.

"Within twenty years," said Baron Meliadus, "the whole of Europe will be ours. Within thirty, all Arabia and the countries that surround it. Within fifty, we shall have the strength to attack that mysterious land on our maps that is called Asiacommunista…"

"An ancient and romantic name," smiled Count Brass, "full of great sorceries, it's said. Is that not where the Runestaff lies?"

"Aye, that's the tale — that it stands on the tallest mountain in the world, where snow swirls and winds howl constantly, protected by hairy men of incredible wisdom and age, who are ten feet high and have the faces of apes." Baron Meliadus smiled. "But there are many places that the Runestaff is said to be — in Amarehk, even."

Count Brass nodded. "Ah, Amarehk — do you include that land in your dreams of empire?" Amarehk was the great continent said to lie across the water to the west, ruled by beings of almost godlike powers. They were reputed to lead lives that were abstracted, tranquil, and remote. Theirs, so the tales went, was the civilization that altogether missed the effects of the Tragic Millennium, when the rest of the world collapsed into various degrees of ruin. Count Brass had jested when he mentioned Amarehk, but Baron Meliadus looked at him sidewise, a gleam in his pale eye.

"Why not?" he said. "I would storm the walls of heaven if I found them."

Disturbed, Count Brass left him shortly thereafter, for the first time wondering if his resolution to remain neutral were as well advised as he'd believed.

Yisselda, though as intelligent as her father, lacked both his experience and his normally good judgment of character. She found even the baron's infamous reputation attractive and at the same time could not believe that all the stories about him were true. For when he spoke to her in his soft, cultivated voice, flattering her beauty and grace, she thought she saw a man of gentle temperament forced to appear grim and ruthless by the conventions of his office and his role in history.

Now, for the third time since his arrival, she slipped at night from her bedchamber to keep an assignation with him in the west tower, which had been unused since the bloody death there of the previous Lord Guardian.

The meetings had been innocent enough — a clasping of her hand, a brushing of her lips with his, the whispering of love words, talk of marriage. Though still unsure of the latter suggestion (for she loved her father and felt it would hurt him deeply if she married Baron Meliadus), she could not resist the attention the baron gave her. Even she was not sure that it was love she felt for him, but she welcomed the sense of adventure and excitement that these meetings gave her.

On this particular night, as she sped light-footed through the gloomy corridors, she did not know that she was being followed. Behind her came a figure in a black cloak, a long dagger in a leather sheath in its right hand.

Heart beating, red lips parted slightly in a half smile, Yisselda ran up the winding steps of the tower until she came to the little turret room where the baron already awaited her.

He bowed low, then caught her in his arms, caressing her soft flesh through the thin, silken nightgown she wore. His kiss was firmer this time, almost brutal, and her breathing became deeper as she returned it, clutching at his broad, leather-clad back. Now his hand moved down to her waist, and then to her thigh, and for a moment she pressed her body closer to his and then tried to tug away as she felt a growing, unfamiliar panic.

He held on to her, panting. A beam of moonlight entered the narrow window and fell across his face, revealing frowning brows and heated eyes.

"Yisselda, you must marry me. Tonight we can leave Castle Brass and be beyond the towers by tomorrow. Your father would not dare follow us to Granbretan.

"My father would dare anything," she said with quiet conviction, "but I feel, my lord, that I have no wish to put him to the trouble."

"What do you mean?"

"I mean that I would not marry without his consent."

"Would he give it?"

"I believe not."

"Then…"

She tried to tug away completely from him, but his strong hands gripped her arms. Now she was frightened, wondering how her former passion could turn so swiftly into fear. "I must go now."

"No! Yisselda, I am not used to my will being opposed. First your obstinate father refuses what I ask — now you! I'd kill you rather than let you leave without promising to come with me to Granbretan!" He pulled her toward him, his lips forcing a kiss from her. She moaned as she tried to resist.

Then the dark, cloaked figure entered the chamber, unsheathing the long dagger from its case. The steel shone in the moonlight, and Baron Meliadus glared at the intruder but did not relinquish his hold on the girl.

"Let her go," said the dark figure, "for if you do not I'll forsake all principle and slay you now."

"Bowgentle!" Yisselda sobbed. "Run for my father — you are not strong enough to fight him!"

Baron Meliadus laughed and threw Yisselda to the corner of the turret room. "Fight? It would not be a fight with you, philosopher — it would be butchery. Stand aside and I'll leave — but I must take the girl."

"Leave alone," Bowgentle replied. "By all means do that, for I have no wish to have your death on my conscience. But Yisselda stays with me."

"She's leaving with me tonight — whether she wills it or no!" Meliadus flung back his own cloak, revealing a short sword high at his waist. "Aside, Sir Bowgentle, for unless you move, I promise that you will not live to write a sonnet about *this* affair!"

Bowgentle stood his ground, dagger held point outward at Baron Meliadus's chest.

The Granbretanian's hand gripped the hilt of the sword and drew it from the scabbard in a blur of movement.

"One last chance, philosopher!"

Bowgentle did not reply. His half-glazed eyes did not blink. Only the hand holding the dagger shook slightly.

Yisselda screamed. The scream was high-pitched and penetrating, echoing through the castle.

Baron Meliadus turned with a grunt of rage, raising the sword.

Bowgentle leaped forward, stabbing clumsily with the dagger, which was deflected by the tough leather the baron wore. Meliadus turned with a laugh of contempt, his sword struck twice at Bowgentle, once at his head and once at his body, and the philosopher-poet fell to the flagstones, his blood staining the floor. Again Yisselda screamed, this time in terror and pity for her father's friend. Baron Meliadus stooped and grabbed the struggling girl by her arm, twisted it so that she gasped, and flung her over his shoulder. Then he left the turret room and began to descend the steps swiftly.

He had to cross the main hall to get to his own quarters, and as he entered it, there came a roar from the other side. By the light of the dying fire he saw Count Brass, clad only in a loose robe, his great broadsword in his hands, blocking the door through which Baron Meliadus meant to go.

"Father!" Yisselda cried, and then the Granbretanian had flung her to one side and brandished his short sword at Count Brass.

"So Bowgentle was right," Count Brass rumbled. "You abuse my hospitality, Baron."

"I want your daughter. She loves me."

"So it seems." Count Brass glanced at Yisselda as she climbed to her feet, sobbing. "Defend yourself, Baron."

Baron Meliadus frowned. "You have a broadsword — my blade's little better than a bodkin. Besides, I've no wish to fight a man of your years. We can make peace, surely…"

"Father — he has killed Bowgentle!"

Count Brass trembled with rage at this. He strode to the wall where a rack of swords was placed, took the largest and best balanced from the rack, and flung it to Baron Meliadus. It clattered on the flagstones. Meliadus dropped his own blade and picked up the broadsword. Now he had the advantage, for he wore stout leather and the count wore only linen.

Count Brass advanced, the broadsword raised, then swung at Baron Meliadus, who met the swipe with a parry. Like men hewing at a great tree, they swung the heavy blades this way and that. The clangour rang through the hall and brought servants scurrying, as well as the baron's men-at-arms, who looked disconcerted and uncertain what to do. By that time, von Villach and his men had arrived; the Granbretanians saw that they were heavily outnumbered and decided to do nothing.

THE JEWEL IN THE SKULL

Sparks scattered into the darkness of the hall as the two big men dueled, the broadswords rising and falling, swinging this way and that, every stroke parried with masterly skill. Sweat covered both faces as the swords swung; both chests heaved with the exertion as they fenced back and forth across the hall.

Now Baron Meliadus cut at Count Brass's shoulder but succeeded only in grazing it. Next Count Brass's sword fell on Baron Meliadus's side but was blocked by the thick leather of the baron's doublet. There was a series of swift strokes in which it seemed both men must be cut to pieces, but when they stepped back and resumed their guard all Count Brass had was a light cut across his forehead and a tear in his gown, and Baron Meliadus's coat was ripped down the front and one arm of it hung in tatters.

The sound of their panting and the scrape of their feet on the floor blended with the great clash of blades as they met again and again.

Then Count Brass tripped over a small table and fell backwards, legs sprawling, one hand losing its grip on the sword. Baron Meliadus smirked and raised his weapon; Count Brass rolled over, swiped at the baron's legs, brought the man thumping down beside him.

The blades forgotten for the moment, they wrestled over and over on the flagstones, fists battering at one another, lips snarling, swords still attached to them by wrist thongs.

Then Baron Meliadus flung himself backward and jumped up, but Count Brass was up again too. He swung his sword suddenly and knocked the baron's blade with such force that the thong snapped and the sword sailed clear across the hall, where it stuck point first in a wooden pillar and thrummed like a metal organ reed.

Count Brass's eyes showed no pity. They held only an intention to kill Baron Meliadus.

"You slew my true and greatest friend," he growled as he raised his broadsword. Baron Meliadus slowly folded his arms across his chest and waited for the blow, eyes downcast, an almost bored expression on his face.

"You slew Bowgentle, and for that I slay you."

"Count Brass!"

The count hesitated, the sword raised above his head.

The voice was Bowgentle's.

"Count Brass, he did not kill me. The flat of his sword stunned me, and the wound in my chest is by no means mortal." Bowgentle came forward through the crowd, his hand on his wound, a livid bruise on his forehead.

Count Brass sighed. "Thank fate for that, Bowgentle. Nonetheless..." He turned to contemplate Baron Meliadus. "This villain has abused my hospitality, insulted my daughter, injured my friend..."

Baron Meliadus raised his eyes to meet the count's. "Forgive me, Count

Brass. Moved by a passion for the beauty of Yisselda as I was, it clouded my brain, possessed me like a demon. I would not beg when you threatened my life, but now I ask you to understand that only honest, human emotions moved me to do what I did."

Count Brass shook his head. "I cannot forgive you, Baron. I'll listen to your insidious words no longer. You must be gone from Castle Brass within the hour and off my lands by morning, or you and yours will perish."

"You'd risk offending Granbretan?"

Count Brass shrugged. "I do not offend the Dark Empire. If they hear anything like the truth of what passed this night, they will punish you for your mistakes, not come against me for having seen justice done. You have failed in your mission. *You* have offended *me* — not I, Granbretan."

Baron Meliadus said no more but, fuming, left to prepare himself for his journey. Disgraced and enraged, he was soon in his bizarre carriage, and the carriage was rolling through the castle gates before half an hour had passed. He made no farewells.

Count Brass, Yisselda, Bowgentle, and von Villach stood in the courtyard watching him leave.

"You were right, Bowgentle," muttered the count. "Both Yisselda and I were beguiled by the man. I'll have no more emissaries from Granbretan visit Castle Brass."

"You realize that the Dark Empire must be fought, destroyed?" Bowgentle asked hopefully.

"I did not say that. Let it do what it will. *We* will have no further trouble from Granbretan or Baron Meliadus."

"You are wrong," Bowgentle said with conviction.

And in his dark carriage, as it bumped through the night toward the northern borders of Kamarg, Baron Meliadus spoke aloud to himself and swore an oath by the most mysterious and sacred object he knew. He swore by the Runestaff (that lost artifact said to contain all the secrets of destiny) that he would get Count Brass into his power by any means possible, that he would possess Yisselda, and that Kamarg would become one great furnace in which all who inhabited it would perish.

This he swore by the Runestaff, and thus the destiny of Baron Meliadus, Count Brass, Yisselda, the Dark Empire, and all who were now and would be later concerned with the events in Castle Brass was irrevocably decided.

The play was cast, the stage set, the curtain raised.

Now the mummers must enact their destiny.

B O O K T W O

Those who dare swear by the Runestaff must then benefit or suffer from the consequences of the fixed pattern of destiny that they set in motion. Some several such oaths have been sworn in the history of the Runestaff's existence, but none with such vast and terrible results as the mighty oath of vengeance sworn by the Baron Meliadus of Kroiden the year before that aspect of the Champion Eternal, Dorian Hawkmoon von Köln, entered into the pages of this ancient narrative.

— *The High History of the Runestaff*

O N E

D O R I A N   H A W K M O O N

Baron Meliadus returned to Londra, gloomy-towered capital of the Dark Empire, and brooded for almost a year before he settled on his plan. Other affairs of Granbretan occupied him in that time. There were rebellions to put down, examples to be made of newly conquered towns, fresh battles to be planned and fought, puppet governors to be interviewed and placed in power.

Baron Meliadus fulfilled all these responsibilities faithfully and with imagination, but his passion for Yisselda and his hatred of Count Brass were never far from his thoughts. Although he had suffered no ignominy for his failure to win the count to Granbretan's cause, he still felt thwarted. Besides, he was constantly finding problems in which the count could have helped him easily. Whenever such a problem arose, Baron Meliadus's brain became clogged with a dozen different schemes of revenge, but none seemed suited to do everything he required. He must have Yisselda, he must get the count's aid in the affairs of Europe, he must destroy Kamarg as he had sworn. They were incompatible ambitions.

In his tall tower of obsidian, overlooking the blood red River Tayme where barges of bronze and ebony carried cargo from the coast, Baron Meliadus paced his cluttered study with its tapestries of time-faded browns, blacks, and blues, its orreries of precious metal and gemstones, its globes and astrolabes of beaten iron and brass and silver, its furniture of dark, polished wood, and its carpets of deep pile the colours of leaves in autumn.

Around him, on all the walls, on every shelf, in every angle, were his clocks. All were in perfect synchronization, and all struck on the quarter, half, and full hour, many with musical effects. They were of various shapes and sizes, in cases of metal, wood, or certain other, less recognizable substances. They were ornately carved, to the extent, sometimes, that it was virtually impossible to tell the time from them. They had been collected from many parts of Europe and the

Near East, the spoils of a score of conquered provinces. They were what Baron Meliadus loved most among his many possessions. Not only this study, but every room in the great tower, was full of clocks. There was a huge four-faced clock in bronze, onyx, gold, silver, and platinum at the very top of the tower, and when its great bells were struck by life-size figures of naked girls holding hammers, all Londra echoed with the din. The clocks rivaled in variety those of Meliadus's brother-in-law, Taragorm, Master of the Palace of Time, whom Meliadus loathed with a deep attachment as rival for his strange sister's perverse and whimful affections.

Baron Meliadus ceased his pacing and picked up a piece of parchment from his desk. It contained the latest information from the province of Köln, a province that, nearly two years previously, Meliadus had made an example of. It seemed now that too much had been done, for the son of the old Duke of Köln (whom Meliadus had personally disemboweled in the public square of the capital) had raised an army of rebellion and almost succeeded in crushing the occupying forces of Granbretan. Had not speedy reinforcements, in the shape of ornithopters armed with long-range flame-lances, been sent, Köln might have been temporarily taken from the Dark Empire.

But the ornithopters had demolished the forces of the young duke, and he had been made prisoner. He was due soon to arrive in Londra to pleasure the nobles of Granbretan with his sufferings. Here again was a situation where Count Brass might have helped, for before he showed himself in open rebellion, the Duke of Köln had offered himself as a mercenary commander to the Dark Empire and had been accepted, had fought well in the service of Granbretan, at Nürnberg and Ulm, winning the confidence of the Empire, gaining command of a force comprised mainly of soldiers who had once served his father, then turning with them and marching back to Köln to attack the province.

Baron Meliadus frowned, for the young duke had provided an example that others might now follow. Already he was a hero in the German provinces, by all accounts. Few dared oppose the Dark Empire as he had done.

If only Count Brass had agreed…

Suddenly Baron Meliadus began to smile, a scheme seeming to spring instantly and complete into his mind. Perhaps the young Duke of Köln could be used in some way, other than in the entertainment of his peers.

Baron Meliadus put down the parchment and pulled at a bellrope. A girl-slave entered, her naked body rouged all over, and fell on her knees to receive his instructions. (All the baron's slaves were female; he allowed no men into his tower for fear of treachery.) "Take a message to the master of the prison catacombs," he told the girl. "Tell him that Baron Meliadus would interview the prisoner Dorian Hawkmoon von Köln as soon as he arrives there."

"Yes, master." The girl rose and backed from the room, leaving Baron Meliadus staring from his window at the river, a faint smile on his full lips.

Dorian Hawkmoon, bound in chains of gilded iron (as befitted his station in the eyes of the Granbretanians), stumbled down the gangplank from barge to quay, blinking in the evening light and staring around him at the huge, menacing towers of Londra. If he had never before needed proof of the congenital insanity of the inhabitants of the Dark Island, he had, to his mind, full evidence now. There was something unnatural about every line of the architecture, every choice of colour and carving. And yet there was also a sense of great strength about it, of purpose and intelligence. No wonder, he thought, it was hard to fathom the psychology of the people of the Dark Empire, when so much of them was paradox.

A guard, in white leather and wearing the white metal death's-head mask that was uniform to the Order he served, pushed him gently forward. Hawkmoon staggered in spite of the lightness of the pressure, for he had not eaten for almost a week. His brain was at once clouded and abstracted; he was hardly aware of the significance of his circumstances. Since his capture at the Battle of Köln, no-one had spoken to him. He had lain most of the time in the darkness of the ship's bilges, drinking occasionally from the trough of dirty water that had been fixed beside him. He was unshaven, his eyes were glazed, his long, fair hair was matted, and his torn mail and breeches were covered in filth. The chains had chafed his skin so that red sores were prominent on his neck and wrists, but he felt no pain. Indeed, he felt little of anything, moved like a sleepwalker, saw everything as if in a dream.

He took two steps along the quartz quay, staggered, and fell to one knee. The guards, now on either side of him, pulled him up and supported him as he approached a black wall that loomed over the quay. There was a small barred door in the wall, and two soldiers, in ruby-coloured pig masks, stood on either side of it. The Order of the Pig controlled the prisons of Londra. The guards spoke a few words to each other in the grunting secret language of their Order, and one of them laughed, grabbing Hawkmoon's arm, saying nothing to the prisoner but pushing him forward as the other guard swung the barred door inward.

The interior was dark. The door closed behind Hawkmoon, and for a few moments he was alone. Then, in the dim light from the door, he saw a mask; a pig mask, but more elaborate than those of the guards outside. Another similar mask appeared, and then another. Hawkmoon was seized and led through the foul-smelling darkness, led down into the prison catacombs of the Dark Empire, knowing, with little emotion, that his life was over.

At last he heard another door open. He was pushed into a tiny chamber; then he heard the door close and a beam fall into place.

The air in the dungeon was fetid, and there was a film of foulness on flagstones and wall. Hawkmoon lay against the wall and then slid gradually to the floor. Whether he fainted or fell asleep, he could not tell, but his eyes closed and oblivion came.

A week before, he had been the Hero of Köln, a champion against the aggressors, a man of grace and sardonic wit, a warrior of skill. Now, as a matter of course, the men of Granbretan had turned him into an animal — an animal with little will to live. A lesser man might have clung grimly to his humanity, fed from his hatred, schemed escape; but Hawkmoon, having lost all, wanted nothing.

Perhaps he would awake from his trance. If he did, he would be a different man from the one who had fought with such insolent courage at the Battle of Köln.

T W O

T H E   B A R G A I N

Torchlight and the glinting of beast-masks; sneering pig and snarling wolf, red metal and black; mocking eyes, diamond white and sapphire blue. The heavy rustle of cloaks and the sound of whispered conversation.

Hawkmoon sighed weakly and closed his eyes, then opened them again as footsteps came nearer and the wolf bent over him, holding the torch close to his face. The heat was uncomfortable, but Hawkmoon made no effort to move away from it.

Wolf straightened and spoke to pig.

"Pointless speaking to him now. Feed him, wash him. Restore his intelligence a little."

Pig and wolf left, closing the door. Hawkmoon closed his eyes.

When he next awoke, he was being carried through corridors by the light of brands. He was taken into a room lighted by lamps. There was a bed covered in rich furs and silks, food laid out on a carved table, a bath of some shimmering orange metal, full of steaming water, two girl-slaves in attendance.

The chains were stripped from him, then the clothes; then he was picked up again and lowered into the water. It stung his skin as the slaves began to lave him, while a man entered with a razor and began to trim his hair and shave his beard. All this Hawkmoon took passively, staring at the mosaic ceiling with blank eyes. He allowed himself to be dressed in fine, soft linen, with a shirt of silk and breeches of velvet, and gradually, a dim feeling of well-being overcame him. But when they first sat him at the table and pushed fruit into his mouth, his stomach contracted and he retched. So they gave him a little drugged milk, then put him on the bed and left him, save for one slave at the door, watching over him.

Some days passed, and gradually Hawkmoon began to eat, began to appreciate the luxury of his existence. There were books in the room, and the women were his, but he still had little inclination to sample either.

Hawkmoon, whose mind had gone to sleep so soon after his capture, took a long time to awaken, and when at length he did, it was to remember his past life as a dream. He opened a book one day, and the letters looked strange, though he could read them well enough. It was simply that he saw no point in them, no importance in the words and sentences they formed, though the book had been written by a scholar once his favourite philosopher. He shrugged and dropped the book onto a table. One of the girl-slaves, seeing this action, pressed herself against his body and stroked his cheek. Gently, he pushed her aside and went to the bed, lying down with his hands behind his head.

At length, he said, "Why am I here?"

They were the first words he had spoken.

"Oh, my lord Duke, I know not — save that you seem an honoured prisoner."

"A game, I suppose, before the Lords of Granbretan have their sport with me?" Hawkmoon spoke without emotion. His voice was flat but deep. Even the words seemed strange to him as he spoke them. He looked out from his inward-turned eyes at the girl, and she trembled. She had long, blonde hair and was well-shaped; a girl from Scandia by her accent.

"I know nothing, my lord, only that I must please you in any way you desire."

Hawkmoon nodded slightly and glanced about the room. "They prepare me for some torture or display, I would guess," he said to himself.

The room had no windows, but by the quality of the air Hawkmoon judged that they were still underground, probably in the prison catacombs somewhere. He measured the passing of time by the lamps; they seemed to be filled about once a day. He stayed in the room for a fortnight or so before he again saw the wolf who had visited him in his cell.

The door opened without ceremony, and in stepped the tall figure, dressed in black leather from head to foot, with a long sword (black-hilted) in a black leather scabbard. The black wolf mask hid the whole head. From it issued the rich, musical voice he had only half-heard before.

"So, our prisoner seems restored to his former wit and fitness."

The two girl-slaves bowed and withdrew. Hawkmoon rose from the bed on which he had lain most of the time since his arrival. He swung his body off the bed and got to his feet.

"Good. Quite fit, Duke von Köln?"

"Aye." Hawkmoon's voice contained no inflection. He yawned unselfconsciously, decided there was little point in standing after all, and resumed his former position on the bed.

"I take it that you know me," said the wolf, a hint of impatience in his voice.

"No."

"You have not guessed?"

Hawkmoon made no reply.

The wolf moved across the room and stood by the table, which had a huge crystal bowl of fruit on it. His gloved hand picked up a pomegranate, and the wolf-mask bent as if inspecting it. "You *are* fully recovered, my lord?"

"It would seem so," answered Hawkmoon. "I have a great sense of well-being. All my needs are attended to, as, I believe, you ordered. And now, I presume, you intend to make some sport with me?"

"That does not seem to disturb you."

Hawkmoon shrugged. "It will end eventually."

"It could last a lifetime. We of Granbretan are inventive."

"A lifetime is not so long."

"As it happens," the wolf told him, tossing the fruit from hand to hand, "we were thinking of sparing you the discomfort."

Hawkmoon's face showed no expression.

"You are very self-contained, my lord Duke," the wolf continued. "Strangely so, since you live only because of the whim of your enemies — those same enemies who slew your father so disgracefully."

Hawkmoon's brows contracted as if in faint recollection. "I remember that," he said vaguely. "My father. The old Duke."

The wolf threw the pomegranate to the floor and raised the mask. The handsome, black-bearded features were revealed. "It was I, Baron Meliadus of Kroiden, who slew him." There was a goading smile on the full lips.

"Baron Meliadus…? Ah… who slew him?"

"All the manliness has gone from you, my lord," Baron Meliadus murmured. "Or do you seek to deceive us in the hope that you may turn traitor upon us again?"

Hawkmoon pursed his lips. "I am tired," he said.

Meliadus's eyes were puzzled and almost angry. "I killed your father!"

"So you said."

"Well!" Disconcerted, Meliadus turned away and paced toward the door, then wheeled around again. "That is not what I came here to discuss. It seems, however, strange that you should profess no hatred or wish for vengeance against me."

Hawkmoon himself began to feel bored, wishing that Meliadus would leave him in peace. The man's tense manner and his half-hysterical expressions discomfited him rather as the buzzing of a mosquito could be distracting to a man wishing to sleep.

"I feel nothing," Hawkmoon replied, hoping that this would satisfy the intruder.

"You have no spirit left!" Meliadus exclaimed angrily. "No spirit! Defeat and capture have robbed you of it!"

"Perhaps. Now, I am tired…"

"I came to offer you the return of your lands," Meliadus went on. "An entirely autonomous state within our Empire. More than we have ever offered a conquered land before."

Now just a trace of curiosity stirred in Hawkmoon. "Why is that?" he said.

"We wish to strike a bargain with you — to our mutual benefit. We need a man who is crafty and war skilled, as you are" — Baron Meliadus frowned in doubt — "or seemed to be. And we need someone who would be trusted by those who do not trust Granbretan." This was not at all the way Meliadus had intended to present the bargain, but Hawkmoon's strange lack of emotion had disconcerted him. "We wish you to perform an errand for us. In return — your lands."

"I would like to go home," Hawkmoon nodded. "The meadows of my childhood…" He smiled in reminiscence.

Shocked by a display of what he mistook for sentimentality, Baron Meliadus snapped, "What you do when you return — whether you make daisy chains or build castles — is of no interest to us. You will return, however, only if you perform your mission faithfully."

Hawkmoon's introverted eyes glanced up at Meliadus. "You think I have lost my reason, perhaps, my lord?"

"I'm not sure. We have means of discovering that. Our sorcerer-scientists will make certain tests…"

"I am sane, Baron Meliadus. Saner, maybe, than I ever was. You have nothing to fear from me."

Baron Meliadus raised his eyes to the ceiling. "By the Runestaff, will no-one take sides?" He opened the door. "We will find out about *you*, Duke von Köln. You will be sent for later today!"

After Baron Meliadus had left, Hawkmoon continued to lie on the bed. The interview was quickly gone from his mind and only half-remembered when, in two or three hours, pig-masked guards entered the chamber and told him to accompany them.

Hawkmoon was led through many passages, marching steadily upward until they reached a great iron door. One of the guards banged on it with the butt of his flame-lance, and it creaked open to admit fresh air and daylight. Waiting beyond the door was a detachment of guards in purple armour and cloaks, with the purple masks of the Order of the Bull covering their faces. Hawkmoon was handed over to them and, looking about him, saw that he stood in a wide courtyard that but for a gravel path was covered by a fine lawn. A high wall, in which was set a narrow gate, surrounded the lawn, and on it paced guards of the Order of the Pig. Behind the wall jutted the gloomy towers of the city.

Hawkmoon was guided along the path to the gate, through the gate, and into a narrow street where a carriage of gilded ebony, fashioned in the shape of a two-headed horse, awaited him. Into this he climbed, accompanied by two silent guards. The carriage began to move. Through a chink in its curtains, Hawkmoon saw the towers as they passed. It was sunset, and a lurid light suffused the city.

Eventually the carriage stopped. Hawkmoon passively allowed the guards to lead him out of it and saw at once that he had come to the palace of the King-Emperor Huon.

The palace rose, tier upon tier, almost out of sight. Four great towers surmounted it, and these towers glowed with a deep golden light. The palace was decorated with bas-reliefs depicting strange rites, battle scenes, famous episodes in Granbretan's long history, gargoyles, figurines, abstract shapes — the whole a grotesque and fantastic structure that had been built over centuries. Every kind of building material had been used in its construction and then coloured, so that the building shone with a mixture of shades covering the entire spectrum. And there was no order to the placing of the colour, no attempt to match or contrast. One colour flowed into the next, straining the eye, offending the brain. The palace of a madman, overshadowing, in its impression of insanity, the rest of the city.

At its gates yet another set of guards awaited Hawkmoon. These were garbed in the masks and armour of the Order of the Mantis, the Order to which King Huon himself belonged. Their elaborate insect masks were covered in jewels, with antennae of platinum wire and eyes faceted with a score or more of different gemstones. The men had long, thin legs and arms and slender bodies encased in insectlike plate armour of black, gold, and green. When they spoke their secret language to each other, it was the rustle and click of insect voices.

For the first time, Hawkmoon felt disturbed as these guards led him into the lower passages of the palace, the walls of which were of deep scarlet metal that reflected distorted images as they moved.

At last they entered a large, high-ceilinged hall whose dark walls were veined, like marble, with white, green, and pink. But these veins moved constantly, flickering and changing course the length and breadth of the walls and ceiling.

The floor of the hall, which was the best part of a quarter of a mile long and almost as wide, was filled at intervals by devices that Hawkmoon took to be machines of some description, though he could not understand their function. Like everything he had seen since arriving in Londra, these machines were ornate, much decorated, built from precious metals and semiprecious stones.

There were instruments set into them unlike anything he knew, and many of the instruments were active, registering, counting, measuring, tended by men who wore the serpent masks of the Order of the Snake — the Order that consisted solely of sorcerers and scientists in the service of the King-Emperor. They were shrouded in mottled cloaks with cowls half-drawn over their heads.

Down the central aisle a figure paced toward Hawkmoon, waving to the guards to dismiss.

Hawkmoon judged this man high in the Order, for his serpent mask was much more ornate than those of the others. He might even be the Grand Constable, by his bearing and general demeanour.

"My lord Duke, greetings."

Hawkmoon acknowledged the bow with a slight one of his own, many of the habits of his former life still being with him.

"I am Baron Kalan of Vitall, Chief Scientist to the King-Emperor. You are to be my guest for a day or so, I understand. Welcome to my apartments and laboratories."

"Thank you. What do you wish me to do?" Hawkmoon asked abstractedly.

"First, I hope you will dine with me."

Baron Kalan signaled graciously for Hawkmoon to precede him, and they walked the length of the hall, passing many peculiar constructions, until they arrived at a door that led to what were obviously the baron's private apartments. A meal was already laid. It was comparatively simple, judged against what Hawkmoon had been eating over the past fortnight, but it was well cooked and tasty. When they had finished, Baron Kalan, who had already removed his mask to reveal a pale, middle-aged face with a wispy white beard and thinning hair, poured wine for them both. They had scarcely spoken during the meal.

Hawkmoon tasted the wine. It was excellent.

"My own invention, the wine," said Kalan, and smirked.

"It is unfamiliar," Hawkmoon admitted. "What grape…?"

"No grape — but grain. A somewhat different process."

"It is strong."

"Stronger than most wines," agreed the baron. "Now, Duke, you know that I have been commissioned to establish your sanity, judge your temperament, and decide whether you are fit to serve His Majesty the King-Emperor Huon."

"I believe that is what Baron Meliadus told me." Hawkmoon smiled faintly. "I will be interested in learning your observations."

"Hmm…" Baron Kalan looked closely at Hawkmoon. "I can see why I was asked to entertain you. I must say that you *appear* to be rational."

"Thank you." Under the influence of the strange wine, Hawkmoon was rediscovering some of his former irony.

Baron Kalan rubbed at his face and coughed a dry, barely heard cough for some several moments. His manner had contained a certain nervousness since he removed the mask. Hawkmoon had already noticed how the people of Granbretan preferred to keep their masks on most of the time. Now Kalan reached toward the extravagant snake mask and placed it over his head. The coughing stopped immediately, and the man's body relaxed visibly. Although Hawkmoon had heard that it was a breach of Granbretanian etiquette to retain one's mask when entertaining a guest of noble station, he affected to show no surprise at the baron's action.

"Ah, my lord Duke," came the whisper from within the mask, "who am I to judge what sanity is? There are those who judge us of Granbretan insane..."

"Surely not."

"It is true. Those with blunted perceptions, who cannot see the grand plan, are not convinced of the nobility of our great crusade. They say, you know, that we are mad, ha, ha!" Baron Kalan rose. "But now, if you will accompany me, we will begin our preliminary investigations."

Back through the hall of machines they went, entering another hall, only slightly smaller than the first. This had the same dark walls, but these pulsed with an energy that gradually shifted along the spectrum from violet to black and back again. There was only a single machine in the hall, a thing of gleaming blue and red metal, with projections, arms, and attachments, a great bell-like object suspended from an intricate scaffold affair that was part of the machine. On one side was a console, attended by a dozen men in the uniform of the Order of the Snake, their metal masks partially reflecting the pulsing light from the walls. A noise filled the hall, emanating from the machine, a faintly heard clatter, a moan, a series of hissings as if it breathed like a beast.

"This is our mentality machine," Baron Kalan said proudly. "This is what will test you."

"It is very large," said Hawkmoon, stepping toward it.

"One of our largest. It has to be. It must perform complex tasks. This is the result of *scientific* sorcery, my lord Duke, none of your hit-and-miss spell singing you find on the Continent. It is our science that gives us our chief advantage over lesser nations."

As the effect of the drink wore off, Hawkmoon became increasingly the man he had been in the prison catacombs. His sense of detachment grew, and when he was led forward and made to stand under the bell when it was lowered, he felt little anxiety or curiosity.

At last the bell completely covered him, and its fleshy sides moved in to mould themselves around his body. It was an obscene embrace and would have horrified the Dorian Hawkmoon who had fought the Battle of Köln, but this new Hawkmoon felt only a vague impatience and discomfort. He began to feel a crawling sensation in his skull, as if incredibly fine wires were entering his head and probing at his brain. Hallucinations began to manifest themselves. He saw bright oceans of colour, distorted faces, buildings and flora of unnatural perspective. It rained jewels for a hundred years, and then black winds blew across his eyes and were torn apart to reveal oceans that were at once frozen and in motion, beasts of infinite sympathy and goodness, women of monstrous tenderness. Interspersed with these visions came clear memories of his childhood, of his life up until the moment he had entered the machine. Piece by piece, the memories built up until the whole of his life had been recalled and presented to him. But still he felt no other emotion save the remembrance of the emotion he had had in that past time. When at last the sides of the bell moved back and the bell itself began to rise, Hawkmoon stood impassively, feeling as if he had witnessed the experience of another.

Kalan was there and took his arm, leading him away from the mentality machine. "The preliminary investigations show you to be rather more than normally sane, my lord Duke — if I read the instruments correctly. The mentality machine will report in detail in a few hours. Now you must rest, and we shall continue our tests in the morning."

The next day Hawkmoon was again given over to the embrace of the mentality machine, and this time he lay full-length within its belly, looking upward while picture after picture was flashed before his eyes and the pictures that they first reminded him of were then flashed onto a screen. Hawkmoon's face hardly altered its expression while all this went on. He experienced a series of hallucinations where he was thrown into highly dangerous situations — an ocean ghoul attacking him, an avalanche, three swordsmen as opponents, the need to leap from the third storey of a building or be burned to death — and in every case he rescued himself with courage and skill, though his reflexes were mechanical, uninspired by any particular sense of fear. Many such tests were made, and he passed through them all without ever once showing any strong emotion of any kind. Even when he was induced by the mentality machine to laugh, weep, hate, love, and so on, the reactions were chiefly physical in expression.

At length Hawkmoon was released by the machine and faced Baron Kalan's snake mask.

"It would seem that you are, in some peculiar way, *too* sane, my lord Duke," whispered the baron. "A paradox, eh? Aye, too sane. It is as if some part of your brain has disappeared altogether or has been cut off from the rest. However, I can only report to Baron Meliadus that you seem eminently suited to his purpose, so long as certain sensible precautions are taken."

"What purpose is that?" Hawkmoon asked with no real interest.

"That is for him to say."

Shortly afterward, Baron Kalan took his leave of Hawkmoon, who was escorted through a labyrinth of corridors by two guards of the Order of the Mantis. At length they arrived outside a door of burnished silver that opened to reveal a sparsely furnished room entirely lined with mirrors on walls, floor, and ceiling, save for a single large window at the far end that opened on to a balcony overlooking the city. Near the window stood a figure in a black wolf mask who could only be Baron Meliadus.

Baron Meliadus turned and motioned for the guards to leave. Then he pulled a cord, and tapestries rippled down the walls to hide the mirrors. Hawkmoon could still look up or down and see his own reflection if he desired. Instead he looked out of the window.

A thick fog covered the city, swirling green-black about the towers, obscuring the river. It was evening, with the sun almost completely set, and the towers looked like strange, unnatural rock formations, jutting from a primordial sea. If a great reptile had risen from it and pressed an eye to the grimy moisture-streaked window it would not have been surprising.

Without the wall mirrors, the room became even gloomier, for there was no artificial source of light. The baron, framed against the window, hummed to himself, ignoring Hawkmoon.

From somewhere in the depths of the city a faint distorted cry echoed through the fog and then faded. Baron Meliadus lifted his wolf mask and looked carefully at Hawkmoon, whom he could now barely see. "Come nearer to the window, my lord," he said. Hawkmoon moved forward, his feet slipping once or twice on the rugs that partially covered the glass floor.

"Well," Meliadus began, "I have spoken to Baron Kalan, and he reports an enigma, a psyche he can hardly interpret. He said it seemed that some part of it had died. What did it die of? I wonder. Of grief? Of humiliation? Of fear? I had not expected such complications. I had expected to bargain with you man to man, trading something you desired for a service I required of you. While I see no reason not to continue to obtain this service, I am not altogether sure, now, how to go about it. Would you consider a bargain, my lord Duke?"

"What do you propose?" Hawkmoon stared beyond the baron, through the window at the darkening sky.

"You have heard of Count Brass, the old hero?"

"Yes."

"He is now Lord Guardian, Protector of the Province of Kamarg."

"I have heard that."

"He has proved stubborn in opposing the will of the King-Emperor, he has insulted Granbretan. We wish to encourage wisdom in him. The way to do this will be to capture his daughter, who is dear to him, and bring her to Granbretan as a hostage. However, he would trust no emissary that we sent nor any common stranger — but he must have heard of your exploits at the Battle of Köln and doubtless sympathizes with you. If you were to go to Kamarg seeking sanctuary from the Empire of Granbretan, he would almost certainly welcome you. Once within his walls, it would not be too difficult for a man of your resourcefulness to pick the right moment, abduct the girl, bring her back to us. Beyond the borders of Kamarg we should, naturally, be able to give you plenty of support. Kamarg is a small territory. You could easily escape."

"That is what you desire of me?"

"Just so. In return we give you back your estates to rule as you please so long as you take no part against the Dark Empire, whether in word or deed."

"My people live in misery under Granbretan," Hawkmoon said suddenly, as if in revelation. He spoke without passion but rather like one making an abstract moral decision. "It would be better for them if I ruled them."

"Ah!" Baron Meliadus smiled. "So my bargain does seem reasonable!"

"Yes, though I do not believe you will keep your part of it."

"Why not? It is essentially to our advantage if a troublesome state can be ruled by someone whom it trusts — and whom we may trust also."

"I will go to Kamarg. I will tell them the tale you suggest. I will capture the girl and bring her to Granbretan." Hawkmoon sighed and looked at Baron Meliadus. "Why not?"

Discomfited by the strangeness of Hawkmoon's manner, unused to dealing with such a personality, Meliadus frowned. "We cannot be absolutely sure that you are not indulging in some complex form of deceit to trick us into releasing you. Although the mentality machine is infallible in the case of all other subjects who have been tested by it, it could be that you are aware of some secret sorcery that confuses it."

"I know nothing of sorcery."

"So I believe — almost." Baron Meliadus's tone became somewhat cheerful. "But we have no need to fear — there is an excellent precaution we can take against any treachery from you. A precaution that will bring you back to us or kill you if we have reason no longer to trust you. It is a device recently discovered by Baron Kalan, though I understand it is not his original invention. It is called the Black Jewel. You will be supplied with it tomorrow. Tonight you will sleep in apartments prepared for you in the palace. Before you leave you will have the honour of being presented to His Majesty the King-Emperor. Few foreigners are granted so much."

With that, Meliadus called to the insect-masked guards and ordered them to escort Hawkmoon to his quarters.

T H R E E

T H E B L A C K J E W E L

Next morning, Dorian Hawkmoon was taken to see Baron Kalan again. The serpent mask seemed to bear an almost cynical expression as it regarded him, but the baron said hardly a word, merely led him through a series of rooms and halls until they reached a room with a door of plain steel. This was opened, to reveal a similar door that, when opened, revealed a third door. This led into a small, blindingly lighted chamber of white metal that contained a machine of intense beauty. It consisted almost entirely of delicate red, gold, and silver webs, strands of which brushed Hawkmoon's face and had the warmth and vitality of human skin. Faint music came from the webs, which moved as if in a breeze.

"It seems alive," said Hawkmoon.

"It is alive," Baron Kalan whispered proudly. "It is alive."

"Is it a beast?"

"No. It is the creation of sorcery. I am not even sure what it is. I built it according to the instructions of a grimoire I bought from an Easterner many years ago. It is the machine of the Black Jewel. Ah, and soon you will become much more intimately acquainted with it, lord Duke."

Deep within him, Hawkmoon felt a faint stirring of panic, but it did not begin to rise to the surface of his mind. He let the strands of red and gold and silver caress him.

"It is not complete," Kalan said. "It must spin the Jewel. Move closer to it, my lord. Move *in* to it. You will feel no pain, I guarantee. It must spin the Black Jewel."

Hawkmoon obeyed the baron, and the webs rustled and began to sing. His ears became confounded, the traceries of red, gold, and silver confused his eyes. The machine of the Black Jewel fondled him, seemed to enter him, become him and he it. He sighed, and his voice was the music of the webs; he moved and his limbs were tenuous strands.

There was pressure from within his skull, and he felt a sense of absolute warmth and softness suffuse his body. He drifted as if bodiless and lost the sense of passing time, but he knew that the machine was spinning something from its own substance, making something that became hard and dense and implanted itself in his forehead so that suddenly he seemed to possess a third eye and stared out at the world with a new kind of vision. Then gradually this faded and he was looking at Baron Kalan, who had removed his mask, the better to regard him.

Hawkmoon felt a sudden sharp pain in his head. The pain vanished almost at once. He looked back at the machine, but its colours had dulled and its webs seemed to have shrunk. He lifted a hand to his forehead and felt with a shock something there that had not been there before. It was hard and smooth. It was part of him. He shuddered.

Baron Kalan looked concerned. "Eh? You are not mad, are you? I was sure of success! You are not mad?"

"I am not mad," Hawkmoon said. "But I think that I am afraid."

"You will become accustomed to the Jewel."

"That is what is in my head? The Jewel?"

"Aye. The Black Jewel. Wait." Kalan turned and drew aside a curtain of scarlet velvet, revealing a flat oval of milky quartz about two feet long. In it, a picture began to form. Hawkmoon saw that the picture was that of Kalan staring into the quartz oval, into infinity. The screen revealed exactly what Hawkmoon saw. As he turned his head slightly, the picture altered accordingly.

Kalan muttered in delight. "It works, you see. What you perceive, the Jewel perceives. Wherever you go we shall be able to see everything and everyone you encounter."

Hawkmoon tried to speak, but he could not. His throat was tight, and there seemed to be something constricting his lungs. Again he touched the warm jewel, so similar to flesh in texture, but so unlike it in every other way.

"What have you done to me?" he asked eventually, his tone as flat as ever.

"We have merely secured your loyalty," chuckled Kalan. "You have taken part of the life of the machine. Should we so desire, we can give all the machine's life to the Jewel, and then…"

Hawkmoon reached out stiffly and touched the baron's arm. "What will it do?"

"It will eat your brain, Duke of Köln."

Baron Meliadus hurried Dorian Hawkmoon through the glittering passages of the palace. Now Hawkmoon had a sword at his side and a suit of clothes and mail much like those he had worn at the Battle of Köln. He was conscious of the jewel in his skull but of little else. The passages widened until they covered the area of a good-sized street. Guards in the masks of the Order of the Mantis were thick along the walls. Mighty doors, a mass of jewels making mosaic patterns, towered ahead of them.

"The throne room," murmured the baron. "Now the King-Emperor will inspect you."

Slowly the doors moved open, to reveal the glory of the throne room. It blazed, half-blinding Hawkmoon with its magnificence. There was glitter and music; from a dozen galleries that rose to the concave roof were draped the shimmering banners of five hundred of Granbretan's noblest families. Lining the walls and galleries, rigid with their flame-lances at the salute, were the soldiers of the Order of the Mantis in their insect-masks and their plate armour of black, green, and gold. Behind them, in a multitude of different masks and a profusion of rich clothing, were the courtiers. They peered curiously at Meliadus and Hawkmoon as they entered.

The lines of soldiers stretched into the distance. There, at the end of the hall, almost out of sight, hung something that Hawkmoon could not at first make out. He frowned. "The Throne Globe," whispered Meliadus. "Now do as I do." He began to pace forward.

The walls of the throne room were of lustrous green and purple, but the colours of the banners ranged the spectrum, as did the fabrics, metals, and precious gems that the courtiers wore. But Hawkmoon's eyes were fixed on the globe.

Dwarfed by the proportions of the throne room, Hawkmoon and Meliadus walked with measured pace toward the Throne Globe while fanfares were played by trumpeters in the galleries to left and right.

Eventually Hawkmoon could see the Throne Globe, and he was astonished. It contained a milky-white fluid that surged about sluggishly, almost hypnotically. At times the fluid seemed to contain iridescent radiance that would gradually fade and then return. In the centre of this fluid, reminding Hawkmoon of a foetus, drifted an ancient man, his skin wrinkled, his limbs apparently useless, his head overlarge. From this head stared sharp, malicious eyes.

Following Meliadus's example, Hawkmoon abased himself before the creature.

"Rise," came a voice. Hawkmoon realized with a shock that the voice came from the globe. It was the voice of a young man in the prime of health — a golden voice, a melodic, vibrant voice. Hawkmoon wondered from what youthful throat the voice had been torn.

"King-Emperor, I present Dorian Hawkmoon, Duke von Köln, who has elected to perform an errand for us. You'll remember, noble sire, that I mentioned my plan to you..." Meliadus bowed as he spoke.

"We go to much effort and considerable ingenuity to secure the services of this Count Brass," came the golden voice. "We trust your judgment is sound in this matter, Baron Meliadus."

"You have reason to trust me on the strength of my past deeds, Great Majesty," Meliadus said, again bowing.

"Has the Duke von Köln been warned of the inevitable penalty he will pay if he does not serve us loyally?" came the youthful, sardonic voice. "Has he been told that we may destroy him in an instant, from any distance?"

Meliadus stroked his sleeve. "He has, Mighty King-Emperor."

"You have informed him that the Jewel in his skull," continued the voice with relish, "sees all that he sees and shows it to us in the chamber of the machine of the Black Jewel?"

"Aye, Noble Monarch."

"And you have made it clear to him that should he show any signs of betraying us — any slight sign, which we may easily detect by watching through his eyes the faces of those he speaks to — we shall give the Jewel its full life? We shall release all the energy of the machine into its sibling. Have you told him, Baron Meliadus, that the Jewel, possessed of its full life, will then eat its way through his brain, devour his mind, and turn him into a drooling, mindless creature?"

"In essence, Great Emperor, he has been so informed."

The thing in the Throne Globe chuckled. "By the look of him, Baron, the threat of mindlessness is no threat at all. Are you sure he's not already possessed of the Jewel's full life?"

"It is his character to seem thus, Immortal Ruler."

Now the eyes turned to peer into those of Dorian Hawkmoon, and the sardonic, golden voice issued from the infinitely aged throat.

"You have contracted a bargain, Duke von Köln, with the immortal King-Emperor of Granbretan. It is a testament to our liberality that we should offer such a bargain to one who is, after all, our slave. You must serve us, in turn, with great loyalty, knowing that you share a part in the destiny of the greatest race ever to emerge on this planet. It is our right to rule the earth, by virtue of our omniscient intellect and omnipotent might, and soon we shall claim this right in full. All who help serve our noble purpose will receive our approval. Go now, Duke, and win that approval."

The wizened head turned, and a prehensile tongue flickered from the mouth to touch a tiny jewel that drifted near the wall of the Throne Globe. The globe began to dim until the foetuslike shape of the King-Emperor, last and immortal descendant of a dynasty founded almost three thousand years before, appeared for a few moments in silhouette. "And remember the power of the Black Jewel," said the youthful voice before the globe took on the appearance of a solid, dull black sphere.

The audience was ended. Abasing themselves, Meliadus and Hawkmoon backed away a few paces and then turned to walk from the throne room. And the audience had served a purpose not anticipated by the baron or his master. Within Hawkmoon's strange mind, in its most hidden depths, a tiny irritation had begun; and the irritation was caused not by the Black Jewel that lay embedded in his forehead, but by a less tangible source.

Perhaps the irritation was a sign of Hawkmoon's humanity returning. Perhaps it marked the growing of a new and altogether different quality; perhaps it was the influence of the Runestaff.

F O U R

J O U R N E Y   T O   C A S T L E   B R A S S

Dorian Hawkmoon was returned to his original apartments in the prison catacombs and there waited for two days until Baron Meliadus arrived, bearing with him a suit of black leather, complete with boots and gauntlets, a heavy black cloak with a cowl, a silver-hilted broadsword in a black leather scabbard, simply decorated with silver, and a black helmet-mask wrought in the likeness of a snarling wolf. The clothes and equipment were evidently modeled on Meliadus's own.

"Your tale, on reaching Castle Brass," Meliadus began, "will be a fine one. You were made prisoner by myself and managed, with the aid of a slave, to drug me and pose as me. In this disguise you crossed Granbretan and all the provinces she controls before Meliadus recovered from the drug. A simple story is the best, and this one serves not only to answer how you came to escape from Granbretan, but also to elevate you in the eyes of those who hate me."

"I understand," Hawkmoon said, fingering the heavy black jacket. "But how is the Black Jewel explained?"

"You were to be the subject of some experiment of mine but escaped before any serious harm could be done to you. Tell the story well, Hawkmoon, for your safety will depend on it. We shall be watching the reaction of Count Brass — and particularly that wily rhyme maker Bowgentle. Though we shall be unable to hear what you say, we can read lips well enough. Any sign of betrayal on your part — and we give the Jewel its full life."

"I understand," Hawkmoon repeated in the same flat tone.

Meliadus frowned. "They will evidently note your strangeness of manner, but with luck they will explain it by the misfortunes you have suffered. It could make them even more solicitous."

Hawkmoon nodded vaguely.

Meliadus looked at him sharply. "I am still troubled by you, Hawkmoon. I am still unsure that you have not by some sorcery or cunning deceived us —

but nonetheless I am certain of your loyalty. The Black Jewel is my assurance." He smiled. "Now, an ornithopter is waiting to take you to Deau-Vere and the coast. Ready yourself, my lord Duke, and serve Granbretan faithfully. If you are successful, you shall soon be master of your own estates again."

The ornithopter had settled on the lawns beyond the city entrance to the catacombs. It was a thing of great beauty, fashioned in the shape of a gigantic griffin, all worked in copper, brass, silver, and black steel, squatting on its powerful lionlike haunches, the forty-foot wings folded on its back. Below the head, in the small cockpit, sat the pilot, dressed in the bird-mask of his Order — the Order of the Crow, which was comprised of all flyers — his gloved hands on the jeweled controls.

With some wariness, Hawkmoon, now clad in the costume that so resembled Meliadus's, climbed in behind the pilot, finding difficulty with his sword as he tried to seat himself in the long, narrow seat. Eventually he settled into a position of comparative comfort and gripped the ribbed metal sides of the flying machine as the pilot depressed a lever and the wings clashed open and began to beat the air with a strange, echoing boom. The whole ornithopter shuddered and listed to one side for an instant before the pilot, cursing, had it under control. Hawkmoon had heard that there were dangers in flying these machines and had seen several that had attacked him at Köln suddenly fold their wings behind them and hurtle to the ground. But in spite of their instabilities, the ornithopters of the Dark Empire had been the chief weapon in conquering so speedily the mainland of Europe, for no other race possessed flying machines of any kind.

Now, with an uncomfortable jerking motion, the metal griffin slowly began to ascend. The wings thrashed the air, a parody of natural flight, and they climbed higher and higher until they had cleared the tops of Londra's tallest towers and were circling toward the south-east. Hawkmoon breathed heavily, disliking the unfamiliar sensation.

Soon the monster had passed above a heavy layer of dark cloud, and sunshine flashed on its metal scales. His face and eyes protected by the mask, through whose jeweled eyes he peered, Hawkmoon saw the sunlight refracted into a million rainbow flashes. He closed his eyes.

Time passed, and he felt the ornithopter begin to descend. He opened his eyes and saw that they were deep within the clouds again, breaking through them to see ash-grey fields, the outline of a turreted city, and the livid, rolling sea beyond.

Clumsily, the machine flapped toward a great, flat stretch of rock that rose from the centre of the city.

It landed with a heavy bumping motion, wings beating frenetically, and at last halted close to the edge of the artificial plateau.

The pilot signaled for Hawkmoon to get out. He did so, feeling stiff, his legs shaking, while the pilot locked his controls and joined him on the ground. Here and there were other ornithopters. As they walked across the rock beneath the lowering sky, one began to flap into the air, and Hawkmoon felt wind slap against his face from the wings as the thing passed close above his head.

"Deau-Vere," the crow-masked pilot said. "A port given over almost wholly to our aerial navies, although ships of war still use the harbour."

Soon Hawkmoon could see a circular steel hatch in the rock ahead of them. The pilot paused beside it and tapped out a complicated series of beats with his booted foot. Eventually the hatch swung downward, revealing a stone stairway, and they descended, while the hatch swung shut above them. The interior was gloomy, with decorations of glowering stone gargoyles and some inferior bas-reliefs.

At last they emerged through a guarded door into a paved street between the square, turreted buildings that filled the city. The streets were crowded with the warriors of Granbretan. Groups of crow-masked flyers rubbed shoulders with the fish- and sea-serpent-masked crews of the men-o'-war, the infantrymen and the cavalry in a great variety of masks, some of the Order of the Pig, others of the Orders of Wolf, Skull, Mantis, Bull, Hound, Goat, and many more. Swords slapped armoured legs, flame-lances clashed in the press, and everywhere was the gloomy jingle of military gear.

Pushing through this throng, Hawkmoon was surprised that it gave way so easily, until he remembered how closely he must resemble Baron Meliadus.

At the gates of the city there was a horse waiting for him, its saddle panniers bulging with provisions. Hawkmoon had already been told about the horse and which road he must follow. He mounted the animal and cantered toward the sea.

Very soon the clouds parted and sunshine broke through them, and Dorian Hawkmoon saw for the first time the Silver Bridge that spanned thirty miles of sea. It flashed in the sunlight, a beautiful thing, seemingly too delicate to withstand the merest breeze but actually strong enough to bear all the armies of Granbretan. It curved away over the ocean, beyond the horizon. The causeway itself measured almost a quarter of a mile across, flanked by quivering networks of silver hawsers supported by pylon archways, intricately moulded in military motifs.

Across this bridge passed to and fro a splendid variety of traffic. Hawkmoon could see carriages of nobles, so elaborate that it was hard to believe they could function; squadrons of cavalry, the horses as magnificently armoured as their riders; battalions of infantry, marching four abreast with unbelievable precision; trading caravans of carts; and beasts of burden with swaying stacks of every conceivable kind of goods — furs, silks, meat carcasses, fruit, vegetables, chests of treasure, candlesticks, beds, whole suites of chairs — much of which, Hawkmoon realized, was loot from states like Köln recently conquered by those same armies who passed the caravans.

War engines, too, he could see — things of iron and copper — with cruel beaks for ramming, high towers for the siege, long beams for hurling massive fireballs and boulders. Marching beside them, in masks of mole and badger and ferret, were the engineers of the Dark Empire, with squat, powerful bodies and large, heavy hands. All these things took on the aspect of ants, dwarfed as they were by the majesty of the Silver Bridge, which, like the ornithopters, had contributed greatly to the ease of Granbretan's conquests.

The guards on the bridge's gateway had been told to let Hawkmoon pass, and the gateway opened as he neared it. He rode straight onto the vibrating bridge, his horse's hooves clattering on the metal. The causeway, seen at this range, lost some of its magnificence. Its surface had been scored and dented by the passage of the traffic. Here and there were piles of horse dung, rags, straw, and less recognizable refuse. It was impossible to keep such a well-used thoroughfare in perfect condition, but somehow the soiled causeway symbolized something of the spirit of the strange civilization of Granbretan.

Hawkmoon crossed the Silver Bridge across the sea and came, after some time, to the mainland of Europe, making his way toward the Crystal City so lately conquered by the Dark Empire; the Crystal City of Parye, where he would rest for a day before beginning his journey south.

But he had more than a day's journey before he came to the Crystal City, no matter how hard he rode. He decided not to stay in Karlye, the city closest to the bridge, but to find a village where he might rest for that night and then continue in the morning.

Just before sunset he reached a village of pleasant villas and gardens that bore the marks of conflict. Indeed, some of the villas were in ruins. The village was strangely quiet, though a few lights were beginning to burn in windows, and the inn, when he reached it, had its doors closed and there were no signs of revelry from within. He dismounted in the inn's courtyard and banged on the door with his fist. He waited for several minutes before the bar was withdrawn and a boy's face peered out at him. The boy looked frightened when he saw the wolf mask. Reluctantly he drew the door open to let Hawkmoon enter. As soon as he was inside, Hawkmoon pushed back the mask and tried to smile at the boy to give him reassurance, but the smile was artificial, for Hawkmoon had forgotten how to move his lips correctly. The boy seemed to take the expression as one of disapproval, and he backed away, his eyes half-defiant, as if expecting a blow at the very least.

"I mean you no harm," Hawkmoon said stiffly. "Only take care of my horse and give me a bed and some food. I'll leave at dawn."

"Master, we have only the humblest food," murmured the boy, partly reassured. The people of Europe in these days were used to occupation by this faction or that, and the conquest of Granbretan was not, in essence, a new experience. The ferocity of the people of the Dark Empire was new, however, and this was plainly what the boy feared and hated, expecting not even the roughest justice from one who was evidently a noble of Granbretan.

"I'll take whatever you have. Save your best food and wine if you will. I seek only to satisfy my hunger and sleep."

"Sire, our best food is all gone. If we —"

Hawkmoon silenced him with a gesture. "I am not interested, boy. Take me literally and you will serve me best."

He looked about the room and noted one or two old men sitting in the shadows, drinking from heavy tankards and avoiding looking at him. He went to the centre of the room and seated himself at a small table, stripping off his cloak and gauntlets and wiping the dust of the road from his face and body. The wolf mask he dumped on the ground beside his chair, a most uncharacteristic gesture for a noble of the Dark Empire. He noticed one of the men glance at him in some surprise, and when a murmur broke out a little later, he realized they had seen the Black Jewel. The boy returned with thin ale and some scraps of pork, and Hawkmoon had the feeling that this was, indeed, their best. He ate the pork and drank the ale and then called to be taken to his room. Once in the sparsely furnished chamber he stripped off his gear, bathed himself, climbed between the rough sheets, and was soon asleep.

During the night he was disturbed, without realizing what had awakened him. For some reason he felt drawn to the window and looked out. In the moonlight he thought he saw a figure on a heavy warhorse, looking up at his window. The figure was that of a warrior in full armour, his visor covering his face. Hawkmoon believed he caught a flash of jet and gold. Then the warrior had turned his horse and disappeared.

Feeling that there was some significance to this event, Hawkmoon returned to his bed. He slept again, quite as soundly as before, but in the morning he was not sure whether he had dreamed or not. If it had been a dream, then it was the first he had had since he had been captured. A twinge of curiosity made him frown slightly as he dressed himself, but he shrugged then and went down to the main room of the inn to ask for some breakfast.

Hawkmoon reached the Crystal City by the evening. Its buildings of purest quartz were alive with colour, and everywhere was the tinkle of the glass decorations that the citizens of Parye used to adorn their houses and public buildings and monuments. Such a beautiful city it was that even the warlords of the Dark Empire had left it almost wholly intact, preferring to take the city by stealth and waste several months, rather than attack it.

But within the city the marks of occupation were everywhere, from the look of permanent fear on the faces of the common folk, to the beast-masked warriors who swaggered the streets, and the flags that flowed in the wind over the houses once owned by Parye's noblemen. Now the flags were those of Jerek Nankenseen, Warlord of the Order of the Fly; Adaz Promp, Grand Constable of the Order of the Hound; Mygel Holst, Archduke of Londra; and Asrovak Mikosevaar, renegade of Muskovia, mercenary Warlord of the Vulture Legion, pervert and destroyer, whose legion had served Granbretan even before her plan of European conquest became evident. A madman to match even those insane nobles of Granbretan he allowed to be his masters, Asrovak Mikosevaar was always at the forefront of Granbretan's armies, pushing the boundaries of Empire onward. His infamous banner, with the words stitched in scarlet on it, *Death to Life!* struck fear into the hearts of all who fought against it. Asrovak Mikosevaar must be resting in the Crystal City, Hawkmoon decided, for it was unlike him to be far from any battle line. Corpses drew the Muskovian as roses drew bees.

There were no children in the streets of the Crystal City. Those who had not been slaughtered by Granbretan had been imprisoned by the conquerors, to ensure the good behaviour of the citizens who remained alive.

The sun seemed to stain the crystal buildings with blood as it set, and Hawkmoon, too weary to ride on, was forced to find the inn Meliadus had told him of and there sleep for the best part of a night and a day before resuming his journey to Castle Brass. There was still more than half of that journey to finish.

Beyond the city of Lyon, the Empire of Granbretan had so far been checked in its conquests, but the road to Lyon was a bleak road, lined with gibbets and wooden crosses on which hung men and women, young and old, girls and boys, and even, perhaps as an insane jest, domestic pets such as cats, dogs, and tame rabbits. Whole families rotted there; entire households, from the youngest baby to the oldest servant, were nailed in attitudes of agony to the crosses.

The stench of decay inflamed Hawkmoon's nostrils as he let his horse plod miserably down the Lyon Road, and the stink of death clogged his throat. Fire had blackened fields and forests, razed towns and villages, turned the very air grey and heavy. All who lived had become beggars, whatever their former station, save those women who had become whores to the Empire's soldiery, or those men who had sworn groveling allegiance to the King-Emperor.

As curiosity had touched him earlier, now disgust stirred faintly in Hawkmoon's breast, but he hardly noticed it. Wolf-masked, he rode on toward Lyon. None stopped him; none questioned him, for those who served the Order of the Wolf were, in the main, fighting in the north, and thus Hawkmoon was safe from any Wolf addressing him in the secret language of the Order.

Beyond Lyon, Hawkmoon took to the fields, for the roads were patrolled by Granbretanian warriors. He stuffed his wolf-mask into one of his now empty panniers and rode swiftly into the free territory where the air was still sweet but where terror still blossomed, save that this was a terror of the future rather than of the present.

In the town of Valence, where warriors prepared to meet the attack of the Dark Empire when it came — discussing hopeless stratagems, building inadequate war engines — Hawkmoon told his story first.

"I am Dorian Hawkmoon von Köln," he told the captain to whom the solders took him.

The captain, one thigh-booted foot on a bench in the crowded inn, stared at him carefully. "The Duke von Köln must be dead by now — he was captured by Granbretan," he said. "I think you are a spy."

Hawkmoon did not protest but told the story Meliadus had given him. Speaking expressionlessly, he described his capture and his method of escape, and his strange tone convinced the captain more than the story itself. Then a swordsman in battered mail pushed through the crowd shouting Hawkmoon's name. Turning, Hawkmoon recognized the insignia on the man's coat as his own, the arms of Köln. The man was one of the few who had fled the Köln battlefield somehow. He spoke to the captain and the crowd, describing the duke's bravery and ingenuity. Then Dorian Hawkmoon was heralded as a hero in Valence.

That night, while his coming was celebrated, Hawkmoon told the captain that he was bound for Kamarg to try to recruit the help of Count Brass in the war against Granbretan. The captain shook his head. "Count Brass takes no sides," he said. "But it is likely he will listen to you rather than anyone else. I hope you are successful, my lord Duke."

Next morning, Hawkmoon rode away from Valence, rode down the trail to the south, while grim-faced men passed him riding north to join forces with those preparing to withstand the Dark Empire.

The wind blew harder and harder as Hawkmoon neared his destination and saw, at length, the flat marshlands of Kamarg, the lagoons shining in the distance, the reeds bent beneath the mistral's force — a lonely, lovely land. When he passed close to one of the tall old towers and saw the heliograph begin to flash, he knew that his coming would be newsed to Castle Brass before he arrived there.

Cold-faced, Hawkmoon sat his horse stiffly as it picked its way along the winding marsh road where shrubs swayed and water rippled and a few birds floated through the sad old skies.

Shortly before nightfall, Castle Brass came in sight, its terraced hill and delicate towers a black-and-grey silhouette against the evening.

F   I   V   E

THE AWAKENING OF HAWKMOON

Count Brass passed Dorian Hawkmoon a fresh cup of wine and murmured, "Please continue, my lord Duke," as Hawkmoon told his story for the second time. In the hall of the Castle Brass sat Yisselda, in all her beauty, Bowgentle, thoughtful of countenance, and von Villach, who stroked his moustache and stared at the fire.

Hawkmoon finished the tale. "And so I sought help in Kamarg, Count Brass, knowing that only this land is secure from the power of the Dark Empire."

"You are welcome here," Count Brass said, frowning. "If refuge is all you seek."

"That is all."

"You do not come to ask us take arms against Granbretan?" It was Bowgentle who spoke, half-hopefully.

"I have suffered enough from doing so myself — for the time being — and would not wish to encourage others to risk meeting a fate I only narrowly missed myself," replied Hawkmoon.

Yisselda looked almost disappointed. It was plain that all in the room, save wise Count Brass, wanted war with Granbretan. For different reasons, perhaps — Yisselda to revenge herself against Meliadus, Bowgentle because he believed such evil must be countered, von Villach simply because he wished to exercise his sword again.

"Good," said Count Brass, "for I'm tired of resisting arguments that I should help this faction or that. Now — you seem exhausted, my lord Duke. Indeed, I have rarely seen a man so tired. We have kept you up too long. I will personally show you to your chambers."

Hawkmoon felt no triumph in having accomplished his deception. He told the lies because he had agreed with Meliadus that he would tell such lies. When the time came for kidnapping Yisselda, he would pursue the task in the same spirit.

Count Brass showed him into a suite consisting of bed-chamber, washing room, and a small study. "I hope it is to your taste, my lord Duke?"

"Completely," Hawkmoon replied.

Count Brass paused by the door. "The jewel," he said, "the one in your forehead — you say that Meliadus was unsuccessful in his experiment?"

"That is so, Count."

"Aha…" Count Brass looked at the floor, then, after a moment, glanced up again. "For I might know some sorcery that could remove it, if it troubles you…"

"It does not trouble me," said Hawkmoon.

"Aha," said the count again, and left the room.

That night, Hawkmoon awoke suddenly, as he had awakened in the inn a few nights since, and thought he saw a figure in the room — an armoured man in jet and gold. His heavy lids fell shut for a moment or two, and when he opened them again the figure was gone.

A conflict was beginning to develop in Hawkmoon's breast — perhaps a conflict between humanity and the lack of it, perhaps a conflict between conscience and the lack of conscience, if such conflicts were possible.

Whatever the exact nature of the conflict, there was no doubt that Hawkmoon's character was changing for a second time. It was not the character he had had on the battlefield at Köln, nor the strange apathetic mood into which he had fallen since the battle, but a new character altogether, as if Hawkmoon were being born again in a thoroughly different mould.

But the indications of this birth were still faint, and a catalyst was needed, as well as a climate in which the birth would be possible.

Meanwhile, Hawkmoon woke up in the morning thinking how he might most speedily accomplish the capture of Yisselda and return to Granbretan to be rid of the Black Jewel and sent back to the land of his youth.

Bowgentle met him as he left his chambers.

The philosopher-poet took his arm. "Ah, my lord Duke, perhaps you could tell me something of Londra. I was never there, though I traveled a great deal when I was younger."

Hawkmoon turned to look at Bowgentle, knowing that the face he saw would be the same as the nobles of Granbretan would see by means of the Black Jewel. There was an expression of frank interest in Bowgentle's eyes, and Hawkmoon decided that the man did not suspect him.

"It is vast and high and dark," Hawkmoon replied. "The architecture is involved, and the decoration complex and various."

"And its spirit? What is the spirit of Londra — what was your impression?"

"Power," said Hawkmoon. "Confidence…"

"Insanity?"

"I am incapable of knowing what is sane and what is not, Sir Bowgentle. You find me a strange man, perhaps? My manner is awkward? My attitudes unlike those of other men?"

Surprised by this turn of the conversation, Bowgentle looked carefully at Hawkmoon. "Why, yes… but what is your reason for asking?"

"Because I find your questions all but meaningless. I say that without — without wishing to insult…" Hawkmoon rubbed his chin. "I find them meaningless, you see."

They began to descend the steps toward the main hall, where breakfast had been laid and where old von Villach was already serving himself to a large steak from a salver held by a servant.

"Meaning," murmured Bowgentle. "You wonder what insanity is — I wonder what meaning is."

"I do not know," Hawkmoon answered. "I only know what I do."

"Your ordeal has driven you into yourself — abolished morality and conscience?" Bowgentle said with sympathy. "It is not an unfamiliar circumstance. Reading ancient texts, one learns of many who under duress lost the same senses. Good food and affectionate company should restore them to you. It was lucky you should come to Castle Brass. Perhaps an inner voice sent you to us."

Hawkmoon listened without interest, watching Yisselda descend the opposite staircase and smile at himself and Bowgentle across the hall.

"Are you well rested, my lord Duke?" she asked.

Before Hawkmoon could reply, Bowgentle said, "He has suffered more than we guessed. It will take our guest a week or two, I should think, before he is fully recovered."

"Perhaps you would like to accompany me this morning, my lord?" Yisselda suggested graciously. "I will show you our gardens. Even in winter they are beautiful."

"Yes," replied Hawkmoon, "I should like to see them."

Bowgentle smiled, realizing that Yisselda's warm heart had been touched by Hawkmoon's plight. There could be no-one better, he thought, than the girl to restore the duke's injured spirit.

They walked through the terraces of the castle gardens. Here were evergreens, there winter-blooming flowers and vegetables. The sky was clear and the sun shone down, and they did not suffer much discomfort from the wind, muffled as they were in heavy cloaks. They looked down on the roofs of the town, and all was at peace. Yisselda's arm was linked in Hawkmoon's, and she conversed lightly, expecting no reply from the sad-faced man at her side. The Black Jewel in his forehead had disturbed her a little at first, until she had decided that it was scarcely different from a jeweled circlet such as she sometimes wore to keep her long hair from her eyes.

She had much warmth and affection in her young heart. It was this affection that had turned to passion for Baron Meliadus, for it needed as many outlets as it could have. She was content to offer it to this strange, stiff hero of Köln and hope that it might heal the wounds of his spirit.

She soon noticed that a hint of expression only came into his eyes when she mentioned his homeland.

"Tell me of Köln," she said. "Not as it is now, but at it was — as one day it might be again."

Her words reminded Hawkmoon of Meliadus's promise to restore his lands. He looked away from the girl and up at the wind-blown sky, folding his arms across his chest.

"Köln," she said softly. "Was it like Kamarg?"

"No..." He turned to stare down at the rooftops far below. "No... for Kamarg is wild and as it has always been since the beginning of time. Köln bore the mark of Man everywhere — in its hedged fields and its straight watercourses — its little winding roads and its farms and villages. It was only a small province, with fat cows and well-fed sheep, with hayricks and meadows of soft grass that sheltered rabbits and fieldmice. It had yellow fences and cool woods, and the smoke from a chimney was never far from sight. Its people were simple and friendly and kind to small children. Its buildings were old and quaint and as simple as the people who lived in them. There was nothing dark in Köln till Granbretan came, a flood of harsh metal and fierce fire from across the Rhine. And Granbretan also put the mark of Man upon the countryside... the mark of the sword and the torch..."

He sighed, an increasing trace of emotion entering his tone. "The mark of the sword and the torch, replacing the mark of the plough and the harrow..." He turned to look at her. "And the cross and gibbet were made from the timber of the yellow fences, and the carcasses of the cows and sheep clogged the watercourses and poisoned the land, and the stones of the farmhouses became ammunition for the catapults, and the people became corpses or soldiers — there was no other choice."

She put her soft hand on his leathern arm. "You speak as if the memory were very distant," she said.

The expression faded from his eyes, and they became cold again. "So it is, so it is — like an old dream. It means little to me now."

But Yisselda looked at him thoughtfully as she led him through the gardens, thinking that she had found a way to reach him and help him.

For his part, Hawkmoon had been reminded of what he would lose if he did not carry the girl to the Dark Lords, and he welcomed her attention for reasons other than she guessed.

Count Brass met them in the courtyard. He was inspecting a large old warhorse and talking to a groom. "Put him out to graze," Count Brass said. "His service is over." Then he came toward Hawkmoon and his daughter. "Sir Bowgentle tells me you are wearier than we thought," he said to Hawkmoon. "But you are welcome to stay at Castle Brass for as long as you like. I hope Yisselda is not tiring you with her conversation."

"No. I find it… restful…"

"Good! Tonight we have an entertainment. I have asked Bowgentle to read to us from his latest work. He's promised to give us something light and witty. I hope you will enjoy it."

Hawkmoon noticed that Count Brass's eyes looked at him acutely, though his manner was hearty enough. Could Count Brass suspect his mission? The count was renowned for his wisdom and judgment of character. But surely if his character had baffled Baron Kalan, then it must also confuse the count. Hawkmoon decided that there was nothing to fear. He allowed Yisselda to lead him into the castle.

That night there was a banquet, with all Castle Brass's best laid out on the large board. Around the table sat several leading citizens of Kamarg, several bull breeders of repute, and several bullfighters, including the now-recovered Mahtan Just, whose life Count Brass had saved a year before. Fish and fowl, red meat and white, vegetables of every kind, wine of a dozen varieties, ale, and many delicious sauces and garnishes were heaped upon the long table. On Count Brass's right sat Dorian Hawkmoon, and on his left sat Mahtan Just, who had become that season's champion. Just plainly adored the count and treated him with a respect that the count seemed to find a trifle uncomfortable. Beside Hawkmoon sat Yisselda, and opposite her, Bowgentle. At the other end of the table was seated old Zhonzhac Ekare, greatest of the famous bull breeders, clad in heavy furs and with his face hidden by his huge beard and thick head of hair, laughing often and eating mightily. Beside him sat von Villach, and the two men seemed to enjoy each other's company a great deal.

When the feast was almost complete and pastries and sweetmeats and rich Kamarg cheese had been cleared, each guest had placed before him three flagons of wine of different kinds, a short barrel of ale, and a great drinking cup. Yisselda, alone, was given a single bottle and a smaller cup, though she had matched the men for drinking earlier and it seemed to be her choice, rather than the form, to drink less.

The wine had clouded Hawkmoon's mind a little and given him what was perhaps a spurious appearance of normal humanity. He smiled once or twice, and if he did not answer his companions jest for jest, at least he did not offend them with a sour expression.

Bowgentle's name was roared by Count Brass. "Bowgentle! The ballad you promised us!"

Bowgentle rose smiling, his face flushed, like the others', with the wine and the good food.

"I call this ballad 'The Emperor Glaucoma' and hope it will amuse you," he said, and began to speak the words.

> The Emperor Glaucoma
> passed the formal
> guardsmen at the far arcade
> and entered the bazaar
> where the ornamental
> remnants of the last war,
> Knights Templar
> and the Ottoman,
> hosts of Alcazar
> and mighty Khan,
> lay in the shade
> of temple palms
> and called for alms.
> But the Emperor Glaucoma
> passed the lazar
> undismayed
> while pipes and tabor
> played
> in honour
> of the Emperor's parade.

Count Brass was looking carefully at Bowgentle's grave face, a wry smile on his own lips. Meanwhile the poet spoke with wit and many graceful flourishes the complex rhyme. Hawkmoon looked about the board and saw some smiling, some looking puzzled, fuddled as they were by the drink. Hawkmoon neither smiled nor frowned. Yisselda bent toward him and murmured something, but he did not hear it.

> The regatta
> in the harbour

                    set off a cannonade
                    when the Emperor
                    displayed
                    stigmata
                    to the Vatican Ambassador

"What does he speak of?" grumbled von Villach.

"Ancient things," nodded old Zhonzhac Ekare, "before the Tragic Millennium."

"I'd rather hear a battle song."

Zhonzhac Ekare put a finger to his bearded lips and silenced his friend while Bowgentle continued.

                    who made
                    gifts of alabaster,
                    Damascus-blade,
                    and Paris plaster
                    from the tomb
                    of Zoroaster
                    where the nightshade
                    and the oleaster
                    bloom.

Hawkmoon hardly heard the words, but the rhythms seemed to have a peculiar effect on him. At first he thought it was the wine, but then he realized that at certain points in the recitation his mind would seem to shudder and forgotten sensations would well up in his breast. He swayed in his chair.

Bowgentle looked hard at Hawkmoon as he continued his poem, gesticulating in an exaggerated way.

                    The poet laureate in laurel
                    and orange brocade
                    chased with topaz
                    and opal
                    and lucent jade,
                    fragrant of pomander,
                    redolent to myrrh
                    and lavender,
                    the treasure

of Samarcand and Thrace,
fell prostrate
in the marketplace,

"Are you well, my lord?" asked Yisselda, leaning toward Hawkmoon and speaking with concern.

Hawkmoon shook his head. "I am well enough, thanks." He was wondering if in some way he had offended the Lords of Granbretan and they were even now giving the Black Jewel its full life. His head was swimming.

insensate,
and while choral
anthems told
his glory,
the Emperor,
majestical,
in slippers of gold
and ivory,
upon him trod
and throngs applaud
the mortal god.

Now all Hawkmoon saw was the figure and face of Bowgentle, heard nothing but the rhythms and the vowel rhymes, and wondered about enchantment. And if Bowgentle were seeking to enchant him, what was his reason?

From windows and towers
gaily arrayed
with garlands of flowers
and fresh bouquets
the children sprayed
showers
of meadow-rue,
roses and nosegays
of hyacinth into
the crossways
where Glaucoma passed.
Down to the causeways
from steeples and parapets

children threw
violets,
plum blossoms, lilies
and peonies,
and, last,
themselves
when Glaucoma passed.

Hawkmoon took a long draft of wine and breathed deeply, staring at Bowgentle as the poet continued with his verse.

The moon
shone dim,
the hot sun swayed
and still delayed
the noon,
the stars bestrewn
with seraphim
upraised
a hymn,
for soon
the Emperor
would stand before the sacred ruin
sublime
and lay his hand upon that door
unknown to time
that he alone
of mortal man may countermand.

Hawkmoon gasped as a man might when plunged into icy water. Yisselda's hand was on his sweat-wet brow, and her sweet eyes were troubled. "My lord…?"

Hawkmoon stared at Bowgentle as the poet went relentlessly on.

Glaucoma passed
with eyes downcast
the grave ancestral portal
inlaid with precious stone
and pearl and bone

and ruby. He passed
the portal and the colonnade while trombone
sounds and trumpets blast
and earth trembles
and above
a host assembles
and the scent of ambergris is
burning in the air.

Dimly, Hawkmoon glimpsed Yisselda's hand touching his face, but he did not hear what she said. His eyes were fixed on Bowgentle, his ears were concentrated on listening to the verse. A goblet had fallen from his hand. He was plainly ill, but Count Brass made no move to help. Count Brass, instead, looked from Hawkmoon to Bowgentle, his face half-hidden behind his wine cup, an ironic expression in his eyes.

Now the Emperor releases
a snow-white dove!
O, a dove
as fair
as peace is,
so rare
that love increases
everywhere.

Hawkmoon groaned. At the far end of the table von Villach banged his wine cup on the table. "I'd agree with that. Why not 'The Mountain Bloodletting'? It's a good..."

The Emperor released
that snow-white dove
and it flew
till none could sight
it, flew through the bright
air, flew through fire,
flew still higher,
still flew higher,
right
into the sun

to die for
the Emperor Glaucoma

Hawkmoon staggered to his feet, tried to speak to Bowgentle, fell across the table, spilling wine in all directions.

"Is he drunk?" von Villach asked in a tone of disgust.

"He is ill!" called Yisselda. "Oh, he is ill!"

"He is not drunk, I think," Count Brass said, leaning over Hawkmoon's body and raising an eyelid. "But he is certainly insensible." He looked up at Bowgentle and smiled. Bowgentle smiled back and then shrugged.

"I hope you are sure of that, Count Brass," he said.

Hawkmoon lay all night in a deep coma and awoke the next morning to find Bowgentle, who acted as physician to the castle, bending over him. Whether what had happened had been caused by drink, the Black Jewel, or Bowgentle, he still could not be sure. Now he felt hot and weak.

"A fever, my lord Duke," Bowgentle said softly. "But we shall cure you, never fear."

Then Yisselda was there, seating herself beside his bed. She smiled at him. "Bowgentle says it is not serious," she told him. "I will nurse you. Soon you will be in good health again."

Hawkmoon looked into her face and felt a great flood of emotion fill him. "Lady Yisselda…"

"Yes, my lord?"

"I… thank you…"

He looked about the room in bewilderment. From behind him he heard a voice speak urgently. It was Count Brass's voice. "Say nothing more. Rest. Control your thoughts. Sleep if you can."

Hawkmoon had not realized Count Brass was in the room. Now Yisselda put a glass to his lips. He drank the cool liquid and was soon asleep again.

The next day the fever was gone, and rather than an absence of emotion, Dorian Hawkmoon felt as if he were numbed physically and spiritually. He wondered if he had been drugged.

Yisselda came to him as he was finishing breakfast and asked if he were ready to accompany her on a walk through the gardens, since the day was fine for the season.

He rubbed his head, feeling the strange warmth of the Black Jewel beneath his hand. With some alarm, he dropped his hand.

"Do you still feel ill, my lord?" asked Yisselda.

"No… I…" Hawkmoon sighed. "I don't know. I feel odd — it's unfamiliar…"

"Some fresh air, perhaps, will clear your head."

Passively, Hawkmoon got up to go with her into the gardens. The gardens were scented with all kinds of pleasant smells, and the sun was bright, making the shrubs and trees stand out sharply in the clear winter air.

The touch of Yisselda's arm linked in his stirred Hawkmoon's feelings further. It was a pleasant sensation, as was the bite of the wind in his face and the sight of the terraced gardens and the houses below. As well as these, he felt fear and distrust — fear of the Black Jewel, for he was sure that it would destroy him if he betrayed any sign of what he was now going through; and distrust of Count Brass and the rest, for he felt that they were in some way deceiving him and had more than an inkling of his purpose in coming to Castle Brass. He could seize the girl now, steal a horse, and perhaps stand a good chance of escaping. He looked at her suddenly.

Sweetly, she smiled up at him. "Has the air made you feel better, my lord Duke?"

He stared down into her face while many emotions conflicted within him. "Better?" he said hoarsely. "Better? I am not sure…"

"Are you tired?"

"No." His head had begun to ache, and again he felt afraid of the Black Jewel. He reached out and grasped the girl.

Thinking that he was falling from weakness, she took his arms and tried to support him. His hands went limp and he could do nothing. "You are very kind," he said.

"You are a strange man," she replied, half to herself. "You are an unhappy man."

"Aye…" He pulled away from her and began to walk over the turf to the edge of the terrace. Could the Lords of Granbretan know what was going on within him? It was unlikely. It was likely, on the other hand, that they were suspicious and might give the Black Jewel its life at any moment. He took a deep breath of the cold air and straightened his shoulders, remembering the voice of Count Brass from the night before. "Control your thoughts," he had said.

The pain in his head was increasing. He turned. "I think we had better return to the castle," he told Yisselda. She nodded and took his arm again, and they walked back the way they had come.

In the main hall, Count Brass met them. His expression was one of kindly concern, and there was nothing in his face to confirm the urgency of tone Hawkmoon had heard last night. Hawkmoon wondered if he had dreamed that or if Count Brass had guessed the nature of the Black Jewel and was acting to deceive it and the Dark Lords who even now watched this scene from the palace laboratories in Londra.

"The Duke von Köln is feeling unwell," Yisselda said.

"I am distressed to hear it," Count Brass answered. "Is there anything you need, my lord?"

"No," Hawkmoon replied thickly. "No — I thank you." He walked as steadily as he could toward the stairs. Yisselda went with him, supporting one arm, until they reached his rooms. At the door he paused and looked down at her. Her eyes were wide and full of sympathy; she lifted a soft hand to touch his cheek for an instant. The touch sent a shudder through him and he gasped. Then she had turned and half-run down the passage.

Hawkmoon entered the room and flung himself on his bed, his breathing shallow, his body tense, desperately trying to understand what was happening to him and what was the source of the pain in his head. At length he slept again.

He awoke in the afternoon, feeling weak. The pain had nearly gone, and Bowgentle was beside the bed, placing a bowl of fruit on a nearby table. "I was mistaken in believing the fever had left you," he said.

"What is happening to me?" Hawkmoon murmured.

"As far as I can tell, a mild fever brought about by the hardships you have suffered and, I am afraid, by our hospitality. Doubtless it was too soon for you to eat rich food and drink so much wine. We should have realized that. You will be well enough in a short time, however, my lord."

Privately, Hawkmoon knew this diagnosis to be wrong, but he said nothing. He heard a cough to his left and turned his head but saw only the open door leading to the dressing room. Someone was within that room. He looked questioningly back at Bowgentle, but the man's face was blank as he pretended an interest in Hawkmoon's pulse.

"You must not fear," said the voice from the next room. "We wish to help you." The voice was Count Brass's. "We understand the nature of the Jewel in your forehead. When you feel rested, rise and go to the main hall, where Bowgentle will engage you in some sort of trivial conversation. Do not be surprised if his actions seem a little strange."

Bowgentle pursed his lips and straightened up. "You will soon be fit again, my lord. I take my leave of you now."

Hawkmoon watched him leave the room and heard another door close also — Count Brass leaving. How could they have discovered the truth? And how would it affect him? Even now the Dark Lords must be wondering about the odd turn of events and suspecting something. They might release the full life of the Black Jewel at any moment. For some reason, this knowledge disturbed him more.

Hawkmoon decided that there was nothing he could do but obey Count Brass's command, though it was just as likely that the count, if he had discovered the purpose of Hawkmoon's presence here, would be as vengeful as the Lords of Granbretan. Hawkmoon's situation was an unpleasant one in all its possibilities.

When the room darkened and evening came, Hawkmoon got up and walked down to the main hall. It was empty. He looked around him in the flickering firelight, wondering if he had not been induced to enter some sort of trap.

Then Bowgentle came through the far door and smiled at him. He saw Bowgentle's lips move, but no sound came from them. Bowgentle then pretended to pause as if listening to Hawkmoon's reply, and Hawkmoon realized then that this was a deception for the benefit of those who watched through the power of the Black Jewel.

When he heard a footfall behind him, he did not turn, but instead pretended to reply to Bowgentle's conversation.

Then Count Brass spoke from behind him. "We know what the Black Jewel is, my lord Duke. We understand that you were induced by those of Granbretan to come here, and we believe we know the purpose of your visit. I will explain…"

Hawkmoon was struck by the oddness of the situation as Bowgentle mimed speech and the count's deep voice came as if from nowhere.

"When you first arrived here at Castle Brass," Count Brass continued, "I realized that the Black Jewel was something more than you said it was — even if you did not yourself realize it. I am afraid that those of the Dark Empire do me little credit, for I have studied quite as much sorcery and science as they, and I have a grimoire in which the machine of the Black Jewel is described. However, I did not know whether you were a knowing or unknowing victim of the Jewel, and I had to discover this without the Granbretanians realizing it.

"Thus on the night of the banquet I asked Sir Bowgentle there to disguise a rune as a pretty set of verses. The purpose of this rune would be to rob you of consciousness — and thus rob the Jewel also — so that we could study you without the Lords of the Dark Empire realizing it. We hoped that they would think you drunk and not connect Bowgentle's pretty rhymes with your own sudden infirmity.

"The rune speaking began, with its special rhythms and cadences designed for your ears. It served its purpose, and you passed into a deep coma. While you slept, Bowgentle and I managed to reach through to your inner mind, which was buried deeply — like a frightened animal that digs a burrow so far underground that it begins to stifle to death. Already certain events had brought your inner mind a little closer to the surface than it had been in Granbretan, and we were able to question it. We discovered most of what had happened to you in Londra, and when I learned of your mission here I almost dispatched you. But then I realized that there was a conflict in you — which even you

HAWKMOON

were scarcely aware of. If this conflict had not been evident, I would have killed you myself or let the Black Jewel do its work."

Hawkmoon, pretending to reply to Bowgentle's non-existent conversation, shuddered in spite of himself.

"However," Count Brass went on, "I realized that you were not to blame for what had occurred and that in killing you I might destroy a potentially powerful enemy of Granbretan. Though I remain neutral, Granbretan has done too much to offend me for me to let such a man die. Thus, we worked out this scheme in order to inform you of what we know and also to say that there is hope. I have the means of temporarily nullifying the power of the Black Jewel. When I have finished, you will accompany Bowgentle down to my chambers, where I will do what must be done. We have little time before the Lords of Granbretan lose patience and release the Jewel's full life into your skull."

Hawkmoon heard Count Brass's footfalls leave the hall, and then Bowgentle smiled and said aloud, "So if you would care to accompany me, my lord, I will show you some parts of the castle you have not as yet visited. Few guests have seen Count Brass's private chambers."

Hawkmoon realized that these words were spoken for the benefit of the watchers in Granbretan. Doubtless Bowgentle was hoping to whet their curiosity and thus gain time.

Bowgentle led the way out of the main hall and into a passage that ended at what appeared to be a solid wall hung with tapestries. Pushing the tapestries aside, Bowgentle touched a small stud set in the stone of the wall, and immediately a section of it began to glow brightly and then faded, to reveal a portal through which, by stooping, a man could pass. Hawkmoon went through, followed by Bowgentle, and found himself in a small room, the walls hung with old charts and diagrams. This room was left and another entered, larger than the first. It contained a great mass of alchemical apparatus and was lined with bookshelves full of huge old volumes of chemistry, sorcery and philosophy.

"This way," murmured Bowgentle, drawing aside a curtain to reveal a dark passage.

Hawkmoon's eyes strained as he tried to peer through the darkness, but it was impossible. He stepped cautiously along the passage, and then it was suddenly alive with blinding white light.

Revealed in silhouette was the looming figure of Count Brass, a strangely wrought weapon in his hands pointed at Hawkmoon's head.

Hawkmoon gasped and tried to leap aside, but the passage was too narrow. There was a crack that seemed to burst his eardrums, a weird, melodious humming sound, and he fell back, losing consciousness.

Awakening in golden half light, Hawkmoon had a sense of astonishing physical well-being. His whole mind and body felt alive as if it had never been alive before. He smiled and stretched. He was lying on a metal bench, alone. He reached up and touched his forehead. The Black Jewel was still there, but its texture had changed. No longer did it feel like flesh; no longer did it possess an unnatural warmth. Instead it felt like any ordinary jewel, hard and smooth and cold.

A door opened, and Count Brass entered, looking down at him with an expression of satisfaction.

"I am sorry if I alarmed you yesterday evening," he said, "but I had to work rapidly, paralyzing the Black Jewel and capturing the life force in it. I now possess that life force, imprisoned by means both physical and sorcerous, but I cannot hold it forever. It is too strong. At sometime, it will escape and flow back into the Jewel in your forehead, no matter where you are."

"So I am reprieved but not saved," Hawkmoon said. "How long does the reprieve last?"

"I am not sure. Six months, almost certainly — perhaps a year — perhaps two. But then again, it could be a matter of hours. I cannot deceive you, Dorian Hawkmoon, but I can give you extra hope. There is a sorcerer in the East who could remove the Black Jewel from your head. He is opposed to the Dark Empire and might help you if you could ever find him."

"What is his name?"

"Malagigi of Hamadan."

"Of Persia, then, this sorcerer?"

"Aye," nodded Count Brass. "So far away as to be almost out of your reach."

Hawkmoon sighed and sat up. "Well, then, I must hope your sorcery lasts long enough to sustain me for just a little while. I will leave your lands, Count Brass, and go to Valence to join the army there. It gathers against Granbretan and cannot win, but at least I will take a few of the King-Emperor's dogs with me, by way of vengeance for all they did to me."

Count Brass smiled wryly. "I give you back your life and you immediately decide to sacrifice it. I would suggest that you think for a while before you take any action of any kind. How do you feel, my lord Duke?"

Dorian Hawkmoon swung his legs off the bench and stretched again. "Awake," he said, "a new man..." He frowned. "Aye — a new man..." he murmured thoughtfully. "And I agree with you, Count Brass. Vengeance can wait until a subtler scheme presents itself."

"In saving you," Count Brass said almost sadly, "I took away your youth. You will never know it again."

S I X

THE BATTLE OF KAMARG

"They spread neither to east nor west," said Bowgentle one morning some two months later, "but carve their way directly south. There is no doubt, Count Brass, that they realize the truth and plan revenge upon you."

"Perhaps their vengeance is directed at me," Hawkmoon said from where he sat in a deep armchair on one side of the fire. "If I were to go to meet them, they might be satisfied. No doubt they think of me as a traitor."

Count Brass shook his head. "If I know Baron Meliadus, he wants the blood of all of us now. He and his wolves lead the armies. They will not stop until they reach our boundaries."

Von Villach turned from the window where he had been looking out over the town. "Let them come. We will blow them away as the mistral blows the leaves from the trees."

"Let us hope so," said Bowgentle doubtfully. "They have massed their forces. For the first time they seem to have ignored their usual tactics."

"Aye, the fools," muttered Count Brass. "I admired them for the way they spread out in a widening semicircle. That way they could always strengthen their rear before advancing. Now they have unconquered territory on both flanks and enemy armies capable of closing off their rear. If we beat them, they'll have a hard time retreating. Baron Meliadus's vendetta against us robs him of his good sense."

"But if they win," Hawkmoon said softly, "they will have built a road from ocean to ocean, and their conquering will be the easier for that."

"Possibly that is how Meliadus justifies his action," Bowgentle agreed. "I fear he could be right in anticipating such an outcome."

"Nonsense!" von Villach grumbled. "Our towers will resist Granbretan."

"They were designed to withstand an attack from land," Bowgentle pointed out. "We did not reckon for the aerial navies of the Dark Empire."

"We have our own army of the air," Count Brass said.

"The flamingoes are not made of metal," Bowgentle replied.

Hawkmoon rose. He still wore the black leather doublet and breeches given him by Meliadus. The leather creaked as he moved. "Within a few weeks at most, the Dark Empire will be at our door," he said. "What preparations must be made?"

Bowgentle tapped the large map he had rolled under his arm. "First, we should study this."

Count Brass pointed. "Spread it on yonder table."

As Bowgentle spread the map, using wine-cups to keep the edges down, Count Brass, von Villach, and Hawkmoon gathered round. The map showed Kamarg and the land surrounding it for some hundred miles.

"They are more or less following the river along its eastern bank," Count Brass said, indicating the Rhone. "From what the messenger said, they should be here"— his finger touched the foothills of the Cevennes — "within a week. We must send out scouts and make sure we know their movements from moment to moment. Then, when they reach our borders, we must have our main force grouped at exactly the right position."

"They might send in their ornithopters ahead," Hawkmoon said. "What then?"

"We'll have our own air scouts circling and be able to anticipate them," von Villach growled. "And the towers will be able to deal with them if the air riders cannot."

"Your actual forces are small," Hawkmoon put in, "so you will be depending heavily on these towers, fighting an almost entirely defensive action."

"That is all we shall need to do," Count Brass told him. "We shall wait at our own borders, with ranks of infantry filling in the spaces between the towers, using heliographers and other signalers to direct the towers to where their power will be most needed."

"We seek only to stop their attack on us," Bowgentle said with a hint of sarcasm. "We have no intention of doing more than withstand them."

Count Brass glanced at him and frowned. "Just so, Bowgentle. We should be fools to press an attack — our few against their many. Our only hope of survival is to depend on the towers and show the King-Emperor and his minions that Kamarg can resist anything he cares to try — whether open battle or long siege — attack from land, sea, or air. To expend men on warfare beyond our borders would be senseless."

"And what say you, friend Hawkmoon?" Bowgentle asked. "You have had experience of battle with the Dark Empire."

Hawkmoon paused, consulting the map. "I see the sense of Count Brass's tactics. I have learned to my cost that any formal battle with Granbretan is out of the question. But it occurs to me that we could weigh the odds further to our advantage if we could pick our own battleground. Where are the defenses strongest?"

Von Villach pointed to an area south-east of the Rhone. "Here, where the towers are thickest and there is high ground where our men could group. At the same time, the ground over which the enemy would have to come is marshy in this season and would cause them some difficulty." He shrugged. "But what point is there in such wishful discussion? They will pick the point of attack, not we."

"Unless they could be *driven* there," Hawkmoon said.

"What would drive them? A storm of knives?" Count Brass smiled.

"I would," Hawkmoon told him. "With the aid of a couple of hundred mounted warriors — never engaging them in open battle, but constantly nibbling at their flanks, we could guide them, with luck, to that spot as your dogs drive your bulls. At the same time, we should have them always in sight and be able to send messages to you so that you would know at all times exactly where they were."

Count Brass rubbed at his moustache and looked at Hawkmoon with some respect. "A tactician after my own heart. Perhaps I'm becoming overcautious, after all, in my old age. If I were younger, I might have conceived a similar scheme. It could work, Hawkmoon, with a great deal of luck."

Von Villach cleared his throat. "Aye — luck and endurance. D'you realize what you're taking on, lad? There'd be scant time for sleeping, you'd have to be on your guard at all hours. It's a grueling task you're considering. Would you be man enough for it? And could the soldiers you take stand it? Then there's the flying machines to consider..."

"We'd only need to keep watch for their scouts," Hawkmoon said, "for we'd strike and run before they could get their main force into the air. Your men know the terrain — know where to hide."

Bowgentle pursed his lips. "There's another consideration. The reason they're following the river is to be near their water-carried supplies. They're using the river to bear provisions, spare mounts, war engines, ornithopters — which is why they move so rapidly. How could they be induced to part company with their barges?"

Hawkmoon thought for a moment, then grinned. "Not too difficult a question to answer. Listen..."

Next day, Dorian Hawkmoon went riding across the wild marshland, the lady Yisselda at his side. They had spent much time together since his recovery, and he was deeply attached to her, though he seemed to show her little attention. Content enough to be near him, she was yet sometimes piqued that he made no demonstration of affection. She did not know that he wanted nothing more than to do so but that he felt a responsibility toward her that made him control his natural desire to court her. For he knew that at any moment of the night or day he might become in the space of a few minutes a mindless, shambling creature bereft of his humanity. He lived constantly in the knowledge that the Black Jewel's power could burst the bonds Count Brass had cast around it and that shortly afterwards the Lords of Granbretan would give the Jewel its full life and it would eat his mind.

So he did not tell her that he loved her and that this love had first stirred his inner mind from its slumber and that because he saw this, Count Brass had spared his life. And she was, for her part, too shy to tell him of her love.

They rode together over the marshes, feeling the wind in their faces, tugging at their cloaks, galloping faster than was wise through the winding, hidden causeways through the lagoons and swamps, disturbing quail and duck, sending them squawking into the skies, coming upon herds of wild horses and stampeding them, alarming the white bulls and their wives, galloping to the long, lonely beaches where the cold surf spread, splashing through the spray, beneath the shadows of the watchful guard towers, laughing up at the lowering clouds, horses' hooves beating on the sand, and at length bringing their steeds to a halt to stare out to sea and shout above the song of the mistral.

"You leave tomorrow, Bowgentle tells me," she called, and the wind dropped for a moment and all was suddenly still.

"Aye. Tomorrow." He turned his sad face to her, then quickly turned away again. "Tomorrow. It will not be long before I return."

"Do not be killed, Dorian."

He laughed reassuringly. "It's not my fate, I think, to be killed by Granbretan. If it were — I'd be dead several times over."

She began to reply, but then the wind came roaring in again, catching her hair and curling it about her face. He leaned over to disentangle it, feeling her soft skin and wishing with all his heart that he could hold her face cupped in his hands and touch her lips with his. She reached up to grasp his wrist and keep his hand where it was, but he withdrew it gently, wheeled his horse, and began to ride inland, toward Castle Brass.

The clouds streamed across the sky, above the flattened reeds and the rippling water of the lagoons. A little rain fell, but hardly enough to dampen their shoulders. They rode back slowly, both lost in their own thoughts.

Clad in chain mail from throat to feet, a steel helm with nasals to protect head and face, a long, tapering broadsword at his side, a shield without insignia, Dorian Hawkmoon raised his hand to bring his men to a halt. The men bristled with weapons — bows, slings, some flame-lances, throwing axes, spears — anything that could be hurled from a distance. They were slung across their backs, over their pommels, tied to the sides of their horses, carried in their hands and at their belts. Hawkmoon dismounted and followed his outrider toward the crest of the hill, bending low and moving cautiously.

Reaching the top, he lay on his belly and looked down into the valley where the river wound. It was his first sight of the full might of Granbretan.

It was like a vast legion out of hell, moving slowly southward, battalion upon battalion of marching infantry, squadron after squadron of cavalry, every man masked so that it seemed that the entire animal kingdom marched against Kamarg. Tall banners sprouted from this throng, and metal standards swayed on long poles. There was the banner of Asrovak Mikosevaar, with its grinning, sword-wielding corpse on whose shoulder a vulture perched; beneath it were stitched the words DEATH TO LIFE! The tiny figure swaggering in his saddle close to this standard must be Asrovak Mikosevaar himself. Next to Baron Meliadus, he was the most ruthless of all the Warlords of Granbretan. Nearby was the cat standard of Duke Vendel, Grand Constable of that Order, the fly banner of Lord Jerek Nankenseen, and a hundred other similar flags of a hundred other Orders. Even the mantis banner was there, though the Grand Constable was absent — he was the King-Emperor Huon. But in the forefront rode the wolf-masked figure of Meliadus, carrying his own standard, the snarling figure of a rampant wolf; even his horse was caparisoned all in armour with fancifully wrought chamfron resembling the head of a gigantic wolf.

The ground shook, even at this distance, as the army moved on, and through the air came the jingle and clatter of its arms, the stench of sweat and of animals.

Hawkmoon did not look for long at the army proper. He concentrated on the river beyond, noting the vast numbers of heavily laden barges that lay side by side, so thick that they almost hid the water. He smiled and whispered to the scout at his side, "It suits our plan, you see? All their watercraft bunched together. Come, we must circle their army and get a good distance behind it.

They ran back down the hill. Hawkmoon climbed into his saddle and waved for his men to move on. Following him, they rode at speed, knowing there was little time to spare.

They rode for the best part of that day until the army of Granbretan was merely a cloud of dust to the south and the river was free of the Dark Empire's ships. Here the Rhone narrowed and became shallow, running through an artificial watercourse of ancient stone, with a low stone bridge spanning it. The ground on one side was flat, and on the other it sloped gently down to form a valley.

Wading through this part of the river as evening came, Hawkmoon looked carefully at the stone banks, looked up at the bridge, and tested the nature of the river bed itself while water rushed around his legs, chilling them as it crept between the links of his mail stockings. The watercourse was in poor condition. It had been built before the Tragic Millennium and hardly repaired since. It had been used to divert the river for some reason. Now Hawkmoon intended to put it to a new use.

On the bank, waiting for his signal, were grouped his flame-lancers, holding their long, unwieldy weapons carefully. Hawkmoon climbed back to the bank and began pointing out certain spots on the bridge and the banks. The flame-lancers saluted and began to move in the directions he had indicated, raising their weapons. Hawkmoon stretched his arm toward the west, where the ground fell away, and called to them. They nodded.

As the sky darkened, red flame began to roar from the tapering snouts of the weapons, cut its way into stone, turned water into boiling steam, until all was heat and tumbling chaos.

Through the night, the flame-lances did their work; then suddenly there was a great groan and the bridge collapsed into the river in a great cloud of spray, sending scalding water in all directions. Now the flame-lancers turned their attention to the western bank, carving out blocks that tumbled down into the dammed river, which was beginning to spread out around the bridge that blocked it.

By morning, water rushed down a new course into the valley, and only a small stream flowed along the original bed.

Tired but satisfied, Hawkmoon and his men grinned at one another and mounted their horses, turning away in the direction whence they had come. They had struck their first blow against Granbretan. And it was an effective blow.

Hawkmoon and his soldiers rested in the hills for a few hours and then went to look at the Dark Empire's army again.

Hawkmoon smiled as he lay beneath the cover of a bush and looked down into the valley at the scene of confusion there.

The river was now a morass of dark mud, and in it, like so many stranded whales, lay the battle barges of Granbretan, some with prows jutting high and sterns buried deep in the stuff of the river bed, some on their sides, some bow-first in the mud, some upside-down, war engines scattered, livestock in panic, provisions ruined. And wading among all this the soldiers attempted to haul the mud-encrusted cargoes to land, free horses from their entangling ropes and straps, and rescue sheep, pigs, and cows that struggled wildly in the morass.

There was a great noise of bellowing animals and shouting men. The uniform ranks that Hawkmoon had seen earlier were now broken. On the banks, proud cavalrymen were being forced to use their horses like dray animals to haul barges closer to firm ground. Elsewhere, camps had been erected as Meliadus had realized the impossibility of moving on until the cargoes were rescued. Although guards had been posted around the camps, their attention was on the river and not on the hills where Hawkmoon and his men waited.

It was coming close to dark, and since the ornithopters could not fly at night, Baron Meliadus would not know the exact reason for the river's sudden drying up until the next day. Then, Hawkmoon reasoned, he would dispatch engineers upriver to try to put right the damage; but Hawkmoon was prepared for this.

Now it was time to ready his men. He crept back down to the depression in the hillside where his soldiers were bivouacked and began to confer with his captains. He had a particular objective in view, one he hoped might help demoralize the warriors of Granbretan.

Nightfall, and by the light of brands the men in the valley continued their work, manhandling the heavy war engines to the bank, dragging cases of provisions up the steep sides of the river bed. Meliadus, whose impatience to reach Kamarg allowed his men no rest, rode among the weary, sweating soldiers urging them on. Behind him, each great circle of tents surrounded the particular standard of its Order, but few of the tents were fully occupied since most of the forces were still at work.

No-one saw the approaching shapes of the mounted warriors whose horses walked softly down from the hills, each man swathed in a dark cloak.

Hawkmoon drew his horse to a halt, and his right hand went to his left side, where the fine sword Meliadus had given him was scabbarded. He swept the sword out, raised it for a moment, then pointed it forward. It was the signal to charge.

Without warcries, their only sound the thunder of their horses' hooves and the clank of their accoutrements, the Kamargians plunged forward, led by Hawkmoon, who leaned across his horse's neck and made straight for a surprised guard. His sword took the man in the throat, and with a gurgling murmur the guard collapsed. Through the first of the tents they went, slashing at guy ropes, cutting down the few armed men who tried to stop them, and still the Granbretanians had no idea who attacked them. Hawkmoon reached the centre of the first circle, and his sword swung in a great arc as he chopped at the standard that stood there — the standard of the Order of the Hound. The pole cracked, groaned, and fell into a cooking fire, sending up a great shower of sparks.

Hawkmoon did not pause; he urged his horse on into the heart of the huge camp. On the riverbank there was no alarm, for the invaders could not be heard over the din the Granbretanians themselves made.

Three half-armoured swordsmen ran toward Hawkmoon. He yanked his horse sideways and swung his broadsword left and right, meeting their blades and striking one from its owner's hand. The other two pressed in, but Hawkmoon chopped at a wrist, severing it. The remaining warrior backed away, and Hawkmoon lunged at him, his sword piercing the man's breast.

The horse reared, and Hawkmoon fought to control it, forcing it through another line of tents, his men following. He broke out across an open space, to see his way blocked by a group of warriors dressed only in nightshirts and armed with swords and bucklers. Hawkmoon shouted an order to his horsemen, and they spread out to charge full tilt at the line, their swords held straight before them. Almost in a single movement they killed or knocked flying the line of warriors and were through into the next circle of tents, guy ropes twisting in the air as they were cut, tents collapsing upon their occupants.

At last, his sword glistening with blood, Hawkmoon fought his way to the centre of this circle, and there stood what he sought — the proud mantis banner of the Order of which the King-Emperor himself was Grand Constable. A band of warriors stood round it, pulling on helmets and adjusting their shields on their arms. Without waiting to see if his men followed, Hawkmoon thundered toward them with a wild yell. A shiver ran up his arm as his sword clanged against the shield of the nearest warrior, but he lifted it again, and the sword split the shield, gashing the face of the man behind it so that he reeled back, spitting blood from his ruined mouth. Another Hawkmoon took in the side, and another's head was shorn off clean. His blade rose and fell like some relentless machine, and now his men joined him, pressing the warriors farther and farther back into a tighter and tighter ring about the mantis banner.

Hawkmoon's mail was ripped by a sword-stroke, his shield was struck from his arm, but he fought on until only one man stood by the banner.

Hawkmoon grinned, leaned forward, tipped the man's helmet off his head with a movement of his sword, and clove the skull in twain. Then he reached out and yanked the mantis banner from the earth, raised it high to display it to his cheering men, and turned his horse about, riding for the hills again, the steed leaping corpses and tangled tents with ease.

He heard a wounded warrior yell from behind him, "Did you see him? He has a Black Jewel embedded in his skull!" — and he knew that before long Baron Meliadus would understand who had raided his camp and stolen his army's most precious standard.

Hawkmoon turned in the direction of the shout, shook the banner triumphantly, and laughed a wild, mocking laugh.

"Hawkmoon!" he cried. "Hawkmoon!" It was the age-old battleshout of his forefathers. It sprang unconsciously to his lips now, bidden by his will to let his great enemy Meliadus, the slayer of his kin, know who opposed him.

The coal-black stallion on which he rode reared up, red nostrils flaring, eyes glaring, was wheeled around on its hindlegs, and plunged through the confusion of the camp.

Behind them came mounted warriors, hastily riding in pursuit, goaded on by Hawkmoon's infuriating laughter.

Hawkmoon and his men soon reached the hills again and headed for the secret encampment they had already prepared. Behind them blundered Meliadus's men. Looking back, Hawkmoon saw that the scene on the dried-up riverbank had turned into even greater confusion. Torches moved hurriedly toward the camp.

Knowing the country as they did, Hawkmoon's men had soon outdistanced their pursuers and at length come to a rocky hillside where they had camouflaged a cave entrance the previous day. Into this cave they now rode, dismounting and replacing the camouflage. The cave was large, and there were even larger caverns beyond it, big enough to take their whole force and stable their horses. A small stream ran through the farthest cave, which held provisions for several days. Other secret camps had been prepared all the way back to Kamarg.

Someone lit brands, and Hawkmoon dismounted, hefting the mantis standard and flinging it into a corner. He grinned at round-faced Pelaire, his chief lieutenant.

"Tomorrow Meliadus will send engineers back to our dam, once his ornithopters have reported. We must make sure they do not destroy our handiwork."

Pelaire nodded. "Aye, but even if we slay one party, he'll send another..."

Hawkmoon shrugged. "And another, doubtless — but I rely upon his impatience to reach Kamarg. At length he should realize the pointlessness in wasting time and men in trying to redivert the river. Then he will press on — and with luck, if we survive, we should be able to drive him south-east to our borders."

Pelaire had begun to count the numbers of the returning warriors. Hawkmoon waited until he had finished, then asked, "What losses?"

Pelaire's face was a mixture of elation and disbelief. "None, master — we have not lost a man!"

"A good omen," Hawkmoon said, slapping Pelaire on the back. "Now we must rest, for we have a long ride in the morning."

At dawn, the guard they had left at the entrance came back to report bad news.

"A flying machine," he told Hawkmoon as the duke washed himself in the stream. "It has been circling above for the last ten minutes."

"Do you think the pilot has guessed something — made out our tracks, perhaps?" Pelaire put in.

"Impossible," Hawkmoon said, drying his face. "The rock would show nothing even to someone on the ground. We must bide our time — those ornithopters cannot remain airborne for long without returning to re-power."

But an hour later the guard returned to say that a second ornithopter had arrived to replace the first. Hawkmoon bit his lip, then reached a decision. "Time is running out. Before the engineers can begin work we must get to the dam. We shall have to resort to a riskier plan than I'd hoped to use..."

Swiftly he drew one of his men aside and spoke to him; then he gave orders for two flame-lancers to come forward, and, last, he told the rest of his men to saddle their horses and be prepared to leave the cavern.

A little later, a single horseman rode out of the cavern entrance and began slowly to ride down the gentle, rocky slope.

Watching from the cave. Hawkmoon saw the sun glance off the body of the great, brazen flying machine as its mechanical wings flapped noisily in the air and it began to descend toward the lone man. Hawkmoon had counted on the pilot's curiosity. Now he made a gesture with his hand, and the flame-lancers brought their long, unwieldy weapons up, their ruby coils already beginning to glow in readiness. The disadvantages of the flame-lance were that it could not be operated instantly and it often grew too hot to hold easily.

Now the ornithopter was circling lower and lower. The hidden flame-lancers raised their weapons. The pilot could be seen, leaning over his cockpit, crow-mask peering downward.

"Now," murmured Hawkmoon.

As one, the red lines of flame left the tips of the lances. The first splashed against the side of the ornithopter and merely heated the armour a little. But the second struck the pilot's body, which almost instantly began to flare. The pilot beat at his burning garments, and his hands left the delicate controls of the machine. The wings flapped erratically, and the ornithopter twisted in the air, keeled to one side, and plunged earthward with the pilot trying to bring the flying machine out of its dive. It struck a nearby hillside and crumpled to pieces, the wings still beating for an instant, the pilot's broken body flung some yards away; then it burst apart with a strange smacking sound. It did not catch fire, but the pieces were scattered widely over the hillside. Hawkmoon did not understand the peculiarities of the power unit used for the ornithopters, but one of them was the manner in which it exploded.

Hawkmoon mounted the black stallion and signaled his men to follow him. Within moments they were galloping down the rocky slope of the hill, heading for the dam they had made the day before.

The winter's day was bright and clear, and the air was exhilarating. They rode with some confidence, cheered by their success of last night. They slowed down, eventually, when the dam was close, saw the river flowing on its new course, watched from the top of the hill as a detachment of warriors and engineers inspected the broken bridge that successfully blocked the water from its earlier course, and then charged down, the mounted flame-lancers in the lead, leaning back in their stirrups while they operated their temperamental weapons.

Ten lines of fire poured toward the surprised Granbretanians, turning men into living brands that ran screaming for the water. Fire swept across the ranks of men in the masks of mole and badger and the protecting force in their vulture masks — Asrovak Mikosevaar's mercenaries. Then Hawkmoon's men had clashed with them, and the air rang with the clangour of their weapons. Bloody axes swung in the air, swords swept back and forth, men screamed in death agonies, horses snorted and whinnied with hooves flailing.

Hawkmoon's horse, protected by chain armour, staggered as a huge man swung a great double-bladed war-axe at it. The horse fell, dragging Hawkmoon down, its body trapping him. The vulture-masked axeman moved in, raising the weapon over Hawkmoon's face. Hawkmoon pulled his arm from beneath the horse, and there was a sword in his hand that swept up just in time to take the main force of the blow. The horse was clambering to its feet again. Hawkmoon sprang up and grabbed its reins while at the same time protecting himself from the swinging axe.

Once, twice, thrice, the weapons met, until Hawkmoon's sword arm ached. Then he slid his blade down the shaft and struck the axeman's fists. Hawkmoon's adversary let go of the weapon with one hand, a muffled oath coming from within the mask. Hawkmoon smashed his sword against the metal mask, denting it. The man groaned and staggered. Hawkmoon got both hands on the grip of the broadsword and brought the blade around to chop deep into the head again. The vulture mask split, and a bloodied face was revealed, the bearded mouth screaming for mercy. Hawkmoon's eyes narrowed, for he loathed the mercenaries more than he loathed the Granbretanians. He delivered a third blow to the head, staving in all of one side so that the man waltzed backward, already dead, and crumpled against one of his fellows who was engaged with a Kamargian horseman.

Hawkmoon remounted and led his men against the last of the Vulture Legion, hacking and thrusting in a fever of bloodletting, until only the engineers, armed with short swords, remained. These presented little opposition and were shortly all slain, their bodies strewn across the dam and drifting down the river they had sought to redivert.

Pelaire glanced at Hawkmoon as they rode away toward the hills. "You have no mercy in you, captain!"

"Aye," Hawkmoon replied distantly, "none. Man, woman, or child, if they be of or for Granbretan, they are my enemies to be slain."

Eight of their number were dead. Considering the strength of the force they had destroyed, they had again known great luck. The Granbretanians were used to massacring their enemies, they were not used to being attacked in this manner.

Perhaps this explained the few losses the men of Kamarg had suffered so far.

Four more expeditions Meliadus sent to destroy the dam, each expedition of increasing numbers. Each was destroyed in turn by sudden attacks from the horsemen of Kamarg, and of the original two hundred riders who followed Dorian Hawkmoon, nearly a hundred and fifty remained to carry out the second part of his plan and harry the armies of Granbretan so that they turned slowly, encumbered as they were by their land-borne war engines and supplies, toward the south-east.

Hawkmoon never afterward attacked by day, when the ornithopters circled the skies, but would creep in by night. His flame-lances burned scores of tents and their occupants, his arrows cut down dozen upon dozen of the men assigned to guard the tents and the warriors who went out by day to seek for the Kamargians' secret camps. Swords scarcely dried before they were wetted again, axes became blunt with their deadly work, and heavy Kamarg spears were in short supply among their original owners. Hawkmoon and his men became haggard and red-eyed, hardly able to keep their saddles at times, often coming within a hairsbreadth of discovery by the ornithopters or search parties. They ensured that the road from the river was lined with Granbretanian corpses — and that that road was the one they chose for the Dark Empire forces to tread.

As Hawkmoon had guessed, Meliadus did not spend the time he should trying to seek out the guerilla riders. His impatience to reach Kamarg dominated even his great hatred for Hawkmoon, and doubtless he reasoned that once he had vanquished Kamarg there would be time enough to deal with Hawkmoon.

Once and only once they came close to confronting one another, as Hawkmoon and his riders moved among the tents and cooking fires, stabbing at random and preparing to leave, since dawn was close. Meliadus, mounted, came up with a group of his wolf cavalry, saw Hawkmoon butchering a couple of men entangled in a fallen tent, and charged toward him.

Hawkmoon looked up, raised his sword to meet Meliadus's, and smiled grimly, pushing the sword gradually backward.

Meliadus grunted as Hawkmoon forced his arm farther and farther back.

"My thanks, Baron Meliadus," said Hawkmoon. "The nurturing you gave me in Londra seems to have improved my strength…"

"Oh, Hawkmoon," Meliadus replied, his voice soft but shaking with rage, "I know not how you escaped the power of the Black Jewel, but you will suffer a fate many thousand times greater than the one you have avoided when I take Kamarg and once again make you my prisoner."

Suddenly Hawkmoon moved his blade in under the brass quillons of Meliadus's sword, turned the point, and sent the other's weapon spinning away.

He raised the broadsword to strike, then realized that too many Granbretanians were coming up.

"Time to be away, Baron, I regret. I'll remember your promise — when you're my prisoner!"

He wheeled his horse about and, laughing, was away, leading his men out of the chaos that was the camp. With an angry motion of his hand, Meliadus dismounted to retrieve his sword. "Upstart!" he swore. "He'll crawl at my feet before the month is past."

The day came when Hawkmoon and his riders made no further attacks on Meliadus's forces but galloped swiftly through the marshy ground that lay below the line of hills where Count Brass, Leopold von Villach, and their army awaited them. The tall, dark towers, almost as ancient as Kamarg itself, loomed over the scene, packed now with more than one guardian, snouts of bizarre weapons jutting from almost every slit.

Hawkmoon's horse climbed the hill, approaching the solitary figure of Count Brass, who smiled with great warmth and relief when he recognized the young nobleman.

"I am glad I decided to let you live, Duke von Köln," he said humorously. "You have done everything you planned — and kept the best part of your force alive. I'm not sure I could have done better myself, in my prime."

"Thank you, Count Brass. Now we must prepare. Baron Meliadus is hardly half a day's march behind us."

Below him now, on the far side of the hill, he could see the Kamargian force, primarily infantry, drawn up.

At most a thousand men, they looked pitifully few compared with the vast weight of warriors marching to meet them. The Kamargians were outnumbered at least twenty to one, probably by twice that amount.

Count Brass saw Hawkmoon's expression.

"Do not fear, lad. We have better weapons than swords with which to resist this invasion."

Hawkmoon had been mistaken in thinking Granbretan would reach the borders in half a day. They had decided to camp before marching on, and it was not until noon of the following day that the Kamargians saw the force approach, moving over the flat plain in a spread-out formation. Each square of infantry and cavalry was made up of a particular Order, each member of the Order pledged to defend every other member whether that member was alive or dead. This system was part of Granbretan's great strength, for it meant that no man ever retreated unless specifically ordered to do so by his Grand Constable.

Count Brass sat on his horse and watched the enemy approach. On one side of him was Dorian Hawkmoon, on the other Leopold von Villach. Here, it was Count Brass who would give the orders. *Now the battle begins in earnest*, thought Hawkmoon, and it was hard to see how they could win. Was Count Brass overconfident?

The mighty concourse of fighting men and machines came eventually to a halt about half a mile away; then two figures broke from the main body and began to ride toward the hill. As they came closer, Hawkmoon recognized the standard as that of Baron Meliadus and realized a moment later that one of the figures was Meliadus himself, riding with his herald. He held a bronze megaphone, symbolizing the wish for a peaceful parley.

"Surely he can't wish to surrender — or expect us to," von Villach said in a tone of disgruntlement.

"I would think not," smiled Hawkmoon. "Doubtless this is one of his tricks. He is famous for them."

Noting the quality of Hawkmoon's smile, Count Brass counseled, "Be wary of that hatred, Dorian Hawkmoon. Do not let it possess your reason the way it possesses Meliadus's."

Hawkmoon stared straight in front of him and did not reply.

Now the herald lifted the heavy megaphone to his lips.

"I speak for Baron Meliadus, Grand Constable of the Order of the Wolf, First Chieftain of the Armies under the most noble King-Emperor Huon, ruler of Granbretan and destined ruler of all Europe."

"Tell your master to lift his mask and speak for himself," Count Brass called back.

"My master offers you honourable peace. If you surrender now, he promises that he will slay nobody and will merely appoint himself as Governor of your province in King Huon's name, to see justice done and order brought to this unruly land. We offer you mercy. If you refuse, all Kamarg will be laid waste, everything shall be burned and the sea let in to flood what remains. The Baron Meliadus says that you well know it is in his power to do all this and that your resistance will be the cause of the deaths of your kin as well as yourselves."

"Tell Baron Meliadus, who hides behind his mask, too abashed to speak since he knows that he is a graceless cur who has abused my hospitality and been beaten by me in a fair fight — tell your master that we may well be the death of him and all his kind. Tell him that he is a cowardly dog and a thousand of his ilk could not bring down one of our Kamarg bulls. Tell him that we sneer at his offer of peace as a trick — a deception that could be seen for what it is by a child. Tell him that we need no governor, that we govern ourselves to our own satisfaction. Tell him..."

Count Brass broke into a jeering laugh as Baron Meliadus angrily turned his horse about and, with the herald at his heels, galloped back toward his men.

They waited for a quarter of an hour, and then they saw the ornithopters rise into the air. Hawkmoon sighed. He had been defeated once by the flying machines. Would he be defeated for a second time?

Count Brass raised his sword in a signal, and there was a great flapping and snapping sound. Looking behind him, Hawkmoon saw the scarlet flamingoes sweeping upward, their graceful flight exceedingly beautiful in comparison with the clumsy motions of the metal ornithopters that parodied them. Soaring into the sky, the scarlet flamingoes, with their riders in their high saddles, each man armed with a flame-lance, wheeled toward the brazen ornithopters.

Gaining height, the flamingoes were in the better position, but it was hard to believe that they would be a match for the machines of metal, however clumsy. Red streamers of flame, hardly visible from this distance, struck the sides of the ornithopters, and one pilot was hit, killed almost instantly and falling from his machine. The pilotless ornithopter flapped on; then its wings folded behind it and it plunged downward, to land, birdlike, prow first, in the swamp below the hill. Hawkmoon saw an ornithopter fire its twin flame-cannon at a flamingo and its rider, and the scarlet bird leaped in the air, somersaulted, and crashed to earth in a great shower of feathers. The air was hot and the flying machines noisy, but Count Brass's attention was now on the Granbretanian cavalry, which was advancing toward the hill at a charge.

Count Brass made no movement at first; he merely watched the huge press of horsemen as they came nearer and nearer. Then he lifted his sword again, yelling: "Towers — open fire!"

The nozzles of some of the unfamiliar weapons turned toward the enemy riders, and there came a shrieking sound that Hawkmoon thought would split his head, but he saw nothing come from the weapons. Then he saw that the horses were rearing, just as they reached the swampland. Every one was bucking now, eyes rolling and foam flecking its lips. Riders were flung off until half the cavalry was crawling in the swamp, slipping on the treacherous mud, trying to control their animals.

Count Brass turned to Hawkmoon. "A weapon that emits an invisible beam down which sound travels. You heard a little of it — the horses experienced its full intensity."

"Shall we charge them now?" Hawkmoon asked.

"No — no need. Wait, curb your impatience."

The horses were falling, stiff and senseless. "It kills them, unfortunately, in the end," Count Brass said.

Soon all the horses lay in the mud while their riders cursed and waded back to firm ground, standing there uncertainly.

Above them, flamingoes dived and circled around the ornithopters, making up in grace for what they lacked in power and strength. But many of the giant birds were falling — more than the ornithopters, with their clanking wings and whirring engines.

Great stones began to crash down near the towers.

"The war machines — they're using their catapults," von Villach growled. "Can't we…?"

"Patience," said Count Brass, apparently unperturbed.

Then a great wave of heat struck them, and they saw a huge funnel of crimson fire splash against the nearest tower. Hawkmoon pointed. "A fire cannon — the largest I've ever seen. It will destroy us all!"

Count Brass was riding for the tower under attack. They saw him leap from his horse and enter the building, which seemed doomed. Moments later the tower began to spin faster and faster, and Hawkmoon realized in astonishment that it was disappearing below the ground, the flame passing harmlessly over it. The cannon turned its attention to the next tower, and as it did so, this tower began to spin and retreat into the ground while the first tower whirled upward again, came to a halt, and let fire at the flame cannon with a weapon mounted on the battlements. This weapon shone green and purple and had a bell-shaped mouth. A series of round white objects flew from it and landed near the flame cannon. Hawkmoon could see them bouncing amongst the engineers who manned the weapon. Then his attention was diverted as an ornithopter crashed close by and he was forced to turn his horse and gallop along the crest of the hill until he was out of range of the exploding power unit. Von Villach joined him. "What are those things?" Hawkmoon asked, but von Villach shook his head, as puzzled as his comrade.

Then Hawkmoon saw that the white spheres had stopped bouncing and that the flame cannon no longer gouted fire. Also the hundred or so people near the cannon were no longer moving. Hawkmoon realized with a shock that they were frozen. More of the white spheres shot from the bell-shaped mouth of the weapon and bounced near the catapults and other war engines of Granbretan. Shortly, the crews of these were also frozen and rocks ceased to fall near the towers.

Count Brass left the tower he had entered and rode back to join them. He was grinning. "We have still other weapons to display to these fools," he said.

"But can they fight such a weight of men?" Hawkmoon asked, for the infantry were now moving forward, their numbers so vast that it seemed not even the mightiest weapons could stop their advance.

"We shall see," Count Brass replied, signaling to a lookout on a nearby tower. The air above them was black with fighting birds and machines, red traceries of fire crisscrossing the sky, pieces of metal and bloody feathers falling all around them. It was impossible to tell which side was winning.

The infantry was almost upon them when Count Brass waved his sword to the lookout and the tower turned wide-muzzled weapons toward the armies of Granbretan. Glass spheres, shimmering blue in the light, hurtled toward the advancing warriors and fell among them. Hawkmoon saw them break formation, begin to run about wildly, flailing at the air and ripping off the masks of their respective Orders.

"What has happened?" he asked Count Brass in amazement.

"The spheres contain a hallucinatory gas," Count Brass told him. "It makes the men see dreadful visions," Now he turned in his saddle and waved his sword to the waiting men below. They began to advance. "The time has come to meet Granbretan with ordinary weapons," he said.

From the remaining ranks of infantry, arrows flew thickly toward them and flame-lances sent searing fire. Count Brass's archers retaliated, and his flame-lancers also returned the attack. Arrows clattered on their armour. Several men fell. Others were struck down by the flame-lances. Through the chaos of fire and flying arrows, the infantry of Granbretan steadily advanced, in spite of depleted numbers. They paused when they came to the swampy ground, choked as it was with the bodies of their horses, and their officers furiously urged them on.

Count Brass ordered his herald forward, and the man approached, bearing the simple flag of his master — a red gauntlet on a white field.

The three men waited as the infantry broke ranks and began to clamber through the mud and over the corpses of the horses, struggling to reach the hill where the forces of Kamarg waited to meet them.

Hawkmoon saw Meliadus some distance in the rear and recognized the barbaric vulture-mask of Asrovak Mikosevaar as the Muskovian led his Vulture Legion on foot and was one of the first to cross the swamp and reach the slopes of the hill.

Hawkmoon trotted his horse forward a little so that he would be directly in the path of Mikosevaar when he approached.

He heard a bellow, and the vulture-mask glared at him with eyes of ruby. "Aha! Hawkmoon! The dog that has worried at us for so long! Now let's see how you conduct yourself in a fair fight, traitor!"

"Call me not 'traitor'," Hawkmoon said angrily. "You sniffer of corpses!"

Mikosevaar hefted his great war axe in his armoured hands, bellowed again, and began to run toward Hawkmoon, who jumped from his horse and, with shield and broadsword, prepared to defend himself.

The axe, shod all in metal, thundered against the shield and sent Hawkmoon staggering back a pace. Another blow followed and split the top edge of the shield. Hawkmoon swung his sword around, and it struck Mikosevaar's heavily armoured shoulder with a great ringing sound, sending up a shower of sparks.

Both men held their ground, giving blow for blow as the battle raged around them. Hawkmoon glanced at von Villach and saw him engaged with Mygel Holst, Archduke of Londra, well-matched in age and strength, and Count Brass was ploughing through the lesser warriors, trying to seek out Meliadus, who had plainly decided to supervise the battle from a distance.

From their advantageous position, the Kamargians withstood the Dark Empire warriors, holding their line firm.

Hawkmoon's shield was a ruin of jagged metal and useless. He flung it from his arm and seized his sword in both hands, swinging it to meet the blow Mikosevaar aimed at his head. The two men grunted with exertion as they maneuvered about in the slippery earth of the hill, now jabbing to try to make the other lose his footing, now slashing suddenly at the legs or torso or battering from above or the side.

Hawkmoon was sweating heavily in his armour, and he grunted with effort. Then suddenly his foot slid from under him and he fell to one knee, Mikosevaar lumbering forward to raise his axe and decapitate his enemy. Hawkmoon flung himself flat, toward Mikosevaar, and grabbed at the man's legs, pulling him down so that both men rolled over and over toward the swamp and the mounds of dead horses.

Punching and cursing, they came to a halt in the filth. Neither had lost his weapon, and now they stumbled to their feet, preparing to continue the fight. Hawkmoon braced himself against the body of a warhorse and swung at the Muskovian. The swing would have broken Mikosevaar's neck had not he ducked, but it knocked the vulture helm from his head, revealing the white, bushy beard and glaring, insane eyes of the Muskovian, who brought his axe upward toward Hawkmoon's belly and had the blow blocked by the sword whistling down.

Releasing his grip on the sword, Hawkmoon pushed with both hands at Mikosevaar's chest, and the man fell backward. As he tried to scramble up, Hawkmoon took a fresh hold of his broadsword, raised it high, and plunged it at the Muskovian's face. The man yelled. The blade rose and descended again. Asrovak Mikosevaar shrieked, and then the sound was suddenly cut off. Hawkmoon lost interest in the groaning thing at his feet and turned to see how the battle went.

It was hard to tell. Everywhere men were falling, and it seemed that the great majority were Granbretanians. The fight in the air was almost over, and only a few ornithopters circled the sky, while there seemed to be many more flamingoes.

Was it possible that Kamarg was winning?

Hawkmoon turned as two warriors of the Vulture Legion ran toward him. Recklessly he stooped to drag up the bloodied mask of Mikosevaar. He laughed at them. "Look! Your Grand Constable is slain — your warlord is destroyed!"

The warriors hesitated, then backed away from Hawkmoon and began to run the way they had come. The Vulture Legion did not have the discipline of the other Orders.

Hawkmoon began to clamber wearily over the bodies of the dead horses, which were now liberally heaped with human corpses. The battle was thin in this area, but he could see von Villach on the hill, kicking the wounded body of Mygel Holst and roaring in triumph as he turned to deal with a group of Holst's warriors who ran at him with spears. Von Villach seemed to need no aid. Hawkmoon began to run as best he could up to the top of the hill, to get a better idea of how the battle turned.

His broadsword was blooded thrice before he could reach his objective and look at the field. The huge army that Meliadus had brought against them was now scarcely a sixth of its former size, while the line of Kamagian warriors still held fast.

Half the banners of the warlords were down, and others were sorely beset. The tight formations of the Granbretanian infantry were largely broken, and Hawkmoon saw that the unprecedented was happening and that the Orders were becoming mixed together, thus throwing their members in confusion, since they were used to fighting side by side with their own brothers.

Hawkmoon saw Count Brass, still mounted, engaged with several swordsmen down the hill. He saw the standard of Meliadus some distance away. It was surrounded by men of the Order of the Wolf. Meliadus had protected himself well. Now Hawkmoon saw several of the commanders — Adaz Promp and Jerek Nankenseen among them — ride toward Meliadus. Evidently they wanted to retreat but must wait for Meliadus's order to do so.

He could guess what the commanders told Meliadus — that the flower of their warriors was being destroyed, that such destruction was not worth suffering for the sake of one tiny province.

But no call came from the trumpets of the heralds who waited nearby. Meliadus was evidently resisting their pleas.

Von Villach came up, riding a borrowed horse. He pushed back his helm and grinned at Hawkmoon. "We're beating them, I think," he said. "Where is Count Brass?"

Hawkmoon pointed. "He is making good account," he smiled. "Should we hold steady or begin to advance — we could if we wished it. I think the Granbretanian warlords are faltering and want to retreat. A push now, and it might make up their minds for them."

Von Villach nodded. "I'll send a messenger down to the count. He must decide."

He turned to a horseman and muttered a few words to him. The man began to race down the hillside, through the confusion of embattled warriors.

Hawkmoon saw him reach the count, saw Count Brass glance up and wave to them, wheel his horse, and begin to return.

Within ten minutes, Count Brass had managed to regain the hill. "Five warlords I slew," he said with a satisfied air. "But Meliadus slunk away."

Hawkmoon repeated what he had said to von Villach, Count Brass agreed with the sense of the plan, and soon the Kamarg infantry began to advance steadily, pushing the Granbretanians down the hill before them.

Hawkmoon found a fresh horse and led the advance, yelling wildly as he chopped about him, striking heads from necks, limbs from torsos, like apples from the bough. His body was covered from head to foot in the blood of the slain. His mail was ragged and threatening to fall from him. His whole chest was a mass of bruises and minor cuts, his arm bled, and his leg ached horribly, but he ignored it all as the bloodlust seized him and he killed man after man.

Riding beside him, von Villach said in a moment of comparative peace, "You seem decided to kill more of the dogs than the rest of our army put together."

"I would not cease if the blood of Granbretan filled this whole plain," Hawkmoon replied grimly. "I would not cease until everything that lived of Granbretan was destroyed."

"Your bloodlust matches theirs," von Villach said ironically.

"Mine is greater," Hawkmoon called, driving forward, "for half theirs is sport."

And, butchering, on he rode.

At last it seemed that his commanders convinced him, for Meliadus's trumpets shouted the retreat and the survivors broke away from the Kamargians and began to run.

Hawkmoon struck down several who threw away their weapons in attitudes of surrender. "I do not care for *living* Granbretanians," he said once as he stabbed a man who had ripped his mask from his young face and begged for mercy.

But at length even Hawkmoon's bitterness was satiated for a while, and he drew up his horse beside those of Count Brass and von Villach and watched as the Granbretanians re-formed their ranks and began to march away.

Hawkmoon thought he heard a great scream of rage rise from the retreating army, thought he recognized the vengeful sound as that of Meliadus, and he smiled.

"We shall see Meliadus again," he said.

Count Brass nodded agreement. "He has found Kamarg invincible to attack by his armies, and he knows that we are too clever to be deceived by his treachery, but he will find some other way. Soon all the lands about Kamarg will belong to the Dark Empire and we shall have to be on our guard the whole time."

When they returned to Castle Brass that night, Bowgentle spoke to the count. "Now do you realize that Granbretan is insane — a cancer that will infect history and will set it on a course that will not only lead to the destruction of the entire human race, but will ultimately result in the destruction of every intelligent or potentially intelligent creature in the universe?"

Count Brass smiled. "You are exaggerating, Bowgentle. How could you know so much?"

"Because it is my calling to understand the forces that go to work to make up what we call destiny. I tell you again, Count Brass, the Dark Empire will infect the universe unless it is checked on this planet — and preferably on this continent."

Hawkmoon sat with his legs stretched out before him, doing his best to work the ache from his muscles. "I have no understanding of the philosophical principles you base your beliefs upon, Sir Bowgentle," he said, "but instinctively I know you to be right. All we think we see is an implacable enemy that means to rule the world — there have been other races like them in the past — but there is something different about the Dark Empire. Forget you not, Count Brass, that I spent time in Londra and was witness to many of their more excessive insanities. You have seen only their armies, which, like most armies, fight fiercely and to win, using conventional tactics because they are the best. But there is little conventional about the King-Emperor, immortal corpse that he is, in his Throne Globe; little conventional about the secret way they have with one another, the sense of insanity that underlies the mood of the entire city…"

"You think we have not, then, witnessed the worst of what they can do?" Count Brass asked seriously.

"That is what I think," Hawkmoon said. "It is not only the need for vengeance that makes me slay them as I do — it is a deeper thing within me that sees them as a threat to the forces of Life itself."

Count Brass sighed. "Perhaps you are right, I do not know. Only the Runestaff could prove you right or wrong."

Hawkmoon got up stiffly. "I have not seen Yisselda since we returned," he said.

"She went to her bed early, I think," Bowgentle told him.

Hawkmoon was disappointed. He had looked forward to her welcome. Had wanted to tell her personally of his victories. It surprised him that she had not been there to greet him.

He shrugged. "Well, I think I'll to mine," he said. "Good night, gentlemen."

They had spoken little of their triumph since returning. Now they were experiencing the reaction of their day's work, and it all seemed a trifle remote, though tomorrow, doubtless, they would celebrate.

When he reached his room it was in darkness, but Hawkmoon sensed something odd and drew his sword before fumbling his way to a table and turning up the lamp that stood there.

Someone lay on his bed, smiling at him. It was Yisselda.

"I heard of your exploits," said she, "and wanted to give you a private welcome. You are a great hero, Dorian."

Hawkmoon felt his breathing become more rapid, felt his heart begin to pound. "Oh, Yisselda…"

Slowly, step by step, he advanced toward the prone girl, his conscience in conflict with his desire.

"You love me, Dorian, I know," she said softly. "Do you deny it?"

He could not. He spoke thickly. "You… are… very… bold…" he said, trying to smile.

"Aye — for you seem extraordinarily shy. I am not immodest."

"I — I am not shy, Yisselda. But no good could come of this. I am doomed — the Black Jewel…"

"What is the Jewel?"

Hesitantly, he told her everything, told her that he did not know how many months Count Brass's sorcerous chains could hold the life force of the Jewel, told her that when its power was released, the Lords of the Dark Empire would be able to destroy his mind.

"So you see — you must not become attached to me… It would be worse if you did."

"But this Malagigi — why do you not seek his aid?"

"The journey would take months. I might waste my remaining time on a fruitless quest."

"If you loved me," she said as he sat down on the bed beside her and took her hand, "you would risk that."

"Aye," he said thoughtfully. "I would. Perhaps you are right…"

She reached up and drew his face toward hers, kissing his lips. The gesture was artless but full of sweetness.

Now he could not restrain himself. He kissed her passionately, held her close. "I will go to Persia," he said at length, "though the way will be perilous, for once I leave the safety of Kamarg, Meliadus's forces will seek me out…"

"You will come back," she said with conviction. "I know you will come back. My love will draw you to me."

"And mine to you?" He stroked her face gently. "Aye — that could be so."

"Tomorrow," she said. "Leave tomorrow and waste no time. Tonight…"

She kissed him again, and he returned her passion fiercely.

B O O K   T H R E E

The histories then tell how, leaving Kamarg, Hawkmoon flew eastward on a giant scarlet bird that bore him a thousand miles or more before it came to the mountains bordering the lands of the Greeks and the Bulgars...

— The High History of the Runestaff

O N E

O L A D A H N

The flamingo was surprisingly easy to ride, as Count Brass had assured him it would be. It responded to commands in the manner of a horse, by means of the reins attached to its curved beak, and was so graceful that never once did Hawkmoon fear falling. In spite of the bird's refusal to fly when it rained, it carried him ten times more swiftly than a horse, needing to rest only for a short time at midday and sleeping, like Hawkmoon, at night.

The high, soft saddle, with its curved pommel, was comfortable, and from it hung panniers of provisions. A harness secured Hawkmoon in this saddle. Its long neck stretched straight before it and its great wings beating slowly, the scarlet bird bore him over mountains, valleys, forests, and plains. Hawkmoon always tried to let the bird come down near rivers or lakes where it could find food to its liking.

Occasionally, Hawkmoon's head would throb, reminding him of the urgency of his mission, but as his winged mount took him farther and farther eastward and the air grew steadily warmer, Hawkmoon's spirits began to rise, and it seemed that the possibilities of returning soon to Yisselda were increasing.

About a week after he had left Kamarg, he was flying over a range of craggy mountains looking for a place to land. It was late evening, and the bird was wearying, dropping lower and lower until the gloomy peaks were all around them and still no water could be seen. Then, suddenly, Hawkmoon saw the figure of a man on the rocky slopes below and, almost instantly, the flamingo screamed, flapping its wings wildly, rocking in the air. Hawkmoon saw a long arrow jutting from its side. A second arrow thudded into the bird's neck, and with a croak, it began to fall rapidly toward the ground. Hawkmoon clung to the pommel of his saddle as the air tore through his hair. He saw the rock rise up, felt a great concussion, and then his head had struck something and he seemed to tumble sickeningly into a black, bottomless well.

Hawkmoon awoke in panic. It seemed that the Black Jewel had been given its life and was even now gnawing at his brain like a rat at a grain sack. He put both hands to his head and felt cuts and bumps, realizing with relief that the pain was physical, resulting from his crash to earth. It was dark, and it seemed that he lay in a cave. Peering forward he saw a flicker of firelight beyond the cave's entrance. He got up and began to make his way toward it.

Near the opening, his foot stumbled against something and he saw his gear piled on the floor. Everything was neatly stacked — saddle, panniers, sword, and dagger. He reached for the sword and softly withdrew it from its scabbard; then he went out.

His face was struck by the heat from the great bonfire a short distance away. Over it, a spit had been constructed, and on the spit turned the huge carcass of the flamingo, trussed, plucked, and bereft of head and claws. Turning the spit by means of a complicated arrangement of leather thongs, which he dampened from time to time, was the stocky figure of a man almost half Hawkmoon's size.

As Hawkmoon approached, the little man turned, saw the blade, yelled and jumped away from the fire. The Duke of Köln was astonished; the creature's face was covered with fine, reddish hair and thicker fur of the same colour seemed to cover his body. He was dressed in a leather jerkin and a leather divided kilt supported by a wide belt. On his feet were boots of soft doeskin, and he wore a cap into which were stuck four or five of the finest flamingo feathers, doubtless purloined from the bird's plumage during the plucking.

He backed away from Hawkmoon, hands raised in a placatory gesture. "Forgive me, master. I am deeply regretful, I assure you. Had I but known that the bird bore a rider, I would not, of course, have shot it. But all I saw was a dinner not to be missed..."

Hawkmoon lowered the sword. "Who are you? Indeed — *what* are you?" He put one hand to his head. The heat from the fire and the exertion had made him dizzy.

"I am Oladahn, kin to the Mountain Giants," began the little man. "Well-known in these parts..."

"Giant? *Giant!*" Hawkmoon laughed hoarsely, swayed, and fell, losing consciousness again.

Next time he awoke, it was to sniff the delicious smell of roasting fowl. He savoured it before he realized what it meant. He had been propped up just within the cave entrance, and his sword had vanished. The little furry man came hesitantly forward, offering him an enormous drumstick.

"Eat, master, and you'll feel better," said Oladahn.

Hawkmoon accepted the great piece of meat. "I suppose I might as well," said he, "since you have robbed me, almost certainly, of everything I desired."

"You were fond of the bird, master?"

"No — but I am in mortal danger, and the flamingo was my only hope of escape." Hawkmoon chewed at the tough flesh.

"Someone pursues you, then?"

"Something pursues me — an unusual and disgusting doom..." And Hawkmoon found himself telling his tale to the creature whose action had brought that doom closer. Even as he spoke, he found it hard to understand why he confided in Oladahn. There was something so grave about his half-human face, something so attentive about the way he cocked his little head, his eyes widening at each new detail, that Hawkmoon's natural reticence was forgotten. "And now here I am," he concluded at last, "eating the bird that was to be my possible salvation."

"It is an ironic tale, my lord," Oladahn sighed, wiping grease from his whiskers, "and it clouds my heart to realize that it was my greedy stomach that brought about this last misfortune. Tomorrow I will do what I can to rectify my mistake and find you a steed of some sort to carry you on to the East."

"Something that can fly?"

"Sadly, no. A goat's the beast I had in mind." Before Hawkmoon could speak, Oladahn continued, "I have a certain influence in these mountains, being regarded as something of a curiosity. I am a crossbred animal, you see, the result of a union between an adventurous youth of peculiar tastes — a sorcerer of sorts — and a Mountain Giantess. Alas, I am an orphan now, for Mother ate Father one hard winter, then Mother was eaten in turn by my Uncle Barkyos — the terror of these parts, largest and fiercest of the Mountain Giants. Since then, I have lived alone, with only my poor father's books for company. I am an outcast — too strange to be accepted either by my father's race or my mother's — living on my wits. If I were not so small, doubtless I should have been eaten, also, by Uncle Barkyos by now..."

Oladahn's face looked so comic in its melancholy that Hawkmoon could no longer bear him even a trace of malice. Besides, he was feeling tired from the heat of the fire and the large meal he had eaten. "Enough, friend Oladahn. Let us forget what cannot be rectified and sleep now. In the morning we must find a new mount for me to ride to Persia."

And they slept, to awaken at dawn to see the fire still flickering under the carcass of the bird and a group of men, in fur and iron, breakfasting off it in some glee.

"Brigands!" Oladahn cried, springing up in alarm. "I should not have left the fire!"

"Where did you hide my sword?" Hawkmoon asked him, but already two of the men, smelling strongly of ancient animal fat, had swaggered toward them, drawing crude swords. Hawkmoon rose slowly to his feet, ready to defend himself as best he could, but Oladahn was already speaking.

"I know you, Rekner," he said, pointing at the largest of the brigands. "And you should know that I am Oladahn of the Mountain Giants. Now that you have had your meal, be off, or my kin will come and slay you."

Rekner grinned, unperturbed, picking his teeth with a dirty fingernail. "I have heard of you, indeed, littlest of giants, and I see nothing to fear, though I've been told that the villagers hereabouts avoid you. But villagers are not brave brigands, eh? Hush now, or we'll kill you slowly instead of quickly."

Oladahn seemed to wilt, but he continued to stare hard at the brigand chieftain. Rekner laughed. "Now, what treasures have you got in that cave of yours?"

Oladahn was swaying from side to side, as if in terror, crooning softly to himself. Hawkmoon looked from him to the brigand and back again, wondering if he could dash into the cave and find his sword in time. Now Oladahn's crooning grew louder, and Rekner paused, the smile freezing on his face and a glassy look coming into his eyes as Oladahn peered into them. Suddenly the little man flung up a hand, pointing and speaking in a cold voice. "Sleep, Rekner!"

Rekner slumped to the ground, and his men cursed, starting forward, then stopping as Oladahn kept his hand raised. "Beware my power, scavengers, for Oladahn is the son of a sorcerer."

The brigands hesitated, glancing at their prone leader. Hawkmoon looked in astonishment at the furry creature who held the warlike men at bay, then ducked into the cave and found his sword rescabbarded. He drew the belt that held it and the dagger about his waist and buckled it, pulling forth the blade and returning to Oladahn's side. The little man muttered from the corner of his mouth, "Bring your provisions. Their steeds are tethered at the bottom of the slope. We'll use them to escape, for Rekner will waken any instant, and I cannot hold them after that."

Hawkmoon got the panniers, and he and Oladahn began to back down the slope, their feet scraping on the loose rock and scrub. Rekner was already stirring. He gave a groan and sat up. His men bent to help him to his feet. "Now," said Oladahn, and turned to run. Hawkmoon followed and there, to his surprise, were half a dozen goats the size of ponies, each animal with a sheepskin saddle. Oladahn swung himself up onto the nearest and held the bridle of another for Hawkmoon. The Duke of Köln hesitated for a moment, then smiled wryly and climbed into the saddle. Rekner and his brigands were racing down the hill toward them. With the flat of his sword, Hawkmoon slapped at the rumps of the remaining goats and they began to spring away.

"Follow me!" cried Oladahn, urging his goat down the mountain toward a narrow trail. But Rekner's men had reached Hawkmoon, and his bright sword met their dull ones as they hacked savagely at him. He stabbed one man through the heart, struck another in the side, managed to slam the side of his blade down on Rekner's pate, then was riding the leaping goat in hot pursuit of the strange little man, the brigands roaring oaths and staggering after him.

The goat moved in a series of leaps, jolting the bones of his body, but soon they had reached the trail and were riding down a tortuous path around the mountain, the cries of the brigands growing fainter and fainter. Oladahn turned with a grin of triumph. "We have our mounts, Lord Hawkmoon, eh? Easier than even I expected. A good omen! Follow me. I'll lead you to your road."

Hawkmoon smiled in spite of himself. Oladahn's company was intoxicating, and his curiosity about the little man, coupled with his growing respect and gratitude for the manner in which he had saved their lives, made Hawkmoon forget almost completely that the furry kin of the Mountain Giants had been the initial cause of his new troubles.

Oladahn insisted on riding with him for several days, all the way through the mountains, until they reached a wide yellow plain and Oladahn pointed, saying, "That is the way you must go."

"I thank you," Hawkmoon said, staring now toward Asia. "It is a shame that we must part."

"Aha!" grinned Oladahn, rubbing at the red fur on his face. "I'd agree with that sentiment. Come, I'll ride with you a way to keep you company on the plain." And with that he urged his goat forward again.

Hawkmoon laughed, shrugged, and followed.

T W O

THE CARAVAN OF AGONOSVOS

It began to rain almost as soon as they reached the plain, and the goats, which had borne them so well through the mountains, were unused to the yielding earth and moved slowly. For a month they traveled, hunched in their cloaks, shivering from the damp that chilled them to their vitals, and Hawkmoon's head throbbed often. When the throbbing came, he would not speak to the solicitous Oladahn but would bury his head in his arms, his face pale and his teeth clenched, tormented eyes staring at nothing. He knew that at Castle Brass the sentience of the Jewel was beginning to break the bonds the count had wrought, and he despaired of seeing Yisselda again.

Rain beat down, and a cold wind blustered, and through the sweeping curtain of water Hawkmoon saw vast stretches of fenland ahead of them, broken by clumps of gorse and black, shrunken trees. He had little idea of his bearings, for most of the time clouds obscured the sky. The only rough indication of direction was in the manner in which the shrubs grew in this part of the world, leaning almost invariably toward the south. He had not expected to meet such country so far to the east, and he gathered that its characteristics were the result of some event that had taken place during the Tragic Millennium.

Hawkmoon brushed his damp hair from his eyes, feeling the hard touch of the Black Jewel embedded in his forehead. He shivered, glancing at Oladahn's miserable face, then back through the rain. There was a dark outline in the distance that might indicate a forest where they would at least have some protection from the rain. The pointed hooves of the goats stumbled through the swampy grass. Hawkmoon's head began to tingle, and again he felt the gnawing sensation in his brain and a nausea in his chest. He gasped, pressing one forearm against his skull while Oladahn looked on in mute sympathy.

At length they reached the low-lying trees. They found the going even slower than it had been and avoided the ponds of dark water that had formed everywhere. The trunks and branches of the trees seemed malformed, twisting toward the ground rather than away from it. The bark was black or dark brown, and at this season there was no foliage. In spite of this, the forest seemed thick and hard to penetrate. At its edge water glinted, a shallow moat protecting the trees.

Their mounts' hooves splashed through the muddy water as they entered the forest, bending low to avoid the curling branches. Even here the ground was swampy, and pools had formed at the bases of the trunks, but there was little shelter, after all, from the perpetually falling rain.

They camped that evening on relatively dry ground, and although Hawkmoon made some attempt to help Oladahn build a fire, he was soon forced to lie with his back against a tree trunk, panting and clutching his head while the little man finished the work.

The next morning they moved on through the forest, Oladahn leading Hawkmoon's mount, for the Duke of Köln was now slumped across its neck. Toward the latter part of the morning they heard human voices and turned their beasts toward the sound.

It was a caravan of sorts, labouring through the mud and water between the trees. Some fifteen wagons, with rain-soaked silk canopies of scarlet, yellow, blue, and green. Mules and oxen strained to haul them, and their feet slipped in mud, and their muscles bulged and rippled as they were goaded on by their drivers, who stood beside them with whips and spiked sticks. At the wheels of the wagons other men sweated to help turn them, and at the backs of the wagons leaned more who pushed with all their might. Yet in spite of this great effort, the wagons hardly moved.

It was not so much this sight that made the two travelers wonder, but the nature of the people of the caravan. Through his clouded eyes, Hawkmoon saw them and wondered.

Without exception they were grotesque. Dwarves and midgets, giants and fat men, men with fur growing all over them (rather like Oladahn, save that the fur of these was unpleasant to look upon), others pale and hairless, one man with three arms, another with one; two cloven-footed people — a man and a woman — children with beards, hermaphrodites with the organs of both sexes, others with mottled skins like snakes, and others with tails, misshapen limbs and warped bodies; faces with features missing or else abnormally proportioned; some hunchbacked, some without necks, some with foreshortened arms and legs, one with purple hair and a horn growing from his forehead. And only in their eyes was there any similarity, for every expression was one of dull despair as the bizarre band toiled to move the caravan a few feet through the wooded marsh.

It seemed that they were in hell and looked upon the damned.

The forest smell of damp bark and wet mould was now mingled with other scents, harder to identify. There was the stink of men and beasts, of heavy perfume and rich spices, but besides these there was something else that lay over them all and made Oladahn shudder. Hawkmoon had raised himself up from his mount's neck and sniffed the air like a wary wolf. He glanced at Oladahn, frowning. The deformed creatures did not seem to notice the newcomers but continued to work in silence. There was only the sound of the wagons creaking and the animals snorting and splashing in their yokes.

Oladahn tugged at his reins, as if to pass the caravan by, but Hawkmoon did not follow his example. He continued to stare thoughtfully at the weird procession.

"Come," said Oladahn. "There is danger here, Lord Hawkmoon."

"We must get our bearings — find out where we are and how far we must travel over this plain," Hawkmoon said in a harsh whisper. "Besides, our provisions are almost gone…"

"We might come upon some game in the forest."

Hawkmoon shook his head. "No. Also I think I know to whom this caravan belongs."

"Who?"

"A man I have heard of but never encountered. A countryman of mine — a kinsman even — who left Köln some nine centuries ago."

"Nine centuries? Impossible!"

"Not so. Lord Agonosvos is immortal — or nearly. If it be he, then he could help us, for I am still his rightful ruler…"

"He would have loyalty to Köln, after nine hundred years?"

"Let us see." Hawkmoon urged his beast toward the head of the caravan, where a tall wagon swayed, its canopy of golden silk, its carriage carved in complicated patterns, painted in bright primaries. Ill at ease, Oladahn followed less rapidly. In the front of the wagon, seated well back to avoid the greater part of the drifting rain, was a figure huddled in a rich bearskin cloak, a plain black helm covering its whole face save for the eyes. It moved as it saw Dorian Hawkmoon regarding it and a thin, hollow sound came from the helm.

"Lord Agonosvos," Hawkmoon said. "I am the Duke von Köln, last of the line begun a thousand years since."

The figure answered in a low, laconic tone. "A Hawkmoon, I can see that. Landless now, eh? Granbretan took Köln, did it not?"

"Aye…"

"And so we are both banished; myself by your ancestor, and you by the conqueror."

"Be that as it may, I am still the last of my line and thus your master." Hawkmoon's tormented face stared hard at the figure.

"Master, is it? Authority over me was renounced when I was sent to the wild lands by Duke Dietrich."

"Not so, as you well know. No man of Köln can ever refuse his prince's will."

"Can he not?" Agonosvos laughed quietly. "Can he not?"

Hawkmoon made to turn away, but Agonosvos raised a thin, slim-fingered hand that was bone-white. "Stay. I have offended you and must make amends. How can I serve you?"

"You admit your loyalty to me?"

"I admit to impoliteness. You seem weary. I will stop my caravan and entertain you. What of your servant?"

"He is not my servant but my friend. Oladahn of the Bulgar Mountains."

"A friend? And not of your race? Still, let him join us." Agonosvos leaned from his wagon to call languidly to his men to stop their labours. Instantly, they relaxed, standing where they were, their bodies limp and their eyes still full of dumb despair.

"What do you think of my collection?" Agonosvos asked when they had dismounted and climbed into the gloom of the wagon's interior. "Such curiosities once amused me, but now I find them dull and they must work to justify their existence. I have one at least of almost every type." He glanced at Oladahn. "Including yours. Some I cross-bred myself."

Oladahn shifted his position uncomfortably. It was unnaturally warm within the confines of the wagon; yet there was no sign of a stove or any other heating apparatus. Agonosvos poured them wine from a blue gourd. The wine, too, was a deep, lustrous blue. The ancient exile of Köln still wore his black, featureless helm, and his black, sardonic eyes looked at Hawkmoon a trifle calculatingly.

Hawkmoon was making a great effort to appear in good health, but it was plain that Agonosvos guessed the truth when he handed him a golden goblet of wine and said, "This will make you feel better, my lord."

The wine did, in fact, revive him, and soon the pain had gone again. Agonosvos asked him how he had come to be in these parts, and Hawkmoon told him a considerable part of his tale. "So," said Agonosvos, "you want my help, eh? For the sake of our ancient kinship, hm? Well, I will brood upon that. In the meantime I will set a wagon aside so that you may rest. We will discuss the matter further in the morning."

Hawkmoon and Oladahn did not sleep immediately. They sat up in the silks and furs Agonosvos had lent them and discussed the strange sorcerer. "He reminds me uncommon much of those Dark Empire Lords you told me of," Oladahn said. "I think he means us ill. Perhaps he wishes to be avenged on you for the wrong he thinks your forefather did him — perhaps he wants to add me to his collection." He shuddered.

"Aye," Hawkmoon said thoughtfully. "But it would be unwise to anger him without reason. He could be useful to us. We'll sleep on it."

"Sleep warily," Oladahn cautioned.

But Hawkmoon slept deeply and awakened to find himself bound in tight leather thongs that had been wrapped round and round his body and then tugged to secure him. He struggled, glaring up at the enigmatic helm that covered the face of his immortal kinsman. There came a soft chuckle from Agonosvos.

"You knew of me, last of the Hawkmoons — but you did not know as much as you should. Know you not that many of my years were spent in Londra, teaching the Lords of Granbretan my secrets? We have long had an alliance, the Dark Empire and I. Baron Meliadus spoke of you when last I saw him. He will pay me anything I desire for your living body."

"Where is my companion?"

"The furry creature? Scampered into the night when he heard our approach. They are all the same, these beast folk — timid and fainthearted friends."

"So you intend to deliver me to Baron Meliadus?"

"You heard me perfectly. Aye, that is just what I intend. I'll leave this clumsy caravan to wend its way as best it can till I return. We'll move on swifter steeds — special steeds I have kept for such a time as this. I have already sent a messenger ahead of me to tell the baron of my catch. You — bear him forth!"

At Agonosvos's command, two midgets hurried forward to pick Hawkmoon up in their long, well-muscled arms and clamber out of the wagon with him into the grey light of early dawn.

A drizzle still fell, and through it Hawkmoon saw two great horses, both with coats of lustrous blue, intelligent eyes, and powerful limbs. He had never seen such fine beasts. "I bred them myself," Agonosvos said, "not for strangeness, in this case, but for speed. We shall soon be in Londra, you and I." He chuckled again as Hawkmoon was slung over the back of one of the steeds and roped to the stirrups.

He climbed into the saddle of the second horse, took the bridle of Hawkmoon's, and spurred forward. Hawkmoon was alarmed at the swift movement of the horse. It moved easily, galloping almost as fast as his flamingo had flown. But where the bird had borne him toward salvation, this horse took him closer to his doom. In an agony of mind, Hawkmoon decided that his lot was hopeless.

They galloped for a long time through the slushy earth of the forest. Hawkmoon's face became coated with mud, and he could see only by blinking heavily and craning his neck up.

Then, much later, he heard Agonosvos curse and shout. "Out of my way — out of my way!" Hawkmoon tried to peer forward but could see nothing save the hindquarters of Agonosvos's horse and a little of the man's cloak. Dimly, he heard another voice but could not distinguish what it said.

"Aaah! May Kaldereen eat your eyes!" Agonosvos now seemed to be reeling in his saddle. The two horses slowed their pace, then halted. Hawkmoon saw Agonosvos sway forward and then fall into the mud, crawling through it and trying to rise. There was an arrow in his side. Helpless, Hawkmoon wondered what new danger had arisen. Was he to be killed here rather than at the Court of King Huon?

A small figure came into view, skipping over the struggling body of Agonosvos and slashing at Hawkmoon's bonds. Hawkmoon dropped from the saddle, holding on to the pommel and rubbing at his numbed arms and legs. Oladahn grinned at him. "You'll find your sword in the sorcerer's baggage," he said.

Hawkmoon grinned in relief. "I thought you'd fled back to your mountains."

Oladahn began to reply, but Hawkmoon gasped a warning. "Agonosvos!" The sorcerer had risen to his feet, clutching at the arrow in his side and staggering toward the little mountain man. Hawkmoon forgot his own pain, ran to the sorcerer's horse, and tore at the man's rolled goods until he found his sword. Oladahn was now wrestling in the mud with Agonosvos.

Hawkmoon sprang at them but dared not risk stabbing at the sorcerer lest he harm his friend. He leaned down and hauled on Agonosvos's shoulder, dragging the enraged man backward. He heard a snarl issue from the helm, and Agonosvos drew his own sword from its scabbard. It whistled through the air as he struck at Hawkmoon. Hawkmoon, still hardly able to stand, met the blow and staggered backward. The sorcerer struck again.

Hawkmoon deflected the blade, swung his sword somewhat weakly at Agonosvos's head, missed, and was just in time to parry the next stroke. Then he saw an opening and drove the blade point-first into the sorcerer's belly. The man shrieked and backed away, curiously stiff-legged, his hands clutching Hawkmoon's sword, which had been wrenched from the Duke of Köln's hands. Then he spread his arms wide, began to speak, and fell sprawling into the dark water of a shallow pool.

Panting, Hawkmoon leaned against the bole of a tree, the pain in his limbs increasing as the circulation returned.

Oladahn rose from the mud, hardly recognizable. A quiver of arrows had been torn loose from his belt, and he picked it up now, inspecting the fletchings. "Some are ruined, but I'll soon replace 'em," he said.

"Where did you get them?"

"Last night, I decided to make my own inspection of Agonosvos's camp. I found the bow and arrows in one of the wagons and thought they might be useful. Returning, I saw Agonosvos enter our wagon and guessed his business, so I remained hidden and followed you."

"But how could you follow such fast horses?" Hawkmoon asked.

"I found an even faster ally," Oladahn grinned, and pointed through the trees. Coming toward them was a grotesque creature with incredibly long legs, the rest of his body of normal size. "This is Vlespeen. He hates Agonosvos and willingly aided me."

Vlespeen peered down at them. "You killed him," he said. "Good."

Oladahn inspected Agonosvos's baggage. He brandished a roll of parchment. "A map. And enough provisions to get us all to the coast." He unrolled the map. "It's not far. Look."

They gathered around the map, and Hawkmoon saw that it was scarcely more than a hundred miles to the Mermian Sea. Vlespeen wandered away to where Agonosvos had fallen; perhaps to gloat over the corpse. A moment later they heard him scream and turned to see the body of the sorcerer, brandishing the sword that had slain him, walking stiffly toward the long-legged man. The sword ripped upward into Vlespeen's stomach, and his legs collapsed under him, jerked like a puppet's, and then were still. Hawkmoon was horrified. From within the helm came a dry chuckle. "Fools! I have lived for nine hundred years. In that time I have learned how to cheat all forms of death."

Without thinking, Hawkmoon leaped at him, knowing it was his one chance to save his life. Even though he had survived a blow that should have been mortal, Agonosvos had evidently been weakened. The two struggled on the edge of the pool, while Oladahn danced around them, jumping at last upon the sorcerer's back and wrenching the tight helm from his head. Agonosvos howled, and Hawkmoon felt nausea overcome him as he stared at the white, fleshless head that was revealed. It was the face of an ancient corpse; a corpse that the worms had chewed upon. Agonosvos covered the face in his hands and staggered away.

As Hawkmoon picked up his sword and made to mount the great blue horse, he heard a voice come calling to him through the woods.

"I shall not forget this, Dorian Hawkmoon. You'll yet make sport for Baron Meliadus — and I shall be there to watch!"

Hawkmoon shuddered and urged the horse southward, where the map had shown the Mermian Sea to lie. Oladahn followed.

Within two days the sky had lightened and a yellow sun shone in blue, and ahead of them was a town beside the glinting sea, where they might take ship for Turkia.

T H R E E

THE WARRIOR IN JET AND GOLD

The heavy Turkian merchantman clove through the calm waters of the ocean, foam breaking over its bow, its single lateen sail stretched like a bird's wing as it took the strong wind. The captain of the vessel, in golden tasseled hat and braided jacket, his long skirts held to his ankles by bands of gold, stood with Hawkmoon and Oladahn in the stern of the ship. The captain jerked his thumb at the two huge blue horses corralled on the lower deck. "Fine beasts, masters. I've never seen the like in these parts." He scratched at his pointed beard. "You would not sell them? I'm part owner of this vessel and could afford a good price."

Hawkmoon shook his head. "Those horses are worth more to me than any riches."

"I can believe it," replied the captain, missing his meaning. He looked up as the man in the topmast yelled and waved, stretching his arm to the west.

Hawkmoon glanced in the same direction and saw three small sails rising over the horizon. The captain raised his spyglass. "By Rakar — Dark Empire ships!" He passed the glass to Hawkmoon. Hawkmoon saw the black sails of the vessels clearly now. Each was emblazoned with the shark symbol of the Empire's warfleet.

"Do they mean us harm?" he asked.

"They mean harm to all not of their own kind," the captain said grimly. "We can only pray they haven't seen us. The sea's becoming thick with their craft. A year ago..." He paused to yell orders to his men. The ship jumped as staysails were added forard. "A year ago there were few of them, and trading peacefully for the most part. Now they dominate the seas. You'll find their armies in Turkia, Syria, Persia — everywhere — spreading insurrection, aiding local revolts. My guess is they'll have the East under their heel as they have the West — give 'em a couple of years."

Soon the Dark Empire ships were below the horizon again, and the captain breathed a sigh of relief. "I'll not be comfortable," said he, "till port's in sight."

The Turkian port was seen at sunset, and they were forced to lie offshore until morning, when they sailed in on the tide and docked.

Not much later, the three Dark Empire warships came into the harbour, and Hawkmoon and Oladahn deemed it expedient to purchase what provisions they could and follow the map eastward, for Persia.

A week later, the great horses had borne them well past Ankara and across the Kizilirmac River, and they were riding through hill country where all seemed turned to yellow and brown by the burning sun. On several occasions they had seen armies pass by but had avoided them. The armies consisted of local troops, often augmented by masked warriors of Granbretan. Hawkmoon was disturbed by this, for he had not expected the Dark Empire's influence to stretch this far. Once, they witnessed a battle from a distance, seeing the disciplined forces of Granbretan easily defeat the opposing army. Now Hawkmoon rode desperately toward Persia.

A month later, as their horses trotted along the shores of a vast lake, Oladahn and Hawkmoon were suddenly surprised by a force of some twenty warriors who appeared over the crest of a hill and came charging toward them. The warriors' masks flashed in the sun, adding to their fierce appearance — the masks of the Order of the Wolf.

"Ho! The two our master seeks!" cried one of the leading horsemen. "The reward is large for the tall one if taken alive."

Oladahn said calmly, "I fear, Lord Dorian, that we're doomed."

"Make them kill you," said Hawkmoon grimly, and drew his sword. If the horses had not been weary, he would have fled the warriors, but he knew that that would be useless now.

Soon the wolf-masked riders were all around them. Hawkmoon had the slight advantage of wishing to kill them, while they wanted him alive. He struck one full in the mask with the pommel of his sword, sheered half-through another's arm, stabbed a third in the groin, and knocked a fourth from his horse. Now they were in the shallows of the lake, the steeds' hooves splashing in the water. Hawkmoon saw Oladahn accounting well for himself, but then the furry little man gave a cry and fell from his saddle. Hawkmoon could not see him for the press, but he cursed and struck about him with a greater will.

Now they closed in so that he hardly had room to swing his sword. He realized, sickeningly, they would take him in a few moments. He struggled and smote on, his ears full of the clang of metal, his nostrils clogged with the smell of blood.

Then he felt the pressure give way and saw through a forest of swords that an ally had joined him. He had seen the figure before — but only in dreams, or visions very similar to dreams. It was the one he had seen in France and later in Kamarg. He was dressed in full armour of jet and gold, a long helm completely enclosing his face. He swung a six-foot broadsword and rode a white battle charger as big as Hawkmoon's. Wherever he struck, men fell, and soon there were only a few wolf warriors still horsed and these at length galloped off through the water, leaving their dead and wounded behind.

Hawkmoon saw one of the fallen riders struggle up. Then he saw another rise beside him and realized it was Oladahn. The little man still had his sword and was defending himself desperately against the Granbretanian. Hawkmoon pushed his horse through the shallows and brought his sword round in a great swing to strike the wolf warrior in the back, shearing through his mail and leather undershirt and cutting deep into his flesh. With a groan the man fell, and his blood joined that already reddening the waters.

Hawkmoon turned to where the Warrior in Jet and Gold sat his horse silently.

"I thank you, my lord," he said. "You have followed me a long way." He resheathed his sword.

"Longer than you know, Dorian Hawkmoon," came the rich, echoing voice of the warrior. "You ride to Hamadan?"

"Aye — to seek the sorcerer Malagigi."

"Good. I will ride with you some of the way. It is not far now."

"Who are you?" Hawkmoon asked. "Who may I thank?"

"I am the Warrior in Jet and Gold. Do not thank me for saving your life. You do not realize yet what I have saved it for. Come." And the warrior led them away from the lake.

A little later, as they rested and ate, the warrior, with one leg crooked beneath him, sat some distance off. Hawkmoon asked him, "Know you much of Malagigi? Will he help me?"

"I know him," said the Warrior in Jet and Gold. "Perhaps he will help you. But know you this — there is civil war in Hamadan. Queen Frawbra's brother, Nahak, schemes against her, and he is aided by many who wear the masks of those we fought at the lake."

F O U R

M A L A G I G I

A week later they looked down on the city of Hamadan, all white and gleaming in the bright sun, with its spires, domes, and minarets chased with gold, silver, and mother-of-pearl.

"I will leave you now," said the mysterious warrior, turning his horse. "Farewell, Dorian Hawkmoon. Doubtless we shall meet again."

Hawkmoon watched him ride away through the hills; then he and Oladahn urged their horses toward the city.

But as they approached the gates they heard a great noise from behind the walls. It was the sound of fighting, the shouts of warriors and the screams of beasts, and suddenly, out of the gates burst a great rabble of soldiers, many of them badly wounded and all much battered. The two men pulled their horses up short but were soon surrounded by the fleeing army. A group of riders charged past them, and Hawkmoon heard one cry — "All is lost! Nahak wins the day!"

Following them came a huge bronze war chariot pulled by four black horses, and in it was a raven-haired woman in blue plate armour who shouted at her men, urging them to turn and fight. The woman was young and very beautiful, with huge, dark, slanting eyes that blazed with anger and frustration. In one hand she held a scimitar, which she brandished high.

She dragged at the reins as she saw the bewildered Hawkmoon and Oladahn. "Who are you? More Dark Empire mercenaries?"

"No — I am an enemy of the Dark Empire," Hawkmoon said. "What is happening?"

"An uprising. My brother, Nahak, and his allies broke through the secret passageways that lead from the desert and surprised us. If you are Granbretan's enemy, then you had best flee now! They have battle beasts with them that..." Then she was yelling again at her men and had moved on.

"We had best return to the hills," Oladahn murmured, but Hawkmoon shook his head.

"I must find Malagigi. He is somewhere in this city. There is little time left."

They pushed their horses through the throng and into the city. Up ahead some men were still fighting in the streets, and the spiked helmets of the local soldiers mingled with the wolf helms of the Dark Empire warriors. Everywhere was carnage. Hawkmoon and Oladahn galloped up a side street where there was little fighting at present and emerged into an open square. On the opposite side they saw gigantic winged beasts, like great black bats but with long arms and curved claws. They were rending at the retreating warriors, and some were already feasting on the corpses. Here and there Nahak's men were trying to urge these battle beasts on, but it was plain the giant bats had already served their purpose.

A bat turned and saw them. Hawkmoon yelled to Oladahn to follow him down a narrow lane, but the bat was already pursuing them, half-running, half-flapping through the air, a disgusting whistling sound coming from its jaws, a dreadful stench exuding from its body. Into the lane they rode, but the bat squeezed between the houses and continued to follow them. Then, from the opposite end of the street, came some half a dozen wolf-masked riders. Hawkmoon drew his sword and charged on. There was little else to do.

He met the first of the riders with a lunge that ripped the man from his saddle. A sword slashed at his shoulder, and he felt it bite home, but he continued to fight in spite of the pain. The battle beast screamed, and the wolf warriors began to back their horses away in panic.

Hawkmoon and Oladahn burst through them and found themselves in a larger square that was empty of the living. Only corpses lay everywhere on cobblestones and pavements. Hawkmoon saw a yellow-robed man dart from a doorway to bend beside a corpse and cut at the purse and jeweled dagger in its belt. The man looked up in panic and tried to dash back into his house when he saw the Duke of Köln, but Oladahn blocked his way. Hawkmoon pressed his sword into the man's cheek. "Which way to Malagigi's house?"

The man pointed a trembling finger and croaked, "That way, masters. The one with the dome that has zodiacal signs inlaid in ebony on a silver roof. Down that street. Do not kill me. I..." He sighed in relief as Hawkmoon turned his great blue horse and rode for the street he had indicated.

The domed house with the zodiacal signs was soon in sight. Hawkmoon stopped at the gate and hammered on it with the pommel of his sword. His head was beginning to throb again, and he knew instinctively that Count Brass's spells could not hold the Black Jewel's life for much longer. He realized that he should have approached the sorcerer's house in a more courteous manner, but there was no time, with Granbretan's soldiers everywhere in the streets of the city. Overhead two of the giant bats flapped, seeking victims.

At last the gate swung open and four huge Negroes armed with pikes and dressed in purple robes barred the way. Hawkmoon saw a courtyard beyond them. He tried to ride forward, but the pikes menaced him immediately. "What business have you with our master, Malagigi?" one of the Negroes asked.

"I seek his help. It is a matter of great importance. I am in peril."

A figure appeared on the steps leading to the house. The man was clad in a simple white toga. He had long grey hair and was clean shaven. His face was lined and old, but the skin had a youthful appearance.

"Why should Malagigi help you?" the man asked. "You are from the West, I see. The people of the West bring war and dissension to Hamadan. Begone I'll have none of you!"

"You are the Lord Malagigi?" Hawkmoon began. "I am a victim of these same people. Help me and I can help you be rid of them. Please, I beg you —"

"Begone. I'll play no part in your internal warring!" The Negroes pressed the two men back, and the gates closed.

Hawkmoon began to bang again on the gates, but then Oladahn gripped his arm and pointed. Up the street toward them came some six wolf-helmed riders led by one whose ornate mask Hawkmoon instantly recognized. It was Meliadus.

"Ha! Your time is near, Hawkmoon!" screamed Meliadus in triumph, drawing his sword and charging forward.

Hawkmoon wrenched his horse about. Although his hatred for Meliadus burned as deeply as ever, he knew he could not fight at that moment. He and Oladahn fled back down the street, their powerful horses outdistancing those of Meliadus's men.

Agonosvos or his messenger must have told Meliadus where Hawkmoon was bound, and the baron must have come here to join his own men, help them take Hamadan, and wreak his personal vengeance on Hawkmoon.

Down one narrow street after another Hawkmoon dashed, until he had for the moment lost his pursuer. "We must escape the city," he shouted to Oladahn. "It is our only chance. Perhaps later we can sneak back and convince Malagigi to help us…" His voice trailed off as one of the gigantic bats swooped suddenly down, to alight immediately in front of them and begin to stalk forward, claws outstretched. Beyond this creature was an open gate and freedom.

So full of desperation was Hawkmoon now, since Malagigi had refused him, that he charged straight at the battle beast, sword slashing at its cruel claws, flinging himself against it. The bat whistled, and the claws struck, clutching Hawkmoon by his already wounded arm. The young nobleman brought his sword up again and again, hewing at the thing's wrist until black blood spurted and the tendon was severed. The beaked mouth clicked open and thrust at Hawkmoon. The horse reared as the head came down, and Hawkmoon thrust his sword up wildly, striking for the huge, beady eye. The sword plunged in. The creature screamed. Yellow mucus began to pour from the wound.

Hawkmoon struck a second time. The thing reeled and began to fall toward him. Hawkmoon managed to pull his horse aside barely in time as the battle beast collapsed. Now he raced for the gate and the hills beyond, Oladahn in his wake calling, "You have killed it, Lord Dorian! This is the stuff of the lays!" And the little man laughed with a fierce joy.

Soon they were in the hills, joining the hundreds of beaten warriors who had survived the battle in the city. They rode slowly now and at length came to a shallow valley where they saw the bronze chariot that the warrior queen had driven earlier and rank after rank of weary soldiery lying down in the tough grass while the raven-haired woman went among them. Near the chariot Hawkmoon saw another figure. It was the Warrior in Jet and Gold, and he seemed to be waiting for Hawkmoon.

Hawkmoon dismounted as he reached the warrior. The woman approached and stood leaning against her chariot, her eyes still glowing with the anger Hawkmoon had noted before.

The Warrior in Jet and Gold's rich voice came from his helmet, faintly laconic. "So Malagigi would not help you, eh?"

Hawkmoon shook his head, looking at the woman without curiosity. Disappointment filled him but was beginning to be replaced with the wild fatalism that had saved his life in his battle with the giant bat. "I am finished now," he said. "But at least I can return and find a way to destroy Meliadus."

"We have that ambition in common," said the woman. "I am Queen Frawbra. My treacherous brother covets the throne and seeks to get it with the aid of your Meliadus and his warriors. Mayhap he already has it. I cannot tell yet — but it would seem we are badly outnumbered, and there's scant chance of retaking the city."

Hawkmoon looked at her thoughtfully. "If there was a slim chance, would you seize it?"

"If there was no chance at all I'd have half a mind to try," the woman replied. "But I'm not sure my warriors would follow me!"

At that moment three more horsemen rode into the camp. Queen Frawbra called to them. "Have you just escaped the city?"

"Aye," one answered. "They are already looting. I have never seen such savage conquerors as those Westerners. Their leader — the big man — has even broken into Malagigi's house and made him prisoner!"

"What!" Hawkmoon cried. "Meliadus has the sorcerer prisoner? Ah, then, there is no hope at all for me."

The Warrior in Jet and Gold said, "Nonsense. There is still hope. So long as Meliadus keeps Malagigi alive — and one might expect him to, since the sorcerer has many secrets Meliadus desires to learn — then you have a chance. You must return to Hamadan with Queen Frawbra's armies, retake the city, and rescue Malagigi."

Hawkmoon shrugged. "But is there time? Already the Jewel shows signs of warmth. That means its life is returning. Soon I will be a mindless creature…"

"Then you have nothing to lose, Lord Dorian," Oladahn put in. He laid a furry hand on Hawkmoon's arm and gave it a friendly squeeze. "Nothing to lose at all."

Hawkmoon laughed bitterly, shrugging off his friend's hand. "Aye, you're right. Nothing. Well, Queen Frawbra, what say you?"

The armoured woman said, "Let us speak to what remains of my force."

A little later, Hawkmoon stood in the chariot and addressed the battle-weary warriors. "Men of Hamadan, I have traveled for many hundreds of miles from the West, where Granbretan holds sway. My own father was tortured to death by the same Baron Meliadus who aids your queen's enemies today. I have seen whole nations reduced to ashes, their populations slain or enslaved. I have seen children crucified and hanging on gibbets. I have seen brave warriors turned to cringing dogs.

"I know that you must feel it is hopeless to resist the masked men of the Dark Empire, but they can be beaten. I, myself, was one of the commanders of an army little more than a thousand strong that put an army of Granbretan more than twenty times its number to flight. It was our will to live that enabled us to do it — our knowledge that even if we fled we should be hunted down and die eventually, ignobly.

"You can at least die courageously like men — and know that there is a chance of defeating the forces that have taken your city today…"

He spoke on in this vein, and gradually the tired warriors rallied. Some cheered him. Then Queen Frawbra joined him in the chariot and cried to her men to follow Hawkmoon back to Hamadan, to strike while the enemy was unwary, while its soldiers were drunk and squabbled over their loot.

Hawkmoon's words had given them cheer; now they saw the logic of Queen Frawbra's words. They began to buckle on their weapons, adjust their armour, look for their horses.

"We'll attack tonight," the queen shouted, "giving them no time to get wind of our plan."

"I'll ride with you, I think," said the Warrior in Jet and Gold. And that night they rode to Hamadan, where the conquering soldiers reveled and the gates still stood open and hardly guarded and the battle beasts slept soundly, their stomachs full of their prey.

F I V E

THE BLACK JEWEL'S LIFE

They had thundered into the city and were striking about them almost before the enemy realized what was happening. Hawkmoon led them. Hawkmoon's head was full of agony, and the Black Jewel had begun to pulse in his skull. His face was taut and white, and there was something about his presence that made soldiers flee before him as his horse reared and he raised his sword and screamed, "Hawkmoon! Hawkmoon!" cutting about him in a hysteria of killing.

Close behind him came the Warrior in Jet and Gold, fighting methodically with an air of detached ease. Queen Frawbra was there, driving her chariot into startled groups of warriors, and Oladahn of the Mountains stood up in his stirrups and shot arrow after arrow into the enemy.

Street by street they drove Nahak's forces and the wolf-helmed mercenaries through the city. Then Hawkmoon saw the dome of Malagigi's house and leaped his horse over the heads of those who blocked his way, reaching the house and standing upon his mount's back to grasp the top of the wall and haul himself over.

He dropped into the courtyard, just missing the sprawled body of one of Malagigi's Negro guards. The door of the house had been broken down, and the interior had been wrecked.

Stumbling through the smashed furniture, Hawkmoon found a narrow stairway. Doubtless this led to the sorcerer's laboratories. He was halfway up the stairs, when a door opened at the top and two wolf-masked guards appeared, running down to meet him, their swords ready. Hawkmoon brought up his own sword to defend himself. His face was set in a death's-head grin as he fought, and his eyes blazed with a madness that was mixed fury and despair. Once, twice, his sword darted forward, and then there were two corpses tumbling down the stairs and Hawkmoon had entered the room at the top, to discover Malagigi strapped to a wall, the marks of torture on his limbs.

Quickly he cut the old man down and lowered him gently to a couch in the corner. There were benches everywhere, with alchemical apparatus and small machines resting on them. Malagigi stirred and opened his eyes.

"You must help me, sir," Hawkmoon said thickly. "I came here to save your life. At least you could try to save mine."

Malagigi raised himself on the couch, wincing in pain. "I told you — I'll do nothing for either side. Torture me if you will, as your countrymen did, but I'll not —"

"Damn you!" Hawkmoon swore. "My head's afire. I'll be lucky if I last till dawn. You must not refuse. I have come two thousand miles to seek your aid. I am as much a victim of Granbretan as you. More. I —"

"Prove that, and perhaps I'll help you," Malagigi said. "Drive the invaders from the city and then return."

"By then it will be too late. The Jewel has its life. At any moment —"

"Prove it," said Malagigi, and sank back on the couch.

Hawkmoon half-raised his sword. In his wild rage and desperation he was ready to strike the old man. But then he turned and ran back down the stairs and out into the courtyard, unbarring the gate and leaping into the saddle of his horse again.

At length he found Oladahn. "How does the battle go?" he yelled over the heads of fighting swordsmen.

"Not too well, I think. Meliadus and Nahak have regrouped and hold a good half of the city. Their main force is in the central square, where the palace stands. Queen Frawbra and your armoured friend are already leading an attack there, but I fear it's hopeless."

"Let's see for ourselves," Hawkmoon said, yanking at his mount's bridle and forcing his way through the embattled warriors, striking here and there at friend or foe, depending on which stood in his path.

Oladahn followed, and they came eventually into the great central square, to find the armies drawn up facing each other. Horsed at the head of their men were Meliadus and the rather foolish-faced Nahak, who was plainly a tool of the Dark Empire baron. Opposite them were Queen Frawbra in her battered war chariot and the Warrior in Jet and Gold.

As Hawkmoon and Oladahn entered the square, they heard Meliadus call through the flickering torchlight that illuminated the armies, "Where is that treacherous coward Hawkmoon? Skulking in hiding, perhaps?"

Hawkmoon broke through the line of warriors, noticing that their ranks were thin. "Here I am, Meliadus. I have come to destroy you!"

Meliadus laughed. "Destroy me? Know you not that you live only by my whim? Do you feel the Black Jewel, Hawkmoon, ready to nibble at your mind?"

Involuntarily, Hawkmoon put his hand to his throbbing forehead, feeling the evil warmth of the Black Jewel, knowing that Meliadus spoke the truth.

"Then why do you wait?" he said grimly.

"Because I am ready to offer you a bargain. Tell these fools their cause is hopeless. Tell them to throw down their arms — and I will spare you the worst."

Now Hawkmoon fully realized that he did, indeed, retain his mind only at the pleasure of his enemies. Meliadus had restrained his desire for immediate vengeance in the hope of forcing Hawkmoon to save Granbretan further losses.

Hawkmoon paused, unable to answer, trying to debate the issues. There was silence from his own ranks as they waited tensely to hear his decision. He knew that the whole fate of Hamadan might now depend on him. As he sat there, his mind in confusion, Oladahn nudged his arm and murmured, "Lord Dorian, take this." Hawkmoon glanced down at the thing the mountain man offered him. It was a helmet. At first he did not recognize it. Then he saw that it was the helm that had been wrenched from the skull of Agonosvos. He remembered the disgusting head that had once reposed in it and shuddered.

"Why? The thing is befouled."

"My father was a sorcerer," Oladahn reminded him. "He taught me secrets. This helm has certain properties. There are circuits built into it which will protect you for a short time from the full force of the Black Jewel's power. Put it on, my lord, I beg you."

"How can I be sure...?"

"Put it on — and find out."

Gingerly Hawkmoon removed his own helmet and donned the sorcerer's. It was a tight fit and he felt stifled by it, but he realized that the Jewel no longer pulsed so fast. He smiled, and a wild feeling of elation filled him. He drew his sword. "This is my answer, Baron Meliadus!" he yelled, and charged full at the startled Lord of Granbretan.

Meliadus cursed and struggled to get his own sword from its scabbard. He had scarcely done so before Hawkmoon's sword had knocked his wolf helm clean from his head and his scowling, bewildered face was revealed. Behind Hawkmoon came the cheering soldiers of Hamadan, led by Oladahn, Queen Frawbra, and the Warrior in Jet and Gold. They clashed with the enemy, forcing them back to the gates of the palace.

From the corner of his eye, Hawkmoon saw Queen Frawbra lean from her chariot and encircle her brother's throat with her arm, dragging him from his saddle. Her hand rose and fell twice, bearing a bloody dagger, and Nahak's corpse dropped to the ground, to be trampled by the horsemen who followed the queen.

Hawkmoon was still driven by wild despair, knowing that the helm of Agonosvos could not protect him for long. He swung his sword rapidly, striking blow after blow at Meliadus, who parried as swiftly. Meliadus's face was twisted in an expression resembling that of the wolf helmet he had lost, and a hatred burned from his eyes that matched Hawkmoon's own.

Their swords clanged rhythmically in warlike harmony, each blow blocked, each blow returned, and it seemed that they would continue in this way until one dropped from weariness. But then a group of fighting warriors backed against Hawkmoon's horse and caused it to rear, throwing him backward so that he lost his footing in his stirrups, and Meliadus grinned and thrust at Hawkmoon's undefended chest. The blow lacked force, but it was enough to push Hawkmoon from his saddle. He fell to the ground below the hooves of Meliadus's horse.

He rolled away as the baron tried to trample him, dragged himself to his feet, and did his best to defend himself from the volley of blows rained down on him by the triumphant Granbretanian.

Twice Meliadus's sword struck the helmet of Agonosvos, denting it badly. Hawkmoon felt the Jewel begin to pulse afresh. He shouted wordlessly and dashed in close.

Astonished by this unexpected move, Meliadus was taken off-guard, and his attempt to block Hawkmoon's thrust was only half-successful. Hawkmoon's sword cut a great furrow along one side of Meliadus's unprotected head, and his whole face seemed to open up and gush blood, his mouth crooked with pain and paralysis. He tried to wipe the blood from his eyes, and Hawkmoon grasped his sword arm and hauled him down to the ground. Meliadus wrenched himself free, stumbled backward, then rushed at Hawkmoon, his sword a blur of metal, striking Hawkmoon's blade with such force that both swords snapped.

For a moment the panting antagonists stood still, glaring at one another; then each drew a long dirk from his belt, and they began to circle, poised to strike. Meliadus's handsome features were handsome no longer, and if he lived, would always bear the mark of Hawkmoon's blow. Blood still came plentifully from the wound, trickling down his breastplate.

Hawkmoon, for his part, was wearying rapidly. The wound he had sustained the day before was beginning to trouble him, and his head was on fire with the pain the Jewel caused. He could hardly see for it, and twice he staggered, only to right himself as Meliadus feinted with his dagger.

Then both men moved and were instantly locked together, grappling desperately to stab the single mortal blow that would end their feud.

Meliadus struck at Hawkmoon's eye but misjudged his blow, and the dagger scraped down the side of the helmet. Hawkmoon's dagger sliced toward Meliadus's throat, but the baron's hand came up, caught Hawkmoon's wrist, and turned it.

The dance of death went on as they wrestled, chest to chest, to deal the finishing cut. Their breath groaned from their throats, their bodies ached with weariness, but fierce hatred glared from both pairs of eyes still and would glare on until one or both became glazed in death.

Around them the battle continued, with Queen Frawbra's forces driving the enemy farther and farther back. Now none fought near the two men and only corpses surrounded them.

Dawn was beginning to touch the sky.

Meliadus's arm trembled as Hawkmoon tried to force it back and make the hand release his wrist. His own free hand was weakening on Meliadus's forearm, for this was his wounded side. Despairingly, Hawkmoon brought his armoured knee up into Meliadus's armoured groin and shoved. The baron staggered. His foot caught in the harness of one of the slain, and he fell. Trying to struggle up, he became worse entangled, and his eyes filled with fear as Hawkmoon slowly advanced, himself only barely able to remain upright.

Hawkmoon raised his dagger. Now his head was swimming. He flung himself down at the baron, then felt a great weakness seize him, and the dagger dropped from his hand.

Blindly, he groped for the weapon, but consciousness was going. He gasped with anger, but even that emotion was ebbing. Fatalistically he knew that Meliadus would now be able to kill him at his very moment of triumph.

S   I   X

SERVANT OF THE RUNESTAFF

Hawkmoon peered through the eyeslits of the helmet, blinking in the bright light. His head still burned, but the anger and desperation seemed to have left him. He turned his neck and saw Oladahn and the Warrior in Jet and Gold staring down at him. Oladahn's face was concerned, but the warrior's face was still hidden by that enigmatic helm.

"I am not... dead?" Hawkmoon said weakly.

"It does not seem so," replied the warrior laconically. "Though perhaps you are."

"Merely exhausted," Oladahn said hastily, darting a disapproving glance at the mysterious warrior. "The wound in your arm has been dressed and is likely to heal quickly."

"Where am I?" Hawkmoon asked now. "A room..."

"A room in Queen Frawbra's palace. The city is hers again and the enemy slain, captured, or fled. We found your body sprawled across that of Baron Meliadus. We thought you both dead at first."

"So Meliadus is dead!"

"It is likely. When we returned to look for his corpse it had vanished. Doubtless it was borne away by some of his fleeing men."

"Ah, dead at last," said Hawkmoon thankfully. Now that Meliadus had paid for his crimes, he felt suddenly at peace, in spite of the pain that still pulsed in his brain. Another thought came to him. "Malagigi. You must find him. Tell him..."

"Malagigi is on his way. When he heard of your exploits he decided to call at the palace."

"Will he help me?"

"I do not know," Oladahn said, glancing again at the Warrior in Jet and Gold.

A little later Queen Frawbra entered, and behind her was the wizen-faced sorcerer carrying an object covered by a cloth. It was about the size and shape of a man's head.

"Lord Malagigi," Hawkmoon murmured, trying to rise from his bed.

"You are the young man who has been pursuing me in recent days? I cannot see your face in that helmet." Malagigi spoke waspishly, and Hawkmoon began to despair again.

"I am Dorian Hawkmoon. I proved my friendship to Hamadan. Meliadus and Nahak are destroyed, their forces gone."

"Hm?" Malagigi frowned. "I have been told of this jewel thing in your head. I know about such creations and their properties. But whether it is *possible* to remove its power I cannot say…"

"I was told you were the only man who could do it," Hawkmoon said.

"Could — yes. Can? I do not know. I am growing old. Physically, I am not sure if…"

The Warrior in Jet and Gold stepped forward and touched Malagigi upon the shoulder. "You know me, sorcerer?"

Malagigi nodded. "Aye, I do."

"And you know the Power I serve?"

"Aye." Malagigi frowned, glancing from one to the other. "But what has that to do with this young man?"

"He, too, serves that Power, though he knows it not."

Malagigi's expression became instantly resolute. "Then I will help him," he said firmly, "even if it means risking my own life."

Again Hawkmoon raised himself on the bed. "What does all this mean? Whom do I serve? I was unaware…"

Malagigi withdrew the cloth from the object he carried. It was a globe covered with little irregularities, each of which glowed a different colour. The colours shifted constantly, making Hawkmoon blink rapidly.

"First you must concentrate," Malagigi told him, holding the strange globe close to his head. "Stare into the device. Stare hard. Stare long. Stare, Dorian Hawkmoon, at all the colours…"

Hawkmoon now found that he was no longer blinking, found that he could not tear his gaze away from the rapidly changing colours in the globe. A peculiar feeling of weightlessness overcame him. A great sensation of well-being. He began to smile, and then all became misty and it seemed he hung in a soft, warm mist, beyond space, beyond time. He was still absolutely conscious in one way, and yet he was unaware of the world around him.

For a long time he remained in this state, knowing vaguely that his body, which no longer seemed very much a part of him, was being moved from one place to another.

The delicate colours of the mist changed sometimes, from a shade of rose-red to shades of sky-blue and buttercup-yellow, but that was all he saw, and he felt nothing at all. He felt at peace, as he had never felt before, save perhaps as a small child in his mother's arms.

Then the pastel shades began to be shot through with veins of darker, grimmer colours, and the sense of peace was gradually lost as lightnings of black and blood-red zigzagged across his eyes. He felt a wrenching sensation, one of terrible agony, and he screamed aloud.

Then he opened his eyes to stare in horror at the machine before him. It was identical to the one he had seen so long ago in the palace laboratories of King Huon.

Was he back in Londra?

The webs of black, gold and silver murmured to him, but they did not caress him as they had done before; instead, they contracted, moving away from him, growing tighter and tighter together until they filled only a fraction of the space. Hawkmoon stared around him and saw Malagigi and beyond him the laboratory where, earlier, he had rescued the sorcerer from the Dark Empire's men.

Malagigi looked exhausted, but there was an expression of great self-satisfaction on his old face.

He stepped forward with a metal box, gathered up the machine of the Black Jewel, and tossed it into the box, closing the lid firmly and locking it.

"The machine," Hawkmoon said thickly. "How did you get it?"

"I made it," Malagigi smiled. "Made it, Duke Hawkmoon, aye! It took a week of intensive effort while you lay there, partly protected from the other machine — the one in Londra — by my spells. I thought for a while that I had lost the struggle, but this morning the machine was complete, save for one element..."

"What was that?"

"Its life force. That was the crucial issue — whether I could time the spell aright. You see, I had to let the whole of the life of the Black Jewel come through and fill your mind, then hope that this machine would absorb it before it could begin to eat."

Hawkmoon smiled in relief. "And it did!"

"It did. You are now free from that fear, at any rate."

"Human dangers I can accept and meet cheerfully," Hawkmoon said, lifting himself from the couch. "I am in your debt, Lord Malagigi. If I can do you any service..."

"Nay — nothing," Malagigi said, almost with a smirk. "I am glad to have this machine here." He tapped the box. "Perhaps it will be of use to me sometime. Besides…" He frowned, staring thoughtfully at Hawkmoon.

"What is it?"

"Ah, nothing." Malagigi shrugged.

Hawkmoon touched his forehead. The Black Jewel was still embedded there, but it was cold. "You did not remove the Jewel?"

"No, though it could be done if you desire. It offers you no danger. It would be a simple matter of surgery to cut it from your head."

Hawkmoon was about to ask Malagigi how this could be arranged, when a thought came to him. "No," he said at length. "No, let it remain — a symbol of my hatred for the Dark Empire. I hope they will soon learn to fear that symbol."

"You intend to carry on the fight against them, then?"

"Aye — with redoubled effort now that you have freed me."

"It is a force that should be countered," Malagigi said. He drew a deep breath. "Now I must sleep. I am very tired. You will find your friends awaiting you in the courtyard."

Hawkmoon walked down the steps of the house into the bright, warm sunshine of the early day, and there was Oladahn, a smile splitting his furry face almost in two. Beside him was the tall figure of the Warrior in Jet and Gold.

"You are completely well?" asked the warrior.

"Completely."

"Good. Then I will leave you. Farewell, Dorian Hawkmoon."

"I thank you for your help," Hawkmoon said as the warrior began to stride toward his great white battle charger. Then, as the warrior began to mount, a memory returned and he said, "Wait."

"What is it?" The helmed head turned to regard him.

"It was you who convinced Malagigi he should remove the power of the Black Jewel. You told him that I serve the Power that you serve. Yet I know of no Power that is my master."

"You will know of it one day."

"What is the Power you serve?"

"I serve the Runestaff," said the Warrior in Jet and Gold, and he rattled the white horse's bridle, urging his mount through the gate and away before Hawkmoon could ask him further questions.

"The Runestaff, is it?" Oladahn murmured, frowning. "A myth, I thought…"

"Aye, a myth. I believe that warrior enjoys mysteries. Doubtless he jokes with us." Hawkmoon grinned, slapping Oladahn on the shoulder. "If we see him again, we'll get the truth from him. I'm hungry. A good dinner…"

"There's a banquet prepared at Queen Frawbra's palace." Oladahn winked.

"The finest I've seen. And I think the queen's interest in you is not sparked merely by gratitude."

"Say you so? Well, I hope I do not disappoint her, friend Oladahn, for I am pledged to a fairer maid than Frawbra."

"Is it possible?"

"Aye. Come, little friend — let's enjoy the queen's food and make preparations to return to the West."

"Must we leave so soon? We're heroes here, and besides, we deserve a rest, surely?"

Hawkmoon smiled. "Stay yourself, if you will. But I've a wedding to attend — my own."

"Oh, well," sighed Oladahn in mock grief, "I could not miss that event. I suppose I will have to cut short my stay in Hamadan."

Queen Frawbra herself escorted them to the gates of Hamadan the next morning. "You'll not think again, Dorian Hawkmoon? I offer you a throne — the throne my brother died trying to win."

Hawkmoon looked to the west. Two thousand miles and several months' journey away, Yisselda awaited him, not knowing whether he had succeeded in his goal or was now a victim of the Black Jewel. Count Brass, too, waited and must be told of Granbretan's further infamy. Bowgentle, doubtless, was even now standing with Yisselda in the turret of the topmost tower of Castle Brass, looking over the wild fenland of Kamarg, trying to console the girl who wondered if the man pledged to wed her would ever return.

He bowed in his saddle and kissed the queen's hand. "I thank you, Your Majesty, and I am honoured that you should think me worthy to rule with you, but there is a pledge I must keep — that I would forfeit twenty thrones to keep — and I must go. Also my blade is needed against the Dark Empire."

"Then go," she said sadly, "but remember Hamadan and her queen."

"I will."

He urged his great blue-coated stallion out across the rocky plain. Behind him, Oladahn turned, blew a kiss to Queen Frawbra, winked, and rode after his friend.

Dorian Hawkmoon, Duke von Köln, rode steadily westward to claim his love and take his vengeance.

THE MAD GOD'S AMULET

For Jim Cawthorn,
for his inspirations and his drawings

B O O K O N E

We have learned now how Dorian Hawkmoon, last Duke of Köln, one aspect of the Champion Eternal, threw off the power of the Black Jewel and saved the city of Hamadan from conquest by the Dark Empire of Granbretan. His arch-enemy, Baron Meliadus, defeated, Hawkmoon set off westward again, bound for besieged Kamarg, where his betrothed, Yisselda, Count Brass's daughter, awaited him. With his boon companion Oladahn, beast-man of the Bulgar Mountains, Hawkmoon rode from Persia toward the Cyprian Sea and the port of Tarabulus, where they hoped to find a ship brave enough to bear them back to Kamarg. But in the Syranian Desert they lost their way and came close to dying of thirst and exhaustion before they saw the peaceful ruins of Soryandum lying at the foot of a range of green hills on which wild sheep grazed...

Meanwhile, in Europe, the Dark Empire extended its terrible rule, while elsewhere the Runestaff pulsed, exerting its influence over thousands of miles to involve the destinies of some several human souls of disparate character and ambitions...

— The High History of the Runestaff

S   O   R   Y   A   N   D   U   M

The city was old, begrimed by time. A place of wind-worn stones and tumbled masonry, its towers tilting and its walls crumbling. Wild sheep cropped the grass that grew between cracked paving stones, bright-plumed birds nested among columns of faded mosaic. The city had once been splendid and terrible; now it was beautiful and tranquil. The two travelers came to it in the mellow haze of the morning, when a melancholy wind blew through the silence of the ancient streets. The hooves of the horses were hushed as the travelers led them between towers that were green with age, passed by ruins bright with blossoms of orange, ochre and purple. And this was Soryandum, deserted by its folk.

The men and their horses were turned all one colour by the dust that caked them, making them resemble statues that had come to life. They moved slowly, looking wonderingly about them at the beauty of the dead city.

The first man was tall and lean, and although weary he moved with the graceful stride of the trained warrior. His long fair hair had been bleached near white by the sun, and his pale blue eyes had a hint of madness in them. But the thing most remarkable about his appearance was the dull Black Jewel sunk into his forehead just above and between the eyes, a stigmata he owed to the perverted miracle workings of the sorcerer-scientists of Granbretan. His name was Dorian Hawkmoon, Duke von Köln, driven from his hereditary lands by the conquests of the Dark Empire, which schemed to rule the world. Dorian Hawkmoon, who had sworn vengeance against the most powerful nation on his war-tormented planet.

The creature who followed Hawkmoon bore a large bone bow and a quiver of arrows on his back. He was clad only in a pair of britches and boots of soft, floppy leather, but the whole of his body, including his face, was covered in red, wiry hair. His head came to just below Hawkmoon's shoulder. This was Oladahn, cross-bred offspring of a sorcerer and a Mountain Giantess from the Bulgar Mountains.

Oladahn patted sand from his fur and looked perplexed. "Never have I seen a city so fair. Why is it deserted? Who could leave such a place?"

Hawkmoon, as was his habit when puzzled, rubbed at the dull Black Jewel in his forehead. "Perhaps disease — who knows? Let's hope that if it was disease, none of it lingers on. I'll speculate later, but not now. I'm sure I hear water somewhere — and that's my first requirement. Food's my second, sleep's my third — and thought, friend Oladahn, a very distant fourth…"

In one of the city's plazas they found a wall of blue-grey rock that had been carved with flowing figures. From the eyes of one stone maiden fell pure spring water that splashed into a hollow fashioned below. Hawkmoon stooped and drank, wiping wet hands over his dusty face. He stepped back for Oladahn to drink, then led the horses forward to slake their thirst.

Hawkmoon reached into one of his saddlebags and took out the cracked and crumpled map that had been given him in Hamadan. His finger crept across the map until it came to rest on the word "Soryandum". He smiled with relief. "We are not too far off our original route," he said. "Beyond these hills the Euphrates flows and Tarabulus lies beyond it by about a week's journey. We'll rest here for today and tonight, then continue on our way. Refreshed, we will travel more rapidly."

Oladahn grinned. "Aye, and you'd explore the city before we leave, I fancy." He splashed water on his fur, then bent to pick up his bow and quiver. "Now to attend to your second requirement — food. I'll not be gone long. I saw a wild ram in the hills. Tonight we'll dine off roast mutton." He remounted his horse and was away, riding for the broken gates of the city while Hawkmoon stripped off his clothes and plunged his hands into the cool spring water, gasping with a sense of utter luxury as he poured the water over his head and body. Then he took fresh clothing from the saddlebag, pulling on a silk shirt given him by Queen Frawbra of Hamadan and a pair of blue cotton britches with flaring bottoms. Glad to be out of the heavier leather and iron he had worn for protection's sake while crossing the desert in case any of the Dark Empire's men were following them, Hawkmoon donned a pair of sandals to complete his outfit. His only concession to his earlier fears was the sword he buckled about him.

It was scarcely possible that he could have been followed here, and besides, the city was so peaceful that he could not believe any kind of danger threatened.

Hawkmoon went to his horse and unsaddled it, then crossed to the shade of a ruined tower to lie with his back against it and await Oladahn and the mutton.

Noon came and went, and Hawkmoon began to wonder what had become of his friend. He dozed for another hour before real trepidation began to stir in him and he rose to resaddle his horse.

It was highly unlikely, Hawkmoon knew, that an archer as skilled as Oladahn would take so long in pursuit of one wild sheep. Yet there seemed to be no possible danger here. Perhaps Oladahn had grown weary and decided to sleep for an hour or two before hauling the carcass back. Even if that were all that was delaying him, Hawkmoon decided, he might need assistance.

He mounted his horse and rode through the streets to the crumbling outer wall of the city and to the hills beyond. The horse seemed to recover much of its former energy as its hooves touched grass, and Hawkmoon had to shorten the rein, riding into the hills at a light canter.

Ahead was a herd of wild sheep led by a large, wise looking ram, perhaps the one Oladahn had mentioned, but there was no sign at all of the little beast-man.

"Oladahn!" Hawkmoon yelled, peering about him. "Oladahn!" But only muffled echoes answered him.

Hawkmoon frowned, then urged his horse into a gallop, riding up a hill taller than the rest in the hope that from this vantage point he would be able to see his friend. Wild sheep scattered before him as the horse raced over the springy grass. He reached the top of the hill and shielded his eyes from the glare of the sun. He stared in every direction, but there was no sign of Oladahn.

For some moments he continued to look around him, hoping to see some trace of his friend; then, as he gazed toward the city, he saw a movement near the plaza of the spring. Had his eyes tricked him, or had he seen a man entering the shadows of the streets that led off the eastern side of the plaza? Could Oladahn have returned by another route? If so, why hadn't he answered Hawkmoon's call?

Hawkmoon had a nagging sense of terror in the back of his mind now, but he still could not believe that the city itself offered any menace.

He spurred his horse back down the hillside and leaped it over a section of ruined wall.

Muffled by the dust, the horse's hooves thudded through the streets as Hawkmoon headed toward the plaza, crying Oladahn's name. But again he was answered only by echoes. In the plaza there was no sign of the little mountain man.

Hawkmoon frowned, almost certain now that he and Oladahn had not, after all, been alone in the city. Yet there was no sign of inhabitants.

He turned his horse toward the streets. As he did so his ears caught a faint sound from above. He looked upward, his eyes searching the sky, certain that he recognized the sound. At last he saw it — a distant black shape in the air overhead. Then sunlight flashed on metal, and the sound became distinct, a clanking and whirring of giant bronze wings. Hawkmoon's heart sank.

The thing descending from the sky was unmistakably an ornate ornithopter, wrought in the shape of a gigantic condor, enameled in blue, scarlet, and green.

No other nation on Earth possessed such vessels. It was a flying machine of the Dark Empire of Granbretan.

Now Oladahn's disappearance was fully explained. The warriors of the Dark Empire were present in Soryandum. It was more than likely, too, that they had recognized Oladahn and knew that Hawkmoon could not be far away. And Hawkmoon was the Dark Empire's most hated opponent.

T W O

H U I L L A M   D ' A V E R C

Hawkmoon made for the shadows of the street, hoping that he had not been seen by the ornithopter.

Could the Granbretanians have followed him all the way across the desert? It was unlikely. Yet what else explained their presence in this remote place?

Hawkmoon drew his great battle blade from its scabbard and then dismounted. In his clothes of thin silk and cotton he felt more than ordinarily vulnerable as he ran through the streets seeking cover.

Now the ornithopter flew only a few feet above the tallest towers of Soryandum, almost certainly searching for Hawkmoon, the man whom the King-Emperor Huon had sworn must be revenged upon for his "betrayal" of the Dark Empire. Hawkmoon might have slain Baron Meliadus at the battle of Hamadan, but without doubt King Huon had swiftly dispatched a new emissary upon the task of hunting down the hated Hawkmoon.

The young Duke of Köln had not expected to journey without danger, but he had not believed that he would be found so soon.

He came to a dark building, half in ruins, whose cool doorway offered shelter. He entered the building and found himself in a hallway with walls of pale, carved stone partly overgrown with soft mosses and blooming lichens. A stairway ran up one side of the hall, and Hawkmoon, blade in hand, climbed the winding, moss-carpeted steps for several flights until he found himself in a small room into which sunlight streamed through a gap in the wall where the stones had fallen away. Flattening himself against the wall and peering around the broken section, Hawkmoon saw a large part of the city, saw the ornithopter wheeling and dipping as its vulture-masked pilot searched the streets.

There was a tower of faded green granite not too distant. It stood roughly in the centre of Soryandum, dominating the city. The ornithopter circled this for some time, and at first Hawkmoon guessed that the pilot believed him to be hidden there, but then the flying machine settled on the flat, battlement-surrounded roof of the tower. From somewhere below other figures emerged to join the pilot.

These men were evidently of Granbretan also. They were all clad in heavy armour and cloaks, with huge metal masks covering their heads, in spite of the heat. Such was the twisted nature of Dark Empire men that they could not rid themselves of their masks whatever the circumstances. They seemed to have a deep-rooted psychological reliance on them.

The masks were of rust red and murky yellow, fashioned to resemble rampant wild boars, with fierce, jeweled eyes that blazed in the sunlight and great ivory tusks curling from the flaring snouts.

These, then, were men of the Order of the Boar, infamous in Europe for its savagery. There were six of them standing by their leader, a tall, slender man whose mask was of gold and bronze and much more delicately wrought — almost to the point of caricaturing the mask of the Order. The man leaned on the arms of two of his companions — one squat and bulky, the other virtually a giant, with naked arms and legs of almost inhuman hairiness. Was the leader ill or wounded? wondered Hawkmoon. There seemed to be something theatrical about the way he leaned on his men. Hawkmoon thought then that he knew who the Boar leader was. It was almost certainly the renegade Frenchman Huillam D'Averc, once a brilliant painter and architect, who had joined the cause of Granbretan long before they had conquered France. An enigma, D'Averc, but a dangerous man for all that he affected illness.

Now the Boar leader spoke to the vulture-masked pilot, who shook his head. Evidently he had not seen Hawkmoon, but he pointed toward the spot where Hawkmoon had abandoned his horse. D'Averc — if it was D'Averc — languidly signed to one of his men, who disappeared below, to re-emerge almost at once with a struggling, snarling Oladahn.

Relieved, Hawkmoon watched as two of the boar-masked warriors dragged Oladahn close to the battlements. At least his friend was alive.

Then the Boar leader signed again, and the vulture pilot leaned into the cockpit of his flying machine and withdrew a bell-shaped megaphone, which he handed to the giant on whose arm the leader still rested. The giant placed this close to the snout of his master's mask.

Suddenly the quiet air of the city was filled with the bored, world-weary voice of the Boar leader.

"Duke von Köln, we know that you are present in this city, for we have captured your servant. In an hour the sun will set. If you have not delivered yourself to us by that time, we must begin to kill the little fellow..."

Now Hawkmoon knew for certain that it was D'Averc. No other man alive could both look and sound like that. Hawkmoon saw the giant hand the megaphone back to the pilot and then, with the help of his squat companion, help his master to the partially ruined battlement so that D'Averc could lean against it and look down into the streets.

Hawkmoon controlled his fury and studied the distance between his building and the tower. By jumping through the gap in the wall he could reach a series of flat roofs that would take him close to a pile of fallen masonry heaped against one wall of the tower. From there he saw that he could easily climb to the battlements. But he would be seen as soon as he left his cover. It would be possible to take that route only at night — and by nightfall they would have begun torturing Oladahn.

Perplexed, Hawkmoon fingered the Black Jewel, sign of his former slavery to Granbretan. He knew that if he gave himself up he would be killed instantly or be taken back to Granbretan and there killed with terrible slowness for the pleasure of the perverted Lords of the Dark Empire. He thought of Yisselda, to whom he had sworn to return, of Count Brass, whom he had sworn to aid in the struggle against Granbretan — and he thought of Oladahn, with whom he had sworn friendship after the little beast-man had saved his life.

Could he sacrifice his friend? Could he justify such an action, even if logic told him that his own life was of greater worth in the fight against the Dark Empire? Hawkmoon knew that logic was of no use here. But he knew, too, that his sacrifice might be useless, for there was no guarantee that the Boar leader would let Oladahn go once Hawkmoon had delivered himself up.

Hawkmoon bit his lips, gripping his sword tightly; then he came to a decision, squeezed his body through the gap in the wall, clung to the stonework with one hand, and waved his bright blade at the tower. D'Averc looked up slowly.

"You must release Oladahn before I come to you," Hawkmoon called. "For I know that all men of Granbretan are liars. You have my word, however, that if you release Oladahn I will deliver myself into your hands."

"Liars we may be," came the languid voice, barely audible, "but we are not fools. How may I trust your word?"

"I am a Duke of Köln," said Hawkmoon simply. "We do not lie."

A light, ironic laugh came from within the boar mask. "You may be naïve, Duke of Köln, but Sir Huillam D'Averc is not. However, may I suggest a compromise?"

"What is that?" Hawkmoon asked warily.

"I would suggest you come halfway toward us so that you are well within the range of our ornithopter's flame-lance, and then I shall release your servant." D'Averc coughed ostentatiously and leaned heavily on the battlement. "What say you to that?"

"Hardly a compromise," called Hawkmoon. "For then you could kill us both with little effort or danger to yourself."

"My dear Duke, the King-Emperor would much prefer you alive. Surely you know that? My *own* interest is at stake. Killing you now would only earn me a baronetcy at most — delivering you alive for the King-Emperor's pleasure would almost certainly gain me a princedom. Have you not heard of me, Duke Dorian? I am the *ambitious* Huillam D'Averc."

D'Averc's argument was convincing, but Hawkmoon could not forget the Frenchman's reputation for deviousness. Although it was true that he was worth more to D'Averc alive, the renegade might well decide it expedient not to risk his gains and might therefore kill Hawkmoon as soon as he came into certain range of the flame-lance.

Hawkmoon deliberated for a moment, then sighed. "I will do as you suggest, Sir Huillam." He poised himself to leap across the narrow street separating him from the rooftops below.

Then Oladahn cried, "No, Duke Dorian! Let them kill me! My life is worthless!"

Hawkmoon acted as if he had not heard his friend and sprang out and down, to land on the balls of his feet on the roof. The old masonry shuddered at the impact, and for a moment Hawkmoon thought he would fall as the roof threatened to crack. But it held, and he began to walk gingerly toward the tower.

Again Oladahn called out and began to struggle in the hands of his captors.

Hawkmoon ignored him, walking steadily on, sword still in one hand but held loosely, virtually forgotten.

Now Oladahn broke free altogether and darted across the tower, pursued by two cursing warriors. Hawkmoon saw him dash to the far edge, pause for a moment, and then fling himself over the parapet.

For a moment Hawkmoon stood frozen in horror, hardly understanding the nature of his friend's sacrifice.

Then he tightened his grip on his sword and raised his head to glare at D'Averc and his men. Bending low, he made for the edge of the roof as the flame cannon began to turn in his direction. There was a great *whoosh* of heat over his head as they sought his range; then he had swung himself over the edge and hung by his hands, peering down into the street far below.

There was a series of stone carvings quite close to him on his left. He inched along until he could grasp the nearest. They ran down the side of the house at an angle, almost to street level. But the stone was plainly rotten. Would the carvings support his weight?

Hawkmoon did not pause. He swung himself down on the first carving. It began to creak and crumble, like a bad tooth. Quickly Hawkmoon dropped to the next and then the next, bits of stone clattering down the sides of the building, to crash in the distant street.

Then at last Hawkmoon was able to leap to the cobbles and land easily in the soft dust that covered them. Now he began to run, not away from the tower — but toward it. He had nothing in his mind but vengeance on D'Averc for driving Oladahn to suicide.

He found the entrance to the tower and entered in time to hear the clatter of metal-shod feet as D'Averc and his warriors descended. He chose a spot on the staircase (which was enclosed) where he would be able to take the Granbretanians one at a time. D'Averc was the first to appear, stopping suddenly as he saw the glowering Hawkmoon, then reaching with gauntleted hand for his long blade.

"You were foolish not to take the chance of escape your friend's silly sacrifice gave you," said the boar-masked mercenary contemptuously. "Now, like it or not, I suppose we shall have to kill you…" He began to cough, doubling up in apparent agony, leaning weakly against the wall. He signed limply to the squat man behind him — one of those Hawkmoon had seen helping D'Averc across the battlements. "Oh, my dear Duke Dorian, I must apologize… my infirmity is liable to seize me at the most inconvenient moments. Ecardo — would you…?"

The powerfully built Ecardo sprang forward grunting and pulling a short-hafted battle-axe from his belt. He tugged out his sword with his free hand and chuckled with pleasure. "Thanks, master. Now let's see how the no-mask prances." He moved like a cat to the attack.

Hawkmoon poised himself, ready to meet Ecardo's first blow.

Then the man sprang with a great feral howl, the battle-axe splashing the air to clang against Hawkmoon's blade. Then Ecardo's short sword ripped upward, and Hawkmoon, already weak from exposure and hunger, barely managed to turn his body in time. Even so, the sword slashed through the cotton of his britches and he felt its cold edge against his flesh.

Hawkmoon's own blade slid from beneath the axe and crashed down on Ecardo's grinning boar mask, wrenching one tusk loose and badly denting the snout. Ecardo cursed, his sword stabbing again, but Hawkmoon leaned against the man's sword arm, trapping it beneath his body and the wall. Then he let go of his own sword so that it hung by its wrist thong, grasped Ecardo's arm, and tried to twist the axe from his hand.

Ecardo's armoured knee drove into Hawkmoon's groin, but Hawkmoon held his position in spite of the pain, tugged Ecardo down the stairs, pushed, and let him fall to the floor under his own momentum.

Ecardo hit the paving stones with a thud that shook the whole tower. He did not move.

Hawkmoon looked up at D'Averc. "Well, sir, are you recovered?"

D'Averc pushed back his ornate mask, to reveal the pale face and pale eyes of an invalid. His mouth twisted in a little smile. "I will do my best," he said.

And when he advanced it was swiftly, with the movements of a man more than ordinarily fit.

This time Hawkmoon claimed the initiative, darting a thrust at his enemy that almost took him by surprise but that he parried with amazing speed. His languid tone belied his reflexes.

Hawkmoon realized that D'Averc was quite as dangerous, in his own way, as the powerful Ecardo. He realized, too, that if Ecardo were merely stunned, he himself might soon be trapped between two opponents.

The swordplay was so swift that the two blades seemed a single blur of metal as both men held their ground. With his great mask flung back, D'Averc was smiling, with an expression of quiet pleasure in his eyes. He looked for all the world like a man enjoying a musical performance or some other passive pastime.

Wearied by his journey through the desert, needing food, Hawkmoon knew that he could not long sustain the fight in this way. Desperately he sought an opening in D'Averc's splendid defense. Once, his opponent stumbled slightly on a broken stair. Hawkmoon thrust swiftly but was parried and had his forearm nicked into the bargain.

Behind D'Averc the warriors of the Boar waited eagerly with swords ready to finish Hawkmoon off once the opportunity was presented to them.

Hawkmoon was tiring rapidly. Soon he was fighting a purely defensive style, barely managing to turn the thrusting steel that drove for his eye, his throat, his heart, or his belly. He took one step backward, then another.

As he took the second step, he heard a groan behind him and knew that Ecardo's senses were returning. It would not be long before the boars butchered him.

Yet he scarcely cared, now that Oladahn was dead. Hawkmoon's swordplay became wilder, and D'Averc's smile grew broader as he sensed his victory coming closer.

Rather than have Ecardo at his back, Hawkmoon sprang suddenly down the steps without turning around. His shoulder bumped against another, and he whirled, prepared to face the brutish Ecardo.

Then his sword almost dropped from his hand in astonishment.

"Oladahn!"

The little beast-man was in the act of raising a sword — the boar warrior's own sword — over the stirring Ecardo's head.

"Aye — I live. But do not ask me how. It's a mystery to me." And he brought the flat of the blade down on Ecardo's helmet with a great clang. Ecardo collapsed again.

There was no more time for talk. Hawkmoon barely managed to block D'Averc's next thrust. There was a look of astonishment in D'Averc's eyes too as he saw the living Oladahn.

Hawkmoon managed to break through the Frenchman's guard, piercing his shoulder armour. Again D'Averc swept the blade aside and resumed the attack. Hawkmoon had lost the advantage of his position. The savage boar mask grinned at him as warriors poured down the stairs.

Hawkmoon and Oladahn backed toward the door, hoping to regain the advantage, but there was little chance of that. For another ten minutes they held their own against the overwhelming odds, killing two Granbretanians, wounding three more. They were wearying rapidly. Hawkmoon could barely hold his sword.

His glazed eyes tried to focus on his opponents as they closed in like brutes for the kill. He heard D'Averc's triumphant "Take them alive!" and then he went down beneath a tide of metal.

T H R E E

T H E   W R A I T H - F O L K

Wrapped in chains so that they could barely breathe, Hawkmoon and Oladahn were borne down innumerable flights of stairs into the depths of the great tower, which seemed to stretch as far below ground as it did above.

At length the boar warriors reached a chamber that had evidently been a storeroom but which now served as an effective dungeon.

There they were flung face down on the coarse rock. They lay there until a booted foot turned them over to blink into the light of a guttering torch held by the squat Ecardo, whose battered mask seemed to snarl in glee. D'Averc, mask still pushed back to expose his face, stood between Ecardo and the huge, hairy warrior Hawkmoon had seen earlier. D'Averc had a brocade scarf to his lips, and he leaned heavily on the giant's arm.

D'Averc coughed musically and smiled down at his prisoners. "I fear I must leave you soon, gentlemen. This subterranean air is not good for me. However, it should do little harm to two such robust young fellows as yourselves. You will not have to stay here more than a day, I assure you. I have sent a request for a larger ornithopter that will be able to bear the two of you back to Sicilia, where my main force is now encamped."

"You have taken Sicilia already?" Hawkmoon asked tonelessly. "You have conquered the isle?"

"Aye. The Dark Empire wastes little time. I, in fact" — D'Averc coughed with mock modesty into his scarf — "am the *hero* of Sicilia. It was my leadership that subjugated the island so swiftly. But that triumph was no special one, for the Dark Empire has many capable captains like myself. We have made excellent gains in Europe these past few months — and in the East, too."

"But Kamarg still stands," Hawkmoon said. "That must irritate the King-Emperor."

"Oh, Kamarg cannot last long besieged," said D'Averc airily. "We are concentrating our *particular* attention on that little province. Why, it may have fallen already…"

"Not while Count Brass lives," Hawkmoon smiled.

"Just so," D'Averc said. "I heard he was badly wounded and his lieutenant von Villach slain in a recent battle."

Hawkmoon could not tell whether D'Averc was lying. He let no emotion show on his face, but the news had shocked him. Was Kamarg ready to fall — and if so, what would become of Yisselda?

"Plainly that news disturbs *you*," D'Averc murmured. "But fear not, Duke, for when Kamarg falls it will be in my safekeeping if all goes well. I plan to claim the province as my reward for capturing you. And these, my boon companions," he continued, indicating his brutish servants, "I will elevate to rule Kamarg when I cannot. They share all aspects of my life — my secrets, my pleasures. It is only fair that they should share my triumph. Ecardo I will make steward of my estates, and I think I shall make Peter here a count."

From within the giant's mask came an animal grunt. D'Averc smiled. "Peter has few brains, but his strength and his loyalty are without question. Perhaps I'll replace Count Brass with him."

Hawkmoon stirred angrily in his chains. "You are a wily beast, D'Averc, but I will not let you goad me to an outburst, if that's what you desire. I'll bide my time. Perhaps I'll escape you yet. And if I do — you may live in terror for the day when our roles are reversed and you are in *my* power."

"I fear you are too optimistic, Duke. Rest here, enjoy the peace, for you'll know none when you get to Granbretan."

With a mocking bow, D'Averc left, his men following. The torchlight faded, and Hawkmoon and Oladahn were left in darkness.

"Ah," came Oladahn's voice after a while. "I find it difficult to take my position seriously after all that has happened today. I am still not even sure whether this be dream, death, or reality."

"What did happen to you, Oladahn?" Hawkmoon asked. "How could you survive the great leap? I had imagined you dashed to death beneath the tower."

"By rights I should have been," Oladahn agreed. "If I had not been arrested by ghosts in midfall."

"Ghosts? You jest."

"Nay. These things — like ghosts — appeared from windows in the tower and bore me gently to earth. They were the size and shape of men but barely tangible…"

"You fell and knocked your head and dreamed this stuff!"

"You could be right." Suddenly Oladahn paused. "But if so, I am dreaming still. Look to your left."

Hawkmoon turned his head, gasping in astonishment at what he saw. There, quite plainly, he could see the figure of a man. Yet, as if through a pool of milk, he could see *beyond* the man and make out the wall behind him.

"A ghost of a classic sort," Hawkmoon said. "Strange to share a dream…"

Faint, musical laughter came from the figure standing over them. "You do not dream, strangers. We are men like you. The mass of our bodies is merely altered a little, that is all. We do not exist in quite the same dimensions as you. But we are real enough. We are the men of Soryandum."

"So you have not deserted your city," Oladahn said. "But how did you attain this… peculiar state of existence?"

The wraith-man laughed again. "By control of the mind, scientific experiment, by a certain mastery of time and space. I regret that it would be impossible to describe how we came to this condition, for we reached it, among other ways, by the creation of an entirely new vocabulary, and the language I would use would mean nothing to you. However, be assured of one thing — we are still able to judge human characters well enough and recognize you as potential friends and those others as actual enemies."

"Enemies of yours? How so?" Hawkmoon asked.

"I will explain later." The wraith-man glided forward until he was leaning over Hawkmoon. The young Duke of Köln felt a strange pressure on his body, and then he was lifted up. The man might have looked intangible, but he seemed far stronger than an ordinary mortal. From the shadows two more of the wraith-people drifted, one to pick up Oladahn and the other to raise his hand and somehow produce a radiance in the dungeon that was mellow yet adequate to illuminate the whole place. Hawkmoon saw that the wraith-men were tall and slender, with thin, handsome faces and blind-seeming eyes.

Hawkmoon had supposed at first that the people of Soryandum were able to pass through solid walls, but now he saw that they had entered from above, for there was a large tunnel about halfway up the wall. Perhaps in the distant past this tunnel has been some kind of chute down which sacks of stores had been rolled.

Now the wraith-people rose into the air toward the tunnel and entered it, drifting up it until light could be seen far ahead — the light of moon and stars.

"Where are you taking us?" Hawkmoon whispered.

"To a safer place where we shall be able to free you of your chains," the man who carried him answered.

When they reached the top of the tunnel and felt the chill of the night air, they paused while the one who had no burden went ahead to make sure that there were no Granbretanian warriors about. He signed to the others to follow, and they drifted out into the ruined streets of the silent city until they came to a simple three storeyed house that was in better condition than the rest but seemed to have no means of entrance at ground level.

The wraith-folk bore Hawkmoon and Oladahn upward again, to the second level, and passed through a wide window into the house.

In a room bare of any ornamentation they came to rest, setting the pair down gently.

"What is this place?" Hawkmoon asked, still unable to trust his senses.

"This is where we live," the wraith-man replied. "There are not many of us. Though we live for centuries, we are incapable of reproducing ourselves. That is what we lost when we became as we are."

Now through the door came other figures, several of them female. All were of the same beautiful and graceful appearance, all had bodies of milky opaqueness; none wore clothes. The faces and bodies were ageless, scarcely human, but they radiated such a sense of tranquillity that Hawkmoon immediately felt relaxed and secure.

One of the newcomers had brought with him a small instrument, scarcely larger than Hawkmoon's index finger, which he now applied to the several padlocks on the chains. One by one the locks sprang open, until at last Hawkmoon and then Oladahn were free.

Hawkmoon sat up, rubbing at his aching muscles. "I thank you," he said. "You have saved me from an unpleasant fate."

"We are happy to have been of use," replied one of their number, slightly shorter than the rest. "I am Rinal, once Chief Councilor of Soryandum." He came forward smiling. "And we wonder if it would interest you that you could be of help to us, also."

"I would be glad to perform any service in repayment of what you have done for me," Hawkmoon said earnestly. "What is it?"

"We, too, are in great danger from those strange warriors with their grotesque beast-masks," Rinal told him. "For they plan to raze Soryandum."

"Raze it? But why? This city offers no threat to them — and it is too remote to be worth their annexing."

"Not so," Rinal said. "For we have listened to their conversations and know that Soryandum is of value to them. They wish to build a great structure here that will house scores and hundreds of their flying machines. The machines can then be sent out to all the surrounding lands to threaten and defeat them."

"I understand," Hawkmoon murmured. "It makes sense. And that is why D'Averc, the ex-architect, was chosen for this particular mission. Building materials already exist here and could be remodeled to form one of their ornithopter bases, and the spot is so remote that few, if any, would note the activity. The Dark Empire would have surprise on their side right up to the moment they wished to launch an attack. They must be stopped!"

"They must be, if only for our sake," Rinal continued. "You see, we are part of this city perhaps more than you can understand. It and we exist as the same thing. If the city were destroyed, we should perish also."

"But how can we stop them?" Hawkmoon said. "And how can I be of use? You must have the resources of a sophisticated science at your disposal. I have only a sword — and even that is in the hands of D'Averc!"

"I told you that we are linked to the city," Rinal said patiently. "And that is exactly the case. We cannot move away from the city. Long ago we rid ourselves of such unsubtle things as machines. They were buried under a hillside many miles from Soryandum. Now we have need for one particular machine, and we cannot ourselves obtain it. You, however, with your mortal mobility, could get it for us."

"Willingly," said Hawkmoon. "If you give us the exact location of the machine we shall bring it to you. Best if we left soon, before D'Averc realizes we have escaped."

"I agree that the thing should be accomplished as soon as possible," Rinal nodded, "but I have omitted to tell you one thing. The machines were placed there by us while we were still able to make short journeys away from Soryandum. To make sure that they were not disturbed, we protected them with a beast-machine — a dreadful contraption designed to frighten off whoever should discover the store. But the metal creature can also kill — will kill any not of our race who dares enter the cavern."

"Then how may we nullify this beast?" Oladahn asked.

"There is but one way for you," Rinal said with a sigh. "You must fight it — and destroy it."

"I see." Hawkmoon smiled. "So I escaped from one predicament to face another scarcely less dangerous."

Rinal raised his hand. "No. We make no demands on you, If you feel that your life would be more useful in the service of some other cause, forget us at once and go your way."

"I owe you my life," Hawkmoon said. "And my conscience would not be clear if I rode away from Soryandum knowing that your city would be destroyed, your race exterminated, and the Dark Empire given the opportunity to wreak even more havoc in the East than it has already. No — I will do what I can, though without weapons it will not be an easy task."

Rinal signed to one of the wraith-folk, who drifted from the room, to return at length with Hawkmoon's battered battle-blade and Oladahn's bow, arrows, and sword. "We found it an easy matter to recover these," smiled Rinal. "And we have another weapon, of sorts, for you." He handed Hawkmoon the tiny device they had used earlier to open the padlocks. "This we retained when we put most of our other machines in store. It is capable of opening any lock — all you must do is point at it. It will help you gain entrance to the main storeroom where the mechanical beast guards the old machines of Soryandum."

"And what is the machine you desire us to find?" Oladahn asked.

"It is a small device, about the size of a man's head. Its colours are those of the rainbow, and it shines. It looks like crystal but feels like metal. It has a base of onyx, and from this projects an octagonal object. There may be two in the storeroom. If you can, bring both."

"What does it do?" Hawkmoon inquired.

"That you will see when you return with it."

"If we return with it," said Oladahn in a tone of philosophical gloom.

F O U R

T H E   M E C H A N I C A L   B E A S T

Having refreshed themselves on food and wine stolen from D'Averc's men by the wraith-folk, Hawkmoon and Oladahn strapped on their weapons and prepared to leave the house.

With two of the men of Soryandum supporting them, they were borne gently down to the ground.

"May the Runestaff protect you," whispered one, as the pair made for the city wall, "for we have heard that you serve it."

Hawkmoon turned to ask him how he had heard this. It was the second time he had been told that he served the Runestaff; yet he had no knowledge that he did. But before he could speak the wraith-man had vanished.

Frowning, Hawkmoon led the way from the city.

Deep in the hills several miles from Soryandum, Hawkmoon paused to get his bearings. Rinal had told him to look for a cairn made out of cut granite, left there centuries before by Rinal's ancestors. At last he saw it, old stone turned to silver by the moonlight.

"Now we go north," he said, and look for the hill from which the granite was cut."

Another half hour and they made out the hill. It looked as if at some time a giant sword had sliced its face sheer. Since that time grass had grown over it again so that the characteristic seemed a natural one.

Hawkmoon and Oladahn crossed springy turf to a place where thick shrubs grew against the side of the hill. Parting these, they discerned a narrow opening in the cliffside. This was the secret entrance to the machine stores of the people of Soryandum.

Squeezing through the entrance, the two men found themselves in a large cave. Oladahn lit the brand they had brought for the purpose, and the flickering light revealed a great, square cavern that had evidently been hewn artificially.

Remembering his instructions, Hawkmoon crossed to the far wall of the cave and looked for a tiny mark at shoulder height. At last he saw it — a sign written in unfamiliar characters, and beneath it a tiny hole. Hawkmoon took from his shirt the instrument they had been given and pointed it at the hole.

He felt a tingling sensation in his hand as he applied slight pressure to the instrument. The rock before him began to tremble. A powerful gust of air made the brand flames stream, threatening to blow them out. The wall began to glow, become transparent, and then disappear altogether. "It will still be there," Rinal had told them, "but temporarily removed to another dimension."

Cautiously, swords in hand, they passed through into a great tunnel full of cool, green light from walls like fused glass.

Ahead of them lay another wall. On it glowed a single red spot, and it was at this that Hawkmoon now pointed the instrument.

Again there was a sudden rush of air. This time it nearly blew them over. Then the wall glowed white, turning to a milky blue before vanishing altogether.

This section of the tunnel was the same milky-blue colour, but the wall ahead of them was black. When it, too, had faded, they entered a tunnel of yellow stone and knew that the main store chamber and its guardian lay ahead of them.

Hawkmoon paused before applying the instrument to the white wall they faced.

"We must be cunning and move swiftly," he told Oladahn, "for the creature beyond this wall will come alive the moment it senses our presence —"

He broke off as a muffled sound reached their ears — a fantastic clashing and clattering. The white wall shuddered as if something on the other side had flung a huge weight against it.

Oladahn looked dubiously at the wall. "Perhaps we should reconsider. After all, if we wasted our lives uselessly we…"

But Hawkmoon was already activating the instrument, and the protecting wall had begun to change colour as the strange, cold wind struck their faces. From behind the wall came an awesome wail of pain and bewilderment. The walls turned to pink, faded — and revealed the machine-beast.

The wall's disappearance seemed to have disturbed it for an instant, for it made no move toward them. It crouched on metal feet, towering over them, its multicoloured scales half-blinding them. The length of its back, save for its neck, was a mass of knife-sharp horns. It had a body fashioned somewhat like an ape's, with short hind legs and long forelegs ending in hands of taloned metal. Its eyes were multifaceted like a fly's, glowing with shifting colours, and its snout was full of razor-sharp metal teeth.

Beyond the mechanical beast they could see great heaps of machinery, stacked in orderly rows about the walls. The room was vast. Somewhere in the middle of it, on his left, Hawkmoon saw the two crystalline devices Rinal had described. Silently, he pointed to them, then made to dash past the monster, into the storeroom.

Their movements as they ran stirred the beast from its daze. It screamed and lumbered after them, exuding a repulsive metallic smell.

From the corner of his eye Hawkmoon saw a gigantic taloned hand clutching at him. He swerved aside, knocking into a delicate machine that toppled and smashed to the floor, scattering bits of glass and broken metal parts. The hand plucked at air an inch from his face, then grabbed again, but Hawkmoon had already sidestepped.

An arrow suddenly struck the beast's snout with a clatter of metal on metal, but it did not scratch the yellow and black scales.

With a roar, the beast sought its other enemy, saw Oladahn, and pounced toward him.

Oladahn scampered backward but not fast enough, for the creature seized him in its paw and drew him towards its gaping mouth. Hawkmoon yelled and struck his sword at the thing's groin. It snorted and flung its prisoner aside. Oladahn lay supine in a corner by the door, either stunned or slain.

Hawkmoon backed away as the creature advanced; then he suddenly changed tactics, ducked, and dashed between the surprised beast's legs. As it began to turn, Hawkmoon dashed back again.

The metal monster snorted in fury, its claws thrashing about it. It leaped into the air and came down with an earsplitting crash, rushing across the floor of the gallery at Hawkmoon, who squeezed down between two machines and, using them for cover, crept closer to the machines he had come to take.

Now the monster began to wrench machines aside in its insensate search for its enemy. Hawkmoon came to a stop by a machine with a bell-shaped nozzle. At the end of its nozzle was a lever. The machine seemed to be some kind of weapon. Without pausing to think, Hawkmoon pulled the lever. A faint noise came from the thing, but nothing else seemed to result.

Now the beast was almost upon him again.

Hawkmoon prepared to make a stand, deciding that he would fling his sword at one of the eyes, since they seemed to be the creature's most vulnerable feature. Rinal had told him that the mechanical beast could not be killed in any ordinary sense; but if it were blinded, he might stand a chance.

But now, as the beast came into direct line of the machine, it staggered and grunted. Evidently some invisible ray was attacking it, possibly interfering with its complicated mechanism. It staggered, and Hawkmoon felt triumphant for an instant, judging the beast defeated. But the creature shook its body and began to advance again with slow, painful movements.

Hawkmoon saw that it was slowly regaining its strength. He must strike now if he was to have any chance at all. He ran toward the beast. It turned its head slowly. But then Hawkmoon had leaped at its squat neck and was climbing up the scales to seat himself on the mechanical beast's shoulders. With a growl it raised its arm to tear Hawkmoon away.

Desperately Hawkmoon leaned forward and with the pommel of his sword struck first at one eye and then at the other. With a sharp, splintering sound, both eyes were dashed to fragments.

The beast screamed, its paws going not to Hawkmoon but to its injured eyes, giving the young duke time to leap from the creature's back and dash for the two boxes he sought.

He pulled a sack from where it was looped over his belt and dropped the two boxes into it.

The mechanical monster was flailing around. Metal buckled and snapped wherever it struck. Blind it might now be, but it had lost none of its strength.

Skipping around the screaming beast, Hawkmoon ran to where Oladahn lay, bundled the little man over his shoulder, and ran for the exit.

Behind him the metal beast had caught the sound of his footsteps and had begun to turn in pursuit. Hawkmoon increased his pace, his heart seeming about to burst from his ribcage with the effort.

Down the corridors he raced, one after the other, until he reached the cave and the narrow opening that led to the outside world. The metal monster would not be able to follow him through such a tiny crack.

As soon as he squeezed through the opening and felt the night air in his lungs, he relaxed and studied Oladahn's face. The little beast-man was breathing well enough, and there seemed to be nothing broken. Only a livid bruise on his head seemed serious, explaining why he was unconscious. Even as he inspected Oladahn's body for worse injuries, the beast-man's eyes began to flutter open. A faint sound came from his lips.

"Oladahn, are you all right?" Hawkmoon asked anxiously.

"Ugh — my head's on fire," Oladahn grunted. "Where are we?"

"Safe. Now try to rise. Dawn is almost here, and we must get back to Soryandum before morning, or D'Averc's men will see us."

Painfully Oladahn pulled himself to his feet. From within the cave came a wild howling and thundering as the mechanical beast sought to reach them.

"Safe?" Oladahn said, pointing to the hillside behind Hawkmoon. "Possibly — but for how long?"

Hawkmoon turned. A great fissure had appeared in the cliff face as the mechanical beast strove to free itself and follow its enemies.

"All the more need for speed," said Hawkmoon, picking up his bundle and beginning to run back in the direction of Soryandum.

They had not gone half a mile before they heard an enormous crash behind them. Looking back, they saw the face of the hill split open and the metal beast emerge, its howling echoing through the hills, threatening to reach all the way to Soryandum.

"The beast is blind," Hawkmoon explained, "so it may not follow us at once. Perhaps if we can reach the city we will be safe from it."

They increased their pace and were soon on the outskirts of Soryandum.

Not much later, as dawn came, they were creeping through the streets seeking the house of the wraith-folk.

F I V E

T H E   M A C H I N E

Rinal and two others met them by the house and hastily bore them up to the entrance window. As the sun rose and light fell through the windows, making the wraith-folk look even less tangible than before, Rinal eagerly took the boxes from Hawkmoon's sack.

"They are as I remember," he murmured, his strange body drifting into the light so that he might look at the objects better. His ghostly hand stroked the octagon set in its onyx base. "Now we need have no fear of the masked strangers. We can escape from them whenever we please..."

"But I thought there was *no* way for you to leave the city," Oladahn said.

"That is true — but with these machines, we can take the whole city with us, if we are lucky."

Hawkmoon was about to question Rinal further, when he heard a commotion in the street outside and sidled to the window to peer cautiously down. There he saw D'Averc, his two brutish lieutenants, and about twenty warriors. One of the warriors was pointing up at the window.

"We have been seen," Hawkmoon said. "We must all leave. We cannot fight so many."

Rinal frowned. "We cannot leave, either. But if we use our machine, it will put you at D'Averc's mercy. I am in a dilemma."

"Use the machine then," Hawkmoon said, "and let us worry about D'Averc."

"We cannot let you die for our sakes! Not after all you have done."

"Use the machine!"

But Rinal still hesitated.

Hawkmoon heard another sound outside and glanced cautiously through the window. "They've brought up ladders. They're about to enter. Use the machine, Rinal."

Another of the wraith-folk, a woman, said softly, "Use the machine, Rinal.

If what we heard was true, then it is unlikely that our friend will come to much harm at D'Averc's hands, not at this moment, anyway."

"What do you mean?" Hawkmoon asked. "How do you know this?"

"We have a friend not of our people," the woman told him, "who sometimes visits us, bringing us news of the outside world. He, too, serves the Runestaff —"

"Is he a warrior in armour of jet and gold?" Hawkmoon interrupted.

"Aye, he told us you —"

"Duke Dorian!" Oladahn cried, pointing. The first of the boar warriors had reached the window.

Hawkmoon whipped his sword from the scabbard, leaped forward, and drove the blade into the throat of the warrior just below his gorget. The man went backward and down with a gurgling scream. Hawkmoon seized the ladder, trying to twist it aside. It was firmly held below. Another warrior came level with the window, and Oladahn swung at his head knocking him sideways, but the man clung on. Hawkmoon relinquished his hold on the ladder and hacked at the man's gauntleted fingers. With a yell he let go and crashed to the ground.

"The machine," Hawkmoon called desperately. "Use it, Rinal. We cannot hold them for long."

From behind him there came a musical thrumming sound, and Hawkmoon felt slightly dizzy as his sword met that of the next attacker.

Then everything began to vibrate rapidly, and the walls of the house turned bright red. Outside in the street the boar warriors were yelling — not in surprise, but in outright fear. Hawkmoon could not understand why the sight terrified them so much.

He could see now that the whole city had turned the same vibrating scarlet and seemed to be shaking itself to pieces in harmony with the thrumming of the machine. Then, abruptly, sound and city vanished and Hawkmoon was falling gently earthward.

He heard the voice of Rinal, faint and disappearing, say, "We have left you the twin of this machine. It is our gift to aid you against your enemies. It has the ability to shift whole areas of the earth into a slightly different dimension of space-time. Our enemies will not have Soryandum now..."

Then Hawkmoon landed on rocky ground, Oladahn close by, and saw that there was not a trace of the city. Instead there was pitted ground that looked as if it had recently been ploughed.

Some distance away were the troops of Granbretan, D'Averc among them, and Hawkmoon could see now why they had screamed in terror.

The machine-beast had come at last to the city and was attacking the boar warriors. Everywhere were the battered and bleeding corpses of Granbretanians.

Urged on by D'Averc, who had his own sword drawn and was joining them in the battle, the Granbretanians were trying to destroy the monster.

Its metal spines shook in fury, its metal teeth clashed in its head, and its metal talons ripped and rent armour and flesh.

"The beast will take care of them," Hawkmoon said. "Look — our horses." About three hundred yards away stood the two bewildered steeds. Hawkmoon and Oladahn ran for them and were soon mounted, riding away from the site of Soryandum and the carnage that the mechanical beast was making of D'Averc's boars.

Now, with the strange gift of the wraith-folk wrapped carefully and placed in Hawkmoon's saddlebag, the two adventurers continued their journey to the coast.

The coarse turf was easier on the horses' hooves, and they made rapid progress over the hills until they came at last to the wide valley where the Euphrates flowed.

By the banks of the broad river they made their camp and debated how best to cross, for the water was fast-flowing at this stretch, and according to Hawkmoon's map, they would have to journey several miles south before they came to a likely fording place.

Hawkmoon stared across the water as the setting sun stained it the colour of poppies. A long, almost silent sigh escaped him, and Oladahn looked up curiously from where he was laying the fire.

"What troubles you, Duke Dorian? One would have thought you in good spirits after our escape."

"It is the future that troubles me, Oladahn. If D'Averc were right and Count Brass lies wounded, with von Villach dead and Kamarg under powerful siege, then I fear we shall return to find nothing but the ashes and mud Baron Meliadus once promised he would make of Kamarg."

"Let us wait until we get there," Oladahn said with attempted cheerfulness, "for it is likely that D'Averc only sought to make you gloomy. Almost certainly your Kamarg still stands. From all you have told me of the great defenses and the mighty valour of the province, I do not doubt that they still hold against the Dark Empire. You will see…"

"But will I?" Hawkmoon's gaze dropped to the darkening ground. "Will I, Oladahn? D'Averc was almost certainly right when he spoke of Granbretan's other conquests. If Sicilia is theirs, then so must be parts of Italia and Espanyia. Don't you see what that means?"

"Outside of the Bulgar Mountains my geography is weak," Oladahn said embarrassedly.

"It means that all routes to Kamarg — by both land and sea — are blocked by the Dark Empire's hordes. Even if we reach the sea and find a ship, what chance will we have of passing unharmed through the Sicilian Channel? The waters there must be thick with Dark Empire ships."

"But do we have to travel that way? What about the route you used to reach the East?"

Hawkmoon frowned. "Much of that territory I flew across, and it would take twice the time to go back that way. Also Granbretan has already made extra gains there."

"But the territories under their control could be circumnavigated," Oladahn said. "At least on land we should stand some chance, while on sea, from what you say, no chance at all."

"Aye," said Hawkmoon thoughtfully. "But it would mean crossing Turkia — a journey of several weeks. But then, perhaps, we could use the Black Sea, which, I hear, is fairly free of Dark Empire ships still." He consulted the map. "Aye — the Black Sea across to Romania — but then it would become increasingly dangerous as we neared France, for the Dark Empire's forces are everywhere thereabouts. Still, you are right — we would have a better chance by that route; might even slay a couple of Granbretanians and use their masks as disguises. One disadvantage that they have is that their faces cannot be recognized as those of friend or foe. If it were not for the secret languages of the various Orders, we could travel safely enough if tricked out in beast-masks and armour."

"Then we change our route," Oladahn said.

"Yes. We go north in the morning."

For a number of long days they followed the Euphrates north, crossing the borders between Syria and Turkia and coming at length to the quiet white town of Birachek, where the Euphrates became the Firat River.

In Birachek a wary innkeeper, suspecting them as servants of the Dark Empire, told them at first that there were no rooms, but then Hawkmoon pointed to the Black Jewel in his forehead and said, "My name is Dorian, last Duke of Köln, sworn enemy of Granbretan," and the innkeeper, even in this remote town, had heard of him and let them in.

Later that night they sat in the public room of the inn, drinking sweet wine and talking to the members of a trading caravan that had arrived in Birachek shortly before them.

The traders were swarthy men with blue-black hair and beards that gleamed with oil. They were dressed in leather shirts and brightly coloured divided kilts of wool; over these clothes they wore woven cloaks, also of wool, in geometric designs of purple, red, and yellow. These cloaks, they told the travelers, showed that they were the men of Yenahan, merchant of Ankara. At their waists were curved sabres with richly decorated hilts and engraved blades, worn unscabbarded. These traders were as used to fighting as they were to bartering.

Their leader, Saleem, hawk-nosed and with piercing blue eyes, leaned forward over the table to speak slowly to the Duke of Köln and Oladahn.

"You have heard that emissaries of the Dark Empire pay court to the Calif of Istanbul and bribe that thriftless monarch to let them station a large force of bull-masked warriors within the city walls?"

Hawkmoon shook his head. "I have little news of the world. But I believe you. It is the way of Granbretan to take with gold rather than take with force. Only if gold is no longer of use will they produce their weapons and armies."

Saleem nodded. "As I thought. You would not, then, think Turkia safe from the Western wolves?"

"Not any part of the world, even Amarehk, is safe from their ambition. They dream of conquering lands that might not even exist, save in fables. They plan to take Asiacommunista, though they must find it first. Arabia and the East are mere camping grounds for their armies."

"But could they have such power?" Saleem asked, astonished.

"They have the power," Hawkmoon said with confidence. "They have a madness, too, which makes them savage, cunning — and inventive. I have seen Londra, capital of Granbretan, and its vast architecture is that of brilliant nightmares made solid. I have seen the King-Emperor himself in his Throne Globe of milky fluid — a wizened immortal with the golden voice of a youth. I have seen the laboratories of the sorcerer-scientists — innumerable caverns of bizarre machines, many whose functions have yet to be rediscovered by the Granbretanians themselves. And I have talked with their nobles, learned of their ambitions, know them to be more insane than anything you or any other normal man could imagine. They are without humanity, have little feeling for each other and none at all for those they regard as lower species — that is, all those not of Granbretan. They crucify men, women, children, and animals to decorate and mark the roads to and from their conquests..."

Saleem leaned back with a wave of his hand. "Ah, come now, Duke Dorian, you exaggerate..."

Hawkmoon said forcefully, glaring into Saleem's eyes, "I tell you this, trader of Turkia — I *cannot* exaggerate the evil of Granbretan!"

Saleem frowned then and shuddered. "I — I believe you," he said. "But I wish that I could not. For how can the little nation of Turkia withstand such might and cruelty?"

Hawkmoon sighed. "I can offer no solution. I would say that you should band together, do not let them weaken you with gold and gradual encroachment in your lands — but I would waste my rhetoric if I tried, for men are greedy and will not see the truth for the gleam of coin. Resist them, I would say, with honour and honest courage, with wisdom and with idealism. Yet those who resist them are vanquished and tortured, see their wives raped and torn apart before their eyes, their children become playthings of warriors and heaped on fires lit to burn whole cities. But if you do not resist, if you escape death in battle, then the same could still happen to you, or you and yours become cringing things, less than human, willing to perform any indignity, any act of evil, to save your skins. I spoke of honesty — and honesty forbids me to encourage you with brave talk of noble battle and warriors' deaths. I seek to destroy them — I am their declared enemy — but I have great allies and considerable luck, and even I feel that I cannot forever escape their vengeance, though I have done so several times. I can only advise those who would save something to resist the minions of King Huon — use cunning. Use cunning, my friend. It is the only weapon we have against the Dark Empire."

"Pretend to serve them, you mean?" Saleem said thoughtfully.

"I did so. I am alive now and comparatively free…"

"I will remember your words, westerner."

"Remember them *all*," Hawkmoon warned him. "For the hardest compromise to make is when you decide to *appear* to compromise. Often the deception becomes the reality long before you realize it."

Saleem fingered his beard. "I understand you." He glanced about the room. The flickering shadows of the torches seemed to take on a sudden menace. "How long, I wonder, will it be…? So much of Europe is already theirs."

"Have you heard anything of the province called Kamarg?" asked Hawkmoon.

"Kamarg. A land of horned werebeasts, is it not, and half-human monsters with mighty powers, who have somehow managed to stand against the Dark Empire. They are led by a metal giant, the Brass Count…"

Hawkmoon smiled. "You have heard much that is legend. Count Brass is flesh and blood, and there are few monsters in Kamarg. The only horned beasts are the bulls of the marshlands and the horses, too. And have they still resisted the Dark Empire? Heard you of how Count Brass fares, or his lieutenant von Villach — or Count Brass's daughter, Yisselda."

"I heard Count Brass was dead and his lieutenant, too. But of a girl I heard nothing — and as far as I know Kamarg still stands."

Hawkmoon rubbed at the Black Jewel. "Your information is not certain enough. I cannot believe that if Count Brass is dead Kamarg still stands. If Count Brass goes down, so does the province."

"Well, I speak only of rumours surrounding other rumours," Saleem said. "We traders are sure of local gossip, but most of what we hear of the West is

HAWKMOON

vague and obscure. You come from Kamarg, do you not?"

"It is my adopted home," Hawkmoon agreed. "If it still exists."

Oladahn put his hand on Hawkmoon's shoulder. "Do not be depressed, Duke Dorian. You said yourself that Trader Saleem's information is barely credible. Wait until we are nearer our goal before you lose hope."

Hawkmoon made an effort to rid himself of the mood, calling for more wine and plates of broiled pieces of mutton and hot unleavened bread. And although he was able to appear more cheerful, his mind was not at rest for fear that all those he loved were indeed dead and the wild beauty of the Kamarg marshlands now turned to a burning waste.

S I X

M A D   G O D ' S   S H I P

Traveling with Saleem and his traders to Ankara and thence to the port of Zonguldak on the Black Sea, Hawkmoon and Oladahn were able, with the help of papers supplied by Saleem's master, to get passage on board the *Smiling Girl*, the only ship ready to take them with it to Simferopol on the coast of a land called Crimia. *Smiling Girl* was not a pretty vessel, and neither did she seem happy. Captain and crew were filthy, and the decks below stank of a thousand different kinds of rot. Yet they were forced to pay heavily for the privilege of passage on the tub, and their quarters were little less noxious than the bilges over which they were positioned. Captain Mouso, with his long, greasy moustachios and shifty eyes, did not inspire their confidence, and neither did the bottle of strong wine that seemed permanently in the mate's hairy paw.

Philosophically, Hawkmoon decided that at least the ship would hardly be worth a pirate's attention — and, for the same reason, a Dark Empire ship's attention — and went aboard with Oladahn shortly before she sailed.

Smiling Girl lumbered away from the quayside on the early-morning tide. As her patched sails caught the wind, every timber in her groaned and creaked; she turned sluggishly north-north-east under a darkening sky that was full of rain. The morning was cool and grey, with a peculiar muted quality to it that dampened sounds and made seeing an effort.

Huddled in his cloak, Hawkmoon stood in the fo'c'sle and watched as Zonguldak disappeared behind them.

Rain had begun to fall in heavy drops by the time the port was out of sight and Oladahn came up from below to move along the heaving deck toward Hawkmoon.

"I've cleaned up our quarters as best I can, Duke Dorian, though we'll not be free of the smell from the rest of the ship — and there's little, I'd guess, that would scare away such fat rats as I saw."

"We'll bear it," Hawkmoon said stoically. "We've borne worse, and the voyage is only for two days." He glanced at the mate, who was reeling out of the wheelhouse. "Though I'd be happier if I thought the ship's officers and crew were a trifle more capable." He smiled. "If the mate drinks any more and the captain lies snoring much longer, we may find ourselves with a command!"

Rather than go below, the two men stood together in the rain, looking to the north and wondering what might befall them on their long journey to Kamarg.

The miserable ship sailed on through the miserable day, tossed on the rough sea, blown by a treacherous wind that ever threatened to become a storm but always stopped just short. The captain stumbled onto the bridge from time to time, to shout at his men, to curse them and beat them into the rigging to reef that sail or loose another. To Hawkmoon and Oladahn, Captain Mouso's orders seemed entirely arbitrary.

Toward evening, Hawkmoon went to join the captain on the bridge. Mouso looked up at him with a shifty expression.

"Good evening, sir," he said, sniffing and wiping his long nose with his sleeve. "I hope the voyage's to your satisfaction."

"Reasonably, thank you. What time have we made — good or bad?"

"Good enough, sir," replied the skipper, turning so that he did not have to look at Hawkmoon directly. "Good enough. Shall I have the galley prepare you some supper?"

Hawkmoon nodded. "Aye."

The mate appeared from below the bridge, singing softly to himself and evidently blind drunk.

Now a sudden squall hit the ship side on, and the ship wallowed over alarmingly. Hawkmoon clung to the rail, feeling that at any moment it would crumble away in his hand. Captain Mouso seemed oblivious of any danger, and the mate was flat on his face, bottle falling from his hand as his body slid nearer and nearer to the side.

"Better help him," Hawkmoon said.

Captain Mouso laughed. "He's all right — he's got a drunkard's luck."

But now the mate's body was against the starboard rail, his head and one shoulder already through. Hawkmoon leaped down the companionway to grab the man and haul him back to safety as the ship heaved again, this time in the other direction, and salt waves washed the deck.

Hawkmoon looked down at the man he had rescued. The mate lay on his back, eyes closed, lips moving in the words of the song he'd been singing.

Hawkmoon laughed, shaking his head, calling up to the skipper, "You're right — he has a drunkard's luck." Then, as he turned his head to port, he thought he saw something in the water. The light was fading fast, but he was sure he had seen a vessel not too far away.

"Captain — do you see anything yonder?" he yelled, going to the rail and peering into the mass of heaving water.

"Looks like a raft of some kind," Mouso called back.

Hawkmoon was soon able to see the thing more closely as a wave swept it nearer. It was a raft, with three men clinging to it.

"Shipwrecked by the look of 'em." Mouso called casually. "Poor bastards." He shrugged his shoulders. "Ah, well, not our affairs…"

"Captain, we must save them." Hawkmoon said.

"We'll never do it in this light. Besides, we're wasting time. I'm carrying no cargo save yourself on this trip and have to be in Simferopol on time to pick up my cargo before someone else does."

"We must save them," Hawkmoon said firmly. "Oladahn — a rope."

The Bulgar beast-man found a coil of rope in the wheelhouse and came hurrying down with it. The raft was still in sight, its burden flat on their faces, clinging to it for dear life. Sometimes it vanished in a great trough of water, reappearing after several seconds, a fair distance from the boat. The gap between them was widening at every moment, and Hawkmoon knew that there was very little time before the raft would be too far away for them to reach it. Lashing one end of the rope to the rail and looping the other about his waist, he stripped off cloak and sword and dived into the foaming ocean.

At once, Hawkmoon realized the danger he was in. The great waves were almost impossible to swim against, and there was every chance of his being dashed against the side of the ship, stunned, and drowned. But he struggled on through the water, fighting to keep it out of his mouth and eyes as he searched about for the raft.

There it was! And now its occupants had seen the ship and were standing up, waving and shouting. They had not seen Hawkmoon swimming toward them.

As he swam, Hawkmoon caught glimpses of the men from time to time, but he could not distinguish them clearly. Two now seemed to be struggling, while the third seemed to be sitting upright watching them.

"Hold on!" Hawkmoon called above the crash of the sea and the moan of the wind. Exerting all his strength, he swam even harder and was soon nearly upon the raft as it was tossed on a wild chaos of black and white water.

Then Hawkmoon caught the edge of the raft and saw that indeed two of the men were fighting in earnest. He saw, too, that they wore the snouted masks of the Order of the Boar. The men were warriors of Granbretan.

For an instant Hawkmoon debated leaving them to their fate. But if he did that, he reasoned, he would be no better than they. He must do his best to save them, then decide what to do with them.

He called up to the fighting pair, but they did not seem to hear him. They grunted and cursed in their struggle, and Hawkmoon wondered if they had not been demented by their ordeal.

Hawkmoon tried to heave himself onto the raft, but the water and the rope around his body dragged him down. He saw the seated figure look up and sign to him almost casually.

"Help me," Hawkmoon gasped, "or I'll not be able to help you."

The figure rose and swayed across the raft until his way was blocked by the fighting men. With a shrug he seized their necks, paused for an instant until the raft dipped in the water, then pushed them into the sea.

"Hawkmoon, my dear friend!" came a voice from within the boar mask. "How happy I am to see you. There — I've helped you. I've lightened our load…"

Hawkmoon made a grab at one of the drowning men who struggled with his companion. In the heavy masks and armour, they were bound to be dragged down in seconds. But he could not reach them. He watched in fascination as, with seeming gradualness, the masks sank below the waves.

He glared up at the survivor, who was leaning down to offer him a hand. "You have murdered your friends, D'Averc! I've a good mind to let you go down with them."

"Friends? My dear Hawkmoon, they were no such thing. Servants, aye, but not friends." D'Averc braced himself as another wave tossed the raft, nearly forcing Hawkmoon to lose his grasp. "They were loyal enough — but dreadfully boring. And they made fools of themselves. I cannot tolerate that. Come along, let me help you aboard my little vessel. It is not much, but…"

Hawkmoon allowed D'Averc to drag him onto the raft, then turned and waved toward the ship, just visible through the darkness. He felt the rope tighten as Oladahn began to haul on it.

"It was fortunate that you were passing," D'Averc said coolly as slowly they were drawn toward the ship. "I had thought myself as good as drowned and all my glorious promise barely fulfilled — and then who should come by in his splendid ship but the noble Duke of Köln. Fate flings us together once again, Duke."

"Aye, but I'll readily fling you away again as you flung your friends, if you do not hold your tongue and help me with this rope," growled Hawkmoon.

The raft plunged through the sea and at last bumped against Smiling Girl's half-rotten side. A rope ladder snaked down, and Hawkmoon began to climb, finally hauling himself with relief over the rail, gasping for breath.

When Oladahn saw the next man's head emerge over the side, he cursed and made to draw his sword, but Hawkmoon stopped him. "He's our prisoner, and we might as well keep him alive, for he could be a useful bargaining counter if we are in trouble later."

"How sensible!" D'Averc exclaimed admiringly, then began coughing. "Forgive me — my ordeal has desperately weakened me, I fear. A change of clothes, some hot grog, a good night's rest, and I'll be myself again."

"You'll be lucky if we let you rot in the bilges," Hawkmoon said. "Take him below to our cabin, Oladahn."

Huddled in the tiny cabin that was dimly lit by a small lantern hanging from the roof, Hawkmoon and Oladahn watched D'Averc strip himself of his mask, armour and sodden undergarments.

"How did you come to be on the raft, D'Averc?" Hawkmoon asked as the Frenchman fussily dried himself. Even he was slightly nonplused by the man's apparent coolness. He admired the quality and even wondered if he did not actually like D'Averc in some strange way. Perhaps it was D'Averc's honesty in admitting his ambition, his unwillingness to justify his actions, even if, as recently, they involved casual murder.

"A long story, my dear friend. The three of us — Ecardo, Peter, and I — left the men to deal with that blind monster you released upon us and managed to reach the safety of the hills. A little later the ornithopter we had sent to collect you arrived and began to circle, evidently puzzled by the disappearance of an entire city — as we were, I must admit; you must explain that to me later. Well, we signaled to the pilot, and he came down. We had already realized the somewhat difficult position we found ourselves in..." D'Averc paused. "Is there any food to be had?"

"The skipper has ordered some supper from the galley," Oladahn said. "Continue."

"We were three men without horses in a rather barren part of the world. As well, we had failed to keep you when we had captured you, and as far as we knew, the pilot was the only living man left who knew that we had done that..."

"You killed the pilot?" Hawkmoon said.

"Just so. It was necessary. Then we boarded his machine with the intention of reaching the nearest base."

"What happened?" Hawkmoon asked. "Did you know how to control the ornithopter?"

D'Averc smiled. "You have guessed correctly. My knowledge is limited. We managed to gain the air, but then the wretched thing would not be steered. Before we knew it, it was carrying us off to the Runestaff knows where. I feared for my safety, I must admit. The monster behaved increasingly erratically, until at last it began to fall. I managed to guide it so that it landed on a soft riverbank, and we were barely hurt. Ecardo and Peter had become hysterical, quarreling among themselves, becoming unbearable in their manners and most hard to control. However, we somehow managed to build a raft with the intention of floating down the river until we came to a town…"

"That same raft?" Hawkmoon asked.

"The same, aye."

"Then how did you come to be at sea?"

"Tides, my good friend," D'Averc said with an airy wave of his hand. "Currents. I had not realized we were so close to an estuary. We were swept along at a most appalling rate, carried far beyond land. On that raft — that damnable raft — we spent the next several days, with Peter and Ecardo whining at one another, blaming one another for their predicament when they should have blamed me. Oh, I cannot tell you what an ordeal it was, Duke Dorian."

"You deserved worse," Hawkmoon said.

There came a knock on the cabin door. Oladahn answered it and admitted a scruffy cabin boy carrying a tray on which were three bowls containing some kind of grey stew.

Hawkmoon accepted the tray and handed D'Averc a bowl and a spoon. For a moment D'Averc hesitated; then he took a mouthful. He seemed to eat with great control. He finished the dish and replaced the empty bowl on the tray. "Delicious," he said. "Quite perfect, for ship's cooking."

Hawkmoon, who had been nauseated by the mess, handed D'Averc his own bowl, and Oladahn, too, proffered his.

"I thank you," said D'Averc. "I believe in moderation. Enough is as good as a feast."

Hawkmoon smiled slightly, once again admiring the Frenchman's coolness. Evidently the food had tasted as foul to him as it had to them, but his hunger had been so great that he had eaten the stuff anyway, and with panache.

Now D'Averc stretched, his rippling muscles belying his claim to invalidism. "Ah," he yawned. "If you will forgive me, gentlemen, I will sleep now. I have had a trying and tiring few days."

"Take my bed," Hawkmoon said, indicating his cramped bunk. He did not mention that earlier he had noticed what had seemed to be a whole catalogue of lice nesting in it. "I'll see if the skipper has a hammock."

"I am grateful," D'Averc said, and there seemed to be a surprising seriousness about his tone that made Hawkmoon wheel away from the door.

"For what?"

D'Averc began to cough ostentatiously, then looked up and said in his old, mocking tone, "Why, my dear Duke, for saving my life, of course."

In the morning the storm had died down, and though the sea was still rough it was much calmer than the previous day.

Hawkmoon met D'Averc on deck. The man was dressed in coat and britches of green velvet but was without his armour. He bowed when he saw Hawkmoon.

"You slept well?" asked Hawkmoon.

"Excellently." D'Averc's eyes were full of humour, and Hawkmoon guessed that he had been bitten a good many times.

"Tonight we should make port," Hawkmoon told him. "You will be my prisoner — my hostage, if you like."

"Hostage? Do you think the Dark Empire cares if I live or die once I have lost my usefulness?"

"We shall see," said Hawkmoon, fingering the Jewel in his skull. "If you attempt to escape, I shall certainly kill you — as coolly as you killed your men."

D'Averc coughed into the handkerchief he carried. "I owe you my life," he said. "So it is yours to take if you would."

Hawkmoon frowned. D'Averc was far too devious for him to understand properly. He was beginning to regret his decision. The Frenchman might prove more of a liability than he had bargained for.

Oladahn came hurrying along the deck. "Duke Dorian," he panted, pointing forward. "A sail — and it's heading directly toward us."

"We're in little danger," Hawkmoon smiled. "We're no prize for a pirate."

But moments later Hawkmoon noticed signs of panic among the crew, and as the captain stumbled past, he caught his arm. "Captain Mouso — what is it?"

"Danger sir," rasped the skipper. "Great danger. Did you not read the sail?"

Hawkmoon peered toward the horizon and saw that the ship carried a single black sail. On it was painted an emblem of some kind, but he could not make out what it was. "Surely they'll not trouble us," he said. "Why should they risk a fight for a tub like this — and you said yourself we're carrying no cargo."

"They care not what we carry or don't carry, sir. They attack anything on the ocean on sight. They're like killer sharks, Duke Dorian — their pleasure is not in taking treasure, but in destruction!"

"Who are they? Not a Granbretanian ship by the look of it," D'Averc said.

"Even one of those would probably not bother to attack us," stuttered Captain Mouso. "No — that is a ship crewed by those belonging to the Cult of the Mad God. They are from Ukrania and in recent months have begun to terrorize these waters."

"They definitely seem to have the intention of attacking," D'Averc said lightly. "With your permission, Duke Dorian, I'll go below and don my sword and armour."

"I'll get my weapons, too," Oladahn said. "I'll bring your sword for you."

"No point in fighting!" It was the mate, gesticulating with his bottle. "Best throw ourselves in the sea now."

"Aye," Captain Mouso nodded, looking after D'Averc and Oladahn as they went to fetch their weapons. "He's right. We'll be outnumbered, and they'll tear us to pieces. If we're captured, they'll torture us for days."

Hawkmoon started to say something to the captain, then turned as he heard a splash. The mate had gone — as good as his word. Hawkmoon rushed to the side but could see nothing.

"Don't bother to help him — follow him," the skipper said, "for he's the wisest of us all."

The ship was bearing down on them now, its black sail painted with a pair of great red wings, and in the centre of them was a huge, bestial face, howling as if in the throes of maniacal laughter. Crowding the decks were scores of naked men wearing nothing but sword belts and metal-studded collars. Drifting across the water came a weird sound that Hawkmoon could not at first make out. Then he glanced at the sail again and knew what it was.

It was the sound of wild, insane laughter; as if the damned of hell were moved to merriment.

"The Mad God's ship," said Captain Mouso, his eyes beginning to fill with tears. "Now we die."

S E V E N

THE RING ON THE FINGER

Hawkmoon, Oladahn, and D'Averc stood shoulder to shoulder by the port rail of the ship as the weird vessel sped closer.

The members of the crew had clustered around their captain, keeping as far as possible from the attackers.

Looking at the rolling eyes and foaming mouths of the madmen in the ship, Hawkmoon decided that their chances were all but hopeless. Grappling irons snaked out from the Mad God's ship and bit into the soft wood of *Smiling Girl's* rail. Instantly the three men hacked at the ropes, severing most of them.

Hawkmoon yelled to the captain, "Get your men aloft — try to turn the ship." But the frightened sailors did not move. "You'll be safer in the rigging!" Hawkmoon shouted. They began to stir but still did nothing.

Hawkmoon was forced to return his attention to the attacking ship and was horrified to see it looming over them, its insane crew clustering against the rail, some already beginning to climb over, ready to leap onto *Smiling Girl's* deck, cutlasses drawn. Their laughter filled the air, and bloodlust shone on their twisted faces.

The first came flying down on Hawkmoon, naked body gleaming, sword raised. Hawkmoon's own blade rose to skewer the man as he fell; another twist of the sword and the corpse dropped down through the narrow gap between the ships, into the sea. Within moments the air was full of naked warriors swinging on ropes, jumping wildly, clambering hand over hand across the grappling lines. The three men stopped the first wave, hacking about them until everything seemed blood-red, but gradually they were forced away from the rail as the madmen swarmed onto the deck, fighting without skill but with a chilling disregard for their own lives.

Hawkmoon became separated from his comrades, did not know if they lived or had been killed. The prancing warriors flung themselves at him, but he clutched his battle blade in both hands and swung it about him in a great arc, this way and that, surrounding himself with a blur of bright steel. He was covered in blood from head to foot; only his eyes gleamed, blue and steady, from the visor of his helmet.

And all the while the Mad God's men laughed — laughed even as their heads were chopped from their necks, their limbs from their bodies.

Hawkmoon knew that eventually weariness would overcome him. Already the sword felt heavy in his hands and his knees shook. His back against a bulkhead, he hacked and stabbed at the seemingly ceaseless wave of giggling madmen whose swords sought to slash the life from him.

Here a man was decapitated, there another dismembered, but every blow drained more energy from Hawkmoon.

Then, as he blocked two swords that struck at him at once, his legs buckled and he went down to one knee. The laughter grew louder, triumphant, as the Mad God's men moved in for the kill.

He hacked upward desperately, gripping the wrist of one of his attackers and wrenching the sword away from him so that now he had two blades. Using the madman's sword to thrust and his own to swing, he managed to regain his footing, kicked out at another man, and scrambled away, to rush up the companionway to the bridge. At the top he turned to fight again, this time with an increased advantage over the howling madmen who crowded up the steps toward him. He saw now that both D'Averc and Oladahn were in the rigging, managing to keep their attackers at bay. He glanced toward the Mad God's ship. It was still held fast by grappling ropes, but it was deserted. Its entire crew was on board the *Smiling Girl*. Hawkmoon at once had an idea.

He wheeled about, running from the warriors, leaped to the rail, and grabbed a rope that trailed from the crosstrees. Then he flung himself into space.

He prayed that the rope would be long enough as he hurtled through the air, then let go, diving, it appeared, over the side of the ship. His grasping hands just managed to catch the rail of the enemy ship as he fell. He hauled himself onto the deck and began slashing at the grappling ropes, yelling "Oladahn — D'Averc! Quickly — follow me!"

From the rigging of the other ship the two men saw him and began climbing higher, to walk precariously along the main mast's yardarm while the men of the Mad God swarmed behind them.

The Mad God's ship was already beginning to slide away, the gap between it and *Smiling Girl* widening rapidly.

D'Averc jumped first, diving for the black-sailed ship's rigging and clutching a rope one-handed, to swing for an instant, threatening to drop to his death.

Oladahn followed him, cutting loose a rope and swinging across the gap, to slide down the rope and land on the deck, where he fell spread-eagled on his face.

Several of the insane warriors tried to follow, and a number actually managed to reach the deck of their own ship. Still laughing, they came at Hawkmoon in a bunch, doubtless judging Oladahn dead.

Hawkmoon was hard put to defend himself. A blade slashed his arm, another caught his face below the visor. Then suddenly, from above, a body dropped into the centre of the naked warriors and began hewing around him, almost as much a maniac as they.

It was D'Averc in his boar-headed armour, streaming with the blood of those he had slain. And now, at the back of their attackers came Oladahn, evidently only winded by his fall, yelling a wild mountain battle cry.

Soon every one of the madmen who had managed to reach the ship was dead. The others were leaping from the deck of *Smiling Girl* into the water, still laughing weirdly, trying to swim after the ship.

Looking back at *Smiling Girl*, Hawkmoon saw that miraculously most of her crew had apparently survived — at the last minute they had climbed to the safety of the mizzen mast.

D'Averc raced forward and took the wheel of the Mad God's ship, cutting the lashings and steering away from the vainly swimming men.

"Well," breathed Oladahn, sheathing his sword and inspecting his cuts, "we seem to have escaped lightly — and with a better ship."

"With luck we'll beat *Smiling Girl* into port," Hawkmoon grinned. "I hope she's still bound for Crimia, for she has all our possessions on board."

Skillfully, D'Averc was turning the ship about toward the north. The single sail bulged as it caught the wind and the boat left the swimming madmen behind. Even as they drowned, they continued to laugh.

After they had helped D'Averc relash the wheel so that the ship continued roughly on course, they began to explore the ship. It was crammed with treasure evidently pillaged from a score of ships, but also there were all kinds of useless things — broken weapons and ships' instruments, bundles of clothing — and here and there a rotting corpse or a dismembered body, all piled together in the holds.

The three men decided to get rid of the corpses first, wrapping them in cloaks or bundling up the various limbs in rags and tossing them overboard. It was disgusting work and took a long time, for some of the remains were hidden under mounds of other things.

Suddenly Oladahn paused as he worked, his eyes fixed on a severed human hand that had become mummified in some way. Reluctantly, he picked it up, inspecting a ring on the little finger. He glanced at Hawkmoon.

"Duke Dorian…"

"What is it? Do not bother to save the ring. Just get rid of the thing."

"No — it is the ring itself. Look — it has a peculiar design…"

Impatiently Hawkmoon crossed the dimly lit hold and peered at the thing, gasping as he recognized it. "No! It cannot be!"

The ring was Yisselda's. It was the ring Count Brass had placed on her finger to mark her betrothal to Dorian Hawkmoon.

Numbed with horror, Hawkmoon took the mummified hand, a look of incomprehension on his face.

"What is it?" Oladahn whispered. "What is it that so disturbs you?"

"It is hers. It is Yisselda's."

"But how could she have come to be sailing this ocean so many hundreds of miles from Kamarg? It is not possible, Duke Dorian."

"The ring is hers." Hawkmoon gazed at the hand, inspecting it eagerly as realization struck him. "But — the hand is not. See, the ring barely fits the little finger. Count Brass placed it on the middle finger, and even then it was a loose fit. This is the hand of some thief." He wrenched the precious ring from the finger and threw the hand down. "Someone who was in Kamarg, perhaps, and stole the ring…" He shook his head. "It's unlikely. But what is the explanation?"

"Perhaps she journeyed this way — seeking you, maybe," Oladahn suggested.

"She'd be foolish if she did. But it is just possible. However, if that's the case, where is Yisselda now?"

Oladahn was about to speak, when there came a low, terrifying chuckling sound from above. They looked up at the entrance to the hold.

A mad, grinning face looked down at them. Somehow one of the insane warriors had managed to catch the ship. Now he prepared to leap down on them.

Hawkmoon just managed to draw his sword as the madman attacked, sword slashing. Metal hit metal.

Oladahn drew his own blade, and D'Averc came rushing up, but Hawkmoon shouted, "Take him alive! We must take him alive!"

As Hawkmoon engaged the madman, D'Averc and Oladahn resheathed their swords and fell on the warrior's back, grasping his arms. Twice he shook them off, but then he went down kicking as they wound length after length of rope around him. And then he lay still, chuckling up at them, his eyes unseeing, his mouth foam-flecked.

"What use is he alive?" D'Averc asked with polite curiosity. "Why not cut his throat and have done with him?"

"This," Hawkmoon said, "is a ring I found just now." He held it up. "It belongs to Yisselda, Count Brass's daughter. I want to know how these men got it."

"Strange," D'Averc said, frowning. "I believe the girl is in Kamarg, nursing her father."

"So Count Brass is wounded?"

D'Averc smiled. "Aye. But Kamarg holds against us. I'd sought to disturb you, Duke Dorian. I do not know how badly Count Brass is hurt, but he still lives. And that wise man of his, Bowgentle, helps him command his troops. The last I heard, it was stalemate between the Dark Empire and Kamarg."

"And you heard nothing of Yisselda? Nothing of her leaving Kamarg?"

"No," said D'Averc, frowning. "But I seem to remember... Ah, yes — a man serving in Count Brass's army. I believe he was approached and persuaded to try to kidnap the girl, but the attempt was unsuccessful."

"How do you know?"

"Juan Zhinaga — the man — disappeared. Presumably Count Brass discovered his perfidy and slew him."

"I find it hard to believe that Zhinaga should be a traitor. I knew the man slightly — a captain of cavalry, he was."

"Captured by us in the second battle against Kamarg." D'Averc smiled. "I believe he was a German, and we had some of his family in our safekeeping..."

"You blackmailed him!"

"He was blackmailed, though do not give me the credit. I merely heard of the plan during a conference in Londra between the various commanders who had been summoned by King Huon to inform him of developments in the campaigns we are waging in Europe."

Hawkmoon's brow furrowed. "But suppose Zhinaga was successful — somehow not managing to reach your people with Yisselda, being stopped on the way by the Mad God's men..."

D'Averc shook his head. "They would never range as far as southern France. We should have heard of them if they had."

"Then what is the explanation?"

"Let us ask this gentleman," D'Averc suggested, prodding at the madman, whose chuckles had died down now so that they were almost inaudible.

"Let us hope we can get sense from him," Oladahn said dubiously.

"Would pain do the trick, do you think?" D'Averc asked.

"I doubt it," Hawkmoon said. "They know no fear. We must try another method." He looked in disgust at the madman. "We'll leave him for a while and hope he calms a little."

They went up on deck, closing the hatch cover. The sun was beginning to set, and the coastline of Crimia was now in sight — black crags sharp against the purple sky. The water was calm and dappled with the fading sunlight, and the wind blew steadily northward.

"I'd best correct our course," D'Averc suggested. "We seem to be sailing a little too far to the north." He moved along the deck to unbind the wheel and spin it several points south.

Hawkmoon nodded absently, watching D'Averc, his great mask flung back from his head, expertly controlling the course of the ship.

"We'll have to anchor offshore tonight," Oladahn said, "and sail in in the morning."

Hawkmoon did not reply. His head was full of unanswered questions. The exertions of the past twenty-four hours had brought him close to exhaustion, and the fear in his mind threatened to drive him to a madness fully as dreadful as that of the man in the hold.

Later that night, by the light of lamps suspended from the ceiling, they studied the sleeping face of the man they had captured. The lamps swung as the ship rocked at anchor, casting shifting shadows on the sides of the hold and over the great piles of booty heaped everywhere. A rat chittered, but the men ignored the sound. They had all slept a little and felt more relaxed.

Hawkmoon knelt down beside the bound man and touched his face. Instantly the eyes opened, staring around dully, no longer mad. They even seemed a little puzzled.

"What is your name?" Hawkmoon asked.

"Coryanthum of Kerch — who are you? Where am I?"

"You should know," Oladahn said. "On board your own ship. Do you not remember? You and your fellows attacked our vessel. There was a fight. We escaped from you, and you swam after us and tried to kill us."

"I remember setting sail," Coryanthum said, his voice bewildered, "but nothing else." Then he tried to struggle up. "Why am I bound?"

"Because you are dangerous," D'Averc said lightly. "You are mad."

Coryanthum laughed, a purely natural laugh. "I mad? Nonsense!"

The three looked at one another, puzzled. It was true that the man seemed to have no hint of madness about him now.

Understanding began to dawn on Hawkmoon's face. "What is the very last thing you remember?"

"The captain addressing us."

"What did he say?"

"That we were to take part in a ceremony — drinking a special drink... Nothing much more." Coryanthum frowned. "We drank the drink..."

"Describe your sail," Hawkmoon said.

"Our sail? Why?"

"Is there anything special about it?"

"Not that I remember. It's canvas — a dark blue. That's all."

"You are a merchant seaman?" Hawkmoon asked.

"Aye."

"And this is your first voyage on this ship?"

"Aye."

"When did you sign on?"

Coryanthum looked impatient. "Last night, my friend — on the Day of the Horse by Kerch reckoning."

"And in universal reckoning?"

The sailor wrinkled his brow. "Oh — the eleventh of the third month."

"Three months ago," said D'Averc.

"Eh?" Coryanthum peered through the gloom at the Frenchman. "Three months? What d'you mean?"

"You were drugged," Hawkmoon explained. "Drugged and then used to commit the foulest acts of piracy every heard of. Do you know anything of the Cult of the Mad God?"

"A little. I heard that it is situated somewhere in Ukrania and that its adherents have been venturing out lately — even onto the high seas."

"Did you know that your sail now bears the sign of the Mad God? That a few hours ago, you raved and giggled in mad bloodlust? Look at your body…" Hawkmoon bent down to cut the bonds. "Feel your neck."

Coryanthum of Kerch stood up slowly, wondering at his own nakedness, his fingers going slowly to his neck and touching the collar there. "I — I don't understand. Is this a trick?"

"An evil trick, and one we did not commit," Oladahn said. "You were drugged until you went insane, then ordered to kill and collect all the loot you could. Doubtless your 'merchant captain' was the only man who knew what would happen to you, and it's almost certain he's not aboard now. Do you remember anything? Any instructions about where you should go?"

"None."

"Without doubt the captain meant to rejoin the ship later and guide it to whatever port he uses," D'Averc said. "Maybe there is a ship in regular contact with the others, if they are all full of such fools as this one."

"There must be a large supply of the drug somewhere aboard," Oladahn said. "Doubtless they fed off it regularly. It was only because we bound this fellow that he did not get the chance to replenish himself."

"How do you feel?" Hawkmoon asked the sailor.

"Weak — drained of all life and feeling."

"Understandable," said Oladahn. "It's sure that the drug kills you in the end. A monstrous plan! Take innocent men, feed them a drug that turns them mad and ultimately destroys them, use them to murder and loot, then collect the proceeds. I've heard of nothing like it before. I'd thought the Cult of the Mad God to be comprised of honest fanatics, but it seems a cooler intelligence controls it."

"On the seas, at any rate," Hawkmoon said. "However, I'd like to find the man responsible for all this. He alone may know where Yisselda is."

"First, I'd suggest we take up the sail," D'Averc said. "We'll drift into the harbour on the tide. Our reception would not be pleasant if they saw our sail. Also, we can make use of this treasure. Why, we are rich men!"

"You are still my prisoner, D'Averc," Hawkmoon reminded him. "But it is true we could dispose of some of the treasure, since the poor souls who owned it are all dead now, and give the rest into the safekeeping of some honest man, to compensate those who have lost relatives and fortunes at the hands of the mad sailors."

"Then what?" asked Oladahn.

"Then we set sail again — and wait for this ship's master to seek her out."

"Can we be sure he will? What if he hears of our visit to Simferopol?" Oladahn asked.

Hawkmoon smiled grimly. "Then doubtless he will still wish to seek us out."

E   I   G   H   T

M A D   G O D ' S   M A N

And so the loot was sold in Simferopol, some of it used to provision the craft and buy new equipment and horses, and the rest given to the safekeeping of a merchant whom all recommended as the most honest in the whole of Crimia. Not much behind the captured ship, *Smiling Girl* limped in, and Hawkmoon hastily bought the captain's silence regarding the nature of the black-sailed ship. He recovered his possessions, including the saddlebag containing Rinal's gift, and, with Oladahn and D'Averc, reboarded the ship, sailing on the evening tide. They left Coryanthum with the merchant to recover.

For more than a week the black ship drifted, usually becalmed, for the wind had dropped to almost nothing. By Hawkmoon's reckoning they were drifting close to the channel that separated the Black Sea from the Azov Sea, near to Kerch, where Coryanthum had been recruited.

D'Averc lounged in a hammock he had hung for himself amidships, occasionally coughing theatrically and remarking on his boredom. Oladahn sat often in the crowsnest, scanning the sea, while Hawkmoon paced the decks, beginning to wonder if his plan had had any substance to it other than his need to know what had become of Yisselda. He was even beginning to doubt that the ring had been hers, deciding that perhaps several such rings had been made in Kamarg over the years.

Then, one morning, a sail appeared on the horizon, coming from the north-west. Oladahn saw it first and called to Hawkmoon to come on deck. Hawkmoon rushed up and peered ahead. It might be the ship they awaited.

"Get below," he called. "Everybody get below."

Oladahn scrambled down the rigging, while D'Averc, suddenly active, swung out of his hammock and strolled to the ladder that led below decks. They met in the darkness of the central hold and waited…

An hour seemed to pass before they heard timber bump against timber and knew that the other ship had drawn alongside. It might still be an innocent vessel curious about a ship drifting apparently unmanned.

Not much later Hawkmoon heard the sound of booted feet on the deck above; a slow, measured tread that went the length of the whole deck and back again. Then there was silence as the man above entered a cabin or climbed to the bridge.

Tension grew as the sound of the footsteps came again, this time walking directly toward the central hold.

Hawkmoon saw a silhouette above, peering down into the darkness where they crouched. The figure paused, then began to descend the ladder. As he did so, Hawkmoon crept forward.

When the newcomer had reached the bottom, Hawkmoon sprang, his arm encircling the man's throat. He was a giant, more than six and a half feet tall, with a huge black bushy beard and plaited hair, wearing a brass breastplate over his shirt of black silk. He growled in surprise and swung around, carrying Hawkmoon with him. The giant was incredibly strong. His huge fingers went up to Hawkmoon's arm and began to prise it loose.

"Quick — help me hold him," Hawkmoon cried, and his friends rushed forward to fling themselves on the giant and bear him down.

D'Averc drew his sword. Wearing his boar mask and the metal finery of Granbretan, he looked dangerous and terrible as he delicately placed the tip of his sword against the giant's throat.

"Your name?" D'Averc demanded, his voice booming in his helmet.

"Captain Shagarov. Where is my crew?"

The black-bearded giant glared up at them, unabashed by his capture. "Where is my crew?"

"You mean the madmen you sent akilling?" Oladahn said. "They are drowned, all but one, and he told us of your evil treachery."

"Fools!" Shagarov cursed. "You are three men. Did you think to trap me — when I have a shipful of fighters aboard my other ship?"

"We have disposed of one shipload, as you'll note," D'Averc told him with a chuckle. "Now that we are used to the work, doubtless we can dispose of another."

For a moment fear crept into Shagarov's eyes; then his expression hardened. "I do not believe you. Those who sailed this ship lived only to kill. How could you...?"

"Well, we did," D'Averc said. He turned his great, helmeted head toward Hawkmoon. "Shall we go on deck and put the rest of our plan into operation?"

"A moment." Hawkmoon bent close to Shagarov. "I want to question him.

Shagarov — did your men capture a girl at any time?"

"They had orders not to kill any girl but to bring them to me."

"Why?"

"I know not — I was ordered to send girls to him — and girls I sent him." Shagarov laughed. "You'll not keep me for long, you know. You'll all three be dead within an hour. The men will get suspicious."

"Why didn't you bring any of them aboard with you? Perhaps because they are not madmen — because even they might be disgusted by what they found?"

Shagarov shrugged. "They'll come when I yell."

"Possibly," said D'Averc. "Rise, please."

"These girls," Hawkmoon continued. "Where did you send them — and to whom?"

"Inland, of course, to my master — the Mad God."

"So you do serve the Mad God — you are not deceiving people into believing these acts of piracy are committed by his followers."

"Aye — I serve him, though I'm no cult member. His agents pay me well to raid the seas and send the booty to him."

"Why this way?"

Shagarov sneered. "The cult has no sailing men. So one of them conceived this plan to raise money — though I know not the purpose for the loot — and approached me." He rose to his feet, towering over them. "Come — let's go up. It will amuse me to see what you do."

D'Averc nodded to the other two, who went back into the shadows and produced long, unlit brands, one for each of them. D'Averc prodded at Shagarov to follow Oladahn up the companionway.

Slowly they climbed to the deck, to emerge at last in the sunlight and see a big, handsome three-master anchored beside them.

The men on board the other ship understood at once what had happened and made to move forward, but Hawkmoon dug his sword into Shagarov's ribs and called, "Do not move, or we will kill your captain."

"Kill me — and they kill you," Shagarov rumbled. "Who gains?"

"Silence," said Hawkmoon. "Oladahn, light the brands."

Oladahn applied flint and tinder to the first brand. It flared into life. He lit the others off it and handed one each to his companions.

"Now," Hawkmoon said. "This ship is covered in oil. Once we touch our brands to it, the whole vessel goes up in flames — and most likely your ship too. So we advise you to make no move toward rescuing your captain."

"So we all burn," Shagarov said. "You're as mad as the ones you slew."

Hawkmoon shook his head. "Oladahn, ready the skiff."

Oladahn went aft to the furthermost hatch, swinging a derrick over it, hauling back the hatch cover, and then disappearing below, taking the cable with him.

Hawkmoon saw the men on the other ship begin to stir and he moved the brand menacingly. The heat from it turned his face dark red, and the flames reflected fiercely in his eyes.

Now Oladahn re-emerged and began to work the specially geared winch with one hand while holding his brand with the other. Slowly something began to appear in the hatch, something that barely cleared the wide opening.

Shagarov grunted in surprise as he saw that it was a large skiff in which three horses were harnessed, looking frightened and bewildered as they were hauled to the deck and then swung out over the sea.

Oladahn stopped his work and leaned back on the winch, panting and sweating, but made sure to keep the brand well away from the timber of the deck.

Shagarov scowled. "An elaborate plan — but you are still only three men. What do you intend to do now?"

"Hang you," said Hawkmoon. "Before the eyes of your crew. Two things motivated me in laying this trap for you. One — I needed information. Two — I determined to give you justice."

"Whose *justice?*" Shagarov bellowed, his eyes full of fear. "Why involve yourselves in the affairs of others? We did no harm to you. Whose justice?"

"Hawkmoon's justice," said the pale-faced Duke of Köln. Caught by the rays of the sun, the sinister Black Jewel in his forehead seemed to glow with life.

"Men!" Shagarov screamed across the water. "Men — rescue me. Attack them."

D'Averc called back, "If you move toward him, we kill him and set the ship ablaze. You gain nothing. If you'd save your own lives and your ship, you'll shove off and leave us. Our quarrel is with Shagarov."

As they had expected, the crew commanded by the pirate did not feel any great loyalty to him and, when their own skins were threatened, felt no great compulsion to come to his help. Yet they did not cast off the grappling irons but waited to see what the three men would do next.

Now Hawkmoon swung up into the crosstrees. He carried a rope with a noose already knotted. When he reached the top, he flung the rope over the arm so that it hung over the water, tied it firmly, and came down again to the deck.

Now there was silence as Shagarov slowly realized that he could expect no assistance from his men.

Up aft, the skiff with its burden of horses and provisions swung slightly in the still air, the davits creaking. The brands flared and puttered in the hands of the three companions.

Shagarov shouted and tried to break away, but three swords stopped him, points at his throat, chest, and belly.

"You cannot…" Shagarov's voice trailed off as he saw the determination on the faces of the three.

Oladahn reached out and hooked the dangling rope with his sword, bringing it to the rail. D'Averc pushed Shagarov forward, Hawkmoon took the noose and widened it to place it over Shagarov's head. Then, as the noose settled around his neck, Shagarov bellowed and struck out at Oladahn, who was perched on the rail. With a shout of surprise, the little man toppled and plunged into the water. Hawkmoon gasped and rushed to see how Oladahn fared. Shagarov turned on D'Averc, knocking the brand from his hand, but D'Averc stepped back and flourished his sword under Shagarov's nose.

The pirate captain spat in his face and leaped to the rail, kicked out at Hawkmoon, who tried to stop him; then the captain leaped into space.

The noose tightened, the yardarm bent, then straightened, and Captain Shagarov's body danced wildly up and down. His neck snapped, and he died.

D'Averc dashed for the fallen brand, but it had already ignited the oil-soaked deck. He began stamping on the flames.

Hawkmoon rushed to fling a rope to Oladahn, who, dripping, climbed up the side of the ship, looking none the worse for his swim.

Now the crew of the other vessel began to mutter and move about, and Hawkmoon wondered why they did not cast off.

"Shove off!" he called, as Oladahn regained the deck. "You cannot save your captain now — and you're in danger from the fire!"

But they did not move.

"The fire, you fools!" Oladahn pointed to where D'Averc was retreating from the flames, which were now leaping high, touching the mast and superstructure.

D'Averc laughed. "Let's to our little boat."

Hawkmoon flung his own brand after D'Averc's and turned. "But why don't they get away?"

"The treasure," said D'Averc as they lowered the skiff to the water, the frightened horses snorting as they sniffed the fire. "They think the treasure's still aboard."

As soon as the skiff was afloat, they clambered down the lines into the boat and cut themselves adrift. Now the black ship was a mass of flame and oily smoke. outlined against the fire, the body of Shagarov swung, twisting this way and that as if trying to avoid the hellish heat.

They let loose the skiff's sail, and the breeze filled it, bearing them away from the blazing vessel. Now, beyond it, they could see the pirate's ship, a sail smouldering as sparks from the other ship caught it. Some of the crew were busy putting it out while others were reluctantly casting off the grappling lines. But now it was touch and go whether the fire would spread through their own ship.

Soon the skiff was too far away for them to see whether the pirate ship was safe or not, and in the other direction, land was in sight. The land of Crimia and, beyond it, Ukrania.

And somewhere in Ukrania they would find the Mad God, his followers, and possibly Yisselda…

B O O K   T W O

Now, while Dorian Hawkmoon and his companions sailed for Crimia's mountainous shore, the armies of the Dark Empire pressed in upon the little land of Kamarg, ordered by Huon, the King-Emperor, to spare no life, energy, and inspiration in the effort to crush and utterly destroy those upstarts who dared resist Granbretan. Across the Silver Bridge that spanned thirty miles of sea came the hordes of the Dark Empire, pigs and wolves, vultures and dogs, mantises and frogs, with armour of strange design and weapons of bright metal. And in his Throne Globe, curled foetuslike in the fluid that preserved his immortality, King Huon burned with hatred for Hawkmoon, Count Brass and the rest who, somehow, he could not contrive to manipulate as he manipulated the rest of the world. It was as if some counterforce aided them — perhaps controlling them as he could not — and this thought the King-Emperor refused to tolerate...

But much depended on those few beyond the power of King Huon's influence, those few free souls — Hawkmoon, Oladahn, perhaps D'Averc, the mysterious Warrior in Jet and Gold, Yisselda, Count Brass, and a handful of others. For on these the Runestaff relied to work its own pattern of destiny...

— *The High History of the Runestaff*

O N E

T H E   W A I T I N G   W A R R I O R

As they neared the bleak crags marking the shore, Hawkmoon glanced curiously at D'Averc, who had flung back his boar-masked helm and was staring out to sea, a slight smile on his lips. D'Averc seemed to sense Hawkmoon's attention and glanced at him.

"You are puzzled, Duke Dorian," he said. "Are you not a little pleased by the outcome of our plan?"

"Aye." Hawkmoon nodded. "But I wonder about you, D'Averc. You joined in this venture spontaneously; yet there is no gain in it for you. I am sure you were not greatly interested in bringing Shagarov his deserts, and you certainly do not share my desperation in wanting to know Yisselda's fate. Also, you have not to my knowledge made any attempt to escape."

D'Averc's smile broadened a little. "Why should I? You do not threaten my life. In fact, you saved my life. At this point, my fortunes seem linked closer to yours than the Dark Empire's."

"But your loyalty is not to me and my cause."

"My loyalty, my dear Duke, as I have already explained, is to the cause most likely to further my own ambition. I must admit I've changed my views about the hopelessness of your own — you seem endowed with such monstrous good luck I am sometimes even inclined to think you might win against the Dark Empire. If that seems possible, I might well join you, and with great enthusiasm."

"You do not bide your time, perhaps, hoping to reverse our roles again and capture me for your masters?"

"No denial would convince you," D'Averc smiled, "so I will not offer you one."

The enigmatic answer set Hawkmoon to frowning again.

As if to change the topic of conversation, D'Averc suddenly doubled up with a coughing fit and lay down, panting, in the boat.

Oladahn called out now from the prow. "Duke Dorian! Look — on the beach!"

Hawkmoon peered ahead. Now, under the looming cliffs, he could make out a narrow strip of shingle. A horseman could be seen on the beach, motionless, looking towards them as if he awaited them with some particular message.

The keel of the skiff scraped the shingle of the beach, and Hawkmoon recognized the horseman who waited in the shadow of the cliff.

Hawkmoon sprang from the boat and approached him. He was clad from head to foot in plate armour, his helmeted head bowed as if in brooding thought.

"Did you know I would be here?" Hawkmoon asked.

"It seemed that you might beach in this particular place," replied the Warrior in Jet and Gold. "So I waited."

"I see." Hawkmoon looked up at him, uncertain what to do or say next. "I see…"

D'Averc and Oladahn came crunching up the beach towards them.

"You know this gentleman?" D'Averc asked lightly.

"An old acquaintance," Hawkmoon said.

"You are Sir Huillam D'Averc," said the Warrior in Jet and Gold sonorously. "I see you still wear the garb of Granbretan."

"It suits my taste," D'Averc replied. "I did not hear you introduce yourself."

The Warrior in Jet and Gold ignored D'Averc, raising a heavy gauntleted hand to point at Hawkmoon. "This is the one I must speak with. You seek your betrothed, Yisselda, Duke Dorian, and you quest for the Mad God."

"Is Yisselda a prisoner of the Mad God?"

"In a manner of speaking, yes. But you must seek the Mad God for another reason."

"Yisselda lives? Does she live?" Hawkmoon said insistently.

"She lives."

The Warrior in Jet and Gold shifted in his saddle. "But you must destroy the Mad God before she can be yours again. You must destroy the Mad God and rip the Red Amulet from his throat — for the Red Amulet is rightfully yours. Two things the Mad God has stolen, and both those things are yours — the girl and the amulet.

"Yisselda is mine, certainly — but I know of no amulet. I have never owned one."

"This is the Red Amulet, and it is yours. The Mad God has no right to wear it, and thus it turned him mad."

Hawkmoon smiled. "If that is the Red Amulet's property, then the Mad God is welcome to it."

"This is not a matter for humour, Duke Dorian. The Red Amulet has turned the Mad God mad because he stole it from a servant of the Runestaff. But if the Runestaff's servant wears the Red Amulet, then he is able to derive great power transmitted from the Runestaff through the amulet. Only a wrongful wearer is turned mad — only the rightful wearer may regain it once another wears it. Therefore, I could not take it from him, nor could any man save Dorian Hawkmoon von Köln, servant of the Runestaff."

"Again you call me servant of the Runestaff; yet I know of no duties I must perform, do not even know if this is a fabric of imaginings and you are some madman yourself."

"Think what you wish. However, there is no doubt, is there, that you seek the Mad God — that you desire nothing greater than to find him?"

"To find Yisselda, his prisoner…"

"If you like. Well, then, I need not convince you of your mission."

Hawkmoon frowned. "There has been a strange series of coincidences since I embarked on the journey from Hamadan. Barely credible."

"There are no coincidences where the Runestaff is concerned. Sometimes the pattern is noticed, sometimes it is not." The Warrior in Jet and Gold turned in his saddle and pointed to a winding path cut into the cliff side. "We can ascend there. Camp and rest above. In the morning we shall begin the journey to the Mad God's castle."

"You know where it lies?" Hawkmoon asked eagerly, forgetting his other doubts.

"Aye."

Then another thought occurred to Hawkmoon. "You did not… did not *engineer* Yisselda's capture? To force me to seek the Mad God?"

"Yisselda was captured by a traitor in her father's army — Juan Zhinaga, who planned to take her to Granbretan. But he was diverted on the way by warriors of the Dark Empire who wished to claim the credit for kidnapping her. While they fought, Yisselda escaped and fled, joining, at length, a refugee caravan through Italia, managing to get passage, sometime later, on a ship sailing the Adriatic Sea, bound, she was told, ultimately for Provence. But the ship was a slaver, running girls to Arabia, and in the Gulf of Sidra was attacked by a pirate vessel from Karpathos."

"It is a hard story to believe. What then?"

"Then the Karpathians decided to ransom her, not knowing that Kamarg was under siege but learning only later of the impossibility of getting money from that quarter. They decided to take her to Istanbul to sell her, but arrived to find the harbour full of Dark Empire ships. Fearing these, they sailed on into the Black Sea, where the ship was attacked by the one you have just burned…"

"I know the rest. That hand I found must have belonged to a pirate who stole Yisselda's ring. But it is a wild tale, Warrior, and barely has the sound of truth. Coincidence…"

"I told you — there are no coincidences where the Runestaff is involved. Sometimes the pattern seems simpler than at other times."

Hawkmoon sighed. "She is unharmed?"

"Relatively."

"What do you mean?"

"Wait until you come to the Mad God's castle."

Hawkmoon tried to question the Warrior in Jet and Gold further, but the enigmatic man remained entirely silent. He sat on his horse, apparently deep in thought, while Hawkmoon went to help D'Averc and Oladahn get the nervous horses out of the boat and unload the rest of the provisions they had brought. Hawkmoon found his battered saddlebag still safe and marveled at his being able to hold on to it through all their adventures.

When they were ready, the Warrior in Jet and Gold silently turned his horse and led the way to the steep cliff path, beginning to climb it without pause.

The three companions, however, were forced to dismount and follow after him at a much slower pace. Several times both men and horses stumbled and seemed about to fall, loose stones dropping away beneath their feet, to hurtle to the shingle that was now far below them. But at last they gained the top of the cliff and looked over a hilly plain that seemed to stretch away forever.

The Warrior in Jet and Gold pointed to the west. "In the morning, we go that way, to the Throbbing Bridge. Beyond that lies Ukrania, and the Mad God's castle lies many days' journey into the interior. Be wary, for Dark Empire troops roam thereabouts."

He watched as they made camp. D'Averc looked up at him. "Won't you join us in our meal, sir?" he said almost sardonically.

But the great, helmeted head remained bowed, and both warrior and horse stood stock still, like a statue, remaining thus all night, as if watching over them — or possibly watching them to make sure they did not leave on their own.

Hawkmoon lay in his tent looking out at the silhouette of the Warrior in Jet and Gold, wondering if the creature were in any way human, wondering if his interest in Hawkmoon was ultimately friendly or malign. He sighed. He wanted only to find Yisselda, save her, and take her back to Kamarg, there to satisfy himself that the province still stood against the Dark Empire. But his life was complicated by this strange mystery of the Runestaff and some destiny he must work out that fitted with the Runestaff's "scheme". Yet the Runestaff was a thing, not an intelligence. Or was it an intelligence? It was the greatest power one could call upon when oath making. It was believed to control all human history. Why, then, he wondered, should it need "servants" if, in effect, all men served it?

But perhaps not all men did. Perhaps there emerged forces from time to time — like the Dark Empire — that were opposed to the Runestaff's scheme for human destiny. Then, perhaps, the Runestaff needed servants.

Hawkmoon became confused. His was not these days the head for profundity of that sort, nor speculative philosophy. Not much later he fell asleep.

T W O

T H E   M A D   G O D ' S   C A S T L E

For two days they rode until they came to the Throbbing Bridge, which spanned a stretch of sea running between two high cliffs some miles apart.

The Throbbing Bridge was an astonishing sight, for it did not seem made of any kind of solid substance at all, but of a vast number of criss-crossed beams of coloured light that seemed somehow to have been plaited. Gold and shining blue were there, and bright, gleaming scarlet and green and pulsing yellow. All the bridge throbbed like some living organ, and below, the sea foamed on sharp rocks.

"What is it?" Hawkmoon asked the Warrior in Jet and Gold. "Surely no natural thing?"

"An ancient artifact," said the warrior, "wrought by a forgotten science and a forgotten race who sprang up sometime between the fall of the Death Rain and the rise of the Princedoms. Who they were and how they were brought into being and died, we do not know."

"Surely you know," D'Averc said cheerfully. "You disappoint me. I had judged you omniscient."

The Warrior in Jet and Gold made no reply. The light from the Throbbing Bridge was reflected on their skins and armour, staining them a variety of hues. The horses began to prance and became difficult to control as they directed them closer to the great bridge of light.

Hawkmoon's horse bucked and snorted, and he tightened its reins, forcing it forward. At last its hooves touched the throbbing light of the bridge and it became calmer as it realized that the bridge would actually bear its weight.

The Warrior in Jet and Gold was already crossing the bridge, his whole body seeming to be ablaze with a multicoloured aura, and Hawkmoon, too, saw the strange light creep around the body of his horse and then immerse him in a weird radiance. Looking back he saw D'Averc and Oladahn shining like beings from another star as they moved slowly over the bridge of throbbing light.

Below, faintly seen through the criss-cross of beams, were the grey sea and the foam-encircled rocks. And in Hawkmoon's ears there grew a humming sound that was musical and pleasant, yet seemed to set his whole frame vibrating gently in time with the bridge itself.

At length they were across, and Hawkmoon felt fresh, as if he had had several days' rest. He mentioned this to the Warrior in Jet and Gold who said, "Aye, that's another property of the Throbbing Bridge, I'm told."

Then they rode on, with only land now between them and the Mad God's lair.

On the third day of their journey it had begun to rain, a fine drizzle that chilled them and lowered their spirits. Their horses plodded across the vast, sodden Ukranian plains, and it seemed that there was no end to the grey world.

On the sixth day of their journey, the Warrior in Jet and Gold raised his head and brought his horse to a halt, signaling for the other three to stop. He appeared to be listening.

Soon Hawkmoon heard the sound too — the drumming of horses' hooves. Then, breasting a slight rise to their left, came some score of riders in sheepskin hats and cloaks, long spears and sabres on their backs.

They seemed in a panic, and not noticing the four onlookers, they rode past at fantastic speed, lashing the rumps of their steeds until blood flew in the air.

"What is it?" Hawkmoon called. "What do you flee from?"

One of the riders turned in his saddle, not lessening his speed. "Dark Empire army!" he called, and dashed on.

Hawkmoon frowned. "Should we continue in this direction?" he asked the warrior. "Or should we find another route?"

"No route is safe," replied the Warrior in Jet and Gold. "We might just as well take this one."

Within half an hour they saw smoke in the distance. It was thick, oily smoke that crept close to the ground, and it stank. Hawkmoon knew what the smoke signified but said nothing until, later, they came to the town that was burning and saw, piled in the square, a huge pyramid of corpses, every one naked — men, women, children, and animals heaped indiscriminately upon one another and burning.

It was this pyre of flesh that gave off the evil-smelling smoke, and there was only one race Hawkmoon knew of who would indulge in such an act as this. The riders had been right. Dark Empire soldiers were nearby. There were signs that a whole battalion of troops had taken the town and razed it.

They skirted around the town, for there was nothing they could do, and in even more sober spirits continued on their journey, wary now for any sign of Granbretanian troops.

Oladahn, who had not witnessed so many of the Dark Empire's atrocities, was the one most visibly moved by the sight they had witnessed.

"Surely," he said, "ordinary mortals could not... could not..."

"They do not regard themselves as ordinary mortals," D'Averc said. "They regard themselves as demigods and their rulers as gods."

"It excuses their every immoral action in their eyes," Hawkmoon said. "And besides, they love to wreak destruction, spread terror, torture and kill. Just as in some beasts, like the wolverine, the urge to kill is stronger even than the urge to live, so it is with those of the Dark Empire. The island has bred a race of madmen whose every thought and action is alien to those not born on Granbretan."

The depressing drizzle continued to fall as they left the town and its blazing pyramid behind.

"It is not far now to the Mad God's castle," said the Warrior in Jet and Gold.

By the next morning they had come to a wide, shallow valley and a small lake on which a grey mist moved. Beyond the lake they saw a black, gloomy shape, a building of rough-hewn stone that lay on the far side of the water.

About midway between the castle and themselves, they could see a collection of rotting hovels clustered on the shore and a few boats drawn up nearby. Nets had been hung out to dry, but there was no sign of the fishers who used them.

The whole day was dark, cold, and oppressive, and there was an ominous atmosphere about lake, village, and castle. The three men followed reluctantly behind the Warrior in Jet and Gold as he made his way around the shore toward the castle.

"What of this Mad God's cult?" Oladahn whispered. "How many men does he command? And are they as ferocious as those we fought on the ship? Does the Warrior underestimate their strength or overestimate our prowess?"

Hawkmoon shrugged, his only thought for Yisselda. He scanned the great black castle, wondering where she was imprisoned.

As they came to the fisherfolk's village they saw why it was so silent. Every last villager had been slain, hacked down by swords or axes. Some of the blades were still buried in skulls of men and women alike.

"The Dark Empire!" said Hawkmoon.

But the Warrior in Jet and Gold shook his head. "Not their work. Not their weapons. Not their way."

"Then... what?" murmured Oladahn, shivering. "The cult?"

The warrior did not answer. Instead, he reined in his horse and dismounted, walking heavily toward the nearest corpse. The others dismounted also, looking warily about them. The mist from the lake curled around them like some malign force that sought to trap them.

The warrior pointed at the corpse. "All these were members of the cult. Some served by fishing to provide the castle with its food. Others lived in the castle itself. Some of these are from the castle."

"They have been fighting among themselves?" D'Averc suggested.

"In a sense, perhaps," replied the warrior.

"How do you mean —?" Hawkmoon began, but then whirled as a chilling shriek came from behind the hovels. All drew their weapons, standing in a hollow circle, prepared for an attack from any side.

But when the attack did come, the nature of the attackers caused Hawkmoon to lower his sword momentarily in astonishment.

They came running between the houses, swords and axes raised. They were dressed in breastplates and kilts of leather, and a ferocious light burned in their eyes. Their lips were drawn back in bestial snarls. Their white teeth gleamed, and foam flecked their mouths.

But this was not what astonished Hawkmoon and his companions. It was their sex that caught them by surprise, for all the maniacally shrieking warriors rushing at them were women of incredible beauty.

As he slowly recovered his defensive stance, Hawkmoon desperately sought among the faces for that of Yisselda and was relieved that he did not find it.

"So this is why the Mad God demanded women be sent to him," D'Averc gasped. "But why?"

"He is a perverse god, I understand," said the Warrior in Jet and Gold as he brought up his blade to meet the attack of the first warrior woman.

Though he defended himself desperately against the blades of the mad-faced women, Hawkmoon found it impossible to counterattack. They left many openings for his sword, and he could have slain several, but every time he had the opportunity to strike, he held back. And it seemed to be the same with his companions. In a moment's respite he glanced around him, and an idea came.

"Retreat slowly," he said to his friends. "Follow me. I've a plan to make this our victory — and a bloodless one."

Gradually the four fell back until they were stopped by the poles on which the stout nets of the fishermen had been hung out to dry. Hawkmoon stepped around the first and seized one end of the net, still battling. Oladahn guessed his scheme and grabbed the other end; then Hawkmoon cried, "Now!" and they flung the thing out over the heads of the women.

The net settled over most of them, entangling them. But some slashed free and came on.

Now D'Averc and the Warrior in Jet and Gold understood Hawkmoon's intention, and they, too, flung a net to trap those who had escaped. Hawkmoon and Oladahn hurled a third net over the group they had originally ensnared. Eventually the women were completely trapped in the folds of several strong nets, and the companions were able to approach them gingerly, grabbing at their weapons and gradually disarming them.

Hawkmoon panted as he raised a sword and flung it into the lake. "Perhaps the Mad God is not so insane. Train women to fight and they'll always have a certain momentary advantage over male soldiers. Doubtless this was part of some larger scheme…"

"You mean his raising money by piracy was to finance a conquering army of women?" Oladahn said, joining him in hurling weapons into the water while the struggles of the women subsided behind them.

"It seems likely," D'Averc agreed, watching them work. "But why did the women kill the others?"

"That we may find out when we reach the castle," said the Warrior in Jet and Gold. "We —" He broke off as part of one of the nets burst and a howling warrior woman came rushing at them, fingers outstretched like claws. D'Averc seized her, encircling her waist with his arms as she kicked and shrieked. Oladahn stepped up, reversed his sword, and struck her on the base of the skull with the pommel.

"Much as it offends my sense of chivalry," D'Averc said, lowering the prone girl to the ground, "I think that you have presented the best scheme for dealing with these pretty murderesses, Oladahn," and he crossed to the nets, to begin languidly and systematically knocking out the struggling women fighters. "At least," he said, "we have not killed them — and they have not killed us. An excellent equilibrium."

"I wonder if they are the only ones," Hawkmoon said broodingly.

"You are thinking of Yisselda?" Oladahn asked.

"Aye, I'm thinking of Yisselda. Come." Hawkmoon swung into his saddle. "Let's to the Mad God's castle." He began to gallop rapidly along the beach toward the great black pile. The others were slower in following, straggling behind him. First came Oladahn, then the Warrior in Jet and Gold, and finally Huillam D'Averc at a leisurely canter, looking for all the world like a carefree youth out for a morning ride.

The castle came closer, and Hawkmoon slowed his mad dash, hauling on his horse's reins and bringing it to a skidding halt as they reached the drawbridge.

Within the castle all was quiet. A little mist curled about its towers. The drawbridge was down, and on it lay the corpses of the guards.

Somewhere, from the tops of one of the highest towers, a raven squawked and flapped away over the water of the lake.

No sun shone through those grey clouds. It was as if no sun had ever shone here, as if no sun ever would shine. It was as if they had left the world for some limbo where hopelessness and death prevailed throughout eternity.

The dark entrance to the castle courtyard gaped at Hawkmoon.

The mist formed grotesque shapes, and there was an oppressive silence everywhere. Hawkmoon took a deep breath of the chill, damp air, drew his blade, kicked at the flanks of his horse, and charged across the drawbridge, leaping the corpses, to enter the Mad God's lair.

T H R E E

H A W K M O O N ' S   D I L E M M A

The great courtyard of the castle was clogged with bodies. Some were of the warrior women, but most were of men wearing the collar of the Mad God. Dried blood caked the cobbles not occupied by corpses in grotesque attitudes.

Hawkmoon's horse snorted in fear as the stench of decaying flesh filled its nostrils, but he urged it on, dreading that he would see Yisselda's face among the dead.

He dismounted, turning over stiff bodies of women, peering at them closely, but none was Yisselda.

The Warrior in Jet and Gold entered the courtyard, Oladahn and D'Averc behind him. "She is not here," said the warrior. "She is alive — within."

Hawkmoon's bleak face rose. His hand trembled as it took the bridle of his horse. "Has — has he done ought to her, Warrior?"

"That you must see for yourself, Sir Champion." The Warrior in Jet and Gold pointed at the castle's main doorway. "Through there lies the court of the Mad God. A short passage leads to the main hall, and there he sits awaiting you…"

"He knows of me?"

"He knows that one day the Red Amulet's rightful wearer must arrive to claim what is his…"

"I care nothing for the amulet, only for Yisselda. Where is she, Warrior?"

"Within. She is within. Go claim your woman and your amulet. Both are important to the Runestaff's scheme."

Hawkmoon turned and ran for the doorway, disappearing into the darkness of the castle.

The interior of the castle was incredibly chill. Cold water dripped from the roof of the passage, and moss grew on the walls. Blade in hand, Hawkmoon crept along it, half-expecting an attack.

But none came. He reached a large wooden door, stretching twenty feet above his head, and paused.

From behind the door came a strange rumbling sound, a deep-voiced murmuring that seemed to fill the hall beyond. Cautiously Hawkmoon pushed against the door, and it yielded. He put his head through the gap and peered in upon a bizarre scene.

The hall was of strangely distorted proportions. In some parts the ceilings were very low, in others they soared upward for fifty feet. There were no windows, and the light came from brands stuck at random in the walls.

In the centre of the hall, on a floor on which one or two corpses lay as they had been cut down earlier, was a great chair of black wood, studded with inlaid plaques of brass. In front of this, swinging from a part of the ceiling that was relatively low, was a large cage, such as would be used for a tame bird, save that this was much bigger. In it, Hawkmoon saw huddled a human figure.

Otherwise, the weird hall was deserted, and Hawkmoon entered, creeping across the floor toward the cage.

It was from this, he realized, that the distressed muttering sound was coming; yet it seemed impossible, for the noise was so great. Hawkmoon decided that it was because the sound was amplified by the peculiar acoustics of the hall.

He reached the cage and could see the huddled figure only dimly, for the light was poor.

"Who are you?" Hawkmoon asked. "A prisoner of the Mad God?"

The moaning ceased, and the figure stirred. From it then came a deep, echoing melancholy voice. "Aye — you could say so. The unhappiest prisoner of all."

Now Hawkmoon could make out the creature better. It had a long, stringy neck, and its body was tall and very thin. Its head was covered in long, straggling grey hair that was matted with filth, and it had a pointed beard, also filthy, that jutted from its chin for about a foot. Its nose was large and aquiline, and its deepset eyes held the light of a melancholy madness.

"Can I save you?" Hawkmoon said. "Can I prise apart the bars?"

The figure shrugged. "The door of the cage is not locked. Bars are not my prison. I have been trapped within my groaning skull. Ah, pity me."

"Who are you?"

"I was once known as Stalnikov, of the great family of Stalnikov."

"And the Mad God usurped you?"

"Aye. Usurped me. Aye, exactly." The prisoner in the unlocked cage turned his huge, sad head to stare at Hawkmoon. "Who are you?"

"I am Dorian Hawkmoon, Duke of Köln."

"A German?"

"Köln was once part of the country called Germania."

"I have a fear of Germans." Stalnikov slid back in the cage, farther away from Hawkmoon.

"You need not fear me."

"No?" Stalnikov chuckled, and the mad sound filled the hall. "No?" He reached into his jerkin and pulled something forth that was attached to a throng about his neck. The thing glowed with a deep red light, like a huge ruby, illuminated from within, and Hawkmoon saw that it bore the sign of the Runestaff. "No? Then you are not the German who has come to steal my power?"

Hawkmoon gasped. "The Red Amulet! How did you obtain it?"

"Why," said Stalnikov, rising and grinning horribly at Hawkmoon, "I obtained it thirty years ago from the corpse of a warrior my retainers set upon and slew as he rode this way." He fondled the amulet, and its light struck Hawkmoon in the eyes so that he could barely see. "*This* is the Mad God. *This* is the source of my madness and my power. *This* is what imprisons me!"

"You are the Mad God! Where is my Yisselda?"

"Yisselda? The girl? The new girl with the blonde hair and the white, soft skin? Why do you ask?"

"She is mine."

"You do not want the amulet?"

"I want Yisselda."

The Mad God laughed, and his laughter filled the hall and reverberated through every cranny of the distorted place. "Then you shall have her, German!"

He clapped his clawlike hands, his whole body moving like a loose-limbed puppet's, the cage swinging wildly. "Yisselda, my girl! Yisselda, come forth to serve your master!"

From the depths of one part of the hall where the ceiling almost touched the floor, a girl emerged. Hawkmoon saw her outlined but could not be fully sure it was Yisselda. He sheathed his sword and moved forward. Yes... the movements, the stance — they were Yisselda's.

A smile of relief began to form on his lips as he stretched out his arms to embrace her.

Then there came a wild animal shriek, and the girl rushed at him, metal-taloned fingers reaching for his eyes, face distorted with bloodlust, every part of her body enclosed in a garment studded with outward-jutting spikes.

"Kill him, pretty Yisselda," chuckled the Mad God. "Kill him, my flower, and we shall reward you with his offal."

Hawkmoon put up his hands to fend off the claws, and the back of one of them was slashed badly. He backed away hastily. "Yisselda, no — it is your betrothed, Dorian…"

But the mad eyes showed no sign of recognition, and the mouth slavered as the girl slashed again with the talons of metal. Hawkmoon leaped away, pleading with his eyes that she might recognize him. "Yisselda…"

The Mad God chuckled, grasping the bars of his cage and looking on eagerly. "Slay him, my chicken. Rip his throat."

Hawkmoon was almost weeping now as he leaped this way and that to avoid Yisselda's gleaming talons.

He called to Stalnikov. "What power is it she obeys that conquers her love for me?"

"She obeys the power of the Mad God, as I obey it," Stalnikov answered. "The Red Amulet makes all its slaves!"

"Only in the hands of an evil creature…" Hawkmoon flung himself aside as Yisselda's talons ripped at him. He scrambled up and darted toward the cage.

"It turns all who wear it evil," Stalnikov replied chuckling as Yisselda's claws ripped at Hawkmoon's sleeve. "All…"

"All but a servant of the Runestaff!"

The voice came from the entrance to the hall, and it belonged to the Warrior in Jet and Gold. It was sonorous and grave.

"Help me," said Hawkmoon.

"I cannot," said the Warrior in Jet and Gold, standing motionless, his huge blade point down on the floor before him, his gauntleted hands resting on the pommel.

Now Hawkmoon stumbled and felt Yisselda's claws digging into his back. He lifted his hands to grab her wrists and yelled in pain as the spikes sank into his palms, but he managed to free himself of the talons and fling her away and dash for the cage where the Mad God gibbered in delight.

Hawkmoon leaped for the bars, kicking at Stalnikov as he did so. The cage swung erratically and began to spin. Yisselda danced below, trying to reach him with her talons.

Stalnikov had withdrawn to the opposite side of the cage, his mad eyes now full of terror, and Hawkmoon managed to drag open the door and fling himself in, pulling it shut behind him. Outside, Yisselda howled in frustrated bloodlust, the light from the amulet turning her eyes scarlet.

Now Hawkmoon wept openly as he darted a glance at the woman he loved; then he turned his hate-filled face on the Mad God.

Stalnikov's deep voice, still mournful, reverberated through the hall. He fingered the amulet, directing its light into Hawkmoon's eyes. "Back, mortal. Obey me — obey the amulet…"

Hawkmoon blinked, feeling suddenly weak. His eyes became fixed on the glowing amulet, and he paused, feeling the power of the thing engulf him.

"Now," said Stalnikov. "Now, you will deliver yourself up to your destroyer."

But Hawkmoon rallied all his determination and took a step forward. The Mad God's bearded chin dropped in astonishment. "I command you in the name of the Red Amulet…"

From the doorway came the sonorous voice of the Warrior in Jet and Gold. "He is the one whom the amulet cannot control. The only one. He is the rightful wearer."

Stalnikov trembled and began to edge around the cage as Hawkmoon, still weak, moved determinedly on.

"Back!" screamed the Mad God. "Leave the cage!"

Below, Yisselda's taloned fingers had grasped the bars and she was hauling her metal-studded body up, her eyes still fixed murderously on Hawkmoon's throat.

"Back!" This time Stalnikov's voice lost some of its force and confidence. He reached the door of the cage and kicked it open.

Yisselda, her white teeth bared, her beautiful face twisted in terrifying madness, had hauled herself up now so that she clung to the outside of the cage. The Mad God's back was toward her, the Red Amulet directed still into Hawkmoon's eyes.

Yisselda's claw darted out, slashing at the back of Stalnikov's head. He screamed and leaped to the floor. Now Yisselda saw Hawkmoon again and made to enter the cage.

Hawkmoon knew there was no time to try to reason with his maddened betrothed. He gathered all his strength and dived past her slashing claw, to land on the uneven flagstones of the floor and lie there for a moment, winded.

Painfully he picked himself up as Yisselda, too, leaped groundward.

The Mad God had scrambled to the great seat opposite the cage, climbing up its back to perch there, the Red Amulet dangling from his neck, casting its strange light again on Hawkmoon's face. Blood streamed down his shoulders from the wound Yisselda's clawed hands had inflicted.

Stalnikov gibbered in terror as Hawkmoon reached the seat and climbed up onto its arm. "I beg you, leave me… I'll do you no harm."

"You've done me much harm already," Hawkmoon said grimly, drawing his blade. "Much harm. Enough to make revenge taste very sweet, Mad God…"

Stalnikov crept as high as he could. He shouted at the girl. "Yisselda — stop! Resume your former character. I command you, by the power of the Red Amulet!"

Hawkmoon turned and saw that Yisselda had paused, looking bemused. Her lips parted in horror as she stared at the things on her hands, the metal spikes that covered her body. "What has happened? What has been done to me?"

"You were hypnotized by this monster here." Hawkmoon waved his sword in the cringing Stalnikov's direction. "But I will avenge the wrongs he has done you."

"No," Stalnikov screamed. "It is not fair!"

Yisselda burst into tears.

Stalnikov looked this way and that. "Where are my minions — where are my warriors?"

"You made them destroy one another for your own perverted sport," Hawkmoon told him. "And those not slain, we captured."

"My army of women! I wanted beauty to conquer all Ukrania. Get me back the Stalnikov inheritance…"

"That inheritance is here," said Hawkmoon, raising his sword.

Stalnikov leaped from the back of the chair and began to run toward the door but swerved aside as he saw that it was blocked by the Warrior in Jet and Gold.

He scuttled into the darkness of the hall, into a cranny where he disappeared from sight.

Hawkmoon got down from the chair and turned to look at Yisselda, who lay in a heap on the floor weeping. He went to her and gently removed the bloodstained talons from her slim, soft fingers.

She looked up. "Oh, Dorian. How did you find me? Oh, my love…"

"Thank the Runestaff," said the voice of the Warrior in Jet and Gold.

Hawkmoon turned, laughing in relief. "You are persistent in your claims, at least, Warrior."

The Warrior in Jet and Gold said nothing but stood like a statue, faceless and tall, by the doorway.

Hawkmoon discovered the fastenings of the grim, spiked suit and began to strip it off the girl.

"Find the Mad God," said the warrior. "Remember, the Red Amulet is yours. It will give you power."

Hawkmoon frowned. "And turn me mad, perhaps?"

"No, fool, it is yours by right."

Hawkmoon paused, impressed by the warrior's tone. Yisselda touched his hand. "I can do the rest," she said.

Hawkmoon hefted his sword and peered into the darkness wherein Stalnikov, the Mad God, had disappeared.

"Stalnikov!"

Somewhere in the deepest recesses of the hall a tiny spot of red light gleamed. Hawkmoon ducked his head and entered the alcove. He heard a sobbing sound. It filled his ears.

Closer and closer crept Hawkmoon to the source of the red brilliance. Greater and greater became the sound of the strange weeping. Then at last the red glow burned very bright, and by its light he saw the wearer of the amulet, standing against a wall of rough-hewn stone, a sword in his hand.

"For thirty years I have waited for you, German," Stalnikov said suddenly, his voice calming. "I knew you must come to ruin my plans, to destroy my ideals, to demolish all I have worked for. Yet I hoped to avert the threat. Perhaps I still can."

With a great scream, he raised the sword and swung it at Hawkmoon.

Hawkmoon blocked the blow easily, turned the blade so that it spun from the Mad God's grasp, brought his own sword forward so that it was presented at Stalnikov's heart.

For a moment Hawkmoon looked gravely and broodingly at the frightened madman. The light from the Red Amulet stained both their faces scarlet. Stalnikov cleared his throat as if to plead; then his shoulders sagged.

Hawkmoon drove the point of his blade into the Mad God's heart. Then he turned on his heel and left both corpse and Red Amulet where they lay.

F O U R

T H E   P O W E R   O F   T H E   A M U L E T

Hawkmoon drew his cloak about Yisselda's naked shoulders. The girl was shivering, sobbing with reaction mixed with joy at seeing Hawkmoon. Nearby stood the Warrior in Jet and Gold, still motionless.

While Hawkmoon embraced Yisselda, the warrior began to move, his huge body crossing the hall and entering the darkness where lay the body of Stalnikov, the Mad God.

"Oh, Dorian, I cannot tell you the horrors I have been through these past months. Captured by this group and that, traveling for hundreds of miles. I do not even know where this hellish place is. I have no memory of recent days, save for a faint remembrance of some nightmare where I struggled with myself against a desire to slay you…"

Hawkmoon hugged her to him. "A nightmare was all it was. Come, we will leave. We will return to Kamarg and safety. Tell me, what has become of your father and the others?"

Her eyes widened. "Did you not know? I had thought you returned there first before coming to seek me."

"I have heard nothing but rumours. How are Bowgentle, von Villach, Count Brass…?"

She lowered her gaze. "Von Villach was killed by a flame-lance in a battle with Dark Empire troops on the northern borders. Count Brass…"

"What is it?"

"When I last saw him, my father lay on a sickbed, and even Bowgentle's healing powers seemed incapable of raising him to health. It is as if he had lost all feelings — as if he no longer wished to live. He said Kamarg must soon fall — he believed you dead when you did not return in the time necessary to have told him you were safe."

Hawkmoon's eyes blazed. "I must get back to Kamarg — if only to give

Count Brass the will again to live. With you gone, he can barely have sustained any kind of energy."

"If he lives at all," she said softly, not wanting to admit the possibility.

"He must live. If Kamarg still stands, then Count Brass lives."

From the passage beyond the hall came the sound of running, booted feet. Hawkmoon pushed Yisselda behind him and again drew his great battle blade.

The door was flung open, and Oladahn stood there panting, D'Averc not far behind.

"Dark Empire warriors," Oladahn said. "More of them than we could fight. They must be exploring the castle and surrounds for survivors and booty."

D'Averc pushed past the little beast-man. "I tried to reason with them — claimed that I had the right to command them, being of greater rank than their leader, but" — he shrugged — "it seems D'Averc has no rank in the legions of Granbretan any more. The damned pilot of the ornithopter lived long enough to tell a search party of my clumsiness in letting you escape. I am as much an outlaw, now, as you…"

Hawkmoon frowned. "Come in, both, and bar that great door. It should hold them if they attack."

"Is it the only exit?" D'Averc asked, appraising the door.

"I think so," Hawkmoon said, "but we must worry about that score later."

From the shadows, the Warrior in Jet and Gold re-emerged. In one gloved hand the Red Amulet dangled from its cord. The cord was stained with blood.

The warrior handled it gingerly, not touching the stone itself, and stretched it out toward Hawkmoon as D'Averc and Oladahn hurried to swing the door shut and bar it.

"Here," said the Warrior in Jet and Gold. "It is yours."

Hawkmoon recoiled. "I do not want it — will not have it. It is an evil thing. It has caused many to die, others to go mad — even that poor creature Stalnikov was its victim. Keep it. Find another fool enough to wear it!"

"You must wear it," came the voice from the helm. "Only you may wear it."

"I will not!" Hawkmoon swept out his hand to point to Yisselda. "That thing drove this gentle girl to become a slavering, killing beast. All those we saw in the fisherfolk's village — all slain by the power of the Red Amulet. All those who came against us — turned insane by its power. All those who died in the courtyard — destroyed by the Red Amulet." He struck the thing from the warrior's hand. "I will not take it. If that is what the Runestaff creates, I will have no part of it!"

"It is what men — fools like yourself — do with it, that makes it corrupt in its influence," the Warrior in Jet and Gold said, his voice still grave and impassive. "It is your duty — as the Runestaff's chosen servant — to take the gift. It will not harm you. It will bring you nothing but power."

"Power to destroy and turn men mad!"

"Power to do good — power to fight the hordes of the Dark Empire!"

Hawkmoon sneered. There came a great crash on the door, and he knew that the warriors of Granbretan had found them. "We are outnumbered," said Hawkmoon. "Will the Red Amulet give us the power to escape them when there is only one way out — through yonder door?"

"It will help you," said the Warrior in Jet and Gold, leaning down to retrieve the fallen amulet, again picking it up by its string.

The door creaked under the pressure of the blows from those on the other side.

"If the Red Amulet can do so much good," Hawkmoon said, "why do you not touch it yourself?"

"It is not mine to touch. It could do to me what it did to the miserable Stalnikov." The warrior moved forward. "Here, take it. It is why you came here."

"It is because of Yisselda I came here — to rescue her. I have done that."

"It is why she came here."

"So it was a trick to lure me...?"

"No. It was part of the pattern. But you say you came to save her, and yet you refuse the means of escaping with her safely from this castle. Once those warriors break in, a score or more of fierce fighters, they will destroy you all. And Yisselda's fate might be worse than yours..."

Now the door was splitting. Oladahn and D'Averc backed away, swords ready, a look of quiet desperation in their eyes.

"Another moment and they will be in here," said D'Averc. "Farewell, Oladahn — and you, too, Hawkmoon. You were less boring companions than some..."

Hawkmoon eyed the amulet. "I do not know..."

"Trust my word," said the Warrior in Jet and Gold. "I have saved you in the past. Would I have done so merely to destroy you now?"

"Destroy me, no — but this will deliver me into some evil power. How do I know you are a messenger for the Runestaff? I have only your word that I serve it and not some darker cause."

"The door is breaking down!" Oladahn yelled. "Duke Dorian, we'll need your aid! Let the Warrior escape with Yisselda if he can!"

"Quick," said the warrior, extending the amulet again to Hawkmoon. "Take it and save the maid, at least."

For an instant, Hawkmoon hesitated; then he accepted the thing. It settled into his hand like a pet in the hand of its master — but an exceedingly powerful pet. Its red light grew in intensity until it flooded the great, grotesquely proportioned chamber. Hawkmoon felt the power surge into him. His whole body became full of a great sense of well-being. When he moved it was with great speed. His brain seemed no longer clouded by the events of the past day. He smiled and placed the blood-stained thong about his neck, bent to kiss Yisselda once and felt a delicious sensation rush through him, turned, sword ready, to face the howling horde that had by now all but demolished the great door.

Then the door fell inward, and there stood crouched the panting beasts of Granbretan, tiger masks gleaming with enameled metal and semiprecious jewels, weapons poised to butcher the pathetic-seeming little group that awaited them.

The leader stepped forward.

"So much exercise for so few. Brothers, we'll make them pay for our efforts."

And then the killing began.

F   I   V   E

T H E   S L A U G H T E R   I N   T H E   H A L L

"Oh, by the Runestaff," murmured Hawkmoon thickly, "the power in me!"

Then he sprang forward, great battle blade howling through the air to snap the enmetalled neck of the leading warrior, slash backhanded at the man to his left and send him reeling, swing around and cut through the armour of the man to his right.

Suddenly there were blood and twisted metal everywhere. The light from the amulet spread scarlet shadows across the masked faces of the warriors as Hawkmoon led his comrades forward in an attack — the last thing the Dark Empire soldiers had expected.

But the amulet's light dazzled them, and they lifted armour-clumsy arms to shield their eyes, weapons held defensively, bewildered by the speed with which Hawkmoon, Oladahn, and D'Averc moved against them. Following the other three came the Warrior in Jet and Gold, his own huge broadsword whistling in a circle of steel death, all his movements apparently effortless.

There was a clattering and a shouting from the men of Granbretan as, with Yisselda behind them at all times, the four drove them into the hall.

Hawkmoon was attacked by some six swearing axemen who tried to press in against him and stop him from wielding his deadly sword, but the young Duke of Köln kicked out at one, elbowed another aside, and brought his blade straight down into the mask-helmet of another, splitting both helm and skull so that brains oozed through the fissure when he'd tugged his sword free. The sword became rapidly blunted with so much work, until at last he was using it more as an axe than anything else. He wrenched a fresh sword from the hand of one of his attackers but kept his own. With the new sword he thrust, with the old he hacked.

"Ah," whispered Hawkmoon. "The Red Amulet is worth its price." It swung at his neck, turning his sweating, vengeful face into a red demon's mask.

Now the last of the warriors tried to flee for the door, but the Warrior in Jet and Gold and D'Averc blocked them, hacking them down as they tried to burst past.

Somewhere, Hawkmoon caught a glimpse of Yisselda. Her face was buried in her hands as she refused to witness the red ruin Hawkmoon and his friends had created. "Oh, it is sweet to slay these carrion," Hawkmoon said. "Yisselda — this is our triumph!" But the girl did not look up.

In many parts of the hall the floors were heaped with the twisted corpses of the slaughtered. Hawkmoon panted, seeking more to slay, but there were none left. He dropped the borrowed blade, sheathed his own, the battle lust leaving him completely. He frowned down at the Red Amulet, raising it up to regard it more closely, studying the simple motif of a runecarved staff.

"So," he murmured. "Your first help is in aiding me to kill. I'm grateful, but I wonder, still, if you're not a force more for evil than for good..." The light from the amulet flickered and began to fade. Hawkmoon looked up at the Warrior in Jet and Gold. "The amulet's dulled — what means that?"

"Nothing," said the warrior. "It draws its power from a great distance off and cannot sustain it at all times. It will grow bright again eventually." He paused, cocking his head toward the passage. "I hear more footsteps — the warriors were not the whole force."

"Then let us go to meet them," D'Averc said with a low bow, waving Hawkmoon before him. "After you, my friend. You seem best equipped to be first."

"No," said the warrior. "I will go. The amulet's power has faded for the while. Come."

Warily they passed through the smashed door, Hawkmoon last with Yisselda. She looked up at him then, her eyes steady. "I am glad you killed them," she said, "though I hate to see death come so gracelessly."

"They live without grace," Hawkmoon said softly, "and they deserve to die without grace. It is the only way to treat those who serve the Dark Empire. Now we must face more of them. Be brave, my love, for we encounter our greatest danger."

Ahead, the Warrior in Jet and Gold had already engaged the first of the fresh force of fighters and was flinging the weight of his great metal-encased body against them so that they stumbled back in the narrow confines of the passage, unnerved, as much as anything, because not one of their opponents seemed hurt by them and because some five and twenty of their comrades appeared to have met their death within.

The Dark Empire soldiers broke out into the corpse-strewn courtyard, shouting and trying to rally themselves. All four who came against them were covered in partly dried blood and brains and made a terrifying sight as they entered the daylight.

The grey rain was still falling and the air was still chill, but it revived Hawkmoon and the others, and their recent victory had made them feel invincible. Hawkmoon, D'Averc, and Oladahn grinned like wolves at their foes — grinned with such complacency, too, that the Dark Empire warriors hesitated before attacking, though they greatly outnumbered Hawkmoon and his companions. The Warrior in Jet and Gold raised a pointing finger to the drawbridge. "Begone," he said in deep, grave tones, "or we shall destroy you as we destroyed your brothers."

Hawkmoon wondered if the warrior were bluffing or if that mysterious entity honestly believed they could beat so many without the power of the Red Amulet to aid them.

But before he could decide, another group of warriors came rushing over the drawbridge. They had retrieved weapons from the hands and bodies of corpses, and they were enraged.

The Mad God's warrior women had escaped from the nets.

"Show them the amulet," the Warrior in Jet and Gold whispered to Hawkmoon. "That is what they are used to obeying. It is that which bemused them in the first place, not the Mad God."

"But its light has faded," Hawkmoon protested.

"No matter. Show them the amulet."

Hawkmoon swept the Red Amulet from his neck and held it up before the howling women.

"Stay. In the name of the Red Amulet, I command you to attack not us — but these…" and he pointed at the wavering Dark Empire warriors. "Come, I will lead you!"

Hawkmoon sprang forward, his blunted sword sweeping out to slash the foremost warrior and slay him before he realized it.

The women easily outnumbered the Dark Empire force, and they worked with a will at their destruction, so well that D'Averc called, "Let them finish — we can escape now."

Hawkmoon shrugged. "This is surely but one pack of Dark Empire hounds. There must be many more about, for it's not their way to spread too far from the mass of their brothers."

"Follow me," said the Warrior in Jet and Gold. "Time, I think, to unloose the Mad God's beasts…"

S I X

THE MAD GOD'S BEASTS

The Warrior in Jet and Gold led them to a section of the courtyard where a pair of great iron trapdoors had been let into the cobblestones. They were forced to drag aside corpses before they could grasp the huge brass rings and heave the doors back. The doors clanged on the stones to reveal a long stone ramp that led down into gloom.

From within came a warm smell that was at once familiar and unfamiliar to Hawkmoon and made him hesitate at the top of the ramp, for he was sure that the scent meant danger.

"Do not be afraid," said the warrior firmly. "Proceed. There lies your method of escaping this place."

Slowly Hawkmoon began to descend, the others following him.

The light coming thinly from above showed him a long room with a large object at the far end. He could not decide what it was and was about to investigate it, when the Warrior in Jet and Gold said from behind him, "Not now. First, the beasts. They are in their stalls."

Hawkmoon realized that the long room was in fact some sort of stable, with stalls on either side. From some of them came stirring sounds and animal grunts, and all at once a door shuddered as a huge bulk was flung against it.

"Not horses," said Oladahn. "Nor bullocks. To me, Duke Dorian, they have the smell of *cats*."

"Aye, that's so," Hawkmoon nodded, fingering the pommel of his sword. "Cats — that's the scent. How can cats aid our escape?"

D'Averc had taken a brand from the wall and was striking a flint to ignite his tinder. Shortly, the brand flamed, and Hawkmoon saw that the object at the far end of the stable was a vast chariot, large enough to accommodate more than their number. Its double shafts had space for four animals.

"Open the stalls," said the Warrior in Jet and Gold, "and harness the cats to the yokes."

Hawkmoon wheeled. "Harness cats to the chariot? Certainly a whim fit for a mad god — but we are sane mortals, Warrior. Besides, those cats are wild, by the sound of their movements. If we open the stalls, they're bound to fall upon us."

As if in confirmation, there came a great yowling roar from one of the stalls, and this was taken up by the other beasts until the stables echoed with the bestial din and it was impossible to make oneself heard over it.

When it had begun to subside, Hawkmoon shrugged and stepped toward the ramp. "We'll find horses above and take our chances with more familiar steeds than these."

"Have you not yet learned to trust my wisdom?" said the warrior. "Did I not speak truth about the Red Amulet and the rest?"

"I have still to test that truth fully," Hawkmoon said.

"Those mad women obeyed the power of the amulet, did they not?"

"They did," Hawkmoon agreed.

"The Mad God's beasts are trained, likewise, to obey he who is master of the Red Amulet. What would I gain, Dorian Hawkmoon, from lying to you?"

Hawkmoon shrugged. "I have grown suspicious of all since I first encountered the Dark Empire. I do not know if you have anything to gain or not. However" — he walked towards the nearest stall and laid his hands on the heavy wooden bar — "I'm tired of bickering and will test your assurances..."

As he flung off the bar, the stable door was swept back from within by a giant paw. Then a head emerged, larger than an ox's, fiercer than a tiger's; a snarling cat's head with slanting yellow eyes and long yellow fangs. As it padded out, a deep growling sound coming from its belly, its glaring eyes regarding them calculatingly, they saw that its back was lined with a row of foot-high spines of the same colour and appearance as its fangs, running down to the base of its tail, which, unlike that of an ordinary cat, was tipped with barbs.

"A legend come to life," gasped D'Averc, losing his detached manner for a moment. "One of the mutant war jaguars of Asiacommunista. An old bestiary I saw pictured them, said that if they had existed at all then it was a thousand years ago, that because they were the products of some perverted biological experiment they could not breed..."

"So they cannot," said the Warrior in Jet and Gold, "but their lifespan is all but infinite."

The huge head now swung toward Hawkmoon, and the barbed tail swished back and forth, the eyes fixing on the amulet at Hawkmoon's throat.

"Tell it to lie down," said the warrior.

"Lie down!" commanded Hawkmoon, and almost at once the beast settled to the floor, its mouth closing, its eyes losing some of their fierceness.

Hawkmoon smiled. "I apologize, Warrior. Very well, let's loose the other three. Oladahn, D'Averc…"

His friends went forward to take out the bars of the remaining stalls, and Hawkmoon put his arm around Yisselda's shoulders.

"That chariot," he said, "will bear us home, my love." Then he remembered something. "Warrior, my saddlebags — still on my horse unless those dogs have stolen them!"

"Wait here," said the warrior, turning and beginning to ascend the ramp. "I will look."

"I will look myself," Hawkmoon said. "I know the —"

"No," said the warrior. "I will go."

Hawkmoon felt a vague suspicion. "Why?"

"Only you, with the amulet, have the power of controlling the Mad God's beasts. If you were not here, they could turn on the others and destroy them."

Reluctantly, Hawkmoon stepped back and watched the Warrior in Jet and Gold move with heavy purposefulness to the top of the ramp and disappear.

Out of their stalls now prowled three more horned cats, similar to the first. Oladahn cleared his throat nervously. "Best remind them that it is you they obey," he said to Hawkmoon.

"Lie down!" Hawkmoon commanded, and slowly the beasts did as he commanded. He went up to the nearest and laid a hand on its thick neck, feeling the wiry, bristling fur, the hard muscle beneath it. The beasts were the height of horses but considerably bulkier and infinitely more deadly. They had not been bred to pull carriages, that was plain, but to kill in battle.

"Move that chariot up," he said, "and let's harness these creatures."

D'Averc and Oladahn dragged the chariot forward. It was of black brass and green gold and smelled of antiquity. Only the leather of the yokes was relatively new. They slipped the harness over the heads and shoulders of the beasts, and the mutant jaguars hardly moved, save for flattening their ears occasionally when the men tightened the straps too rapidly.

When all was ready, Hawkmoon signed to Yisselda to enter the chariot. "We must wait for the Warrior to return," he said. "Then we may set off."

"Where is he?" D'Averc asked.

"Gone to find my gear," Hawkmoon explained.

D'Averc shrugged and lowered his great helm over his face. "It is taking him long enough. I for one will be glad when we leave this place behind. It stinks of death and evil."

Oladahn pointed upward, at the same time drawing his sword. "Is that what you smelled, D'Averc?"

At the top of the ramp stood six or seven more Dark Empire warriors of the

Order of the Weasel, their long-snouted masks seeming to tremble in anticipation of killing the men below.

"Into the chariot, quick," Hawkmoon ordered as the weasels descended.

In the front of the chariot was a raised block on which the driver could stand, and beside it, in a rack once used for javelins, a long-handled whip. Hawkmoon sprang onto the block, seized the whip, and cracked it over the heads of the beasts. "Up, beauties! Up!" The cats climbed to their feet. "And now — forward!"

The chariot jumped forward with a great lurch as the powerful animals dragged it up the ramp. The weasel-masked warriors screamed as the gigantic horned cats raced toward them. Some leaped from the ramp, but most were too late and went down screaming, crushed by clawed feet and iron-rimmed wheels.

Out into the grey daylight the bizarre chariot broke, scattering more weasel warriors come to investigate the open trapdoors.

"*Where is the Warrior?*" Hawkmoon cried above the din of howling men. "Where are my saddlebags?"

But the Warrior in Jet and Gold was nowhere to be seen, and neither could they locate Hawkmoon's horse.

Now Dark Empire swordsmen hurled themselves against the chariot, and Hawkmoon lashed out at them with his whip while behind him Oladahn and D'Averc held them back with their own blades.

"Drive through the gate!" D'Averc cried. "Hurry — at any moment they'll overwhelm us!"

"Where is the Warrior?" Hawkmoon looked wildly about him.

"Doubtless he awaits us outside!" D'Averc shouted desperately. "Drive, Duke Dorian, or we're doomed!"

Suddenly Hawkmoon saw his horse over the heads of the milling warriors. It had been stripped of its saddlebags, and he had no way of knowing who had taken them.

In panic he shouted again, "Where is the Warrior in Jet and Gold? I must find him. The contents of those saddlebags could mean life or death for Kamarg!"

Oladahn gripped his shoulder and said urgently, "And if you do not drive us from this place it means our deaths — and maybe worse for Yisselda!"

Hawkmoon was nearly out of his mind with indecision, but then, as Oladahn's words at last entered his consciousness, he gave a great yell and whipped up the beasts, sending them springing through the gate and across the drawbridge, to gallop along the lakeside with what seemed like all the hordes of Granbretan behind them.

Moving far more rapidly than horses could move, the Mad God's beasts dragged the bouncing chariot over the ground and away from the dark castle and the mist-covered lake, away from the village of hovels and the place of corpses, into the foothills beyond the lake, down a muddy road that led between gloomy cliffs, and onto the wide plains again. There the road petered out and the ground became soft, but the mutant jaguars had no effort in crossing it.

"If I have a complaint," remarked D'Averc, as he clung for dear life to the side of the chariot and was bounced about horribly, "it is that we are moving a trifle too rapidly…"

Oladahn tried to grin through gritted teeth. He was crouched in the bottom of the vehicle, holding Yisselda and trying to protect her from the worst of the bumps.

Hawkmoon made no response. He clenched the reins tight in his hands and did not reduce the speed of their flight. His face was pale and his eyes blazed with anger, for he was sure he had been duped by the man who claimed to be his chief ally against the Dark Empire — duped by the apparently incorruptible Warrior in Jet and Gold.

S E V E N

E N C O U N T E R   I N   A   T A V E R N

"Hawkmoon, stop, for the Runestaff's sake! Stop, man! Are you possessed!" D'Averc, more troubled than anyone had ever seen him, tugged at Hawkmoon's sleeve as the man lashed at the panting beasts. The chariot had been moving for hours now, had splashed across two rivers without stopping, and was now tearing through a forest as night fell. At any moment it might strike a tree and kill them all. Even the powerful horned cats were tiring, but Hawkmoon mercilessly lashed them on.

"Hawkmoon! You are mad!"

"I am betrayed!" answered Hawkmoon. "Betrayed! I had the salvation of Kamarg in those saddlebags, and the Warrior in Jet and Gold stole them. He tricked me. Gave me a trinket with limited powers in exchange for a machine with powers that were unlimited for my purposes! On, beasts, on!"

"Dorian, listen to him. You will kill us all!" Yisselda spoke tearfully. "You will kill yourself — and then how will you aid Count Brass and Kamarg?"

The chariot leaped into the air and came down with a crash. No normal vehicle could have stood such a shock, and it jarred the passengers to their bones.

"Dorian! You have gone mad. The Warrior would not betray us. He has helped us. Perhaps he was overwhelmed by Dark Empire men — the saddlebags stolen from him!"

"No — I sensed some betrayal when he left the stables. He has gone — my gift from Rinal with him."

But Hawkmoon's rage and bafflement were beginning to pass, and he no longer whipped at the flanks of the straining beasts.

Gradually the pace of the chariot slowed as the tired beasts, free from the whip, gave in to their instinct to rest.

D'Averc took the reins from Hawkmoon's hands, and the young warrior did not resist, merely sank to the bottom of the chariot and buried his head in his hands.

D'Averc brought the beasts to a halt, and they fell at once to the ground, panting noisily.

Yisselda stroked Hawkmoon's hair. "Dorian — all Kamarg needs is you to save it. I do not know what this other thing was, but I am sure we have no use for it. And you have the Red Amulet. That will be of some use, surely."

It was night now, and moonlight fell through a lattice of tree branches. D'Averc and Oladahn dismounted from the chariot, rubbing their bruised bodies, and went off to look for wood for a fire.

Hawkmoon looked up. The light from the moon struck his pale face and the Black Jewel embedded in his forehead. He regarded Yisselda with melancholy eyes, though his lips tried to smile. "I thank you, Yisselda, for your faith in me, but I fear it *will* need more than Dorian Hawkmoon to win the fight against all Granbretan, and the Warrior's perfidy has made me despair the more..."

"There is no proof of perfidy, my dear."

"No — but I knew instinctively that he planned to leave us, taking the machine with him. He sensed my knowledge, too. I do not doubt he has it and is far away by now. I do not necessarily suspect that he takes it for an ignoble purpose. Possibly his purpose is of greater importance than mine, yet I cannot excuse his actions. He deceived me. He betrayed me."

"If he served the Runestaff, he may know more than you. He may wish to preserve this thing, may think it dangerous to you."

"I have no proof he serves the Runestaff. For all I know, he may serve the Dark Empire and I am their tool!"

"You have become oversuspicious, my love."

"I have been forced to become so," Hawkmoon sighed. "I will be so until Granbretan is defeated or I am destroyed." And he held her close to him, burying his weary head in her bosom, and slept that way all night.

In the morning the sun was bright though the air cold. Hawkmoon's gloomy spirits had departed with the deep sleep, and they all appeared in a better mood. All were ravenous, including the mutant beasts, whose tongues lolled and whose eyes were greedy and fierce. Oladahn had fashioned himself a bow and some arrows early and had gone off into the deeper reaches of the forest to seek game.

D'Averc coughed theatrically as he polished his huge boar-helm with a piece of cloth he had found in the bottom of the chariot.

"This western air does not do my weak lungs any good," he said. "I would rather be in the East again, perhaps in Asiacommunista, where I have heard a noble civilization exists. Perhaps such a civilization would appreciate my talents, elevate me to some high estate."

216   HAWKMOON

"You have given up hope of any reward from the King-Emperor?" Hawkmoon asked with a grin.

"The reward I'll get is the same he's promised you," D'Averc said mournfully. "If that damned pilot had not lived... and then my being seen fighting with you at the castle... No, friend Hawkmoon, I am afraid my ambitions as far as Granbretan go are now seen to be somewhat unrealistic."

Oladahn appeared, staggering under the weight of two deer, one on each shoulder. They jumped up to help him.

"Two with two shots," he said proudly. "And the arrows were hastily made at that."

"We cannot eat all of one, let alone two," D'Averc said.

"The beasts," Oladahn said. "They need feeding or I'll warrant, Red Amulet or no Red Amulet, they'll feed on us before the day's done."

They quartered the larger deer and flung it to the mutant cats, who gulped the meat down swiftly, growling softly. Then they set about making a spit on which to roast the second animal.

When they were eating at last, Hawkmoon sighed and smiled. "They say that good food banishes all care," he said, "but I had not believed it until now. I feel a new man. That is the first good meal I have eaten in months. Fresh-killed venison eaten in the woods — ah, the pleasure of it!"

D'Averc, who was wiping his fingers fastidiously and had eaten delicately an enormous amount of meat, said, "I admire health such as yours, Hawkmoon. I wish I had your hearty appetite."

"And I wish I had yours," said Oladahn, laughing, "for you've eaten enough to last you a week."

D'Averc looked at him reproachfully.

Yisselda, who was still wrapped only in Hawkmoon's cloak, shivered a little and put down the bone on which she had been chewing. "I wonder," said she, "if we could seek out a town as soon as possible. There are things I would purchase..."

Hawkmoon looked embarrassed. "Of course, Yisselda, my dear, though it will be difficult... If Dark Empire warriors are thick in these parts, it would be better to drive on farther south and west toward Kamarg. Perhaps in Carpathia a town can be found. We must be almost upon her borders now."

D'Averc pointed his thumb to the chariot and the beasts. "We'd get a poor reception arriving at a town in that unearthly thing," he said. "Perhaps if one of us went into the nearest settlement...? But then, what would we use for money?"

"I have the Red Amulet," Hawkmoon said. "It could be traded..."

"Fool," said D'Averc, suddenly deadly serious and glaring at him. "That amulet is your life — and ours — our only protection, the only means of controlling our beasts there. It seems to me that it is not the amulet you hate, but the responsibility it implies."

Hawkmoon shrugged. "Maybe. Perhaps I was a fool to suggest it. Still, I like not the thing. I saw what you did not — I saw what it had done to a man who had worn it thirty years."

Oladahn interrupted. "There is no need for this dispute, friends, for I anticipated our need and while you, with great ferocity, were finishing off our foes in the Mad God's hall, Duke Dorian, I dug a few eyes from the Dark Empire men..."

"Eyes!" Hawkmoon said in revulsion, then relaxed and smiled as he saw Oladahn holding up a handful of jewels he had prised from the Granbretanians' masks.

"Well," said D'Averc, "we need provisions desperately, and the Lady Yisselda needs some clothing. Who'll stand least chance attracting attention if he goes into a town when we get to Carpathia?"

Hawkmoon gave him a sardonic glance. "Why, you, of course, Sir Huillam, without your Dark Empire accessories. For I, as I am sure you would have pointed out, have this damned Black Jewel to label me, and Oladahn has his furry face. But you are still my prisoner..."

"I am aggrieved, Duke Dorian. I thought us allies — united against a common enemy, united by blood, by saving each other's lives..."

"You have not saved mine, as I recall."

"Not specifically, I suppose. Still..."

"And I am not disposed to give you a handful of jewels and set you free," Hawkmoon continued, adding in a more sombre tone, "Besides, I'm not in a trusting mood today."

"You would have my word, Duke Dorian," D'Averc said lightly, though his eyes seemed to harden slightly.

Hawkmoon frowned.

"He has proved himself our friend in several fights," Oladahn said softly.

Hawkmoon sighed. "Forgive me, D'Averc. Very well, when we reach Carpathia, you will buy us what we need."

D'Averc began to cough. "This damnable air. It will be the death of me."

They rode on, the horned cats loping at a more gentle pace than the previous day's but still making faster speed than any horse. They left the great forest by midday and by evening saw in the distance the mountains of Carpathia at the same time as Yisselda pointed north, indicating the tiny figures of riders approaching them.

"They've seen us," Oladahn said, "and seem to be planning to ride at an angle to cut us off."

Hawkmoon flicked his whip over the flanks of the huge beasts drawing the chariot. "Faster!" he shouted, and almost at once the chariot began to gather speed.

A little later D'Averc called above the rumble and rattle of the wheels, "They're Dark Empire riders — no doubt of that. Order of the Walrus if I'm not mistaken."

"The King-Emperor must be planning a serious invasion of Ukrania," Hawkmoon said. "There's no other reason for so many bands of Dark Empire warriors here. That means he has almost certainly consolidated all conquests farther west and south."

"Save for Kamarg, I hope," said Yisselda.

The race continued, with the horsemen gradually drawing nearer, riding, as they were, at an angle to the chariot's course.

Hawkmoon smiled grimly, letting the riders think they were catching them. "Ready with your bow, Oladahn," he said. "Here's an opportunity for target practice."

As the horsemen, in grotesque, grinning walrus masks of ebony and ivory, drew close, Oladahn nocked an arrow to string and let fly. A rider fell, and a few javelins hurtled toward the chariot but dropped short. Three more members of the Walrus Order died from Oladahn's arrows before they were outdistanced and the jaguars were hauling their burden into the first foothills of the Carpathian Mountains.

Within two hours it was dark and they decided it was safe to camp.

Three days later they contemplated the rocky side of a mountain and knew that they would have to abandon both beasts and chariot if they were to cross the range at all. They would have to travel on foot; there was no alternative.

The terrain had become increasingly difficult for the mutant jaguars, and the mountainside ahead was impossible for them to climb dragging the chariot. They had tried to find a pass, had wasted two days looking for one, but there was none.

Meanwhile, if they were pursued, their pursuers would be almost upon them by now. There was no doubt in their minds that Hawkmoon had been recognized as the man whom the King-Emperor Huon had sworn to destroy. Therefore, Dark Empire warriors, interested in elevating themselves in the eyes of their master, would be eager to seek him out.

So they began to climb, stumbling up the steep face of the mountain, leaving the unharnessed beasts behind them.

When they were nearing a ledge that seemed to extend for some distance around the mountain and offer a relatively easy path, they heard the rattle of weapons and hooves and saw the same walrus-masked riders who had pursued them on the plain come riding from behind some rocks below.

"Their javelins are bound to get us at this range," D'Averc said grimly. "And there's no cover."

But Hawkmoon smiled thinly. "There is still one thing," he said, and raised his voice. "At them, my beasts — kill them, my cats! Obey me, in the name of the amulet!"

The mutant cats turned their baleful eyes on the newcomers, who were so jubilant at seeing their victims exposed that they hardly noticed the horned jaguars. The leader raised his javelin.

And the cats leaped.

Yisselda did not look back as the terrified screams filled the air and the bloodcurdling snarls echoed through the quiet mountains as the Mad God's beasts first killed and then fed.

By the next day they had crossed the mountains and come to a green valley with a little red town that was very peaceful.

D'Averc looked down at the town and held out his hand to Oladahn. "The jewels, if you please, friend Oladahn. By the Runestaff, I feel naked in just shirt and britches!" He took the jewels, tossed them in his palm, winked at Hawkmoon, and set off for the village.

They lay in the grass and watched him walk down whistling and enter the street; then he disappeared.

They waited for four hours. Hawkmoon's face began to grow grim, and he glanced resentfully at Oladahn, who pursed his lips and shrugged.

And then D'Averc reappeared, but he had others with him. With a shock, Hawkmoon realized they were Dark Empire troops. Men of the feared Order of the Wolf, Baron Meliadus's old Order. Had they recognized D'Averc and captured him? But no — on the contrary, D'Averc seemed quite friendly with them. He waved, turned on his heel, and began to walk up the hill to where they were hidden, a large bundle on his back. Hawkmoon was puzzled, for the wolf masks had gone back into the village, allowing D'Averc to go free.

"He can talk, can D'Averc," grinned Oladahn. "He must have convinced them he was an innocent traveler. Doubtless the Dark Empire is still using the soft approach in Carpathia."

"Perhaps," said Hawkmoon, not entirely convinced.

When D'Averc came back he flung down his bundle and pulled it open, displaying several shirts and a pair of britches, as well as a number of different foodstuffs — cheeses, bread, sausages, cold meat, and the like. He handed back most of Oladahn's jewels to him. "I purchased them relatively cheaply," he said, then frowned as he saw Hawkmoon's expression. "What is it, Duke Dorian? Not satisfied? I could not get the Lady Yisselda a gown, I regret, but the britches and shirt should fit her."

"Dark Empire men," said Hawkmoon, jerking his thumb at the village. "You seemed very friendly with them."

"I was worried, I'll admit," D'Averc said, "but they seem to be cautious of violence. They are in Carpathia to tell the folk of the benefits of Dark Empire rule. Apparently the King of Carpathia is entertaining one of their nobles. The usual technique — gold before violence. They asked me a few questions but were not unduly suspicious. They say they're warring in Shekia, have almost subdued that nation but for a key city or two."

"You did not mention us?" Hawkmoon said.

"Of course not."

Half-satisfied, Hawkmoon relaxed a little.

D'Averc picked up the cloth in which he'd wrapped his bundle. "Look — four cloaks with hoods, such as the holy men in these parts wear. They'll hide our faces well enough. I heard there's a larger town about a day's walk further south. It's a town where they trade horses. We can get there by tomorrow and buy steeds. Is it a good idea?"

Hawkmoon nodded slowly. "Aye. We need horses."

The town was called Zorvanemi, and it bustled with folk of all sorts come to sell and to buy horses. Just outside the main town were the stockyards, and here were many kinds of horseflesh, from thoroughbreds to plough horses.

They arrived too late in the evening to buy, and they put up at an inn on the edge of town, close to the stockyards, so that they could buy what they wanted and be away early in the morning. Here and there they saw small groups of Dark Empire soldiers, but the soldiers paid no attention to the cowled holy men who mingled with the crowd; there were several deputations from different monasteries in the area, and one more went unnoticed.

In the warmth of the inn's public room they ordered hot wine and food and consulted a map they had bought, speaking softly, discussing their best route through to southern France.

A little later the door of the inn was pushed open, and the cold night air swept in. Over the sounds of conversation and occasional laughter, they heard the coarse tones of a man yelling for wine for himself and his comrades and suggesting to the landlord that girls should be found for them as well.

Hawkmoon glanced up and was instantly on his guard. The men who had entered were soldiers in the Order of the Boar, the Order that D'Averc had belonged to. With their squat, armoured bodies and heavy helmet masks, they looked, in the half-light, exactly like the animals they represented, as if so many boars had learned to talk and walk on their hind legs.

The landlord was plainly nervous, clearing his throat several times and asking them what wine they preferred.

"Strong wine, plentiful wine," shouted the leader. "And the same goes for the women. Where are your women? I hope they're lovelier than your horses. Come man, be quick. We've spent all day buying horseflesh and helping this town's prosperity — now you'll do us a favour."

The boar warriors were evidently here to buy steeds for the Dark Empire troops — probably those bent on conquering Shekia, which lay just across the border.

Hawkmoon, Yisselda, Oladahn, and D'Averc drew their cowls surreptitiously about their heads and sipped at their wine without looking up.

There were three serving wenches in the public room, as well as two men and the landlord himself. As one passed, the boar warrior grabbed her and pressed the snout of his mask against her cheek.

"Give an old pig a kiss, little girl," he roared.

She wriggled and tried to get free, but he held her tight. Now there was silence everywhere else in the tavern, and tension.

"Come outside with me," the boar leader continued. "I'm in a rutting mood."

"Oh no, please let me go," the girl sobbed. "I'm to be married next week."

"Married, eh?" guffawed the warrior. "Well, let me teach you a thing or two for you to teach your husband."

The girl screamed and continued to resist. No-one else in the tavern moved.

"Come on," the warrior said hoarsely. "Outside..."

"I won't," wept the girl. "I won't until I'm married."

"Is that all?" The boar-masked man laughed. "Well, then — I'll marry you if that's what you want." He turned suddenly and glared at the four who sat in the shadows. "You're holy men, aren't you? One of you can marry us." And before Hawkmoon and the rest had realized what was happening, he had grabbed Yisselda, who sat on the outside of the bench, and hauled her to her feet. "Marry us, holy man, or — By the Runestaff! What sort of a holy man are you?" Yisselda's cowl had fallen back, revealing her lovely hair.

Hawkmoon stood up. There was nothing for it now but to fight. Oladahn and D'Averc stood up.

As one, they drew the swords hidden under their robes. As one, they launched themselves at the armoured warriors, yelling for the women to flee.

The boar warriors were drunk and surprised, and the three companions were neither. It was their only advantage. Hawkmoon's blade slipped between breastplate and gorget of the leader and killed him before he could draw his own sword, while Oladahn's swipe to another's barely protected legs hamstrung him. D'Averc managed to slice off the hand of one who had stripped off his gauntlets.

Now they fought back and forth across the tavern floor as men and women made hastily for the stairs and doors, many to crowd to the gallery above to watch.

Oladahn, forsaking normal swordplay in the narrow room, had leaped onto the back of a huge opponent and, dirk in hand, was trying to stab him through the eyeholes of his mask while the man clumsily tried to dislodge him, staggering about half-blind.

D'Averc was fencing with a swordsman of some skill who was driving him back steadily toward the stairs, while Hawkmoon was desperately defending himself against a man with a huge axe that, every time it missed him, chopped chunks out of the woodwork.

Hawkmoon, hampered by his cloak, was trying to get out of it and at the same time duck the blows from the axe. He stepped to one side, tripped in the folds of the cloak, and fell. Above, the axeman snorted and raised the axe for the final blow.

Hawkmoon rolled just in time as the axe came down and sheared through the cloth of his gown. He leaped up as he tugged the axe from the hard wood of the floor and swung his sword round to clang against the back of the axeman's neck. The man groaned and fell, dazed, to his knees. Hawkmoon kicked back the mask, revealing a red twisted face, and stabbed into the gaping mouth, driving the sword deep into the throat so that the jugular was cut and blood shot from the helm. Hawkmoon withdrew his blade and the helm clanged shut.

Nearby, Oladahn was struggling, half-off his man, who had now got a grip on his arm and was tugging him away from his neck. Hawkmoon jumped forward and with both hands drove his sword into the man's belly, piercing armour, leather underjerkin, and flesh. The man screamed and crumpled to the floor, to lie there writhing.

Then together Oladahn and Hawkmoon took D'Averc's man from behind, both swords slashing at him, until he, too, lay dead on the floor.

There was nothing left but to finish off the handless man who lay propped against a bench, weeping and trying to stick his hand back on.

Panting, Hawkmoon looked about the tavern room at the carnage they had wrought. "Not a bad night's work for holy men," he said.

D'Averc looked thoughtful. "Maybe," he said softly, "it is time to change our disguise to a more useful one."

"What do you mean?"

"There are enough pieces of boar armour here to furnish all four of us, particularly since I still have mine. I speak the secret language of the Order of the Boar. With luck we could travel disguised as those we fear most — as Dark Empire men. We have been wondering how to get through the countries where Granbretan has consolidated her gains. Well — here's our way."

Hawkmoon thought deeply. D'Averc's suggestion was a wild one, but it had possibilities, particularly since D'Averc himself knew all the rituals of the Order.

"Aye," said Hawkmoon. "Perhaps you're right, D'Averc. We could then go where the Dark Empire forces are thickest and stand a chance of getting to Kamarg faster. Very well, we'll do it."

They began stripping the armour from the corpses.

"We can be sure of the landlord's and townspeople's silence," said D'Averc, "for they'll not want it known that six Dark Empire warriors were killed here."

Oladahn watched them work, nursing his twisted arm. "A pity," he said with a sigh. "It was an exploit that should be recorded."

E   I   G   H   T

T H E   D A R K   E M P I R E   C A M P

"Brood of the Mountain Giants! I'll stifle to death before we've gone a mile!" The muffled voice of Oladahn came from within the grotesque helmet as he tried to tug himself free of its engulfing weight. They sat, all four, in their room above the tavern, trying on the captured armour.

Hawkmoon, too, was finding the stuff uncomfortable. Apart from the fact that it did not fit him properly, it made him feel distinctly claustrophobic. He had worn something like it some time before, when disguised in the wolf armour of Baron Meliadus's Order, but if anything, the boar armour was even heavier and far less comfortable. It must be that much worse for Yisselda. Only D'Averc was used to it and had donned his own, to look with some relish and amusement at their first encounter with the uniform of his Order.

"No wonder you claim ill health," Hawkmoon told him. "I know of nothing less healthy. I'm tempted to forget the whole plan."

"You'll become more used to it as we ride," D'Averc assured him. "A little chaffing, a little stuffiness; then you'll find you'll feel naked without it."

"I'd rather be naked," Oladahn protested, yanking off the leering boar mask at last. It fell with a clatter to the floor.

"Careful with it." D'Averc wagged a finger. "We don't want to damage any more."

Oladahn gave the helmet an extra kick.

A day and a night later, they were riding deep into Shekia. There was no doubt that the Dark Empire had conquered the province, for towns and villages were everywhere laid waste, crucified corpses hung along every road, carrion birds were thick in the air and even thicker on the ground where they feasted. The night had been as light as if the sun were permanently on the horizon, lit by the funeral pyres of villages, farms, towns, villas, and cities. And the black hordes of the Island Empire of Granbretan, brands in one hand, swords in the other, rode like demons from hell, howling and shrieking across the broken land.

Survivors hid, cringing from the four as they rode in disguise through this world of terror, galloping as fast as they could, for none suspected them. They were just one small pack of murderers and looters among many, and neither friend nor foe had any suspicion of their real identities.

Now it was morning, a morning overcast with black smoke, warmed by distant fires, a morning of ash-covered fields and trampled crops, of broken flowers and bloody corpses, a morning like any other morning in a land under the heel of Granbretan.

Along the churned mud of the road, a group of riders came toward them, swathed in great canvas night cloaks that covered their bemasked heads as well as their bodies. They rode powerful black horses and were hunched in their saddles as if they had been riding for many days.

As they drew close, Hawkmoon murmured, "Dark Empire men for certain, and they seem to be taking an interest in us..."

The leader pushed back his canvas cowl and revealed a huge boar mask, larger and more ornate than even D'Averc's. He reined in his black stallion, and his men came to a halt behind him.

"Silence, all three," murmured D'Averc, leading them up to the waiting warriors. "I'll speak."

Now from the leader of the boar warriors came a peculiar snorting, snuffling, and whining voice that must be speaking, thought Hawkmoon, the secret language of the Order of the Boar.

He was surprised to hear similar sounds begin to issue from D'Averc's throat. The conversation continued for some time, D'Averc pointing back down the road, the boar leader jerking his helm mask in the other direction. Then the leader urged his horse on, and he and his men filed past the nervous three and continued on up the road.

"What did he want?" Hawkmoon asked.

"Wanted to know if we'd seen any livestock. They're a foraging party of some sort, out to locate provisions for the camp ahead."

"What camp's that?"

"A big one, he said, about four miles further on. They're getting ready to attack one of the last cities still standing against them — Bradichla. I know the place. It had beautiful architecture."

"Then we are close to Osterland," Yisselda said, "and beyond Osterland lies Italia, and beyond Italia, Provence... home."

"True," said D'Averc. "Your geography is excellent. But we are not home yet, and the most dangerous part of the journey has still to be encountered."

"What shall we do about this camp," Oladahn said, "skirt it or try to ride through it?"

"It's a vast camp," D'Averc told him. "Our best chance would be to go through the middle, possibly even spend the night in it and try to learn something of the Dark Empire's plans — whether they have heard we are nearby, for instance."

Hawkmoon's muffled voice came from the helmet. "I am not sure it is not too dangerous," he said doubtfully. "Yet if we try to skirt the camp, we might arouse suspicion. Very well, we go through it."

"Will we not have to remove our masks, Dorian?" Yisselda asked him.

"No fear of that," D'Averc said. "The native Granbretanian often sleeps in his mask, hates to reveal his face."

Hawkmoon had noticed the weariness in Yisselda's voice and knew that they must rest soon; it would have to be in the Granbretanian camp.

They had expected the camp to be huge, but not as vast as this. In the distance beyond it was the walled city of Bradichla, its spires and facades visible even from here.

"They are remarkably beautiful," said D'Averc with a sigh. He shook his head. "What a pity they must fall tomorrow. They were fools to resist this army."

"It is of incredible size," said Oladahn. "Surely unnecessary to defeat that town?"

"The Dark Empire aims at speed of conquest," Hawkmoon told him. "I have seen larger armies than this used on smaller cities. But the camp covers a great distance, and organization will not be perfect. I think we can hide here."

There were canopies, tents, even huts built here and there, cooking fires on which food of all descriptions was being prepared, and corrals for horses, bullocks, and mules. Slaves hauled great war machines through the mud of the camp, goaded on by men of the Order of the Ant. Banners fluttered in the breeze, and the standards of a score of military Orders were stuck here and there in the ground. From a distance, it seemed like some primeval concourse of beasts as a line of wolves tramped across a ruined field or a gathering of moles (one of the engineering Orders) groaned about a cooking fire, while elsewhere could be seen wasps, ravens, ferrets, rats, foxes, tigers, boars, flies, hounds, badgers, goats, wolverines, otters, and even a few mantises, select guards whose Grand Constable was King Huon himself.

Hawkmoon himself recognized several of the banners — that of Adaz Promp, fat Grand Constable of the Order of the Hound; Brenal Farnu's ornate flag, showing him to be a baron of Granbretan and the Rats' Grand Constable; the fluttering standard of Shenegar Trott, Count of Sussex. Hawkmoon guessed that this city must be the last to fall in a sustained campaign and that was why the army was so large and attended by so many high-ranking warlords. He made out Shenegar Trott himself, being borne in a horse litter toward his tent, his robes covered in jewels, his pale silver mask wrought in the parody of a human face.

Shenegar Trott seemed like a soft-living, soft-brained aristocrat, ruined by rich living, but Hawkmoon had seen Shenegar Trott do battle at the Ford of Weizna on the Rhine, had seen him deliberately sink himself and horse under water and ride along the river bottom, to emerge on the enemy's bank. It was the puzzling thing about all Dark Empire noblemen. They seemed soft, lazy, and self-indulgent; yet they were as strong as the beasts they pretended to be and were often braver. Shenegar Trott was also the man who had hacked off the limb of a screaming child and eaten a bite from it while its mother was forced to watch.

"Well," said Hawkmoon, taking a deep breath, "let's ride through and camp as near to the far side as we can. I hope we'll be able to slip away in the morning."

They rode slowly through the camp. From time to time a boar would greet them and D'Averc would answer for them. Eventually they came to the farthest edge of the camp and dismounted. They had brought the gear stolen from the men they had killed in the tavern, and now they set it up without suspicion, for it bore no special insignia. D'Averc watched the others work. It would not do, he had told them, for one of his obvious rank to be seen helping his men.

A group of engineers of the Badger Order came tramping around with a cartload of spare axeheads, sword pommels, arrowheads, spear tips, and the like. They also had a sharpening machine.

"Any work for us, brother boars?" they grunted, pausing beside the little camp.

Hawkmoon boldly drew his blunted blade. "This needs sharpening."

"Aye, and I've lost a bow and a quiver of arrows," Oladahn said, eyeing a batch of bows in the bottom of the cart.

"What about your mate?" said the man in the badger mask. "He's got no sword at all." He indicated Yisselda.

"Then give him one, fool," barked D'Averc in his most lordly tone, and the badger hastily obeyed.

When they had been re-equipped and had their weapons freshly sharpened, Hawkmoon felt his confidence come back. He was pleased at the coolness of his deception.

Only Yisselda seemed downhearted. She hefted the great sword she had been forced to strap around her waist. "Much more weight," she said, "and I'll fall to my knees."

"Best get inside the tent," Hawkmoon said, "there you'll be able to take off some of the gear, at least."

D'Averc seemed unsettled, watching Hawkmoon and Oladahn prepare a cooking fire.

"What ails you, D'Averc?" Hawkmoon asked, looking up and peering through the eyeslits of his helmet. "Sit down. The food will not be long."

"I smell something wrong," D'Averc murmured. "I am not altogether happy that we are in no danger."

"Why? Do you think the badgers suspected us?"

"Not at all." D'Averc looked across the camp. Evening darkened the sky, and the warriors were beginning to settle down; there was less movement now. On the walls of the distant city, soldiers lined the battlements, ready to resist an army that none had resisted to date, save for Kamarg. "Not at all," D'Averc repeated, half to himself, "but I would feel relieved if…"

"If what?"

"I think I will walk about the camp a little, see what gossip I can hear."

"Is that wise? Besides, if we are approached by others of the Boar Order, we'll not be able to speak the language."

"I'll not be gone long. Get into your tents as soon as you can."

Hawkmoon wanted to stop D'Averc, but he did not know how to without attracting unwanted attention. He watched D'Averc stride off through the camp.

Just then a voice said from behind them, "A nice-looking piece of sausage you have there, brothers."

Hawkmoon turned. It was a warrior in the mask of the Order of the Wolf.

"Aye," said Oladahn quickly. "Aye — will you have a piece… brother?" He cut a slice of sausage and handed it to the man in the wolf mask. The warrior turned, lifted his mask, popped the food into his mouth, lowered his mask quickly, and turned back again.

"Thanks," he said. "I've been traveling for days on next to nothing. Our commander drives you hard. We just came in. Riding faster than a flying Frenchman." He laughed. "All the way from Provence."

"From Provence?" Hawkmoon said involuntarily.

"Aye. Been there?"

"Once or twice. Have we won Kamarg yet?"

"As good as. Commander thinks it's a matter of days. They're virtually leaderless, running out of provisions. Those weapons they've got have killed a million of us, but they won't kill many more before we ride over them!"

"What happened to Count Brass, their leader?"

"Dead, I heard — or as good as. Their morale's getting worse every day. By the time we get back, I should think it'll be all over there. I'll be glad. I've been pitched there for months. This is the first change of scenery since we began the damned campaign. Thanks for the sausage, brothers. Good killing tomorrow!"

Hawkmoon watched the wolf warrior stamp away into the night that was now lit by a thousand campfires. He sighed and entered the tent. "You heard that?" he asked Yisselda.

"I heard." She had removed her helmet and greaves and was combing her hair. "It seems my father still lives." She spoke in an overcontrolled tone, and Hawkmoon, even in the darkness of the tent, could see tears in her eyes.

He took her face in his hands and said, "Do not fear, Yisselda. A few days more and we shall be at his side."

"If he lives that long…"

"He awaits us. He will live."

Later Hawkmoon went outside. Oladahn sat by the dying fire, arms around his knees.

"D'Averc has been gone too long," said Oladahn.

"Aye," said Hawkmoon distantly, staring at the faraway walls of the city. "Has he come to harm? I wonder."

"Deserted us, more likely —" Oladahn broke off as several figures emerged from the shadows.

Hawkmoon saw, with sinking heart, that they were boar-masked warriors. "Into your tent, quickly," he murmured to Oladahn.

But it was too late. One of the boars was already talking to Hawkmoon, addressing him in the guttural secret tongue of the Order. Hawkmoon nodded and raised a hand as if acknowledging a greeting, hoping that that was all it was, but the boar's tone became more insistent. Hawkmoon tried to enter his tent, but an arm restrained him.

Again the boar spoke to him. Hawkmoon coughed, pretending illness, pointing at his throat. but then the boar said, "I asked you, *brother*, if you drink with us. Take off that mask!"

Hawkmoon knew that no member of any Order would demand of another that he remove his mask — unless he suspected him of wearing it illicitly. He stepped back and drew his sword.

"I regret I should not like to drink with you, *brother*. But I'll happily fight with you."

Oladahn sprang up beside him, his own sword ready.

"Who are you?" growled the boar. "Why wear the armour of another Order? What sense does that make?"

Hawkmoon flung back his helm, revealing his pale face and the Black Jewel that shone there. "I am Hawkmoon," he said simply, and leaped forward into the mass of astonished warriors.

The pair took the lives of five of the Dark Empire men before the noise of the fight brought others running from all over the camp. Riders galloped up. All around him Hawkmoon was aware of shouts and the babble of voices. His arm rose and fell in the darkness of the press, but soon it was gripped by a dozen hands and he felt himself borne down. A spear haft caught him a buffet in the back of his neck, and he fell into the mud of the field.

Dazed, he was dragged upright and hauled before a tall, black-armoured figure seated on a horse some distance away from the main mass. His mask was lifted back, and he peered up at the horseman.

"Ah, this is pleasant, Duke of Köln," came the deep, musical voice from within the horseman's helm, a voice edged with evil and with malice; a voice Hawkmoon recognized dimly but could not believe in his recognition.

"My long journey has not been wasted," said the horseman, turning to his mounted companion.

"I am glad, my lord," was the reply. "I trust I am now reinstated in the eyes of the King-Emperor?"

Hawkmoon's head jerked up to look at the other man. His eyes blazed as he recognized the elaborate mask-helm of D'Averc.

Thickly, Hawkmoon cried, "So you have betrayed us? Another betrayal! Are all men traitors to Hawkmoon's cause?" He tried to break free, to grab with his hands at D'Averc, but the warriors held him back.

D'Averc laughed. "You are naïve, Duke Dorian..." He began to cough weakly.

"Have you got the others?" the horseman asked. "The girl and the little beast-man?"

"Aye, your excellency," answered one of the men.

"Then bring them to my camp. I want to inspect them all closely. This is a very satisfying day for me."

N   I   N   E

T H E   J O U R N E Y   S O U T H

A storm had begun to rumble over the camp as Hawkmoon, Oladahn, and Yisselda were dragged through the mud and the filth, past the bright, curious eyes of the warriors, through the noise and confusion, to where a great banner fluttered in the newly come wind.

Lightning suddenly split a jagged gulf in the sky, and thunder growled, then exploded. More lightning came, fast on the thunder's heels, illuminating the scene before them. Hawkmoon gasped as he recognized the banner, tried to speak to Oladahn or Yisselda, but was then bundled into a large pavilion where a masked man sat on a carved chair, D'Averc standing beside him. The man in the chair wore the mask of the Order of the Wolf. The banner had proclaimed him Grand Constable of that Order, one of the greatest nobles in all Granbretan, First Chieftain of the Armies of the Dark Empire under the King-Emperor Huon, a Baron of Kroiden — a man Hawkmoon thought dead, was sure he had slain him himself.

"Baron Meliadus!" he grunted. "You did not die at Hamadan."

"No, I did not die, Hawkmoon, though you wounded me sorely. I escaped that battlefield."

Hawkmoon smiled thinly. "Few of your men did. We defeated you — routed you."

Meliadus turned his ornate wolf mask and spoke to a captain who stood nearby. "Bring chains. Bring many chains, strong and of great weight. Heap them on these dogs and rivet them. I want no locks that might be picked. This time I will be sure they are brought to Granbretan."

He left his chair and descended, to peer through the eyeslits in his mask at Hawkmoon's face. "They have discussed you often at King Huon's Court, have devised such exquisite, such elaborate, such splendid punishments for you, traitor. Your dying will take a year or two, and each moment will be agony of mind, spirit, and body. All our ingenuity, Hawkmoon, we have squandered on you."

He stepped back and reached out a black gauntlet to cup Yisselda's hate-twisted face. She turned her head, eyes filled with anger and despair. "And as for you — I offered you all honours to become my wife. Now you will have no honour, but a husband I shall be to you until I tire of you or your body breaks." The wolf head moved slowly to regard Oladahn. "And as for this creature, unhuman, yet upstart enough to walk on two legs, he shall crawl and whine like the animal he is, be trained to behave like a proper beast…"

Oladahn spat at the jeweled mask. "I'll have an excellent model in you," he said.

Meliadus whirled, cloak swirling, and limped heavily back to his chair.

"I'll save all until we've presented ourselves at the Throne Globe," Meliadus said, his voice slightly unsteady. "I've been patient and will remain so for a few more days. We move off at first light, returning to Granbretan. But we shall take a slight detour in order that you may witness the final destruction of Kamarg. I have been there for a month, you know, and watched its men die daily, watched the towers fall, one by one. There are not many left. I have told them to hold off the last assault until I return. I thought you would like to see your homeland… raped." He laughed, putting his grotesquely masked head on one side to look at them again. "Ah! Here are the chains."

Members of the Order of the Badger were coming in, bearing huge iron chains, a brazier, hammers, and rivets.

Hawkmoon, Yisselda, and Oladahn struggled as the badgers bound them, but soon they were forced down to the floor by the weight of the iron links.

Then the red-hot rivet nails were hammered home, and Hawkmoon knew that no human being could possibly hope to escape such bonds.

Baron Meliadus came to look down at him when the work was done. "We'll journey by land to Kamarg and from there to Bordeaux, where a ship will be waiting for us. I regret I cannot offer you a flying machine — we are using most of them to level Kamarg."

Hawkmoon closed his eyes; the only gesture he could make to display his contempt for his captor.

Bundled into an open wagon the next morning, the three were given no food before Baron Meliadus's heavily guarded caravan set off. From time to time Hawkmoon caught a glimpse of his enemy, riding near the head of the column with Sir Huillam D'Averc by his side.

The weather was still stormy and oppressive, and a few heavy drops of rain splashed on Hawkmoon's face and fell into his eyes. He was so heavily bound that he could barely shake his head to rid it of the moisture.

The wagon bumped and jerked away, and in the distance the Dark Empire troops were marching against the city.

It seemed to Hawkmoon that he had been betrayed on all sides. He had trusted the Warrior in Jet and Gold and had had his saddlebags stolen; he had trusted D'Averc and found himself delivered into the hands of Baron Meliadus. Now he sighed, not sure that even Oladahn would not betray him, given the opportunity...

He found himself slipping almost comfortably into the mood that had possessed him months before after his defeat and capture by Granbretan when he had led an army against Baron Meliadus in Germany. His face became frozen, his eyes dull, and he ceased to think.

Sometimes Yisselda would speak and he would answer with an effort, having no words of comfort because he knew that there were none that would convince her. Sometimes Oladahn would try to make a cheerful comment, but the others did not reply, and eventually he, too, lapsed into silence. Only when, from time to time, food was pushed into their mouths did they show any signs of life.

So the days passed as the caravan trundled southward towards Kamarg.

They had all anticipated this homecoming for months, but now they looked forward to it without joy. Hawkmoon knew he had failed in his chosen mission, failed to save Kamarg, and he was full of self-contempt.

Soon they were passing through Italia, and Baron Meliadus called out one day, "Kamarg we'll reach before a couple of nights have passed. We are just crossing the border into France!" And he laughed.

T   E   N

"Sit them up," said Baron Meliadus, "so they can see."

On horseback, he leaned over to look into the wagon. "Get them up straight," he told his sweating men who were wrestling with the three bodies still clad in armour and made heavier by the great weight of chains about them. "They do not look well," he added. "And I thought them such hardy spirits!"

D'Averc rode up beside Baron Meliadus, coughing, hunched a little in his saddle. "And you're still in poor condition, D'Averc. Did not my apothecary mix you the medicine you asked for?"

"He did, my lord Baron," D'Averc said weakly, "but it does me little good."

"It should have done, the mixture of herbs you had him put in it." Meliadus returned his attention to the three prisoners. "See, we have stopped on this hill so that you could look at your homeland."

Hawkmoon blinked in the midday sunlight, recognizing the marshlands of his beloved Kamarg stretching and shining away to the horizon.

But closer he saw the great, sombre watchtowers of Kamarg, the strength of Kamarg with their strange weapons of incredible power, whose secrets were known only to Count Brass. And camped near them, a black mass of men, like so many million ants ready to sweep in, were the gathered forces of the Dark Empire.

"Oh!" sobbed Yisselda. "They can never withstand so many!"

"An intelligent estimate, my dear," said Baron Meliadus. "You are quite right."

He and his party had come to a rest on the slopes of a hill that led gradually down to the plain where the troops of Granbretan massed. Hawkmoon could see infantry, cavalry, engineers, rank upon rank of them; he saw war engines of enormous size, huge flame-cannon, ornithopters flapping through the skies in such numbers that they blotted out the sun as they passed over the heads of the onlookers. All manner of metal had been brought against peaceful Kamarg, brass and iron and bronze and steel, tough alloys that could resist the bite of the flame-lance, gold and silver and platinum and lead. Vultures marched beside frogs, and horses beside moles; there were wolves and boars and stags and wildcats, eagles and ravens and badgers and weasels. Silk banners fluttered in the moist, warm air, bright with the colours of two score of nobles from all corners of Granbretan. There were yellows and purples and blacks and reds, blues and greens and flashing pink, and the sun caught the jewels of a hundred thousand eyes and made them flash, malevolent and grim.

"Aha," laughed Baron Meliadus. "That army I command. If Count Brass had not refused to aid us that day, you would all be honoured allies of the Dark Empire of Granbretan. But because you resisted us — you will be punished. You thought your weapons and your towers and the stoic bravery of your men were enough to stand against the might of Granbretan. Not enough, Dorian Hawkmoon, not enough! See — my army, raised by me to commit my vengeance. See, Hawkmoon, and know what a fool you and the rest were!" He flung back his head and laughed for a long time. "Tremble, Hawkmoon — and you, too, Yisselda — tremble as your fellows are trembling now within their towers, for they know those towers must fall, they know Kamarg will be ashes and mud before tomorrow's sunset. I will destroy Kamarg if it means sacrificing my entire army!"

And Hawkmoon and Yisselda did tremble, though it was with grief at the threat of the destruction foreseen by mad Baron Meliadus.

"Count Brass is dead," said Baron Meliadus, turning his horse to ride to the head of his company, "and now dies Kamarg!" He waved his arm, "Forward. Let them see the carnage!"

The wagon began to move again, bumping down the hill road to the plain, its prisoners propped in it with stricken faces and miserable eyes.

D'Averc continued to ride beside the wagon coughing ostentatiously. "The baron's medicine's not bad," he said at length. "It should cure the ills of all his men." And with that enigmatic pronouncement he urged his horse into a gallop to reach the head of the column and ride beside his master.

Hawkmoon saw strange rays flash from the towers of Kamarg and strike into the gathered ranks that came against them, leaving scars of smoking ground where men had been. He saw the cavalry of Kamarg begin to move up to take its positions, a thin line of battered guardians, riding their horned horses, flame-lances on their shoulders. He saw ordinary townsfolk from the settlements, armed with swords and axes, coming in the wake of the cavalry. But he did not see Count Brass, he did not see von Villach, and he did not see the philosopher Bowgentle. The men of Kamarg marched leaderless to this last battle.

He heard the faint sounds of their battle shouts, coming over the howls and roars of the attackers, the crack of cannon and the shriek of flame-lances; heard the clatter of armour and the creak of metal; smelled beast and man and weapon, marching through the mud. And then he saw the black hordes pause as a wall of fire rose into the air before them and scarlet flamingoes flew over it, riders aiming flame-lances at the clanking ornithopters.

Hawkmoon ached to be free, to have the feel of a sword in his hand and a horse between his legs, to rally the men of Kamarg, who, even leaderless, could still resist the Dark Empire, though their numbers were a fraction of the enemy's. He writhed in his chains, and he cursed in his fury and frustration.

Evening came, and the battle went on. Hawkmoon saw an ancient black tower struck by a million flames from the Dark Empire cannon, saw it sway, topple, and fall, crashing down to become rubble suddenly. And the black hordes cheered.

Night fell, and the battle went on. The heat of it reached even to the three in the wagon and brought sweat to their faces. Around them the wolf guards sat laughing and talking, certain of victory. Their master had ridden his horse into the thick of his troops, the better to see how the battle went, and they brought out a skin of wine with long straws jutting from it so that they could suck the stuff through their masks. As the night grew longer, their talk and their laughter subsided until, strangely, they all slept.

Oladahn remarked on it. "Not like the vigilant wolves to sleep so hard. They must be confident."

Hawkmoon sighed. "Aye, but it does us no good. These damned chains are riveted so fast that we have no hope of escaping."

"What's this?" The voice was D'Averc's. "No longer optimistic, Hawkmoon? I find it hard to believe!"

"Away with you, D'Averc," Hawkmoon said as the man emerged from the darkness to stand beside the wagon. "Back to lick the boots of your master."

"I had brought this," D'Averc said in a mock-aggrieved tone, "to see if it would serve you." He displayed a bulky object in his hand. "After all, it was my medicine that drugged the guards."

Hawkmoon's eyes narrowed. "What's that in your hand?"

"A rarity I found on the battleground. Some great commander's I'd judge, for there are few of them to be found these days. It's a kind of flame-lance, though small enough to be carried in one hand."

"I've heard of them," Hawkmoon nodded. "But what use is it to me? I'm in chains, as you see."

"Aye, I noted that. If you'd take a risk, however, it might be that I could release you."

"Is this a new trap, D'Averc, that you and Meliadus have concocted between you?"

"I'm hurt, Hawkmoon. Why should you think that?"

"Because you betrayed us into Meliadus's hands. You must have prepared the trap well ahead, when you spoke to those wolf warriors in that Carpathian village. You sent them to find their master and arranged to lead us to that camp where we could be most easily captured."

"Why, it sounds possible," agreed D'Averc. "Though you could see it another way — the wolf warriors recognized me then and followed us, going later to warn their master. I heard the rumour at the camp that Meliadus had come to find you, decided to tell Meliadus I had led you into this trap so that one of us would be free at least." D'Averc paused. "How does that sound?"

"Glib."

"Well, yes, it does sound glib. Now, Hawkmoon, there is not much time. Shall I see if I can burn your chains without burning you, or would you rather keep your seats for fear of missing a development in the battle?"

"Burn the damned chains," Hawkmoon said, "for at least with my hands free I'll have a chance to choke you if you lie!"

D'Averc brought the little flame-lance up and directed it at an angle to Hawkmoon's fettered arms. Then he touched a stud, and a beam of intense heat sprang from the muzzle. Hawkmoon felt pain sear his arm, but he gritted his teeth. The pain got worse until he felt he must cry out, and then there was a clatter as one of the links fell to the bottom of the wagon and he felt some of the weight leave him. An arm was free, his right arm. He rubbed it and almost yelled as he touched a part where the armour had been burned clean through.

"Hurry," murmured D'Averc. "Here, hold up another length of chain. It will be easier now."

At last Hawkmoon was free of the chain, and they set about releasing Yisselda and then Oladahn. D'Averc was becoming noticeably more nervous by the time they had finished.

"I have your swords here," he said, "and new masks and horses, You must follow me. And hurry, before Meliadus comes back. I had, to tell you the truth, expected him before now."

They crept through the darkness to where the horses were tethered, donned the masks, strapped the swords to their waists, and climbed into their saddles.

Then they heard other steeds galloping up the hill road toward them, heard confused shouts and an angry bellow that could only be Meliadus's.

"Quick," D'Averc hissed. "We must ride — ride for Kamarg!"

They kicked their horses into a wild gallop and began to career down the hill toward the main battlefield. "Make way!" D'Averc screamed. "Make way! The force must move through. Reinforcements for the front!"

Men leaped aside for their horses as they thundered through the thick of the camp, cursing the four figures who rode so heedlessly.

"Make way!" D'Averc yelled. "A message for the Grand Commander!" He found time to turn his head and call to Hawkmoon, "It bores me to sustain the same lie!" He yelled again, "Make way! The potion for the plague-struck!"

Behind them they heard other horses as Meliadus and his men came in pursuit.

Ahead they could now see that the fighting still continued, but not with the intensity it had had earlier.

"Make way!" bellowed D'Averc. "Make way for Baron Meliadus!"

The horses leaped knots of men, swept around war engines, galloped through fires, drawing nearer and nearer to Kamarg's towers, while behind them they could hear Meliadus yelling.

Now they reached a point where the horses galloped over corpses, the fallen of Granbretan, and the main force was now behind them.

"Get the masks off," D'Averc called. "It's our only chance. If the Kamargians recognize you and Yisselda in time, they'll hold their fire. If not…"

From out of the darkness came the bright beam of a flame-lance, narrowly missing D'Averc. Behind them other flame-lances shot their searing death, aimed doubtless by Meliadus's men. Hawkmoon grappled with the straps of his mask helm, managed at last to unloose it and fling it behind him.

"Stop!" The voice was Meliadus's, gaining on them now. "You'll perish by your own forces! Fools!"

More flame-lances had opened up from the Kamarg side, illuminating the night with ruddy light. The horses rode over the dead, finding it hard going. D'Averc had his head down over his horse's neck, and Yisselda and Oladahn were crouching low, too, but Hawkmoon drew his sword and yelled, "Men of Kamarg! It is Hawkmoon! Hawkmoon has returned!"

The flame-lances did not cease, but they were getting closer and closer to one of the towers now. D'Averc straightened in his saddle.

"Kamargians! I bring you Hawkmoon, who will —" and fire splashed him. He flung up his arms, cried out, and began to topple from his saddle. Hawkmoon hastily drew alongside, steadying the body. The armour was red-hot, melted in places, but D'Averc seemed not wholly dead. A faint laugh came from the blistered lips. "A piece of serious misjudgment, linking my fortunes with yours, Hawkmoon…"

The other two came to a halt, their horses stamping in confusion. Behind them, Baron Meliadus and his men drew closer.

"Take the reins of his horse, Oladahn," Hawkmoon said. "I'll steady him in his saddle, and we'll see if we can get closer to the tower."

Flame shot out again, this time from the Granbretanian side. "Stop, Hawkmoon!"

Hawkmoon ignored the command and moved on, slowly picking his way through the mud and death all around him, trying to support D'Averc.

Hawkmoon shouted as a great beam of light sprang from the tower. "Men of Kamarg! It is Hawkmoon — and Yisselda, Count Brass's daughter."

The light faded. Closer now came the horses of Meliadus. Yisselda, too, was swaying in her saddle from exhaustion. Hawkmoon prepared to meet the wolves of Meliadus.

Then, bursting down an incline, streamed a score of armoured guardians, the white, horned horses of Kamarg under them, and they surrounded the four.

One of the guardians peered close into Hawkmoon's face, then his eyes lit with joy. "It is my lord Hawkmoon! It is Yisselda! Ah — now our luck will change!"

Some distance away Meliadus and his men had paused when they saw the Kamargians. Then they turned and rode into the darkness.

They came to Castle Brass in the morning, when the pale sunlight fell on the lagoons and wild bulls looked up from where they drank and watched them pass. A wind stirred the reeds, making them roll like the sea, and the hill overlooking the town was rich with grapes and other fruits just beginning to ripen. On top of the hill stood Castle Brass, solid and old and seemingly unchanged by the wars that had raged on the borders of the province it protected.

They rode up the curling white road to the castle, crossed into the courtyard, where joyous stewards rushed out to take their horses, then entered the hall, which was full of Count Brass's trophies. It was strangely cold and silent, and a single figure stood by the great fireplace waiting for them. Although he smiled, his eyes were fearful and his face had aged much since Hawkmoon had last seen him — wise Sir Bowgentle, the philosopher-poet.

Bowgentle embraced Yisselda, then gripped Hawkmoon's hand.

"How is Count Brass?" Hawkmoon asked.

"Physically well, but he has lost the will to live." Bowgentle signed for stewards to help D'Averc. "Take him to the room in the northern tower — the sickroom. I'll attend to him as soon as I can. Come," he said. "See for yourselves…"

They left Oladahn to stay with D'Averc and climbed the old stone staircase to the landing where Count Brass's apartments still were. Bowgentle opened a door and they entered the bedroom.

There was a simple soldier's bed, big and square, with white sheets and plain pillows. On the pillows lay a great head that seemed carved from metal. The red hair had a little more grey, the bronzed face was a trifle paler, but the red moustache was the same. And the heavy brow that hung like a ledge of rock over the cave of the deepset golden brown eyes, that, too, was the same. But the eyes stared at the ceiling without blinking, and the lips did not move, were set in a hard line.

"Count Brass," murmured Bowgentle. "Look."

But the eyes remained fixed. Hawkmoon had to come forward, peer straight into the face, and make Yisselda do likewise. "Count Brass, your daughter, Yisselda, has returned, and Dorian Hawkmoon, too."

From the lips now came a rumbling murmur, "More illusions. I'd thought the fever past, Bowgentle."

"So it is, my lord — these are not phantoms."

The eyes moved now to look at them. "Am I dead at last and joined with you, my children?"

"You are on earth, Count Brass!" Hawkmoon said.

Yisselda bent and kissed her father on the lips. "There, Father — an earthly kiss."

Gradually the hard line of the lips began to melt, until a smile was there, then a wide grin. Then the body heaved under the clothes, and suddenly Count Brass was sitting upright. "Ah! It's true. I'd lost hope! Fool that I am, I'd lost hope!" He laughed now, suddenly alive with vitality.

Bowgentle was astonished. "Count Brass — I thought you but a pace from the door of death!"

"So I was, Bowgentle — but I've leaped back from it, as you see. Leaped a long way. How goes the siege, Hawkmoon?"

"Badly for us, Count Brass, but better, I'll wager, now we three are together again!"

"Aye. Bowgentle, have my armour brought. And where is my sword?"

"Count Brass — you must still be weak…"

"Then bring me food — a great deal of food — and I'll fortify myself as we talk." And Count Brass sprang from his bed to embrace his daughter and her betrothed.

In the hall they ate while Dorian Hawkmoon told Count Brass all that had befallen him since leaving the castle so many months before. Count Brass, in turn, told of his tribulations with, it had seemed, the entire might of the Dark Empire to contend with. He told of von Villach's last battle and how the old man had died bravely, at the cost of a score of Dark Empire lives, how he, himself, had been wounded, how he had learned of Yisselda's disappearance and lost the will to live.

Oladahn came down then and was introduced. He said that D'Averc was badly hurt but that Bowgentle thought he would recover.

On the whole it was a cheerful homecoming, but marred by the knowledge that on the borders the guardians were fighting for their lives, almost certainly fighting a losing battle.

Count Brass had by this time donned his armour of brass and strapped on his huge broadsword. He towered above the others as he stood up and said, "Come, Hawkmoon, Sir Oladahn, we must to the battlefield and lead our men to victory."

Bowgentle sighed. "Two hours ago I thought you all but dead — now you ride to battle. You are not well enough, sir."

"My sickness was of the spirit, not the flesh, and that's cured now," roared Count Brass. "Horses! Tell them to bring our horses, Sir Bowgentle!"

Though himself weary, Hawkmoon found renewed vigour as he followed the old man from the castle. He blew a kiss to Yisselda, and then they were in the courtyard, mounting the horses that would bear them to the battlefield.

They rode hard, the three of them, through the secret pathways of the marshlands, with huge clouds of giant flamingoes passing through the air over their heads, herds of wild horned horses galloping away from them. Count Brass waved a gloved hand. "Such a land is worth defending with all we have. Such peace is worth protecting."

Soon they heard the sounds of warfare and came to where the Dark Empire drove against the towers. They reined in when they saw the worst.

Count Brass spoke in a stricken whisper. "Impossible," he said.

But it was true.

The towers had fallen. Each lay broken, a pile of smoking masonry. The survivors were even now being pressed back, though they battled bravely.

"This is the fall of Kamarg," said Count Brass in the voice of an old man.

E L E V E N

R E T U R N   O F   T H E   W A R R I O R

Now one of the captains saw them and came riding up. His armour was in tatters and his sword broken, but there was joy in his face. "Count Brass! At last! Come sir, we must rally the men — drive the Dark Empire dogs away!"

Hawkmoon saw Count Brass force himself to smile, draw his great broadsword, and say, "Aye, captain. See if you can find a herald or two to tell all that Count Brass is back!"

A cheer went up from the hard-pressed Kamargians as Count Brass and Hawkmoon appeared, and they held their ground, even pushed the Granbretanians back in places. Count Brass, with Hawkmoon and Oladahn following, rode into the thick of his men, once again the invincible man of metal. "Aside, lads!" he called. "Aside and let me get at the enemy!"

Count Brass grabbed his own battered standard from a nearby rider, and with this balanced in the crook of his arm, his sword waving, he drove forward at the mass of beast-masks ahead.

Hawkmoon rode up beside him, and they made a menacing, almost supernatural pair, the one in his flaming armour of brass and the other with the Black Jewel embedded in his forehead, their swords rising and falling on the heads of the tightly packed Granbretanian infantry. And when another figure joined them, a stocky man with fur covering his face and a flashing sabre striking here and there like lightning, they seemed a trio out of mythology, unnerving the beast warriors of Granbretan so that they fell back.

Hawkmoon searched about for Meliadus, swearing that he would certainly kill him this time, but he could not see him for the moment.

Gauntleted hands tried to drag him from his saddle, but his sword slipped through eyeholes, split helms, and sliced heads from their shoulders.

The day wore on, and the fighting continued without respite. Hawkmoon swayed in his saddle now, battle-weary and half-dazed with pain from a dozen minor cuts and a great many bruises. His horse was killed, but the weight of men surrounding him was so great that he sat it for half an hour before he realized it was dead. Then he sprang off it and continued fighting on foot.

He knew that no matter how many he and the others killed, they were outnumbered and ill-equipped. Gradually they were being driven farther and farther back.

"Ah," he murmured to himself, "if only we had a few hundred fresh troops, we might win the day. By the Runestaff, we need aid!"

Suddenly a strange electric sensation ran through his body, and he gasped, recognizing what was happening to him, realizing that he had unconsciously invoked the Runestaff. The Red Amulet, which now glowed at his neck, spreading red light on the armour of his enemies, was now transmitting power into his body. He laughed and began to hew around him with fantastic strength, cutting back the circle of warriors attacking him. His sword snapped, but he grabbed a lance from a horseman riding at him, dragged its owner from his saddle, and, swinging the lance like a sword, jumped onto the horse and resumed the attack.

"Hawkmoon! Hawkmoon!" he cried using the old battlecry of his ancestors. "Hai — Oladahn — Count Brass!" He gouged his way through the beast-masked warriors between himself and his friends. Count Brass's standard still swayed in its owner's hand.

"Drive them back!" Hawkmoon yelled. "Drive them back to our borders!"

Then Hawkmoon was everywhere, a whirling bringer of death. He raced through the ranks of Granbretan, and where he passed there were only corpses. A great muttering went up from the enemy then, and they began to falter.

Soon they were falling back, some actually running from the field. And then the figure of Baron Meliadus appeared, crying out to them to turn to stand and to fight.

"Back!" he cried. "You cannot fear so few!" But the tide was completely on the turn now, and he himself was caught by it, borne back by his retreating men.

They fled in terror from the pale-faced knight whose sword fell everywhere, in whose skull a black jewel shone and at whose throat hung an amulet of scarlet fire, whose fierce horse reared over their heads. They had heard, too, that he shouted the name of a dead man — that he, himself, was a dead man, Dorian Hawkmoon, who had fought against them at Köln and almost defeated them there, who had defied the King-Emperor himself, who had nearly slain Baron Meliadus and had, in fact, defeated him more than once. Hawkmoon! It was the only name the Dark Empire feared.

"Hawkmoon! Hawkmoon!" The figure held its sword high as its horse reared again. "Hawkmoon!"

Possessed of the power of the Red Amulet, Hawkmoon chased the fleeing army, and he laughed wildly with a mad triumph. Behind him rode Count Brass, terrible in his red-gold armour, his huge blade dripping with the blood of his foes; Oladahn, grinning through his fur, bright eyes gleaming, sabre slick with gore; and behind them the jubilant forces of Kamarg, a handful of men jeering at the mighty army they had routed.

Now the power of the amulet began to fade from Hawkmoon, and he felt his pains return, felt the weariness again, but now it did not matter, for they had come to the border, marked by the ruined towers, and watched their enemies in flight.

Oladahn laughed. "Our victory, Hawkmoon."

Count Brass frowned. "Aye — but not one we can sustain. We must withdraw, regroup, find some safer ground to stand, for we will not beat them again in the open field."

"You are right," nodded Hawkmoon. "Now that the towers have fallen we need to find another spot well defended — and there is only one I can think of…" He glanced at the count.

"Aye — Castle Brass," agreed the old man. "We must send word to all the towns and villages of Kamarg to tell the people to bring their goods and stock to Aigues-Mortes under the protection of the castle…"

"Will we be able to sustain so many for a long siege?" Hawkmoon asked.

"We shall see," Count Brass replied, watching the distant army beginning to regroup. "But at least they will have some protection when the Dark Empire troops flood over our Kamarg."

There were tears in his eyes as he turned his horse and began to ride back to the castle.

From the balcony of his rooms in the eastern tower, Hawkmoon watched the people driving their livestock into the protection of the old town of Aigues-Mortes. Most of them were corralled in the amphitheatre at one end of the town. Soldiers brought in provisions and helped folk with their loaded carts. By evening all but a few had entered the safety of the walls, crowding into houses or camping in the streets. Hawkmoon prayed that plague or panic might not set in, for such a crowd might be hard to control.

Oladahn joined him on the balcony, pointing to the north-east.

"Look," he said. "Flying machines." And Hawkmoon saw the ominous shapes of Dark Empire ornithopters flapping over the horizon, a certain sign that the army of Granbretan was on the move.

By nightfall, they could see the cooking fires of the nearest troops.

"Tomorrow," said Hawkmoon. "It could be our last battle."

They went down to the hall, where Bowgentle talked to Count Brass. Food had been prepared, as lavishly as ever. The two men turned as Hawkmoon and Oladahn entered the hall.

"How is D'Averc?" Hawkmoon asked.

"Stronger," Bowgentle said. "He has an excellent constitution, says he would like to get up to eat tonight. I said he might."

Yisselda came through the outer door. "I've spoken to the women," she said, "and they say all are within the walls. We have enough provisions to last as much as a year, if we slaughter the stock..."

Count Brass smiled sadly. "It will take less than a year to decide this battle. And how is the spirit in the town?"

"Good," she said, "now that they have heard of your victory today and know you both to be alive."

"It is as well," Count Brass said heavily, "that they do not know that tomorrow they die. Or if not tomorrow, the next day. We cannot stand against such a weight of soldiers for long, my dear. Most of our flamingoes are dead, so we have virtually no protection in the air. Most of our guardians are dead, and the troops we have left are all but untrained."

Bowgentle sighed. "And we thought Kamarg could never fall..."

"You are too certain that it will," said a voice from the stairs, and there was D'Averc, pale and dressed in a loose, fawn-coloured gown, limping down to the hall. "In such spirits you are bound to lose. You could try to talk of victory, at least."

"You are right, Sir Huillam." Count Brass changed his mood with an effort of will. "And we could eat some of this good food here to give us energy for tomorrow's struggle."

"How are you, D'Averc?" Hawkmoon asked as they seated themselves at the board.

"Well enough," said D'Averc lightly. "I think I can manage some small refreshments." And he began to heap his plate with meat.

They ate in silence, for the most part, relishing the meal that many felt would be their last.

When Hawkmoon looked from his window the next morning, it was to see the marshlands overlaid with men. In the night, the Dark Empire had crept up close to their walls, and now it was readying itself for the assault.

Quickly Hawkmoon donned clothes and armour and went down to the hall, where he found D'Averc already encased in his patched armour, Oladahn cleaning his blade, and Count Brass discussing some feature of the coming campaign with two of his remaining captains.

There was an atmosphere of tension in the hall, and the men spoke to one another in murmurs.

Yisselda appeared and called to him softly, "Dorian..." He turned and ran up the stairs to the landing on which she stood, taking her in his arms and holding her close, kissing her gently on the forehead. "Dorian," she said, "let us be married before…"

"Aye," he said quietly. "Let us find Bowgentle."

They found the philosopher in his quarters reading a book. He looked up as they entered and smiled at them. They told him what they wanted, and he laid down his book. "I had hoped for the grand ceremony," he said, "but I understand."

And he made them join hands and kneel before him while he spoke the words of his own composition that had always been used in marriages since he and his friend the count had come to Castle Brass.

When it was done, Hawkmoon stood up and kissed Yisselda again. Then he said, "Look after her, Bowgentle," and left the room to join his friends, who were already leaving the hall for the courtyard.

As they mounted their horses a great shadow suddenly darkened the courtyard, and they heard the creaking and clattering overhead that could only be a Dark Empire ornithopter. A bolt of flame leapt from it and splashed on the cobbles, narrowly missing Hawkmoon and causing his horse to rear, nostrils flaring and eyes rolling.

Count Brass brought up the flame-lance with which he had already equipped himself and touched the stud, and red fire struck upwards at the flying machine. They heard the pilot scream and saw the thing's wings cease to work. It glided out of sight, and they heard it crash at last on the side of the hill.

"I must station flame-lancers in the towers," Count Brass said. "They'll have the best chance of striking back at the ornithopters. Come, gentlemen — let's to the battle."

And as they left the castle walls and rode down to the town, they saw the huge tide of men was already washing at the walls of the town where Kamarg warriors fought desperately to drive it back.

Ornithopters, fashioned like grotesque metal birds, wheeled over the town, pouring down flame into the streets, and the air became filled with the screams of the townsfolk, the roar of flame-lances, and the clash of metal against metal. Black smoke hung over Aigues-Mortes, and in places houses were already burning.

Hawkmoon led the charge down to the town and pushed through frightened women and children to gain the walls and join in the fight. Elsewhere were Count Brass, D'Averc, and Oladahn, helping to resist the force that tried to crush the town.

There came a desperate roar from one portion of the wall and an echoing cheer of triumph, and Hawkmoon began to run in that direction, seeing that a hole had been breached in the defenses and Dark Empire warriors, in helms of wolf and bear, were gushing through.

Hawkmoon met them, and they wavered instantly, remembering his earlier exploits. He was no longer equipped with superhuman strength, but he used the pause to cry his ancestral battleshout, "Hawkmoon! Hawkmoon!" and leap at them, sword meeting metal, flesh, and bone and driving them back through the breach.

So they fought all day, holding the town even as their numbers rapidly dropped, and when the night fell and the Dark Empire troops withdrew, Hawkmoon knew, as they all knew, that the next morning must bring defeat.

Wearily, Hawkmoon, Count Brass, and the others led their horses back up the winding road to the castle, their hearts heavy as they thought of all the innocents slaughtered that day and of all the innocents who would be slaughtered tomorrow — if they were lucky enough to die.

Then they heard a galloping horse behind them and turned on the slope, swords ready, to see the strange figure of a tall rider coming up the hill toward the castle. He had a long helm that completely encased his face, and his armour was wrought all in jet and gold. Hawkmoon scowled. "What does that traitorous thief want?" he said.

The Warrior in Jet and Gold pulled up his big horse nearby. His deep, vibrant voice came from within his helmet then. "Greetings, defenders of Kamarg, I see the day goes badly for you. Baron Meliadus will defeat you tomorrow."

Hawkmoon wiped his forehead with a rag. "No need to make so much of the obvious, Warrior. What have you come to steal this time?"

"Nothing," said the warrior. "I have come to deliver something." He reached behind him and produced Hawkmoon's battered saddlebags.

Hawkmoon's spirits rose, and he leaned forward to take the saddlebags, opening one to look inside. There, wrapped in a cloak, was the object he had been given so long ago by Rinal. It was safe. He pulled back the cloak and saw the crystal unshattered.

"But why did you take it in the first place?" he asked.

"Let us go to Castle Brass, and there I will explain all to you," said the warrior.

In the hall the warrior stood up by the fireplace while the others sat in various positions around him, listening.

"At the Mad God's castle," began the warrior, "I left you because I knew that with the aid of the Mad God's beasts you could soon be safely away from there. But I knew other hazards lay ahead of you and suspected that you might be captured. Therefore, I decided to take the object Rinal gave you and keep it safe until you should return to Kamarg."

"And I had thought you a thief!" Hawkmoon said. "I am sorry, Warrior."

"But what is the object?" Count Brass asked.

"An ancient machine," the warrior said, "produced by one of the most sophisticated sciences ever to emerge on this earth."

"A weapon?" Count Brass asked.

"No. It is a device which can warp whole areas of time and space and shift them into other dimensions. While the machine exists, it can exert this power, but should it, by mischance, be destroyed, then the area it has warped falls immediately back into the time and space original to it."

"And how is it operated?" Hawkmoon asked, remembering suddenly that he had no such knowledge.

"It is difficult to explain, since you would recognize none of the words I would use," said the Warrior in Jet and Gold. "But Rinal has taught me its use, among other things, and I can work it."

"But for what purpose?" D'Averc asked. "To shift the troublesome baron and his men to some limbo where they will not bother us again?"

"No," said the warrior. "I will explain —"

The doors burst open, and a battered soldier rushed into the hall. "Master," he cried to Count Brass, "it is Baron Meliadus under a flag of truce. He would parley with you at the town walls."

"I have nothing to say to him," Count Brass said.

"He says that he intends to attack at night. That he can have the walls down within an hour, for he has fresh troops held back for the purpose. He says that if you deliver your daughter, Hawkmoon, D'Averc, and yourself into his hands, he will be lenient with the rest."

Count Brass thought for a moment, but Hawkmoon broke in, "It is useless to consider such a bargain, Count Brass. We both know of Meliadus's penchant for treachery. He seeks only to demoralize the folk to make his victory easier."

Count Brass sighed. "But if what he says is true, and I cannot doubt that it is, he will have the walls down shortly and we all perish."

"With honour, at least," said D'Averc.

"Aye," said Count Brass with a somewhat sardonic smile. "With honour, at least." He turned to the courier. "Tell Baron Meliadus that we still do not wish to speak with him."

The courier bowed. "I will, my lord." He left the hall.

"We had best return to the walls," said Count Brass, rising wearily just as Yisselda entered the room.

"Ah, Father, Dorian — you are both safe."

Hawkmoon embraced her. "But now we must go back," he said softly. "Meliadus is about to launch another attack."

"Wait," said the Warrior in Jet and Gold. "I have yet to describe my plan to you."

T W E L V E

E S C A P E   T O   L I M B O

Baron Meliadus smiled when he heard the courier's message.

"Very well," he said to his stewards, "let the whole town be destroyed and as many of its inhabitants taken alive to give us sport on our victory day." He turned his horse back to where his fresh troops awaited him.

"Move forward," he said, and watched as they began to flow towards the doomed town and the castle beyond.

He saw the fires on the town walls, the few soldiers waiting, knowing with certainty that they would die. He saw the graceful outlines of the castle that had once protected the town so well, and he chuckled. There was a warmth inside him, for he had longed for this victory ever since he had been ejected from the castle some two years earlier.

Now his troops had nearly reached the walls, and he kicked his horse's flanks to make it move down so that he could see the battle better.

Then he frowned. There seemed something wrong with the light, for the outline of town and castle had apparently wavered in a most alarming fashion.

He opened his mask and rubbed at his eyes, then looked again.

The silhouette of Castle Brass and Aigues-Mortes seemed to glow, first pink, then pale red, then scarlet, and Baron Meliadus felt lightheaded. He licked his dry lips and feared for his sanity.

The troops had paused in their attack, muttering to themselves and backing away from the place. The entire town and the hillside and castle it surrounded were now a flaming blue. The blue began to fade, and fading with it went Castle Brass and Aigues-Mortes. A wild wind blew, knocking Baron Meliadus back in his saddle.

He cried out, "Guards! What has happened?"

"The place has — has vanished, my lord," came a nervous voice.

"Vanished! Impossible. How can a whole town and a hill vanish? It is still there. They have erected some kind of screen around the place."

Baron Meliadus rode wildly down to where the town walls had been, expecting to meet a barrier, but none blocked him, and his horse trampled over only mud that looked as if it had been recently ploughed.

"They have escaped me!" he howled. "But how? What science aids them? What power can they have that is greater than mine?"

The troops had begun to turn back. Some were running. But Baron Meliadus dismounted from his horse, hands outstretched, trying to feel for the vanished town. He screamed with fury and wept with impotent rage, falling at last to his knees in the mud and shaking his fist at where Castle Brass had been.

"I will find you, Hawkmoon — and your friends. I will bring all the scientific knowledge of Granbretan to bear on this search. And I will follow you, if needs be, to whatever place you have escaped to, whether it be on this earth or beyond it, and you will know my vengeance. By the Runestaff, I swear this!"

And then he looked up as he heard the thump of a horse's hooves riding past him, thought he saw a figure flash by in armour of jet and gold, thought he heard ghostly ironic laughter, and then the rider, too, had vanished.

Baron Meliadus rose up from his knees and looked around him for his horse.

"Oh, Hawkmoon," he said through clenched teeth. "Oh, Hawkmoon, I will catch thee!"

Again he had sworn by the Runestaff, as on that fateful morning two years before. And his action had set in motion a new pattern of history. His second oath strengthened that pattern, whether it favoured Meliadus or Hawkmoon, and hardened all their destinies a little more strongly.

Baron Meliadus found his horse and returned to his camp. Tomorrow he would leave for Granbretan and the labyrinthine laboratories of the Order of the Snake. Sooner or later he would be bound to find a way through to the vanished Castle Brass, he told himself.

Yisselda looked through the window in wonderment, her face alight with joy. Hawkmoon smiled down at her and hugged her to him.

Behind them, Count Brass coughed and said, "To tell you the truth, my children, I'm a little disturbed by all this — this *science*. Where did that fellow say we were?"

"In some other Kamarg, Father," said Yisselda.

The view from the window was misty. Though the town and the hillside were solid enough, the rest was not. Beyond it they could see, as if through a blue radiance, shining lagoons and waving reeds, but they were of transformed colours, no longer of simple greens and yellows, but of all the colours of the rainbow and without the substance of the castle and its surrounds.

"He said we might explore it," said Hawkmoon. "So it must be more tangible than it looks."

D'Averc cleared his throat. "I'll stay here and in the town, I think. What say you, Oladahn?"

Oladahn grinned. "I think so — until I'm more used to it, at least."

"Well, I'm with you," said Count Brass. He laughed. "Still, we're safe, eh? And our people, too. We've that to be grateful for."

"Aye," said Bowgentle thoughtfully. "But we must not underestimate the scientific prowess of Granbretan. If there is a way of following us here, they will find it — be sure of that."

Hawkmoon nodded. "You are right, Bowgentle." He pointed to Rinal's gift, which lay now in the centre of the empty dining table, outlined in the strange, pale blue light that flooded through the windows. "We must keep that in our safest vault. Remember what the Warrior said — if it is destroyed, we find ourselves back again in our own space and time."

Bowgentle went over to the machine and gently picked it up. "I will see that it is safe," he said.

When he had left, Hawkmoon turned again to look through the window, fingering the Red Amulet.

"The Warrior said that he would come again with a message and a mission for me," he said. "I am in no doubt now that I serve the Runestaff, and when the Warrior comes, I shall have to leave Castle Brass, leave this sanctuary, and return again to the world. You must be prepared for that, Yisselda."

"Let us not speak of it now," she said, "but celebrate, instead, our marriage."

"Aye, let us do that," he said with a smile. But he could not shut entirely from his mind the knowledge that somewhere, separated from him by subtle barriers, the world still existed and was still in danger from the Dark Empire. Though he appreciated the respite, the time to spend with the woman he loved, he knew that soon he must return to that world and do battle once more with the forces of Granbretan.

But for the moment, he would be happy.

THE SWORD OF THE DAWN

For Ed and Leigh Brackett Hamilton

B   O   O   K   O   N   E

When that aspect of the Eternal Champion called Dorian Hawkmoon, last Duke of Köln, ripped the Red Amulet from the throat of the Mad God and made that powerful thing his own, he returned with Huillam D'Averc and Oladahn of the Mountains to Kamarg where Count Brass, his daughter Yisselda, his friend Bowgentle the philosopher and all their people underwent siege from the hordes of the Dark Empire led by Hawkmoon's old enemy Baron Meliadus of Kroiden.

So powerful had the Dark Empire grown that it threatened to destroy even the well-protected province of Kamarg. If that happened, it would mean that Meliadus would take Yisselda for his own and slay slowly all the rest, turning Kamarg to a waste of ash. Only by the mighty force released by the ancient machine of the wraith-folk which could warp whole areas of time and space were they saved by shifting into another dimension of the Earth.

And so they found sanctuary. Sanctuary in some other Kamarg, where the evil and horror of Granbretan did not exist; but they knew that if ever the crystal machine were destroyed, they would be plunged back into the chaos of their own time and space.

For a while they lived in joyful relief at their escape, but gradually Hawkmoon began to finger his sword and wonder at the fate of his own world...

— *The High History of the Runestaff*

T H E   L A S T   C I T Y

The grim riders spurred their battle-steeds up the muddy slopes of the hill, coughing as their lungs took in the thick black smoke rising from the valley.

It was evening, the sun was setting, and their grotesque shadows were long. In the twilight, it seemed that gigantic beast-headed creatures rode the horses.

Each rider bore a banner, stained by war, each wore a huge beast-mask of jeweled metal and heavy armour of steel, brass and silver, emblazoned with its wearer's device, battered and bloodied, and each gauntleted right hand gripped a weapon on which was encrusted the remains of a hundred innocents.

The six horsemen reached the top of the hill and dragged their snorting mounts to a halt, stabbing their banners into the earth where they flapped like the wings of birds of prey in the hot wind from the valley.

Wolf-mask turned to stare at Fly-mask, Ape glanced at Goat, Rat seemed to grin at Hound — a grin of triumph. The Beasts of the Dark Empire, each a Warlord of thousands, looked beyond the valley and beyond the hills to the sea, looked back at the blazing city below them where, faintly, they could hear the wails of the slaughtered and the tormented.

The sun set, night fell and the flames burned brighter, reflected in the dark metal of the masks of the Lords of Granbretan.

"Well, my lords," said Baron Meliadus, Grand Constable of the Order of the Wolf, Commander of the Army of Conquest, his deep, vibrant voice booming from within his great mask, "well, we have conquered all Europe now."

Mygel Holst, skeletal Archduke of Londra, head of the Order of the Goat, veteran of Kamarg, from which he had barely escaped with his life, laughed. "Aye — all Europe. Not an inch of it is not ours. And now great parts of the East belong to us also." The Goat helm nodded as if in satisfaction, the ruby eyes catching the firelight, flashing malignantly.

"Soon," merrily growled Adaz Promp, Master of the Order of the Hound, "all the world will be ours. All."

The Barons of Granbretan, masters of a continent, tacticians and warriors of ferocious courage and skill, careless of their own lives, corrupt of soul and mad of brain, haters of all that was not in decay, wielders of power without morality, force without justice, chuckled with gloomy pleasure as they watched the last European city to withstand them crumble and die. It had been an old city. It had been called Athena.

"All," said Jerek Nankenseen, Warlord of the Order of the Fly, "save hidden Kamarg…"

And Baron Meliadus lost his humour then, made almost as if he would strike his fellow warlord.

Jerek Nankenseen's bejeweled Fly mask turned a little to regard Meliadus and the voice from within the mask was baiting. "Is it not enough that you have chased them away, my lord Baron?"

"No," snarled the Wolf of Wolves. "Not enough."

"They can offer us no menace," murmured Baron Brenal Farnu of the Rat helm. "From what our scientists divined, they exist in a dimension beyond Earth, in some other time or space. We cannot reach them and they cannot reach us. Let us enjoy our triumph, unmarred by thoughts of Hawkmoon and Count Brass…"

"I cannot!"

"Or is it another name that haunts thee, brother baron?" Jerek Nankenseen mocked the man who had been his rival in more than one amorous encounter in Londra. "The name of the fair one, Yisselda? Is it love that moves you, my lord? Sweet love?"

For a moment the Wolf did not reply, but the hand that gripped the sword tightened as if in fury. Then the rich, musical voice spoke and it had recovered its composure, was almost light in tone.

"Vengeance, Baron Jerek Nankenseen, is what motivates me…"

"You are a most passionate man, Baron…" Jerek Nankenseen said dryly.

Meliadus sheathed his sword suddenly and reached out to grasp his banner, wrenching it from the earth. "They have insulted our King-Emperor, our land — and myself. I will have the girl for my pleasure, but in no soft spirit will I take her, no weak emotion will motivate me…"

"Of course not," murmured Jerek Nankenseen, a hint of patronage in his voice.

"… And as for the others, I will have my pleasure with them, also — in the prison vaults of Londra. Dorian Hawkmoon, Count Brass, the philosopher Bowgentle, the unhuman one, Oladahn of the Bulgar Mountains, and the traitor Huillam D'Averc — all these shall suffer for many years. That I have sworn by the Runestaff!"

There was a sound behind them. They turned to peer through the flickering light and saw a canopied litter being borne up the hill by a dozen Athenan prisoners of war who were chained to its poles. In the litter lounged the unconventional Shenegar Trott, Count of Sussex. Count Shenegar almost disdained the wearing of a mask at all, and as it was he wore a silver one scarcely larger than his head, fashioned to resemble, in caricature, his own visage. He belonged to no Order and was tolerated by the King-Emperor and his Court because of his immense richness and almost superhuman courage in battle — yet he gave the appearance, in his jeweled robes and lazy manner, of a besotted fool. He, even more than Meliadus, had the confidence (such as it was) of the King-Emperor Huon, for his advice was almost always excellent. He had plainly heard the last part of the exchange and spoke banteringly.

"A dangerous oath to swear, my lord Baron," said he softly. "One that could, by all counts, have repercussions on he who swears it…"

"I swore the oath with that knowledge," replied Meliadus. "I shall find them, Count Shenegar, never fear."

"I came to remind you, my lords," said Shenegar Trott, "that our King-Emperor grows impatient to see us and hear our report that all Europe is now his property."

"I will ride for Londra instantly," Meliadus said. "For there I may consult our sorcerer-scientists and discover a means of hunting out my foes. Farewell, my lords."

He dragged at his horse's reins, turning the beast and galloping back down the hill, watched by his peers.

The beast-masks moved together in the firelight. "His singular mentality could destroy us all," whispered one.

"What matter?" chuckled Shenegar Trott, "so long as all is destroyed with us…"

The answering laughter was wild, ringing from the jeweled helms. It was insane laughter, tinged as much with self-hatred as with hatred of the world.

For this was the great power of the Lords of the Dark Empire, that they valued nothing on all the Earth, no human quality, nothing within or without themselves. The spreading of conquest and desolation, of terror and torment, was their staple entertainment, a means of employing their hours until their spans of life were ended. For them, warfare was merely the most satisfactory way of easing their ennui…

T W O

THE FLAMINGOES' DANCE

At dawn, when clouds of giant scarlet flamingoes rose from their nests of reeds and wheeled through the sky in bizarre ritual dances, Count Brass would stand on the edge of the marsh and stare over the water at the strange configurations of dark lagoons and tawny islands that seemed to him like hieroglyphs in some primeval language.

The ontological revelations that might exist in these patterns had always intrigued him, and of late he had taken to studying the birds, reeds and lagoons, attempting to divine the key to this cryptic landscape.

The landscape, he thought, was coded. In it he might find the answers to the dilemma of which even he was only half-conscious; find, perhaps, the revelation that would tell him what he needed to know of the growing threat he felt was about to engulf him both psychically and physically.

The sun rose, brightening the water with its pale light, and Count Brass heard a sound, turned, and saw his daughter Yisselda, golden-haired madonna of the lagoons, an almost preternatural figure in her flowing blue gown, riding bareback her white horned Kamarg horse and smiling mysteriously as if she, too, knew some secret that he could never fully comprehend.

Count Brass sought to avoid the girl by stepping out briskly along the shore, but already she was riding close to him and waving.

"Father — you're up early! Not for the first time recently."

Count Brass nodded, turned again to contemplate the waters and the reeds, looked up suddenly at the dancing birds as if to catch them by surprise, or by some instinctive flash of divination learn the secret of their strange, almost frenetic gyrations.

Yisselda had dismounted and now stood beside him. "They are not our flamingoes," she said. "And yet they're so like them. What do you see?"

Count Brass shrugged and smiled at her. "Nothing. Where's Hawkmoon?"

"At the castle. He's still asleep."

Count Brass grunted, clasping his great hands together as if in desperate prayer, listening to the beating of the heavy wings overhead. Then he relaxed and took her by the arm, guiding her along the bank of the lagoon.

"It's beautiful," she murmured. "The sunrise."

Count Brass made a small gesture of impatience, "You don't understand..." he began, and then paused. He knew that she would never see the landscape as he saw it. He had tried once to describe it to her, but she had lost interest quickly, had made no effort to understand the significance of the patterns he detected everywhere — in the water, the reeds, the trees, the animal life that filled this Kamarg in abundance, as it had filled the Kamarg that they had left.

To him it was the quintessence of order, but to her it was simply pleasurable to look at — something "beautiful", to admire, in fact, for its "wildness".

Only Bowgentle, the philosopher-poet, his old friend, had an inkling of what he meant and even then Bowgentle believed that it reflected not on the nature of the landscape but on the particular nature of Count Brass's mind.

"You're exhausted, disorientated," Bowgentle would say. "The ordering mechanism of the brain is working too hard, so you see a pattern to existence that, in fact, only stems from your own weariness and disturbance..."

Count Brass would dismiss this argument with a scowl, don his armour of brass and ride away on his own again, to the discomfort of his family and friends. He had spent a long while exploring this new Kamarg that was so much like his own save that there was no evidence of mankind's ever having existed here.

"He is a man of action, like myself," Dorian Hawkmoon, Yisselda's husband, would say. "His mind turns inward, I fear, for want of some real problem with which to engage itself."

"The real problems seem insoluble," Bowgentle would reply, and the conversation would end as Hawkmoon, too, went off by himself, his hand on the hilt of his sword.

There was tension in Castle Brass, and even in the village below, the folk were troubled, glad of their escape from the terror of the Dark Empire, but not sure that they were permanently settled in this new land so like the one they had left. At first, when they had arrived, the land had seemed a transformed version of Kamarg, its colours those of the rainbow, but gradually those colours had changed to more natural ones, as if their memories had imposed themselves on the landscape, so that now there was little difference. There were herds of horned horses and white bulls to tame, scarlet flamingoes that might be trained to bear riders, but at the back of the villagers' minds was always the threat of the Dark Empire somehow finding a way through even to this retreat.

To Hawkmoon and Count Brass — perhaps to D'Averc, Bowgentle and Oladahn, too — the idea was not so threatening. There were times when they would have welcomed an assault from the world they had left.

While Count Brass studied the landscape and sought to divine its secrets, Dorian Hawkmoon would ride at speed along the lagoon trails, scattering herds of bulls and horses, sending the flamingoes flapping into the sky, looking for an enemy.

One day, as he rode back on a steaming horse from one of his many journeys of exploration along the shores of the violet sea (sea and terrain seemed without limit), he saw the flamingoes wheeling in the sky, spiraling upwards on the air currents and then drifting down again. It was afternoon and the flamingo dance took place only at dawn. The giant birds seemed disturbed and Hawkmoon decided to investigate.

He spurred his horse along the winding path through the marsh until he was directly below the flamingoes, saw that they wheeled above a small island covered in tall reeds. He peered intently at the island and thought that he glimpsed something among the reeds, a flash of red that could be a man's coat.

At first Hawkmoon decided that it was probably a villager snaring duck, but then he realized that if that had been so the man would have hailed him — at least waved him away to ensure he would not disturb the fowl.

Puzzled, Hawkmoon spurred his horse into the water, swimming it across to the island and on to the marshy ground. The animal's powerful body pushed back the tough reeds as it moved and again Hawkmoon saw a flash of red, became convinced that he had seen a man.

"Ho!" he cried. "Who's there!"

He received no answer. Instead the reeds became more agitated as the man began to run through them without caution.

"Who are you?" Hawkmoon cried, and it came to him then that the Dark Empire had broken through at last, that there were men hidden everywhere in the reeds ready to attack Castle Brass.

He thundered through the reeds in pursuit of the red-jerkined man, saw him clearly now as he flung himself into the lagoon and began to swim for the bank.

"Stop!" Hawkmoon called, but the man swam on.

Hawkmoon's horse plunged again into the water and it foamed white. The man was already wading onto the opposite bank, glanced back to see that Hawkmoon was almost upon him, turned right round and drew a bright, slender sword of extraordinary length.

But it was not the sword that astonished Hawkmoon most — it was the impression that the man had no face! The whole of the head beneath the long, fair, dirty hair was blank. Hawkmoon gasped, drawing his own sword. Was it some alien inhabitant of this world?

Hawkmoon swung himself from his saddle, sword ready, as the horse clambered onto the bank, stood legs astraddle facing his strange antagonist,

HAWKMOON

laughed suddenly as he realized the truth. The man was wearing a mask of light leather. The mouth and eye slits were very thin and could not be distinguished at a distance.

"Why do you laugh?" the masked man asked in a braying voice, his sword on guard. "You should not laugh, my friend, for you are about to die."

"Who are you?" Hawkmoon asked. "I know you for a boaster only."

"I am a greater swordsman than you," replied the man. "You had best surrender now."

"I regret I can't accept your word on the quality of my swordsmanship or your own," Hawkmoon replied with a smile. "How is it that such a master of the blade is so poorly attired, for instance?"

With his sword he indicated the man's patched red jerkin, his trousers and boots of cracked leather. Even his bright sword had no scabbard, but had been drawn from a loop of cord attached to a rope belt on which also dangled a purse that bulged. On the man's fingers were rings of obvious glass and paste and the flesh of his skin looked grey and unhealthy. The body was tall but stringy, half-starved by the look of it.

"A beggar, I'd guess," mocked Hawkmoon. "Where did you steal the sword, beggar?"

He gasped as the man thrust suddenly, then withdrew. The movement had been incredibly rapid and Hawkmoon felt a sting on his cheek, put up his hand to his face and discovered that it bled.

"Shall I prick you thus to death?" sneered the stranger. "Put down your heavy sword and make yourself my prisoner."

Hawkmoon laughed with real pleasure. "Good! A worthy opponent after all. You do not know how much I welcome you, my friend. It has been too long since I heard the ring of steel in my ears!" And with that he lunged at the masked man.

His adversary deftly defended himself with a parry that somehow became a thrust which Hawkmoon barely managed to block in time. Feet planted firmly in the marshy ground, neither moved an inch from his position, both fought skillfully and unheatedly, each recognizing in the other a true master of the sword.

They fought for an hour, absolutely matched, neither giving nor sustaining a wound, and Hawkmoon decided on different tactics, began gradually to shift back down the bank towards the water.

Thinking that Hawkmoon was retreating, the masked man seemed to gain confidence and his sword moved even more rapidly than before so that Hawkmoon was forced to exert all his energy to deflect it.

Then Hawkmoon pretended to slip in the mud, going down on one knee. The other sprang forward to thrust and Hawkmoon's blade moved rapidly, the flat striking the man's wrist. He yelled and the sword fell from his hand. Quickly Hawkmoon jumped up and placed his boot upon the weapon, his blade at the other's throat.

"Not a trick worthy of a true swordsman," grumbled the masked man.

"I am easily bored," Hawkmoon replied. "I was becoming impatient with the game."

"Well, what now?"

"Your name?" Hawkmoon replied. "I'll know that first — then see your face — then know your business here — then, and perhaps most important, discover how you came here."

"My name you will know," said the man with undisguised pride. "It is Elvereza Tozer."

"I do know it, indeed!" remarked the Duke of Köln in some surprise.

T H R E E

E L V E R E Z A   T O Z E R

Elvereza Tozer was not the man Hawkmoon would have expected to meet if he had been told in advance that he was to encounter Granbretan's greatest playwright — a writer whose work was admired throughout Europe, even by those who in all other ways loathed Granbretan. The author of *King Staleen*, *The Tragedy of Katine and Carna*, *The Last of the Braldurs*, *Annala, Chirshil and Adulf*, *The Comedy of Steel* and many more, had not been heard of of late, but Hawkmoon had thought this due to the wars. He would have expected Tozer to have been rich in dress, confident in every way, poised and full of wit. Instead he found a man who seemed more at ease with a sword than with words, a vain man, something of a fool and a popinjay, dressed in rags.

As he propelled Tozer with his own sword along the marsh trails towards Castle Brass, Hawkmoon puzzled over this apparent paradox. Was the man lying? If so, why should he claim to be, of all things, an eminent playmaker?

Tozer walked along, apparently undisturbed by his change of fortune, whistling a jaunty tune.

Hawkmoon paused. "A moment," he said, and reached to grasp the reins of his horse, which had been following him. Tozer turned. He still wore his mask. Hawkmoon had been so astonished at hearing the name that he had forgotten to order Tozer to remove the leather from his face.

"Well," Tozer said, glancing about him. "It is a lovely country — though short in audiences, I would gather."

"Aye," replied Hawkmoon, nonplused. "Aye…" He gestured towards the horse. "We'll ride pillion, I think. Into the saddle with you, Master Tozer."

Tozer swung up onto the horse and Hawkmoon followed him, taking the reins and urging the horse into a canter.

In this manner they rode until they came to the gates of the town, passed through them, and proceeded slowly through the winding streets, up the steep road to the walls of Castle Brass.

Dismounting in the courtyard, Hawkmoon gave the horse to a groom and indicated the door to the main hall of the castle. "Through there, if you please," he told Tozer.

With a small shrug, Tozer sauntered through the door and bowed to the two men who stood there by the great fire which blazed in the hall. Hawkmoon nodded to them. "Good morning, Sir Bowgentle — D'Averc. I have a prisoner…"

"So I see," D'Averc said, his gaunt, handsome features brightening a little with interest. "Are the warriors of Granbretan at our gates again?"

"He is the only one, so far as I can judge," Hawkmoon replied. "He claims to be Elvereza Tozer…"

"Indeed?" The ascetic Bowgentle's quiet eyes took on a look of curiosity. "The author of *Chirshil and Adulf*? It is hard to believe."

Tozer's thin hand went to the mask and tugged at the thongs securing it. "I know you, sir," he said. "We met ten years hence when I came with my play to Malaga."

"I recall the time. We discussed some poems you had recently published and which I admired." Bowgentle shook his head. "You *are* Elvereza Tozer, but…"

The mask came loose and revealed an emaciated, shifty face sporting a wispy beard which did not hide a weak, receding chin and which was dominated by a long, thin nose. The flesh of the face was unhealthy and bore the marks of a pox.

"And I recall the face — though it was fuller then. Pray, what has happened to you, sir?" Bowgentle asked faintly. "Are you a refugee seeking escape from your countrymen?"

"Ah," Tozer sighed, darting Bowgentle a calculating look. "Perhaps. Would you have a glass of wine, sir? My encounter with your military friend here has left me thirsty, I fear."

"What?" put in D'Averc. "Have you been fighting?"

"Fighting to kill," Hawkmoon said grimly. "I feel that Master Tozer did not come to our Kamarg on an errand of good will. I found him skulking in the reeds to the south. I think he comes as a spy."

"And why should Elvereza Tozer, greatest playwright of the world, wish to *spy*?" The words were delivered by Tozer in a disdainful tone that yet somehow lacked conviction.

Bowgentle bit his lip and tugged a bell rope for a servant.

"That is for you to tell us, sir," Huillam D'Averc said with some amusement in his voice. He coughed ostentatiously. "Forgive me — a slight chill, I think. The castle is full of draughts…"

"And I'd wish the same for myself," Tozer said, "if a *draught* could be found."

He looked at them expectantly. "A draught to help us forget the draught, if you understand me. A draught…"

"Yes, yes," said Bowgentle hastily and turned to the servant who had entered. "A jug of wine for our guest," he requested. "And would you eat, Master Tozer?"

"'I would eat the bread of Babel and the meat of Marakhan…'" Tozer said dreamily. "'For all such fruits as fools supply are merely…'"

"We can offer some cheese at this hour," D'Averc interrupted sardonically.

"*Annala*, Act VI, Scene V," Tozer said. "You'll remember the scene?"

"I remember," D'Averc nodded. "I always felt that section somewhat weaker than the rest."

"Subtler," Tozer said airily. "Subtler."

The servant re-entered with the wine and Tozer helped himself, pouring a generous amount into the goblet. "The concerns of literature," he said, "are not always obvious to the common herd. A hundred years from now and people will see the last act of *Annala* not, as some stupid critics have said, as hastily written and poorly conceived, but as the complex structure it really is…"

"I had reckoned myself as something of a writer," Bowgentle said, "but I must confess, I did not see subtleties… Perhaps you could explain."

"Some other time," Tozer told him, with an insouciant wave of the hand. He drank off the wine and helped himself to another full goblet.

"In the meanwhile," Hawkmoon said firmly, "perhaps you could explain your presence in Kamarg. After all, we had thought ourselves inviolate and now…"

"You are still inviolate, never fear," Tozer said, "save to myself, of course. By the power of my brain I propelled myself hither."

D'Averc skeptically rubbed his chin. "By the power of your — *brain*? How so?"

"An ancient discipline taught me by a master philosopher who dwells in the hidden valleys of Yel…" Tozer belched and poured more wine.

"Yel is that south-western province of Granbretan is it not?" Bowgentle asked.

"Aye. A remote, barely inhabited land, peopled by a few dark-brown barbarians who live in holes in the ground. After my play *Chirshil and Adulf* had incurred the displeasure of certain elements at Court, I deemed it wise to retire there for a while, leaving my enemies to take for themselves all goods, monies, and mistresses I left behind. What know I of petty politics? How was I to realize that certain portions of the play seemed to reflect the intrigues then current at the Court?"

"So you were disgraced?" Hawkmoon said, looking narrowly at Tozer. The story could be part of the man's deception.

"More — I almost lost my life. But the rural existence near killed me as it was…"

"You met this philosopher who taught you how to travel through the dimensions? Then you came here seeking refuge?" Hawkmoon studied Tozer's reaction to these questions.

"No — ah, yes…" said the playwright. "That is to say, I did not know exactly where I was coming…"

"I think that you were sent here by the King-Emperor to destroy us," Hawkmoon said. "I think, Master Tozer, that you are lying to us."

"Lying? What is a lie? What is truth?" Tozer grinned glassily up at Hawkmoon and then hiccuped.

"Truth," Hawkmoon replied evenly, "is a coarse noose about your throat. I think we should hang you." He fingered the dull Black Jewel embedded in his forehead. "I am not unfamiliar with the tricks of the Dark Empire. I have been their victim too often to risk being deceived again." He looked at the others. "I say we should hang him now."

"But how do we know if he is really the only one who can reach us?" D'Averc asked sensibly. "We cannot be too hasty, Hawkmoon."

"I am the only one, I swear it!" Tozer spoke nervously now. "I admit, good sir, that I was commissioned to come here. It was that or lose my life in the prison catacombs of the Great Palace. When I had the old man's secret, I returned to Londra thinking that my power would enable me to bargain with those at Court who were displeased with me. I wished only to be returned to my former status and know that I had an audience to write for once again. However, when I told them of my new-found discipline, they instantly threatened my life unless I came here and destroyed that which enabled you to enter this dimension… so I came — glad, I must admit, to escape them. I was not particularly willing to risk my skin in offending you good folk but…"

"They did not ensure, in some way, that you would perform the task they set you?" Hawkmoon asked. "That is strange."

"To tell you the truth," Tozer said, downcast, "I do not think they altogether believed in my power. I think they merely wished to test that I had it. When I agreed to go and left instantly, they must have been shocked."

"Not like the Dark Empire lords to allow such an oversight," mused D'Averc, his aquiline face frowning. "Still, if you did not win our confidence, there's no reason you should have won theirs. Nonetheless, I am not altogether convinced that you speak the truth."

"You told them of this old man?" Bowgentle said. "They will be able to learn his secret for themselves!"

"Not so," Tozer said with a leer. "I told them I had struck upon the power myself, in my months of solitude."

"No wonder they did not take you seriously!" D'Averc smiled.

Tozer looked hurt and took another draught of wine.

"I find it difficult to believe that you were able to travel here by exercise of your will alone," Bowgentle admitted. "Are you sure you employed no other means…?"

"None."

"I like this not at all," Hawkmoon said darkly. "Even if he tells the truth, the Lords of Granbretan will wonder where he found his power by now, will learn all his movements, will almost certainly discover the old man — and then they will have the means to come through in strength and we shall be doomed!"

"Indeed, these are difficult times," Tozer said, filling his goblet yet again. "Remember your *King Staleen*, Act IV, Scene II — 'Wild days, wild riders, and the stink of warfare across the world!' Aha, I was a visionary and knew it not!" He was now evidently drunk.

Hawkmoon stared hard at the weak-chinned drunkard, still finding it almost impossible to believe that this was the great playwright Tozer.

"You wonder at my poverty, I see," Tozer said, speaking with slurred tongue. "The result of a couple of lines in *Chirshil and Adulf*, as I told you. Oh, the wickedness of fate! A couple of lines, penned in good faith, and here I am today, with the threat of a noose about my gullet. You remember the scene of course, and the speech? 'Court and king, alike corrupt…?' Act I, Scene I? Pity me, sir, and do not hang me. A great artist destroyed by his own mighty genius."

"This old man," Bowgentle said. "What was he like? Where exactly did he live?"

"The old man…" Tozer forced more wine down his throat. "The old man reminded me somewhat of Ioni in my *Comedy of Steel*. Act II, Scene VI…"

"What was he like?" Hawkmoon asked impatiently.

"'Machine-devoured, all his hours were given o'er to that insidious circuitry, and old grew he, unnoticing, in the service of his engines.' He lived only for his science, you see. He made the rings…" Tozer put his hand to his mouth.

"Rings? What rings?" D'Averc said swiftly.

"I feel that you must excuse me," Tozer said, rising in a parody of dignity, "for the wine has proved too rich for my empty stomach. Your pity, if you please…"

It was true that Tozer's face had taken on a greenish tinge.

"Very well," Bowgentle said wearily. "I will show you."

"Before he leaves," came a new voice from near the door, "ask him for the ring he wears on the middle finger of his left hand." The tone was slightly muffled, a little sardonic. Hawkmoon recognized it at once and turned.

Tozer gasped and clamped his hand over the ring.

"What do you know of this?" he said. "Who are you?"

"Duke Dorian here," said the figure with a gesture towards Hawkmoon, "calls me the Warrior in Jet and Gold."

Taller than any of them, covered all in armour and helm of black and gold, the mysterious warrior raised an arm and pointed a metal-clad finger at Tozer. "Hand him that ring."

"The ring is of glass, nothing more. It is of no value…"

D'Averc said. "He mentioned rings. Is the ring, then, what actually transported him here?"

Tozer still hesitated, his face stupid with drink and with anxiety. "I said that it was glass, of no value…"

"By the Runestaff, I command thee!" rumbled the warrior in a terrible voice.

With a little nervous movement, Elvereza Tozer drew off the ring and flung it onto the flagstones. D'Averc stooped and caught it up, inspecting it. "It's a crystal," he said, "not glass. A familiar kind of crystal, too…"

"It is of the same substance from which the device that brought you here was carved," the Warrior in Jet and Gold told him. He displayed his own gauntleted hand and there, on the middle finger, reposed an identical ring. "And it possesses the same properties — can transport a man through the dimensions."

"As I thought," Hawkmoon said. "It was no mental discipline that enabled you to come here, but a piece of crystal. Now I'll hang you assuredly! Where did you get the ring?"

"From the man — from Mygan of Llandar. I swear that is the truth. He has others — can make more!" Tozer cried. "Do not hang me, I pray you. I will tell you exactly where to find the old man."

"That we shall have to know," Bowgentle said thoughtfully, "for we shall have to get to him before the Dark Empire lords do. We must have him and his secrets — for our security."

"What? Must we journey to Granbretan?" D'Averc said in some astonishment.

"It would seem necessary," Hawkmoon told him.

F   O   U   R

F L A N A   M I K O S E V A A R

At the concert, Flana Mikosevaar, Countess of Kanbery, adjusted her mask of spun gold and glanced absently about her, seeing the rest of the audience only as a mass of gorgeous colours. The orchestra in the centre of the ballroom played a wild and complex melody, one of the later works of Granbretan's last great musician, Londen Johne, who had died two centuries earlier.

The countess's mask was that of an ornate heron, its eyes faceted with a thousand fragments of rare jewels. Her heavy gown was of luminous brocade that changed its many colours as the light varied. She was Asrovak Mikosevaar's widow, he who had died under Dorian Hawkmoon's blade at the first Battle of Kamarg. The Muskovian renegade, who had formed the Vulture Legion to fight on the European mainland and whose slogan had been *Death to Life*, was not mourned by Flana of Kanbery and she bore no grudge against his killer. He had been her twelfth husband, after all, and the fierce insanity of the bloodlover had served her pleasure long enough before he had set off to make war on Kamarg. Since then she had had several lovers and her memory of Asrovak Mikosevaar was as cloudy as all her other memories of men, for Flana was an inturned creature who barely distinguished between one person and another.

It was her habit, on the whole, to have husbands and lovers destroyed when they became inconvenient to her. An instinct, rather than any intellectual consideration, stopped her from murdering the more powerful ones. This was not to say that she was incapable of love, for she could love passionately, doting entirely on the object of her love, but she could not sustain the emotion for long. Hatred was unknown to her, as was loyalty. She was for the most part a neutral animal, reminding some of a cat and others of a spider — though in her grace and beauty she was more reminiscent of the former. And there were many who bore her hatred, who planned vengeance against her for a husband stolen or a brother poisoned, who would have taken that vengeance had she not been the Countess of Kanbery and cousin to the King-Emperor Huon, that immortal monarch who dwelt eternally in his womblike Throne Globe in the huge throne room of his palace. She was the centre of other attentions, also, since she was the only surviving kin of the monarch, and certain elements at Court considered that with Huon destroyed she could be made Queen-Empress and serve their interests.

Unaware of any plots concerning her, Flana of Kanbery would have been unperturbed had she been told of them, for she had not the faintest curiosity about the affairs of any one of her species, sought only to satisfy her own obscure desires, to ease the strange, melancholy longing in her soul which she could not define. Many had wondered about her, sought her favours with the sole object of unmasking her to see what they could learn in her face, but her face, fair-skinned, beautiful, the cheeks slightly flushed always, the eyes large and golden, held a look remote and mysterious, hiding far more than could any golden mask.

The music ceased, the audience moved, and the colours became alive as the fabrics swirled and masks turned, nodded, gestured. The delicate masks of the ladies could be seen gathering around the warlike helms of those recently returned captains of Granbretan's great armies. The countess rose but did not move towards them. Vaguely she recognized some of the helms — particularly that of Meliadus of the Wolf Order, who had been her husband five years earlier and who had divorced her (an action she had hardly noticed). There, too, was Shenegar Trott, lounging on heaped cushions, served by naked mainland slave-girls, his silver mask a parody of a human face. And she saw the mask of the Duke of Lakasdeh, Pra Flenn, barely eighteen and with ten great cities fallen to him, his helm a grinning dragon head. The others she thought she knew, and she understood that they were all the mightiest warlords, back to celebrate their victories, to divide up the conquered territories between them, to receive the congratulations of their emperor. They laughed considerably, stood proudly as the ladies flattered them, all but her ex-husband Meliadus, who appeared to avoid them and conferred instead with his brother-in-law Taragorm, Master of the Palace of Time, and the serpent-masked Baron Kalan of Vitall, Grand Constable of the Order of the Snake and chief scientist to the King-Emperor. Behind her mask, Flana frowned, remembering distantly that Meliadus normally avoided Taragorm...

F I V E

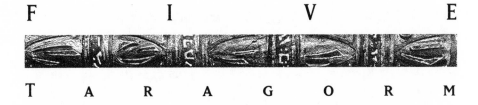

T A R A G O R M

"And how have you fared, Brother Taragorm?" asked Meliadus with forced cordiality.

The man who had married his sister replied shortly: "Well." He wondered why Meliadus should approach him thus when it was common knowledge that Meliadus was profoundly jealous of Taragorm's having won his sister's affections. The huge mask lifted a little superciliously. It was constructed of a monstrous clock of gilded and enameled brass, with numerals of inlaid mother-of-pearl and hands of filligreed silver, the box in which hung its pendulum extending to the upper part of Taragorm's broad chest. The box was of some transparent material, like glass of a bluish tint, and through it could be seen the golden pendulum swinging back and forth. The whole clock was balanced by means of a complex mechanism so as to adjust to Taragorm's every movement. It struck the hour, half-hour and quarter-hour and at midday and midnight chimed the first eight bars of Sheneven's *Temporal Antipathies*.

"And how," continued Meliadus in this same unusually ingratiating manner, "do the clocks of your palace fare? All the ticks ticking and the tocks tocking, mmm?"

It took Taragorm a moment to understand that his brother-in-law was, in fact, attempting to joke. He made no reply.

Meliadus cleared his throat.

Kalan of the serpent mask said: "I hear you are experimenting with some machine capable of traveling through time, Lord Taragorm. As it happens, I, too, have been experimenting — with an engine…"

"I wished to ask you, brother, about your experiments," Meliadus said to Taragorm. "How far advanced are they?"

"Reasonably advanced, brother."

"You have moved through time already?"

"Not personally."

"My engine," Baron Kalan continued implacably, "is capable of moving ships at enormous speeds across vast distances. Why, we could invade any land on the globe, no matter how far away…"

"When will the point be reached," Meliadus asked, moving closer to Taragorm, "when a man can journey into the past or future?"

Baron Kalan shrugged and turned away. "I must return to my laboratories," he said. "The King-Emperor has commissioned me urgently to complete my work. Good day, my lords."

"Good day," said Meliadus absently. "Now, brother, you must tell me more of your work — show me, perhaps, how far you have progressed."

"I must," Taragorm replied facetiously. "But my work is secret, brother. I cannot take you to the Palace of Time without the permission of King Huon. That you must seek first."

"Surely it is unnecessary for me to seek such permission?"

"None is so great that he can act without the blessing of our King-Emperor."

"But the matter is of extraordinary importance, brother," Meliadus said, his tone almost desperate, almost wheedling. "Our enemies have escaped us, probably to another era of the Earth. They offer a threat to Granbretan's security!"

"You speak of that handful of ruffians whom you failed to defeat at the Battle of Kamarg?"

"They were almost conquered — only science or sorcery saved them from our vengeance. No-one blames me for my failure…"

"Save yourself? You do not blame yourself?"

"No blame to me, at all, from any quarter. I would finish the matter, that's all. I would rid the Empire of her enemies. Where's the fault in that?"

"I have heard it whispered that your battle is more private than public, that you have made foolish compromises in order to pursue a personal vendetta against those who dwell in Kamarg."

"That is an opinion, brother," Meliadus said, restraining with difficulty his chagrin. "But I fear only for our Empire's well-being."

"Then tell King Huon of this fear and he may permit you to visit my palace." Taragorm turned away. As he did so, his mask began to boom out the hour. Further conversation was momentarily impossible. Meliadus made to follow him, then changed his mind, walking, fuming, from the hall.

Surrounded now by young lords, each seeking to attract her deadly attentions, Countess Flana Mikosevaar watched Baron Meliadus depart.

By the impatient manner of his gait, she assumed him to be in uneven temper. Then she forgot him as she returned her attention to the flatteries of her attendants, listening not to the words (which were familiar to her) but to the voices themselves which were like old, favourite instruments.

Taragorm, now, was conversing with Shenegar Trott.

"I am to present myself to the King-Emperor in the morning," Trott told the Master of the Palace of Time. "Some commission, I believe, that is at this moment a secret known only to himself. We must keep busy, Lord Taragorm, eh?"

"Indeed, we must, Count Shenegar, lest boredom engulfs us all."

S I X

T H E   A U D I E N C E

Next morning Meliadus waited impatiently outside the King-Emperor's throne room. He had requested an audience the previous evening and had been told to present himself at eleven o'clock. It was now twelve and the doors had not yet opened to admit him. The doors, towering into the dimness of the huge roof, were encrusted with jewels that made up a mosaic of images of ancient things. The fifty mantis-masked guards who blocked them stood stock still with flame-lances ready at a precise angle. Meliadus strode up and down before them; behind him, the glittering corridors of the King-Emperor's hallucinatory palace.

Meliadus attempted to fight back his feelings of resentment that the King-Emperor had not granted him an immediate audience. After all, was he not paramount Warlord of Europe? Had it not been under his direction that the armies of Granbretan had conquered a continent? Had he not taken those same armies into the Middle East and added further territories to the domain of the Dark Empire? Why should the King-Emperor seek to insult him in this manner? Meliadus, first of Granbretan's warriors, should have priority over all lesser mortals. He suspected a plot against him. From what Taragorm and the others had said, they judged him to be losing his grip. They were fools if they did not realize the threat that Hawkmoon, Count Brass and Huillam D'Averc offered. Let them escape their deserved reckoning and it would inflame others to rebel, make the work of conquest less speedy. Surely King Huon had not listened to those who spoke against him? The King-Emperor was wise, the King-Emperor was objective. If he were not, then he was unfit to rule...

Meliadus dismissed the thought in horror.

At last the jeweled doors began to move open until they were wide enough to admit a single man — and through this crack strode a jaunty, corpulent figure.

"Shenegar Trott!" exclaimed Meliadus. "Is it you who has kept me waiting so long?"

Trott's silver mask glinted in the light from the corridors. "My apologies, Baron Meliadus. My deep apologies. There were many details to discuss. But I am finished now. A mission, my dear baron — I have a mission! Such a mission, ha, ha!"

And before Meliadus could tax him further on the nature of his mission, he had swept away.

From within the throne room now issued a youthful, vibrant voice, the voice of the King-Emperor himself.

"You may join me now, Baron Meliadus."

The mantis warriors parted their ranks and allowed the baron to pass through them and into the throne room.

Into that gigantic hall of blazing colour, where hung the bright banners of Granbretan's five hundred noblest families, which was lined on either side by a thousand statue-still mantis guards, stepped Baron Meliadus of Kroiden and abased himself.

Ornate gallery upon ornate gallery stretched upwards and upwards to the concave ceiling of the hall. The armour of the soldiers of the Order of the Mantis shone black and green and gold, and in the distance, as he rose to his feet, Baron Meliadus saw his King-Emperor's Throne Globe, a white speck against the green and purple of the walls behind it.

Walking slowly, it took Meliadus twenty minutes to reach the globe and once again abase himself. The globe contained a sluggishly swirling liquid that was milk-white but which was sometimes streaked with iridescent veins of blood-red and blue. At the centre of this fluid was curled King Huon himself, a wrinkled, ancient, immortal foetuslike creature in which the only living things seemed the eyes, black, sharp and malicious.

"Baron Meliadus," came the golden voice that had been torn from the throat of a beautiful youth to furnish King Huon with speech.

"Great Majesty," murmured Meliadus. "I thank you for your graciousness in permitting this audience."

"And for what purpose did you desire the audience, Baron?" The tone was sardonic, a trifle impatient. "Do you seek to hear us praise again your efforts in Europe on our behalf?"

"The accomplishment is enough, noble sire. I seek to warn you that danger still threatens us in Europe…"

"What? You have not made the continent wholly ours?"

"You know that I have, Great Emperor, from one coast to the other, to the very borders of Muskovia and beyond. Few live who are not totally our slaves. But I refer to those who fled us…"

"Hawkmoon and his friends?"

"The same, Mighty King-Emperor."

"You chased them away. They offer us no threat."

"While they live, they threaten us, noble sire, for their escape could give others hope, and hope we must destroy in all we conquer lest we are troubled by risings against your discipline."

"You have dealt with risings before. You are used to them. We fear, Baron Meliadus, that you may be forsaking your King-Emperor's interests in favour of personal interests…"

"My personal interests are your interests, Great King-Emperor, your interests are my personal interests — they are indivisible. Am I not the most loyal of your servants?"

"Perhaps you believe yourself to be so, Baron Meliadus…"

"What do you mean, Powerful Monarch?"

"We mean that your obsession with the German Hawkmoon and that handful of villains he has as friends could not necessarily be in our interest. They will not return — and if they should dare return, why, we can deal with them then. We fear that it is vengeance alone which motivates you and that you have rationalized your thirst for vengeance into a belief that the whole Dark Empire is threatened by those you would be avenged upon."

"No! No, Prince of All! I swear that is not so!"

"Let them stay where they are, Meliadus. Deal with them only if they reappear."

"Great King, they offer a potential threat to the Empire. There are other powers involved who support them — else where could they have obtained the machine which plucked them away when we were about to destroy them? I cannot offer positive evidence now — but if you would let me work with Taragorm to use his knowledge to discover the whereabouts of Hawkmoon and his company — then I will find that evidence and you will believe me!"

"We are dubious, Meliadus!" There was a grim note now in the melodious voice. "But if it does not interfere with the other duties at Court we intend to give you, you may visit Lord Taragorm's palace and seek his assistance in your attempts to locate your enemies…"

"Our enemies, Prince of All…"

"We shall see, Baron, we shall see."

"I thank you for your faith in me, Great Majesty. I will —"

"The audience is not ended, Baron Meliadus, for we have not yet told you of those duties we mentioned."

"I shall be honoured to perform them, noble sire."

"You spoke of our security being in peril from Kamarg. Well, we believe that we may be threatened from other quarters. To be precise we are anxious that the East may promise us a fresh enemy that could be as powerful as the Dark Empire itself. Now, this could have something to do with your own suspicions concerning Hawkmoon and his supposed allies, for it is possible that we entertain representatives of those allies this day at our Court…"

"Great King-Emperor, if that be so…"

"Let us continue, Baron Meliadus!"

"I apologize, noble sire."

"Last night there appeared at the gates of Londra two strangers who claimed to be emissaries from the Empire of Asiacommunista. Their arrival was mysterious — indicating to us that they have methods of transport unknown to us, for they told us they had left their capital not two hours before. It is our opinion that they have come here, as we would visit others in whose territories we were interested, to spy out our strength. We, in turn, must try to gauge *their* power, for the time must come, even if it is not soon, when we shall be in conflict with them. Doubtless our conquests in the Near and Middle East have become known to them and they are nervous. We must discover all we can about them, try to convince them that we mean them no harm, try to persuade them to let us return emissaries to their domain. Should that prove possible, we should want you, Meliadus, to be one of those emissaries, for you have greater experience of such diplomacy than any other among our servants."

"This is disturbing news, Great Emperor."

"Aye, but we must take what advantage we can from the events. You will be their guide, treat them courteously, try to draw them out, make them expand upon the extent of their power and the size of their territories, the number of warriors their monarch commands, the power of their weaponry and the capabilities of their transports. This visit, Baron Meliadus, offers, as you can see, a much more important potential threat than any which may come from the vanished castle of Count Brass."

"Perhaps, noble sire…"

"No — *certainly*, Baron Meliadus!" The prehensile tongue flickered from the wrinkled mouth. "That is to be your most important task. If you have any time to spare, that can be devoted to your vendetta against Dorian Hawkmoon and the rest."

"But, Mighty King-Emperor…"

"Bide our instructions well, Meliadus. Do not disappoint us." The tone was one of menace. The tongue touched the tiny jewel that floated near the head and the globe began to dull until it had the appearance of a solid, black sphere.

Baron Meliadus could still not rid himself of the feeling that his King-Emperor had lost trust in him, that King Huon was deliberately finding means of curtailing his own schemes regarding the inhabitants of Castle Brass. True the king had made a convincing case for Meliadus's need to involve himself with the strange emissaries from Asiacommunista, had even flattered him by hinting that only Meliadus could deal with the problem, and would have the opportunity, later, of becoming not only the First Warrior of Europe, but also Paramount Warlord of Asiacommunista. But Meliadus's interest in Asiacommunista was not as great as his interest in Castle Brass — for he felt that there was evidence for believing Castle Brass to be a considerable threat to the Dark Empire, whereas his monarch had no evidence to suppose that Asiacommunista threatened them.

Clad in his finest mask and most sumptuous garments, Meliadus made his way through the shining corridors of the palace towards the hall where the previous day he had sought out his brother-in-law Taragorm. Now the hall was to be used for another reception — to welcome, with due ceremony, the visitors from the East.

As the King-Emperor's deputy, Baron Meliadus should have considered himself fully honoured, for it gave him prestige second only to King Huon's; but even this knowledge did not entirely ease his vengeful mind.

He entered the hall to the sound of fanfares from the galleries that ran around the walls. All the noblest of Granbretan were assembled here, their finery splendid and dazzling. The emissaries from Asiacommunista had not yet been announced. Baron Meliadus walked to the dais on which were placed three golden thrones, mounted the steps and seated himself on the throne in the middle. The sea of nobles bowed before him and the hall was silent in anticipation. Meliadus himself had not yet met the emissaries. Captain Viel Phong of the Order of the Mantis had been their escort up to now.

Meliadus looked about the hall, noting the presence of Taragorm, of Flana,

Countess of Kanbery, of Adaz Promp and Mygel Holst, of Jerek Nankenseen and Brenal Farnu. He was puzzled for a moment, wondering what was wrong. Then he realized that of all the great warrior nobles, only Shenegar Trott was missing. He remembered that the fat count had spoken of a mission. Had he left to fulfill it already? Why had not he, Meliadus, been informed of Trott's expedition? Were they keeping secrets from him? Had he truly lost the trust of his King-Emperor? His brain in turmoil, Meliadus turned as the fanfares sounded again and the doors of the hall opened to admit two incredibly garbed figures.

Automatically Meliadus rose to greet them, astonished at the sight of them, for they were barbaric and grotesque — giants of over seven feet high, walking stiffly like automatons. Were they, indeed, human? he wondered. It had not occurred to him that they would not be. Were these some monstrous creation of the Tragic Millennium? Were the folk of Asiacommunista not men at all?

Like the people of Granbretan, they wore masks (he assumed those constructions on their shoulders were masks) so that it was impossible to tell if human faces were within them. They were tall things, roughly oblong in shape, of brightly painted leather in blues, greens, yellows and reds, swirling patterns on which had been painted devil features — glaring eyes and teeth-filled mouths. Bulky fur cloaks hung to the ground and their clothes were leather, painted to travesty human limbs and organs, reminding Meliadus of the coloured sketches he had once seen in a medical text.

The herald announced them:

"The Lord Kominsar Kaow Shalang Gatt, Hereditary Representative of the President Emperor Jong Mang Shen of Asiacommunista and Prince Elect of the Hordes of the Sun."

The first of the emissaries stepped forward, his fur cloak drifting back to reveal shoulders that were at least four feet in width, the sleeves of his coat of bulky multicoloured silk, his right hand holding a staff of gem-encrusted gold that might have been the Runestaff itself, the care he took of it.

"The Lord Kominsar Orkai Heong Phoon, Hereditary Representative of the President Emperor Jong Mang Shen of Asiacommunista and Prince Elect of the Hordes of the Sun."

The second man (if man he was) stepped forward, similarly garbed but without a staff.

"I welcome the noble emissaries of the President Emperor Jong Mang Shen and let them know that all Granbretan is at their disposal to do with as they wish." Meliadus spread his arms wide.

The man with the staff paused before the dais and began to speak in a strange, lilting accent as if the language of Granbretan, and indeed all Europe and the Near East, was not native to him.

"We thank you most graciously for your welcome and would beg to know what mighty man addresses us."

"I am the Baron Meliadus of Kroiden, Grand Constable of the Order of the Wolf, Paramount Warlord of Europe, Deputy to the Immortal King-Emperor Huon the Eighteenth, Ruler of Granbretan, of Europe and all the Realms of the Middle Sea, Grand Constable of the Order of the Mantis, Controller of Destinies, Moulder of Histories, Feared and Powerful Prince of All. I greet you as he would greet you, speak as he would speak, act in accord with all his wishes, for you must know that, being immortal, he cannot leave the mystic Throne Globe which preserves him and which is protected by the Thousand who guard him night and day." Meliadus thought it best to dwell for a moment upon the invulnerability of the King-Emperor, to impress the visitors, should it have occurred to them, that an attempt on King Huon's life was impossible. Meliadus indicated the twin thrones on either side of him. "I ask you — be seated, be entertained."

The two grotesque creatures mounted the steps and, with some difficulty, placed themselves in the golden chairs. There would be no banquet, for the people of Granbretan regarded eating, on the whole, as a personal matter, for it could necessitate the removal of their masks and the horror of displaying their naked faces. Only thrice a year did they shed in public their masks and garments in the security of the Throne Room itself where they would indulge in a week-long orgy before the greedy eyes of King Huon, taking part in disgusting and bloody ceremonies with names existing only in the languages of their various Orders and which were never referred to save upon those three occasions.

Baron Meliadus clapped his hands for the entertainments to begin, the courtiers parted like a curtain and took their places on the two sides of the hall, then on came the acrobats and the tumblers, the Harlequins, Pierrots and Columbines, while wild music sounded from the gallery above. Human pyramids swayed, bent and suddenly collapsed to re-form again in even more complex assemblages, clowns capered and played upon one another the dangerous jokes that were expected of them, while the acrobats and tumblers cavorted around them at incredible speeds, walking on wires stretched between the galleries, performing on trapezes suspended high above all the heads of the audience.

Flana of Kanbery did not watch the tumblers and failed to see any humour in the actions of the clowns. Instead she turned her beautiful heron mask in the direction of the strangers and regarded them with what was for her unusual curiosity, thinking dimly that she would like to know them better, for they offered the possibility of a unique diversion, particularly if, as she suspected, they were not entirely manlike.

Meliadus, who could not rid himself of the suspicion that he was being prejudiced against by his king and plotted against by his fellow nobles, made a mighty attempt to be civil to the visitors. When he wished, he could impress strangers (as he had once impressed Count Brass) with his dignity, his wit and his manliness, but this night it was an effort and he feared that the effort could be detected in his tone.

"Do you find the entertainment to your liking, my lords of Asiacommunista?" he would say — and be met with a slight inclination of the huge heads. "Are the clowns not amusing?" — and there would be a movement of the hand from Kaow Shalang Gatt, who bore the golden staff — or: "Such skill! We brought those conjurers from our territories in Italia — and those tumblers were once the property of a duke of Krahkov — you must have entertainers of equal skill at your own emperor's court..." and the other, called Orkai Heong Phoon, would move his body in its seat, as if in discomfort. The result was to increase Baron Meliadus's sense of impatience, make him feel that these peculiar creatures somehow judged themselves above him or were bored by his attempts at civility, and it became more and more difficult for him to continue the light conversation that was the only conversation possible while the music played.

At length he rose and clapped his hands. "Enough of them. Dismiss these entertainers. Let us have more exotic sport." And he relaxed a trifle as the sexual gymnasts entered the hall and began to perform for the delight of the depraved appetites of the Dark Empire. He chuckled, recognizing some of the performers, pointing them out to his guests. "There's one who was a prince of Magyaria — and those two, the twins, were the sisters of a king in Turkia. I captured the blonde one there myself — and the stallion you see — in a Bulgarian stable. Many of them I personally trained." But though the entertainment relaxed the tortured nerves of Baron Meliadus of Kroiden, the emissaries of the President Emperor Jong Mang Shen seemed as unmoved and as taciturn as ever.

At last the performance was over and the entertainers retired (to the emissaries' relief, it seemed). Baron Meliadus, much refreshed, wondering if the creatures were of flesh and blood at all, gave the order for the ball to commence.

"Now gentlemen," said he rising, "shall we circulate about the floor so that you may meet those who have assembled to honour you and be honoured by you."

Moving stiffly, the emissaries of Asiacommunista followed Baron Meliadus, towering over the heads of even the tallest in the hall.

"Would you dance?" asked the baron.

"We do not dance, I regret," said Kaow Shalang Gatt tonelessly, and since etiquette demanded that the guests dance before the others could, no dancing was done. Meliadus fumed. What did King Huon expect of him? How could he deal with these automata?

"Do you not have dances in Asiacommunista?" he said, his voice trembling with suppressed anger.

"Not of the sort I suppose you to prefer," replied Orkai Heong Phoon, and though there was no inflection in his voice, again Baron Meliadus was given to think that such activities were beneath the dignity of the Asiacommunistan nobles. It was becoming, he thought grimly, exceedingly difficult to remain polite toward these proud strangers. Meliadus was not used to suppressing his feelings where mere foreigners were concerned and he promised himself the pleasure of dealing with these two in particular should he be given the privilege of leading any army that conquered the Far East.

Baron Meliadus paused before Adaz Promp who bowed to the two guests. "May I present one of our mightiest warlords, the Count Adaz Promp, Grand Constable of the Order of the Hound, Prince of Parye and Protector of Munchein, Commander of Ten Thousand." The ornate dog mask inclined itself again.

"Count Adaz led the force that helped us conquer all the European mainland in two years when we had allowed for twenty," Meliadus said. "His hounds are invincible."

"The baron flatters me," said Adaz Promp, "I am sure you have mightier legions in Asiacommunista, my lords."

"Perhaps, I do not know. Your army sounds as fierce as our dragon-hounds," Kaow Shalang Gatt said.

"Dragon-hounds? And what are they?" Meliadus enquired, remembering at last what his king had desired him to do.

"You have none in Granbretan?"

"Perhaps we call them by another name? Could you describe them?"

Kaow Shalang Gatt made a movement with his staff. "They are about twice the height of a man — one of our men — with seventy teeth that are like ivory razors. They are very hairy and have claws like a cat's. We use them to hunt those reptiles we have not yet trained for war."

"I see," Meliadus murmured, thinking that such warbeasts would require special tactics to defeat. "And how many such dragon-hounds have you trained for battle?"

"A good number," said his guest.

They moved on, meeting other nobles and their ladies, and each was prepared with a question such as Adaz Promp had asked, to give Meliadus the opportunity of extracting information from the emissaries. But it became plain that although they were willing to indicate that their forces and weaponry were mighty, they were too cautious to provide details as to numbers and capacity. Meliadus realized that it would take more than one evening to gather that sort of information, and he had the feeling that it would be hard to get it at all.

"Your science must be very sophisticated," he said as they moved through the throng. "More advanced than ours, perhaps?"

"Perhaps," said Orkai Heong Phoon, "but I know so little of your science. It would be interesting to compare such things."

"Indeed it would," agreed Meliadus. "I heard, for instance, that your flying machine brought you several thousand miles in a very short space of time."

"It was not a flying machine," said Orkai Heong Phoon.

"No? Then how…?"

"We call it an Earth Chariot — it moves through the ground…"

"And how is it propelled? What moves the earth away from it?"

"We are not scientists," put in Kaow Shalang Gatt. "We do not pretend to understand the workings of our machines. We leave such things to the lowlier castes."

Baron Meliadus, feeling slighted again, came to a halt before the beautiful heron mask of the Countess Flana Mikosevaar. He announced her and she curtsied.

"You are very tall," she said in her throaty murmur. "Yes, very tall."

Baron Meliadus attempted to move on, embarrassed by the countess as he had half-suspected he would be. He had only introduced her to fill the silence following the visitor's last remark. But Flana reached and touched Orkai Heong Phoon's shoulder. "And your shoulders are very broad," she said. The emissary made no reply, but stood stock still. Had she insulted him? Meliadus wondered. He would have felt some satisfaction if she had. He did not expect the Asiacommunistan to complain, for he realized it was as much in the man's interests to remain on good terms with Granbretan's nobles as it was in Granbretan's interests, at this stage, to remain on good terms with them. "May I entertain you in some way?" asked Flana, gesturing vaguely.

"Thank you, but I can think of nothing at this moment," said the man, and they moved on.

Astonished, Flana watched them continue their progress. She had never been rejected thus before and she was intrigued. She decided to explore these possibilities further, when she could find a suitable time. They were odd, these taciturn creatures, with their stiff movements. They were like men of metal, she thought. Could anything, she wondered, produce a human emotion in them?

Their great masks of painted leather swayed above the heads of the crowd as Meliadus introduced them to Jerek Nankenseen and his lady, the Duchess Falmoliva Nankenseen who, in her youth, had ridden to battle with her husband.

And when the tour was completed, Baron Meliadus returned to his golden throne wondering, with increased frustration, where his rival, Shenegar Trott, had disappeared to, and why King Huon should have deigned not to trust him with the information of Trott's movements. He wanted urgently to rid himself of his charges and hurry to Taragorm's laboratories to discover what progress the Master of the Palace of Time had made and whether there was any possibility of discovering the whereabouts in time or space of the hated Castle Brass.

E I G H T

MELIADUS AT THE PALACE OF TIME

Early next morning, after an unsatisfactory night in which he had given up sleep and failed to find pleasure, Baron Meliadus left to visit Taragorm at the Palace of Time.

In Londra there were few open streets. Houses, palaces, warehouses and barracks were all connected by enclosed passages which, in the richer sections of the city, were of bright colours as if the walls were made of enameled glass or, in the poorer sections, of oily, dark stone.

Meliadus was borne through these passages in a curtained litter by a dozen girl-slaves, all naked and with rouged bodies (the only kind of slaves Meliadus would have to serve him). His intention was to visit Taragorm before those boorish nobles of Asiacommunista were awake. It could be, of course, that they did represent a nation helping Hawkmoon and the rest, but he had no proof. If his hopes of Taragorm's discoveries were realized, he might gain that proof, present it to King Huon, vindicate himself and perhaps, too, rid himself of the troublesome task of playing host to the emissaries.

The passages widened and strange sounds began to be heard — dull booms and regular, mechanical noises. Meliadus knew that he heard Taragorm's clocks.

As he neared the entrance to the Palace of Time, the noise became deafening as a thousand gigantic pendulums swung at a thousand different rates, as machinery whirred and shifted, as jacks struck bells and gongs and cymbals, mechanical birds cried and mechanical voices spoke. It was an incredibly confusing din for, although the palace contained some several thousand clocks of differing sizes, it was itself a gigantic clock, the chief regulator for the rest, and above all the other sounds came the slow, ponderous, echoing clack of the massive escapement lever, far above near the roof, and the hissing of the monstrous pendulum as it swung through the air in the Hall of the Pendulum where Taragorm conducted most of his experiments.

Meliadus's litter arrived at last before a relatively small set of bronze doors and mechanical men sprang forward to block the way, a mechanical voice cutting through the din of the clocks to demand:

"Who visits Lord Taragorm at the Palace of Time?"

"Baron Meliadus, his brother-in-law, with the permission of the King-Emperor," replied the baron, forced to shout.

The doors remained closed for a good deal longer, Meliadus thought, than they should have done, then opened slowly to admit the litter.

Now they passed into a hall with curved walls of metal, like the base of a clock, and the noise increased. The hall was full of *ticks* and *clacks* and *whirrs* and *booms* and *thumps* and *swishes* and *clangs* and, had not the baron's head been encased in its wolf helm, he would have pressed his hands to his ears. As it was he began to be convinced that shortly he would become deaf.

They passed through this hall into another swathed in tapestries (inevitably representing in highly formalized design a hundred different time-keeping devices) which muffled the worst of the noise. Here the girl-slaves lowered the litter and Baron Meliadus pushed back the curtains with gauntleted hands and stood there to await the coming of his brother-in-law.

Again he felt he had to wait an unconscionable time before the man appeared, stepping sedately through the doors at the far end of the hall, his huge clock mask nodding.

"It is early, brother," said Taragorm. "I regret I kept you waiting, but I had not breakfasted."

Meliadus reflected that Taragorm had never had a decent regard for the niceties of etiquette, then he snapped: "My apologies, brother, but I was anxious to see your work."

"I am flattered. This way, brother."

Taragorm turned and left through the door he had entered, Meliadus close on his heels.

Through more tapestried passages they moved until at last Taragorm pressed his weight against the bar locking a huge door. The door opened and the air was suddenly full of the sound of a great wind; the noise of a gigantic drum sounding a painfully slow beat.

Automatically Meliadus looked up and saw the pendulum hurtling through the air above him — its bob fifty tons of brass fashioned in the form of an ornate, blazing sun, creating a draught that fluttered all the tapestries in the halls behind them and raised Meliadus's cloak like a pair of heavy silken wings. The pendulum supplied the wind and the hidden escapement lever, high above, supplied the sound like a drum. Across the vast Hall of the Pendulum was stretched an array of machines in various stages of construction, of benches containing laboratory equipment, of instruments of brass and bronze and silver, of clouds of fine golden wires, of webs of jeweled thread, of timekeeping instruments — water-clocks, pendulum movements, lever movements, ball movements, watches, chronometers, orreries, astrolabes, leaf-clocks, skeleton clocks, table clocks, sun dials — and working on all these were Taragorm's slaves, scientists and engineers captured from a score of nations, many of them the finest of their lands.

Even as Meliadus watched, there would come a flash of purple light from one part of the hall, a shower of green sparks from another, a gout of scarlet smoke from elsewhere. He saw a black machine crumble to dust and its attendant cough, tumble forward into the dust and vanish.

"And what was that?" came a laconic voice from nearby. Meliadus turned to see that Kalan of Vitall, Chief Scientist to the King-Emperor, was also visiting Taragorm.

"An experiment in accelerated time," said Taragorm. "We can create the process, but we cannot control it. Nothing, so far, has worked. See there…" he pointed to a large ovoid machine of yellow, glassy substance… "That creates the opposite effect and again, unfortunately, cannot be controlled as yet. The man you see beside it," he indicated what Meliadus had taken to be a lifelike statue (some mechanical figure from a clock being repaired), "has been frozen thus for weeks!"

"And what of traveling through time?" Meliadus said.

"Over there," Taragorm replied. "You see the set of silver boxes? Each of those houses an instrument we have created that can hurl an object through time, either back or forth — we are not sure for what distances. Living things, however, suffer much when undergoing the same journey. Few of the slaves or animals we have used have lived, and none have not suffered considerable agonies and deformities."

"If only we had believed Tozer," Kalan said, "perhaps then we might have discovered the secret of traveling through time. We should not have made such a joke of him — but, really, I could not believe that that scribbling buffoon had truly discovered the secret!"

"What's that? What?" Meliadus had heard nothing of Tozer. "Tozer the playwright. I thought him dead! What did he know of time travel?"

"He reappeared, trying to reinstate himself in the King-Emperor's graces with a story that he had learned how to journey through time from an old man in the West — a mental trick, he said. We brought him here, laughingly asked him to prove the truth of his words by traveling through time. Whereupon, Baron Meliadus, he vanished!"

"You — you made no effort to hold him?"

"It was impossible to believe him," Taragorm put in. "Would you have?"

"I would have been more careful in testing him."

"It was in his interest to return, we thought. Besides, brother, we were not clutching at straws."

"What do you mean by that — brother?" retorted Meliadus.

"I mean that we are working in the spirit of pure scientific research, whereas you require immediate results in order to continue your vendetta against Castle Brass."

"I, brother, am a warrior — a man of action. It does not suit me to sit about and play with toys or brood over books." Honour satisfied, Baron Meliadus returned his attention to the subject of Tozer.

"You say the playwright learned the secret from an old man in the West?"

"So he said," replied Kalan. "But I think he was lying. He told us it was a mental trick he had developed, but we did not think him capable of such discipline. Still, the fact remains, he faded and vanished before our eyes."

"Why was I not told of this?" Meliadus moaned in frustration.

"You were still on the mainland when it took place," Taragorm pointed out. "Besides, we did not think it was of interest to a man of action like yourself."

"But his knowledge could have clarified your work," Meliadus said. "You seem so casual about having lost the opportunity."

Taragorm shrugged. "What can we do about it now? We are progressing little by little..." somewhere there was a bang, a man screamed and a mauve and orange flash illuminated the room... "and we shall soon have tamed time as we are taming space."

"In a thousand years, perhaps!" snorted Meliadus. "The West — an old man in the West? We must locate him. What is his name?"

"Tozer told us only that he was called Mygan — a sorcerer of considerable wisdom. But, as I said, I believe he was lying. After all, what's in the West save desolation? Nothing has lived there but malformed creatures since the Tragic Millennium."

"We must go there," Meliadus said. "We must leave no stone unturned, no chance overlooked..."

"I'll not journey to those bleak mountains on a wild goose chase," said Kalan with a shudder. "I have my work to do here, fitting my new engines into ships enabling us to conquer the rest of the world as swiftly as we conquered Europe. Besides, I thought you, too, had responsibilities at home, Baron Meliadus — our visitors..."

"Damn the visitors. They cost me precious time."

"Soon I shall be able to offer you all the time you require, brother," Taragorm told him. "Give us a little while..."

"Bah! I can learn nothing here. Your crumbling boxes and exploding machines make spectacular sights, but they are useless to me. Play your games, brother, as you please. I'll bid you good morning!"

Feeling relieved that he no longer had to be polite to his hated brother-in-law, Meliadus turned and stalked out of the Hall of the Pendulum, through the tapestried corridors and halls, back to his litter.

He flung himself into it, grunted for the girls to bear him away.

As he was borne back to his own palace, Meliadus considered the new information.

At the first opportunity he would rid himself of his charges and journey to the West, to see if he could retrace Tozer's steps and discover the old man who held not only the secret of time, but also the means of his at last exacting his full vengeance upon Castle Brass.

N   I   N   E

INTERLUDE   AT   CASTLE   BRASS

At Castle Brass, in the courtyard, Count Brass and Oladahn of the Bulgar Mountains, straddled their horned horses and rode out, through the red-roofed town, and away to the fens, as was their habit now every morning.

Count Brass had lost some of his brooding manner and had begun to desire company again since the visit of the Warrior in Jet and Gold.

Elvereza Tozer was held captive in a suite of rooms in one of the towers and had seemed content when Bowgentle had given him supplies of paper, pens and ink and told him to earn his keep with a play, promising him an appreciative, if small audience.

"I wonder how Hawkmoon fares," he said, as they rode together in pleasurable companionship. "I regret that I did not draw the straw which would have enabled me to accompany him."

"I, too," said Oladahn. "D'Averc was lucky. A shame there were only two rings that could be used — Tozer's and the Warrior's. If they return with the rest, then we'll all be able to make war on the Dark Empire…"

"It was a dangerous idea, friend Oladahn, to suggest, as the Warrior suggested, they visit Granbretan itself and try to discover Mygan of Llandar in Yel."

"I have heard it said that it is often safer to dwell in the lion's lair than outside it," Oladahn said.

"Safer still to live in a land where there are no lions," Count Brass retorted with a quirk of his lips.

"Well, I hope the lion does not devour them, that is all, Count Brass," said Oladahn frowning. "It may be perverse of me, but I still envy him his opportunity."

"I have a feeling that we shall not long have to put up with this inaction," Count Brass said, guiding his horse along the narrow track between the reeds, "for it seems to me that our security is threatened from not one quarter but many…"

"It is not a possibility that worries *me* overmuch," said Oladahn, "but I fear for Yisselda, Bowgentle and the ordinary folk of the town, for they have no relish for the sort of activity we enjoy."

The two men rode on to the sea, enjoying the solitude and at the same time yearning for the din and the action of battle.

Count Brass began to wonder if it were not worth smashing the crystal device that was their security, plunging Castle Brass back into the world they had left, and making a fight of it, even though there was no chance of defeating the hordes of the Dark Empire.

T H E   S I G H T S   O F   L O N D R A

The ornithopter's wings thrashed at the air as the flying machine hovered over the spires of Londra.

It was a large machine, built to carry four or five people, and its metal bulk gleamed with scrollwork and baroque designs.

Meliadus bent his head over the side and pointed downward. His guests leaned forward also, barely polite. It seemed that their tall, heavy masks would fall from their shoulders if they leaned any further.

"There you see the palace of King Huon where you are staying," Meliadus said, indicating the crazy magnificence of his King-Emperor's domicile. It towered above all the other buildings and was set apart from them, in the very centre of the city. Unlike most other buildings, it could not be reached by a series of corridors. Its four towers, glowing with a light of deep gold, were even now above their heads, though they sat in the ornithopter, well above the tops of the other buildings. Its tiers were thick with bas-reliefs depicting all manner of dark activities beloved of the Empire. Gigantic and grotesque statues were placed on corners of parapets, seeming about to topple into the courtyards far, far below. The palace was blotched with every imaginable colour and all the colours clashed in such a way as to make the eye ache in a matter of seconds.

"The Palace of Time," said Meliadus, indicating the superbly ornamented palace that was also a giant clock, and then: "My own palace." This was brooding black, faced with silver. "The river you see is, of course, the River Tayme." The river was thick with traffic. Its blood-red waters bore barges of bronze, ebony and teak ships emblazoned with precious metal and semi-precious jewels, with huge white sails on which designs had been sewn or printed.

"Further to your left," said Baron Meliadus, deeply resenting this silly task, "is our Hanging Tower. You will see that it appears to hang from the sky and is not rooted upon the ground. This was the result of an experiment of one of our sorcerers who managed to raise the tower a few feet but could raise it no further.

Then, it appeared, he could not recall it to Earth — so it has remained thus ever since."

He showed them the quays where the great, garnet-burnished battleships of Granbretan dispensed their stolen goods; the Quarter of the Unmasked where lived the scum of the city; the dome of the huge theatre where once Tozer's plays had been performed; the Temple of the Wolf, headquarters of his own Order, with a monstrous and grotesque stone wolf head dominating the curve of the roof, and the various other temples with similarly grotesque beast heads carved in stone and weighing many tons.

For a dull day they flew over the city, stopping only to refuel the ornithopter and change pilots, with Meliadus growing hourly impatient. He showed them all the wonders that filled that ancient and unpleasant city, seeking, as his King-Emperor had demanded, to impress the visitors with the Dark Empire's might.

As evening came and the setting sun stained the city with unhealthy shades, Baron Meliadus sighed with relief and instructed the pilot to direct the ornithopter to the landing stage on the roof of the palace.

It landed with a great flurry of metal wings, a wheezing and a clattering and the two emissaries climbed stiffly out; like the machine, they remained semblances of natural life.

They walked to the hooded entrance of the palace and moved down the winding ramp until they were at last again in the corridors of shifting light, to be met by their guard of honour, six high-ranking warriors of the Order of the Mantis, their insect masks reflecting the brightness from the walls, who escorted them back to their own chambers where they would rest and eat.

Leaving them at the door of their apartments, Baron Meliadus bowed and hurried away, having promised that tomorrow they should discuss matters of science, and compare the progress of Asiacommunista with the achievements of Granbretan.

Flinging himself through the hallucinatory passages he almost bowled over the King-Emperor's relative, Flana, Countess of Kanbery.

"My lord!"

He paused, made to pass her, stopped. "My lady — my apologies."

"You are in a hurry, my lord!"

"I am, Flana."

"You are in uneven temper, it seems."

"My temper is poor."

"You would console yourself?"

"I have business to attend to..."

"Business should be conducted with a cool head, my lord."

"Perhaps."

"If you would cool your passion…"

He started to continue his progress, then stopped again. He had experienced Flana's methods of consolation before. Perhaps she was right. Perhaps he did need her. On the other hand he needed to make preparations for his expedition to the West as soon as the emissaries had departed. Still, they would be here for some days at least. Also, the previous night had proved unsatisfactory and his morale was low. At least he could prove himself a lover.

"Perhaps…" he said again, this time more thoughtfully.

"Then let us make haste to my apartments, my lord," said she with a trace of eagerness.

With mounting interest, Meliadus took her arm.

"Ah, Flana," he murmured. "Ah, Flana."

E L E V E N

THOUGHTS OF THE COUNTESS FLANA

Flana's motives in seeking the company of Meliadus had been mixed, for it was not the baron in whom she was chiefly interested, but in his charges, the two stiff-limbed giants from the East.

She asked him about them as they lay in their sweat in her enormous bed and he confided his frustrations, his hatred of his task and his hatred of the emissaries, told her of his real ambition, which was to avenge himself of his enemies, the slayers of her husband, the inhabitants of Castle Brass, told her of his discovery that Tozer had found an old man in the West, in the forgotten province of Yel, who might have the secret of reaching his foes.

And he murmured of his fears that he was losing his power, his prestige (though he knew he should not speak such secret thoughts to Flana of all women) and that the King-Emperor was these days trusting others, such as Shenegar Trott, with the knowledge that he once only gave to Meliadus.

"Oh, Flana," he said, shortly before he fell into a moody sleep, "if you were queen, together we could fulfill our Empire's mightiest destiny."

But Flana scarcely heard him, was scarcely thinking, merely lay there and moved her heavy body from time to time, for Meliadus had failed to ease the aching in her soul, had barely eased the craving in her loins, and her mind was on the emissaries who lay sleeping only two tiers above her head.

At length she rose from the bed, leaving Meliadus snoring and moaning in his sleep, and dressed herself again in gown and mask, and slipped from her room to glide along the corridors, up the ramps, until she came at last to the doors that were guarded by the Mantis warriors. The insect masks turned questioningly.

"You know who I am," said she.

They did know and they withdrew from the doors. She chose one and pressed it open, entering the exciting darkness of the emissaries' apartments.

T W E L V E

A R E V E L A T I O N

Moonlight alone illuminated the room, falling on a bed in which a figure stirred, showing her the discarded ornaments, armour and mask of the man who lay there.

She moved closer.

"My lord?" she whispered.

Suddenly the figure shot up in the bed and she saw his startled face, saw his hands fly up to cover his features, and she gasped in recognition.

"I know you!"

"Who are you?" He leapt from beneath the silken sheets, naked in the moonlight, ran forward to seize her. "A woman!"

"Aye…" purred she. "And you are a man." She laughed softly. "Not a giant at all, though of goodly height. Your mask and armour made you seem more than a foot taller."

"What do you want?"

"I sought to entertain you, sir — and be entertained. But I am disappointed, for I believed you to be other than human. Now I know you to be the man I saw in the throne room two years ago — the man Meliadus brought before the King-Emperor."

"So you were there that day." His grip tightened on her and his hand rose to yank off her mask and cover her mouth. She nibbled the fingers; stroked the muscles of the other arm. The hand on her mouth relaxed.

"Who are you?" he whispered. "Do others know?"

"I am Flana Mikosevaar, Countess of Kanbery. None suspects you, daring German. And I will not call in the guards, if that is what you expect, for I have no interest in politics and no sympathy with Meliadus. Indeed, I am grateful to you, for you rid me of troublesome spouse."

"You are Mikosevaar's widow?"

"I am. And you I knew immediately by the Black Jewel in your forehead which you sought to hide when I entered. You are Duke Dorian Hawkmoon von Köln, here in disguise, no doubt, to learn the secrets of your enemies."

"I believe I shall have to kill you, madam."

"I have no intention of betraying you, Duke Dorian. At least, not at once. I came to offer myself for your pleasure, that is all. You have rid me of my mask." She turned her golden eyes upward to regard his handsome face. "Now you may rid me of the rest of my garb…"

"Madam," he said hoarsely. "I cannot. I am married."

She laughed. "As am I — I have been married countless times."

There was sweat on his forehead as he returned her gaze and his muscles tensed. "Madam — I — I cannot…"

There was a sound and they both turned.

The door separating the apartments opened and there stood a gaunt, good-looking man who coughed a little ostentatiously and then bowed. He, too, was completely naked.

"My friend, madam," said Huillam D'Averc, "is of a somewhat rigid moral disposition. However, if I can assist…"

She moved toward him, looking him up and down. "You seem a healthy fellow," she said.

He turned his eyes away. "Ah, madam, it is kind of you to say so. But I am not, not a well man. On the other hand," he reached out and took her shoulder, guiding her into his chamber, "I will do what little I can to please you before this failing heart gives up on me…"

The door closed, leaving Hawkmoon trembling.

He sat on the edge of his bed, cursing himself for not having slept in his cumbersome disguise, but the exhausting tour of the day had made him dispense with caution of that kind. When the Warrior in Jet and Gold had put the plan to them, it had seemed unnecessarily dangerous. The logic had been sound enough — they must discover if the old man from Yel had been found before they went off searching for him in western Granbretan. But now it seemed their chances of getting such information were dashed.

The guards must have seen the countess enter. Even if they killed her or imprisoned her, the guards would suspect something. They were in a city that was, to a man, totally dedicated to their destruction. They had no allies and there was no possible hope of escape once their real identities became known.

Hawkmoon racked his brains for a plan that would at least enable them to flee the city before it became alerted, but all seemed hopeless.

Hawkmoon began to pile on his heavy robes and armour. The only weapon he had was the golden baton which the warrior had given him. He hefted it, wishing he had a sword or some other power over his crystal ring.

Pacing the room, he continued to try to think of a feasible plan of escape, but nothing came.

He was still pacing when morning came and Huillam D'Averc put his head through the door and grinned. "Good morning, Hawkmoon. Have you had no rest, man? I sympathize. Neither have I. The countess is a demanding creature. However I am glad to see you ready for a journey. We must hurry."

"What do you mean, D'Averc? I have tried all night to conceive a plan, but I can think of nothing…"

"I have been questioning Flana of Kanbery and she has told me everything we need to know, for Meliadus, apparently, has confided much in her. She has also agreed to help us escape."

"How?"

"Her private ornithopter. It is ours for the taking."

"Can you trust her?"

"We must. Listen — Meliadus has not yet had time to seek out Mygan of Llandar. By good fortune, it was our arrival kept him here. But he knows of him — knows, at least, that Tozer learned his secret from an old man in the West — and means to find him. We have the chance to find Mygan first. We can go part of the way by Flana's ornithopter which I shall attempt to fly and continue the rest of the journey on foot."

"But we are weaponless — without proper clothes!"

"Weapons and clothes I can obtain from Flana — masks also. She has a thousand trophies of past conquests in her chambers."

"We must go to her chambers now!"

"No. We must wait for her to return here."

"Why?"

"Because, my friend, Meliadus may still be sleeping in her apartments. Have patience. We are in luck. Pray that it will hold!"

Not much later Flana returned, took off her mask and kissed D'Averc almost hesitantly, as a young girl might kiss a lover. Her features seemed softer and her eyes less haunted, as if she had found some quality in D'Averc's lovemaking that she had not experienced before — possibly gentleness, which was not a quality of the men of Granbretan.

"He is gone," she said. "And I have half a mind, Huillam, to keep you here, for myself. For many years I have contained a need which I could not express, never satisfy. You have come close to satisfying it…"

He bent and kissed her lightly on the lips and his voice seemed sincere when he said: "And you, too, Flana, have given me something…" He straightened stiffly, having donned his heavy, built-up garments. He placed his tall mask upon his head. "Come, we must hurry, before the palace wakes."

Hawkmoon followed D'Averc's example, donning his own helmet, and once again the two resembled strange, half-human creatures, the emissaries from Asiacommunista.

Now Flana led them from the apartments, past the Mantis guards, who fell in behind them, and through the twisting, shining corridors until her own apartments were reached. They ordered the guards to remain outside.

"They will report that they followed us here," D'Averc said. "You will be suspected, Flana!"

She doffed her heron mask and smiled. "No," she said and crossed the deep carpet to a polished chest set with diamonds. She raised the lid and took out a long pipe, at the end of which was a soft bulb. "This bulb contains a poison spray," she said. "Once inhaled, the poison turns the victim mad so that he runs wild and berserk before dying. The guards will run through many corridors before they perish. I have used it before. It always works."

She spoke so sweetly of murder that Hawkmoon was forced to shudder.

"All I need do, you see," she continued, "is to push the hollow rod through the keyhole and squeeze the bulb."

She placed the apparatus on the lid of the chest and led them through several splendid, eccentrically furnished rooms, until they came to a chamber with a huge window that looked out onto a broad balcony. There on the balcony, its wings neatly folded, fashioned to resemble a beautiful scarlet and silver heron, was Flana's ornithopter.

She hurried to another part of the room and drew back a curtain. There, in a great pile, was her booty — clothes, masks and weapons of all her departed lovers and husbands.

"Take what you need," she murmured, "and hurry."

Hawkmoon selected a doublet of blue velvet, hose of black doe-skin, a sword-belt of brocaded leather which held a long, beautifully balanced blade and a poignard. For his mask he took one of his slain enemy's — Asrovak Mikosevaar's — glowering vulture masks.

D'Averc dressed himself in a suit of deep yellow with a cloak of lustrous blue, boots of deerhide and a blade similar to Hawkmoon's. He, too, took a vulture mask, reasoning that two of the same Order would be likely to be traveling together. Now they looked fully great nobles of Granbretan.

Flana opened the window and they stepped out into the cold, foggy morning.

"Farewell," whispered Flana. "I must get back to the guards. Farewell, Huillam D'Averc. I hope we shall meet again."

"I hope so, also, Flana," replied D'Averc with unusual gentleness of tone. "Farewell."

He climbed into the cockpit of the ornithopter and started the motor. Hawkmoon hastily got in behind him.

The thing's wings began to beat at the air and with a clatter of metal it rose into the gloomy sky of Londra, turning west.

Many emotions conflicted in Baron Meliadus as he entered the throne room of his King-Emperor, abased himself and began the long trudge toward the Throne Globe.

The white fluid of the globe surged more agitatedly than usual, alarming the baron. He was at once furious that the emissaries had disappeared, nervous of his monarch's wrath, anxious to pursue his quest for the old man who could give him the means of reaching Castle Brass. Also he feared lest he lose his power and his pride and (the king had been known to do it before) be banished to the Quarter of the Unmasked. His nervous fingers brushed his wolf helm and his step faltered as he neared the Throne Globe and looked anxiously up at the foetuslike shape of his monarch.

"Great King-Emperor. It is your servant Meliadus."

He fell to his knees and bowed to the ground.

"Servant? You have not served us very well, Meliadus!"

"I am sorry, Noble Majesty, but…"

"But?"

"But I could have no knowledge that they planned to leave last night, returning by the means with which they came…"

"It should have been your business to sense their plans, Meliadus."

"Sense? *Sense* their plans, Mighty Monarch…?"

"Your instinct is failing you, Meliadus. Once it was exact — you acted according to its dictates. Now your silly plans for vengeance fill your brain and being and make you blind to all else. Meliadus, those emissaries slew six of my best guards. How they killed them, I know not — perhaps a mental spell of some kind — but kill them they did, somehow leaving the palace and returning to whatever machine brought them here. They have discovered much about us — and we, Meliadus, have discovered virtually nothing about them."

"We know a little of their military equipment…"

"Do we? Men can lie, you know, Meliadus. We are displeased with you. We charged you to perform a duty and you performed it only partially and without your full attention. You spent time at Taragorm's palace, left the emissaries to their own devices when you should have been entertaining them. You are a fool, Meliadus. A fool!"

"Sire, I —"

"It is your stupid obsession with that handful of outlaws who dwell in Castle Brass. Is it the girl you desire? Is that why you seek them with such single-mindedness?"

"I fear they threaten the Empire, noble sire…"

"So does Asiacommunista threaten our Empire, Baron Meliadus — with real swords and real armies and real ships that can travel through the earth. Baron, you must forget your vendetta against Castle Brass or, we warn you, you had best be wary of our displeasure."

"But, sire…"

"We have warned you, Baron Meliadus. Put Castle Brass from your mind. Instead, try to learn all you can of the emissaries, discover where their machine met them, how they managed to leave the city. Redeem yourself in our eyes, Baron Meliadus — restore yourself to your old prestige…"

"Aye, sire," Baron Meliadus said through gritted teeth, controlling his anger and chagrin.

"The audience is at an end, Meliadus."

"Thank you," said Meliadus, blood pounding in his head, "sire."

He backed away from the Throne Globe.

He turned on his heel and began to pace the long hall.

He reached the jeweled doors, pushed past the guards and strode down the gleaming corridors of shifting light.

On he marched, and on, his pace rapid and his movements stiff, his hand white on the hilt of his sword which it gripped tightly.

He paced until he had reached the great reception hall of the palace where waited the nobles craving audience with the King-Emperor, descended the steps that led to the gates opening on the outer worlds, signed for his girls to come forward with his litter, clambered into it and, dumping himself heavily on its cushions, allowed himself to be borne back to his black and silver palace.

Now he hated his King-Emperor. Now he loathed the creature who had humiliated him so, thwarted him so, insulted him so. King Huon was a fool not to realize the potential danger offered by Castle Brass. Such a fool was not fit to reign, not fit to command slaves, let alone Baron Meliadus, Grand Constable of the Order of the Wolf.

Meliadus would not listen to King Huon's stupid orders, would do what he thought best and, if the King-Emperor objected, then he would defy him.

A little later, Meliadus left his palace on horseback. He rode at the head of twenty men. Twenty hand-picked men whom he could trust to follow him anywhere — even to Yel.

T H I R T E E N

K I N G   H U O N ' S   D I S P L E A S U R E

The Countess Flana's ornithopter dropped closer and closer to the ground, its belly brushing the tops of tall pines, its wings narrowly missing becoming entangled with the branches of birches, until at last it landed on the wiry heather beyond the forest.

The day was cold and a sharp wind whistled across the heath, biting through their flimsy costumes.

Shivering, they clambered from the flying machine and looked warily about them. No-one was in sight.

D'Averc reached into his jerkin and produced a scrap of thin leather on which a map was scrawled.

He pointed. "We go in that direction. Now we must get the ornithopter into the woods and hide it."

"Why cannot we leave it? The chances of anyone finding it for a day or so are slim," Hawkmoon said.

But D'Averc spoke seriously. "I do not wish any harm to come to Countess Flana, Hawkmoon. If the machine were discovered, it could be ill for her. Come."

And so they tugged and shoved at the metal machine until it was in the pinewood and thickly covered with brush. It had borne them as far as it could until its fuel gave out. They had not expected it to carry them the whole way to Yel.

Now they must continue on foot.

For four days they walked through woods and across heaths, the terrain gradually becoming less and less fertile as they neared the borders of Yel.

Then one day Hawkmoon paused and pointed. "Look, D'Averc — the Mountains of Yel."

And there they were in the distance, their purple peaks in cloud, the plain and the foothills beneath them all tawny yellow rock.

It was a wild, beautiful landscape, such as Hawkmoon had never seen before.

He gasped. "So there are some sights in Granbretan not entirely offensive to the eye, D'Averc."

"Aye, it is pretty," D'Averc agreed. "But daunting also. We have to find Mygan there somewhere. Judging by the map, Llandar is still many miles into those mountains."

"Then let us press on." Hawkmoon adjusted his sword belt. "We had a small advantage over Meliadus to begin with, but it is possible that even now he is on his way to Yel in hot quest of Mygan."

D'Averc stood on one leg and ruefully rubbed his foot. "True, but I fear these boots will not last the distance. I picked them from pride, for their prettiness, not for their sturdiness. I am learning my mistake."

Hawkmoon clapped him on the shoulder. "I've heard wild ponies roam these parts. Pray we find a couple we can tame."

But no wild ponies could be found and the yellow ground was hard and rocky and the sky above became full of a livid radiance. Hawkmoon and D'Averc began to realize why the folk of Granbretan were so superstitious of this region, for there did seem to be something unnatural about both land and sky.

At last the mountains were entered.

Seen close to, these were also of a yellowish colour, though with streaks of dark red and green, all glassy and grim. Strange-looking beasts skittered away from their path as they clambered on over jagged rocks and peculiar man-like creatures, with hairy bodies topped by completely hairless heads, measuring less than a foot high, regarded them from cover.

"They were once men, those creatures," D'Averc said. "Their ancestors dwelt in these parts. But the Tragic Millennium did its work here well."

"How do you know this?" Hawkmoon asked him.

"I have read my books. It was in Yel, worse than any other part of Granbretan, that the Tragic Millennium's effects were felt. That is why it is so desolate, for people will not come here any longer."

"Save Tozer — and the old man, Mygan of Llandar."

"Aye — if Tozer spoke the truth. We could still be on a wild goose chase, Hawkmoon."

"But Meliadus had the same story."

"Perhaps Tozer is merely a consistent liar?"

It was close to nightfall when the mountain creatures came scuttling from their caves high above and attacked Hawkmoon and D'Averc.

They were covered in oily fur, with the beaks of birds and the claws of cats, huge eyes blazing, beaks parting to reveal teeth, emitting a horrible hissing sound. There were three females and about six males as far as they could tell in the semi-darkness.

Hawkmoon drew his sword, adjusting his vulture mask as he would adjust an ordinary helm, and set his back to a wall of rock.

D'Averc took up a position beside him. Then the beasts were on them.

Hawkmoon slashed at the first, carving a long, bloody scar across its chest. It recoiled with a shriek.

A second was taken by D'Averc, stabbed through the heart. Hawkmoon neatly slit the throat of a third, but a fourth's claws were gripping his left arm. He struggled, muscles straining as he tried to turn his dagger upward to stab the creature's wrist. Meanwhile he slashed at one trying to take him from the other side.

Hawkmoon coughed and felt nauseous, for the beasts stank horribly. He at last wrenched his hand round and dug the point of his dagger into its forearm. It grunted and let go.

Instantly Hawkmoon drove the blade of the dagger deep into one staring eye and left the weapon there as he turned to deal with the next creature.

It was dark now and hard to make out how many of the beasts were left. D'Averc was holding his own, shouting filthy insults at the creatures as his blade moved rapidly this way and that.

F O U R T E E N

T H E   W A S T E S   O F   Y E L

Hawkmoon's foot slipped on blood and he staggered, catching the small of his back on a spur of rock. With a hiss another beaked beast was on him, clutching him in a bearlike grip, pinning both arms to his sides, the beak snapping at his face and closing with a snap on the vulture visor.

Hawkmoon sweated to break the grip, tore his head from the mask, leaving it in the creature's beak, wrenched the thing's arms apart and punched it heavily in the chest. It staggered in surprise, not realizing that the vulture mask had not been part of Hawkmoon's body.

Quickly Hawkmoon drove his sword into its heart and turned to assist D'Averc, who had two of the things on him.

Hawkmoon lopped one's head completely from its shoulders and was about to attack the next when it released D'Averc and screamed, rushing off into the night, clutching part of his jerkin.

They had accounted for all but one of their disgusting attackers.

D'Averc was panting, wounded slightly in the chest where the claws had ripped his jerkin away. Hawkmoon ripped up a piece of his cloak and padded the wound.

"No great harm done," said D'Averc. He yanked off his battered vulture mask and flung it away. "Those came in useful, but I'll wear mine no longer since I see you've discarded yours. That jewel in your forehead is unmistakable, so there's no point in my continuing to disguise myself!" He grinned. "I told you the Tragic Millennium had produced some ugly creatures, friend Hawkmoon."

"I believe you," smiled Hawkmoon. "Come, we had best find a place to camp for the night. Tozer marked a safe resting spot on his map. Bring it out into the starlight so we can read it."

D'Averc reached into his jerkin and then his jaw dropped in horror. "Oh, Hawkmoon! We are not so lucky!"

"Why so, my friend?"

"That section of my jerkin the creature carried off contained the pocket in which I had the map supplied by Tozer. We are lost, Hawkmoon!"

Hawkmoon cursed, sheathed his sword and frowned.

"There's nothing for it," he said. "We must trail the beast. It was slightly wounded and might have left a trail of blood. Perhaps it has dropped the map on its way back to its lair. Failing that we shall have to follow it all the way to where it lives and find a means of getting back our map when we arrive!"

D'Averc frowned. "Is it worth it? Can we not remember where we are bound?"

"Not well enough. Come, D'Averc."

Hawkmoon began to clamber over the sharp rocks in the direction in which the creature had disappeared and D'Averc came reluctantly after him.

Luckily the sky was clear and the moon bright and Hawkmoon at last saw some gleaming patches on the rocks that must have been blood. A bit further on he saw more patches.

"This way, D'Averc," he called.

His friend sighed, shrugged and followed.

The search went on until dawn, when Hawkmoon lost the trail and shook his head. They were high up on a mountain slope, with a good view of two valleys below them. He ran his hand through his blond hair and he sighed.

"No sign of the thing. And yet I was sure…"

"Now we are worse off," D'Averc said absently, rubbing his weary eyes. "No map — and no longer, even, on our original trail…"

"I am sorry, D'Averc. I thought it the best plan." Hawkmoon's shoulders sagged. Then suddenly he brightened and pointed.

"There! I saw something moving. Come on." And he was sprinting along the shelf of rock to disappear from D'Averc's sight.

D'Averc heard a shout of surprise and then a sudden silence.

The Frenchman drew his sword and followed after his friend, wondering what he had met with.

Then he saw the source of Hawkmoon's amazement. There, far below in a valley, was a city all made of metal, with shiny surfaces of red, gold, orange, blue and green, with curving metal roadways and sharp metal towers. It was plain to see, even from here, that the city was deserted and falling to pieces, with rusting walls and adornments.

Hawkmoon stood looking down at it. He pointed. There was their remaining antagonist of the night before, sliding down the rocky sides of the mountain toward the city.

"That must be where he lives," Hawkmoon said.

"I like not to follow him down there," D'Averc murmured. "There could be poison air — the air that makes your flesh crumple from your face, that causes vomiting and death…"

"The poison air does not exist any more, D'Averc, and you know it. It only lasts for a while and then disappears. Surely there has been no poison air here for centuries." He began to clamber down the mountain in pursuit of his foe who still clutched the piece of jerkin containing Tozer's map.

"Oh, very well," groaned D'Averc. "Let's seek death together!" And once again he began to follow in his friend's wake. "You are a wild, impatient gentleman, Duke von Köln!"

While loose stones rattled down and made the creature they pursued run all the faster towards the city, Hawkmoon and D'Averc gave chase as best they could, for they were unused to mountainous terrain and D'Averc's boots were almost in shreds.

They saw the beast enter the shadows of the metal city and disappear.

A few moments later they, too, had reached the city and looked up, in some trepidation, at the huge metal structures that loomed into the sky, creating menacing shadows below.

Hawkmoon noticed some more bloodstains and threaded his way between the struts and pylons of the city, peering with difficulty in the murky light.

And then suddenly there was a clicking sound, a hissing sound, a peculiar kind of subdued growl —

— and the creature was upon him, its claws about his throat, digging deeper and deeper. He felt one pierce, then another. He whipped up his own hands and tried to prise the clawed fingers away, felt the beak snap at the back of his neck.

Then there was a wild shriek and a yell and the claws released his throat.

Hawkmoon staggered round to see D'Averc, sword in hand, looking down at the body of the beaked beast.

"The disgusting creature had no brains," said D'Averc lightly. "What a fool it was to attack you and leave me free to slay it from behind." He extended his arm and delicately skewered the missing piece of cloth that had fallen from the dead thing's claw. "Here's our map, as good as ever!"

Hawkmoon wiped blood from his throat. The claws had not pierced too deeply. "The poor thing," he said.

"No softness now, Hawkmoon! You know how it alarms me to hear you speaking thus. Remember the creatures attacked us."

"I wonder why. There should be no shortage of their natural prey in these mountains — there are all kinds of edible creatures. Why feast on us?"

"Either we were the nearest meat they saw," D'Averc suggested, looking about him at the lattice of metal everywhere, "or else they have learned to hate men."

D'Averc re-sheathed his sword with a flourish and began to make his way through the forest of metal struts that supported the towers and streets of the city above them. Refuse lay everywhere and there were bits of dead animals, offal; rotting, unidentifiable stuff.

"Let's explore this city while we're here," D'Averc said, climbing up one girder. "We could sleep in it."

Hawkmoon consulted the map. "It's marked," he said. "Halapandur's its name. Not too far to the east of where our mysterious philosopher has his cavern."

"How far?"

"About a day's march in these mountains."

"Let's rest and press on tomorrow," D'Averc suggested.

Hawkmoon frowned for a moment. Then he shrugged. "Very well." He, too, began to clamber up through the girders until they reached one of the strange, curving metal streets.

"We'll strike out for yonder tower," suggested D'Averc.

They began to walk along the gently sloping ramp towards a tower that gleamed turquoise and sultry scarlet in the sunshine.

F I F T E E N

T H E   D E S E R T E D   C A V E R N

At the base of the tower was a small door that had been driven inwards as if by the punching of a giant fist. Clambering through the aperture, Hawkmoon and D'Averc tried to peer through the gloom to see what the tower contained.

"There," said Hawkmoon. "A stairway — or something very like one."

They stumbled over rubble and discovered that it was not a stairway leading up into the higher parts of the tower, but a ramp, not unlike the ramps that connected one building to another in the city itself.

"From what I've read this place was built only shortly before the Tragic Millennium," D'Averc told Hawkmoon as they continued up the ramp. "It was a city wholly given over to scientists — a Research City, I believe they called it. Every kind of scientist came here from all parts of the world. The idea was that new discoveries would be made by cross-fertilization. If my memory serves me, the legends say that many strange inventions were created here, though most of their secrets are now completely lost."

Up they went until the ramp led them onto a wide platform which was completely surrounded by windows of glass. Most of the windows were cracked or completely blown out, but from this platform it was possible to see the whole of the rest of the city.

"Almost certainly this was used to view the goings on all over Halapandur," Hawkmoon said. He looked about him. Everywhere were the remains of instruments whose function he could not recognize. They bore the stamp of things prehistoric; all in dull, plain cases with austere characters engraved on them, totally unlike the baroque decoration and flowing numerals and letters of modern times. "Some sort of room controlling the functions of the rest of Halapandur."

D'Averc pursed his lips and pointed. "Aye — you can observe its uses at once. Look, Hawkmoon."

Some distance away, on the opposite side of the city from the one they had entered, could be seen a line of horsemen in the helmets and armour of Dark Empire troops. They could make out no details from this height.

"My guess is that Meliadus leads them," Hawkmoon said, fingering his sword. "He cannot know exactly where Mygan is, but he can have discovered that Tozer was in this city at some time, and he'll have trackers with him who'll soon discover Mygan's cave. We cannot afford to rest here now, D'Averc. We must press on at once."

D'Averc nodded. "A shame."

They ran back down the ramp to the entrance of the tower. Risking being seen by the Dark Empire warriors, they dashed along the large, outer ramps as fast as they could, then swung back again down the girders and out of sight.

"I don't think we were seen," D'Averc said. "Come on — we go this way for Mygan's lair."

They began to race up the side of the mountain, slithering and sliding in their anxiety to reach the old sorcerer before Meliadus.

Night came, but they moved on.

They were starving, for they had eaten practically nothing since they had set out for Llandar Valley, and they were beginning to weaken.

But they struggled on and just before dawn came to the valley marked on the map. The valley where the sorcerer Mygan was said to live.

Hawkmoon began to smile. "Those Dark Empire riders will have camped for the night, almost certainly. We'll have time to see Mygan, get his crystals, and be away before they ever arrive!"

"Let's hope so," said D'Averc, thinking privately that Hawkmoon needed rest, for his eyes were a little feverish. But he followed him down to the valley and consulted the map. "Up there," he said. "That's where Mygan's cave's supposed to be, but I see nothing."

"The map has it halfway up yonder cliff," said Hawkmoon. "Let us climb up and see."

They crossed the floor of the valley, leaping over a small, clear stream that ran down a fissure in the rock the length of the valley. Here there were, indeed, signs of Man, for there was a path down to the river and a wooden apparatus that had evidently been used for drawing up water from the stream.

They followed the path to the side of the cliff. Now they found old, worn handholds in the rock. They had not been carved recently, but had been there, it appeared, for ages, well before Mygan had been born.

They began to climb.

The going was difficult, but at last they reached a ledge of rock on which a huge boulder stood, and there, behind the boulder, was the dark entrance to a cavern!

Hawkmoon went forward, eager to enter, but D'Averc put a cautionary hand on his shoulder. "Best take care," he said and drew his sword.

"An old man cannot harm us," Hawkmoon said.

"You are tired, my friend, and exhausted, otherwise you would realize that an old man of the wisdom Tozer claimed for him will possibly have weapons which could harm us. He has no liking for men, from what Tozer said, and there is no reason why he should think us anything more than enemies."

Hawkmoon nodded, drew his own blade, and then advanced.

The cavern was dark and seemingly empty, but then they saw a glimmer of light from the back. Approaching the source of this light, they discovered a sharp bend in the cavern.

Rounding the bend they saw that the first cavern led on to a second, much larger. This was fitted up with all sorts of things, instruments of the kind they had seen in Halapandur, a couple of cots, cooking materials, chemical equipment and much more. The source of the light was a globe in the centre of the cave.

"Mygan!" called D'Averc, but there was no reply.

They searched the cave, wondering if there was yet another extension, but found nothing.

"He has gone!" Hawkmoon said in desperation, his nervous fingers rubbing at the Black Jewel in his forehead. "Gone, D'Averc, and who knows where. Perhaps after Tozer left him, he decided that it was no longer safe to remain and has moved on."

"I think not," D'Averc said. "He would have taken some of this stuff with him, would he not?" He looked around the cave. "And that cot looks recently slept in. There is no dust anywhere. Mygan has probably gone off on some local expedition and will be back soon. We must wait for him."

"And what of Meliadus — if that was Meliadus we saw?"

"We must simply hope he moves slowly on the trail and takes some time to discover this cave!"

"If he's eager as Flana told you, then he'll not be far behind us," Hawkmoon pointed out. He went to a bench on which there were various dishes of meat, vegetables and herbs, helping himself greedily. D'Averc followed his example.

"We'll rest here and wait," D'Averc said. "It is all we can do now, my friend."

A day passed, and a night, and Hawkmoon hourly grew impatient as the old man did not return.

"Suppose he has been captured," he suggested to D'Averc. "Suppose Meliadus found him wandering in the mountains."

"If so, then Meliadus is bound to bring him back here and we shall win the old man's gratitude by rescuing him from the baron," D'Averc replied with forced cheerfulness.

"There were twenty men we saw, armed with flame-lances if I was not mistaken. We cannot take twenty, D'Averc."

"You are in low spirits, Hawkmoon. We have taken twenty before — more!"

"Aye," Hawkmoon agreed, but it was plain that the journey had taken much out of him. Perhaps, too, the deception at the Court of King Huon had been a greater strain on him than on D'Averc, for D'Averc appeared to relish deception of that kind.

At length, Hawkmoon strode to the outer cave and onto the ledge beyond. Some instinct seemed to draw him out, for he looked into the valley and saw them.

Now it was close enough to be sure.

The leader of the men was, indeed, Baron Meliadus. His ornate wolf mask glinted ferociously as it turned up and saw Hawkmoon at the instant Hawkmoon looked down.

The great, roaring voice echoed through the mountains. It was a voice full of mingled rage and triumph, the voice of a wolf that has scented its prey.

"Hawkmoon!" came the cry. "Hawkmoon!"

Meliadus flung himself from his saddle and began to scale the cliff. "Hawkmoon!"

Behind him came his well-armed men and Hawkmoon knew there was little chance of fighting them all off. He called back into the cavern. "D'Averc — Meliadus is here. Quickly man, he'll trap us in these caves. We must reach the top of the cliff."

D'Averc came running from the cavern, buckling on his sword belt, glanced down, thought for a moment, then nodded. Hawkmoon ran to the face of the cliff, seeking handholds on the rough surface, hauling himself upward.

A flame-lance beam splashed against the rock close to his hand, singeing the hairs on his wrist. Another landed beneath him, but he climbed on.

Perhaps at the top of the cliff he could stand and make a fight, but he needed to protect his life and D'Averc's for as long as possible, for the security of Castle Brass could depend on it.

"Haaawkmoooon!" came the echoing cry of the vengeful Meliadus. "Haaaawkmoooooon!"

Hawkmoon climbed on, scraping his hands on the rock, gashing his leg, but not pausing, taking incredible risks as he clambered up the cliff face, D'Averc close behind him.

At last they reached the top and saw a plateau stretching away from them. If they attempted to cross it, the flame-lances were bound to cut them down.

"Now," Hawkmoon said grimly, drawing his sword, "we stand and fight."

D'Averc grinned. "At last. I thought you were losing your nerve, my friend."

They glanced over the edge of the cliff and saw that Baron Meliadus had reached the ledge by Mygan's cavern and was darting in, sending his men on ahead in pursuit of his two hated foes. Doubtless he hoped to find some of the others there — Oladahn, Count Brass — or even, perhaps, Yisselda, whom Hawkmoon knew was loved by the baron, however much he refused to admit it.

Soon the first of the wolf warriors had reached the cliff and Hawkmoon delivered a jarring kick to his helmet. He did not fall, however, but reached out and clutched Hawkmoon's foot, either trying to drag himself back to safety or drag Hawkmoon with him over the cliff.

D'Averc sprang forward, stabbing the man in the shoulder. He grunted, released the grip on Hawkmoon, sought to grasp a spur of rock on the cliff edge, missed and tumbled backwards, arms flailing, to yell one long yell all the way to the floor of the valley, far, far below.

But now others were clambering over the edge. D'Averc engaged one, while Hawkmoon suddenly found himself with two to contend with.

Back and forth along the edge of the cliff they fought, the valley hundreds of feet below them.

Hawkmoon took one in the throat, between helm and gorget, neatly skewered another through the belly, where his armour did not reach, but two more quickly took their place.

They fought for an hour thus, keeping back as many as they could from gaining the top of the cliff, engaging with their swords those they could not dissuade from getting to the top.

Then they were surrounded, the swords pressing in on them like the teeth of some gigantic shark, until their throats were threatened by a band of blades and Meliadus's voice came from somewhere, full of gloating malice. "Surrender, gentlemen, or you'll be butchered, I promise."

Hawkmoon and D'Averc lowered their swords, glancing hopelessly at each other.

They both knew that Meliadus hated them with a terrible, consuming hatred. Now they were his prisoners in his own land. There was no possibility of escape.

Meliadus seemed to realize this, too, for he cocked his wolf mask on one side and chuckled.

"I do not know how you came to Granbretan, Hawkmoon and D'Averc, but I do know you now for a pair of fools! Were you too seeking the old man? Why, I wonder? You already have what he has."

"Perhaps he has other things," said Hawkmoon, deliberately attempting to obscure the matter as much as possible, for the less Meliadus knew, the more chance they had of deceiving him.

"Other things? You mean he has other devices useful to the Empire? Thanks for telling me, Hawkmoon. The old man himself will doubtless be more specific."

"The old man has left, Meliadus," said D'Averc smoothly. "We warned him you might be coming."

"Left, eh? If that's the case, you'll know where he has gone, Sir Huillam."

"Not I," said D'Averc, looking peeved as the warriors bound him and Hawkmoon together and tied a noose under their arms.

"We'll see." Meliadus chuckled again. "I appreciate the excuse you offer me to begin a little torture here and now. A soupçon of vengeance for the moment. We'll explore the full possibilities when we return to my palace. Then, too, perhaps I'll have the old man and his secret of traveling through the dimensions..." Privately he told himself that he was bound, in this way, to reinstate himself with the King-Emperor and achieve Huon's forgiveness for leaving the city without permission.

His gauntleted hand reached out to stroke Hawkmoon's face almost lovingly. "Ah, Hawkmoon — soon you shall feel my punishment; soon..."

Hawkmoon shuddered to the roots of his being, then spat full into the grinning wolf mask.

Meliadus recoiled, hand going up to mask, then sweeping out and striking Hawkmoon across the mouth. He growled in rage. "Another moment of anguish for that, Hawkmoon. And those moments, I promise you, will seem to last for aeons!"

Hawkmoon turned his head away in disgust and pain, was thrust roughly forward by the guards and pushed, together with Sir Huillam D'Averc, over the edge of the cliff.

The rope around their bodies stopped them from falling far, but they were lowered un-gently to the ledge and Meliadus joined them shortly.

"I must still find the old man," said the baron. "I suspect he's lurking somewhere hereabouts. We'll leave you well bound in the cavern, put a couple of guards at the entrance just in case you somehow free yourselves from your bonds, and set off to look for him. There is no escape for you now, Hawkmoon, none for you either, D'Averc. You are both mine at last! Drag them inside. Bind them with all the rope you can find. Remember — guard them well, for they are Meliadus's playthings!"

He watched as they were trussed and dragged into the nearer cavern. Meliadus placed three men at the entrance of the cavern and began to clamber back down the cliff in high spirits.

It would not be much longer, he promised himself, before all his enemies were in his power, all their secrets had been tortured from them, and then the King-Emperor would know that he had spoken the truth.

And if the King-Emperor did not think well of him — what matter?

Meliadus had plans to right that error, also.

S I X T E E N

M Y G A N   O F   L L A N D A R

Night fell outside the cavern and Hawkmoon and D'Averc lay in the shadow cast by the light from the second cave.

The broad backs of the guards filled the entrance and the ropes of their bonds were tight-bound and considerable.

Hawkmoon tried to struggle, but his movements were virtually restricted to moving his mouth, his eyes and his neck a little. D'Averc was in a similar position.

"Well, my friend, we were not cautious enough," D'Averc said with as light a tone as he could muster.

"No," Hawkmoon agreed. "Starvation and weariness makes fools of even the wisest of men. We have only ourselves to blame…"

"We deserve our suffering," D'Averc said, somewhat doubtfully. "But do our friends? We must think of escape, Hawkmoon, no matter how hopeless it seems."

Hawkmoon sighed. "Aye, if Meliadus should succeed in reaching Castle Brass…"

He shuddered.

It seemed to him from his brief encounter with the Granbretanian nobleman, that Meliadus was even more deranged than previously. Was it his defeat, several times, by Hawkmoon and the folk of Castle Brass? Was it the thwarting of his victory when Castle Brass had been spirited away? Hawkmoon could not guess. He only knew that his old enemy seemed less in control of his mind than earlier. There was no telling what he would do in such an unbalanced condition.

Hawkmoon turned his head, frowning, thinking he had heard a noise from within the far cavern. From where he lay, he could see a little of the lighted cave.

He craned his neck, hearing the sound again. D'Averc murmured, very softly so that the guards should not hear, "There is someone in there, I'll swear..."

And then a shadow fell across them and they stared up into the face of a tall, old man with a great, rugged face that seemed carved from stone and a mane of white hair that helped his leonine appearance.

The old man frowned, looking the bound men up and down. He pursed his lips and peered out to where the three guards stood at attention, glanced back at Hawkmoon and D'Averc. He said nothing, simply folded his arms across his chest. Hawkmoon saw that there were crystal rings on his fingers — all but the little finger of the left hand bore rings, even the thumbs. This must be Mygan of Llandar! But how had he got into the cave?

Hawkmoon looked at him desperately, mouthing his pleas for help.

The giant smiled again and bent forward a little so that he could hear Hawkmoon's whisper.

"Please, sir, if you be Mygan of Llandar, know that we are friends to you — prisoners of your enemies."

"And how do I know you speak truth?" said Mygan, also in a whisper.

One of the guards stirred outside, beginning to turn, doubtless sensing something. Mygan withdrew into the cavern. The guard grunted.

"What are you two muttering about? Discussing what the baron will do with ye, eh? Well, you can't imagine what entertainments he's got fixed up for you, Hawkmoon."

Hawkmoon made no reply.

When the guard had turned back, chuckling, Mygan bent closer again.

"You're Hawkmoon?"

"You've heard of me?"

"Something. If you're Hawkmoon, you may be speaking the truth, for though I be of Granbretan, I hold no brief for the lords who rule in Londra. But how do you know who my enemies are?"

"Baron Meliadus of Kroiden has learned of the secret you imparted to Tozer who was your guest here not long ago..."

"Imparted! He wheedled it from me, stole one of my rings when I slept, used it to escape. Wanted to ingratiate himself with his masters in Londra, I gather..."

"You are right. Tozer told them of a power, boasted that it was a mental attribute, demonstrated his power and turned up in Kamarg..."

"Doubtless by accident. He had no conception of how to use the ring properly."

"So we gathered."

"I believe you, Hawkmoon, and I fear this Meliadus."

"You'll free us? We can attempt to escape from here. Protect you against him?"

"I doubt if I need your protection."

Mygan disappeared from Hawkmoon's view.

"What does he plan, I wonder," said D'Averc, who had deliberately remained silent until now.

Hawkmoon shook his head.

Mygan reappeared with a long knife in his hand. He stretched out and began slicing through Hawkmoon's bonds until at last the Duke von Köln was able to free himself, keeping a wary eye on the guards outside.

"Hand me the knife," he whispered, and took it from Mygan's hand. He began cutting away D'Averc's ropes.

From outside they heard voices.

"Baron Meliadus is returning," one of the guards said. "He sounds in an evil temper."

Hawkmoon darted an anxious glance at D'Averc and they sprang up.

Alerted by the movement, one of the guards turned, crying out in surprise.

The two men darted forward. Hawkmoon's hand stopped the guard from drawing his sword. D'Averc's arm went round another's throat and drew his sword for him. The sword rose and fell even before the guard could scream.

While Hawkmoon wrestled with the first guard, D'Averc engaged the third. The clang of swords began to sound in the air and they heard Meliadus's shout of surprise.

Hawkmoon threw his opponent to the ground and placed a knee in his groin, drew the dagger that was still sheathed at his side, prised back the mask and struck the man in the throat.

Meanwhile, D'Averc had despatched his man, stood panting over the corpse.

Mygan called from the back of the cavern. "I see you wear crystal rings, like those I have. Do you know how to control them?"

"We know only how to return to Kamarg! A turn to the left..."

"Aye. Well, Hawkmoon, I would help you. You must turn the crystals first to the right and then to the left. Repeat the movement six times and then..."

The great bulk of Meliadus loomed in the entrance to the cavern.

"Oh, Hawkmoon — you plague me still. The old man! Seize him!"

The rest of Meliadus's warriors began to surge into the cavern. D'Averc and Hawkmoon fell back before them, desperately fighting.

The old man shouted in fury: "Trespassers. Back!" He rushed forward with his long knife raised.

"No!" cried Hawkmoon. "Mygan — let us do the blade work. Keep away. You are defenseless against such as these!"

But Mygan did not retreat. Hawkmoon tried to reach him, saw him go down before a blow from a wolf sword, struck out at the one who had struck Mygan.

The cavern was in confusion as they retreated back into the inner cave. The sound of the swords echoed, counterpointed by Meliadus's enraged shouts.

Hawkmoon dragged the wounded Mygan back to the second cave, warding off the blows that fell upon them both.

Now Hawkmoon faced the singing blade of Meliadus himself, who swung his sword two-handed.

Hawkmoon felt a numbing shock in his left shoulder, felt blood begin to soak his sleeve. He parried a further blow, then struck back, taking Meliadus in the arm.

The baron groaned and staggered.

"Now, D'Averc!" called Hawkmoon. "Now, Mygan! Turn the crystals! It is our only hope of escape!"

He turned the crystal in his ring first to the right and then to the left, then six times more to right and left. Meliadus growled and came at him again. Hawkmoon raised his sword to block the blow.

And then Meliadus had vanished.

So had the cavern, so had his friends.

He stood alone upon a plain that stretched flat in all directions. It was noon, for a huge sun hung in the sky. The plain was turf of a kind that grew close to the ground and the smell it gave off reminded Hawkmoon of spring.

Where was he? Had Mygan tricked him? Where were the others?

Then the figure of Mygan of Llandar began to materialize close by, lying on the turf and clutching at his worst wound. He was covered in a dozen sword cuts, his leonine face pale and twisted with pain. Hawkmoon sheathed his sword and sprang towards him. "Mygan…"

"Ah, I'm dying, I fear, Hawkmoon. But at least I've served in the shaping of your destiny. The Runestaff…"

"My destiny? What do you mean? And what of the Runestaff? I've heard so much of that mysterious artifact, and yet no-one will tell me exactly how it concerns me…"

"You'll learn when it's time. Meanwhile…"

Suddenly D'Averc appeared, staring around him in astonishment. "The things work! Thank the Runestaff for that. I'd thought us all surely slain."

"You — you must seek…" Mygan began to cough. Blood spurted from between his teeth, falling down his chin.

Hawkmoon cradled his head in his arms. "Do not try to speak, Mygan. You are badly wounded. We must find help. Perhaps if we returned to Castle Brass…"

Mygan shook his head. "You cannot."

"Cannot return? But why? The rings worked to bring us here. A turn to the left…"

"No. Once you have shifted in this way, the rings must be re-set."

"How shall we set them?"

"I will not tell you!"

"Will not? You mean cannot?"

"No. It was my intention to bring you through space to this land where you must fulfill part of your destiny. You must seek — ah, ah! The pain!"

"You have tricked us, old man," said D'Averc. "You wish us to play some role in a scheme of your own. But you are dying. We cannot help you now. Tell us how to return to Castle Brass and we shall get someone to doctor you."

"It was no selfish whim that instructed me to bring you here. It was knowledge of history. I have traveled to many places, visited many eras, by means of the rings. I know much. I know what you serve, Hawkmoon, and I know that the time has come for you to venture here."

"Where?" Hawkmoon said desperately. "In what time have you deposited us? What is the land called? It seems to consist entirely of this flat plain!"

But Mygan was coughing blood again and it was evident that death was close.

"Take my rings," he said, breathing with difficulty. "They could be useful. But seek first Narleen and the Sword of the Dawn — that lies to your south. Then turn north, when that's done, and seek the city of Dnark — and the Runestaff." He coughed again, then his body shook with a great spasm and life fled him.

Hawkmoon looked up at D'Averc.

"The Runestaff? Are we then in Asiacommunista where the thing is supposed to dwell?"

"It would be ironic, considering our earlier ruse," said D'Averc, dabbing with his kerchief at a wound on his leg. "Perhaps that is where we are. I care not. We are away from that boorish Meliadus and his bloodthirsty pack. The sun above is warm. Save for our wounds, we are considerably better off than we might have been."

Looking about him, Hawkmoon sighed. "I am not sure. If Taragorm's experiments are successful, he could find a way through to our Kamarg. I would rather be there than here." He fingered his ring. "I wonder…"

D'Averc put out his hand. "No, Hawkmoon. Do not tamper with it. I'm inclined to believe the old man. Besides, he seemed well-disposed toward you. He must have meant you well. Probably he intended to tell you where this was, give you more explicit directions as to how to reach the places — presuming they were places — he spoke of. If we try to work the rings now, there's no telling where we'll find ourselves — possibly even back in that unpleasant company we left in Mygan's cave!"

Hawkmoon nodded. "Perhaps you're wise, D'Averc. But what do we do now?"

"First we do as Mygan said, and remove his rings. Then we head south — to that place — what did he call it?"

"Narleen. It could be a person. A thing."

"South, at any rate, we go, to find out if this Narleen be place, person or thing. Come." He bent beside the corpse of Mygan of Llandar and began to strip the crystal rings from his fingers. "From what I saw of his cavern, it's almost certain that he found these in the city of Halapandur. That equipment he had in his cave evidently came from there. These must have been one of the inventions of those people before the onset of the Tragic Millennium..."

But Hawkmoon was barely listening to him. Instead he was pointing out across the plain.

"Look!"

The wind was blowing up.

In the distance something gigantic and reddish purple came rolling, emitting lightnings.

B O O K T W O

As the Champion Eternal served the Runestaff, so had Mygan of Llandar (though knowingly) and the philosopher of Yel had seen fit to deposit Hawkmoon in a strange, unfriendly land, giving him little information, in order, as he saw it, to further the Runestaff's cause. So many destinies were interlinked now — Kamarg's with Granbretan's, Granbretan's with Asiacommunista, Asiacommunista's with Amarehk — Hawkmoon's with D'Averc's, D'Averc's with Flana's, Flana's with Meliadus's, Meliadus's with King Huon's, King Huon's with Shenegar Trott's, Shenegar Trott's with Hawkmoon's; and all this on only one of Earth's many planes — so many destinies weaving together to do the Runestaff's work which was begun when Meliadus swore upon the Runestaff his great oath of vengeance against the inhabitants of Castle Brass and thus set the pattern of events. Paradoxes and ironies were all apparent in the fabric, would become increasingly clearer to those whose fates were woven into it. And while Hawkmoon wondered where he was placed in time or space, King Huon's scientists perfected more powerful war machines that helped the armies of the Dark Empire spread faster and further across the globe, to stain the map with blood...

— *The High History of the Runestaff*

Z H E N A K - T E N G

Hawkmoon and D'Averc watched the strange sphere approach and then wearily drew their swords.

They were in rags, their bodies all bloody, their faces pale with the strain of the fight, and there was little hope in their eyes.

"Ah, I could do with the amulet's power now," said Hawkmoon of the Red Amulet which, on the warrior's advice, he had left behind at Castle Brass.

D'Averc smiled wanly. "I could do with some ordinary mortal energy," he said. "Still, we must do our best, Duke Dorian." He straightened his shoulders.

The thundering sphere came closer, bouncing over the turf. It was a huge thing, full of flashing colours and there was no question of swords being useful against it.

It rolled to a halt with a dying, growling noise and stopped close by, towering over them.

Then it began to hum and a split appeared at its centre, widening out until it seemed the sphere would split in two. From it appeared white, delicate smoke drifting in a cloud to the ground.

The cloud now began to disperse and a tall, well-proportioned figure was revealed, his long fair hair held from his eyes by a silver coronet, his bronzed body clad in a short divided kilt of light brown colour. He appeared to have no weapons.

Hawkmoon looked at him warily.

"Who are you?" he said. "What do you want?"

The occupant of the sphere smiled. "That's a question I should ask you," he said in a peculiar accent. "You have been in a fight, I see one of your number is dead. He seems old to have been a warrior."

"Who are you?" Hawkmoon asked again.

"You are single-minded, warrior. I am Zhenak-Teng of the family of Teng. Tell me who you fought here. Was it the Charki?"

"The name means nothing. We fought no-one here," D'Averc said. "We are travelers. Those we fought are a great distance away now. We came here fleeing them…"

"And yet your wounds look fresh. You will accompany me back to Teng-Kampp?"

"That is your city?"

"We do not have cities. Come. We can help you — dress your wounds, perhaps even revive your friend."

"Impossible. He is dead."

"We can revive the dead as often as not," the handsome man said airily. "Will you come with me?"

Hawkmoon shrugged. "Why not?" He and D'Averc lifted the body of Mygan between them and advanced towards the sphere, Zhenak-Teng leading the way.

They saw that the interior of the sphere was, in fact, a cabin in which several men could sit comfortably. Doubtless the thing was a familiar form of transport here, for Zhenak-Teng made no effort to help them, leaving them to work out for themselves where they should sit and how they should position themselves.

He waved his hand over the control board of the sphere and the crack in the side began to seal itself. Then they were off, rolling smoothly over the turf at a fantastic speed, seeing dimly the landscape they passed.

The plain stretched on and on. Never once did they see trees or rocks or hills or rivers. Hawkmoon began to wonder if it were not, in fact, artificial — or had been artificially leveled at some time in the past.

Zhenak-Teng had his eyes pressed close to an instrument through which, presumably, he could see his way. His hands were on a lever attached to a wheel which he swung in one direction or another from time to time, doubtless steering the strange vehicle.

Once they passed at a distance a group of moving objects that they could not define through the shifting walls of the sphere. Hawkmoon pointed them out.

"Charki," Zhenak-Teng said. "With luck, they will not attack."

They seemed to be grey things, the colour of dark stone, but with many legs and waving protuberances. Hawkmoon could not decide whether they were creatures or machines, or neither.

An hour passed and at last the sphere began to slow. "We are nearing Teng-Kampp," Zhenak-Teng said.

A little later the sphere rolled to a halt and the bronzed man leant back, sighing with relief. "Good," he said. "I found what I set out looking for. That force of Charki is feeding in a south-westerly direction and should not come too close to Teng-Kampp."

"What are the Charki?" D'Averc asked, gasping as he moved and his wounds began to hurt again.

"The Charki are our enemies, created to destroy human life," Zhenak-Teng replied. "They feed from above ground, sucking up energy from the hidden Kampps of our people."

He touched a lever and with a jolt the globe began to descend into the ground.

The earth seemed to swallow them up and then close above them. The globe continued to descend for a few moments and then stopped. A bright light came on suddenly and they saw they were in a small underground chamber, barely large enough to hold the sphere.

"Teng-Kampp," said Zhenak-Teng laconically, touching a stud in the control panel which caused the sphere to split again.

They descended to the floor of the chamber, carrying Mygan with them, ducking to pass under an archway and emerge in another chamber where men dressed similarly to Zhenak-Teng hurried forward, presumably to service the sphere.

"This way," the tall man said, leading them into a cubicle which began to spin slowly. Hawkmoon and D'Averc leant against the sides of the cubicle, feeling dizzy, but at last the experience was over and Zhenak-Teng led them out into a richly carpeted room full of simple, comfortable looking furniture.

"These are my apartments," he said. "I'll send now for the medical members of my family who may be able to help your friend. Excuse me." He disappeared into another room.

A little later he came back smiling. "My brothers will be here soon."

"I hope so," said D'Averc fastidiously. "I've never been greatly fond of the company of corpses..."

"It will not be long. Come, let us go into another room where refreshment awaits you."

They left the body of Mygan behind and entered a room where trays of food and drink seemed to drift unsupported, in the air above piled cushions.

Following Zhenak-Teng's example, they seated themselves on the cushions and helped themselves to the food. It was delicious and they found themselves eating tremendous quantities of it.

As they ate, two men, of a similar appearance to Zhenak-Teng, entered the room.

"It is too late," said one of them to Zhenak-Teng. "I am sorry, brother, but we cannot revive the old man. The wounds, and the time involved..."

Zhenak-Teng looked apologetically at D'Averc and Hawkmoon. "There — you have lost your comrade for good, I fear."

"Then perhaps you can give him a good departure," said D'Averc, almost relieved.

"Of course. We shall do what is necessary."

The other two withdrew for about half-an-hour and then returned just as Hawkmoon and D'Averc finished eating. The first man introduced himself as Bralan-Teng and the second announced himself as Polad-Teng. They were both brothers of Zhenak-Teng and practitioners of medicine. They inspected Hawkmoon's and D'Averc's wounds and applied dressings. Very shortly the two men began to feel improved.

"Now you must tell me how you came to the land of the Kampps," Zhenak-Teng said. "We have few strangers on our plain, because of the Charki. You must tell me of events in the other parts of the world…"

"I am not sure that you would understand the answer to your first enquiry," Hawkmoon told him, "or that we can help you with news of our world." And he explained, as best he could, how they had come here and where their world was. Zhenak-Teng listened with careful attention.

"Aye," he said, "you are right. I can understand little of what you tell me. I have never heard of any 'Europe' or 'Granbretan' and the device you describe is not known to our science. But I believe you. How else could you have turned up so suddenly in the land of Kampps?"

"What are the Kampps?" D'Averc asked. "You said they were not cities."

"So they are not. They are family houses, belonging to one clan. In our case, the underground house belongs to the Teng family. Other nearby families are the Ohn, the Sek and the Neng. Years ago there were more — many more — but the Charki found them and destroyed them…"

"And what are the Charki?" Hawkmoon put it.

"The Charki are our age-old enemies. They were created by those who once sought to destroy the houses of the plain. That enemy destroyed himself, ultimately, with some kind of explosive experiment, but his creatures — the Charki — continue to wander the plain. They have unwholesome means of defeating us so that they may feed off our life-energy." Zhenak-Teng shuddered.

"They feed off your life-energy?" D'Averc said with a frown. "What is that?"

"Whatever gives us life — whatever life is, they take it and leave us drained, useless, dying slowly, unable to move…"

Hawkmoon began another question, then changed his mind. Evidently the subject was painful to Zhenak-Teng. Instead he asked, "And what is this plain? It does not seem natural to me."

"It is not. It was the site of our landing fields, for we of the One Hundred

Families were once mighty and powerful — until the coming of he who created the Charki. He wanted our artifacts and our sources of power for himself. He was called Zhenadar-vron-Kensai and he brought the Charki with him from the East, their vocation being entirely to destroy the Families. And destroy them they did, save for the handful that still survives. But gradually, through the centuries, the Charki sniff them out..."

"You seem to have no hope," said D'Averc, almost accusingly.

"We are merely realistic," Zhenak-Teng replied without rancour.

"Tomorrow we should like to be on our way," said Hawkmoon. "Have you maps — something that will help us reach Narleen?"

"I have a map — though it is crude. Narleen used to be a great trading city on the coast. That was centuries ago. I do not know what it might be today."

Zhenak-Teng rose. "I will show you to the room I have had prepared for you. There you may sleep tonight and begin your long journey in the morning."

T W O

T H E   C H A R K I

Hawkmoon awoke to the sounds of battle.

He wondered for a moment if he had dreamed and he was back in the cave and D'Averc was still engaged with Baron Meliadus. He sprang from his bed reaching for the sword that lay on a nearby stool with his tattered clothes. He was in the room where Zhenak-Teng had left them the previous night, and on the other bed D'Averc was awake, his features startled.

Hawkmoon began to struggle into his clothes. From behind the door came yells, the clash of swords, strange whining sounds and moans. When he was dressed, he went swiftly to the door and opened it a crack.

He was astonished. The bronzed, handsome folk of Teng-Kampp were busily at work trying to destroy one another — and it was not swords, after all, that were making the clashing sound, but meat cleavers, iron bars and a weird collection of domestic and scientific tools utilized as weapons. Snarls, bestial and alarming, were on all faces, and foam flecked lips, while eyes stared madly. The same insanity possessed them all!

Dark blue smoke began to pour along the corridor; there was a stink Hawkmoon could not define, the sound of smashing glass and torn metal.

"By the Runestaff, D'Averc," he gasped. "They seem possessed!"

A knot of battling men suddenly pressed against the door, pushing it inwards and Hawkmoon found himself in the middle of them. He pushed them back, sprang aside. None attacked him or D'Averc. They continued to butcher one another as if unaware of the spectators.

"This way," Hawkmoon said, and left the room, sword in hand. He coughed as the blue smoke entered his lungs and stung his eyes. Everywhere was ruin. Corpses lay thick in the corridor.

Together they struggled along the passages until they reached Zhenak-Teng's apartments. The door was locked. Frantically, Hawkmoon beat upon it with the pommel of his blade.

"Zhenak-Teng, it is Hawkmoon and D'Averc! Are you within?"

There was a movement from the other side of the door, then it sprang open and Zhenak-Teng, his eyes wild with terror, beckoned them in, then hastily closed and locked the door again.

"The Charki," he said. "There must have been another pack roaming elsewhere. I have failed in my duty. They took us by surprise. We are doomed."

"I see no monsters," D'Averc said. "Your kinsmen fight among themselves."

"Aye — that's the Charki's way of defeating us. They emit waves — mental rays of some description — that turn us mad, make us see enemies in our closest friends and brothers. And while we fight, they enter our Kampp. They will soon be here!"

"The blue smoke — what is that?" D'Averc asked.

"Nothing to do with the Charki. It comes from our smashed generators. We have no power now, even if we could rally."

From somewhere above came terrible thumps and crashes that shook the room.

"The Charki," murmured Zhenak-Teng. "Soon their rays will reach me, even me..."

"Why have they not reached you already?" Hawkmoon demanded.

"Some of us are more able to resist them. You, plainly, do not suffer from them at all. Others are quickly overcome."

"Can we not escape?" Hawkmoon glanced about the room. "The sphere we came in...?"

"Too late, too late..."

D'Averc grasped Zhenak-Teng by the shoulder. "Come man, we can escape if we're quick. You can drive the sphere!"

"I must die with my family — the family I helped destroy." Zhenak-Teng was barely recognizable as the self-contained, civilized man they had spoken to the day before. All the spirit had left him. Already his eyes were glazed and it seemed to Hawkmoon that soon the man would succumb to the strange power of the Charki.

He came to a decision, raised his sword and struck swiftly. The pommel connected with the base of the Zhenak-Teng's skull and he collapsed.

"Now, D'Averc," Hawkmoon said grimly. "Let's get him to the sphere. Hurry!"

Coughing as the blue smoke grew thicker, they stumbled from the room and into the passages, carrying Zhenak-Teng's unconscious body between them. Hawkmoon remembered the way to the place where they had left the sphere and directed D'Averc.

Now the whole passage shook alarmingly until they were forced to stop to keep their balance. Then...

"The wall! It's crumbling!" howled D'Averc, staggering back. "Quickly, Hawkmoon — the other way!"

"We must get to the sphere!" Hawkmoon called back. "We must go on!"

Now pieces of the ceiling began to fall and a grey, stonelike creature crept through the crack in the wall and into the passage. On the end of the creature was what resembled a sucker such as an octopus would possess, moving like a mouth seeking to kiss them.

Hawkmoon shuddered in horror and stabbed at the thing with his sword. It recoiled; then, pouting a little, as if only a trifle offended by his gesture and willing to make friends, it advanced again.

This time Hawkmoon chopped at it and there was a grunt and a shrill hiss from the other side of the room. The creature seemed surprised that something was resisting it. Heaving Zhenak-Teng onto his shoulder, Hawkmoon struck another blow at the tentacle, then leapt over it and began to race down the crumbling passage.

"Come on, D'Averc! To the sphere!"

D'Averc skipped over the wounded tentacle and followed. Now the wall gave way altogether, and it revealed a mass of waving arms, a pulsing head and a face that was a parody of human features, grinning a placatory, idiot's grin.

"It wants us to pet it!" D'Averc cried with grim humour as he avoided a reaching tentacle. "Would you hurt its feelings so, Hawkmoon?"

Hawkmoon was busily opening the door that led to the chamber of the sphere. Zhenak-Teng, who lay on the floor near him, was beginning to moan and clutch his head.

Hawkmoon got the door open, hefted Zhenak-Teng onto his shoulder again, and passed through into the chamber where the sphere lay.

No noise came from it now and its colours were muted, but it was opened sufficient to admit them. Hawkmoon climbed the ladder and dumped Zhenak-Teng in the control seat as D'Averc joined him.

"Get this thing moving," he told Zhenak-Teng, "or we'll all be devoured by the Charki you see there..." He pointed with his sword to the giant thing that was squeezing its way through the door of the chamber.

Several tentacles crept up the sides of the sphere towards them. One touched Zhenak-Teng lightly on the shoulder and he moaned. Hawkmoon yelled and chopped at it. It flopped to the floor. But others were now waving all around him and had fastened on the bronzed man who seemed to accept the touch with complete passivity. Hawkmoon and D'Averc screamed at him to get the sphere moving while they hacked desperately at the dozens of waving limbs.

Hawkmoon reached out with his left hand to grasp the back of Zhenak-Teng's neck. "Close the sphere, Zhenak-Teng! Close the sphere."

With a jerky movement, Zhenak-Teng obeyed, depressing a stud which made the sphere murmur and hum and begin to glow with all kinds of colours.

The tentacles tried to resist the steady motion of the walls as the aperture closed. Three leapt through D'Averc's defense and fastened themselves on Zhenak-Teng who groaned and went limp. Again Hawkmoon slashed at the tentacles as the sphere finally closed and began to rise upwards.

One by one the tentacles disappeared as the sphere rose and Hawkmoon sighed in relief. He turned to the bronzed man. "We are free!"

But Zhenak-Teng stared dully ahead of him, his arms limp at his sides.

"It is no good," he said slowly. "It has taken my life…" And he slumped to one side, falling to the floor.

Hawkmoon bent beside him, putting his hand to the man's chest to feel his heartbeat. He shuddered in horror.

"He's cold, D'Averc — incredibly cold!"

"And does he live?" the Frenchman asked.

Hawkmoon shook his head. "He is entirely dead."

The sphere was still rising rapidly and Hawkmoon sprang to the controls, looking at them in despair, not knowing one instrument from another, not daring to touch anything lest they descend again to where the Charki feasted on the life-energy of the people of Teng-Kampp.

Suddenly they were in the open air and bounding over the turf. Hawkmoon seated himself in the control seat and took the lever as he had seen Zhenak-Teng take it the day before. Gingerly he pushed it to one side, and had the satisfaction of seeing the sphere begin to roll in that direction.

"I think I can steer it," he told his friend. "But how one stops it or opens it, that I cannot guess!"

"As long as we are leaving those monsters behind, I am not entirely depressed," D'Averc said with a smile. "Turn the thing to the south, Hawkmoon. At least we will be going in the direction we intended."

Hawkmoon did as D'Averc suggested and for hours they rolled over the flat plain until, at length, a forest came in sight.

"It will be interesting," said D'Averc, when Hawkmoon pointed out the trees to him, "to see how the sphere behaves when it reaches the trees. It was plainly not designed for such terrain."

T H R E E

THE SAYOU RIVER

The sphere struck the trees with a great sound of snapping wood and tortured metal.

D'Averc and Hawkmoon found themselves flung to the far side of the control chamber, keeping company with the unpleasantly cold corpse of Zhenak-Teng.

Next they were flung upwards, then sideways, and had not the walls of the sphere been well padded, they would have died of broken bones.

At last the sphere rolled to a halt, rocked for a few moments, then suddenly split apart, tumbling Hawkmoon and D'Averc to the ground.

D'Averc groaned. "What an unnecessary experience for one as weak as myself."

Hawkmoon grinned, partly at his friend's drollery, partly in relief.

"Well," he said, "we have escaped more easily than I'd dared hope. Rise up, D'Averc, we must strike on — strike for the South!"

"I think a rest is called for," D'Averc said, stretching and looking up at the green branches of the trees. Sun slanted through them, turning the forest to emerald and gold. There was the sharp scent of pine and the earthier scent of the birch and from a branch above them a squirrel looked down, its bright black eyes sardonic. Behind them the wreckage of the sphere lay amongst tangled roots and branches. Several small trees had been torn up and others snapped. Hawkmoon realized that their escape had been very lucky indeed. He began to shake, now, with reaction, and understood the sense of D'Averc's words. He sat down on a grassy hillock, averting his eyes from the wreck and the corpse of Zhenak-Teng that could just be seen to one side of the sphere.

D'Averc lay down nearby and rolled over onto his back. From within his tattered jerkin he drew a tightly wadded piece of parchment, the map that Zhenak-Teng had given him shortly before they retired the night before.

D'Averc opened the parchment and studied it. It showed the plain in considerable detail, marked the various Kampps of Zhenak-Teng's people and what appeared to be the hunting trails of the Charki. Against most of the sites of the underground dwellings were crosses, presumably showing which the Charki had destroyed.

He pointed to a spot near the corner of the map. "Here," he said. "Here's the forest — and just to the north here is marked a river — the Sayou. This arrow points south to Narleen. From which I can gather, the river will lead us to the city."

Hawkmoon nodded. "Then let's head for the river when we're recovered. The sooner we reach Narleen, the better — for there at least we may discover where we are in space and time. It was unlucky that the Charki should have attacked when they did. By questioning Zhenak-Teng longer, we might have been able to learn from him where we were."

They slept in the peace of the forest for an hour or more, then rose up, adjusted their worn gear and ragged clothes, and set off towards the north and the river.

As they progressed, the undergrowth grew thicker and the trees more dense, and the hills on which the trees clung became steeper, so that by evening they were weary and in ill-temper, barely speaking to one another.

Hawkmoon sorted through the few objects in the purse on his belt, found a tinder box of ornate design. They walked on for another half-hour until they came to a stream that fed a pool set between high banks on three sides. Beside this was a small clearing and Hawkmoon said: "We'll spend the night here, D'Averc, for I cannot continue any longer."

D'Averc nodded and flung himself down beside the pool, drinking greedily the clear water. "It looks deep," he said, rising and wiping his lips.

Hawkmoon was building a fire and did not reply.

Soon he had a good blaze going.

"We should, perhaps, hunt for game," D'Averc said lazily. "I am becoming hungry. Do you know anything of forest lore, Hawkmoon?"

"Some," said Hawkmoon, "but I am not hungry, D'Averc."

And with that he lay down and went to sleep.

It was night, it was cold, and Hawkmoon was suddenly awakened by a terrified yell from his friend.

He was up instantly, staring in the direction D'Averc pointed, sword leaping from his scabbard. He gasped in horror at what he saw.

Rising from the waters of the pool, water rushing from its huge sides, was a reptilian creature with blazing eyes and scales as black as the night. Only its mouth, which now gaped wide, contained the whiteness of pointed teeth. With a great slopping sound it was heaving itself through the water toward them.

Hawkmoon staggered back, feeling dwarfed by the monster. Its head darted down and forward, its jaws snapping inches from his face, its loathsome breath almost asphyxiating him.

"Run, Hawkmoon, run!" yelled D'Averc, and together they began to stumble back into the woods.

But the creature was out of the water now and giving chase. From its throat came a terrible croaking noise that seemed to fill the forest. Hawkmoon and D'Averc clutched at one another's hands to keep together as they stumbled through the undergrowth, almost blind in the blackness of the night.

Again the croaking noise and this time a long, soft tongue whistled like a whip through the air and encircled D'Averc's waist.

D'Averc screamed. He slashed at the tongue with his blade. Hawkmoon yelled and sprang forward, stabbing out at the black thing with all his might, while hanging on to D'Averc's hand and holding his ground as best he could.

Inexorably, the tongue drew them towards the gaping mouth of the water-beast. Hawkmoon could see that it was hopeless to try to save D'Averc in this way. He let go of D'Averc's hand and leapt to one side, slashing at the thick, black tongue.

Then he took his sword in both hands, raised it above his head and chopped down with all his strength.

The beast croaked again and the ground shook, but the tongue parted slowly and foul blood gushed from it. Then there came a hideous cry and the trees began to part and snap as the water-thing lumbered at them. Hawkmoon grabbed D'Averc and hauled him to his feet, pushing aside the sticky flesh of the severed tongue.

"Thanks," D'Averc panted as they ran. "I'm beginning to dislike this land, Hawkmoon — it seems more full of perils than our own!"

Crunching and croaking and crying out with insensate rage, the thing from the pool pursued them.

"It's nearly on us again!" shouted Hawkmoon. "We can't escape it!"

They turned, peering through the blackness. All they could see now were the two blazing black eyes of the creature. Hawkmoon hefted his sword in his hand, getting its balance. "There's only one chance," he called, and flung his sword straight at the malevolent orbs.

There was another croaking scream and a great threshing sound amongst the trees, then the blazing orbs disappeared and they heard the beast crashing away, back to the pool.

Hawkmoon gasped with relief. "I didn't kill it, but it doubtless decided we were not the easy prey it originally took us for. Come, D'Averc, let's get to that river as soon as we can. I want to leave this forest behind!"

"And what makes you think the river is any less perilous?" D'Averc asked him sardonically as they began to move through the forest again, taking their direction from the side of the trees on which moss grew.

Two days later they broke out of the forest and stood on the sides of a hill that went steeply down to a valley through which a broad river flowed. It was without doubt the River Sayou.

They were covered in filth, unshaven, their clothes ragged to the point of disintegration. Hawkmoon had only a dagger for a weapon, and D'Averc, at last rid of his torn jerkin, was naked to the waist.

They ran down the hill, stumbling over roots, struck by branches, careless of any discomfort in their haste to reach the river.

Where the river would take them, they knew not. They wished only to leave the forest and its dangers. Though they had encountered nothing as dreadful as the creature from the pool, they had seen other monsters from a distance, discovered the spoor of more.

They flung themselves into the water and began to wash the mud and filth from their bodies, grinning at one another.

"Ah, sweet water!" exclaimed D'Averc. "You lead to towns and cities and civilization. I care not what that civilization offers us — it will be more familiar and even more welcome than the worst this dirty *natural* place presents to us!"

Hawkmoon smiled, not entirely sharing D'Averc's sentiments, but understanding his feelings.

"We'll build a raft," he said. "We're lucky that the current flows south. All we need do, D'Averc, is let the current bear us to our goal!"

"And you can fish, Hawkmoon — get us tasty meals. I'm not used to the simple fare we've lived on the past two days — berries and roots, ugh!"

"I'll teach you how to fish, too, D'Averc. The experience might be useful to you if you find yourself in a similar situation in the future!" And Hawkmoon laughed, slapping his friend on the back.

F O U R

V A L J O N   O F   S T A R V E L

Four days later the raft had borne them many miles down the great river. Forests no longer lined the banks, but instead there were gentle hills and seas of wild corn on both sides of them.

Hawkmoon and D'Averc lived off the fat fish they caught in the river, together with corn and fruit found on the banks, and they became more relaxed as the raft drifted on toward Narleen.

They had the appearance of shipwrecked sailors, with their ragged clothes and beards that grew thicker daily, but their eyes no longer had the wild look of hunger and exposure and they were in better spirits than they had been.

It was late in the afternoon of the fourth day that they saw the ship coming up behind them and leapt to their feet, waving to attract its attention.

"Perhaps the ship is from Narleen!" cried Hawkmoon. "Perhaps they'll let us work a passage to the city!"

The ship was high-prowed, made of wood painted with rich colours. Principally it was red, with gold, yellow and blue scrollwork along its sides. Although rigged like a two-masted schooner it also possessed oars which were now being used to propel it toward them. It flew a hundred brightly coloured flags and the men on its decks wore clothes to match.

The ship struck her oars and pulled alongside. A heavily bearded face peered down at them. "Who are you?"

"Travelers — strangers in these parts — can we sign aboard to work our passage to Narleen?" D'Averc asked.

The bearded man laughed. "Aye, that you can. Come up, gentlemen."

A rope ladder was thrown down and Hawkmoon and D'Averc climbed gratefully up it to stand on the ornamental deck of the ship.

"This is the *River Wind*," the bearded man told them. "Heard of her?"

"I told you — we're strangers," said Hawkmoon.

"Aye... Well, she's owned by Valjon of Starvel — you've heard of *him* no doubt."

"No," said D'Averc. "But we're grateful to him for sending a ship our way," he smiled. "Now, my friend, what do you say to our working our passage to Narleen?"

"Well, if you've no money..."

"None..."

"We'd best find out from Valjon himself what he wants done with you."

The bearded man escorted them up the deck to the poop where a thin man, pale and in black, stood brooding, not looking at them.

"Lord Valjon?" said the bearded man.

"What is it, Ganak?"

"The two we took aboard. They've no money — wish to work their passage, they say."

"Why, then let them, Ganak, if that's what they desire." Valjon smiled wanly.

He did not look directly at Hawkmoon and D'Averc and his melancholy eyes continued to stare out over the river. With a wave of his hand he dismissed them.

Hawkmoon felt uncomfortable, looked about him. All the crew were looking on silently, faint smiles on their faces. "What's the joke?"

"Joke?" Ganak said. "There's none. Now, gentlemen, would you pull an oar to get you to Narleen?"

"If that's the work that will get us to the city," said D'Averc with some reluctance.

"It looks somewhat strenuous work," Hawkmoon said. "But it's not far to Narleen, if our map was in order. Show us to our oars, friend Ganak."

Ganak took them along the deck until they reached the catwalk between the rowers. Here Hawkmoon was shocked when he saw the condition of the oarsmen. All looked half-starved and filthy. "I don't understand..." he began.

Ganak laughed. "Why, you will soon."

"What are these rowers?" D'Averc asked in dismay.

"They are slaves, *gentlemen* — and slaves you are, too. We take nothing aboard the *River Wind* that will not profit us and, since you have no money, and ransom seems unlikely, why we'll make you slaves to work our oars for us. Get down there!"

D'Averc drew his sword and Hawkmoon his dagger, but Ganak sprang back signaling to his crewmen. "Come, lads. Teach them new tricks, for they seem not to understand what slaves must do."

Behind them, along the catwalk, clambered a great weight of sailors, all with bright blades in their hands, while another mass of men came at their front.

D'Averc and Hawkmoon prepared to die taking a good quantity of the sailors with them, but then from above a figure came hurtling, down a rope from the crosstrees, to strike once, twice upon their heads with a hardwood club and knock them into the oarpits.

The figure grinned and bounced on the catwalk, putting away his club. Ganak laughed and clapped him on the shoulder. "Good work, Orindo. That trick's always the best one and saves much spilt blood."

Others sprang down to relieve the stunned men of their weapons and rope their wrists to an oar.

When Hawkmoon awoke, he and D'Averc sat side by side on a hard bench and Orindo was swinging his legs from the catwalk above them. He was a boy of perhaps sixteen, a cocky smile on his face.

He called back to someone above whom they could not see. "They're awake. We can start moving now — back to Narleen."

He winked at Hawkmoon and D'Averc. "Commence, gentlemen," he said. "Commence rowing, if you please." He seemed to be imitating a voice he had heard. "You're lucky," he added. "We're going downstream. Your first work will be easy."

Hawkmoon gave a mock bow over his oar. "Thank you, young man. We appreciate your concern."

"I'll give you further advice from time to time, for that's my kindly nature," said Orindo springing up, gathering his red and blue coat about him and bouncing along the catwalk.

Ganak's face peered down next. He prodded at Hawkmoon's shoulder with a sharp boathook. "Pull well, friend, or you'll feel the bite of this in your bowels." Ganak disappeared. The other rowers bent to their task and Hawkmoon and D'Averc were forced to follow suit.

For the best part of a day they pulled, with the stink of their own and others' bodies in their nostrils, with a bowl of slops to eat at midday. The work was back-breaking, though it was a sign of what upstream rowing was like when the other slaves murmured with gratitude for the ease of their task!

At night, they lay over their oars, barely able to eat their second bowl of nauseating mess which was, if anything, worse than the first.

Hawkmoon and D'Averc were too weary to talk, but made some attempt to rid themselves of their bonds. It was impossible for they were too weak to get free of such tightly knotted ropes.

Next morning Ganak's voice awoke them. "All port rowers get pulling. Come on you, scum! That means you, gentlemen! Pull! Pull! There's a prize in sight and if we miss it, you'll suffer the Lord Valjon's wrath!"

The emaciated bodies of the other rowers instantly became active at this threat and Hawkmoon and D'Averc bent their backs with them, hauling the huge boat round against the current.

From above were the sounds of footfalls as men rushed about, preparing the ship for battle. Ganak's voice roared from the poop as he issued instructions in the name of his master, the Lord Valjon.

Hawkmoon thought he would die with the effort of rowing, felt his heart pound and his muscles creak with the agony of the exertion. Fit he might be, but this effort was unusual, placing strain on parts of his body that had never had to take such strain before. He was covered in sweat and his hair was pasted to his face, his mouth open as he gasped for breath.

"Oh, Hawkmoon…" panted D'Averc. "This — was — not — meant to — be — my role — in life…"

But Hawkmoon could not reply for the pain in his chest and arms.

There was now a sharp jarring as the boat met another and Ganak yelled: "Port rowers, drop oars!"

Hawkmoon and the others obeyed instantly and slumped over their oars as the sounds of battle commenced above. There was the noise of swords, of men in agony, of killing and of dying, but it seemed only like a distant dream to Hawkmoon. He felt that if he continued to row in Lord Valjon's galley, he would shortly perish.

Then suddenly he heard a guttural cry above him and felt a great weight fall upon him. The thing struggled, crawled over his head and fell in front of him. It was a brutish looking sailor, his body covered in red hair. There was a large cutlass sticking from the middle of his body. He gasped, quivered, then died, the knife falling from his hand.

Hawkmoon stared at the corpse dully for a while until his brain began to work. He extended his feet and found he could touch the fallen knife. Gradually, with several pauses, he drew it towards him until it was under his bench. Exhausted, he again fell over his oar.

Meanwhile the sounds of fighting died down and Hawkmoon was recalled to reality by the smell of burning timber, looked about him in panic, then realized the truth.

"It's the other ship that's burning," D'Averc told him. "We're aboard a pirate, friend Hawkmoon." He smiled sardonically. "What an unworthy occupation — and my health so frail…"

Hawkmoon reflected, with some self-judgment, that D'Averc seemed to be reacting better to their situation than was he.

He drew a deep breath and straightened his shoulders as best he could.

"I have a knife…" he began in a whisper. But D'Averc nodded rapidly.

"I know. I saw you. You're not in such bad condition, after all."

Hawkmoon said: "Rest tonight, until just before dawn. Then we'll escape."

"Aye," agreed D'Averc. "Save as much strength as we can. Courage, Hawkmoon — we'll soon be free men again!"

For the rest of the day they pulled rapidly downriver, pausing only at noon for their bowl of slops. Once Ganak squatted on the catwalk and tickled Hawkmoon's shoulder with his boathook.

"Another day and you'll have your desire. We'll be docking at Starvel tomorrow."

"And what's Starvel?" croaked Hawkmoon.

Ganak looked at him astonished. "You must be from far away if you've not heard of Starvel. It's part of Narleen — the most favoured part. The walled city where the great princes of the river dwell — and of whom Lord Valjon is the greatest."

"Are they all pirates?" asked D'Averc.

"Careful, stranger," Ganak said frowning. "We help ourselves by right to whatever's on the river. The river belongs to Lord Valjon and his peers."

He straightened up and strode away. They rowed on until nightfall and then, at Ganak's order, ceased their work. Hawkmoon had found the work easier, now that his muscles and body had become used to it, but he was still tired.

"We must sleep in shifts," he murmured to D'Averc as they ate their slops. "You first, then I."

D'Averc nodded and slumped down almost instantly.

The night grew cold, and Hawkmoon could barely stop from falling asleep. He heard the first watch sounded, then the second. With relief, he nudged at D'Averc until he was awake.

D'Averc grunted and Hawkmoon was instantly asleep, remembering D'Averc's words. By dawn, with luck, they would be free. Then would come the difficult part — of leaving the ship unseen.

He awoke feeling strangely light in the body and realized with mounting spirits that his hands were free of the oars. D'Averc must have worked in the night. It was almost dawn.

He turned to his friend who grinned at him and winked. "Ready?" D'Averc murmured.

"Aye..." replied Hawkmoon with a great sigh. He looked with envy at the long knife D'Averc held.

"If I had a weapon," he said, I would repay Ganak for a few indignities..."

"No time for that now," D'Averc pointed out. "We must escape as silently as possible."

Cautiously they rose up from the benches and poked their heads up over the catwalk. At the far end, a sailor stood on watch; and on the poop deck above this man, stood Lord Valjon, his posture brooding and abstracted, his pale face staring into the darkness of the river night.

The sailor's back was towards them. Valjon did not seem about to turn. The two men heaved themselves onto the catwalk, making stealthily for the prow.

But it was then that Valjon's sepulchral voice sounded:

"What's this? Two slaves escaping?"

Hawkmoon shuddered. The man's instinct was uncanny, for it was plain he had not seen them, perhaps had only heard them for a moment. His voice, though deep and quiet, somehow carried the length of the ship. The sailor on watch wheeled and yelled. Lord Valjon's deathly pale face also glared at them.

From below decks several sailors appeared, blocking their way to the side. They wheeled and Hawkmoon ran toward the poop and Lord Valjon. The sailor drew his cutlass, struck at him, but Hawkmoon was desperate and could not be stopped. He ducked beneath the blow, grasped the man by the waist and heaved him up, hurling him to the deck where he lay winded. Hawkmoon picked up the unwieldly blade and struck off the man's head. Then he turned to stare at Lord Valjon.

The pirate lord seemed undisturbed by the closeness of danger. He continued to glare back at Hawkmoon from his pale, bleak eyes.

"You are a fool," he said slowly. "For I am the Lord Valjon."

"And I am Dorian Hawkmoon, Duke von Köln! I have fought and defeated the Dark Lords of Granbretan. I have resisted their most powerful magic as this stone in my skull testifies. I do not fear you, Lord Valjon, the pirate!"

"Then fear those," murmured Valjon, pointing a bony finger behind Hawkmoon.

Hawkmoon spun on his heel and saw a great number of sailors bearing down on him and D'Averc. And D'Averc was armed only with a knife.

Hawkmoon flung him the cutlass. "Hold them off, D'Averc!" And he leapt for the poop, grasped the rail and hauled himself over it as Lord Valjon, an expression of mild surprise on his face, took a step or two backward.

Hawkmoon advanced toward him, hands outstretched. From under his loose robe Valjon drew a slim blade which he pointed at Hawkmoon, making no attempt to attack but continuing to back away.

"Slave," murmured Lord Valjon, his grim features baffled. "Slave."

"I'm no slave, as you'll discover." Hawkmoon ducked past the blade and tried to grab the strange pirate captain. Valjon stepped aside swiftly, still keeping the long sword before him.

Evidently Hawkmoon's attack on him was unprecedented, for Valjon hardly knew what to do. He had been disturbed from some brooding trance and stared at Hawkmoon as if he were not real.

Hawkmoon leapt again, avoiding the extended sword. Again Valjon sidestepped.

Below, D'Averc had his back to the poop deck, was just able to hold off the sailors who crammed the narrow catwalk. He called to Hawkmoon:

"Hurry up with your business, friend Hawkmoon — or I'll have a dozen skewers in me before long!"

Hawkmoon aimed a blow at Valjon's face, felt his fist connect with cold, dry flesh, saw the man's head snap back and the sword fall from his hand. Hawkmoon swept up the sword, admiring its balance, and heaved the unconscious Valjon to his feet, directing the sword at his vitals.

"Back, scum, or your master dies!"

In astonishment the sailors began to move away, leaving three of their number dead at D'Averc's feet. Ganak came hurrying up behind them. He was wearing only a kilt, a naked cutlass in his hand. His jaw dropped when he saw Hawkmoon.

"Now, D'Averc, perhaps you'd care to join me." Hawkmoon spoke almost merrily.

D'Averc circled the poop and climbed the ladder to the deck. He grinned at Hawkmoon. "Good work, friend."

"We'll wait until dawn!" Hawkmoon called. "And then you'll guide this ship to the shore. When that's done, and we're free, perhaps I'll let your master live."

Ganak scowled. "You are a fool to handle Lord Valjon thus. Know you not that he is the most powerful river prince in Starvel."

"I know nothing of your Starvel, friend, but I have dared the dangers of Granbretan, have ventured into the Dark Empire's very heart, and I doubt if you can offer dangers more sophisticated than theirs. Fear is an emotion I rarely feel, Ganak. But mark you this — I would be revenged on you. Your days are numbered."

Ganak laughed. "Your luck makes you stupid, slave! Vengeance taking will be the Lord Valjon's prerogative!"

Dawn was already beginning to lighten the horizon. Hawkmoon ignored Ganak's jibe.

It seemed a century before the sun finally rose and began to dapple the distant trees of the riverbank. They were anchored close to the left bank of the river, not far from a small cove that could just be made out about half a mile away.

"Give the order to row, Ganak!" Hawkmoon called. "Make for the left shore."

Ganak scowled and made no effort to obey.

Hawkmoon's arm encircled Valjon's throat. The man was beginning to blink awake. Hawkmoon tapped his stomach with his sword. "Ganak! I could make Valjon die slowly!"

Suddenly, from the throat of the pirate lord there came a tiny, ironic chuckle. "Die slowly…" he said. "Die slowly…"

Hawkmoon stared at him, puzzled. "Aye — I know where best to strike to give you the maximum time and maximum pain a-dying."

Valjon made no other sound, merely stood passively with his throat still gripped by Hawkmoon's arm.

"Now, Ganak! Give the instructions!" D'Averc called.

Ganak took a deep breath. "Rowers!" he cried, and began to issue orders. The oars creaked, the backs of the oarsmen bent, and slowly the ship began to ride toward the left bank of the wide Sayou River.

Hawkmoon watched Ganak closely, for fear the man would attempt to trick them, but Ganak did not move, merely scowled.

As the bank came closer and closer, Hawkmoon began to relax. They were almost free. On land they could avoid any pursuit by the sailors who would, anyway, be reluctant to leave their ship.

Then he heard D'Averc yell and point upward. He stared up to see a figure come whizzing down a rope above his head.

It was the boy Orindo, a hardwood club in his hand, a wild grin on his lips.

Hawkmoon released Valjon and raised his arms to protect himself, unable to do the obvious thing which was to use his blade to strike Orindo as he descended. The club fell heavily on his arm and he staggered back. D'Averc rushed forward and grasped Orindo round the waist, imprisoning his arms.

Valjon, suddenly swift-footed, darted down the companionway screaming a strange, wordless scream.

D'Averc pushed Orindo after him with an oath.

"Taken by the same trick twice, Hawkmoon. We deserve to die for that!"

Growling sailors led by Ganak were coming up the companionway now. Hawkmoon struck out at Ganak, but the bearded sailor blocked the blow, aiming a huge swing at Hawkmoon's legs. Hawkmoon was forced to leap back and then Ganak scuttled up to the poop and faced him, a sneering grin on his lips.

"Now, slave, we'll see how you fight a man!" Ganak said.

"I do not see a man," Hawkmoon replied. "Only some kind of beast." He laughed as Ganak struck at him again. He thrust swiftly with the marvelously balanced sword he had taken from Valjon.

Back and forth across the deck they fought, while D'Averc managed to hold the others at bay. Ganak was a master swordsman, but his cutlass was no match for the shining sword of the pirate lord.

Hawkmoon took him in the shoulder with a darting thrust, reeled back as the cutlass collided with the hilt of his blade, feeling the weapon almost fall from his hand, recovered himself to thrust again and wound Ganak in the left arm.

The bearded man howled like an animal and came on with renewed ferocity.

Hawkmoon thrust again, this time piercing Ganak's right arm. Blood drenched both brawny arms and Hawkmoon was unwounded. Ganak flung himself at Hawkmoon again, now in a kind of fierce panic.

Hawkmoon's next thrust was to the heart, to put Ganak out of further misery. The point of the blade bit through flesh, scraped against bone, and the life was gone from Ganak.

But now the other sailors had forced D'Averc back and he was surrounded, hacking about him with the cutlass. Hawkmoon left the corpse of Ganak and leapt forward, taking one in the throat and another under the ribs before they were aware of his presence.

Back to back now, Hawkmoon and D'Averc held off the sailors, but it seemed they must soon expire for more were running to join their comrades.

Soon the poop was heaped with corpses and Hawkmoon and D'Averc were covered with cuts from a dozen blades, their bodies all bloody. Still they fought. Hawkmoon caught a glimpse of the Lord Valjon standing by the mainmast watching from out of his deepset eyes, staring fixedly at him as if he wished to have a clear impression of his face for the rest of his life if need be.

Hawkmoon shuddered, then returned his full attention to the attacking seamen. The flat of a cutlass caught him a blow on the head and he reeled against D'Averc, sending his friend off-balance. Together they collapsed to the deck, struggled to rise up, still fighting. Hawkmoon took one man in the stomach, struck another's lowering face with his fist, heaved himself to his knees.

Then suddenly the sailors stepped back, their eyes fixed to port. Hawkmoon sprang up, D'Averc with him.

The sailors were watching in concern as a new ship came swimming from the cove, its white, schooner-rigged sails billowing with the fresh breeze from the south, its rich black and deep blue paint, trimmed with gold, all agleaming in the early morning sunshine, its sides lined with armed men.

"A rival pirate, no doubt," D'Averc said, and used his advantage to cut down the nearest sailor and run for the rail of the poop. Hawkmoon followed his example and, with backs pressed against the rail they fought on, though half their enemies were running down the companionway to present themselves to Lord Valjon for his orders.

A voice called across the water, but it was too far away for the words to be clear.

Somehow in the confusion, Hawkmoon heard Valjon's deep, world-weary voice speak a single word, a word containing much loathing.

The word was "Bewchard!"

Then the sailors were upon them again and Hawkmoon felt a cutlass nick his face, turned blazing eyes on his attacker and thrust out his sword to catch him through the mouth, driving the sharp blade upwards for the brain, hearing the man scream a long, horrible scream as he died.

Hawkmoon felt no mercy, yanked his sword back and stabbed another in the heart.

And thus they fought, while the black and midnight blue schooner sailed closer and closer.

For a moment, Hawkmoon wondered if the ship would be friend or foe. Then there was no more time for wondering as the vengeful sailors pressed in, their heavy cutlasses rising and falling.

F   I   V   E

P A H L   B E W C H A R D

As the black and blue ship crashed alongside, Hawkmoon heard Valjon's voice calling.

"Forget the slaves! Forget them! Stand by to hold off Bewchard's dogs!"

The remaining sailors backed warily away from the panting Hawkmoon and D'Averc. Hawkmoon made a thrust at them that sent them away faster, but he had not the energy to pursue them for the moment.

They watched as sailors, all dressed in jerkins and hose that matched the paint of the ship, came sailing on ropes to land on the deck of the *River Wind.* They were armed with heavy war-axes and sabres and fought with a precision that the pirates could not imitate, though they did their best to rally.

Hawkmoon looked for Lord Valjon, but he had disappeared — probably below decks.

He turned to D'Averc. "Well, we've done our share of blood-letting this day, my friend. What say you to a less lethal action — we could free the poor wretches at the oars!" And with that he leapt the poop rail to land on the catwalk and lean down to slash the knotted ropes binding the slaves to their oars.

They looked up in surprise, not realizing, most of them, what Hawkmoon and D'Averc were doing for them.

"You're free," Hawkmoon told them.

"Free," D'Averc repeated. "Take our advice and leave the ship while you can, for there's no knowing how the battle will go."

The slaves stood up, stretching their aching limbs, and then, one by one, they hauled themselves to the side of the ship and began to slide into the water.

D'Averc watched them go with a grin.

"A shame we can't help those on the other side," he said.

"Why not?" asked Hawkmoon indicating a hatch let into the side under the catwalk. "If I'm not mistaken, this leads under the deck."

He put his back to the side of the ship and kicked at the hatch. Several kicks and it sprang open. They entered the darkness and crept under the boards, hearing the sounds of fighting immediately above them.

D'Averc paused, slicing open a bundle with his much-blunted blade. Jewels poured out of the bundle. "Their loot," he said.

"No time for that now," Hawkmoon warned, but D'Averc was grinning.

"I didn't plan to keep it," he told his friend, "but I'd hate Valjon to escape with it if the fight goes well for him. Look…" and he indicated a large circular object set into the bottom of the hold. "If I'm not mistaken, this will let a little of the river into the ship!"

Hawkmoon nodded. "While you work on that, I'll make haste to free the slaves."

He left D'Averc to his task and reached the far hatch, stripping out the pegs holding it in position.

The hatch burst inwards, bringing two struggling men with it. One wore the uniform of the attacking ship, the other was a pirate. With a quick movement, Hawkmoon despatched the pirate. The uniformed man looked at him in surprise. "You're one of the men we saw fighting on the poop deck!"

Hawkmoon nodded. "What's your ship?"

"It's Bewchard's ship," replied the man wiping his forehead; he spoke as if the name were sufficient explanation.

"And who is Bewchard?"

The uniformed man laughed. "Why, he's Valjon's sworn enemy, if that's what you need to know. He saw you fighting. He was impressed by your swordsmanship."

"So he should have been," grinned Hawkmoon, "for I fought my best today. And why not? I was fighting for my life!"

"That often makes excellent swordsmen of us all," agreed the man. "I'm Culard — and your friend if you're Valjon's foe."

"Best warn your comrades, then," said Hawkmoon. "We're sinking the ship — look." He pointed through the dimness to where D'Averc was wrestling with the circular bung.

Culard nodded swiftly and ducked out into the slave pit again. "I'll see you after this is over, friend," he called as he left. "If we live!"

Hawkmoon followed him, creeping along the aisle to cut the slaves' bonds.

Above him the men of Bewchard's ship seemed to be driving Valjon's pirates back. Hawkmoon felt the ship move suddenly, saw D'Averc come hastily out of the hatch.

"I think we'd best make for the shore," said the Frenchman with a smile, jerking his thumb at the slaves who were disappearing over the side. "Follow our friends' example."

Hawkmoon nodded. "I've warned Bewchard's men of what's happening. We've repaid Valjon now, I think." He tucked Valjon's sword under his arm. "I'll try not to lose this blade — it's the finest I've ever used. Such a blade would make an outstanding swordsman of anyone!"

He clambered up to the side and saw that Bewchard's men had driven the pirate sailors back to the other side of the ship but were now withdrawing.

Culard had evidently spread the news.

Water was bubbling through the hatch. The ship would not last long afloat. Hawkmoon turned and looked back. There was barely space between the ships to swim. The best method of escape would be to cross the deck of Bewchard's schooner.

He informed D'Averc of his plan. His friend nodded and they poised themselves on the rail, leaping out to land on the deck of the other ship.

There were no rowers present and Hawkmoon realized that Bewchard's oarsmen must be free men, part of the fighting complement of the ship. This, it seemed to him, was a more sensible scheme — less wasteful than the use of slaves. It also gave him cause to pause and, as he paused, a voice called from the *River Wind.*

"Hey, my friend. You with the black gem in your forehead. Have you plans for scuttling my ship, too?"

Hawkmoon turned and saw a good looking young man, dressed all in black leather with a high-collared bloodstained blue cloak thrown back from his shoulders, a sword in one hand and an axe in the other, raising his sword to him from the rail of the doomed galley.

"We're on our way," called Hawkmoon. "Your ship's safe from us..."

"Stay a moment!" The black-clad man leapt up and balanced himself on the *River Wind's* rail. "I'd like to thank you for doing half our work for us."

Reluctantly Hawkmoon waited until the man had leapt back to his own ship and approached them along the deck.

"I'm Pahl Bewchard and the ship's mine," he said. "I've waited many weeks to catch the *River Wind* — might not have done so, had you not taken on the best part of the crew and given me time to sneak out of the cove..."

"Aye," said Hawkmoon. "Well, I want no further part in a quarrel between pirates..."

"You do me a disservice sir," Bewchard replied easily. "For I'm sworn to rid the river of the Pirate Lords of Starvel. I am their fiercest enemy."

Bewchard's men were swarming back into their own ship, cutting loose the mooring ropes as they came. The *River Wind* swung round in the current, her stern now below the water-line. Some of the pirates leapt overboard, but there was no sign of Valjon.

"Where did their leader escape to!" D'Averc asked, studying the ship.

"He's like a rat," Bewchard answered. "Doubtless he slipped away as soon as it was plain the day was lost for him. You have helped me greatly, gentlemen, for Valjon is the worst of the pirates. I am grateful."

And D'Averc, never at a loss where courtesy and his own interests were concerned, replied, "And we are grateful to you, Captain Bewchard — for arriving when things were lost for us. The debt is settled." He smiled pleasantly.

Bewchard inclined his head. "Thank you. However, if I may make a somewhat direct statement, you seem in need of something to aid your recovery. Both of you are wounded, your clothes are plainly not what you, as gentlemen, would normally choose to wear... I mean, in short, that I would be honoured if you would accept the hospitality of my ship's galley, such as it is, and the hospitality of my mansion when we dock."

Hawkmoon frowned thoughtfully. He had taken a liking to the young captain. "And where do you plan to dock, sir?"

"In Narleen," replied Bewchard. "Where I live."

"We were, in fact, traveling to Narleen before we were trapped by Valjon," Hawkmoon began.

"Then you must certainly travel with me. If I can be of assistance..."

"Thank you, Captain Bewchard," Hawkmoon said. "We should appreciate your aid in reaching Narleen. And perhaps on the way you would be able to supply us with some information which we lack."

"Willingly." Bewchard gestured toward a door set beneath the poop deck. "My cabin is this way, gentlemen."

S I X

N A R L E E N

Through the portholes of Captain Bewchard's cabin, they saw the spray fly as the ship flung itself downriver under full sail.

"If we should meet a couple of pirates," Bewchard told them, "we should have little chance. That is why we make such speed."

The cook brought in the last of the dishes and laid it before them. There were several kinds of meat, fish and vegetables, fruit and wine. Hawkmoon ate as sparingly as possible, unable to resist at least a sample of everything on the table, but aware that his stomach might not yet be ready for such rich food.

"This is a celebration meal," Bewchard told them cheerfully, "for I have been hunting Valjon for months."

"Who is Valjon?" Hawkmoon asked between munches. "He seems a strange individual."

"Unlike any pirate I ever imagined," D'Averc put in.

"He is a pirate by tradition," Bewchard told them. "His ancestors have always been pirates, preying on the river traffic for centuries. For a long time the merchants paid huge taxes to the Lords of Starvel, but some years ago they began to resist and Valjon retaliated. Then a group of us decided to build fighting ships, like the pirates', and attack them on the water. I command such a ship. A merchant by trade, I have turned to more military pursuits until Narleen is free of Valjon and his like."

"And how are you faring?" asked Hawkmoon.

"It is hard to say. Valjon and the other lords are still impregnable in their walled city — Starvel is a city within a city, within Narleen — and so far we have only been able to curb their piracy a little. As yet there has been no major test of strength for either side."

"You say Valjon is a pirate by tradition…" D'Averc began.

"Aye, his ancestors came to Narleen many hundreds of years ago. They were powerful and we were relatively weak. Legend says that Valjon's ancestor, Batach Gerandiun, had sorcery to aid him. They built the wall around Starvel, the quarter of the city they took for themselves, and have been there ever since."

"And how does Valjon answer you when you attack his ships as we saw today?" Hawkmoon took a long draught of wine.

"He retaliates with every possible means, but we are beginning to make them warier of venturing onto the river these days. There is still much to do. I would slay Valjon if I could. That would break the power of the whole pirate community, I am sure, but he always escapes. He has an instinct for danger — is always able to avoid it even before it threatens."

"I wish you luck in finding him," Hawkmoon said. "Captain Bewchard, know you anything of a blade called 'The Sword of the Dawn' — we were told that we should find it in Narleen?"

Bewchard looked surprised. "Aye, I've heard of it. It is connected with the legend I told you of — concerning Valjon's ancestor Batach Gerandiun. Batach's sorcerous power was said to be contained in the blade. Batach has become a god since — the pirates have deified him and worship him at their temple which is named after him — the Temple of Batach Gerandiun. They are a superstitious breed, those pirates. Their minds and manners are often unfathomable to the practical merchant kind, like myself."

"And where is the blade?" D'Averc asked.

"Why, it is the sword the pirates worship in the Temple. It represents their power to them, as well as Batach's. Do you seek to make the blade your own, then, gentlemen?"

"I do not…" began Hawkmoon, but D'Averc interrupted smoothly.

"We do, captain. We have a relative — a very wise scholar from the North — who heard of the blade and wished to inspect it. He sent us here to see if it could be bought…"

Bewchard laughed heartily. "It could be bought, my friends — with the blood of half a million fighting men. The pirates would fight to the last man to defend the Sword of the Dawn. They value it above all other things."

Hawkmoon felt his spirits sink. Had the dying Mygan sent them on an impossible quest?

"Ah, well." D'Averc shrugged philosophically. "Then we must hope that you eventually defeat Valjon and the others and put their property up for auction."

Bewchard smiled. "That day will not come in my lifetime. It will take many years before Valjon is finally defeated." He rose from his table. "Excuse me for a few moments, I must see how things are on deck."

He left the cabin with a brief, courteous bow.

When he had gone Hawkmoon frowned. "What now, D'Averc? We are stranded in this strange land, unable to get that which we sought." He took Mygan's rings from his pouch and jingled them on the palm of his hand. There were eleven there now, for he and D'Averc had taken their own off. "We are lucky to have these still. Perhaps we should use them — leap at random into the dimensions in the hope of finding a way back to our Kamarg?"

D'Averc snorted. "We might find ourselves suddenly at King Huon's Court, or in peril of our lives from some monster. I say we go to Narleen and spend some time there — see just how difficult it will be to obtain the pirate sword."

Pahl Bewchard came back through the door. He was smiling.

"Less than an hour, my friends — and we shall be berthing in Narleen," he told them. "I think you will like our city." Then he added with a grin: "At least, that part which is not inhabited by the Pirate Lords."

Hawkmoon and D'Averc stood on the deck of Bewchard's ship and watched as it was skillfully brought into harbour. The sun was hot in a clear, blue sky, making the city shine. The buildings were for the most part quite low, rarely more than four storeys, but they were richly decorated with rococo designs that seemed very old. All the colours were muted, weathered, but nonetheless still clear. Much wood was used in the construction of the houses — pillars, balconies and frontages were all of carved wood — but some had painted metal railings and even doors.

The quayside was crowded with crates and bales which were being loaded or unloaded onto the myriad ships crowding the harbour. Men worked with derricks to swing them into hatches or onto the quays, hauled them along gangplanks, sweating in the heat of the day, stripped to the waist.

Everywhere was noise and bustle which Bewchard seemed to relish as he escorted Hawkmoon and D'Averc down the gangplank of his schooner and through the crowd which had begun to gather.

Bewchard was greeted on all sides.

"How did you fare, captain?"

"Did you find Valjon?"

"Have you lost many men?"

At last Bewchard paused, laughing good-humouredly.

"Well, fellow citizens of Narleen," he shouted. "I must tell you, I see, or you shall not let us pass. Aye, we sank Valjon's ship..."

There was a gasp from the crowd and then silence. Bewchard sprang up onto a packing case and raised his arms.

"We sank Valjon's ship, the *River Wind*, but it would have likely escaped us altogether had it not been for my two companions here."

D'Averc glanced at Hawkmoon in embarrassment. The citizens stared at the two in surprise, as if unable to believe that two such ragged starvelings could be anything but lowly slaves.

"These two are your heroes, not I," Bewchard continued. "Single-handed they resisted the whole pirate crew, killed Ganak, Valjon's lieutenant, and made the ship easy prey to our attack. Then they scuttled the *River Wind!*"

There was a great cheer now from the crowd.

"Know their names, citizens of Narleen. Remember them as friends of this city and deny them nothing. They are Dorian Hawkmoon of the Black Jewel and Huillam D'Averc. You have not seen braver souls nor finer swordsmen!"

Hawkmoon was genuinely embarrassed by all this and frowned up at Bewchard, trying to signal that he should stop.

"And what of Valjon?" called a member of the crowd. "Is he dead?"

"He escaped us," Bewchard replied regretfully. "He ran like a rat. But we shall have his head one day.

"Or he yours, Bewchard!" The speaker was a richly dressed man who had pushed forward. "All you have done is anger him! For years I paid my river taxes to Valjon's men and they let me ply the river in peace. Now you and your like say 'Pay no taxes' and I do not — but I know no peace these days, cannot sleep without fear of what Valjon will do. Valjon is bound to retaliate. And it might not be only you on whom he takes his vengeance! What of the rest of us — those who want peace of mind and not glory? You endanger us all!"

Bewchard laughed. "It was you, Veroneeg, if I'm not mistaken, who first began to complain about the pirates, said you could not stand the high levies they demanded, supported us when we formed the league to fight Valjon. Well, Veroneeg, we are fighting him, and it is hard, but we shall win, never fear!"

The crowd cheered again, but this time the cheer was a little more ragged and the people were beginning to disperse.

"Valjon will take his vengeance, Bewchard," Veroneeg repeated. "Your days are numbered. There are rumours that the Pirate Lords are gathering their strength, that they have only been playing with us up to now. They could raze Narleen if they wished!"

"Destroy the source of their livelihood! That would be foolish of them!" Bewchard shrugged as if to dismiss the middle-aged merchant.

"Foolish, perhaps — as foolish as your actions," wheezed Veroneeg. "But make them hate us enough and their hatred might cause them to forget that it is we who feed them!"

Bewchard smiled and shook his head. "You should retire, Veroneeg. The rigours of merchant life are too much for you."

The crowd had almost completely vanished now and there were looks of anxiety on many of the faces which only lately had been cheering the heroes.

Bewchard jumped down from the box and put his arms around his companions' shoulders. "Come, my friends, let's listen no longer to poor old Veroneeg. He would make any triumph sour with his gloomy prattling. Let's to my mansion and see if we can find you raiment more befitting gentlemen — then, tomorrow, we can go about the city and buy new outfits for you both!"

He led them through the teeming streets of Narleen, streets that wound an apparently logic-less course, that were narrow and smelling of a million mingled odours, that were crowded with sailors and swordsmen and merchants and quay workers, old women, pretty girls, stallkeepers selling their wares and riders picking their way among those on foot. He led them over the cobbles, up a steep hill and out into a square with one side clear of houses. And there was the sea.

Bewchard paused for a moment to stare at the sea. It sparkled in the sunlight.

D'Averc gestured toward it. "You trade beyond that ocean?"

Bewchard unpinned his heavy cloak and threw it over his arm. He opened the collar of his shirt and shook his head, smiling. "Nobody knows what lies beyond the sea — probably nothing. No, we trade along the coast for about two or three hundred miles in each direction. This area is thick with rich cities that did not suffer too badly the effects of the Tragic Millennium."

"I see. And what do you call this continent? Is it, as we suspect, Asiacommunista?"

Bewchard frowned. "I have not heard it called that, though I'm no scholar. I have heard it called variously 'Yarshai', 'Amarehk' and 'Nishtay'." He shrugged. "I am not even sure where it lies in relation to the legendary continents said to exist elsewhere in the world…"

"Amarehk!" Hawkmoon exclaimed. "But I had always thought it the legendary home of superhuman creatures…"

"And I had thought the Runestaff in Asiacommunista!" D'Averc laughed. "It does not do, friend Hawkmoon, to place too much faith in legends! Perhaps, after all, the Runestaff does not exist!"

Hawkmoon nodded. "Perhaps."

Bewchard was frowning. "The Runestaff — legends — what do you speak of, gentlemen?"

"A point this scholar we mentioned made," D'Averc said hastily. "It would be boring to explain."

Bewchard shrugged. "I hate to be bored, my friends," he said diplomatically, and led them on through the streets.

They were now beyond the trading part of the city and on a hill in which the houses were much richer and less crowded together. High walls surrounded gardens that could be seen to contain flowering trees and fountains.

It was outside the gates of one such walled house that Bewchard at last stopped.

"Welcome to my mansion, my good friends." He rapped on the gate.

A covered grille was opened and eyes peered at them. Then the gate was pulled wide and a servant bowed to Bewchard. "Welcome home, master. Was the voyage successful? Your sister awaits you."

"Very successful, Per! Aha — so Jeleana is here to greet us. You will like Jeleana, my friends!"

S E V E N

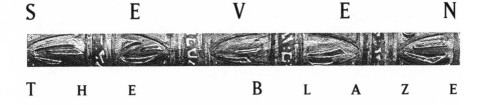

T H E   B L A Z E

Jeleana was beautiful, a young, raven-haired girl with a vivacious manner that instantly captivated D'Averc. At dinner that night he flirted with her and was delighted when she cheerfully responded.

Bewchard smiled to see them play so wittily, but Hawkmoon found it hard to watch, for he was reminded painfully of his own Yisselda, his wife who waited for him thousands of miles across the sea and perhaps hundreds of years across time (for he had no way of knowing if the crystal rings had brought him only through space).

Bewchard seemed to detect a melancholy look in Hawkmoon's eye and sought to cheer him up with jokes and anecdotes concerning some of his lighter and more amusing encounters while fighting the pirates of Starvel.

Hawkmoon responded bravely, but he still could not rid his mind of thoughts of his beloved girl, Count Brass's daughter, and how she fared.

Had Taragorm perfected his machines for traveling through time? Had Meliadus found another means of reaching Castle Brass?

The more the evening wore on, the less able Hawkmoon was to continue a light conversation. At length he rose and bowed politely. "I do apologize, Captain Bewchard," he murmured, "but I am very weary. The time spent in the galley — the fighting today…"

Jeleana Bewchard and Huillam D'Averc did not notice him rise, for they were engrossed with one another.

Bewchard stood up quickly, a look of concern on his handsome face. "Of course. I apologize, Master Hawkmoon, for my thoughtlessness…"

Hawkmoon smiled wanly. "You have not been thoughtless, captain. Your hospitality is magnificent. However…"

Bewchard's hand made a movement toward the bell pull, but before he could summon a servant there came a sudden banging on the door. "Enter!" Bewchard commanded.

The servant who had admitted them to the garden earlier that day stood panting in the doorway. "Captain Bewchard! There is a fire at the quayside — a ship is burning."

"A ship? Which ship?"

"Your ship, captain — the one you came home in today!"

Instantly Bewchard was making for the door, Hawkmoon and D'Averc following rapidly behind him, Jeleana behind them.

"A carriage, Per," he ordered. "Hurry, man!"

Within moments an enclosed carriage drawn by four horses was brought round to the front of the house and Bewchard climbed in, waiting impatiently for Hawkmoon and D'Averc to join him. Jeleana tried to enter, but he shook his head. "No, Jeleana. We do not know what is happening on the quays. Wait here!"

Then they were off, bumping over the cobbles at an alarming rate, making for the dockside.

The narrow streets were lit with torches stuck in brackets attached to the sides of houses and the carriage flung a black shadow on the walls as it passed, bumping and crashing through the streets.

At last the quayside was reached, illuminated by more than torches, for in the harbour a schooner blazed. Everywhere was confusion as masters of vessels arrived to bully their men aboard their own craft and move them away from Bewchard's schooner, for fear that they, too, would be set afire.

Bewchard leapt from the carriage, closely followed by Hawkmoon and D'Averc. He ran for the quayside, elbowing his way through the crowd, but once by the water he paused and hung his head.

"It's hopeless," he murmured in despair. "She's gone. This could only have been Valjon's work…"

Veroneeg, his face sweating and red in the glare from the burning ship, burst from the crowd. "You see, Bewchard — Valjon is taking his vengeance! I warned you!"

They turned at the sound of galloping hooves, saw a rider rein in his horse close by. "Bewchard!" the man cried. "Pahl Bewchard who claims to have sunk the *River Wind!*"

Bewchard looked up. "I am Bewchard. Who are you?"

The rider was clad in bizarre finery and in his left hand he clutched a scroll which he brandished. "I am Valjon's man — his messenger!" He threw the scroll toward Bewchard who let it lie where it had fallen.

"What is it?" Bewchard said between gritted teeth.

"It is a bill, Bewchard. A bill for fifty men and forty slaves, for a ship and all furnishings, plus twenty-five thousand smaygars' worth of treasure. Valjon, too, can play the merchant game!"

Bewchard glared at the messenger. The light from the blazing ship sent shadows flickering across his face. He spurned the scroll with his foot, kicking it into the debris-filled water.

"You seek to frighten me with this melodrama, I see!" he said firmly. "Well, tell Valjon I do not intend to pay his bill and that I am not frightened. Tell him — if he wishes to 'play the merchant game' — that he and his greedy ancestors owe the people of Narleen considerably more than the amount on his bill. I will continue to reclaim that debt."

The rider opened his mouth as if to speak, then changed his mind, spat on the cobbles and wheeled his horse about, galloping away into the darkness.

"He will kill you now, Bewchard," said Veroneeg almost triumphantly. "He will kill you. I hope he realizes that not all of us are as foolish as you!"

"And I hope that we are not all as foolish as you, Veroneeg," answered Bewchard contemptuously. "If Valjon is threatening me, it means that I have succeeded — partially at least — in unnerving him!"

He stalked toward his carriage and stood aside while Hawkmoon and D'Averc climbed in. Then he entered, slammed the door and tapped with the hilt of his sword on the roof, signaling the driver to return to the mansion.

"Are you sure that Valjon is as weak as you suggest?" Hawkmoon asked hesitantly.

Bewchard smiled at him grimly.

"I am sure that he is stronger than I suggest — stronger perhaps than Veroneeg thinks. My own opinion is that Valjon is still somewhat surprised that we have had the temerity to attack his ship as we did today, that he has not yet marshaled all his resources. But it would not do to tell Veroneeg that, would it, my friend."

Hawkmoon looked at Bewchard admiringly. "You have much courage, captain."

"Desperation, possibly, friend Hawkmoon."

Hawkmoon nodded. "I know what you mean, I think."

The rest of the return journey was made in thoughtful silence.

At the mansion the garden gate was open and they drove straight into the drive. At the main door to the house Jeleana awaited them pale-faced.

"Are you unharmed, Pahl?" she asked as he descended from the carriage.

"Of course," replied Bewchard. "You seem unduly frightened, Jeleana."

She turned and walked back into the house, back into the dining room where their supper still lay on the table.

"It — it was not the burning ship that made me thus," she told him trembling. She looked at her brother, then at D'Averc, lastly at Hawkmoon. Her eyes were wide. "We had a visitor while you were gone."

"A visitor? Who was it?" Bewchard asked, putting his arm around her shaking shoulders.

"He — he came alone..." she began.

"And what is so remarkable about a visitor coming alone? Where is he now?"

"It was Valjon, Pahl — Lord Valjon of Starvel himself. He..." She put her hand to her face. "He stroked my face — he looked at me from those bleak, inhuman eyes of his, he spoke in that voice..."

"And what did he say?" Hawkmoon asked suddenly, his tone grim. "What did he say, Lady Jeleana?"

Again her eyes went from one to the other, to return to Hawkmoon.

"He said that he is merely playing with Pahl, that he is too proud to spend all his time and strength in pursuing a vendetta against him, that, unless Pahl proclaims in the city square tomorrow that he will cease bothering the Pirate Lords, Pahl will be punished in a way that will be suitable to his particular misdemeanour. He said that he expects to hear that the proclamation has been made by midday tomorrow."

Bewchard frowned. "He came here, to my own house, to display his contempt for me, I suppose. The burning of the ship was just a demonstration — and a diversion to get me to the quayside. He spoke to you, Jeleana, to show that he can reach my nearest and most beloved whenever he chooses." Bewchard sighed. "There is no question now that he not only threatens my life, but the lives of those close to me. It is a trick that I should have expected — did half-expect, yet..."

He looked up at Hawkmoon, his eyes suddenly tired.

"Perhaps I have been a fool, after all, Master Hawkmoon. Perhaps Veroneeg was right. I cannot fight Valjon — not while he fights from the security of Starvel. I have no weapons such as those he employs against me!"

"I cannot advise you," said Hawkmoon quietly. "But I can offer you my services — and D'Averc's here — in your struggle, should you wish to continue it."

Bewchard looked directly into Hawkmoon's face then and he laughed, straightening his shoulders.

"You do not advise me, Dorian Hawkmoon of the Black Jewel, but you do indicate to me what I should think of myself if I refused the aid of two such swordsmen as yourself. Aye — I'll fight on. Indeed, tomorrow I shall spend relaxing, ignoring Valjon's warning. You, Jeleana, I will have guarded here. I will send for our father and ask him to bring his guards to protect you. Hawkmoon, D'Averc and myself — why — we'll shop tomorrow." He indicated the borrowed clothes that the two men wore. "I promised you new suits — and a good sheath, I think, Master Hawkmoon, for your borrowed sword — Valjon's sword. We will be casual tomorrow. We will show Valjon — and, more important, the people of this city — that we are not frightened by Valjon's threats."

D'Averc nodded soberly. "It is the only way, I think, if the spirit of your fellow citizens is not to be destroyed," he said. "Then, even if you die, you die a hero — and inspire those who follow you."

"I hope I do not die," Bewchard smiled, "for I have a great love for life. Still, we shall see, my friends."

E   I   G   H   T

T H E   W A L L S   O F   S T A R V E L

Next day dawned as hot as the previous day and Pahl Bewchard sauntered out with his friends.

As they moved through the streets of Narleen, it was plain that many already knew of Valjon's ultimatum and were wondering what Bewchard would do.

Bewchard did nothing. Nothing but smile at all he met, kiss the hands of a few ladies, greet a couple of acquaintances, leading Hawkmoon and D'Averc toward the centre of the town where he had recommended a good outfitter.

That the outfitter's shop was barely a stone's throw from the walls of Starvel suited Bewchard's purpose.

"After midday," he said, "we shall visit the outfitter's. But before then we will take lunch at a tavern I can vouch for. It lies close to the central square and many of our leading citizens drink there. We shall be seen to be relaxed and untroubled. We will talk of small things and not mention Valjon's threats at all, no matter how many efforts are made to bring the subject up."

"You are asking a great deal, Captain Bewchard," D'Averc pointed out.

"Perhaps," Bewchard answered, "but I have a feeling that much hangs on this day's events — more than I understand at this moment. I am gambling on those events — for it could be that the day could mean victory or defeat for me."

Hawkmoon nodded but made no comment. He, too, sensed something in the air and could not question Bewchard's instinct.

The tavern was visited, food eaten, wine drunk, and they pretended not to notice that they were the centre of attention, cleverly avoiding all attempts to quiz them on what they intended to do about Valjon's ultimatum.

The hour of noon came and went and Bewchard sat and chatted with his friends for a further hour before rising, putting down his wine cup and saying, "Now gentlemen, this outfitter I mentioned…"

The streets were unusually lacking in crowds as they walked casually through them, getting closer and closer to the middle of the city. But there were many curtains that moved as they passed, many faces seen at windows, and Bewchard grinned, as if relishing the situation.

"We are the only actors on the stage today, my friends," he said. "We must play our parts well."

Then at last Hawkmoon saw his first glimpse of the walls of Starvel. They rose above the rooftops, white and proud and enigmatic, seemingly without gates.

"There are a few small gates," Bewchard told Hawkmoon, "but they are rarely used. Instead they have huge underground waterways and docks. These, of course, lead directly to the river."

Bewchard led them into a sidestreet and indicated a sign about halfway down. "There, my friends — there's our outfitter."

They entered the shop crammed with bales of cloth, with heaps of cloaks and jerkins and britches, swords and daggers of all description, fine harness, helmets, hats, boots, belts and everything else that a man could possibly want to wear. The owner of the shop was serving another customer as they entered. The owner was a middle-aged man, well-built and genial, with a red face and pure white hair. He smiled at Bewchard and the customer turned — a youth whose eyes widened when he saw the three standing in the doorway of the shop. The youth muttered something and made to leave.

"You do not want the sword, master?" the outfitter asked in surprise. "I would drop my price by half a smaygar, but not more."

"Another time, Pyahr, another time," answered the youth hurriedly, bowed swiftly to Bewchard and left the shop.

"Who was that?" asked Hawkmoon with a smile.

"Veroneeg's son, if I remember right," Bewchard replied. He laughed. "He has inherited his father's cowardice!"

Pyahr came up. "Good afternoon, Captain Bewchard. I had not expected to see you here today. You did not make the announcement?"

"No, Pyahr, I did not."

Pyahr smiled. "I had a feeling you wouldn't, captain. However, you are in considerable danger now. Valjon will have to pursue the matter, will he not?"

"He will have to try, Pyahr."

"He will try soon, captain. He will waste no time. Are you sure it is wise to come so close to the walls of Starvel?"

"I have to show that I am not afraid of Valjon," Bewchard answered. "Besides, why should I change my plans for him? I promised my friends here that they could choose clothing from the finest outfitter in Narleen and I am not a man to forget a promise like that!"

Pyahr smiled and made a dismissive gesture with his hand. "I wish you luck, captain. Now, gentlemen, what do you see that you like?"

Hawkmoon picked up a cloak of rich scarlet, fingering its golden clasp. "I see much that I like. You have a fine shop, Master Pyahr."

While Bewchard chatted with the shopkeeper, Hawkmoon and D'Averc wandered slowly around the shop, picking out a shirt here and a pair of boots there. Two hours passed before they had finally made up their minds.

"Why do you not go into my dressing rooms and try on the clothes?" Pyahr suggested. "I think you have chosen well, gentlemen."

Hawkmoon and D'Averc retired into the dressing rooms. Hawkmoon had a shirt of silk in a deep lavender shade, a jerkin of soft, light-coloured brushed leather, a scarf of purple and fine, flaring breeches that were also silk and matched the scarf, which he knotted about his neck. These breeches he tucked into boots of the same leather as the jerkin, which he left unbuttoned. He drew a wide leather belt about his waist and then clasped a cloak of deep blue over his shoulders.

D'Averc had taken for himself a scarlet shirt and matching britches, a jerkin of shining black leather and boots that were also of black leather and reached almost to his knees. Over this he drew a cloak of stiff silk, coloured deep purple. He was reaching for his sword belt when there came a shout from the shop.

Hawkmoon parted the curtains of the dressing room.

The shop was suddenly full of men — evidently pirates from Starvel. They had surrounded Bewchard who had not had time to draw his sword.

Hawkmoon wheeled and picked up his sword from the pile of discarded clothing, rushing into the shop to collide with Pyahr who was staggering back, blood pumping from his throat.

Even now the pirates were backing out of the shop and Bewchard could not even be seen.

Hawkmoon stabbed a pirate directly in the heart, defended himself from another's thrust.

"Do not try to fight us," snarled the pirate who had tried to stab him, "we want only Bewchard!"

"Then you must kill us before you take him," cried D'Averc who had joined Hawkmoon.

"Bewchard goes to find his punishment for insulting our Lord Valjon," the pirate told him and slashed at him.

D'Averc leapt back, bringing his sword up in a flickering movement that knocked the pirate's blade from his hand. The man snarled, hurling the dagger that was in his other hand, but D'Averc deflected this also, thrusting out to take the man in the throat.

Now half the pirates had detached themselves from their fellows and advanced on Hawkmoon and D'Averc who were pressed backward into the shop.

"They're escaping with Bewchard," Hawkmoon said desperately. "We must aid him."

He thrust savagely at his attackers, trying to cut his way through them to go to Bewchard's assistance, but then he heard D'Averc yell from behind him.

"More of them — coming through the back exit!"

That was the last he heard before he felt a sword hilt slam against the base of his skull and he fell forward onto a heap of shirts.

He awoke feeling smothered and rolled over onto his back. It was getting dark inside the shop and it was strangely silent now.

He staggered up, his sword still in his hand. The first thing he saw was Pyahr's corpse sprawled near the curtains of the dressing room.

The second thing he saw was what seemed to be D'Averc's corpse lying stretched across the bale of orange cloth, blood covering most of his features.

Hawkmoon went to his friend, put his hand inside his jerkin and with relief heard his heart beating. Like him, it seemed, D'Averc had only been stunned. Doubtless the pirates had left them behind intentionally, wanting someone to tell the citizens of Narleen what befell those who, like Pahl Bewchard, offended the Lord Valjon.

Hawkmoon stumbled to the back of the shop and found a pitcher of water. He carried it back to where his friend lay and put the pitcher to D'Averc's lips, then he tore off a strip from the bale of cloth and bathed the face. The blood had come from a broad but shallow cut across the temple.

D'Averc began to stir, opened his eyes and looked directly into Hawkmoon's.

"Bewchard," he said. "We must rescue him, Hawkmoon."

Hawkmoon nodded bleakly. "Aye. But he is in Starvel by now."

"No-one knows that but us," D'Averc said rising stiffly to a sitting position. "If we could rescue him and bring him back, then tell the city the story, think what that would do for the citizens' morale."

"Very well," said Hawkmoon. "We shall pay a visit to Starvel — and pray that Bewchard still lives." He sheathed his sword. "We must climb those walls somehow, D'Averc. We shall need equipment."

"Doubtless we'll find all we want in this shop," D'Averc replied. "Come, let us move swiftly. It is already nightfall."

Hawkmoon fingered the Black Jewel set in his forehead. His thoughts went again to Yisselda, to Count Brass, Oladahn and Bowgentle, wondering about their fate. His whole impulse was to forget about Bewchard, forget about Mygan's instructions, the legendary Sword of the Dawn and the equally legendary

Runestaff, to steal one of the ships from the harbour and set off across the sea to try to find his beloved. But then he sighed and straightened his back. They could not leave Bewchard to his fate. They must try to rescue him or die.

He thought of the walls of Starvel that lay so close. Perhaps no-one had tried to scale them before, for they were very steep and doubtless well-guarded. Perhaps it could be done, however. They would have to try.

N   I   N   E

THE   TEMPLE   OF   BATACH   GERANDIUN

Each with more than a score of daggers stuck in their belts, Hawkmoon and D'Averc began to scale the walls of Starvel.

Hawkmoon went first, wrapping cloth around the hilt of a dagger and then searching for a crack in the stone into which to insert the point, tap it gently into place, praying that no-one above would hear him and that the dagger would hold.

Slowly they ascended the wall, testing the daggers as they went. Once Hawkmoon felt a blade begin to give beneath his foot, clung to the dagger he had just inserted above his head as he felt that too begin to work loose. A hundred feet below was the street. Desperately he took another dagger from his belt and hunted for a crack in the stone, found one and plunged the blade in. It held, while the dagger supporting his foot fell away. He heard a thin clatter as it landed in the street. Now he hung, unable to move up or down, as D'Averc tried to insert another dagger into the crack. At last he succeeded and Hawkmoon breathed with relief. They were near the top of the wall now. Only a few more feet to go — and no idea what awaited either on the wall or beyond it.

Perhaps their efforts were useless? Perhaps Bewchard was already dead? There was no point in thinking such thoughts now.

Hawkmoon went even more cautiously as he reached the top. He heard a footfall above him and knew that a guard was passing. He paused in his work. Only one more dagger and he would be able to gain the top of the wall. He glanced down, saw D'Averc's face grim in the moonlight. The footfalls died away and he continued tapping in the dagger.

Then, just as he was heaving himself upwards the footsteps came back, moving much more rapidly than before. Hawkmoon looked up — directly into the face of a startled pirate.

Instantly Hawkmoon risked everything, sprang for the top of the wall, grasped it as the man drew his blade, flung himself upwards and struck with all his might at the man's legs.

The pirate gasped, tried to regain his balance, and then fell soundlessly.

Breathing rapidly, Hawkmoon reached down and helped D'Averc to the top of the wall. Running along it now came two more guards.

Hawkmoon rose, drew his sword and prepared to meet them.

Metal clashed on metal as D'Averc and Hawkmoon engaged the two pirates. The exchange was short, for the two companions had little time to waste and were desperate. Almost as one their blades struck for the hearts of the pirate guards, sank into flesh and were withdrawn. Almost as one the guards collapsed and lay still.

Hawkmoon and D'Averc glanced up and down the length of the wall. It seemed that they had not yet been detected by others. Hawkmoon pointed to a stairway leading down to the ground. D'Averc nodded and they made their way toward it, descending softly and as rapidly as they dared, hoping no-one would come up.

It was dark and quiet below. It seemed a city of the dead. Far away, in the centre of Starvel, a beacon gleamed, but elsewhere all was in darkness, save for a little light that escaped from the shutters of windows or through cracks in doors.

As they drew nearer to the ground they heard a few sounds from the houses — of coarse laughter and roistering. Once a door opened showing a crowded, drunken scene inside, and a pirate staggered drunkenly out cursing something, falling flat on his face on the cobbles. The door closed, the pirate did not stir.

The buildings of Starvel were simpler than those beyond the wall. They did not have the rich decoration of Narleen and, if Hawkmoon had not known better, he would have thought that Starvel was the poorer city. But Bewchard had told him that the pirates only displayed their wealth on their ships, their backs and in the mysterious Temple of Batach Gerandiun where the Sword of the Dawn was said to hang.

They crept into the streets, swords ready. Even assuming Bewchard was still alive, they had no idea where he was being held prisoner, but something drew them towards the beacon in the centre of the city.

Then, when they were quite close to the light, the sonorous boom of a drum suddenly filled the air, echoing through the dark, empty streets. Then they heard the tramp of feet, the clatter of horses' hooves nearby.

"What's that?" hissed D'Averc. He peered cautiously around a building and then rapidly withdrew his head. "They're coming towards us," he said. "Get back!"

Torchlight began to flicker and huge shadows swam into the street ahead of them. Hawkmoon and D'Averc backed away into the darkness, watching as a procession began to file past.

It was led by Valjon himself, his pale face stark and rigid, his eyes staring straight ahead of him as he rode a black horse through the streets towards the place where the beacon burned. Behind him were drummers, beating out a slow, monotonous rhythm, and behind them another group of armed horsemen, all richly clad. These must be the other Lords of Starvel. Their faces, too, were set and they sat in their saddles as stiffly as statues. But it was that which came behind these Pirate Lords which caught the watchers' main attention.

It was Bewchard.

His arms and legs were stretched out on a great frame of whalebone fixed upright upon a wheeled platform drawn by six horses led by liveried pirates. He was pale and his naked body was covered in sweat. He was evidently in great pain, but his lips were pressed grimly together. On his torso strange symbols had been painted and there were similar markings on his cheeks. His muscles strained as he struggled to free himself from the cords biting into his ankles and wrists; but he was securely bound.

As D'Averc made a movement to spring forward Hawkmoon restrained him. "No," he whispered. "Follow them. We might have a better chance to save him later."

They let the rest of the procession pass and then crept after it. It moved slowly on until it entered a wide square lit by a great beacon glowing over the doorway of a tall building of strange, asymmetrical architecture which seemed to have been formed naturally out of some glassy, volcanic stuff. It was an ominous construction.

"The Temple of Batach Gerandiun without question," Hawkmoon murmured. "I wonder why they take him there?"

"Let us find out," D'Averc said as the procession filed into the temple.

Together, they darted across the square and crouched in the shadows near the door. It was half-open. Apparently no attempt had been made to guard it. Perhaps the pirates believed that no-one would dare enter such a place unless it was their right.

Looking about him to see if they were observed, Hawkmoon crept toward the door and pushed it slowly open. He was in a dark passage. From round a corner came a reddish glow and the sound of chanting. D'Averc close behind him, Hawkmoon began to move down the corridor.

Hawkmoon paused before he reached the corner. A strange smell was in his nostrils, a disgusting smell that was at once familiar and unfamiliar. He shuddered and took a step back. D'Averc's face wrinkled in nausea. "Ugh — what is it?"

Hawkmoon shook his head. "Something about it — the smell of blood, perhaps. Yet not just blood…"

D'Averc's eyes were wide as he looked at Hawkmoon. It seemed that he was about to suggest that they go no further; then he squared his shoulders and took a stronger grip on his sword. He pulled off the scarf around his throat and pressed it to nose and lips in an ostentatious gesture reminding Hawkmoon much more of D'Averc's normal self, and making him grin, but he followed D'Averc's action and unwound his own scarf and placed it to his face.

Then they moved forward again, turning the corner of the passage.

The light grew brighter, a rosy radiance not unlike the colour of fresh blood. It emanated from a doorway at the far end of the corridor, seeming to pulse to the rhythm of the chanting which now grew louder and held a note of terrible menace. The stench, too, grew worse as they advanced.

Once a figure crossed the space from which the pulsing radiance poured. Hawkmoon and D'Averc stood stock still but were unseen. The silhouette vanished and they continued to advance.

Just as the stench assailed their nostrils, so the chanting began to offend their ears. There was something weirdly off-key about it, something that grated on their nerves. With their eyes half-blinded by the rosy light, it seemed that all their senses were under attack at once. But still they pressed on until they stood only a foot or two from the entrance.

They stared and they shuddered.

The hall was roughly circular, but with a roof whose height varied enormously. In this it resembled the outward appearance of the building, seeming to be less artificial than organic, rising and falling in a purely arbitrary way as far as Hawkmoon could tell. All the glassy walls reflected the rosy radiance so that the whole scene was stained red.

The light came from a place high in the roof and it drew Hawkmoon's wincing gaze upward.

He recognized it immediately, recognized the thing hanging there, dominating the hall. It was without doubt the thing that, with his dying breath, Mygan had sent him here to find.

"The Sword of the Dawn," whispered D'Averc. "The foul thing can have no part in our destinies, surely!"

Hawkmoon's face was grim. He shrugged. "That is not what we are here to take. He is what we have come for…" and he pointed.

Below the sword were stretched a dozen figures, all on the whalebone frames, arranged in a semi-circle. Not all the men and women on the frames were dead, but most were dying.

D'Averc turned his face away from the sight but then, his expression one of purest horror, forced himself to look back again.

"By the Runestaff!" he gasped. "It's barbaric!"

Veins had been cut in the naked bodies and from those veins the lifeblood pumped slowly.

The wretches on the bone frames were being bled to death. Those who lived had faces twisted in anguish and their struggles weakened gradually as their blood dripped, dripped into the pit below them, a pit that had been carved from the obsidian rock.

It was a pit, too, in which things moved, rising to the surface to lap at the fresh blood as it fell, then darting down again. Dark shapes moving in the deep pool of blood.

How deep was the pool? How many thousands had died to fill it? What peculiar properties did the pool contain so that the blood did not congeal?

Around the pool were clustered the Pirate Lords of Starvel, chanting and swaying, their faces lifted up to the Sword of the Dawn. Immediately below the sword, his body straining on the frame, Bewchard hung.

There was a knife in Valjon's hand and there could be no doubting the use he intended to make of it. Bewchard stared down at him with loathing and said something Hawkmoon could not hear. The knife glistened as if already wet with blood, the chanting grew louder and Valjon's hollow tones could be heard through it.

"Sword of the Dawn, in which the spirit of our god and ancestor dwells; Sword of the Dawn, which made Batach Gerandiun invincible and won us all we have; Sword of the Dawn, which makes the dead come alive, causes the living to remain living, which draws its light from the lifeblood of Men; Sword of the Dawn accept this, our latest sacrifice, and continue to know that you shall be worshipped for all time while you stay in the Temple of Batach Gerandiun; then Starvel shall never fall! Take this thing, this enemy of ours, this upstart, take this Pahl Bewchard of that coarse caste who call themselves merchants!"

Bewchard spoke again, his lips writhing, but his voice could not be heard above the hysterical chanting of the other Pirate Lords.

The knife began to move toward Bewchard's body and Hawkmoon could not restrain himself. The battle-cry of his ancestors came automatically to his lips and he screamed the wild bird-cry and voiced the words:

"Hawkmoon! Hawkmoon!"

And he dashed forward at the gathered ghouls, at the noisome pit and its terrible denizens, the frames on which the dead and dying were stretched below the shining, awesome sword.

"Hawkmoon! Hawkmoon!"

The Pirate Lords turned, their chanting over. Valjon's eyes widened in rage and he cast back his robe to reveal a sword that was the twin to the one

Hawkmoon carried. He cast the knife into the pit of blood and drew his blade.

"Fool! It is a truth that no stranger who enters Batach's Temple ever leaves until his body is drained of its blood!"

"It is your body will bleed tonight, Valjon!" cried Hawkmoon, and he struck at his enemy. But suddenly there were twenty men blocking his way to Valjon, twenty blades against his one.

He lashed at them in fury, his throat clogged with the dreadful stench, his eyes dazzled by the light from the sword, catching glimpses of Bewchard struggling in his bonds. He stabbed and a man died, he slashed and another staggered back into the pit to be dragged down by whatever dwelt there, he hacked and another pirate lost a hand. D'Averc, too, did well and they held the pirates at bay.

For a while it seemed their fury would carry them through all the pirates to Bewchard and save him. Hawkmoon hacked his way into the group and managed to reach the edge of the terrible bloodfilled pit, tried to cut Bewchard's bonds while he fought off the pirates at the same time. But then his foot slipped on the edge of the pool and he sank into it up to his ankle. He felt something touch his foot, something sinuous and disgusting, withdrew as fast as he could and found his arms clutched by pirates.

He flung back his head and called: "I am sorry, Bewchard — I was impetuous — but there was no time, no time!"

"You should not have followed me!" Bewchard cried in misery. "Now you, too, shall suffer my fate and feed the monsters of the pit! Oh, you should not have followed me, Hawkmoon!"

T E N

A Friend from the Shadows

"I am afraid, friend Bewchard, that your generosity was wasted on us!"

Even in this predicament D'Averc could not resist the irony.

He and Hawkmoon were spreadeagled on either side of Bewchard. Two of the dead sacrificial victims had been cut down and they had replaced them. Below the black things rose and dived restlessly in the pool of blood. Above the light from the Sword of the Dawn cast a red glow throughout the hall, cast a glow upon the upturned, expectant faces of the Pirate Lords, upon Valjon's face as his brooding eyes stared with a kind of triumph at their stripped bodies which, like Bewchard's, had been daubed with peculiar symbols.

There were strange plopping noises below as the creatures in the pit swam about in the blood, waiting, no doubt, for the fresh blood to fall into their pool. Hawkmoon shuddered and barely restrained himself from vomiting. His head ached and his limbs felt weak and incredibly painful. He thought of Yisselda, of his home and his efforts to wage war on the Dark Empire. Now he would never see his wife again, never breathe the air of Kamarg, never aid in the downfall of Granbretan, should that time ever come. And he had lost all that in a vain effort to save a stranger, a man he hardly knew, whose fight was remote and unimportant compared with the fight against the Dark Empire.

Now it was too late to consider those things, for he was going to die. He would die in a terrible way, bled like a pig, feeling his strength ebbing from him with every pulse of his heart.

Valjon smiled.

"You do not call out a bold battle-cry now, my slave friend. You seem silent. Have you nothing to ask me? Would you not beg for your life — beg to be made my slave again? Would you not apologize for sinking my ship, for killing my men, for insulting me?"

Hawkmoon spat at him.

Valjon gave a slight shrug. "I wait for a new knife. When that is brought and properly blessed, then I shall slit your veins here and there, making sure that you die very slowly, that you will be able to see your blood feeding the ones below. Your bloodless corpses will be sent to the Mayor of Narleen — Bewchard's uncle if I'm not mistaken — as evidence that we of Starvel do not expect to be disobeyed."

A pirate came through the hall and kneeled at Valjon's feet, offering him a long, sharp knife. Valjon accepted it and the pirate backed away.

Valjon now murmured words over the knife, looking often up at the Sword of the Dawn, then he took the knife in his right hand and raised it until its tip was almost touching Hawkmoon's groin.

"Now we shall begin again," said Valjon, and slowly he started to chant the litany Hawkmoon had heard earlier.

Hawkmoon tasted bile in his mouth as he tried to break free of the cords that bound him. The words droned on, the chanting rose in volume and in hysterical pitch.

"... Sword of the Dawn, which makes the dead come alive, causes the living to remain living..."

The tip of the knife stroked Hawkmoon's thigh.

"... which draws its light from the lifeblood of Men..."

Absently, Hawkmoon wondered if, indeed, the rosy sword did derive its light, in some peculiar way, from blood. The knife touched his knee and he shuddered again, cursing at Valjon, struggling wildly in the bonds.

"... know that you shall be worshipped for all time..."

Suddenly Valjon paused in his chanting and gasped, looking beyond Hawkmoon to a spot above his head. Hawkmoon craned his neck back and gasped, too.

The Sword of the Dawn was descending from the roof!

It came slowly and then Hawkmoon could see that it hung in a kind of web of metallic ropes — and there was something else in the web, now — the figure of a man.

The man wore a long helmet that hid all his face. His armour and trappings were all black and golden and at his side he bore a huge broadsword.

Hawkmoon could not believe it. He recognized the man — if man it was.

"The Warrior in Jet and Gold!" he cried.

"At your service," said a sardonic voice from within the helm.

Valjon snarled with rage and flung the knife at the Warrior in Jet and Gold. It clattered on his armour and fell into the pool.

The warrior hung by one gauntleted hand to the pommel of the Sword of the Dawn and carefully cut at the thongs holding Hawkmoon's wrists.

"You desecrate our most holy object," Valjon said unbelievingly. "Why are you not punished? Our god, Batach Gerandiun, will have his vengeance. The sword is his, it contains his spirit."

"I know better," said the warrior. "The sword is Hawkmoon's. The Runestaff saw fit, once, to use your ancestor Batach Gerandiun for its purposes, giving him power over this rosy blade, but now you have lost the power and Hawkmoon here has it!"

"I do not understand you," Valjon said baffled. "And who are you? Where do you come from? Are you — could you be — Batach Gerandiun?"

"I could be," murmured the warrior. "I could be many things, many men."

Hawkmoon prayed that the warrior would be finished in time. Valjon would not remain so dazed forever. He clung to the frame as his wrists came free, took the knife the warrior handed him, began gingerly to cut at the thongs binding his ankles.

Valjon shook his head.

"This is impossible. A nightmare." He turned to his fellow pirates. "Do you see it, too — the man who hangs from our sword?"

They nodded dumbly. One of them began to run back towards the entrance of the hall. "I'll fetch men. Men to aid us…"

Hawkmoon sprang then — sprang for the nearest Pirate Lord and grasped him by the throat. The man cried out, tried to wrench Hawkmoon's hands away, but Hawkmoon bent back his head until the neck snapped, swiftly drew the sword from the corpse's scabbard and let the body drop.

There he stood, naked in the glow from the great sword, while the Warrior in Jet and Gold cut at the bonds of his friends.

Valjon backed away, his eyes disbelieving. "It cannot be. It cannot be…"

Now D'Averc swung down to stand beside Hawkmoon, then Bewchard joined him. Both were unarmed and naked.

Nonplused by their leader's indecision, the other pirates made no move. Behind the naked trio, the Warrior in Jet and Gold swung on the great sword, dragging it nearer to the floor.

Valjon screamed and grabbed for the blade, wrenching it from its web of metal. "It is mine! It is mine by right!"

The Warrior in Jet and Gold shook his head. "It is Hawkmoon's by right!"

Valjon clutched the sword to him. "He shall not have it! Destroy them!"

Now men were rushing into the hall, bearing brands, and the Pirate Lords drew their swords, began to advance on the four who stood by the pool. The Warrior in Jet and Gold drew his own great blade and swept it before him like a scythe, driving the pirates back, killing several.

"Take up their swords," he told Bewchard and D'Averc. "Now we must fight."

Bewchard and D'Averc did as the warrior instructed and, following behind him, pushed forward.

But now it seemed that a thousand men filled the hall. They had gleaming eyes which lusted for their lives.

"You must take that sword from Valjon, Hawkmoon," shouted the warrior above the din of battle. "Take it — or we shall all perish!"

Again they were pressed back to the edge of the bloody pit and behind them there came a slobbering sound. Hawkmoon darted a look into the pit and cried out in horror. "They are rising from the pool!"

And now the creatures swam toward the edge and Hawkmoon saw that they were like the tentacled creature they had encountered in the forest, but smaller. Evidently they were of the same breed, brought here centuries before by Valjon's ancestors, gradually adapting from an environment of water to an environment of human blood!

He felt a tentacle touch his naked flesh and he shuddered in cold terror. The peril at his back gave him extra strength and he drove with all his might at the pirates, seeking out Valjon who stood nearby, clutching at the Sword of the Dawn which engulfed him in its weird, red radiance.

Seeing his danger, Valjon moved his hand to the hilt of the sword, called out something and waited expectantly. But what he expected to happen did not occur and he gasped, running at Hawkmoon with the sword raised high.

Hawkmoon sidestepped, blocked the blow and staggered, half-blinded by the light. Valjon screamed and swung the rosy sword again. Hawkmoon ducked beneath the swing and brought his own blade in, catching Valjon in the shoulder. With a great, bewildered cry Valjon struck again, and again his blow was avoided by the naked man.

Valjon paused, studying Hawkmoon's face, his expression one of mingled terror and astonishment. "How can it be?" he murmured. "How can it be?"

Hawkmoon laughed then. "Do not ask me, Valjon, for all this is as much a mystery to me as it is to you. But I was told to take your sword, and take it I shall!" And with that he aimed another thrust at Valjon which the Pirate Lord deflected with a sweeping motion of the Sword of the Dawn.

Now Valjon's back was toward the pit and Hawkmoon saw that the things, blood streaming down their scaly sides, were beginning to crawl onto the floor. Hawkmoon drove the Pirate Lord further and further toward the dreadful creatures. He saw a tentacle reach out and catch Valjon's leg, heard the man scream in fear and try to hack at the tentacle with his blade.

Hawkmoon stepped forward then, aimed a blow at Valjon's face with his fist and, with his other hand, wrenched the sword from the Pirate Lord's hand.

Then he watched grimly as Valjon was dragged slowly into the pool.

Valjon stretched out his hands to Hawkmoon. "Save me — please save me, Hawkmoon."

But Hawkmoon's eyes were bleak and he did nothing, simply stood with his hands on the pommel of the Sword of the Dawn as Valjon was dragged closer and closer to the pit of blood.

Valjon said nothing further but covered his face with his hands as first one leg and then the other was drawn into the pool.

There came a long, despairing scream and Valjon disappeared beneath the surface of the pool.

Hawkmoon turned now, hefting the heavy sword and marveling at the light which shone from it. He took it in both hands and looked to see how his friends were faring. They stood in a tight group, fighting off scores of enemies and it was plain that they would have been overwhelmed by now had it not been for the fact that the pool was disgorging its terrible contents.

The warrior saw that he had the blade and cried out something, but Hawkmoon could not hear it. He was forced to bring the sword up to defend himself as a knot of pirates came at him, drove them back and cut through them in an effort to join his friends.

The things from the pit were crowding the edge now, slithering over the floor, and Hawkmoon realized that their position was virtually hopeless, for they were trapped between a horde of swordsmen on one hand and the creatures of the pool on the other.

Again the Warrior in Jet and Gold tried to cry out, but still Hawkmoon could not hear him. He battled on, desperately trying to reach the warrior, hacking off a head here, a limb there and slowly coming closer and closer to his mysterious ally.

The warrior's voice sounded again and this time Hawkmoon heard the words.

"Call for them!" he boomed. "Call for the Legion of the Dawn, Hawkmoon, or we're lost!"

Hawkmoon frowned. "What do you mean?"

"It is your right to command the Legion. Summon them. In the name of the Runestaff, man, *summon them!*"

Hawkmoon parried a thrust and cut down the man who attacked him. The blade's light seemed to be fading, but it could have been that it was now in competition with the scores of torches blazing in the hall.

"Call for your men, Hawkmoon!" cried the Warrior in Jet and Gold desperately.

Hawkmoon shrugged and disbelievingly cried out: "I summon the Legion of the Dawn!"

Nothing happened. Hawkmoon had expected nothing. He had no faith in legends, as he had said before.

But then he noticed that the pirates were screaming and that new figures had appeared from nowhere — strange figures who blazed with rosy light, who struck about them ferociously, chopping down the pirates.

Hawkmoon drew a deep breath and wondered at the sight.

The newcomers were dressed in highly ornamental armour somehow reminiscent of a past age. They were armed with lances decorated with tufts of dyed hair, with huge notched clubs covered with ornate carvings and they howled and shouted and killed with incredible ferocity, driving many pirates from the hall within moments.

Their bodies were brown, their faces covered in paint from which huge black eyes stared, and from their throats came a strange, moaning dirge.

The pirates fought back desperately, striking down the shining warriors. But as a man died, his body would vanish and a new warrior would appear from nowhere. Hawkmoon tried to see where they came from, but he was never able to do so — he would turn his head and when he looked back a new warrior would be standing there.

Panting, Hawkmoon joined his friends. The naked bodies of Bewchard and D'Averc were cut in a dozen places, but not badly. They stood and watched as the Legion of the Dawn slaughtered the pirates.

"These are the soldiers who serve the sword," said the Warrior in Jet and Gold. "With them, because it then suited the Runestaff's scheme of things, Valjon's ancestor made himself feared throughout Narleen and its surrounds. But now the sword turns against Valjon's people, to take from them what it gave them!"

Hawkmoon felt something touch his ankle, turned and shouted in horror. "The things from the pit! I had forgotten them!" He hacked at the tentacle.

Instantly there were a dozen of the shining warriors between him and the monsters. The tufted lances rose and fell, the clubs battered and the monsters tried to retreat. But the Soldiers of the Dawn would not let them retreat. They surrounded them, stabbing and hacking until all that remained was a black mess staining the floor of the hall.

"It is done," Bewchard said incredulously. "We are the victors. The power of Starvel is broken at last." He stooped and picked up a brand. "Come, friend Hawkmoon, let us lead your ghostly warriors forward into the city. Let us kill all we find. Let us burn."

"Aye…" Hawkmoon began, but the Warrior in Jet and Gold shook his head.

"No — it is not for killing pirates that the Legion is yours, Hawkmoon. It is yours so that you may do the Runestaff's work."

Hawkmoon hesitated.

The warrior placed a hand on Bewchard's shoulder. "Now that most of the Pirate Lords are dead and Valjon destroyed, there will be nothing to stop you and your men returning to Starvel to finish the work we began tonight. But Hawkmoon and his blade are needed for greater things. He must leave soon."

Hawkmoon felt anger come then. "I am grateful to you, Warrior in Jet and Gold, for what you have done to aid me. But I would remind you that I would not be here at all had it not been for your schemings and those of dead Mygan of Llandar. I need to return home — to Castle Brass and my beloved. I am my own man, Warrior. I will decide my fate."

And then the Warrior in Jet and Gold laughed. "You are still an innocent, Dorian Hawkmoon. You are the Runestaff's man, believe me. You thought you came to this temple merely to help a friend who needed you. But it is the Runestaff's way to work thus! You would not have dared the Pirate Lords had you simply been trying to get the Sword of the Dawn, in whose legend you did not believe, but you did dare them to rescue Bewchard here. The web the Runestaff weaves is a complicated web. Men are never aware of the purposes of their actions where the Runestaff is concerned. Now you must continue on the second part of your mission in Amarehk. You must journey north — you can go round the coast, for Bewchard, I am sure, will lend you a ship — and find Dnark, the City of the Great Good Ones who will need your aid. There you will find proof that the Runestaff exists."

"I am not interested in mysteries, Warrior. I want to know what has become of my wife and friends. Tell me — do we exist in the same era?"

"Aye," said the warrior. "This time is concurrent with the time you left in Europe. But as you know, Castle Brass exists elsewhere..."

"I know that." Hawkmoon frowned thoughtfully. "Well, Warrior, perhaps I will agree to take Bewchard's ship and go on to Dnark. Perhaps..."

The warrior nodded. "Come," he said, "let us leave this unclean place and make our way back to Narleen. There we can discuss with Bewchard the matter of a ship."

Bewchard smiled. "Anything, Hawkmoon, that I have is yours, for you have done much for me and the whole of my city. You saved my life and you were responsible for destroying Narleen's age-old enemies — you may have twenty ships if you wish them."

Hawkmoon was thinking deeply. He had it in mind to deceive the Warrior in Jet and Gold.

E L E V E N

T H E   P A R T I N G

Bewchard escorted them next afternoon to the quayside. The citizens were celebrating. A force of soldiers had invaded Starvel and routed out every last pirate.

Bewchard put his hand on Hawkmoon's arm. "I wish that you would stay, friend Hawkmoon. We shall be having celebrations for a week yet — and you and your friends should be here. It will be sad for me, celebrating without your company — for you are the true heroes of Narleen, not I."

"We were lucky, Captain Bewchard. It was our good fortune that our fates were linked. You are rid of your enemies — and we have obtained that which we sought." Hawkmoon smiled. "We must leave now."

Bewchard nodded. "If you must, you must." He looked frankly at Hawkmoon and grinned. "I do not suppose that you still believe I am entirely convinced by your story of a 'scholar relative' interested in that sword you now wear?"

Hawkmoon laughed. "No — but on the other hand, captain, I can give you no better story. I do not know why I had to find the sword…" He patted the scabbard that now held the Sword of the Dawn. "The Warrior in Jet and Gold here says that it is all part of a larger destiny. Yet I am an unwilling slave to that destiny. All I seek is a little love, a little peace, and to be revenged upon those who have ravaged my homeland. Yet here I am, on a continent thousands of miles away from where I desire to be, off to seek another legendary object — and reluctantly. Perhaps we shall all understand these matters in time."

Bewchard looked at him seriously. "I think you serve a great purpose, Hawkmoon. I think your destiny is a noble one."

Hawkmoon laughed. "And yet I do not pine for a noble destiny — merely a secure one."

"Perhaps," said Bewchard. "My friend, my best ship is prepared for you and well-provisioned. Narleen's finest sailors have begged to sail with you and now man her. Good luck in your quest, Hawkmoon — and you, too, D'Averc."

D'Averc coughed into his hand. "If Hawkmoon is an unwilling servant of this 'greater destiny', then what does that make me? A great fool, perhaps? I am unwell, I have a chronically poor constitution, and yet find myself dragged about the world in the service of this mythical Runestaff. Still, it kills time, I suppose."

Hawkmoon smiled, then turned almost anxiously to mount the gangplank of the ship. The Warrior in Jet and Gold moved impatiently.

"Dnark, Hawkmoon," he said. "You must seek the Runestaff itself in Dnark."

"Aye," said Hawkmoon. "I heard you, Warrior."

"The Sword of the Dawn is needed in Dnark," continued the Warrior in Jet and Gold, "and you are needed to wield it."

"Then I shall do as you desire, Warrior," Hawkmoon replied lightly. "Do you sail with us?"

"I have other matters to attend to."

"We shall meet again, doubtless."

"Doubtless."

D'Averc coughed and raised his hand. "Then, farewell, Warrior. Thanks for your aid."

"Thank you for yours," replied the warrior enigmatically.

Hawkmoon gave the order for the gangplank to be raised and the oars to be unshipped.

Soon the ship was pulling out of the bay and into the open sea. Hawkmoon watched the figures of Bewchard and the Warrior in Jet and Gold become smaller and smaller and smaller and then he turned and smiled at D'Averc.

"Well, D'Averc, do you know where we are going?"

"To Dnark, I take it," D'Averc replied innocently.

"To Europe, D'Averc. I care not for this destiny. I wish to see my wife again. We are going to sail across the sea, D'Averc — for Europe. There we may use our rings to take us back to Castle Brass. I would see Yisselda again."

D'Averc said nothing, merely turned his head to look upward as the white sails billowed and the ship began to gather speed.

"What do you say to that, D'Averc?" Hawkmoon asked with a grin, slapping his friend on the back.

D'Averc shrugged. "I say that it would be a welcome rest to spend some time in Castle Brass again."

"There is something about your tone, friend. Something a trifle sardonic..." Hawkmoon frowned. "What is it?"

D'Averc gave him a sidelong glance that matched his tone. "Maybe I am not as sure as you, Hawkmoon, that this ship will find its way to Europe. Perhaps I have a greater respect for the Runestaff."

"You believe in such legends? Why, Amarehk was supposed to be a place of godlike people. It was far from that, eh?"

"I think you insist on the Runestaff's non-existence too much. I think your anxiety to see Yisselda must influence you considerably."

"Possibly."

D'Averc stared out to sea. "Time will tell us how strong the Runestaff is."

Hawkmoon gave him a puzzled look before he shrugged, walking away down the deck.

D'Averc smiled, shaking his head as he watched his friend.

Then he turned his attention to the sails, wondering privately if he would ever see Castle Brass again.

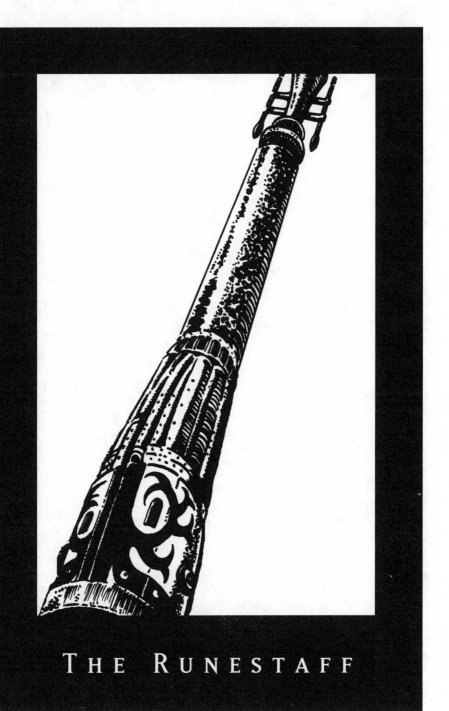

THE RUNESTAFF

For Nik Turner

B O O K O N E

Tacticians and warriors of ferocious courage and skill; careless of their own lives; corrupt of soul and mad of brain; haters of all that was not in decay; wielders of power without morality — force without justice; the Barons of Granbretan carried the standard of their King-Emperor Huon across the continent of Europe and made that continent their property; carried the banner to West and East to other continents to which they also laid claim. And it seemed that no force, either natural or supernatural, was strong enough to halt the insane and deadly tide.

Indeed, none now resisted them at all. With chuckling pride and cold contempt they demanded whole nations as tribute and the tribute was paid.

In all the subdued lands few hoped. Of those, fewer dared express hope — and among those few hardly a single soul possessed the courage to murmur the name symbolizing that hope.

The name was Castle Brass.

Those who spoke the name understood its implications, for Castle Brass was the only stronghold to remain unvanquished by the warlords of Granbretan, and Castle Brass housed heroes; men who had fought the Dark Empire, whose names were loathed and hated by the brooding Baron Meliadus, Grand Constable of the Order of the Wolf, Commander of the Army of Conquest, for it was known that Baron Meliadus fought a private feud with those heroes, particularly the legendary Dorian Hawkmoon von Köln who was married to the woman Meliadus desired, Yisselda, daughter of Count Brass of Castle Brass.

But Castle Brass had not defeated the armies of Granbretan, it had merely evaded them, disappearing by means of a strange, ancient crystal machine into another dimension of the Earth, where those heroes, Hawkmoon, Count Brass, Huillam D'Averc, Oladahn of the Bulgar Mountains and their handful of Kamargian men-at-arms, now sheltered, and most folk felt that the heroes of Kamarg had deserted them forever. They did not blame them, but their hope waned fainter with every day that passed and the heroes did not return.

In that other Kamarg, sundered from its original by mysterious dimensions of time and space, Hawkmoon and the rest were faced with fresh problems, for it seemed that the sorcerer-scientists of the Dark Empire were close to discovering means either of breaking through into their dimension or of recalling them. The enigmatic Warrior in Jet and Gold had sent Hawkmoon and D'Averc on a quest to a strange new land to seek the legendary Sword of the Dawn, which would be of aid to them in their struggle, and which would in turn aid the Runestaff, which, the warrior insisted, Hawkmoon, manifestation of the Champion Eternal, served. Having won the rosy sword, Hawkmoon was then informed he must travel by sea around the coast of Amarehk to the city of Dnark, where the services of the blade were required. But Hawkmoon demurred. He was anxious to return to Kamarg and see his beautiful wife Yisselda again. In a ship supplied by Bewchard of Narleen, Hawkmoon set sail for Europe, against the dictates of the Warrior in Jet and Gold who had told him that his duty to the Runestaff, that mysterious artifact said to control all human destinies, was greater than his duty to his wife, friends and adopted homeland. With the foppish Huillam D'Averc by his side, Hawkmoon headed out to sea.

Meanwhile in Granbretan Baron Meliadus fumed at what he considered his King-Emperor's foolishness in not allowing him to pursue his vendetta against Castle Brass. When Shenegar Trott, Count of Sussex, seemed to be favoured over him by a King-Emperor growing steadily more mistrustful of his unstable conquistador, Meliadus became rebellious, pursuing his prey to the Wastes of Yel, losing them, and returning with redoubled hatred to Londra, there to scheme not only against the heroes of Castle Brass, but also against his immortal ruler, Huon, the King-Emperor...

— *The High History of the Runestaff*

O   N   E

AN EPISODE IN KING HUON'S THRONE ROOM

The vast doors parted and Baron Meliadus, but lately returned from Yel, walked into the throne room of his King-Emperor, to report his failures and his discoveries.

As Meliadus entered the room, whose roof seemed so tall as to be one with the heavens and whose walls were so distant as to seem to encompass an entire country, his way was blocked by a double line of guards. These guards, members of the King-Emperor's own Order of the Mantis and wearing the great jeweled insect masks belonging to that Order, seemed reluctant to let him pass through.

Meliadus controlled himself with difficulty and waited while the ranks drew back to admit him.

Then he strode on into the hall of blazing colour, whose galleries were hung with the gleaming banners of Granbretan's five hundred greatest families and whose walls were encrusted with a mosaic of precious gems depicting Granbretan's might and history, along an aisle made up on either side by a thousand mantis warriors, each statue-still, towards the Throne Globe more than a mile distant.

Half-way to the globe, he abased himself in a somewhat peremptory fashion.

The solid black sphere seemed to shudder momentarily as Baron Meliadus rose, then the black became shot through with veins of scarlet and white which slowly spread through the darker shade until it had vanished altogether. The mixture like milk and blood swirled and cleared to reveal a tiny foetuslike shape curled in the centre of the sphere. From this twisted figure peered eyes that were hard, black and sharp, containing an old — indeed, an immortal — intelligence. This was Huon, King-Emperor of Granbretan and the Dark Empire, Grand Constable of the Order of the Mantis, wielder of absolute power over tens of millions of souls, the ruler who would live forever and in whose name Baron Meliadus had conquered the whole of Europe and beyond.

The voice of a golden youth now issued from the Throne Globe (the golden youth to whom it had belonged had been dead a thousand years):

"Ah, our impetuous Baron Meliadus..."

Again Meliadus bowed and murmured, "Your servant, Prince of All."

"And what have you to report to us, hasty lord?"

"Success, Great Emperor. Proof of my suspicions..."

"You have found the missing emissaries from Asiacommunista?"

"I regret not, noble sire..."

Baron Meliadus did not know that it had been in this disguise that Hawkmoon and D'Averc had penetrated the capital of the Dark Empire. Only Flana Mikosevaar, who had helped them escape, knew that.

"Then why are you here, Baron?"

"I discovered that Hawkmoon, whom I insist is still the greatest threat to our security, has been visiting our island. I went to Yel and there found him and the traitor Huillam D'Averc, as well as the magician Mygan of Llandar. They know the secret of traveling through the dimensions." Baron Meliadus did not mention that they had escaped from him. "Before we could apprehend them they vanished before our eyes. Mighty Monarch, if they can come and go from our land at will, surely it is plain that we can never be safe until they are destroyed. I would suggest we begin immediately to direct all the efforts of our scientists — of Taragorm and Kalan in particular — to finding these renegades and finishing them. They threaten us from within..."

"Baron Meliadus. What news of the emissaries from Asiacommunista?"

"None, so far, Mighty King-Emperor, but..."

"A few guerillas, Baron Meliadus, this empire may contend with, but if our shores are threatened by a force as great, if not greater, than our own, by a force, moreover, that is possessed of scientific secrets unknown to us, that we may not survive, you see..." The golden voice spoke with acid patience.

Meliadus frowned. "We have no proof that such an invasion is planned, Monarch of the World..."

"Agreed. Neither have we proof, Baron Meliadus, that Hawkmoon and his band of terrorists have the power to do us any great harm." Streaks of ice blue suddenly appeared in the Throne Globe's fluid.

"Great King-Emperor. Give me the time and the resources..."

"We are an expanding empire, Baron Meliadus. We wish to expand still further. It would be pessimistic, would it not, to stand still? That is not our way. We are proud of our influence upon the Earth. We wish to extend it. You seem uneager to carry out the principles of our ambition which is to spread a great, laughing terror to the corners of the world. You are becoming small-minded, we fear..."

"But by refusing to counter those subtle forces that might wreck our schemes, Prince of All, we could betray our destiny also!"

"We resent dissension, Baron Meliadus. Your personal hatred of Hawkmoon and, we have heard, your desire for Yisselda of Brass, represent dissension. We have your self-interest at heart, Baron, for if you continue in this course, we shall be obliged to elect another over you, to dismiss you from our service — aye, even to dismiss you from your Order..."

Instinctively, Baron Meliadus's gauntleted hands leapt fearfully to his mask. *To be unmasked!* The greatest disgrace — the greatest horror of them all! For that was what the threat implied. To join the ranks of the lowest scum in Londra — the caste of the unmasked ones! Meliadus shuddered and could hardly bring himself to speak.

At last he murmured, "I will reflect on your words, Emperor of the Earth..."

"Do so, Baron Meliadus. We would not wish to see such a great conqueror destroyed by a few clouded thoughts. If you would regain all our favour, you will find for us the means by which the Asiacommunistan emissaries left."

Baron Meliadus fell to his knees, his great wolf mask nodding, his arms outspread. Thus the conqueror of Europe abased himself before his lord, but his brain flared with a dozen rebellious thoughts and he thanked the spirit of his Order that the mask hid his face so that his fury did not show.

He backed away from the Throne Globe while the beady, sardonic eyes of the King-Emperor regarded him. Huon's prehensile tongue darted out to touch a jewel floating near the shrunken head and the milky fluid swirled, flashed with rainbow colours, then gradually turned black once more.

Meliadus wheeled and began the long march back to the gigantic doors, feeling that every eye behind the unmoving mantis masks watched him with malevolent humour.

When he had passed through the doors, he turned to the left and strode through the corridors of the twisted palace, seeking the apartments of the Countess Flana Mikosevaar of Kanbery, widow of Asrovak Mikosevaar, the Muskovian renegade who had once headed the Vulture Legion. Countess Flana not only was now titular head of the Vulture Legion, but also cousin to the King-Emperor — his only surviving kin.

T W O

HUMAN THOUGHTS OF THE COUNTESS FLANA

The Heron mask of spun gold lay on the lacquered table before her as she stared through the window, over the curling, crazy spires of the city of Londra, her pale, beautiful face full of sadness and confusion.

As she moved, the rich silks and jewels of her gown caught the light from the red sun. She went to a closet and opened it. There were the strange costumes she had kept since those two visitors had left her apartments so many days before. The disguises that Hawkmoon and D'Averc had used when posing as princes from Asiacommunista. Now she wondered where they were — particularly D'Averc whom she knew loved her.

Flana, Countess of Kanbery, had had a dozen husbands and more lovers, had disposed of them in one way or another as a woman might dispose of a useless pair of stockings. She had never experienced love, never had the emotion known to most others, even the rulers of Granbretan.

But somehow D'Averc, that dandified renegade who claimed to be permanently ill, had aroused these feelings in her. Perhaps she had remained so remote heretofore because she was sane, while those surrounding her at court were not, because she was gentle and capable of selfless love, whereas the Lords of the Dark Empire understood nothing of such feelings. Perhaps D'Averc, gentle, subtle, sensitive, had awakened her from an apathy induced not by lack of soul, but by a greatness of soul — such greatness that it could not bear to exist in the mad, selfish, perverse world of the Court of King Huon.

But now that the Countess Flana was awake, she could not ignore the horror of her surroundings, the despair she felt that her lover of a single night might never return, that he might even be already dead.

She had taken to her apartments, avoiding contact with the rest, but while this ruse afforded her some surcease from understanding of her circumstances, it only allowed her sorrow silence in which to grow.

Tears fell down Flana's perfect cheeks and she stopped their flow with a scented silken scarf.

A maidservant entered the room and hesitated on the threshold. Automatically Flana reached for her heron mask.

"What is it?"

"The Baron Meliadus of Kroiden, my lady. He says he has to speak with you. A matter of paramount urgency."

Flana slipped her mask over her head and settled it on her shoulders.

She considered the girl's words for a moment and then shrugged. What did it matter if she saw Meliadus for a few moments? Perhaps he had some news of D'Averc, whom she knew he hated. By subtle means she might discover what he knew.

But what if Meliadus wished to make love to her, as he had on previous occasions?

Why, she would turn him away, as she had turned him away before.

She inclined the lovely heron mask a fraction.

"Admit the baron," she said.

T H R E E

H A W K M O O N   A L T E R S   H I S   C O U R S E

The great sails curved in the wind as the ship sped over the surface of the sea. The sky was clear and the sea was calm, a vast expanse of azure. Oars had been shipped and the helmsman now looked to the main deck for his course. The bosun, clad in orange and black, climbed to the deck where Hawkmoon stood staring across the ocean.

Hawkmoon's golden hair streamed in the wind and his cloak of wine-coloured velvet whipped out behind him. His handsome features were battle-hardened and weather beaten and were only marred by the existence, embedded in his forehead, of a dull, black stone. Gravely, he acknowledged the bosun's salute.

"I've given orders to sail around the coast, heading due east, sir," the bosun said.

"Who gave you that course, bosun?"

"Why, nobody, sir. I just assumed that since we were heading for Dnark..."

"We are not heading for Dnark, tell the helmsman."

"But that strange warrior — the Warrior in Jet and Gold you called him — he said..."

"He is not my master, bosun. No — we sail out to sea now. For Europe."

"For Europe, sir! You know that after you saved Narleen we would take you anywhere, follow you anywhere, but have you any understanding of the distances we must sail to reach Europe — the seas we should have to cross, the storms...?"

"Aye, I understand. But we still sail for Europe."

"As you say, sir." Frowning, the bosun turned away to give his orders to the helmsman.

From his cabin below the main deck, D'Averc now emerged and began to climb the ladder. Hawkmoon grinned at him. "Did you sleep well, friend D'Averc?"

"As well as possible aboard this rocking tub. I am inclined to suffer from insomnia at the best of times, Hawkmoon, but I snatched a few moments. The most, I suppose, I may expect."

Hawkmoon, laughed. "When I looked in on you an hour ago, you were snoring."

D'Averc raised his eyebrows. "So! You heard me breathing heavily, eh? I tried to keep as quiet as possible, but this cold of mine — contracted since coming aboard — is giving me a certain amount of difficulty." He raised a tiny square of linen to the tip of his nose.

D'Averc was dressed in silk, with a loose blue shirt, flowing scarlet breeks, a heavy broad leather belt supporting his sword and a dirk. Around his bronzed throat was wound a long scarf of purple and his long hair was held back by a band matching his breeks. His fine, almost ascetic features bore their usual sardonic expression.

"Did I hear aright below?" D'Averc asked. "Were you instructing the bosun to head for Europe?"

"I was."

"So you still intend to try to reach Castle Brass and forget what the Warrior in Jet and Gold said of your destiny — that it was to take that blade there," D'Averc pointed to the great red broadsword at Hawkmoon's side, "to Dnark, thus serving the Runestaff?"

"I owe allegiance to myself and my kin before I will serve an artifact in whose existence I gravely doubt."

"You would not have believed before in the powers of the Sword of the Dawn," D'Averc remarked wryly, "yet you saw it summon warriors from thin air to save our lives."

An obstinate look passed over Hawkmoon's features. "Aye," he agreed reluctantly. "But I still intend to return to Castle Brass, if that is possible."

"There's no telling if it's in this dimension or another."

"I can only hope that it is in this dimension." Hawkmoon spoke with finality, showing his unwillingness to discuss the matter further. D'Averc raised his eyebrows for a second time, then descended to the deck and strolled along it whistling.

For five days they sailed on through the calm ocean, every sail unfurled to give them maximum speed.

On the sixth day the bosun came up to Hawkmoon, who was standing in the prow of the ship, and pointed ahead.

"See the dark sky on the horizon, sir. We're heading straight for a storm."

Hawkmoon peered in the direction the bosun indicated. "A storm, you say. Yet it has a peculiar look to it."

"Aye, sir. Shall I reef the sails?"

"No, bosun. We sail on until we have a better idea of what we are heading into."

"As you say, sir." The bosun walked back down the deck, shaking his head.

A few hours later the sky ahead became a lurid wall across the sea, from horizon to horizon, its predominant colours dark red and purple. It towered upwards and yet the sky above them was as blue as it ever had been and the sea was perfectly calm. Only the wind had dropped slightly. It was as if they sailed in a lake, enclosed on all sides by mountains whose peaks disappeared into the heavens. The crew was disconcerted and there was a note of fear in the bosun's voice when he next confronted Hawkmoon.

"Do we sail on, sir? I have never heard of such a phenomenon as this before; I've never experienced anything like it. The crew's nervous, sir, and I'll admit that I am, also."

Hawkmoon nodded sympathetically. "It's peculiar, right enough, seeming to be more supernatural than natural."

"That's what the crew's saying, sir."

Hawkmoon's own instinct was to press on and face whatever it was, but he had a responsibility to the crew, each member of which had volunteered to sail with him in gratitude for his ridding their home city, Narleen, of the power of the Pirate Lords.

Hawkmoon sighed. "Very well, bosun. We'll take in all sail and wait the night. With luck, the phenomenon will have passed by morning."

The bosun was relieved. "Thank you, sir."

Hawkmoon acknowledged his salute then turned to stare up at the huge walls. Were they cloud or were they something else? A chill had come into the air and although the sun still shone down, its rays did not seem to touch the massed clouds.

All was still. Hawkmoon wondered if he had made a wise decision in heading away from Dnark. None, to his knowledge, save the ancients had ever sailed these oceans. Who was to tell what uncharted terrors inhabited them?

Night fell, and in the distance the vast, lurid walls could still be seen, their dark reds and purples piercing the blackness of the night. And yet the colours hardly seemed to have the usual properties of light.

Hawkmoon began to feel perturbed.

In the morning the walls seemed to have drawn in much closer and the area of blue sea seemed much smaller. Hawkmoon wondered if they had not been caught in a trap set by giants.

Clad in a thick cloak that did not keep out much of the chill, he paced the deck at dawn.

D'Averc was next to emerge, wearing at least three cloaks and shivering ostentatiously. "A fresh morning, Hawkmoon."

"Aye," murmured the Duke of Köln. "What do you make of it, D'Averc?"

The Frenchman shook his head. "It's a grim sort of stuff, isn't it? Here comes the bosun."

They both turned to greet the bosun. He, too, was wrapped up heavily in a great leather cloak normally used for protection when sailing through a storm.

"Any thoughts on this, bosun?" D'Averc asked.

The bosun shook his head and addressed Hawkmoon. "The men say that whatever happens, sir, they are yours. They will die in your service if necessary."

"They're in a gloomy mood, I gather," smiled D'Averc. "Well, who's to blame them?"

"Who indeed, sir." The bosun's round, honest face looked despairing. "Shall I give the order to sail on, sir?"

"It would be better than waiting here while the stuff closes in," Hawkmoon said. "Let go the sails, bosun.

The bosun shouted orders and men began to climb through the rigging, letting down the sails and securing their lines. Gradually the sails filled and the ship began to move, seemingly reluctantly, towards the strange cliffs of clouds.

Yet even as they moved forward, the cliffs began to swirl and become agitated. Other, darker colours crept in and a wailing noise drifted towards the ship from all sides. The crew could barely contain its panic, many men standing frozen in the rigging as they watched. Hawkmoon peered forward anxiously.

Then, instantly, the walls had vanished!

Hawkmoon gasped.

Calm sea lay on all sides. Everything was as before. The crew began to cheer, but Hawkmoon noticed that D'Averc's face was bleak. Hawkmoon, too, felt that perhaps the danger was not past. He waited, poised at the rail.

Then from the sea erupted a huge beast.

The crew's cheers changed to screams of fear.

Other beasts began to emerge all around them. Gigantic, reptilian monsters with gaping red jaws and triple rows of teeth, the water streaming from their scales and their blazing eyes full of mad, rolling evil.

There was a deafening flapping noise and one by one the giant reptiles climbed into the air.

"We are done for, Hawkmoon," said D'Averc philosophically as he drew his sword. "It's a pity not to have had one last sight of Castle Brass, nor one last kiss from the lips of those women we love."

Hawkmoon barely heard him. He was full of bitterness at the fate which had decided he should meet his end in this wet and lonely place. Now none would know where or how he had died...

F O U R

O R L A N D   F A N K

The shadows of the gigantic beasts swept back and forth over the deck and the noise of their wings filled the air. Looking upwards in cold detachment as a monster dropped towards him, its maw distended, the Duke of Köln knew his life had ended. But then the monster had soared again, having snapped once at the high mast.

Nerves tense, muscles taut, Dorian Hawkmoon drew the Sword of the Dawn, the blade which no other man could wield and live. Even this supernatural broadsword would be useless against the dreadful beasts; they need not even attack the crew directly, need only strike the ship a few blows to send those aboard to the bottom.

The ship rocked in the wind created by the vast wings and the air stank of their foetid breath.

D'Averc frowned. "Why are they not attacking? Are they playing a game with us?"

"It seems likely." Hawkmoon spoke between clenched teeth. "Maybe it pleases them to play with us for a while before destroying us."

As a great shadow descended, D'Averc leapt up and slashed at a creature which had flapped into the air again before D'Averc's feet returned to the deck. He wrinkled his nose. "Ugh! The stink! It can do my lungs no good."

Now, one by one, each of the creatures descended and struck the ship a few thwacks with its leathery wings. The ship shuddered. Men screamed as they were flung from the rigging to the deck. Hawkmoon and D'Averc staggered, clinging to the rail to save themselves from toppling.

"They're turning the ship!" D'Averc cried in puzzlement. "We're being forced round!"

Hawkmoon stared grimly at the terrifying monsters and said nothing. Soon the ship had been turned by about eighty degrees. Then the beasts rose higher into the sky, wheeling above the ship as if debating their next action. Hawkmoon looked at their eyes, trying to discern intelligence there, trying to discover some hint of their intentions, but it was impossible. The creatures began to flap away until they were far to sternward. And then they began to come back.

In formation the beasts flapped their wings until such a wind was created that Hawkmoon and D'Averc could no longer keep their footing and they were pressed down to the planks of the deck.

The sails of the ship bent in this wind and D'Averc cried out in astonishment. "They're driving the ship the way they want it to go! It's incredible!"

"We're heading towards Amarehk," Hawkmoon said, struggling to rise. "I wonder..."

"What can their diet be?" D'Averc shouted. "Certainly they eat nothing intended to sweeten the breath! Phew!"

Hawkmoon grinned in spite of their plight.

The crew were now all huddled in the oar-wells, staring up fearfully at the monstrous reptiles as they flapped overhead, filling the sails with wind.

"Perhaps their nest is in this direction," Hawkmoon suggested. "Perhaps their young are to be fed and they prefer live meat?"

D'Averc looked offended. "What you say is likely, friend Hawkmoon. But it was still tactless of you to suggest it..."

Again Hawkmoon gave a wry grin.

"There's a chance, if their nests are on land, of getting to grips with them," he said. "On the open sea we had no chance of survival at all."

"You're optimistic, Duke of Köln..."

For more than an hour the extraordinary reptiles propelled the ship over the water at breakneck speed. Then at last Hawkmoon pointed ahead, saying nothing.

"An island!" exclaimed D'Averc. "You were right about that, at any rate!"

It was a small island, apparently bare of vegetation, its sides rising sharply to a peak, as if the tip of a drowned mountain had not been entirely engulfed.

It was then that a fresh danger alerted Hawkmoon!

"Rocks! We're heading straight for them! Crew! To your positions. Helmsman..." But Hawkmoon was already dashing for the helm, had grabbed it, was desperately trying to save the ship from running aground.

D'Averc joined him, lending his own strength to turn the craft. The island loomed larger and larger and the sound of the surf boomed in their ears — a drumbeat to herald disaster.

Slowly the ship turned as the cliffs of the island towered over them and the spray drenched them, but then they heard a terrible scraping sound which became a scream of tortured timbers and they knew that the rocks were ripping into the starboard side beneath the waterline.

"Every man for himself!" Hawkmoon cried and ran for the rail, D'Averc closely behind him. The ship lurched and reared like a living thing and all were flung back against the port rails of the craft. Bruised but still conscious, Hawkmoon and D'Averc pulled themselves to their feet, hesitated for a moment, then dived into the black and seething waters of the sea.

Weighted by his great broadsword, Hawkmoon felt himself being dragged to the bottom. Through the swirling water he saw other shapes drifting and the noise of the surf was now dull in his ears. But he would not release the Sword of the Dawn. Instead he fought to scabbard it and then use all his energy to strike up to the surface, dragging the heavy blade with him.

At last he broke through the waves and got a dim impression of the ship above him. The sea seemed much calmer and eventually the wind dropped altogether, the boom of the surf diminished to a whisper and a strange silence took the place of the cacophony of a few moments earlier. Hawkmoon headed for a flat rock, reached it, and dragged himself on to land.

Then he looked back.

The reptilian monsters were still wheeling in the sky, but so high they did not disturb the air with their wing beats. Suddenly they rose still higher, hovered for a moment, then dived headlong toward the sea.

One by one they struck the waves with a great smashing noise. The ship groaned as the wash hit it and Hawkmoon was almost sluiced from his place of safety.

Then the monsters were gone.

Hawkmoon wiped water from his eyes and spat out the brine from his mouth.

What would they do next? Was it their intention to keep their prey alive, to pick them off when they needed fresh meat? There was no way of telling.

Hawkmoon heard a cry and saw D'Averc and half-a-dozen others come staggering along the rocks toward him.

D'Averc looked bewildered. "Did you see the beasts leave, Hawkmoon?"

"Aye. Will they be back, I wonder?"

D'Averc glanced grimly in the direction in which the beasts had disappeared. He shrugged.

"I suggest we strike inland, saving what we can from the ship," Hawkmoon said. "How many of us left alive?" He turned enquiringly to the bosun who stood behind D'Averc.

"Most of us, I think, sir. We were lucky. Look." The bosun pointed beyond the ship to where the major part of the crew was assembling on the shore.

"Send some men back to her before she breaks up," Hawkmoon said. "Rig lines to the shore and start getting provisions to dry land."

"As you say, sir. But what if the monsters return?"

"We'll have to deal with them when we see them," Hawkmoon said.

For several hours Hawkmoon watched as everything possible was carried from the ship and piled on the rocks of the island.

"Can the ship be repaired, do you think?" D'Averc asked.

"Maybe. Now that the sea is calm, there's little chance of her breaking up. But it will take time." Hawkmoon fingered the dull, black stone in his forehead. "Come, D'Averc, let's explore inland."

They began to climb up over the rocks, heading up the slope to the summit of the island. The place seemed completely devoid of life. The best they could hope to find would be pools of fresh water and there might be shellfish on the shore. It was a bleak place. Their hopes of survival, if the ship could not be refloated, seemed very slight, particularly with the prospect of the monsters returning.

They reached the summit at last and paused, breathing heavily from their exertions.

"The other side's as barren as this," D'Averc said, gesturing downward. "I wonder..." He broke off and gasped. "By the Eyes of Berezenath! A man!"

Hawkmoon looked in the direction D'Averc indicated.

Sure enough, a figure was strolling along the shore below. As they stared, he looked up and waved cheerfully, gesturing them towards him.

Certain they were suffering hallucinations, the two began slowly to climb down until they were close to him. He stood there, fists on his hips, feet wide apart, grinning at them. They paused.

The man was dressed in a peculiar and archaic fashion. Over his brawny torso was stretched a jerkin of leather, leaving his arms and chest bare. He wore a woolen bonnet on his mop of red hair and a pheasant's tailfeather was stuck jauntily into it. His breeks were of a strange chequered design and he wore battered buckled boots on his feet. Secured over his back by a cord was a gigantic battle-axe, its steel blade streaked with dirt and battered by much use. His face was bony and red and his pale blue eyes were sardonic as he stared at them.

"Well, now — you'd be the Hawkmoon and the D'Averc," he said in a strange accent. "I was told you'd likely come."

"And who are you, sir?" D'Averc asked somewhat haughtily.

"Why, I'm Orland Fank, didn't you know? Orland Fank — here at your service, good sirs."

"Do you live on this island?" Hawkmoon asked.

"I have lived on it, but not at the moment, don't you know." Fank removed his bonnet and wiped his forehead with his arm. "I'm a traveling man, these days. Like yourselves, I understand."

"And who told you of us?" Hawkmoon asked.

"I've a brother. Given to wearing somewhat fancy metal of black and gold…"

"The Warrior in Jet and Gold!" Hawkmoon exclaimed.

"He's called some such foppish title, I gather. He would not have mentioned his rough and ready brother to you, I don't doubt."

"He did not. Who are you?"

"I'm called Orland Fank. From Skare Brae — in the Orkneys, you know…"

"The Orkneys!" Hawkmoon's hand went to his sword. "Is that not part of Granbretan? Island to the far north!"

Fank laughed. "Tell an Orkney man that he belongs to the Dark Empire, and he'll tear the throat from you with his teeth!" He gestured apologetically, and as if in explanation said, "It's the favourite way of dealing with a foe out there, you know. We're not a sophisticated folk."

"So the Warrior in Jet and Gold is also from the Orkneys D'Averc began.

"Save you, no man! Him from the Orkneys, with his fancy suit of armour and his fine manner!" Orland Fank laughed heartily. "No. He's no Orkney man!" Fank wiped tears of laughter from his eyes with his battered bonnet. "Why should you think that?"

"You said he was your brother."

"So he is. Spiritually, you might say. Perhaps even physically. I've forgotten. It's been many years, you see, since we first came together."

"What brought you together?"

"A common cause, you might say. A shared ideal."

"And would the Runestaff be the source of that cause?" Hawkmoon murmured, his voice hardly louder than the whisper of the surf below them.

"It might."

"You seem close-mouthed, suddenly, friend Fank," said D'Averc.

"Aye. In Orkney, we're a close-mouthed folk," smiled Orland Fank. "Indeed, I'm considered something of a babbler there." He did not seem offended.

Hawkmoon gestured behind him. "Those monsters. The strange clouds we saw earlier. Would that be to do with the Runestaff?"

"I saw no monsters. No clouds. I've but recently arrived here myself."

"We were driven to this island by gigantic reptiles," Hawkmoon said. "And now I begin to see why. They, too, served the Runestaff, I do not doubt."

"That's as may be," Fank replied. "It's not my business, you see, Lord Dorian."

"Was it the Runestaff that caused our boat to be wrecked?" Hawkmoon asked fiercely.

"I could not say," Fank replied, replacing his bonnet on his mop of red hair and scratching at his bony chin. "I only know that I'm here to give you a boat and tell you where you might find the nearest habitable land."

"You have a boat for us?" D'Averc was astonished.

"Aye. Not a splendid one, but a seaworthy craft nonetheless. It should take the two of you."

"We have a crew of fifty!" Hawkmoon's eyes blazed. "Oh, if the Runestaff wishes me to serve it, it should arrange things better! All it has succeeded in doing so far is to anger me fiercely!"

"Your anger will only weary you," Orland Fank replied mildly. "I had thought you bound for Dnark in the Runestaff's service. My brother told me..."

"Your brother insisted I go to Dnark. But I have other loyalties, Orland Fank — loyalties to the wife I have not seen for months, to the father-in-law who awaits my return, to my friends..."

"The folk of Castle Brass? Aye, I've heard of them. They are safe, for the moment, if that comforts you."

"You know this for certain?"

"Aye. Their lives are pretty much without event, save for the trouble with one Elvereza Tozer."

"Tozer! What of the renegade?"

"He has vanished from Kamarg, I gather." Orland Fank made a flying gesture with his hand.

"For where?"

"Who knows?"

"They are well rid of Tozer, at any rate."

"I do not know the man."

"A talented playwright," Hawkmoon said, "with the morals of a — of a..."

"A Granbretanian?" offered Fank.

"Exactly." Hawkmoon frowned then and stared hard at Orland Fank. "You would not deceive me? My kin and friends are safe?"

"Their security is not for the moment threatened."

Hawkmoon sighed. "Where is this boat? And what of my crew?"

"I have some small skill as a shipwright. I'll help them mend their ship so that they can return to Narleen."

"Why cannot we go with them?" D'Averc asked.

"I understood you were an impatient pair," Fank said innocently, "and that you would be off the island as soon as you could. It will take many days to repair the large craft."

"We'll take your little boat," Hawkmoon said. "It seems that if we did not, the Runestaff — or whatever power it was that really sent us here — would see to it that we were further inconvenienced."

"I understand that would be likely," Fank agreed, smiling a little to himself.

"And how will you leave the island if we take your boat?" D'Averc asked.

"I'll sail with the seamen of Narleen. I have a great deal of time to spare."

"How far is it to the mainland?" Hawkmoon asked. "And by what shall we sail? Have you a compass to lend us?"

Fank shrugged. "It's of no great distance and you'll not need a compass. You need only wait for the right sort of wind."

"What do you mean?"

"The winds in these parts are somewhat peculiar. You will understand what I mean."

Hawkmoon shrugged in resignation.

They followed as Orland Fank led the way around the shore.

"It would seem that we are not quite as much the masters of our destinies as we should like," murmured D'Averc sardonically as the small boat came in sight.

F I V E

A City of Glowing Shadows

Hawkmoon lay scowling in the small boat and D'Averc whistled a tune as he stood in the prow, the spray lashing his face. For a whole day now the wind had guided the craft, blowing them on what was plainly a particular course.

"Now I understand what Fank meant about the wind," growled Hawkmoon. "This is no natural breeze. I resent the feeling of being the puppet of some supernatural agency."

D'Averc grinned and pointed ahead. "Well, perhaps we'll have a chance to voice our complaints to the agency itself. See — land in sight."

Hawkmoon rose reluctantly. There were faint signs of land on the horizon.

"And so we return to Amarehk!" D'Averc laughed.

"If only it were Europe and Yisselda were there." Hawkmoon sat down again.

"Or even Londra, and Flana to comfort me." D'Averc shrugged and began to cough theatrically. "Still, it is best this way, lest she find herself pledged to a sick and dying creature…"

Gradually they made out features on the shoreline: irregular cliffs, hills and beaches; some trees. Then, to the south, they saw a peculiar aura of golden light — light which throbbed as if in concert to a gigantic heart.

"More disturbing phenomena." D'Averc frowned.

The wind blew harder and the little boat turned toward the golden light.

"And we're heading directly for it," groaned Hawkmoon. "I am becoming tired of such things!"

Now it was clear they sailed into a bay formed by the mainland and a long island jutting out between the two shores. It was from the far end of this island that the golden light was pulsing.

The land on either side seemed pleasant, consisting of beaches and wooded hills, though there were no signs of habitation.

As they neared the source of the light, it began to fade until only a faint glow filled the sky and the boat's speed diminished. They still sailed directly towards the light. They saw it, then, and were amazed...

It was a city of such grace and beauty it robbed them of speech. As huge as Londra, if not larger, its buildings were symmetrical spires and domes and turrets, all glowing with the same strange light, but coloured in delicate, pale shades that lurked behind the gold — pink, yellow, blue, green, violet and cerise — like a painting created in light and then washed with gold. Its magnificent beauty did not seem a proper habitation for human creatures, but for gods.

Now the ship sailed into a harbour stretching out from the city, its quays shifting with the same subtle shades of the buildings.

"It is like a dream..." Hawkmoon murmured.

"A dream of heaven." D'Averc's cynicism had vanished before the vision.

The little boat drifted to a set of steps that led down to the water, which was dappled with the reflections of the colours, and came to a halt.

D'Averc shrugged. "I suppose this is where we disembark. The boat could have borne us to a less pleasant place."

Hawkmoon nodded gravely and then said: "Are the rings of Mygan still in your pouch, D'Averc?"

D'Averc patted his pouch. "They are safe. Why?"

"I wanted to know that if the danger was too great for us to face with our swords and there was time to use the rings, we could use them."

D'Averc nodded his understanding and then his forehead creased. "Strange that we did not think of using them on the island..."

Hawkmoon's face showed his astonishment. "Aye — aye..." And then he pursed his lips in disgust. "Doubtless that was the result of supernatural interference with our brains! How I hate the supernatural!"

D'Averc merrily put his fingers to his lips and put on an expression of mock disapproval. "What a thing to say in a city such as this!"

"Aye — well, I hope its inhabitants are as pleasant as its appearance."

"If it has any inhabitants," replied D'Averc, glancing around him.

Together they climbed the steps and reached the quayside. The strange buildings were ahead of them and between the buildings ran wide streets.

"Let's enter the city," Hawkmoon said resolutely, "and find out why we have been taken here as soon as we can. Then, perhaps, we shall be allowed to return to Castle Brass!"

Entering the nearest street, it seemed to them that the shadows cast by the buildings actually glowed with a life and colour of their own. At close hand the tall towers were hardly tangible and when Hawkmoon reached out to touch one the substance of it was unlike anything he had touched before. It was not stone and it was not timber; not steel even, for it gave slightly under his fingers and made them tingle. He was also surprised by the warmth that ran through his arm and suffused his body.

He shook his head. "It is more like flesh than stone!"

D'Averc reached out now and was equally astonished. "Aye — or like vegetation of some kind. Organic — living stuff!"

They moved on. Every so often the long streets would broaden out into squares. They crossed the squares, choosing another street at random, looking up at the buildings which gave the appearance of infinite height, which disappeared into the strange, golden haze.

Their voices were hushed; they feared to disturb the silence of the great city.

"Have you noticed," murmured Hawkmoon, "that there are no windows?"

"And no doors." D'Averc nodded. "I am certain that this city was not built for human use — and that humans did not build it!"

"Perhaps some beings created in the Tragic Millennium," Hawkmoon suggested. "Beings like the wraith-folk of Soryandum."

D'Averc nodded his head in agreement.

Now ahead of them the strange shadows seemed to gather closer together and they passed into them, an impression of great well-being overcoming them. Hawkmoon smiled in spite of his fears, and D'Averc, too, answered his smile. The glowing shadows swam around them. Hawkmoon began to wonder if perhaps these shadows were, in fact, the inhabitants of the city.

They passed out of the street and stood in a huge square at the very centre of the city. Rising from the middle of this square was a cylindrical building. In spite of being the largest building in the city it also seemed the most delicate. Its walls moved with coloured light and Hawkmoon noticed something at its base.

"Look, D'Averc — steps leading to a door!"

"What should we do, I wonder," whispered his friend.

Hawkmoon shrugged. "Enter, of course. What have we to lose?"

"Perhaps we shall discover the answer to that question within. After you, Duke of Köln!"

The two mounted the steps and climbed until they reached the doorway. It was relatively small — of human size in fact and within it they could see more of the glowing shadows.

Hawkmoon stepped bravely forward with D'Averc immediately behind him.

S I X

J E H A M I A   C O H N A H L I A S

Their feet seemed to sink into the floor and the glowing shadows wrapped themselves around them as they advanced into the scintillating darkness of the tower.

A sweet sound now filled the corridors — a gentle sound like an unearthly lullaby. The music increased their sense of well-being. They pressed deeper into the strangely organic construction.

And then suddenly they stood in a small room, full of the same golden, pulsing radiance they had seen earlier from the boat.

And the radiance came from a child.

He was a boy, of oriental appearance, with a soft, brown skin, clad in robes on to which jewels had been stitched so that the fabric was completely hidden.

He smiled and his smile matched the gentle radiance surrounding him. It was impossible not to love him.

"Duke Dorian Hawkmoon von Köln," he said sweetly, bowing his head, "and Huillam D'Averc. I have admired both your painting and your buildings, sir."

D'Averc was astonished. "You know of those?"

"They are excellent. Why do you not do more?"

D'Averc coughed in embarrassment. "I — I lost the knack, I suppose. And then the War…"

"Ah, of course. The Dark Empire. That is why you are here."

"I would gather so —"

"I am called Jehamia Cohnahlias." The boy smiled again. "And that is the only direct information about myself I can offer you, in case you were going to ask me anything further. This city is called Dnark and its inhabitants are called in the outer world the Great Good Ones. You have encountered some of them already, I believe."

"The glowing shadows?" Hawkmoon asked.

"Is that how you perceive them?"

"Are they sentient?" Hawkmoon queried.

"They are indeed. More than sentient, perhaps."

"And this city, Dnark," Hawkmoon said. "It is the legendary City of the Runestaff."

"It is."

"Strange that all those legends should place its position not on the continent of Amarehk, but in Asiacommunista," said D'Averc.

"Perhaps it is not a coincidence," smiled the boy. "It is convenient to have such legends."

"I understand."

Jehamia Cohnahlias smiled quietly.

"You have come to see the Runestaff, I gather?"

"Apparently," said Hawkmoon, unable to feel anger in the presence of the child. "First the Warrior in Jet and Gold told us to come here and then when we demurred we were introduced to his brother — one Orland Fank..."

"Ah, yes," smiled Jehamia Cohnahlias. "Orland Fank. I have a special affection for that particular servant of the Runestaff. Well, let us go." He frowned slightly. "Ah, first you will want to refresh yourselves and meet a fellow traveler. One who preceded you here by only a matter of hours."

"Do we know him?"

"I believe you have had some contact in the past."

The boy seemed almost to float down from his chair. "This way."

"Who can it be?" murmured D'Averc to Hawkmoon. "Who would we know who would come to Dnark?"

S E V E N

A W E L L - K N O W N T R A V E L E R

They followed Jehamia Cohnahlias through the winding, organic corridors of the building. Now they were lighter, for the glowing shadows — the Great Good Ones as the boy had described them — had vanished. Presumably their task had been to help guide Hawkmoon and D'Averc to the child.

At last they entered a larger hall in which had been set a long table, presumably made of the same substance as the walls, and benches also of the same stuff. Food had been laid on the table — relatively simple fare: fish, bread and green vegetables.

But it was the figure at the far end of the hall who attracted their attention, who made their hands go automatically to their swords while their faces assumed expressions of angry astonishment.

It was Hawkmoon who got the words out at last, between clenched teeth.

"Shenegar Trott!"

The fat figure moved heavily towards them, his plain, silver mask apparently a parody of the features beneath it.

"Good afternoon, gentlemen. Dorian Hawkmoon and Huillam D'Averc, is it not?"

Hawkmoon turned to the boy. "Do you realize who this creature is?"

"An explorer from Europe," he said.

"He is the Count of Sussex — one of King Huon's righthand men. He has raped half of Europe! He is second only to Baron Meliadus in the evil he has wrought!"

"Come now," Trott said, his voice soft and amused. "Let us not begin by insulting each other. We are on neutral ground here. The issues of war are another matter. Since they do not at the moment concern us, then I suggest we behave in a civilized manner — and not insult our young host here…"

Hawkmoon glowered. "How did you come to Dnark, Count Shenegar?"

"By ship, Duke of Köln. Our Baron Kalan — whom I understand you have met…" Trott chuckled as Hawkmoon automatically put his hand to the Black Jewel Kalan had earlier placed there… "invented a new kind of engine to propel our ships at great speed over the sea. Based on the engine that gives power to our ornithopters, I gather, but more sophisticated. I was commissioned by our wise King-Emperor to journey to Amarehk, there to make friendly advances to the powers dwelling here…"

"To discover their strengths and weaknesses before you attacked, you mean!" Hawkmoon shouted. "It is impossible to trust a servant of the Dark Empire!"

The boy spread his hands and a look of sorrow crossed his face. "Here in Dnark we seek only equilibrium. That, after all, is the goal and reason for existence of the Runestaff, which we are here to protect. Save your disputes, I beg you, for the battlefield and join together to eat the food we have prepared."

"But I must warn you," Huillam D'Averc said in a lighter tone than Hawkmoon had used, "that Shenegar Trott is not here to bring peace. Wherever he goes, he brings evil and disruption. Be prepared — for he is considered to be the most cunning lord in all Granbretan."

The boy seemed embarrassed and merely gestured again to the table. "Please be seated."

"And where is your fleet, Count Shenegar?" D'Averc asked as he sat down on the bench and pulled a plate of fish towards him.

"Fleet?" Trott replied innocently, "I did not mention a fleet — only my ship, which is moored with its crew a few miles away from the city."

"Then it must be a large ship indeed," murmured Hawkmoon, biting at a hunk of bread, "for it is unlike a count of the Dark Empire to make a journey unprepared for conquest."

"You forget that we are scientists and scholars, too, in Granbretan," Trott said, as if mildly offended. "We seek knowledge and truth and reason. Why, our whole intention in uniting the warring states of Europe was to bring a rational peace to the world, so that knowledge could progress the faster."

D'Averc coughed ostentatiously but said nothing.

Trott now did something that in a Dark Empire noble was virtually unprecedented, for he cheerfully pushed back his mask and began to eat. In Granbretan it was considered gross indecency both to display the face and to eat in public. Trott, Hawkmoon knew, had always been thought eccentric in Granbretan, tolerated by the other nobles only by virtue of his vast private fortune, his skill as a general and, in spite of his flabby appearance, a warrior of considerable personal courage.

The face revealed was the one caricatured on the mask. It was white, plump and intelligent. The eyes were without expression, but it was plain Shenegar Trott could put whatever expression he chose into them.

They ate in relative silence. Only the boy touched none of the food, though he sat with them.

At length Hawkmoon gestured to the count's bulky silver armour. "Why do you travel in such heavy accoutrement, Count Shenegar, if you are on a peaceful mission of exploration?"

Shenegar Trott smiled. "Why — how was I to anticipate what dangers I should have to face in this strange city? Surely it is logical to travel well prepared?"

D'Averc changed the subject as if he realized they would receive nothing but smooth answers from the Granbretanian. "How goes the War in Europe?" he asked.

"There is no war in Europe," Trott answered.

"No war! Then why should we be here — exiles from our own lands?" Hawkmoon said.

"There is no war, because all of Europe is now at peace under the patronage of our good King Huon," Shenegar Trott said, and then he gave a faint wink — almost a comradely wink — which made it impossible for Hawkmoon to reply.

"Save for Kamarg, that is," Trott continued. "And that, of course, has vanished altogether. My fellow peer Baron Meliadus was quite enraged by that."

"I'm sure he was," said Hawkmoon. "And does he still continue his vendetta against us?"

"Indeed he does. In fact when I left Londra, he was in danger of becoming a laughing stock at court."

"You seem to feel little affection for Baron Meliadus," D'Averc suggested.

"You understand me well," Count Shenegar told him. "You see we are not all such insane and greedy men as you would think. I have many disputes with Baron Meliadus. Though I am loyal to my motherland and my leader, I do not agree with everything done in their names — indeed, what I myself have done. I follow my orders. I am a patriot." Shenegar Trott shrugged his bulky shoulders. "I would prefer to stay at home, reading and writing. I was once thought a promising poet, you know."

"But now you write only epitaphs — and those in blood and fire," Hawkmoon said.

Count Shenegar did not seem hurt. Instead he replied reasonably. "You have your point of view, I have mine. I believe in the ultimate sanity of our cause — that the unification of the world is of maximum importance, that personal ambitions, no matter how noble, must be sacrificed to the larger principles."

"That is the usual bland Granbretanian answer," Hawkmoon said, unconvinced. "It is the argument that Meliadus used to Count Brass shortly before he attempted to rape and carry off his daughter Yisselda!"

"I have already disassociated myself from Baron Meliadus," Count Shenegar said. "Every court must have its fool, every great ideal must attract some who are motivated only by self-interest."

Shenegar Trott's answers seemed more directed at the quietly listening boy than at Hawkmoon and D'Averc themselves.

The meal finished, Trott pushed back his plate and resettled his silver mask over his face. He turned to the boy. "I thank you, sir, for your hospitality. Now — you promised me I might look upon and admire the Runestaff. It will give me great joy to stand before that legendary artifact…"

Hawkmoon and D'Averc glanced warningly at the boy, but he did not appear to notice.

"It is late, now," said Jehamia Cohnahlias. "We shall all visit the Hall of the Runestaff tomorrow. Meanwhile rest here. Through that little door" he gestured across the room, "you will find sleeping accommodation. I will call for you in the morning."

Shenegar Trott rose and bowed. "I thank you for your offer, but my men will become agitated if I do not return to my ship tonight. I will rejoin you here tomorrow."

"As you wish," the boy said.

"We would be grateful to you for your hospitality," Hawkmoon said. "But again let us warn you that Shenegar Trott may not be what he would have you believe."

"You are admirable in your tenacity," Shenegar Trott said. He waved a gauntleted hand in a cheerful salute and strode jauntily from the hall.

"I fear we shall sleep poorly knowing that our enemy is in Dnark," said D'Averc.

The boy smiled. "Fear not. The Great Good Ones will help you rest and protect you from any harm. Goodnight, gentlemen. I shall see you tomorrow."

The boy walked lightly from the room and D'Averc and Hawkmoon went to inspect the cubicles containing bunks and bedding that were let into the side of the walls.

"Shenegar Trott means the boy harm," Hawkmoon said.

"We had best make it our business to look after him, if we can," D'Averc replied. "Goodnight, Hawkmoon."

After D'Averc had ducked into his cubicle, Hawkmoon entered his own. It was full of glowing shadows and the soft music of the unearthly lullaby he had heard earlier. Almost immediately he was sound asleep.

E I G H T

A N   U L T I M A T U M

Hawkmoon awoke late feeling thoroughly rested, but then he noticed that the glowing shadows seemed agitated. They had turned to a cold, blue colour and were swirling around as if in fear!

Hawkmoon rose quickly and buckled on his sword belt. He frowned. Was the danger he had anticipated about to come — or had it come already? The Great Good Ones seemed incapable of human communication.

D'Averc came running into Hawkmoon's cubicle.

"What do you think is the matter, Hawkmoon?"

"I do not know. Is Shenegar Trott scheming invasion? Is the boy in trouble?"

All at once the glowing shadows had wrapped themselves chillingly around the two men and they felt themselves whisked from the cubicle, through the room in which they had eaten, and along the corridors at incredible speed until they broke out of the building altogether and were whirled upward into the golden light.

Now the speed of the Great Good Ones decreased and Hawkmoon and D'Averc, still breathless at the sudden action of the glowing shadows, hovered in the air high above the main square.

D'Averc looked pale, for his feet were planted on nothing and the glowing shadows seemed to have taken on even less substance. Yet they did not fall.

Down in the square tiny figures could be seen moving in towards the cylindrical tower.

"It is an entire army!" Hawkmoon gasped. "There must be thousands of them. So much for Shenegar Trott's claims for the peaceful nature of his mission. He has invaded Dnark! But why?"

"Isn't it obvious to you, my friend," said D'Averc grimly. "He seeks the Runestaff itself. With that in his power, he would doubtless rule the world!"

"But he does not know its location!"

"That is probably why he is attacking the tower. See — there are warriors already inside!"

Surrounded by the flimsy shadows, and with golden light on all sides, the two men looked at the scene in dismay.

"We must descend," Hawkmoon said finally.

"But we are only two against a thousand!" D'Averc pointed out.

"Aye — but if the Sword of the Dawn will again summon the Legion of the Dawn, then we might succeed against them!" Hawkmoon reminded him.

As if they had understood his words, the Great Good Ones began to descend. Hawkmoon felt his heart enter his throat as they dropped rapidly towards the square, now thickly clustered with masked Dark Empire warriors — members of the terrible Falcon Legion which, like the Vulture Legion, was a mercenary force made up of renegades who were, if anything, more evil than the native Granbretanians. Falcon eyes had stared up in anticipation of the feast of blood Hawkmoon and D'Averc offered; they had beaks ready to tear the flesh of the two enemies of the Dark Empire, and their swords, maces, axes and spears were like talons poised to rend.

As the glowing shadows deposited D'Averc and the Duke of Köln near the entrance to the tower they just had time to draw their blades before the Falcons attacked.

But then Shenegar Trott appeared at the entrance of the tower and called to his men.

"Stop, my Falcons. There is no need for bloodshed. I have the boy!"

Hawkmoon and D'Averc saw him lift the child, Jehamia Cohnahlias, by his robes and hold him struggling before them.

"I know that this city is full of supernatural creatures who would seek to stop us," the count announced, "and thus I have taken the liberty of insuring our safety while we are here. If we are attacked, if one of us is touched, I shall slit the little boy's throat from ear to ear." Shenegar Trott chuckled. "I take this step only to avoid unpleasantness on all sides…"

Hawkmoon made to move, to summon the Legion of the Dawn, but Trott wagged his finger chidingly. "Would you be the cause of a child's death, Duke of Köln?"

Glowering, Hawkmoon dropped his swordarm, addressing the boy. "I warned you of his perfidy!"

"Aye…" The boy struggled, half-choking in his robes. "I fear I should have — paid more — attention to you, sir."

Count Shenegar laughed, his mask flashing in the golden light. "Now — tell me where the Runestaff is kept."

The boy pointed back into the tower. "The Hall of the Runestaff is within."

"Show me!" Shenegar Trott turned to his men. "Watch this pair. I'd rather have them alive, since the King-Emperor will be well pleased if we can return with two heroes of Kamarg as well as the Runestaff. If they move, shout to me and I'll take off an ear or two." He drew his dirk and held it near the boy's face. "Most of you — follow me."

Shenegar Trott disappeared once more into the tower and six of the falcon warriors stayed to guard Hawkmoon and D'Averc while the rest followed their leader.

Hawkmoon scowled. "If only the boy had paid heed to what we said!" He moved slightly and the Falcons stirred warningly. "Now how are we to save him — and the Runestaff — from Trott?"

Suddenly the Falcons looked upward in astonishment and D'Averc's gaze followed theirs.

"It seems we are to be rescued," smiled D'Averc.

The glowing shadows were returning.

Before the Falcons could move or speak, the shadows had wrapped themselves around the two men and were once again lifting them upwards.

Disconcerted, the Falcons slashed at their feet as they ascended, and then turned to run into the tower, to warn their leader of what had happened.

Higher and higher rose the Great Good Ones, carrying Hawkmoon and D'Averc with them. Into the golden haze that became a thick, golden mist so that they could no longer see each other, let alone the buildings of the city.

They seemed to travel for hours before they became aware of the golden mist thinning.

N   I   N   E

T   H   E   R   U   N   E   S   T   A   F   F

As the golden mist diminished, Hawkmoon blinked his eyes, for they were now assailed by all manner of colours — waves and rays making strange configurations in the air — and all emanating from a central source.

Narrowing his eyes against the light, he peered around him. They hovered near the roof of a hall whose walls seemed constructed of sheets of translucent emerald and onyx. At the centre of the hall rose a dais, reached by steps from all sides. It was from the object on this dais that the configurations of light originated. The patterns — stars, circles, cones and more complex figures — shifted constantly, but their source was always the same. It was a small staff, about the length of a short sword, of a dense black, dull and apparently discoloured in a few places. The discolorations were of a deep, mottled blue.

Could this be the Runestaff? Hawkmoon wondered. It seemed unimpressive for an object of such legendary powers. He had imagined it taller than a man, of brilliant colours — but that thing he could carry in one hand!

Suddenly, from the side of the hall, men thrust themselves in. It was Shenegar Trott and his Falcon Legion. The little boy still struggled in Trott's grasp and now the laughter of the Count of Sussex began to fill the hall.

"At last! And it is mine! Even the King-Emperor will not dare to deny me anything once the Runestaff itself is in my hands."

Hawkmoon sniffed. There was a fragrant, bitter-sweet smell in the air. And now a mellow humming sound filled the hall. The Great Good Ones began to lower himself and D'Averc until they stood high on the steps, just below the Runestaff. And then Count Shenegar saw them.

"How…?"

Hawkmoon glared down at him, raised his left arm to point directly at him. "Release the child, Shenegar Trott!"

The Count of Sussex chuckled again, recovering quickly from his astonishment. "First tell me how you arrived here before me."

"By means of the help of the Great Good Ones — those supernatural creatures you feared. And we have other friends, Count Shenegar."

Trott's dirk leapt to within a hairsbreadth of the boy's nose. "I would be a fool, then, to release my only chance of freedom — not to say success!"

Hawkmoon lifted up the Sword of the Dawn. "I warn you, Count, this blade I bear is no ordinary instrument! See how it glows with rosy light!"

"Aye — it is very pretty. But can it stop me before I pluck one of the boy's eyes from his skull, like a plum from the jar?"

D'Averc glanced about the strange room, at the constantly changing patterns of light, at the peculiar walls, and the glowing shadows now high above and seemingly looking on. "It's stalemate, Hawkmoon," he murmured. "We can get no further help from the glowing shadows. Evidently there are powerless to take a part in human affairs."

"If you'd release the boy, I'd consider letting you leave Dnark unharmed." Hawkmoon said.

Shenegar Trott laughed. "Indeed? And you would chase an army from the city, you two?"

"We are not without allies," Hawkmoon reminded him.

"Possibly. But I suggest you lay down your own swords and pass me the Runestaff there. When I have that, you may have the boy.

"Alive?"

"Alive."

"How can we trust Shenegar Trott of all men?" D'Averc said. "He will kill the boy and then dispose of us. It is not the way of the nobles of Granbretan to keep their word."

"If only we had some guarantee," whispered Hawkmoon desperately.

At that moment a familiar voice spoke from behind them and they turned in surprise.

"You have no choice but to release the child, Shenegar Trott!" The voice boomed from within a helm of jet and gold.

"Aye, my brother speaks the truth…" From the other side of the dais Orland Fank now emerged, his gigantic war-axe on his leather-clad shoulder.

"How did you get here?" Hawkmoon asked in astonishment.

"I might ask the same," grinned Fank. "At least you now have friends with whom to debate this dilemma."

HAWKMOON

S P I R I T   O F   T H E   R U N E S T A F F

Shenegar Trott, Count of Sussex, chuckled again and shook his head. "Well, there are now four of you, but it does not alter the situation a scrap. I have thousands at my back. I have the boy. You will kindly step aside, gentlemen, while I take the Runestaff for my own."

Orland Fank's rawboned face split in a huge grin, while the Warrior in Jet and Gold merely shifted his armoured feet a little. Hawkmoon and D'Averc looked questioningly at them. "I think there is a weakness in your argument, my friend," said Orland Fank.

"Oh, no sir — there is none." Shenegar Trott began to move forward.

"Aye — I'd say that there was."

Trott paused. "What is it, then?"

"You are assuming you can hold yon boy, are you not?"

"I could kill him before you could take him."

"Aye — but you're assuming the child has no means of escaping from you, are you not?"

"He can't wriggle free!" Shenegar Trott held the child up by the slack of his garments and began to laugh loudly. "See!"

And then the Granbretanian yelled in astonishment as the boy seemed to flow from his grasp, streaking out across the hall in a long strip of light, his features still visible but oddly elongated. The music swelled in the hall and the odour increased.

Shenegar Trott made ineffectual grabbing motions at the boy's thinning substance but it was as impossible to grasp him as it was to grasp the glowing shadows now pulsing in the air above them.

"By Huon's Globe — he is *not* human!" screamed Trott in frustrated anger. "He is not human!"

"He did not claim to be," Orland Fank said mildly and winked cheerfully at Hawkmoon. "Are you and your friend ready for a good fight?"

"We are," grinned Hawkmoon. "We are indeed!"

Now the boy — or whatever it was — was stretching out over their heads to touch the Runestaff. The configurations changed rapidly and many more of them filled the hall so that all their faces were crossed with shifting bars of colour.

Orland Fank watched this with great attention and it seemed that as the boy was actually absorbed into the Runestaff the Orkneyman's face flooded with regret.

Soon there was no trace of the boy in the hall and the Runestaff glowed a brighter black, seemed to have sentience.

Hawkmoon gasped. "Who was he, Orland Fank?"

Fank blinked. "Who? Why, the spirit of the Runestaff. He rarely materializes in human form. You were especially honoured."

Shenegar Trott was screaming in fury. Then he broke off as a great voice boomed from the closed helm of the Warrior in Jet and Gold. "Now you must prepare yourself for death, Count of Sussex."

Trott laughed crazily. "You are still mistaken. There are four of you — thousands of us. You shall die, and then I shall claim the Runestaff!"

The warrior turned to Hawkmoon. "Duke of Köln, would you care to summon some aid?"

"With pleasure," grinned Hawkmoon and he raised the rosy sword high in the air. "*I summon the Legion of the Dawn!*"

A rosy light filled the hall, flooding over the colourful patterns in the air. And there stood a hundred fierce warriors, each framed in his own scarlet aura.

The warriors had a barbaric appearance, as if they came from an earlier, more primitive age. They bore great spiked clubs decorated with ornate carvings, lances bound with tufts of dyed hair. Their brown bodies and faces were smeared with paint and clad in loincloths of bright stuff. On their arms and legs were strapped wooden discs for protection. Their large black eyes were full of a remote sorrow and they gave voice to a mournful, moaning dirge.

These were the Warriors of the Dawn.

Even the hardened members of the Falcon Legion cried out in horror as the warriors appeared from nowhere. Shenegar Trott took a step backward.

"I would advise you to lay down your weapons and make yourselves our prisoners," Hawkmoon advised grimly.

Trott shook his head. "Never. There are still more of us than there are of you!"

"Then we must begin our battle," Hawkmoon said, and he moved down the steps towards his enemies.

Now Shenegar Trott drew his own great battle blade and dropped to a fighting position. Hawkmoon swung at him with the Sword of the Dawn, but Trott dodged aside, swinging at Hawkmoon and barely missing gouging a line across his stomach. Hawkmoon was at a disadvantage, for Trott was fully armoured, while Hawkmoon wore only silk.

The dirge of the Soldiers of the Dawn changed to a great howl as they rushed down the steps behind Hawkmoon and began to hack and stab about them with clubs and lances. The fierce Falcon fighters met them valiantly, giving as good as they received, but were plainly demoralized when they discovered that for every Warrior of the Dawn that they slew another appeared from nowhere to take his place.

D'Averc, Orland Fank and the Warrior in Jet and Gold moved more slowly down the steps, swinging their blades in unison before them and driving back the Falcons with three pendulums of steel.

Shenegar Trott struck again at Hawkmoon and ripped the sleeve of his shirt. Hawkmoon flung out his swordarm and the Sword of the Dawn met Trott's mask, denting it so that the features took on an even more grotesque appearance.

But then, as Hawkmoon leapt backward, poised to continue the fight, he felt a sudden blow on the back of his head, half-turned and saw a Falcon warrior had struck him with the haft of an axe. He tried to recover, but then began to fall. As he lost his senses, he saw the Warriors of Dawn fade into oblivion. Desperately he tried to recover, for the Warriors of Dawn, it seemed, could not exist unless he had control of his senses.

But it was too late. As he fell to the steps, he heard Shenegar Trott chuckling.

E L E V E N

A B R O T H E R   S L A I N

Hawkmoon heard the distant din of battle, shook his head and peered through a haze of red and black. He tried to rise, but at least four corpses pinned him down. His friends had taken good account of themselves.

Struggling up, he saw that Shenegar Trott had reached the Runestaff. And there stood the Warrior in Jet and Gold, evidently badly wounded, hacked at by a hundred blades, attempting to stop the Granbretanian. But Shenegar Trott raised a huge mace and brought it down on the warrior's helm. He staggered and the helm crumpled.

Hawkmoon gathered his breath to cry hoarsely: "Legion of the Dawn! Return to me! Legion of the Dawn!"

At last the barbaric warriors reappeared, lashing about them at the startled Falcons.

Hawkmoon staggered up the steps to the warrior's aid, unable to see if any of the others lived. But then the huge weight of the jet and gold armour began to fall towards him, knocking him backwards. He supported it as best he could, but he knew by the feel of it that there was no life in the body within.

He forced back the visor, weeping for the man he had never considered a friend until now, curious to see the features of the one who had guided his destiny for so long, but the visor would hardly move an inch, Shenegar Trott's mace had buckled it so.

"Warrior..."

"The Warrior is dead!" Shenegar Trott had flung off his mask and was reaching for the Runestaff, triumphantly staring over his shoulder at Hawkmoon. "As shall you be in a trice, Dorian Hawkmoon!"

With a shout of fury, Hawkmoon dropped the warrior's corpse and flew up the steps towards his enemy. Disconcerted, Trott turned, raising the mace again.

Hawkmoon ducked the blow and closed with Trott, grappling with him on the topmost step while red carnage spread all around them.

As he struggled with the count, he saw D'Averc, halfway up the steps, his shirt a mass of bloody rags, one arm limp at his side, tackling five of the Falcon warriors — and higher up Orland Fank was still alive, whirling his battle-axe around his head and giving voice to a strange, skirling cry.

Trott's breath wheezed from between his fat lips and Hawkmoon was astonished at his strength. "You will die, Hawkmoon — you must die if the Runestaff is to be mine!"

Hawkmoon panted as he wrestled with the count. "It will never be yours. It can be possessed by no man!"

With a sudden heave, he broke Trott's guard and punched him full in the face. The count screamed and came forward again, but Hawkmoon raised his booted foot and kicked him in the chest, sending him reeling back against the dais. Then Hawkmoon recovered his sword and when Shenegar Trott ran at him again, blind with anger, he ran directly on to the point of the Sword of the Dawn, dying with an obscene curse on his lips and one last, backward look at the Runestaff.

Hawkmoon tugged the sword free and looked about him. His Legion of the Dawn were finishing their work, clubbing down the last of the Falcons, and D'Averc and Fank were leaning exhaustedly against the dais beneath the Runestaff.

Soon a few groans were cut short as spiked clubs fell on heads, and then there was silence save for the faint, melodic humming and the heavy breathing of the three survivors.

As the last Granbretanian died, the Legion of the Dawn vanished.

Hawkmoon stared down at the fat corpse of Shenegar Trott and he frowned. "We have slain one — but if one has been sent here, then others will follow. Dnark is no longer safe from the Dark Empire."

Fank sniffed and wiped his nose with his forearm. "It is for you to make sure that Dnark is safe — that the rest of the world is safe."

Hawkmoon smiled sardonically. "And how may I do that?"

Fank began to speak and then his eyes lighted on the huge corpse of the Warrior in Jet and Gold and he gasped: "Brother!" and began to stagger down the steps, to drop his battle-axe and gather the armoured figure in his arms. "Brother...?"

"He is dead," Hawkmoon said softly. "He died by Shenegar Trott's hand, defending the Runestaff. I slew Trott..."

Fank wept.

*

At length they stood together, the three of them, looking about at the carnage. The whole hall of the Runestaff was full of corpses. Even the patterns in the air seemed to have taken on a reddish colouring and the bitter-sweet odour could not disguise the stink of death.

Hawkmoon scabbarded the Sword of the Dawn. "What now, I wonder?" he said. "We've done the work we were asked to do. We've defended the Runestaff successfully. Now do we return to Europe?"

Then a voice spoke from behind them; it was the sweet voice of the child, Jehamia Cohnahlias. Turning, Hawkmoon saw that he stood beside the Runestaff, holding it in one hand.

"Duke of Köln, you take what you have rightfully earned," said the boy, his slanting eyes full of warm humour. "You take the Runestaff with you back to Europe, there to decide the destiny of the Earth."

"To Europe! I thought it could not be removed from its place."

"You, as the chosen one of the Runestaff, may take it." The boy stretched out towards Hawkmoon, and in his hand was the Runestaff. "Defend it. And pray it defends you."

"And how shall we use it?" D'Averc enquired.

"As your standard. Let all men know that the Runestaff rides with you — that the Runestaff is on your side. Tell them that it was the Baron Meliadus who dared swear an oath on the Runestaff and thus set into motion these events which will destroy completely one protagonist or the other. Whatever happens, it will be final. Carry your invasion to Granbretan if you can, or else die in the effort. The last great battle between Meliadus and Hawkmoon is soon to be fought, and over it the Runestaff will preside!"

Hawkmoon mutely accepted the staff. It felt cold, dead and very heavy, though the patterns still blazed about it.

"Put it inside your shirt, or wrap it in a cloth," advised the boy, "and none will observe those betraying forces until you should wish them revealed."

"Thank you," said Hawkmoon quietly.

"The Great Good Ones will help you return to your home," the boy continued. "Farewell, Hawkmoon."

"Farewell? Where do you go now?"

"Where I belong."

And suddenly the boy began to change again, turning into a streamer of golden light still bearing some semblance of human shape, pouring itself into the Runestaff which immediately became warm, vital and light in Hawkmoon's grasp.

With a slight shudder, Hawkmoon tucked the Runestaff inside his shirt.

As they walked out of the hall, D'Averc observed that Orland Fank was still weeping softly.

"What disturbs you, Fank?" D'Averc asked. "Do you still grieve for the man who was your brother?"

"Aye — but I grieve for my son the more."

"Your son? What of him?"

Orland Fank jerked his thumb at Hawkmoon, who wandered behind, his head bowed in thought. "He has him."

"What do you mean?"

Fank sighed. "It must be, I know that. But still, I am a man, I can weep. I speak of Jehamia Cohnahlias."

"The boy! The spirit of the Runestaff?"

"Aye. He was my son — or myself — I have never quite understood these things…"

B O O K   T W O

As it is written: "Those who swear by the Runestaff must then benefit or suffer from the consequences of the fixed pattern of destiny that they set in motion." And Baron Meliadus of Kroiden had sworn such an oath, had sworn vengeance against all of Castle Brass, had sworn that Yisselda, Count Brass's daughter, would be his. On that day, many months earlier, he had fixed the pattern of fate; a pattern that had involved him in strange, destructive schemes, that had involved Dorian Hawkmoon in wild and uncanny adventures in distant places, and that was now nearing its terrible resolution.

— *The High History of the Runestaff*

O N E

WHISPERING IN SECRET ROOMS

The verandah overlooked the blood-red River Tayme, making its sluggish way through the very heart of Londra, between gloomy, crazy towers.

Above them the occasional ornithopter, a bright bird of metal, clanked past, and on the river the barges of bronze and ebony carried cargo to and from the coast. Those cargoes were rich; full of stolen goods and stolen men, women and children brought as slaves to Londra. An awning of heavy purple velvet hung with tassels of scarlet silk protected the occupants of the verandah from view from above and the awning's shadow made it impossible for them to be seen from the river.

A table of brass and two golden chairs upholstered in blue plush stood on the verandah. A richly decorated platinum tray on the table bore a wine jug of dark green glass and two matching goblets. On either side of the door leading on to the verandah stood a naked girl, with face, breasts and genitals heavily rouged. Anyone familiar with the Court of Londra would have recognized the slave-girls as belonging to Baron Meliadus of Kroiden, for he had only female slaves and their only livery was the rouge he insisted they wear. Of the girls, who stared fixedly out at the river, one was a blonde, almost certainly from Köln in Germany, the baron's possession by right of conquest. The other girl was dark, doubtless from some province in the Middle East Baron Meliadus had added, by means of a bloodied sword, to his estates.

In one golden chair sat a woman, clad from head to foot in rich brocade and wearing a silver mask, delicately fashioned to resemble a heron. Next to her sat a figure dressed in bulky black leather, his shoulders crowned by a huge mask representing a black, snarling wolf. He inserted a golden tube into his goblet and stuck the other end through a tiny aperture in the mask, sucking slowly at the wine.

There was silence between the pair and the only sound came from beyond the verandah — from the wake of the barges slapping at the wall, from a distant tower as someone screamed and laughed at once, from an ornithopter high above, its metal wings flapping slowly as it sought to land on the flat top of one of the towers.

And then, at length, the figure in the wolf mask began to speak in a low, thrilling voice. The other figure did not move its head or appear to hear but continued to stare out over the blood-red water whose strange colour was attributed to the effluvia which poured from outlets near its bed.

"You are under some slight suspicion yourself, you know, Flana. King Huon thinks you might have had something to do with the mysterious madness which overwhelmed the guards the night the Asiacommunistans escaped. Doubtless I am not helping my own cause by seeing you thus, but I think only of our beloved homeland — only of the glory of Granbretan."

The speaker paused as if expecting a reply. He received none.

"It is plain, Flana, that the present situation of the Court is not in the best interests of the Empire. I delight in eccentricity, of course, as a true son of Granbretan, but there is a difference between eccentricity and senility. You take my meaning?"

Flana Mikosevaar said nothing.

"I am suggesting," continued the other, "that we need a new ruler — an Empress. There is only one alive who is a direct blood relative of Huon — only one all would accept as rightful liege; legal inheritor to the throne of the Dark Empire."

Again no reply.

The figure in the wolf mask bent forward. "Flana?"

The heron mask turned to regard the snarling wolf visage.

"Flana — you could be Queen-Empress of Granbretan. With myself as Regent, we could ensure the security of our nation and our territories, make Granbretan greater — make the whole world ours!"

"And what would be done with the world once we owned it, Meliadus?" For the first time Flana Mikosevaar spoke.

"Enjoy it, Flana! Use it!"

"Cannot one tire of rape and murder? Of torture and destruction?"

Meliadus seemed puzzled by her comment. "One can become bored by anything, of course, but there are other things — there are Kalan's experiments — and Taragorm's for that matter. With the resources of the world at their disposal, our scientists could make anything. Why, they could build us ships to sail through space, as the ancients did. We could journey to new worlds and conquer them — pitting wits and skill against a universe! Granbretan's adventure could last a million years!"

"And is adventure and sensation all we should seek, Meliadus?"

428   HAWKMOON

"Aye — why not? All is chaos, there is no meaning to existence, there is only one advantage to living one's life and that is to discover all the sensations the human mind and body is capable of feeling. That will take at least a million years, surely?"

Flana nodded. "That is our creed, true." She appeared to sigh. "Therefore I suppose I can agree to your plans, Meliadus, for what you suggest I do is doubtless no more boring than anything else." She shrugged. "Very well, I will be your queen when you need me — and if Huon discovers our perfidy, why, it will be a relief to die."

Slightly unnerved by this, Meliadus rose from the table. "You will say nothing to anyone until the time comes, Flana?"

"I will say nothing."

"Good. Now I must visit Kalan. He is attracted to my scheme, since it means more scope for his experiments if we succeed. Taragorm, too, is with me…"

"You trust Taragorm? Your rivalry is well-known."

"Aye — I hate Taragorm, it is true, and he hates me, but it is a mellow sort of hatred now, for you'll remember that our rivalry began over Taragorm's marriage to my sister whom I had previously intended to wed myself. But my sister compromised herself — with a jackass, I heard — and Taragorm discovered it. Whereupon, as you no doubt heard, my sister had her slaves slaughter her and the ass in some strange manner. Taragorm and I disposed of the slaves jointly and during that episode we rediscovered something of our old comradeship. My brother-in-law may be trusted. He feels Huon hampers his researches too much."

All this time their voices had not risen above a murmur so that even the slave-girls by the door could not hear them.

Meliadus bowed to Flana, snapped his fingers at the girls so that they ran to prepare his litter and carry him back through the corridors to his own home, and left.

Flana continued to stare out over the water, hardly thinking of Meliadus's scheme, but dreaming instead of the handsome D'Averc and of days in the future when they might meet again and D'Averc would take her away from Londra and all its intrigues — take her perhaps to his own rural estates in France which she, if she were queen, would be able to give back to him.

Perhaps there would be an advantage to her becoming Queen-Empress, then? That way she could choose her husband and that husband would be, of course, D'Averc. She could pardon him for his crimes against Granbretan, perhaps even pardon his companions — Hawkmoon and the rest.

But no, Meliadus might agree to D'Averc's reprieve — he would not agree to sparing all the rest.

Perhaps her scheme was foolish. She sighed. She did not altogether care. There was even doubt that D'Averc was still alive. In the meantime she saw no reason for not taking at least a passive part in Meliadus's treason, although even she had some inkling of the awful consequences of failure, of the magnitude of Meliadus's scheme. He must be desperate indeed to consider overthrowing his hereditary ruler. In all the two thousand years of his rule, no Granbretanian had previously dared think of deposing Huon. Flana did not even know if it were possible.

She shuddered. If she were made queen, she would not choose immortality — particularly if it meant becoming a wizened thing like Huon.

Conversation Beside the Mentality Machine

Kalan of Vitall fingered his serpent mask with pale, old hands on which the veins stood out, resembling, themselves, so many curling blue snakes. Ahead was the main laboratory — a great, low-ceilinged hall in which many experiments were being performed by men dressed in the uniforms and masks of the Order of the Serpent, of which Baron Kalan was Grand Constable. Strange machines gave off stranger sounds and stenches and miniature coloured lightnings flashed and cracked around them so that the entire area resembled some hellish workshop presided over by devils. Here and there human beings of both sexes and varying ages had been strapped out or fitted into machines as the scientists tested their experiments on the human mind and body. Most had been silenced in some way, but a few screamed or moaned or cried out in peculiar insane voices, often to the annoyance of the distracted scientists who would stuff rags into the mouths or sever vocal chords or find some other swift method of achieving a measure of quiet while they worked.

Kalan put one hand on Meliadus's shoulder and pointed to a machine standing unattended nearby.

"You'll remember the mentality machine? The one we used to test Hawkmoon's mind?"

"Aye," Meliadus grumbled. "That's the one led you to believe we could trust Hawkmoon."

"We reckoned without factors we could not anticipate," Kalan said by way of defense. "Well, that is not why I mentioned my little invention. I was asked to use it this morning."

"By whom?"

"By the King-Emperor himself. He summoned me to the throne room and told me he wished to test a member of the Court."

"Who?"

"Who d'you think, my lord?"

"Myself!" Meliadus spoke with outrage.

"Exactly. I think he suspects your loyalty in some way, lord Baron."

"How much, do you think?"

"Not much. All that appears to be in Huon's mind is that you may be concentrating too much on your personal schemes and not enough on the interests of his own plans. I think he would merely like to know how strong your loyalty is and if you have given up your personal plans."

"Do you intend to obey his orders, Kalan?"

Kalan shrugged. "Do you suggest I ignore them?"

"No — but what shall we do?"

"I will have to put you in the mentality machine, of course, but I think I can obtain the results that would be most in our interest." Kalan chuckled, a hollow whisper of a sound from within his mask. "Shall we begin, Meliadus?"

Meliadus moved reluctantly forward, looking nervously at the gleaming machine of red and blue metal, with its mysterious projections, its heavy, jointed arms and attachments of unknown application. Its main feature, however, was the huge bell hanging above the rest of the machine, depending from an intricate scaffold.

Kalan threw a switch and gestured apologetically. "We once kept this machine in a hall of its own, but space has become so limited of late. That is one of my chief complaints. We are asked for so much and given so little room in which to achieve it." From the machine came a sound like the breathing of some gigantic beast. Meliadus took a step backward. Kalan chuckled again and signaled for serpent-masked servitors to come to help him operate the device.

"If you will kindly stand beneath the bell, Meliadus, we will lower it at once," Kalan suggested.

Slowly, suspiciously, Meliadus took his place. The bell began to descend until it had covered him, its fleshy sides writhing until they had moulded themselves completely to his body. Then Meliadus felt as if hot wires had been inserted into his skull and that they were probing into his brain. He tried to yell, but was muffled. Hallucinations began — visions and memories of his past life — mainly of battles and bloodshed, though the hated face of Dorian Hawkmoon, twisted into a million fearful shapes, swam often before his eyes, as did the sweetly beautiful face of the woman he desired above everything, Yisselda of Brass. Gradually, through an eternity, his whole life began to be built up until he had recalled all that had ever happened to him, everything he had ever thought or dreamed of, not sequentially, but in order of importance. Riding over everything was his desire for Yisselda, his hatred of Hawkmoon and his schemes for ousting Huon from power.

Then the bell was rising and Meliadus looked once again upon the mask of

Kalan. Meliadus felt mentally purged and in high spirits.

"Well, Kalan, what did you discover?"

"Nothing, at this stage, that I did not already know. The full results will take an hour or two to process." He giggled. "The emperor would be much amused to see them."

"Aye. He will not see them, I hope."

"He will see something, Meliadus, that will show that your hatred for Hawkmoon is diminishing and that your love for the emperor is abiding and deep. Do not they tell us that love and hate are close together. Therefore your hatred of Huon will become love, with a little doctoring on my part."

"Good. Now let us discuss the rest of our project. First we must find a way of bringing Castle Brass back to this dimension — or else of finding a way through ourselves — secondly we must discover a means of reactivating the Black Jewel in Hawkmoon's skull and thus getting him into our power again. Lastly we must devise weapons and so forth to enable us to overcome Huon's forces."

Kalan nodded. "Of course. There are already the new engines I invented for the ships..."

"The ships that Trott left with?"

"Aye. The engines drive vessels faster and farther than anything ever before invented. Trott's ships are the only ones so far equipped with them. Trott should be reporting to us soon."

"Where did he go?"

"I am not sure. Only he and King Huon knew — but it must have been a good distance away — several thousand miles at the least. Perhaps to Asiacommunista."

"That seems likely," Meliadus agreed. "Still, let us forget Trott and discuss the details of our plan. Taragorm, also, is working on a device which might help us reach Castle Brass."

"Perhaps it would be best for Taragorm to concentrate on that line of research, since it is his speciality, while I try to find a means of activating the Black Jewel," Kalan suggested.

"Perhaps," murmured Meliadus. "First, I think, I will consult my brother-in-law. I'll leave you now and return shortly."

With that, Meliadus summoned his slaves who brought his litter. He climbed into it, waved farewell to Kalan, and directed the girls to take him to the Palace of Time.

T H R E E

Taragorm of the Palace of Time

In Taragorm's strange palace, shaped like a gigantic clock, the air was full of clanks and whirrs and the whistling of pendula and balance wheels and Taragorm, in his huge clock mask which told the time as accurately as the other clocks in the palace, took Meliadus's arm and guided him through the Hall of the Pendulum where, a short distance above Meliadus's head, the huge brass bob, made to resemble an ornate, blazing sun, flung its fifty ton weight back and forth across the hall.

"Well, brother," Meliadus shouted above the noise, "you sent me a message that you said I would be pleased to hear, but the message only told me to come to see you."

"Aye, I felt it best to tell you in private. Come." Taragorm led Meliadus through a short passage and into a small room in which stood only one ancient clock. Taragorm closed the door and there was relative silence. He indicated the clock. "It is probably the oldest clock in the world, brother — a 'grandfather' it was called and it was made by Thomas Tompion."

"I have not heard the name."

"A master craftsman — the greatest of his age. He lived well before the onset of the Tragic Millennium."

"Indeed? And has this something to do with your message?"

"Of course not." Taragorm clapped his hands and a side door opened. A lean, ragged figure stepped through, his face covered by a cracked, plain leather mask. He bowed extravagantly to Meliadus.

"Who is this?"

"It is Elvereza Tozer, brother. You remember the name?"

"Of course! The man who stole Mygan's ring and then vanished!"

"Exactly. Tell my brother Baron Meliadus where you have been, Master Tozer."

Again Tozer bowed and then sat himself down on the edge of the table, spreading his arms wide. "Why, I've been to Castle Brass, my lord!"

Suddenly Meliadus sprang across the room to grab the startled Tozer by the slack of his shirt. "You've been *where!*" he growled.

"C-Castle B-Brass, your honour."

Meliadus shook Tozer, lifting him clear of the ground. "How?"

"I reached the place by accident — I was captured by Hawkmoon of Köln — I was held prisoner — my ring taken from me — without ring could not remain — escaped — arrived b-back here..." Tozer gasped in fright.

"He brought some information with him that's more interesting," Taragorm said. "Tell him, Tozer."

"The machine which protects them — which keeps them in that other dimension — it's in the dungeons of the castle — kept carefully protected. A crystal thing they got from a place called Soryandum. It took them there and it ensures their safety."

Taragorm laughed. "It is true, Meliadus. I've tested him a dozen times. I've heard of this crystal machine but did not suspect it existed still. And with the rest of the information Tozer has given me, I think I can achieve some results."

"You can get us through to Castle Brass?"

"Oh, much more convenient than that, brother — within a short time I am fairly certain that I will bring Castle Brass back to us."

Meliadus looked silently at Taragorm for a moment and then began to laugh. His laughter was so great then that it threatened to drown the noise of the clocks.

"At last! At last! Thank you, brother! Thank you, Master Tozer! Destiny is patently upon my side!"

F O U R

A M I S S I O N F O R M E L I A D U S

It was on the following day, however, that Meliadus was summoned to King Huon's throne room.

As he made his way to the palace, Meliadus scowled in concentration. Had Kalan betrayed him? Had the scientist told King Huon the true results of the mentality machine's test? Or had King Huon guessed for himself? After all, the monarch was immortal. He had lived for two thousand years and had doubtless learned much. Were Kalan's faked records too clumsy to deceive Huon? Meliadus felt panic rise within him. Was this the end of everything? When he arrived in the throne room would Huon order the Mantis Guard to destroy him?

The great gates swung open. The mantis warriors confronted him. At the far end was the Throne Globe, black and mysterious.

Meliadus began to walk towards the Throne Globe. Eventually he reached it and bowed before it, but for a long while it remained solid, mysterious black. Was Huon playing with him?

At length it began to swirl dark blue, then green, then pink and then white, revealing the foetus shape with its sharp, malevolent eyes staring down at Meliadus.

"Baron…"

"Noblest of Rulers."

"We are pleased with you."

Meliadus looked up in astonishment. "Great Emperor?"

"We are pleased with you and we wish to honour you."

"Noble Prince?"

"You know of course that Shenegar Trott left on a special expedition."

"I do, Mighty Monarch."

"And you know where he went."

"I do not, Light of the Universe."

"He went to Amarehk, there to discover what he could about the continent — to see if we should meet resistance if we landed a force there."

"It would seem, then, that he did meet resistance, Immortal Ruler...?"

"Aye. He should have reported back a week or more ago. We are concerned."

"You think he is dead, Noble Emperor?"

"We should like to discover that — and also discover who slew him if that is the case, Baron Meliadus. We wish to entrust you with the second expedition."

At first Meliadus was filled with fury. Meliadus play second to that fat buffoon Trott! Meliadus waste time questing about on the coasts of a continent in the hope of discovering Trott's droppings! He would have none of it! He would attack the Throne Globe now, if that senile fool above him would not be sure to have him cut down in an instant. He swallowed his temper and a new scheme began to form in his skull.

"I am honoured, King of All!" he said with mock humility. "Do I choose my crews?"

"If you wish."

"Then I'll take men who I can be sure of. Members of the Order of the Wolf and the Order of the Vulture."

"But these are not sailors. They are not even marines!"

"The Vultures have sailors among them, Emperor of the World, and those are the men I will select."

"As you say, Baron Meliadus."

Meliadus was astonished to discover Trott had sailed to Amarehk. It made him even more resentful — Huon had entrusted the Count of Sussex with an assignment rightfully his. Another score to settle, he told himself. He was glad now that he had bided his time and accepted — or appeared to have accepted — the king's orders. His opportunity, in fact, seemed to have been handed to him by the creature he now considered to be his arch enemy after Hawkmoon.

Meliadus pretended to think for a moment. "If you believe the Vultures to be untrustworthy, Monarch of Space and Time, then may I suggest I take with me their chief...?"

"Their chief? Asrovak Mikosevaar is dead — killed by Hawkmoon!"

"But his widow inherited the Constabulary..."

"Flana! A woman!"

"Aye, Great Emperor. She will control them."

"I would not have thought that the Countess of Kanbery could control a rabbit, she is so vague, but if that is your wish, my lord, then so be it."

For a further hour they discussed the details of the plan and the king gave Meliadus all possible information relating to Trott's first expedition.

Then Meliadus left, his hidden eyes full of triumph.

F   I   V   E

THE FLEET AT DEAU-VERE

Overlooked by the turreted city of Deau-Vere, flanked on three sides by quays of scarlet stone, the small fleet lay at anchor in a livid sea. On the wide roofs of the buildings stood thousands of ornithopters, fancifully fashioned to resemble birds and mythical beasts, their wings folded; and in the streets below their pilots swaggered in masks of Crow and Owl, mingling with the sailors in their Fish and Sea Serpent helms and in the infantry and cavalry — Pig, Bear, Hound, Goat and Bull — who were preparing to cross the Channel not by ship but by the famed Silver Bridge Across The Sea which could be seen on the other side of the city, its great curve disappearing into the distance, all delicate and shining and loaded constantly with traffic coming to and from the Continent.

The men-o'-war in the harbour were crowded with soldiers clad in Wolf and Vulture helms and armed to the teeth with swords, spears, bows, quivers of arrows and flame-lances and the flagship bore the banners both of the Grand Constable of the Order of the Wolf and of the Grand Constable of the Order of the Vulture which had once been simply the Vulture Legion but which had been raised to the status of an Order by King Huon for the fighting it had done in Europe and to honour the death of its bloodthirsty chieftain Asrovak Mikosevaar.

The ships themselves were remarkable in that they had no sails but were instead mounted with huge paddle wheels at their sterns. They were built of a mixture of wood and metal — the wood ornately carved and the metal wrought in baroque designs. There were panels in their sides, each carrying an intricate painting depicting some earlier sea victory for Granbretan. Gilded figureheads decorated the forward parts of the ship, representing the terrifying ancient gods of Granbretan — *Jhone, Jhorg, Phowl, Rhunga*, who were said to have ruled the land before the Tragic Millennium — *Chirshil*, the Howling God; *Bjrin Adass*, the Singing God; *Jeajee Blad*, the Groaning God; *Jh'Im Slas*, the Weeping God and *Aral Vilsn*, the Roaring God, Supreme God, father of *Skvese* and *Blansacredid* the Gods of Doom and Chaos.

The *Aral Vilsn* was the flagship and on the flagship's bridge stood the brooding figure of Baron Meliadus, beside him Countess Flana Mikosevaar. Below the bridge, in Wolf and Vulture masks, the captains of the ships began to assemble, having been summoned to the flagship by Meliadus.

They looked up expectantly as Meliadus cleared his throat.

"You are doubtless wondering about our destination, gentlemen — and wondering, too, about the nature of these strange ships we sail in. The ships are no mystery — they are equipped with engines similar to those powering our ornithopters and are the invention of that genius of Granbretan, Baron Kalan of Vitall. They can bear us swifter than sail across continents of water and do not need to wait on the will of the wind. As to our destination, that I will reveal in private. This ship is the *Aral Vilsn*, named after the Supreme God of ancient Granbretan, who made this nation into what she is today. Her sister ships are the *Skvese* and the *Blansacredid*, which are the old words for Doom and for Chaos. But they are also the sons of *Aral Vilsn* and represent the glory of Granbretan, the old dark glory, the gloomy glory, the bloody and terrible glory of our land. A glory of which I am sure you are all rightly proud." Meliadus paused. "Would you see it lost, gentlemen?"

The answer roared back. *No! No! By Aral Vilsn, by Skvese and Blansacredid — NO! NO!*

"And would you do anything to make sure that Granbretan retained her black might and her lunatic glory?"

"AYE! AYE! AYE!"

"And would you all unite with me in an insane adventure such as those embarked upon by *Aral Vilsn* and his peers?"

"AYE! Tell us what is it! Tell us!"

"You would not shrink from it? You would follow it through to the end?"

"AYE!" shouted more than a score of voices.

"Then follow me to my cabin and I will detail the plan. But be warned, once you have entered that cabin, you will have to follow me forever. Any who holds back will not leave the cabin alive."

Then Meliadus swung down from the bridge and strode into his cabin below it. He was followed by every one of the captains who stood before him and every one of them was to leave the cabin alive.

Baron Meliadus stood before them, his dark cabin lighted only by a dim lamp. There were maps on his table, but he did not consult them. He spoke in a low, vibrant voice to his men.

"I shall not waste time further, gentlemen, but will tell you at once the nature of this adventure. We are embarking upon treason." He cleared his throat. "We are about to rebel against our hereditary ruler, Huon the King-Emperor."

There were many gasps from around the cabin as the Wolf and Vulture masks stared intently at Baron Meliadus.

"King Huon is insane," Meliadus told them quickly. "It is not personal ambition drives me to this scheme, but a love for our nation. Huon is mad — his two thousand years of life has clouded his brain rather than given him wisdom. He is trying to make us expand too rapidly. This expedition, for instance, was to go to Amarehk to see if the land could be conquered, while we have barely crushed the whole Middle East and there are still parts of Muskovia that are not entirely ours."

"And you would rule in Huon's place, eh, Baron?" a Vulture captain suggested cynically.

Meliadus shook his head. "Not at all. Flana Mikosevaar would be your queen. Vulture and Wolf would take the place of the Mantis in the royal favour. Yours would be the supreme Orders."

"But the Vultures are a mercenary Order," a Wolf captain pointed out.

Meliadus shrugged. "They have proved loyal to Granbretan. And it could be argued that many of our own Orders are moribund, that fresh blood is needed in the Dark Empire."

Another Vulture captain spoke thoughtfully. "So Flana would be our Queen-Empress — and you, Baron?"

"Regent and Consort. I shall marry Flana and aid her rule."

"You would be the King-Emperor in all but name," said the same Vulture captain.

"I would be powerful, it is true — but Flana is of the royal blood, not I. She is your Queen-Empress by right of ancestry. I shall be merely Supreme Warlord and leave the other affairs of state to her — for war's my life, gentlemen, and I seek only to improve the manner in which our wars are conducted."

The captains seemed satisfied.

Meliadus continued: "So instead of sailing to Amarehk on the morning tide, we sail around the coast a little, biding our time, then make for the Tayme estuary, sailing upriver to Londra and arriving in the heart of the city before anyone can guess our intent."

"But Huon is well-protected. His palace is impossible to storm. There will be legions in the city loyal to him, surely," said another Wolf captain.

"We will have allies in the city. Many of the legions will be with us. Taragorm is on our side and he is hereditary commander of several thousand warriors since his cousin's death. The Order of the Ferret is a small one, to be sure, but it has many legions in Londra, while other legions are in Europe, defending our possessions. All the nobles likely to remain loyal to Huon are abroad at this moment. It is a perfect time to strike. Baron Kalan is also with us — he can aid us with new weapons and his Serpents to operate them. If we achieve a swift victory — or at least make quick gains — then it is likely that many others will join us, for few will discover love for King Huon once Flana is on the throne."

"I feel a loyalty for King Huon," admitted a Wolf captain. "It is bred into us."

"And so is a loyalty to the spirit of *Aral Vilsn* — to all that Granbretan stands for. Is that not a loyalty even more deeply bred into us?"

The captain deliberated for a moment before nodding. "Aye — you are right. With a new ruler of the blood royal on the throne, then perhaps our whole greatness will come to us."

"Oh, it will, it will!" promised Meliadus fiercely, his black eyes gleaming from his snarling helm.

S I X

THE RETURN TO CASTLE BRASS

In the great hall of Castle Brass Yisselda, Count Brass's daughter, wept and wept.

She wept for joy, hardly able to believe that the man before her was her husband whom she loved with such passion, hardly daring to touch him lest he proved a phantom. Hawkmoon laughed and strode forward, putting his arms around her and kissing at her tears. Then she, too, began to laugh, her face becoming radiant.

"Oh, Dorian! Dorian! We feared you killed in Granbretan!"

Hawkmoon grinned. "Considering everything, Granbretan was the safest place we saw in our travels! Is that not so, D'Averc?"

D'Averc coughed into his kerchief. "Aye — and maybe the healthiest, too."

The thin and kindly-faced Bowgentle shook his head in mild astonishment. "But how did you return from Amarekh in that dimension to Kamarg in this?"

Hawkmoon shrugged his shoulders. "Ask me not, Sir Bowgentle. The Great Good Ones brought us here, that is all I know. The journey was swift, taking but a few minutes."

"The Great Good Ones! Never heard of 'em!" Count Brass spoke gruffly, stroking his red moustachios and trying to hide the tears in his eyes. "Spirits of some sort, eh?"

"Aye of some sort, father." Hawkmoon stretched out his hand to his father-in-law. "You are looking well, Count Brass. Your hair's as red as ever."

"That's not a sign of youth," Count Brass complained. "That's rust! I'm rotting here while you enjoy yourself chasing about the world."

Oladahn, the little son of a giantess of the Bulgar Mountains, stepped shyly forward. "I'm glad to see you back, friend Hawkmoon. And in good health, it seems." He grinned, offering Hawkmoon a goblet of wine. "Here — drink this as a welcome cup!"

Hawkmoon smiled back and accepted the goblet, quaffing it in a single draught. "Thanks, friend Oladahn. How's it with you?"

"Boring. We are all bored — and afraid you would not return."

"Well, I am back and I think I have enough stories of my adventures to dispel your boredom for a few hours. And I have news of a mission for us all which will bring you relief from the inactivity you have been suffering."

"Tell us!" Count Brass roared. "For all our sakes — tell us at once!"

Hawkmoon laughed easily. "Aye — but give me a moment to look at my wife." He turned and stared into Yisselda's eyes and he saw that they were now perturbed.

"What is it, Yisselda?"

"I see something in your manner," said she. "Something that tells me, my lord, that you are soon to risk your life again."

"Perhaps."

"If it must be, then it must be." She took a deep breath and smiled at him. "But it will not be tonight, I hope."

"Nor for several nights. We have many plans to make."

"Aye," she said softly, glancing at the stones of the hall. "And I have much to tell you."

Count Brass stepped forward gesturing to the far end of the hall where the servants were laying the table with food. "Let's eat. We have saved our best for this homecoming."

Later as they sat with full bellies by the fire and Bowgentle had finished recounting how Tozer had suddenly vanished, Hawkmoon showed them the Sword of the Dawn and the Runestaff, which he drew from his shirt. At once the hall was illuminated with whirling flames making patterns in the air and the strange bittersweet scent filled the hall.

The others looked at the thing in silent awe until Hawkmoon replaced it. "That is our standard, my friends. That is what we now serve when we go out to fight the whole Dark Empire."

Oladahn scratched at the fur on his face. "The whole Dark Empire, eh?"

Hawkmoon smiled gently. "Aye."

"Are there not several million warriors on the side of Granbretan?" Bowgentle asked innocently.

"There are *several* million, I believe."

"And we have about five hundred Kamargians left at Castle Brass," murmured Count Brass wiping his lips on his sleeve and giving a mock frown. "Let me compute that..."

D'Averc now spoke. "We have more than five hundred. You forget the Legion of the Dawn." He pointed at Hawkmoon's sword which lay scabbarded beside his chair.

"How many in that mysterious legion?" Oladahn asked.

"I do not know — perhaps an infinite number, perhaps not."

"Say a thousand," Count Brass mused. "To be conservative of course. Making fifteen hundred warriors against —"

"Several million," supplied D'Averc.

"Aye, several million, equipped with all the resources of the Dark Empire, including scientific knowledge we cannot match."

"We have the Red Amulet and the rings of Mygan," Hawkmoon reminded him.

"Ah, yes, those…" Count Brass seemed to scowl. "We have those, too. And we have right on our side — is that an asset, Duke Dorian?"

"Perhaps. But if we use the rings of Mygan to take us back to our own dimension and we fight a couple of small battles close to home, freeing the oppressed, we can begin to raise some kind of peasant army."

"A peasant army, you say. Hm…"

Hawkmoon sighed. "I know it seems impossible odds, Count Brass."

Then Count Brass suddenly broke into a beaming, golden smile. "That's right, lad. You've guessed!"

"What do you mean?"

"They're just the sort of odds I like. I'll get the maps and we can begin to plan our initial campaigns!"

While Count Brass was away, Oladahn said to Hawkmoon, "Elvereza Tozer could have returned to Londra and revealed our plans and our position. We are very vulnerable at this moment, friend Hawkmoon."

Count Brass came back with the maps. "Now, let's see…"

An hour later Hawkmoon got up and took Yisselda's hand, bid goodnight to his friends and followed his wife to their apartments.

Five hours later they were still awake, lying in each other's arms. It was then that she told him they were to have a child.

He accepted the news in silence, merely kissed her and held her closer. But when she was asleep, he got up and went to the window, staring out over the reeds and lagoons of Kamarg, thinking to himself that now he had something even more important to fight for than an ideal.

He hoped he would live to see his child.

He hoped his child would be born even if he did not live.

S   E   V   E   N

THE   BEASTS   BEGIN   TO   SQUABBLE

Meliadus smiled behind his mask and his hand tightened on Flana Mikosevaar's shoulder as the towers of Londra came in sight upriver.

"It is going so well," he murmured. "Soon, my dear, you will be queen. They do not suspect. They cannot suspect. There has been no uprising such as this for hundreds of centuries! They are unprepared. How they will curse the architects who sited the barracks on the waterfront!" He laughed softly.

Flana was tired of the thrumming of the engines and the rumble of the paddle wheel as it pushed the ship along. One of the virtues of a sailing ship, she now realized, was that it was silent. These noisy things would not be allowed in sight of Londra once their purpose was served and she ruled. But the irritation was slight and the decision unimportant. Again she turned her thoughts inward and forgot Meliadus, forgot that the only reason she had agreed to his plan was because she did not care what became of her. She was thinking again of D'Averc.

The captains on board the leading ships knew what to do. As well as Kalan's engines, they were now equipped with Kalan's flame cannon and they knew their targets — the military barracks of the Orders of the Pig and the Rat and the Fly and others lining the river close to the outskirts of Londra.

Softly Baron Meliadus instructed his ship's captain to raise the appropriate colour, the flag that would give the signal to begin the bombardment.

Londra was silent and still in the morning, as gloomy as ever, as darkly bizarre as usual, with her crazy towers leaning into the sky, like the clutching fingers of a million madmen.

It was early. None but the slaves would be awake. None, that is, save Taragorm and Kalan, waiting for the sounds of strife so that they could move their men into position. The intention was to slay as many as possible, then drive the rest towards the palace, bottling them in, containing them so that they should have not several objectives but, by the afternoon, one.

Meliadus knew that even if they succeeded in this plan the real fighting would begin with the attack on the palace and they would be hard put to take it before reinforcements arrived.

Meliadus's breathing quickened. His eyes gleamed. From the bronze snouts of the cannon flame spewed, shrieking towards the unsuspecting barracks. Within the first few seconds the morning air was split by a tremendous explosion as the first of the buildings blew up.

"What luck!" Meliadus exclaimed. "This is a splendid omen. I had not thought to have such success so soon!"

A second explosion — a barracks on the other side of the water — and from the remaining buildings ran terrified men, some so alarmed that they had even left their masks behind! As they scurried out the flame cannon caught them, burning them to cinders. Their yells and screams echoed among the sleeping towers of Londra — the first warning most of the citizens had had.

Wolf mask turned to Vulture helm in expressions of silent satisfaction as they witnessed the carnage on the banks. Pigs and Rats scuttled for cover — Flies flung themselves behind the nearest buildings and the few who had managed to bring flame-lances with them opened fire.

The beasts had begun to squabble.

It was part of that pattern of destiny fixed by Meliadus when, on leaving Castle Brass in disgrace, he had called upon the Runestaff.

Yet none could say how finally that pattern would resolve itself and who would be the ultimate victor — Huon, Meliadus or Hawkmoon.

E   I   G   H   T

T A R A G O R M ' S   I N V E N T I O N

By midmorning the barracks had been completely wiped out and the survivors were fighting in the streets near the centre of the city. They had been reinforced with several thousand Mantis warriors. It was probable that Huon still had no idea of what was really happening. Perhaps he thought the attack was by Asiacommunistans disguised as Granbretanians. Meliadus smiled as he disembarked with Flana Mikosevaar and made his way to the Palace of Time on foot, flanked by a dozen Vultures and Wolves. The surprise had been complete. His men had remained in the few open streets and had not ventured into the maze of corridors linking most of the towers. As the warriors had emerged, Meliadus's men had picked them off. Now they were bottling them in, for there were few windows from which Huon's soldiers could fight. Windows were not a feature of Londra's architecture, for the Granbretanians had little liking for fresh air or daylight. What windows there were tended to be placed so high as to be useless to snipers. Even the ornithopters, unequipped for fighting in a city such as Londra, were proving to be a smaller threat than Meliadus had anticipated. He was well pleased as he entered the Palace of Time and discovered Taragorm in a small chamber.

"Brother! Our plans go well — better than I had expected."

"Aye," answered Taragorm with a nod to Flana to whom, like Meliadus, he had been married for a short time. "My Ferrets have hardly needed to do anything as yet. But doubtless they'll be useful in flushing out those who stay in the tunnels. I plan to use them to come up on the enemy from behind as soon as we have properly located the main pockets."

Meliadus nodded his approval. "But you sent a message for me to meet you here. Why is that?"

"I believe I have discovered the means of bringing your friends of Castle Brass back to their natural environment," Taragorm murmured, his voice full of quiet satisfaction.

Meliadus gave a deep groan and it was a moment before Flana realized he was voicing his extreme pleasure. "Oh, Taragorm! At last the rabbits are mine!"

Taragorm laughed. "I am not entirely certain that my machine will work, but I feel it might since it is based on an old formula I discovered in the same book as the one which mentioned the crystal machine of Soryandum. Would you care to see it?"

"Aye! Lead me to it, brother, I beg you!"

"This way."

Taragorm led Meliadus and Flana through two short corridors full of the noise of clocks and arrived at last outside a low door which he opened with a small key.

"In here." He took a torch from the bracket outside and used it to light the dungeon he had opened. "There. It is on roughly the same level as the crystal machine at Castle Brass. Its voice can carry through the dimensions."

"I hear nothing," Meliadus said with some disappointment.

"You hear nothing because there is nothing to hear — in this dimension. But it makes a goodly sound, I guarantee, in some other space and time."

Meliadus moved towards the object. It was like a great brass skeleton clock the size of a man. Its pendulum swung beneath it, working the escapement lever moving the hands. It had springs and cogs and looked in every respect like an ordinary clock made huge. On its back was mounted a gong-like affair with a striking arm. Even as they watched the hands touched the half-hour and the arm moved slowly up to fall suddenly upon the gong. They could see the gong vibrating but did not hear a whisper of sound.

"Incredible!" whispered Meliadus. "But how does it work?"

"I have still to adjust it a little to ensure that it is operating in exactly the correct dimension of space and time which, with the help of Tozer, I have managed to locate. When midnight comes, our friends at Castle Brass should experience something of an unwelcome surprise."

Meliadus sighed with pleasure. "Oh, noble brother! You shall be the richest and most honoured man in the Empire!"

Taragorm's weird clock mask bowed slightly in recognition of Meliadus's promise. "It is only fitting," he murmured, "but I thank you, brother."

"You are sure it will work?"

"If it does not, then I shall not be the richest and most honoured man in the Empire," Taragorm said with some humour. "Doubtless, in fact, you shall see to it that I am rewarded in a less pleasant fashion."

Meliadus flung his arms around his brother-in-law's shoulders. "Do not speak of such a thing, brother! Oh, do not speak of it!"

N   I   N   E

HUON CONFERS WITH HIS CAPTAINS

"Well, well, gentlemen. Some sort of civil disturbance, we gather." The golden voice came from the wizened throat and the sharp black eyes darted this way and that at the gathered masks before them.

"It is treason, Noble Monarch," a Mantis mask said. His uniform was untidy and his mask singed by a flame-lance.

"Civil War, Great Emperor," another emphasized.

"And very nearly a *fait accompli*," murmured the man next to him, almost to himself. "We were totally unprepared, Excellent Ruler."

"Indeed you were, gentlemen. We blame you all — and ourselves. We were deceived."

The eyes moved more slowly over the assembled captains. "And is Kalan amongst you?"

"He is not, Grand Sire."

"And Taragorm?" purred the sweet voice.

"Taragorm is not present, King of All."

"So… And some thought you saw Meliadus on the flagship…"

"With Countess Flana, Magnificent Emperor."

"That is logical. Yes, we have been very much deceived. But no matter — the palace is well defended, we assume?"

"Only a very large force could possibly hope to take it, Lord of the World."

"But perhaps they have a very large force? And if they have Kalan and Taragorm with them, they have other powers. Were we prepared for siege, captain?" Huon addressed the captain of the Mantis Guard who bowed his head.

"After a fashion, Excellent Prince. But such a thing is without precedent."

"Indeed it is. Perhaps we should seek reinforcements, then?"

"From the Continent," said a captain. "All the loyal barons are there —

Adaz Promp, Brenal Farnu, Shenegar Trott..."

"Shenegar Trott is not on the Continent," King Huon said politely.

"... Jerek Nankenseen, Mygel Holst..."

"Yes, yes, yes — we know the names of our barons. But can we be sure that these are loyal?"

"I would assume so, Great King-Emperor, for their men perished today. If they were in league with Meliadus, they would have given him those loyal to their Order, surely?"

"Your guess is probably accurate. Very well — recall the Lords of Granbretan. Tell them to bring all available troops to squash this uprising as quickly as possible. Tell them that it is inconvenient to us. The messenger had best leave from the roof of the palace. We understand that several ornithopters are available."

From somewhere, muffled and distant, there was a roar as if from a flame cannon and the throne room seemed to tremble very slightly.

"Extremely inconvenient," sighed the King-Emperor. "What did you estimate as Meliadus's gains in the past hour?"

"Almost the entire city save the palace, Excellent Monarch."

"I always knew he was the best of my generals."

T E N

A L M O S T   M I D N I G H T

Baron Meliadus sat in his own chambers watching the fires of the city. He especially enjoyed the spectacle of an ornithopter crashing in flames over the palace. The night sky was clear and the stars were bright. It was an exceptionally pleasant evening. To make it perfect he had a quartette of girl-slaves, once well-known musicians in their own lands, play him the music of Londen Johne, Granbretan's finest composer.

The counterpoint of explosions, of screams and the clash of metal was exquisite to Meliadus's ear. He sipped his wine and consulted his maps, humming to the music.

There was a knock on his door and a slave opened it. His Chief of Infantry, Vrasla Beli, entered and bowed.

"Captain Beli?"

"I must report, sir, that we are becoming very short of men. We have achieved a miracle on very few, sir, but we cannot ensure our gains without reinforcements. Either that, or we must regroup..."

"Or leave the city altogether and choose the ground on which we fight — is that it, Captain Beli?"

"Exactly, sir."

Meliadus rubbed at his mask. "There are detachments of Wolves, Vultures and even Ferrets on the mainland. Perhaps if they were recalled..."

"Would there be time, sir?"

"Well, we should have to make time, captain."

"Aye, sir."

"Offer all prisoners a change of mask," Meliadus suggested. "They can see that we are winning and might wish to join a new Order."

Beli saluted. "King Huon's palace is superbly defended, sir."

"And it will be superbly taken, captain, I am sure."

The music of Johne continued and the firing continued and Meliadus felt sure that all was going perfectly. It would take time to capture the palace, but he was confident that it would be taken, Huon destroyed, Flana put in his place and Meliadus the most powerful man in the land.

He glanced at the clock on the wall. It was nearing eleven o'clock. He got up and clapped his hands, silencing the girls. "Fetch my litter," he ordered. "I journey to the Palace of Time."

The same four girls returned with his litter and he climbed in to sink among the cushions.

As they moved slowly along the corridors, Meliadus could still hear the music of the flame cannon, the shouts of men in conflict. Admittedly victory had not yet been accomplished and even if he slew King Huon there might be barons who would not accept Flana as Queen-Empress. He would need a few months in which to consolidate — but it would help if he could unite them all into turning their hatred against Kamarg and Castle Brass.

"Hurry," he called to the naked girls. "Faster! We must not be late!"

If Taragorm's machine worked, then he would have the double advantage of being able to reach his enemies and unite his nation.

Meliadus sighed with pleasure. Everything was working so perfectly.

B O O K   T H R E E

And now the resolution was imminent. The heroes of Kamarg plotted in Castle Brass — Baron Meliadus plotted in Taragorm's Palace of Time — the King-Emperor Huon plotted in his throne room — and all the plots that were made began to influence each other. The Runestaff, too, centrepiece of the drama, was beginning to exert its influence upon the players. And now the Dark Empire was divided — divided because of Meliadus's hatred of Hawkmoon whom he had planned to use as his puppet but who had been strong enough to turn against him. Perhaps it was then — when Meliadus had chosen Hawkmoon to use against Castle Brass — that the Runestaff had made its first move. It was a tightly woven drama — so tightly woven that certain threads were close to snapping...

— *The High History of the Runestaff*

O N E

T H E   S T R I K I N G   O F   T H E   C L O C K

There was a chill in the air. Hawkmoon drew his heavy cloak about him and turned his sombre head to regard his comrades. Each face looked at the table. The fire in the hall was burning low, but the objects on the table could be clearly seen.

First there was the Red Amulet, its ruddy light staining their faces as if with blood. This was Hawkmoon's strength, giving its owner more than natural energy. Then there were the crystal rings of Mygan which could transport those who wore them through the dimensions. These were their passports back to their own space and time. Beside the rings was the scabbarded Sword of the Dawn. In this lay Hawkmoon's army. And finally, wrapped in a length of cloth, there was the Runestaff, Hawkmoon's standard and his hope.

Count Brass cleared his throat. "Even with all these powerful objects can we defeat an empire as great as Granbretan?"

"We have the security of our castle," Oladahn reminded him. "From it we can go through the dimensions at will and return at will. By this means we can fight a prolonged guerilla action until we have worn down the enemy's resistance."

Count Brass nodded. "What you say is true, but I am still doubtful."

"With respect, sir, you are used to fighting classic battles," D'Averc reminded him. D'Averc's pale face was framed by the collar of a dark leather cloak. "And you would be happier with a direct confrontation, drawn up in ranks of lancers, archers, cavalry, infantry and so on. But we have not the men to fight such battles. We must strike from the dark, therefore — from behind, from cover — at least initially."

"You are right, I suppose, D'Averc." Count Brass sighed.

Bowgentle poured wine for them all. "Perhaps we should get to our beds, my friends. There is more planning to do and we should be fresh."

Hawkmoon strode to the far end of the table where the maps had been laid out. He rubbed at the Black Jewel in his forehead. "Aye, we must plan our first campaigns carefully." He studied the map of Kamarg. "There is a chance there is a permanent camp surrounding the place where Castle Brass stood — perhaps waiting for its return."

"But did you not feel that perhaps Meliadus's power is waning?" D'Averc said. "Shenegar Trott seemed to think so."

"If that is the case," Hawkmoon agreed, "then it is possible that Meliadus's legions are now deployed elsewhere, since there seems to be some sort of contention at the Court of Londra as to whether we are very important as a threat or not."

Bowgentle made a movement to speak but then cocked his head to one side. Now they all felt a slight tremor run through the floor.

"It's damned cold," Count Brass grumbled and went to the fire to fling on another log. Sparks flew and the log caught quickly, the flames sending red shadows skipping through the hall. Count Brass had wrapped his bull-like body in a simple woolen robe and now he tugged at this as if regretting he had not worn something more substantial. He glanced at the rack at the far end of the hall. The rack contained spears, bows, arrows, maces, swords — and his own broadsword, and his armour of brass. His great, bronzed face was clouded.

Again a tremor shook the building and the arms decorating the walls rattled.

Hawkmoon glanced at Bowgentle, noticing in the philosopher's eyes the same sense of inexplicable doom he felt. "A mild earthquake, perhaps?"

"Perhaps," murmured Bowgentle, plainly unconvinced. "To me it is as if the gears of some vast machine were grinding into motion."

Now they heard a sound — a long, distant note, reverberating endlessly, like the booming of a gong, but so low as to be almost inaudible. They rushed to the doors of the hall and Count Brass hesitated for a moment before flinging them open and looking up at the night.

The sky was black, but the clouds seemed dark blue, swirling in considerable agitation as if the dome of the sky were about to crack.

The reverberation came again, this time plainly audible. The voice of a huge, low bell or a gong. It hummed in their ears.

"It's like being in the bell-tower of the castle as the clock strikes," Bowgentle said, his eyes full of alarm.

Every face was pale — every face tense. Hawkmoon began to stride back into the hall, walking with arm outstretched towards the Sword of the Dawn. D'Averc called to him. "What do you suspect, Hawkmoon? Some kind of attack by the Dark Empire?"

"By the Dark Empire — or by something supernatural," Hawkmoon answered.

A third stroke sounded filling the night, echoing over the flat marshes of Kamarg, over the lagoons and the reeds. Flamingoes, disturbed by the noise, began to squawk from the darkness.

A fourth followed, louder still — a great booming bell of doom.

A fifth. And Count Brass went to the rack and took up his broadsword.

A sixth. D'Averc covered his ears as the sound increased. "This is sure to bring on at least a mild migraine," he complained languidly.

Yisselda ran down the stairs in her nightclothes. "What is it, Dorian? Father — what's the sound? It is like the striking of a clock. It threatens to burst my eardrums..."

Oladahn looked up gloomily. "It seems to me that it threatens our very existence," he said. "Though I do not know why I think that..." A seventh stroke sounded and plaster fell from the ceiling as the castle shook to its foundations.

"We had better close the doors," Count Brass said as the echo died sufficiently for him to make himself heard. Slowly they moved inside and Hawkmoon helped Count Brass push the doors together and replace the heavy iron bar.

An eighth stroke filled the hall and made them all press their palms to their ears. A huge shield, there since time immemorial, clattered from the wall, fell to the flagstones and rolled about noisily until it crashed to rest near the table.

In panic, the servants came running into the hall.

A ninth stroke and windows cracked, the glass splintering. This time Hawkmoon felt as if he were on a ship at sea that had struck suddenly a hidden reef, for the whole castle shuddered and they were flung about. Yisselda began to fall, but Hawkmoon managed to save her, hanging on to a pillar to stop himself from toppling. The sound made him feel sick and his vision was blurred.

For the tenth time the great gong reverberated, as if the whole world shook, as if the universe itself were filled with the sound signaling the end of everything.

Bowgentle keeled over and fell upon the flagstones in a faint. Oladahn reeled about, his palms pressing at his head. He collapsed to the floor. Hawkmoon clung to Yisselda grimly, barely able to retain his grip. He was filled with nausea and his head pounded. Count Brass and D'Averc had staggered across the room to the table and were hanging on to it as it shook. The stroke died. Hawkmoon heard D'Averc call: "Hawkmoon — look at this!"

Supporting Yisselda, Hawkmoon managed to reach the table and stared down at the rings of Mygan. He gasped. Every one of the crystals had shattered.

"So much for our scheme of guerilla raids," D'Averc said hoarsely. "So much, perhaps, for all our schemes..."

The eleventh stroke sounded. It was deeper and louder than the one before and the whole castle shuddered and flung them to the floor. Hawkmoon screamed in pain as the sound roared in his skull and seemed to sear his brain, but he could not hear his scream above the noise. Everything was shaking and he rolled about on the floor at the mercy of whatever force it was making the castle quake.

As it faded, he crawled on his hands and knees towards Yisselda, desperately trying to reach her. Tears of pain streamed down his face and he knew by the warmth that his ears were bleeding. Dimly he saw Count Brass trying to rise by clutching at the table. The count's ears gouted gore that matched his hair. "We are destroyed," he heard the old man say. "Destroyed by some cowardly enemy we cannot even see! Destroyed by a force against which our swords are useless!"

Hawkmoon continued to crawl towards Yisselda who lay prone on the floor.

Now the twelfth stroke sounded, louder and more terrible than the rest. The stones of the castle threatened to crack. The wood of the table split and the thing collapsed with a crash. Flagstones suddenly broke in twain or shattered to fragments. The castle was tossed like a cork in a gale and Hawkmoon roared with pain as the tears in his eyes were now replaced with blood, as the veins in his body threatened to burst.

Then the deep note was counterpointed by another — a high-pitched scream — and colours began to flood the hall. First came violet, then purple, then black. A million tiny bells seemed to ring in unison and this time it was possible to locate the sound as it came from below them, from the dungeon.

Weakly, Hawkmoon attempted to rise and then fell face down on the stones. The note boomed gradually away, the colours began to fade, the ringing sound subsided quite suddenly.

So there was silence.

T W O

T H E   B L A C K E N E D   M A R S H

"The crystal is destroyed…"

Hawkmoon shook his head and blinked his eyes. "Eh?"

"The crystal is destroyed." D'Averc knelt beside him trying to help him to his feet.

"Yisselda?" Hawkmoon said. "How is she?"

"No worse than you. We have put her to bed. The crystal is destroyed."

Hawkmoon dug dried blood from ears and nostrils. "You mean the rings of Mygan?"

"D'Averc — tell him more clearly." It was Bowgentle's voice. "Tell him that the machine of the wraith-folk is broken."

"Broken?" Hawkmoon heaved himself to his feet. "Was that the final shattering sound I heard?"

"That was it." Now Count Brass stood nearby, leaning wearily on a table and mopping at his face. "The vibrations destroyed the crystals."

"Then —?" Hawkmoon glanced questioningly at Count Brass who nodded.

"Aye — we're back in our own dimension."

"And not under attack?"

"It does not seem so."

Hawkmoon took a deep breath and began to walk slowly to the main doors of the hall. Painfully he drew back the iron bar and tugged the doors open.

It was still night. The stars in the sky remained the same but the swirling blue clouds had vanished and there was an uncanny silence hanging over the area, a strange smell in the air. But no flamingoes squawked, no wind sighed through the reeds.

Slowly, thoughtfully, Hawkmoon closed the doors again.

"Where are the legions?" D'Averc asked. "One would have thought they were waiting for us — at least a few!"

Hawkmoon frowned. "We'll have to wait until morning before we can guess the answer to that. Perhaps they are out there, planning to take us by surprise."

"Do you think that sound was sent by the Dark Empire?" Oladahn asked.

"Without doubt," Count Brass answered. "They have succeeded in their object. They have brought us back to our own dimension." He sniffed the air. "I wish I could identify that smell."

D'Averc was sorting things from the wreckage of the table. "It is a miracle that we are alive," he said.

"Aye," said Hawkmoon. "That noise seemed to affect inanimate things worse than us."

"Two of the older servants are dead," Count Brass said quietly. "Their hearts could not stand it, I suppose. They are being buried now, in case it is not possible in the morning. In the inner courtyard."

"What of the castle?" Oladahn asked.

Count Brass shrugged. "It's hard to tell. I've been down to the dungeons. The crystal machine is completely smashed and some of the stonework is cracked. But this is a strong old castle. She seems to have fared not too badly. No window glass, of course. No glass of any sort intact. Otherwise…" He shrugged as if his beloved castle had ceased to matter to him, "… otherwise we are still standing as firm as we did before."

"Let's hope so," murmured D'Averc. He held the Sword of the Dawn by its scabbard and the Red Amulet by its chain. He offered them to Hawkmoon. "You'd best don these for it is certain that you will soon have need of them."

Hawkmoon put the amulet around his neck and buckled the scabbard to his belt. Then he stopped and picked up the swaddled Runestaff.

"This does not seem to be bringing us the luck I had hoped," he said and sighed.

Dawn came at last. It came slowly and it came grey and chill, the horizon white as an old corpse and the clouds the colour of bone.

Five heroes watched it rise. They stood outside the gates of Castle Brass, on the hill, and their hands were on their swords, their grips tightening as they saw the scene below.

It was the Kamarg they had left, but it was a Kamarg wasted by war. The smell they had spoken of earlier was the smell of carnage, of a burnt land. For as far as they could see, all was black ruin. The marshes and lagoons had all been dried up by the fire of the flame cannon. The flamingoes, the horses and the bulls had been destroyed or fled. The watchtowers which had guarded the borders were flattened. It seemed as if the whole world were a sea of grey ash.

"It is all gone," said Count Brass in a low voice. "All gone, my beloved Kamarg, my people, my animals. I was their elected Lord Guardian and I failed in my task. Now there is nothing to live for save vengeance. Let me reach the gates of Londra and see the city taken. Then I will die. But not before."

T H R E E

D A R K   E M P I R E   C A R N A G E

By the time they reached the borders of Kamarg, Hawkmoon and Oladahn were covered from head to foot in clinging ash which stung their nostrils and was harsh in their throats. Their horses, too, were covered in the stuff and their eyes were as red as their riders'.

Now the sea of ash gave way to sparse, yellow grassland and still they had found no sign of the legions of the Dark Empire.

A little watery sunshine broke through the layers of cloud as Hawkmoon drew his horse to a halt and consulted his map. He pointed due east. "The village of Verlin lies yonder. Let's ride cautiously and see if Granbretanian troops still occupy it."

The village came in sight at last and when he saw it Hawkmoon began to gallop faster. Oladahn called from behind him:

"What is it, Duke Dorian? What has happened?"

Hawkmoon did not reply for, as they neared the village, it could be seen that half the buildings lay in ruins, that corpses choked the streets. And still no sign of the Dark Empire troops.

Many of the buildings had been blackened by flame-lance fire and some of the corpses had been slain by flame-lances. Here and there lay the body of a Granbretanian, an armoured figure with its mask tilting skyward.

"They were all Wolves here, by the look of it," Hawkmoon murmured. "Meliadus's men. It seems they fell upon the villagers and the villagers attacked them back. See — that Wolf was stabbed by a reaping hook — that one died from the blow of the spade still in his neck…"

"Maybe the villagers rose up against them," Oladahn suggested, "and the Wolves retaliated."

"Then why did they leave the village?" Hawkmoon pointed out. "They were garrisoned here."

They guided their horses over the bodies of the fallen. The stink of death was still heavy in the air. It was plain that this carnage had been wreaked only recently. Hawkmoon pointed out gutted stores and the corpses of cattle, horses, even dogs.

"They left nothing alive. Nothing which could be used for food. It is as if they were in retreat from some more powerful enemy!"

"Who is more powerful than the Dark Empire?" Oladahn said with a shudder. "Have we some new enemy to face, friend Hawkmoon?"

"I hope not. Yet this sight is puzzling."

"And disgusting," Oladahn added. There were not only men dead in the streets, but children too and every woman, young or old, bore signs of having been raped before she had been slain, mostly by means of a cut throat, for the Granbretanian soldiery liked to slay their victims as they raped them.

Hawkmoon sighed. "It is the sign of the Dark Empire, everywhere you venture."

He looked up, bending his head to catch a small sound carried on the chill wind. "A cry! Someone still lives, perhaps."

He turned his horse and followed the sound until he entered a sidestreet. Here a door had been broken open and a girl's body lay half in the doorway, half in the street. The cry was stronger. Hawkmoon dismounted and walked cautiously towards the house. It came from the girl. Quickly he knelt down and raised her in his arms. She was almost naked, her body covered with a few strips of torn clothing. There was a red line across her throat as if a blunt dagger had been drawn across it. She was about fifteen, with tangled fair hair and glazed blue eyes. Her body was a mass of blue-black bruises. She gasped as Hawkmoon lifted her.

Hawkmoon lowered her gently and went to his saddle, returning with a flask of wine. He put the flask to her lips and she drank, gasping, her eyes suddenly widening in alarm.

"Do not fear," Hawkmoon said softly. "I am an enemy of the Dark Empire."

"And you live?"

Hawkmoon smiled sardonically. "Aye — I live. I am Dorian Hawkmoon, the Duke of Köln."

"Hawkmoon von Köln? But we thought you dead — or flown forever…"

"Well I have returned and your village shall be revenged, I swear. What happened here?"

"I am not altogether sure, my lord, save that the beasts of the Dark Empire intended to leave none alive." She looked up suddenly. "My father and mother — my sister…"

Hawkmoon glanced inside the house and shuddered. "Dead," he said. It had been an understatement. They had been disgustingly mutilated. He picked up the girl as she sobbed and took her to his horse. "I will carry you back to Castle Brass," he said.

F O U R

N E W H E L M S

She lay in the softest bed in Castle Brass, tended by Bowgentle, comforted by Yisselda and Hawkmoon who sat beside her bed. But she was dying. She was dying not from her injuries but from sorrow. She wished to die. They respected that wish.

"For several months," she murmured, "the Wolf troops occupied our village. They took everything while we starved. We heard that they were part of an army left to guard Kamarg, though we could not think what there was to guard of that wasteland."

"They were awaiting our return most likely," Hawkmoon told her.

"That would seem likely," the girl said gravely.

She continued: "Then yesterday an ornithopter arrived at the village and its pilot went straight to the commander of the garrison. We heard it rumoured that the soldiers were being recalled to Londra and we were overjoyed. An hour later the soldiers of the garrison fell upon the village, killing, looting, raping. They had orders to leave nothing alive so that when they returned they would not meet resistance, so that any others who came upon the village should not find food. An hour afterwards, they were gone."

"So they plan to return," Hawkmoon mused. "But I wonder why they left…"

"Some invading enemy, perhaps?" Bowgentle suggested, bathing the girl's brow.

"That was my guess — and yet it does not seem to fit." Hawkmoon sighed. "It is puzzling — frightening that we know so little."

There came a knock upon the door and D'Averc entered. "An old friend is here, Hawkmoon."

"An old friend? Who?"

"The Orkneyman — Orland Fank."

Hawkmoon rose. "Perhaps he can enlighten us."

As he walked towards the door Bowgentle spoke quietly. "The girl is dead, Duke Dorian."

"She knows she will be avenged," Hawkmoon said flatly and he left to descend the stairs to the hall.

"Something is in the wind, I agree, friend," Orland Fank was saying to Count Brass as they stood together beside the fire. He waved his hand as Hawkmoon joined them. "And how d'you fare, Duke Dorian?"

"Well enough, in the circumstances. Do you know why the legions are leaving, Master Fank?"

"I was telling the good Count Brass here that I do not."

"Ah, and I thought you omniscient, Master Fank."

Fank grinned sheepishly, tugging off his bonnet to wipe his face with it. "I still need time to gather information and I've been busy the while since you left Dnark. I've brought gifts for all the heroes of Castle Brass."

"You are kind."

"They're not from me, you understand, but from — well, the Runestaff, I suppose. I'll give you them later. They've little practical use, you might think, but then it's hard to say what is practical and what is not in the fight against the Dark Empire."

Hawkmoon turned to D'Averc. "What did you discover on your ride?"

"Much the same as you," D'Averc replied. "Razed villages, all the inhabitants hastily slain. Signs of an overswift departure on the part of the troops. I gather that there are still some garrisons in the large towns, but they are skeleton staffed — mainly artillery and no cavalry at all."

"This seems insane," murmured Count Brass.

"If they are insane, then we may yet take advantage of their lack of rationality," Hawkmoon said with a grim smile.

"Well spoken, Duke Dorian." Fank clapped his red, brawny hand on Hawkmoon's shoulder. "Now can I bring in the gifts?"

"By all means, Master Fank."

"Lend me a couple of servants to help, if you will, for there's six of 'em and they're powerful heavy. I brought them on two horses."

A few moments later the servants came in, each holding two wrapped objects, one in each hand. Fank himself brought in the remaining two. He laid them on the flagstones at their feet. "Open them, gentlemen."

Hawkmoon bent and pulled back the cloth that wrapped one of the gifts. He blinked as the light struck his eyes and he saw his own face reflected perfectly back at him. He was puzzled, dragging off the rest of the cloth to stare in astonishment at the objects before him. The others, too, were murmuring in surprise.

The objects were battle helmets designed to cover the whole head and rest on the shoulders. The metal of their manufacture was unfamiliar, but it was polished more finely than the finest mirror Hawkmoon had ever seen. With the exception of two eye slits the fronts of the helms were completely smooth, without decoration of any sort so that whoever stared at them saw a complete image of himself. The backs were crested in the same metal, with clean, simple decoration. It struck Hawkmoon how useful they could be in battle, for the enemy would be confused by his own reflection, would have the impression that he was fighting himself!

Hawkmoon laughed aloud. "Why, whoever invented these must be a genius! They are the finest helms I have ever seen."

"Try them on," Fank said, grinning back. "You'll find they fit well. They are the Runestaff's answer to the beast-masks of the Dark Empire."

"How do we know which is ours?" Count Brass said.

"You will know," Fank told him. "The one you have opened. The one with the crest the colour of brass."

Count Brass smiled and lifted the helm to place it upon his shoulders. Hawkmoon looked at him and saw his own face, the dull Black Jewel in the centre of his forehead, staring back in amused surprise. Hawkmoon lifted his helm over his head. His had a golden crest. Now when he turned to regard Count Brass it seemed at first that the count's helm gave no reflection, until Hawkmoon realized that there were an infinity of reflections.

The others had put their helms on their shoulders. D'Averc's had a blue crest and Oladahn's a scarlet one. They laughed with pleasure.

"A goodly gift, Master Fank," Hawkmoon said, removing his helmet. "An excellent gift. But what of the other two helms?"

Fank smiled mysteriously. "Ah — ah, yes — they would be for those who would desire them."

"For yourself?"

"Not for myself, no — I must admit I tend to disdain armour. It is cumbersome stuff and it makes it harder for me to wield my old battle-axe here." He jerked this thumb behind him at the axe secured by a cord on his back.

"Then who are the other two helms for?" Count Brass said, removing his own helm.

"You will know when you know," Fank said. "And then it will seem obvious to you. How are the folk of Castle Brass faring?"

"You mean the villagers of the hill?" Hawkmoon said. "Well, some of them were slain by the striking of the great gong recalling us to our own dimension.

A few buildings fell, but all in all they survived well enough. The remaining Kamargian cavalry has survived."

"About five hundred men," said D'Averc. "Our army."

"Aye," Fank said with a sidelong glance at the Frenchman. "Aye. Well, I must be away about my business."

"And what business would that be, Master Fank?" Oladahn asked.

Fank paused. "In the Orkneys, my friend, we are not asking of each other's business," he said chidingly.

"Thank you for the gifts," Oladahn said with a bow, "and forgive my curiosity."

"I accept your apology," Fank said.

"Before you leave, Master Fank, I thank you on behalf of us all for these welcome gifts," Count Brass told him. "And could we bother you with a final question?"

"You are all prone to too much questioning in my own opinion," Fank said. "But then we're close-mouthed in the Orkneys. Ask away, friend, and I'll do my level best to answer, if the question is not too personal."

"Do you know how the crystal machine came to be shattered?" Count Brass asked. "What caused it?"

"I would gather that Lord Taragorm, Master of the Palace of Time in Londra, discovered the means of breaking your machine once he understood its source. He has many old texts which would tell him such things. Doubtless he built a clock whose striking would travel through the dimensions and be of such a pitch and volume as to shatter the crystal. It was, I believe, the one remedy of the enemies of the folk of Soryandum who gave you the machine."

"So it was the Dark Empire brought us back," Hawkmoon said. "But if that was so, then why were they not waiting for us?"

"Perhaps a domestic crisis of some sort," Orland Fank said. "We shall see. Farewell, my friends. I have the feeling we will meet again shortly."

FIVE HEROES AND A HEROINE

As the gates closed behind Fank, Bowgentle descended the stairs and there was an odd expression on his kindly features. He walked stiffly, and his eyes had a distant look.

"What is it, Bowgentle," Count Brass said in concern, moving forward to grip his old friend by the arm. "You seem disturbed."

Bowgentle shook his head. "Not disturbed — resolute. I have reached a decision. It is many years since I have wielded a weapon larger than a pen, borne anything weightier than a difficult problem in philosophy. Now I will bear arms against Londra. I will ride with you when you set out against the Dark Empire."

"But Bowgentle," Hawkmoon said, "you are not a warrior. You comfort us, sustain us with your kindness and your wisdom. All these things give us strength and are as useful as any comrade in arms."

"Aye — but this fight will be the last fight, win or lose," Bowgentle reminded him. "If you do not return, then you'll have no need of wisdom — and if you do return, you'll have but little inclination to seek my advice, for you'll be the men who broke the Dark Empire. So I will take up a blade. One of yonder mirror helms will fit me, I know. The one with the black crest."

He stood aside as Bowgentle went to the helm and picked it up. Slowly he lowered it over his head. It fitted perfectly. Reflected in the helm they could see what Bowgentle saw — their own faces at once admiring and grim.

D'Averc was the first to step forward with his hand outstretched. "Very well, Bowgentle. It will be a pleasure to ride with someone of sophisticated wit for a change!"

Hawkmoon frowned. "It is agreed. If you wish to, Bowgentle, we shall all be happier for your riding with us. But who is the other helm for, I wonder?"

"It is for me."

The voice was low, firm, sweet. Hawkmoon turned slowly to stare at his wife.

"No, it is not for you, Yisselda…"

"How can you be sure?"

"Well…"

"Look at it — the helm with the white crest. Is it not smaller than the others? Suitable for a boy — or a woman?"

"Aye," Hawkmoon answered reluctantly.

"Am I not Count Brass's daughter?"

"You are."

"And cannot I ride as well as any of you?"

"You can."

"And did I not fight in the bullring as a girl — and win honour there? And did I not train with the guardians of Kamarg in the arts of the axe, the sword and the flame-lance? Father?"

"It is true, she was proficient in all these arts," Count Brass said soberly. "But proficiency is not all that is required of a warrior…"

"Am I not strong?"

"Aye — for a woman…" answered the lord of Castle Brass. "Soft and as strong as silk, I believe a local poet said." He glanced sardonically at Bowgentle, who blushed.

"Is it stamina, then, that I lack?" Yisselda asked, her eyes flashing with a mixture of defiance and humour.

"No — you have more than enough stamina," Hawkmoon said.

"Courage? Do I lack courage?"

"There is none more courageous than you, my child," Count Brass agreed.

"Then what quality do I lack that a warrior has?"

Hawkmoon shrugged his shoulders. "None, Yisselda — save that you are a woman and — and —"

"And women do not fight. They merely remain at the fireside to mourn their lost kin, is that it?"

"Or welcome them back…"

"Or welcome them back. Well, I have no patience with that scheme of things. Why should I remain behind at Castle Brass? Who will protect me?"

"We will leave guards."

"A few guards — guards you will need in your battle. You know very well that you will want every man with you."

"Aye, that's true," Hawkmoon said. "But there is one other factor. Yisselda. Do you forget that you carry our child?"

"I do not forget. I carry our child. Aye, and I'll carry it into battle — for if we are defeated there will be nothing for it to inherit save disaster — and if we win then it will know the thrill of victory even before it comes into the world.

But if we are all slain — then we shall die together. I'll not be Hawkmoon's widow and I'll not bear Hawkmoon's orphan. I will not be safe at Castle Brass alone, Dorian, I'll ride with you." She went to the mirror helm with the white crest and she picked it up. She drew it over her head and spread her soft arms triumphantly.

"See — it fits perfectly. It was plainly made for me. We will ride together, the six of us, and lead the Kamargians against the massed might of the Dark Empire — five heroes — and, I hope, one heroine!"

"So be it," murmured Hawkmoon moving forward to embrace his wife. "So be it."

S   I   X

A   N E W   A L L Y

The Wolves and the Vultures had fought their way back from the Continent and were now pouring into Londra. Coming into Londra, too, were the Flies, the Rats, the Goats and the Hounds and all the other bloodthirsty beasts of Granbretan.

From a high tower, now his command headquarters, Meliadus of Kroiden watched them arrive, flooding in by every gate and battling as they came. One group puzzled him and he strained his eyes to see it better. It was a large detachment of troops riding under a black and white striped banner signifying neutrality. The banner carried beside it now became easier to see.

Meliadus frowned.

The banner was that of Adaz Promp, Grand Constable of the Order of the Hound. Did the neutral flag mean that he had not yet decided on whose side to fight? Or did it mean he planned a complicated trick? Meliadus rubbed his lips thoughtfully. With Adaz Promp on his side he could begin an assault on the palace itself. He reached for his wolf helm and stroked the metal head.

For the past few days as the battle for Londra had reached deadlock Meliadus had become pensive — the more so because he did not know if Taragorm's device had succeeded and brought Castle Brass back to its own dimension. His earlier good humour, based on his success in the initial fighting, had been replaced by a nervousness resulting from several uncertainties.

The door opened. Automatically Meliadus reached for his helm, donning it as he turned.

"Ah, it's you, Flana. What do you want?"

"Taragorm is here."

"Taragorm, eh? Has he something positive to tell me?"

The clock mask appeared behind Flana's heron mask.

"I had hoped that you would have some positive news, brother," Taragorm said acidly. "After all, we have made no great gains for the past few days."

"The reinforcements are arriving," Meliadus said petulantly, waving his gauntleted hand at the window. "Wolves and Vultures pouring in — and even some Ferrets."

"Aye — reinforcements for Huon, too — and seemingly in larger numbers than ours."

"Kalan should have his new weapons ready soon," Meliadus said defensively. "That will give us an advantage."

"If they work." Taragorm spoke sardonically. "I am beginning to wonder if I have not made a mistake, joining you. You struck too impetuously…"

"Brother! We must not quarrel, or we're finished. There is no time now!"

"Aye, that I'll grant you. If Huon wins we're all doomed."

"Huon will not win."

"We need a million men to attack the palace and succeed."

"We'll find a million men. If only we can make a little headway, others will come over to our side."

Taragorm ignored this statement and turned instead to Flana. "It is a shame, Flana. You would have made a beautiful queen…"

"She will still make a queen," Meliadus said savagely, restraining himself from striking Taragorm. "Your pessimism amounts to treachery, Taragorm!"

"And will you slay me for my treachery, brother? With all my knowledge. Only I know all the secrets of Time."

Meliadus shrugged. "Of course I will not slay you. Let us cease this arguing and concentrate instead on winning the palace."

Bored by the quarrel, Flana left the room.

"I must see Kalan," Meliadus said. "He has suffered a setback, having to remove all his equipment to a new site so hastily. Come, Taragorm, we'll visit him together."

They summoned their litters, climbed in and had their slaves carry them through the dimly lit corridors of the tower, down twisting ramps to the rooms Kalan had adapted as laboratories. A door opened and foul-smelling heat struck their bodies. Meliadus could feel it through his mask. He coughed as he left his litter and walked into the chamber where Kalan stood, his scrawny body naked to the waist and only his mask on his head, supervising the serpent-masked scientists who toiled for him.

Kalan greeted them impatiently. "What do you want? I have no time for conversation!"

"We wondered what progress you were making, Baron," Meliadus yelled over the boiling sound.

"Good progress, I hope. The facilities are ridiculously primitive. The weapon is almost ready."

Taragorm glanced at the tangle of tubes and wires from which all the noise and heat and stink was issuing. "That's a weapon?"

"It will be, it will be."

"What will it do?"

"Bring me men to mount it on our roof and I'll show you in a few hours."

Meliadus nodded. "Very well. You realize what depends on your success, Kalan?"

"Aye, that I do. I'm beginning to curse myself for joining you, Meliadus, but I'm in with you now and can only continue. Please leave — I'll send word when the weapon's ready."

Meliadus and Taragorm walked back through the corridors, their litters following behind.

"I hope Kalan has not lost all sanity," Taragorm said icily. "For if he has, that thing might destroy us."

"Or destroy nothing," Meliadus said gloomily.

"Now who is the pessimist, brother?"

Returning to his apartments, Meliadus discovered that he had a visitor. A fat visitor clad in gaudy silk-covered armour with a brightly painted helm representing a savage and grinning hound.

"Baron Adaz Promp," said Flana Mikosevaar, emerging from another room. "He arrived shortly after you left, Meliadus."

"Baron," Meliadus said, bowing formally. "I am honoured."

Adaz Promp's smooth tones came from the helm. "What are the issues, Meliadus? What are the goals?"

"The issues — our plans of conquest. The goals — to put a more rational monarch on the throne of Granbretan. One who will respect the advice of experienced warriors such as ourselves."

"Respect your advice, you mean!" Promp chuckled. "Well, I have to admit that I thought you insane, my lord, not Huon. Your pursuing this wild vendetta against Hawkmoon and Castle Brass, for instance. I suspected that it was motivated only by your private lust and vengeance."

"You no longer believe that?"

"I do not care. I am beginning to share your opinion that they represent the greatest danger to Granbretan and that they should be exterminated before we think of anything else."

"Why have you changed your mind, Adaz?" Meliadus leaned forward eagerly. "Why? You have some evidence not known to me?"

"More a suspicion or two," Adaz Promp said slowly, flatly. "A hint of this, a hint of that."

"What sort of hints?"

"A ship we encountered and boarded in the northern seas as we were returning from Scandia to answer our emperor's call. A rumour from France. Nothing more."

"What of the ship? What ship was it?"

"One like those anchored on the river, only much larger — with the strange contraption on its arse and no sails. It was battered, drifting and had two men aboard, both wounded. They died before we could transfer them to our own vessel."

"Shenegar Trott's ship. From Amarehk.

"Aye — that's what they told us."

"But what has it to do with Hawkmoon?"

"It appears they met Hawkmoon in Amarehk. It seems they received their wounds from Hawkmoon in some bloody battle in a city called Dnark. According to these men — and they were raving — the issue of the dispute was the Runestaff itself."

"And Hawkmoon won the dispute."

"Indeed he did. There were two thousand of them, we were told — Trott's men, that is — and only four, including Hawkmoon, against them."

"And Hawkmoon won!"

"Aye — aided by supernatural warriors according to he who lived long enough to babble the tale. It all sounds like truth mixed with fantasy, but it is plain that Hawkmoon defeated a force much larger than his own and that he personally slew Shenegar Trott. It does seem, also, that he has certain scientific powers at his disposal of which we know little. This is confirmed by the manner in which they managed to escape from us the last time. Which brings me to my second tale, picked up from one of your own Wolves as we marched to Londra."

"What's that?"

"He had heard that Castle Brass has reappeared, that Hawkmoon and the rest took a town to the north of Kamarg and destroyed every man of ours occupying it. "It's a rumour and hard to believe. Where could Hawkmoon have raised an army at such short notice?"

"Such rumours are common in times of war," Meliadus mused, "but it is possible. You believe Hawkmoon a larger threat than Huon thought?"

"It's a guess — but I feel it's an informed one. I'm motivated by other considerations, Meliadus. I think that the sooner we end this fight the better, for if Hawkmoon has an army — recruited, perhaps, in Amarehk — then the sooner we should clear it up. I'm with you, Meliadus; I can put half a million

Hounds at your disposal within the next day."

"Have you enough now to take the palace with those that I command?"

"Possibly, with artillery cover."

"That you shall have."

Meliadus pumped Promp's hand. "Oh, Baron Adaz, I believe we shall have victory by the morrow!"

"But how many of us will be alive to see it, I wonder," Promp said. "To take the palace will cost a few thousand lives — perhaps even a few hundred thousand."

"It will be worth it, Baron. Believe me."

Meliadus's spirits were rising at the prospect of victory over Huon, but mainly he gloated that he might soon have Hawkmoon in his power again — particularly if Kalan could really find a way of re-activating the Black Jewel as he had promised he would.

S E V E N

THE BATTLE FOR HUON'S PALACE

Meliadus watched them mount the contraption on the roof of his headquarters. They were high above the streets and close to the palace where the fighting raged. Promp had not yet brought up his Hounds but was waiting to see what Kalan's machine would do before he made an open attack on the palace gates. The huge building seemed capable of withstanding any attack — it looked as if it could survive the end of the world. It rose, tier upon magnificent tier, into the lowering sky. Flanked by four vast towers glowing with a peculiar golden light, encrusted with grotesque bas-reliefs depicting Granbretan's ancient glory, shining with a million clashing colours, protected by gigantic gates of steel thirty foot thick, the palace appeared to look down contemptuously at the embattled factions.

Even Meliadus felt momentary doubt as he stared at it, then returned his attention to Kalan's weapon. From the mass of wires and tubes projected a great funnel, like the bell of a monstrous trumpet and this was turned toward the palace walls crowded with hosts of soldiers, primarily of the Orders of the Mantis, the Pig and the Fly. Outside the city the ranks of other Orders were preparing to assault Meliadus's forces from the rear and he knew the time element was crucial, that if he won a victory at the palace gates others would come over to his side.

"It is ready," Kalan told him.

"Then use it," Meliadus growled. "Use it on the troops manning the walls."

Kalan nodded and his Serpents trained the weapon. Kalan stepped forward and seized a great lever. He turned his masked face to the lurid skies as if in prayer, then he pulled the lever down.

The machine trembled. Steam rose from it. It rumbled and quivered and roared and from the trumpet grew a gigantic, pulsing green bubble that gave off intense heat. The thing broke loose from the muzzle of the weapon and began to move slowly down towards the walls.

Fascinated, Meliadus watched it drift, watched it reach the wall and settle upon a score of warriors. With satisfaction he heard their screams break off as they writhed in the hot, green stuff and then vanished completely. The ball of green heat began to roll along the wall, gobbling its human prey until suddenly it burst and green liquid boiled down the sides of the wall in viscous streamers.

"It has broken. It does not work!" Meliadus yelled in rage.

"Patience, Meliadus," Kalan shouted. His men were repositioning the weapon by a few degrees. "Watch!" Again he pulled down the lever, again the machine shook and hissed and slowly another gigantic green bubble formed at its snout. The bubble drifted to the wall, rolled over another group of men and rolled again. This one rolled longer until there was hardly a warrior left on the wall when it eventually burst.

"Now we send them over the wall," Kalan chuckled and pulled the lever once more. This time he did not wait. As one boiling green bubble left the muzzle, he would bring another into being until at least a score of the things had drifted over the walls and into the courtyard beyond. He worked furiously, totally absorbed in his work, as the machine shuddered and hissed and threw off almost unbearable heat.

"That mixture will corrode anything!" Kalan yelled excitedly. "Anything!" He paused for a moment to point. "Look what it is doing to the walls!"

Sure enough the viscous stuff was eating its way into the stone. Huge pieces of highly decorated rock fell into the street below, forcing the attackers to back off. The mixture ate through the stone as boiling oil might eat through ice, leaving huge jagged gaps in the defenses.

"But how will our men get through?" Meliadus complained. "That stuff will not care what it eats!"

"Have no fear," Kalan chuckled. "The mixture only has a potency of a few minutes." Again he pulled the lever, sending another huge green bubble of heat over the wall. As he did so, a whole section of the wall near the gates collapsed completely and when the smoke from the rubble cleared, Meliadus could see that there was now a way through. He was elated.

A sudden whine now came from Kalan's machine and Kalan began to fiddle with the improvised controls — leaping about from part to part giving hasty directions to his men.

Taragorm emerged on the roof and saluted Meliadus. "I underestimated Kalan, I see." He moved towards the Serpent scientist. "Congratulations, Kalan."

Kalan was waving his arms and screaming with pleasure. "You see, Taragorm! You see! Here — why don't you try it. You merely depress this lever."

Taragorm gripped the lever in both hands, his clock mask turning to look at the wall through which it was now possible to see Huon's troops retreating into the palace itself, pursued by the rolling spheres of death. But then suddenly from the palace a flame-cannon roared. Huon's men had at last succeeded in positioning their artillery within the palace itself. Several bolts of fire shot over their heads and others splashed harmlessly on the walls below. Kalan chuckled in triumph. "Those things are useless against my weapon. Aim it at them, Taragorm. Send a bubble — *there!*" — and his finger stabbed towards the windows where the guns were positioned.

Taragorm seemed as absorbed in the machine as Kalan and it amused Meliadus to watch the two scientists playing like schoolboys with a new toy. He felt in a tolerant mood now. It was obvious Kalan's weapon was turning the battle in his favour. It was time to join Adaz Promp and lead in the troops.

He descended the steps that took him to the interior of the tower and called for his litter. Once in it, he leaned back comfortably, feeling already a certain sweet triumph.

Then overhead he heard a mighty explosion that shook the whole tower. He leapt from his litter and began to run back the way he had come. As he neared the roof he was driven back by an intense heat and saw Kalan, his mask twisted and buckled, staggering through the steam towards him. "Get back!" Kalan screamed. "The machine exploded. I was near the entrance or I should have been killed. It's spilling my mixture all over the tower. Get away or we'll all be eaten by the stuff."

"Taragorm!" Meliadus said. "What of Taragorm?"

"There can be nothing left of him," Kalan said. "Quickly — we'll have to leave the tower as fast as we can. Hurry, Meliadus!"

"Taragorm dead? And so soon after he had served my purpose?" Meliadus followed Kalan down the ramps. "I had known he would give me trouble after Huon was defeated. I had wondered how to cope with him. But now my problem is solved! My poor brother!"

Meliadus roared with laughter as he ran.

E I G H T

F L A N A   O B S E R V E S   T H E   B A T T L E

From the safety of her own tower, Flana Mikosevaar watched the soldiers pour through the breached wall of the palace as the tower which had lately been Meliadus's headquarters toppled, tilted and fell with a crash upon the lower sections of the city.

For a moment she had thought Meliadus destroyed when the tower fell, but now she could see his banner leading the warriors into battle. She also saw the banner of Adaz Promp beside it and knew that Wolf and Hound, traditional rivals, attacked King Huon together.

She sighed. The noise of the battle had intensified and she could find no escape from it. The flame cannon vainly attempted to shorten range, to fire down into the courtyard at the warriors as they rushed towards the great gates of the palace in which the green bubbles had eaten gaping holes. But the artillery was useless. It had been positioned anticipating a long siege and now it could not be moved down in time. A few flame-lances fired from the broken gates, but no large artillery.

The sound of the battle seemed to fade, as did the sight of it, as Flana thought again of D'Averc and wondered if he would come. Adaz Promp's news had raised her hopes, for if Hawkmoon were alive then D'Averc was likely to be also.

But would she ever see D'Averc? Would he die in some skirmish, vainly attempting to resist the might of Granbretan? Even if he did not die at once he was destined to live the life of a hunted bandit, for none could ever hope to do battle with the Dark Empire and succeed. She supposed that Hawkmoon, D'Averc and the rest would die on some distant battlefield. They might reach the coast before they were destroyed, but they could not possibly come close to her, for the sea separated them and the Silver Bridge Across The Sea would not be open to the Kamargian guerillas.

Flana considered taking her own life, but it did not seem worth it at present. When all hope was gone, then she would kill herself, but not before. And if she were queen, she would have some power. There was a slight chance that Meliadus would spare D'Averc, for D'Averc in some ways was the least of Meliadus's hates, though the Frenchman was considered a traitor.

She heard a great shout go up and looked again towards the palace. Meliadus and Adaz Promp were riding into Castle Huon. Victory was clearly in sight.

N I N E

THE SLAYING OF KING HUON

Baron Meliadus rode his black charger full tilt through the echoing corridors of King Huon's palace. He had been here many times before and always in humility or apparent humility. Now his snarling wolf visor was proud and a battle-cry roared from Meliadus's throat as he drove his way through the Mantis Guards whom once he had been forced to fear. He struck about him with the great black broadsword he had wielded so well in Huon's service. He made his horse rear and its hooves, which had trampled the ground of a score of conquered lands, struck down on insect helms and made long necks snap.

Meliadus laughed. Meliadus roared. Meliadus galloped for the throne room where the remnants of the defenders were gathering. He saw them at the far end of the corridor attempting to bring up a flame-cannon. With a dozen mounted Wolves behind him he did not pause but struck directly at the cannon before its surprised operators could move. Six heads flew from their necks in as many seconds and all the artillerymen were dead. Flame-lance beams shrieked around the black wolf helm, but Meliadus ignored them. The eyes of his horse were red with battle-madness and it plunged forward at the foe.

Meliadus pressed back the Mantis Guards, hacking them down. They died convinced that he had supernatural powers.

But it was wild energy, the elation of war, driving Meliadus of Kroiden through the massive gates of the throne room to find the few remaining guards in confusion. All possible men had been used to defend the gates. Now as the Mantis warriors advanced cautiously, spears outraised, Meliadus shouted his laughter at them and rode through them before they could move, galloping towards the Throne Globe where earlier he had crawled.

The black globe shimmered and gradually the wizened shape of the immortal King-Emperor became visible. The little foetus shape wriggled like a malformed fish, dashing back and forth across the confining bowl that was its life. It was undefended. It was helpless. It had never believed that it would need to protect itself against such treachery. Even it, in all its two thousand years of wisdom, had not been able to conceive that a Granbretanian noble would turn against his hereditary ruler.

"Meliadus…" There was fear in the golden voice. "Meliadus — you are insane. Listen — it is your King-Emperor speaking to you. I order you to leave this place, to withdraw your troops, to swear your loyalty to me, Meliadus!"

The black eyes, once so sardonic, were now full of animal fear. The prehensile tongue flickered like that of a snake, the enfeebled, useless hands and feet flapped.

"Meliadus!"

Shaking with triumphant laughter Meliadus drew back his great broadsword and struck at the Throne Globe. He felt a shock run the length of his body as the blade crashed into the globe. There was a white explosion, a wailing cry, a sound of shards falling to the floor and the splattering of fluid against Meliadus's body.

He blinked his eyes, expecting to look down upon the twisted, tiny frame of his slain King-Emperor. He saw nothing but deep blackness.

His laughter changed to a scream of terror.

"By Huon's Teeth! *I AM BLIND!*"

T E N

T H E   H E R O E S   R I D E   O U T

"The fort burns well," said Oladahn, turning back in his saddle to look for the last time upon the garrison. It had contained a force of Rat infantry but now not one lived save the commander who would take his time in dying for the citizens of the town had crucified him on the scaffold where he had crucified so many of their husbands, wives and children.

Six mirror helms now looked forward to the horizon as Hawkmoon, Yisselda, Count Brass, D'Averc, Oladahn and Bowgentle rode away from the town at the head of five hundred Kamargian flame-lancers.

Their first encounter since leaving Kamarg had been a complete victory. With surprise on their side they had wiped out the skeleton garrison in less than half an hour.

Feeling little elation, but with no sense of exhaustion, Hawkmoon led his comrades on towards the next town where they had heard they might find more Granbretanians to kill.

But then he reined in his horse as he saw a rider galloping towards them and realized that it was Orland Fank, his battle-axe bouncing on his brawny back.

"Greetings, friends! I have some news for you — an explanation. The beasts have fallen upon each other. There is civil war in Granbretan. Londra itself is the main battleground with Baron Meliadus in arms against King Huon. Thousands have been slain so far."

"So that is why there are so few here," Hawkmoon said, removing his mirror helm and wiping his forehead with a silken kerchief. He had worn armour rarely in the past months and he had not yet got used to the discomfort. "They have all been recalled to defend King Huon."

"Or to fight with Meliadus. It is to our advantage, don't you think?"

"I do," Count Brass broke in gruffly, his voice more excited than usual, "for that means they are killing each other and improving the odds a little in our favour. While they battle, we move swiftly to the Silver Bridge, crossing it and reaching the very shores of Granbretan herself! Luck is with us, Master Fank."

"Luck — or fate — or destiny," Fank said lightly, "call it what you will."

"Then had we best not ride swiftly to the sea?" Yisselda said.

"Aye," Hawkmoon said. "Swiftly — to take advantage of their confusion."

"A sensible idea," Fank nodded. "And being a sensible man myself, I believe I will ride with you."

"You are most welcome, Master Fank."

E L E V E N

N E W S   O F   S E V E R A L   S O R T S

Meliadus lay gasping on the stretcher as Kalan bent over him probing at his blind eyes with his instruments. His voice was a mixture of pain and fury. "What is it, Kalan?" he groaned. "Why am I blind?"

"Simply the intensity of the light released during the explosion," Kalan said. "Your sight should be restored in a day or so."

"In a day or so! I need to see. I need to consolidate my gains. I need to make sure that there are no counterplots hatched against me. I need to convince the other barons to swear loyalty to Flana now and then to find out what Hawkmoon is up to. My plans — my plans — are they to be all destroyed!"

"Most of the barons have decided to support your cause," Kalan told him. "There is little they can do. Only Jerek Nankenseen and the Flies represent a serious threat and Brenal Farnu is with him — but Farnu virtually has no Order left. Most of the Rats died in the early fighting. Adaz Promp is even now chasing Rats and Flies from the city."

"No Rats left," said Meliadus, suddenly thoughtful. "How many dead in all, d'you think, Kalan?"

"About half the fighting men of Granbretan."

"Half? Have I destroyed half our warriors? Half our strength?"

"Was it not worth it for the victory you have won?"

Meliadus's blind face stared up at the ceiling. "Aye — I suppose so…"

Now he sat upright on the stretcher. "But I must justify the deaths of those who fell, Kalan. I did it for Granbretan — to rid the world of Hawkmoon and the scum from Castle Brass. I must succeed or, Kalan, I cannot justify weakening the Dark Empire's fighting force to such a degree!"

"Have no fear on that score," Kalan told him with a faint smile, "for I have been working on another of my machines."

"A new weapon?"

"An old one, made to function again."

"What is that?"

Kalan chuckled. "The Machine of the Black Jewel, Baron Meliadus. Hawkmoon shall soon feel the power of the Black Jewel as it begins to eat his brain."

A slow, satisfied smile crossed Meliadus's lips. "Oh, Kalan — at last!"

Kalan pressed Meliadus back against the stretcher. He began to rub ointment on the baron's blind eyes. "Rest now and dream of your revenge, old friend. We shall enjoy it together."

Kalan looked up suddenly. A courier had entered the small room. "What is it? What news?"

The courier was panting. "I have come from the mainland, your excellency. I have news of Hawkmoon and his men."

"What of them?" Again Meliadus rose up from the stretcher, the ointment dripping down his cheeks, careless that a minion should see him unmasked. "What of Hawkmoon?"

"They ride for the Silver Bridge, my lord."

"They plan to invade Granbretan?" Meliadus was incredulous. "How many men have they? What is the size of their army?"

"Five hundred horsemen, my lord."

Meliadus began to laugh.

TWELVE

THE NEW QUEEN

Kalan led Meliadus up the steps towards a throne now replacing the sinister globe. On the throne sat Flana Mikosevaar in a jeweled heron mask, a crown upon her head, the robes of state upon her body. And before Flana Mikosevaar knelt all those nobles loyal to her.

"Behold," Meliadus said in a voice booming coarse and proud through the vast hall, "your new queen. Under Queen Flana you will be great — greater than you have dreamed. Under Queen Flana a new age will bloom — an age of laughing madness and roaring pleasure, the sort of pleasure we of Granbretan hold dear. The world shall be our toy!"

The ceremony progressed, with each noble in turn swearing his allegiance to Queen Flana. And when at length it was finished, Baron Meliadus spoke again. "Where is Adaz Promp, Chief Warlord of the Armies of Granbretan?"

Promp spoke up. "Here I am, my lord, and I thank you for the honour you do me." This was the first time Meliadus had mentioned Promp's reward — command over all other commanders, save Meliadus himself.

"Will you report how the rebels fare, Adaz Promp?"

"There are few left, my lord. Those Flies we have not swatted are dispersed and their Grand Constable, Jerek Nankenseen, is dead. I slew him myself. Brenal Farnu and the few remaining Rats have bolted into holes somewhere in Sussex and will soon be flushed out. All others have united in their loyalty to Queen Flana."

"That is satisfactory, Adaz Promp, and I am pleased. And what of Hawkmoon's laughable force? Does it still progress towards us?"

"So our ornithopter scouts report, my lord. They will soon be ready to cross the Silver Bridge."

Meliadus chuckled. "Let them cross. Let them come at least half the distance, then we shall wipe them out. Kalan, how do you manage with the machine?"

"It is almost ready, my lord."

"Good. Now we must set off for Deau-Vere to welcome Hawkmoon and his friends. Come, my captains, come."

And Meliadus was led back down the steps by Kalan and along the hall until he came to the great gates — the gates guarded not by Mantis warriors, but by Wolves and Vultures. Meliadus regretted he could not see them and thus savour his triumph the more.

After the doors had closed behind him, Flana sat frozen on her throne and thought of D'Averc. She had tried to speak of him to Meliadus, but he had not heard her. Would he be killed? she wondered.

She thought, also, of what had befallen her. Alone among the nobles of Granbretan, save Shenegar Trott, she had read many old texts, some of which were legends and alleged histories of the years before the Tragic Millennium. She believed, whatever became of herself and Meliadus, that she now presided over a court entering its last stages of decadence. The wars of expansion, the internal strife — all were signs of a nation in its death throes, and though that death might not come for another two hundred years, or five hundred, or a thousand, she knew that the Dark Empire was doomed.

She prayed that something better would emerge to take its place.

T H I R T E E N

" W H A T   D O   Y O U   S E E ? "

Meliadus held the reins of his herald's horse. "You must not leave me, boy. You must tell me what you see and I must plan the battle accordingly."

"I will tell you, my lord."

"Good. Are the troops all assembled?"

"They are, my lord. They await your signal."

"And is that cur Hawkmoon in sight yet?"

"Figures have been seen riding towards us across the Silver Bridge. They will ride directly into our ranks, unless they flee."

Meliadus grunted. "They will not flee — not Hawkmoon — not now. Can you see them yet?"

"I see a flash like silver — like a heliograph signal — one — two — three, four — five — six. The sun makes them shine so. Six silver mirrors. I wonder what it can mean?"

"The sun on polished spears?"

"I think not, my lord."

"Well, we shall soon know."

"Yes, my lord."

"What now?"

"Now I see six riders, my lord, at the head of a mass of cavalry. Each rider is crowned with flashing silver. Why, my lord, it is their helmets that shine!"

"Are they well-polished, then?"

"They are helms. They cover their faces. I — I can hardly bear to look upon them, they are so bright."

"Strange. Still, doubtless the helmets will break quickly enough beneath our weapons. You have told them that Hawkmoon must be taken alive but they can kill the rest?"

"I have, my lord."

"Good."

"And I told them what you said — that if Hawkmoon should clutch at his head and begin to act strangely they should tell you at once."

"Excellent." Meliadus chuckled. "Excellent. I shall have my vengeance, either way."

"They have almost reached the end of the bridge, my lord. They have seen us but they are not stopping."

"Then give the signal to charge," Meliadus said. "Blow your trumpet, herald."

"Aye, my lord."

"Are they charging, herald?"

"They are, my lord."

"And what now? Have the armies met?"

"They have engaged, my lord."

"And what is happening?"

"I am — I am uncertain, my lord — what with the flashing of those helmets and some — there is a peculiar red light spreading over the scene — there seem to be more men in Hawkmoon's army than we at first thought. Infantry — and some cavalry. By Huon's Teeth — I beg your pardon, my lord — by Flana's Breasts! They are the strangest warriors I have ever seen!"

"What do they look like?"

"Barbaric — primitive — and yet so fierce! They are driving into our forces like hot coals through cream!"

"What? It cannot be! We have five thousand troops and they have five hundred. All the reports confirmed that number."

"There are more than five hundred, my lord. Many more."

"Have all the scouts lied, then? Or are we all going mad? These barbarian warriors, they must have come with Hawkmoon from Amarehk. What now? What now? Are our forces rallying?"

"They are not, my lord."

"What are they doing, then?"

"They are falling back, my lord."

"Retreating? Impossible!"

"They appear to be falling back rapidly, my lord. Those that live."

"What do you mean? How many remain of our five thousand?"

"I would say about five hundred infantry, my lord, and a scattered hundred of cavalry."

"Tell the pilot of my ornithopter to prepare his machine, herald."

"I will, my lord."

"Is the pilot ready to fly, herald?"

"He is, my lord."

"And what of Hawkmoon and his band? What of the men in the silver helms?"

"They are pursuing the remains of our force, my lord."

"I have been deceived in some way, herald."

"As you say, my lord. There are many dead. But now the barbarian warriors slaughter the infantry. Only the cavalry escape."

"I cannot believe it. O, curse this blindness! I feel as if I dream!"

"I will lead you to the ornithopter, my lord."

"Thank you, herald. Now, pilot — to Londra. Hurry. I must consider fresh plans!"

As the ornithopter beat its way up into the pale blue sky, Meliadus felt a great silver flash pass across his eyes and he blinked, looking down. And he could see. He could see the six flashing helmets the herald had mentioned, he could see the slaughtered legions he had known would destroy Hawkmoon's force, he saw the remains of his cavalry scurrying wildly for their lives. And he heard distant laughter he recognized as belonging to his most hated enemy.

He shook his fist. "Hawkmoon! Hawkmoon!"

Silver flashed as a helmet turned to look upward.

"No matter what tricks you use, Hawkmoon, you will perish by the night. I know you will. I know!"

He looked again, seething as Hawkmoon laughed on. He looked for the barbarians who had routed his soldiers. They had vanished.

It was a nightmare, he thought. Or had the herald been in league with Hawkmoon? Or were Hawkmoon's barbarians invisible to his eyes?

Meliadus rubbed at his face. Perhaps the blindness, so recently left him, was still troubling him in some obscure form. Perhaps the barbarians were on another part of the field.

But no, there were no barbarians.

"Hurry, pilot," he called through the sound of the metallic wings flapping at the air. "Hurry — we must return to Londra as fast as we can!"

Meliadus began to think that Hawkmoon's defeat was not going to be as easy as he had guessed. But then he remembered Kalan and the Machine of the Black Jewel, and he smiled.

F O U R T E E N

T H E   P O W E R   R E T U R N S

Slightly overawed by a victory in which they had lost only twelve killed and twenty slightly wounded, the six removed their mirror helms and stared after the retreating horsemen.

"They were not expecting the Legion of the Dawn!" Count Brass smiled. "Unprepared, they were startled and could hardly resist. But they will be better prepared by the time we reach Londra."

"Aye," Hawkmoon said, "and Meliadus will put a good many more warriors in the field next time." He fingered the Red Amulet about his throat and glanced at Yisselda who was shaking out her blonde hair.

"You fought well, my lord," she said. "You fought like a hundred men."

"That is because this amulet gives me the strength of fifty men and your love gives me the strength of another fifty," he smiled.

She laughed lightly. "You never flattered me so during our courtship."

"Perhaps it is because I have come to love you even more than before," he replied.

D'Averc cleared his throat. "We'd best camp a mile or two on, away from all this death."

"I'll tend to the wounded," Bowgentle said and turned his horse back to where the Kamargian cavalry were grouped, squatting beside their horses and talking among themselves.

"You did well, lads," Count Brass called back. "It is like the old days, eh? When we fought across Europe! Now we fight to save Europe."

Hawkmoon started to speak and then gave a terrible shriek. The helmet fell from his grasp and he pressed both hands to his head, his eyes rolling in pain and horror. He swayed in his shadow and would have fallen had not Oladahn caught him.

"What is it, Duke Dorian?" Oladahn asked in alarm.

"Why do you cry, my love?" Yisselda dismounted swiftly, helping Oladahn support him.

Through clenched teeth and pale lips Hawkmoon managed to utter a few words. "The Jewel… The Black Jewel — it is gnawing at my brain again! The power has returned!" He swayed and fell into their arms, his limbs swinging loosely and his face a terrible white. As his hands dropped from his head they saw he spoke truth. The Black Jewel was crawling with life. It had regained its malevolent lustre.

"Oladahn, is he dead?" Yisselda cried in panic.

The little man shook his head. "No — he lives. But for how long, I cannot tell. Bowgentle! Sir Bowgentle! Come quickly."

Bowgentle hurried up and took Hawkmoon in his arms. This was not the first time he had seen the Duke of Köln thus. He shook his head. "I can try to work a temporary remedy, but I have not the materials that I had at Castle Brass."

In panic, Yisselda and Oladahn, and later Count Brass and D'Averc, watched Bowgentle work. And at last Hawkmoon stirred, opening his eyes.

"The Jewel," he said. "I dreamed it was eating my brain again…"

"So it will if we cannot find a way of blocking it soon," murmured Bowgentle. "The power has gone for the moment, but we do not know when it will return again and in what force."

Hawkmoon hauled himself to his feet. He was pale and could hardly stand. "We must press on, then — to Londra while there is time. If there is time."

"Aye, if there is time."

F I F T E E N

T H E   G A T E S   O F   L O N D R A

The troops were massed outside the gates of Londra as the six riders mounted the crest of the hill at the head of their cavalry.

Hawkmoon, ill with pain, fingered the Red Amulet. This alone was keeping him alive, helping him fight the power of the Black Jewel. Somewhere in the city Kalan was operating the machine that fed life to the Jewel. To reach Kalan he had to take the city, had to beat the multitude of warriors that, with Meliadus at their head, now awaited them.

Hawkmoon did not hesitate. He knew he could not hesitate, for every second of his life was precious. He drew the rosy Sword of the Dawn and gave the order to charge.

Gradually the Kamargian cavalry topped the hill and began to thunder down on a force many times their number.

Flame-lances spat from the Granbretanian ranks and were answered by the fire of the Kamargians. Hawkmoon judged the moment right and flung his swordarm skyward. *"The Legion of the Dawn! I summon the Legion of the Dawn!"* and then he groaned as the pain filled his skull and he felt the heat of the Jewel in his forehead. Yisselda beside him had time to cry out, "Are you all right, my love?" but he could not give an answer.

And then they were in the thick of the battle. Hawkmoon's eyes were so glazed with pain he could hardly see the enemy, could not tell at first if the Legion of the Dawn had materialized. But there they were now, their rosy auras lighting the sky. He felt the power of the Red Amulet fill him as it fought the power of the Black Jewel and he felt his strength gradually returning. But how long would it last?

Now he was in the middle of a mass of fear-crazed horses, striking about him at Vulture-helmeted warriors who bore long-handled maces with heads like the stretched claws of hunting birds. He blocked a blow and struck back, his great sword cutting through the warrior's armour and into his chest. He swung in the saddle to take another foe in the neck, ducked a whistling mace and stabbed its owner in the groin.

The fight was noisy and the fighting hot and hysterical. The air stank of fear and Hawkmoon had soon decided that this was the worst battle he had ever fought, for, in their shock at the appearance of the Legion of the Dawn, the Dark Empire warriors had lost their nerve and were fighting wildly, had broken their ranks, had abandoned their commanders.

Hawkmoon knew that it was to be a messy fight and one in which there would be few left alive at the end. He began to suspect that he would not see the finish, for the pain in his skull was growing stronger again.

Oladahn died unseen by his comrades, lonely and without dignity, hacked to pieces by a dozen war-axes wielded by Pig infantry.

But Count Brass died in this manner:

He encountered three barons. Adaz Promp, Mygel Holst and Saka Gerden (the latter of the Order of the Bull). They recognized him not by his helm, which was plain save for its crest, but by his body and his armour of brass. And they rode at him in a pack — Hound, Goat and Bull — with their swords raised to chop him down.

But Count Brass, looking up from the body of his last opponent (who had slain his steed and thus left the count on foot), saw the three barons riding down on him and took his broadsword in both hands and, as their horses reached him, he swung the sword, cutting the legs of the horses from under them so that each baron was flung forward over his horse's head and landed in the churned mud of the battlefield, whereupon Count Brass dispatched Adaz Promp in a very undignified position in the rear, lopped off the head of Mygel Holst (whom he had almost slain once before) as the Goat baron begged to be spared, and by this time had only the Bull, Saka Gerden, to deal with. Baron Saka had time to get to his feet and assume a decent fighting stance though he shook his head several times as Count Brass's mirror mask blinded him. Upon seeing this, Count Brass ripped off his silver helm and threw it to one side, displaying his bristling red hair and moustache in all its pride and battle-anger. "I took two in an unfair manner," growled the count, "so it is only fair to give you the chance to slay me."

Saka Gerden charged like the fierce Bull of his Order and Count Brass sidestepped him, bringing his sword around in a swing to split Saka Gerden's helm down the middle and split Saka Gerden's skull, also. As the baron fell, the count smiled and a spear was driven completely through his neck by a goat rider. Even then Count Brass turned, wrenching the spear from his assailant's grasp, and flung his broadsword to catch the Goat in the throat, thus giving as good as he had received. That was how Count Brass died.

Orland Fank saw it happen. He had left the party before the battle but had joined them later and had done considerable damage with his battle-axe. He saw how Count Brass died. It was at about the moment when the Dark Empire forces, lacking three of their leaders, began to regroup closer to the gates and were only stopped from retreating behind the gates by Baron Meliadus who was most fearsome in his black armour, his black Wolf helm and his great black broadsword.

But then even Baron Meliadus was pressed back as Hawkmoon, Yisselda, D'Averc, Bowgentle and Orland Fank led their few surviving Kamargians and the strange, dirge-calling Legion of the Dawn, against the beasts of Granbretan.

There was no time to close the gates before the heroes of Kamarg had entered the city and Baron Meliadus realized he had always estimated Hawkmoon's power correctly and only now, overconfident, had underestimated it. There was nothing for it but to bring up as many reinforcements as possible and get Kalan to increase the power of the Black Jewel.

Then his heart lifted. He saw Hawkmoon sway in his saddle, his hands going to the silver helm, saw the strange man in the bonnet and the chequered breeks grasp him and then reach behind him for the roll of cloth attached to his saddle.

Fank murmured to Hawkmoon, "Try to listen, man, will you? It is time to use the Runestaff. Time to bring out our standard. Do it now, Hawkmoon, or you'll live less than a minute more!"

Hawkmoon felt the power gnawing at his brain like a rat in a cage, but he grasped the Runestaff as Fank handed it to him, raised it high in his left hand and saw the waves and rays begin to fill the air around him.

Fank yelled: "The Runestaff! The Runestaff! We fight for the Runestaff!" And Fank laughed and laughed as the Granbretanians fell back in fear, so demoralized now, in spite of their numbers, that Hawkmoon already felt the victor.

But Baron Meliadus was not prepared to be the conquered. He screamed at his men. "That is nothing! It is only an object! It cannot harm you! You fools — take them."

Then the heroes of Kamarg rode forward with Hawkmoon swaying in his saddle, managing to bear the Runestaff aloft, through the gates of Londra and into the city where still there were a million men to stop them.

Now, as if in a dream, Hawkmoon led his supernatural legion against the enemy, the Sword of the Dawn in one hand and the Runestaff in the other, guiding his horse with his knees.

The press was so solid, as Pig and Goat infantry tried to tear them from their saddles, they could hardly move at all. Hawkmoon saw one of the mirror-helmed figures fighting valiantly as a dozen beasts dragged it from its horse and he feared it was Yisselda. Energy flooded into him and he turned, trying to reach his comrade, but another mirror-helmed horsemen was already there, hacking about it, and he realized it had not been Yisselda in peril but Bowgentle and that Yisselda had come to his rescue.

To no avail. Bowgentle disappeared and the weapons of the beasts, of the Goats and the Pigs and the Hounds, rose and fell above his body until eventually one held aloft a bloodied silver helm — held it aloft only for a moment, for then Yisselda's slim sword had sliced off the wrist so that blood fountained from the arm.

Another searing charge of pain. Kalan was increasing the power. Hawkmoon gasped and his vision dimmed, but he managed to protect himself from the weapons whistling around him, managed to hold up the Runestaff still.

As his vision cleared for the moment, he saw that D'Averc was leaping his horse through the Granbretanians, his sword whirling in all directions as he cut a road through them. Then Hawkmoon realized where D'Averc was going. To the palace — to reach the woman he loved, Queen Flana.

And this is how D'Averc died:

D'Averc managed somehow to reach the palace which was still in the half-ruined condition it had been in after Meliadus had taken it. He was able to ride through the breach in the wall and dismount at the outer steps to run at the guards on the door. They had flame-lances. He had only a sword. He flung himself flat as the flames shrieked past his head, rolled over to take cover in a ditch cut by the green fluid from one of Kalan's bubbles and found a flame-lance there which he poked over the edge and used to cut down all the guards before they could know what had happened.

D'Averc sprang up. He began to run through the tall corridors, his boots echoing loudly. He ran until at last he came to the doors of the throne room where a score of guards saw him and turned their weapons upon him, but he used his own flame-lance again and cut them down, being singed only slightly in his right shoulder. He pushed open the doors a crack and looked into the throne room. A mile away was the dais, but he could not see if Flana sat on it. Otherwise the hall was empty.

D'Averc began to run towards the distant throne.

And he shouted her name as he ran. "Flana! Flana!"

Flana had been daydreaming on her throne and looked up to see the tiny figure advancing. She heard her name taken up by a thousand echoes in the huge hall. "Flana! Flana! Flana!"

And she recognized the voice but thought that she had probably not yet woken up.

The figure came closer and it had a helmet that shone like polished silver, like a mirror. But the body — was the body not recognizable?

"Huillam?" she murmured uncertainly. "Huillam D'Averc?"

"Flana!" The figure wrenched off its mask and flung it from him so that it clattered across the great marble floor. "Flana!"

"Huillam!" She stood up and began to descend the steps towards him.

He opened his arms, smiling with joy.

But they never touched in life again, for a flame beam descended like a stroke of lightning from a gallery high above and burned off his face so that he screamed in agony and fell to his knees, then burned into his back so that he slumped forward and died at her feet while she sobbed great, strangled sobs that shook her body.

And the voice of a guard from the gallery called in great self-approval, "You are safe now, madam."

S I X T E E N

T H E F I N A L F I G H T

The Dark Empire forces were still swarming from every rathole in their maze city and Hawkmoon noted with despair that the Legion of the Dawn was getting thinner. Now when a warrior was slain another did not always take his place. Around him the air was full of the bitter sweet scent of the Runestaff and strange patterns in the air.

Then, as Hawkmoon saw Meliadus, a wave of pain gnawed again at his brain and he fell from his horse.

Meliadus dismounted from his black charger and walked slowly towards Hawkmoon. The Runestaff had fallen from his hand and the Sword of the Dawn was only loosely held.

Hawkmoon stirred, groaning. Around him the battle still raged, but it did not seem to be anything to do with him. He felt the energy leaving him, felt the pain increasing, opened his eyes and saw Meliadus approaching, the helm snarling as if in triumph. Hawkmoon's throat was dry and he tried to move, tried to reach the Runestaff which lay on the cobbles of the street.

Meliadus said softly, "Ah, Hawkmoon, at last. And you are in pain, I see. You are weak, I see. My only disappointment is that you will not live to witness your ultimate defeat and Yisselda in my power." Meliadus spoke almost with pity, with concern. "Can you not rise, Hawkmoon? Is the Jewel eating your brain behind that silver mask of yours? Shall I let it finish you, or shall I give myself the pleasure? Can you answer, Hawkmoon? Would you care to beg for mercy?"

Hawkmoon grabbed convulsively for the Runestaff. His hand went around it and tightened. Almost immediately power seemed to flow into him — not much, but enough to enable him to stagger to his feet and stand there swaying. His body was bowed. His breathing came in great panting sobs. He stared blearily at Meliadus as the baron lifted his sword to finish him.

Hawkmoon tried to raise his own sword, but failed.

Meliadus hesitated. "So you cannot fight. I grieve for you, Hawkmoon." He reached forward. "Give me that little staff, Hawkmoon. It was upon it I swore my oath of vengeance upon Castle Brass. And my vengeance is almost complete now. Let me hold it, Hawkmoon."

Hawkmoon took two staggering paces backward, shaking his head, unable to speak for the weakness in his body.

"Hawkmoon — give it to me."

"You — shall — not — have — it..." croaked the Duke of Köln.

"Then I shall have to kill you first." Meliadus raised his battle blade. The Runestaff suddenly pulsed with brighter light and Meliadus stared full into his own Wolf-helmed eyes as Hawkmoon's mask reflected his image back. It startled Meliadus. He hesitated.

And Hawkmoon, drawing further energy from the Runestaff, raised his sword knowing he had only enough strength for one blow and that blow must slay the man who stood transfixed before him, mesmerized by his own image.

And Hawkmoon brought up the Sword of the Dawn and he brought it down again and Meliadus gave a great, agonized cry as the blade bit through his shoulder bone and down into his heart. And his last words, which came with his last painful breath, were:

"Curse the Runestaff! It has brought ruin upon Granbretan!"

And Hawkmoon collapsed to the ground knowing that now he would die, that Yisselda would die and that Orland Fank would die, for there were few Kamarg warriors left and the Dark Empire soldiers were many.

S E V E N T E E N

T H E   S A D   Q U E E N

Hawkmoon awoke in alarm, staring full into the Serpent mask of Baron Kalan of Vitall. He sprang upright on the bench, groping for a weapon.

Kalan shrugged, turning to the group of people who stood in the shadows. "I told you I could do it. His brain is restored, his energy is restored, his whole foolish personality is restored and now, Queen Flana, I would beg your permission to continue with what I was doing when you interrupted me."

Hawkmoon recognized the heron mask. It nodded once and Kalan shuffled into the next room and carefully closed the door. The figures stepped forward and Hawkmoon saw with joy that one of them was Yisselda. He hugged her in his arms and kissed her soft cheek.

"Oh, I feared that Kalan would trick us," she said. "It was Queen Flana who found you, after she had ordered her troops to cease fighting. We were the last alive, Orland Fank and I, and we thought you dead. But Kalan brought you back to life, removed the Jewel from your skull and dismantled the machine so that none may ever fear the power of the Black Jewel again."

"And what business did you interrupt him in, Queen Flana?" Hawkmoon asked. "Why was he so disgruntled?"

"He was about to kill himself," Flana said flatly. "I threatened to keep him alive forever if he did not do what I demanded."

"D'Averc?" Hawkmoon said, puzzled. "Where is D'Averc?"

"Dead," said the sad queen in the same flat voice. "Slain in the throne room by an over-zealous guard."

Hawkmoon's joy turned to gloom. "And are they all dead, then — Count Brass, Oladahn, Bowgentle?"

"Aye," said Orland Fank, "but they died for a great cause and they freed millions from slavery. Until this day Europe has known only strife. Now perhaps people will seek peace, for they can see where strife leads."

"Count Brass wished for peace in Europe more than anything," Hawkmoon said. "But I wish he could have lived to see it."

"Perhaps his grandson will see it," Yisselda said.

"You need fear nothing from Granbretan as long as I am queen," Flana told them. "I intend to leave Londra dismantled and meanwhile make my own town of Kanbery the capital. The wealth of Londra — which is almost certainly greater than all the wealth of the rest of the world — shall be used in rebuilding the towns of Europe, in restocking the farms, in making good, as best we can, the evil we have done." She drew off her mask, revealing that great, sad, beautiful head. "And, also, I shall abolish the wearing of masks."

Orland Fank seemed skeptical, but he said nothing. "The power of Granbretan is broken for ever," he said, "and the Runestaff's work is done." He patted the bundle under his arm. "I'm taking the Sword of the Dawn, the Red Amulet and the Runestaff itself into safe-keeping, but if there should ever come a time, friend Hawkmoon, when you have a mutual need to rejoin each other, then you shall rejoin each other, I promise."

"I hope the time does not come, Orland Fank."

Fank sighed. "The world does not change, Dorian Hawkmoon. There is merely the occasional shift in equilibrium and if that shift goes too far in one direction, then the Runestaff attempts to right it. Perhaps the days of extremes are over for a century or two? I do not know."

Hawkmoon laughed. "But you should — you are omniscient."

Fank smiled. "Not I, my friend, but that which I serve — the Runestaff."

"Your son — Jehamia Cohnahlias..."

"Ah, there's the mystery even the Runestaff will not answer." Fank rubbed his long nose and looked at them over it. "Well, I'll say farewell, what's left of you. You fought well and you fought for justice."

"Justice?" Hawkmoon called after him as he left the room. "Is there such a thing?"

"It can be manufactured in small quantities," Fank told him. "But we have to work hard, fight well and use great wisdom to produce just a tiny amount."

"Aye," Hawkmoon nodded. "Perhaps you are right."

Fank laughed. "I know I am right." And then he was gone. And his voice came back to Hawkmoon with just one last observation. "Justice is not the Law, it is not Order, as human beings normally speak of it; it is Equilibrium, the Correction of the Balance. Remember that, Sir Champion Eternal!"

Hawkmoon put his arm around Yisselda's shoulders. "Aye, I will," he murmured. "And now we return to Castle Brass, to make the springs flow again, to bring back the reeds and the lagoons, to bring back the bulls and the horses and the flamingoes. To make it our Kamarg once more."

"And the power of the Dark Empire will never threaten it again." Queen

Flana smiled.

Hawkmoon nodded. "I am sure of that. But if some other evil should come to Castle Brass, I shall be ready for it, no matter how powerful it shall be, or in what form it will come. The world is still wild. The justice Fank spoke of has hardly been manufactured at all. We must try to make a little more. Farewell, Flana."

Flana watched them leave and she was weeping.

THE END
OF THE THIRD VOLUME

BETWEEN THE RANKS OF MANTIS-GUARDS WITH READY FLAME-LANCES, BETWEEN THE MURMURING CROWDS OF COURTIERS AND PETITIONERS, HAWKMOON AND MELIADUS PACED TO AN AUDIENCE WITH THE IMMORTAL KING-EMPEROR, **HUON.**

He had not reckoned on the
flamingoes: they swept up from
the Towers in scarlet clouds:
Flame-lances blazed!

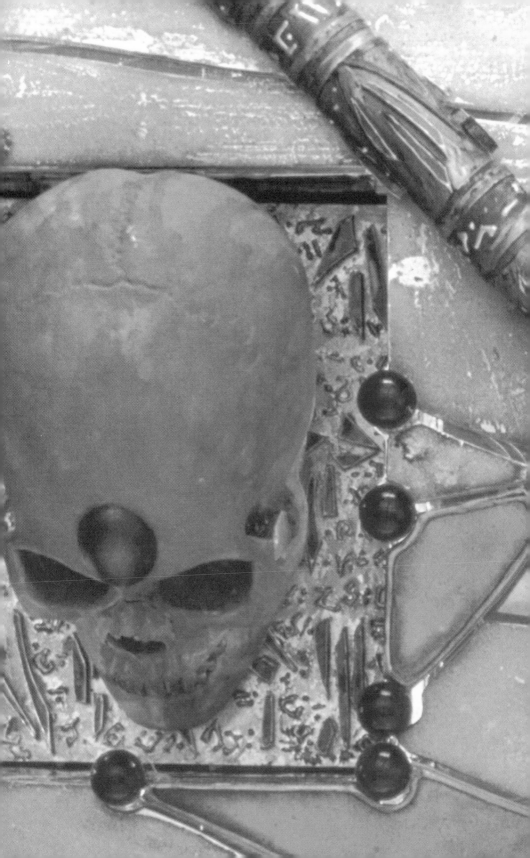